About the Author

Dr Jennifer Browne (PhD) is one of Western Australia's most published and respected educators and academic authors.

Following a teaching and writing career spanning forty years, and culminating as an Associate Professor and Head of School of Arts and Humanities Education at Edith Cowan University, Jennifer became a founding Director of two acclaimed educational publishing businesses, B&G Resources and Innovative Business Resources. In the process, Jennifer authored and co-authored more than a hundred books and manuals, particularly in post-compulsory education, and especially in small business management and physical education.

Sarjan was her first venture into fiction.

After struggling to engage a mainstream publisher, Jennifer initially self-published *Sarjan* in 2002, and it turned out to be such a resounding success that *Sarjan* has been re-released in 2009.

Although now officially retired to her beachside home in Perth, with her partner, and their four-legged children, Jennifer continues to write.

SARJAN

An Historical Novel

JENNIFER BROWNE

Sarjan's Legacy
www.sarjan.com.au

Published by *Sarjan's Legacy* **2009**
PO Box 314, North Beach, Western Australia 6020
Tel: +(61) 428 819456
Fax: +(618) 92431021
Email: admin@sarjan.com.au
Website: www.sarjan.com.au

First published by B&G Resources 2002

National Library of Australia
Cataloguing-in-Publication data:

Browne, Jennifer 1937-
Sarjan
ISBN 978-0-9806054-1-9
1.Title.
A823.4

Cover Design by Lauren Wilhelm, Designmine
Maps by Regina Gaujers

Portion of item 5041 P for cover page reproduced courtesy of Battye Library. Portion of lower photograph facing page 49, from The World of the First Australians, reproduced for the cover courtesy of the Estate of RM. and C.H. Berndt.

Printed by Salmat Print On Demand, Bassendean, Western Australia

ACKNOWLEDGEMENTS

Lauren Wilhelm for designing a cover that captured the essence of the book and expressed my feelings perfectly.

Dr Anne Harris for taking on the time-consuming final edit as a favour. Her meticulous attention to detail and careful analysis was appreciated immensely.

Trudy Graham for her enthusiastic support and assessment of the first draft. Stan Richards for his ongoing interest and suggestions.

Dr Neville Green for his encouragement, particularly in the early stages of research.

Library staff at Edith Cowan University and the Royal WA Historical Society, especially Graham Connell and Jennifer Marshall.

Dr Rica Erickson (dec'd) for her permission to modify the map of early Fremantle from *The Dempsters*.

Mollie Farmers (nee Elizabeth Lane) for providing me with a copy of the diary written by Captain IT Ellis during his voyage to the Swan River Colony.

With a gestation period of over twenty years, *Sarjan* needed more than the usual amount of support. To my editors and proofreaders, sincere thanks for your time and encouragement.

To my loyal and cherished friends and supporters, I express my sincere appreciation for your kindness and generosity of spirit. To those who have subsequently read and enjoyed *Sarjan*, and urged me to come up with a sequel, I will do my best not to disappoint you.

INTRODUCTION

When I purchased an old holiday house at Mandurah, seventy-two kilometres south of Perth, Western Australia, in 1978, I discovered that the property was only a hundred metres from the site of the original *Mandurah House*, the residence of Thomas Peel who transported the first settlers to Western Australia in 1829. A bronze plaque cemented into the southern footpath of Mandurah Terrace marks the position of Mandurah House.

My holiday home was situated in a depression and had very rich soil, and a water table only inches below the surface. Seashells were abundant in the earth. A long time ago the area was a tidal swamp and more recently part of the original Peel Farm. And so evolved an interest in the history of the area, which ultimately led to the writing of *Sarjan*.

In my attempts to provide an historical background that was as accurate as possible, my research for the novel was ongoing and intensive. However, a writer cannot enter the minds of historical figures, and eventually their motives for action can only be inferred from an interpretation of their previous and later exploits as history records them. The fictional players, such as the (early European settlers) Andrews, Blairs and Roberts, and (Aboriginals) Yeddi, Mandu and Odern, take over the story, but are portrayed within an historical context.

I pored over hundreds of books, journals and early Perth newspapers in an attempt to maintain authenticity for the period of history covered in the story, especially as it related to Australia, England and the Cape Colony (South Africa).

The references relating to early European settlement, that I found to be most useful, were Alexandra Hasluck's meticulously researched *Thomas Peel of Swan River* (1965); Ronald Richards' comprehensive history of *The Murray District of Western Australia: A History* (1978); George Fletcher Moore's day-to-day descriptions of colonial life in *Diary of Ten*

Years Eventful Life of an Early Settler in Western Australia (1978); *Broken Spears* (1984), Neville Green's account of the impact of early European settlement on the Nyoongar Aboriginals; Pamela Statham's *Dictionary of Western Australia* (1979); J. K. Hitchcock's snippets of information in *The History of Fremantle* (1929); and J Flett's *A Pictorial History of the Victorian Goldfields* (1977). *The Dempsters* by Rica Erickson (1978) was particularly useful in developing a picture of early Fremantle and Rottnest.

Information relating to Aboriginal culture for the story is a synthesis of information provided from many sources, including a course in the local hills to 'Discover the Nyoongar Way'.

The books referred to most frequently were: George Fletcher Moore's *Diary of Ten Years Eventful Life of an Early Settler in Western Australia* (1978); Jesse Hammond's *Winjan's People* (1933); Neville Green's *Broken Spears* (1984); *Aboriginal Perth* by Daisy Bates, edited by P. J. Bridge (1992), and: *The Native Tribes of Western Australia*, by Daisy Bates and edited by Isobel White (1984).

The chapter detailing Yeddi's trial drew extensively from the proceedings of the trial of Weewar as reported in the *Inquirer: A Western Australian Journal of Politics and Literature* (12 January, 1842).

Because of perceptions over time, discrepancies in interpreting language, and perceived differences by writers of aspects of customs between tribes and within tribal groups, accounts varied from reference to reference. The possibility of seeking contemporary opinions was considered and discarded because, whether it was the viewpoint of anthropologists, historians, or local Aboriginal elders, I was convinced there would be significant disparities of conviction between and within such groups. So I went it alone, and hope my descriptions, explanations and interpretations will not offend.

Jennifer Browne

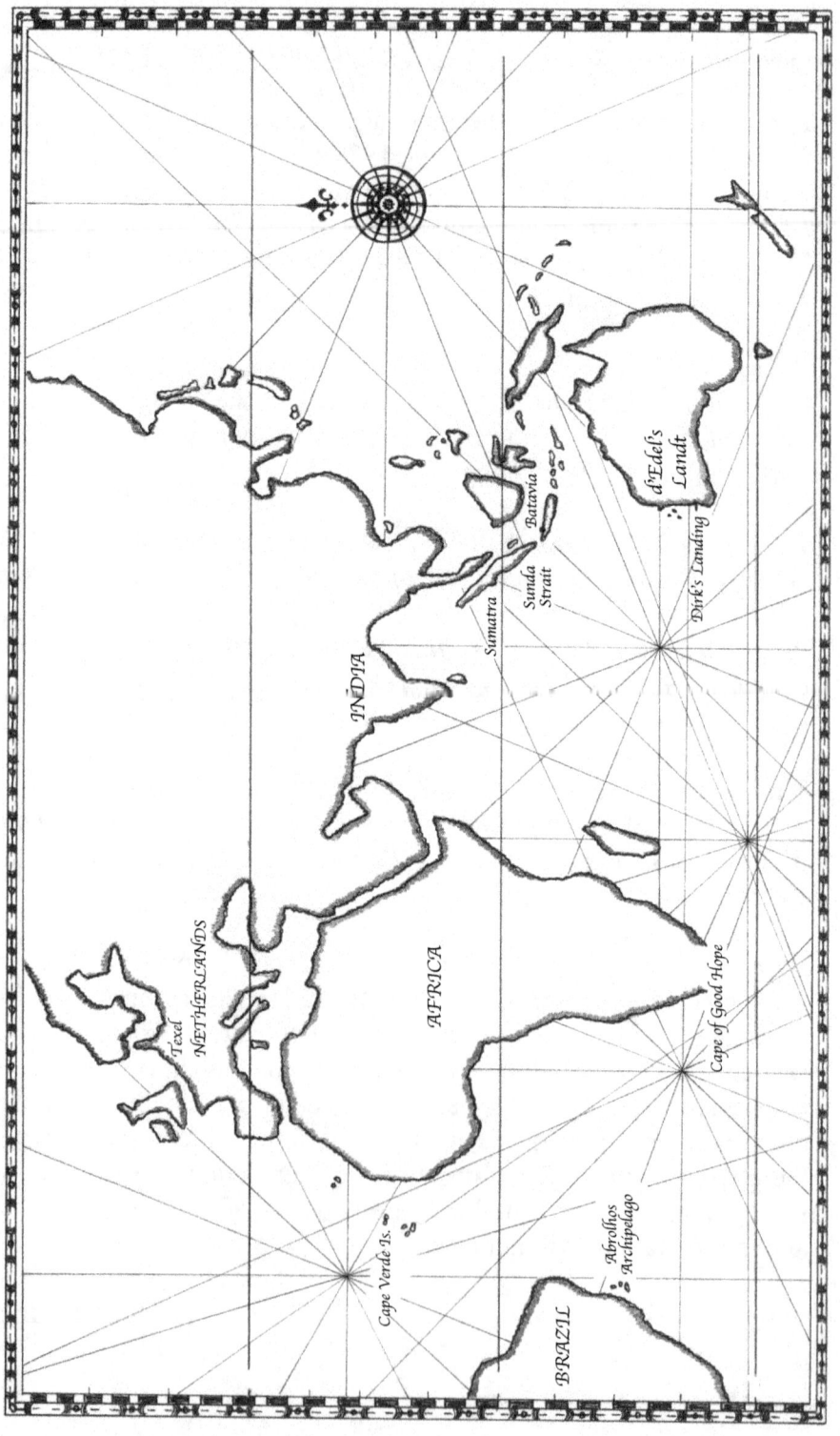

Prologue
Connections

A° 1659

Journal by me Abraham Phillipsz of the voyage of the Delft made from the Island of Texel in the Netherlands and bound for Batavia in the East Indies in the year Anno 1659. May it please God Almighty to give hereto His Blessing to this voyage. Amen.

On 3rd January A° 1659 in the morning at last finding a fair wind raised our anchors and went under sail from the Island of Texel of the Fatherland. Good weather with smooth water. Wind north by north-east topsails breeze. Sailed 36 mijlen through North Sea.

* * * * *

On 4th April in the morning sailed toward land and anchored in 22 fathoms where wait for breeze to take ship safely into Table Bay. At noon observed latitude 33 degrees 50 minutes longitude 15 degrees 40 minutes. One glass being out in afternoon watch with wind from north-west sailed into Bay and dropped anchor. Sent Uppersteersman Matys Haas ashore in ship's boat to gain permission to land sickly persons. Afflicted being put ashore such trips taken as necessary. 28 persons in all unable to walk and placed in care. Fresh fruit, vegetables, meat and water brought to ship for those still aboard. Crew not on watch went ashore. Great rejoicing on our safe arrival. May the Lord be praised. Double rations of arrack allowed during dog watch. Commandeur van Riebeeck sent greetings to ship.

On 5th d° in the morning went ashore with Uppermerchant Purmer to meet with Commandeur Riebeeck. Exchanged greetings and messages. Discussed matters. Estimated 10 days for sick to heal and fresh stores and water to be loaded aboard. Ordered to follow V O C directive and look for survivors of the Vergulde Draeck. Cape settlement increasing in size and now sufficient in most things. Gave rope, musket shot and Spanish wine as requested. Winds light from north-west. Good weather.

* * * * *

On 12th May in the morning good weather. Wind steady with topsails breeze. At noon observed latitude 32 degrees 40 minutes longitude 115 degrees 10 minutes. Drifting rockweed and seabirds seen. Estimated 960 mijlen sailed from Cape of Good Hope. A man kept continuously on watch for the South Land. Scurvy affecting all crew and passengers. May God speed this ship. Sailed 46 mijlen.

* * * * *

With barely controlled impatience, Captain Phillipsz leaned forward, strong brown hands gripping a salt-stained rail. Peering intently into the pinkish dawn, constantly sniffing the air, he was now certain he could smell vegetation. The signs of proximity to land were unmistakable. Light-coloured water, floating seaweed and increasing numbers of birds had been pointed out by the crew with great enthusiasm. The watch had been doubled the previous day.

Immediately land was sighted, he would set a course north for the Sunda Strait and another long haul to Batavia would soon be over. But at what cost! It made him miserable to think about the slow deterioration of the crew. The inevitability of it all on every voyage was a nightmare. Not even five months had elapsed since their departure from the Netherlands and already forty-two men had succumbed to fever, scurvy or the dreaded dysentery. Some poor bastards had suffered them all. The stench emanating from the forward sections of the ship was appalling.

Phillipsz began pacing the half deck, his hands clasped behind his back. He was an impressive figure of a man, tall, broad-backed, with swarthy skin - the trademark of a sailor. Strong features were accentuated by a flared moustache and full beard, which he stubbornly maintained against the dictates of fashion. Scratching his crotch, as he strode, he cursed the inevitable crabs. I've about had enough of this life, he thought. My savings are sound and in safe-keeping and my family grow up without me. Perhaps one more voyage will do it.

"Ahoy below! Ahoy below!" The excited cry came from the lookout perched high in the crows-nest and the Captain's head jerked upwards to attend the call.

"Land ho! Land ho!" The sailor was pointing eastward. Phillipsz grabbed for his telescope and brought the heavy instrument into focus with practised ease. White beaches and low dunes topped with grey-green vegetation came into view. The sun was rising blood red from behind a line of distant hills.

"Reduce sail!", Phillipsz directed the waiting Boatswain and gave an audible sigh of relief. "Thank the Lord", he said to no one in particular.

"All hands on deck!" The Boatswain repeated the shouted command until the crew, some still pulling on overshirts, appeared from below decks and clambered groggily up the rigging.

"Furl topsails" was the call and within minutes, the ship slowed noticeably.

Phillipsz scanned the ocean to the east for breakers. As every Captain sailing to the Indies, he feared this treacherous coastline. The disaster of the *Batavia* wrecked in 1629, with the massacre of crew and passengers by the mutinous Cornelisz, was still discussed in hushed tones by Amsterdam society.

Only three years ago, the *Vergulde Draeck*, on her second voyage to Batavia, had run aground on a submerged reef. Over a hundred lives and a rich cargo of goods and coin went to the bottom. but the ship's longboat miraculously made it to Batavia. Three rescue expeditions had failed to find the remaining sixty-eight lost souls keeping their vain vigil on the barren coast. It was for survivors of the *Vergulde Draeck* that Phillipsz had been asked to keep watch.

"Boatswain, take the ship through 60 points and head north."

The helmsman glanced anxiously at the compass before pulling the whipstaff across to its full extent. The *Delft* resisted the manoeuvre momentarily, timbers creaking and groaning, as the bowsprit turned slowly northwards. Leaning away from the light sea breeze, the ship began a northerly reach. Excited soldiers, awakened by the shouting, hung over the railing, pointing and laughing.

Captain Phillipsz was joined by Uppermerchant Cornelius Purmer on the half deck. The senior representative of the Dutch East India Company was tall and thin with a sallow complexion, long nose and Vandyke beard. It gave his face a wedge shape. His perpetually sad expression reminded Phillipsz of a predikant preparing for a funeral. As always, he wore the black suit, top coat and tall hat favoured by the Company.

"What have we here, Captain?" His bleary eyes roamed the horizon.

"The great South Land, Mynheer. A very dangerous coastline indeed. As you would well know, we have lost precious lives and cargo on the hidden outlying reefs. Every precaution will be taken to safeguard the ship as we make our run to the Sunda Strait."

Purmer's eyes narrowed as he considered the Captain's words. "Is there any likelihood of fresh food and water in this land?"

"I do not know, Mynheer. No one has reported on this particular section of coast. It is charted but unexplored."

The Uppermerchant's cheek muscles twitched with worry. The wretched stomach ulcer was now paining constantly. His seriously ill wife and three daughters were confined to their cabin with bleeding gums, loose teeth and suppurating sores covering their bodies. The food was repulsive and the water foul. The chattering and laughter usual at home in Amsterdam had stilled during the voyage. He blamed himself and wished he had never accepted this last honour. To head the Council of the Indies was the final accolade of a brilliant career in the Company. None of it would be worthwhile if he were to serve it alone. He cleared his throat.

"Captain, I would remind you of the orders of Commandeur Riebeeck at the Cape which expressly requested that we seek out evidence of the fate of the *Vergulde Draeck*. Further, that a share of any goods acquired from the wreck would be apportioned to the finder. I would suggest a small landing party to investigate. At the same time fresh provisions could be sought." He paused significantly, fixing his gaze on the far shore. "My family is sorely in need of fresh food."

Phillipsz was no fool. Although in charge of the ship, he was subservient to Commandeur Purmer in all other matters. If his superior wanted a shore party, he would have a shore party. What was one more day in a journey of six months? The reward was also a tantalising thought.

"An excellent idea, Mynheer." He turned to the Boatswain. "Furl the sails and stand by to drop anchors. Arrange a small landing party as soon as the crew has broken fast."

As the Boatswain gave the orders to furl the sails, a young man wiping the sleep from his eyes emerged from a rear cabin. "Good morning, Mynheer. Good morning, Captain." He nodded to his two superiors. "It appears I am missing the action. The Spanish wine imbibed last evening seems to have induced a degree of somnolence." He held his head. "And a headache."

A smile flickered across Phillipsz's face causing his whiskers to lift. He liked this extroverted young fellow. At least he was pleasant company. "Good morning, Mynheer Witsen. The excitement is just beginning. At the sunrise is the great South Land. Perhaps you would like to join the shore party being arranged. It seeks survivors of the *Vergulde Draeck* and fresh food and water."

The young man looked towards the shore, shading his eyes. "Indeed I would, Captain. It will be a refreshing change of scenery." Not to mention relief from a rolling ship infested with lice, fleas, cockroaches and rats.

Phillipsz addressed the Boatswain. "Drop anchors."

Anchors splashed into a deep blue sea and as they gripped the ocean bed, the *Delft* swung into the south-westerly breeze. Shortly afterwards, the ship's boat with four empty water casks was lowered and the landing party clambered down the rope ladder, each with a Beardman jug and a bag of biscuits slung around his neck. Within minutes, with sail raised, the dinghy ploughed towards land through the light chop.

The group comprised Understeersman Abel Jonas, a burly, taciturn man, in charge of the expedition, who handled the tiller with consummate ease; Hans Pietersz, a mariner, who set the sails; Claas Willemsz, a soldier nervously clasping his musket and acting as guard; and passenger Dirk Witsen, fair-haired and handsome, except for a prominent jaw and lower lip, which his father had told him in confidence was some obscure and not to be discussed connection with the royal House of Hapsburg. Dressed in fawn suede breeches and doublet, he wore a baldric with sword and viewed himself as an intrepid adventurer. The others viewed him as an affable young upstart.

Dirk observed the antics of terns gliding over the waves, then soaring for height to plunge like stones on some aquatic prey. Flying fish skimmed the water and dolphins raced the boat on either side of the prow. It was indeed an exciting and beautiful morning.

He sighed in anticipation. There was much to relate to Anneken, his betrothed, awaiting him in Batavia. Although it was an arranged marriage, her portraits depicted her a beauty. Dirk furtively reached under his jacket to feel the leather belt fastened snugly around his waist. Each partition held a number of coins: twelve gold ducats minted in Amsterdam; six Spanish pieces of eight; four German thalers; and twenty English gold unites. The partition closest to the buckle contained two solid gold rings and two fine gold rings studded with rubies and emeralds. The only son of Jeronimus Witsen was assured of a wedding commensurate with his father's standing in Amsterdam, particularly since the Governor-General was to give the bride away.

Abel scowled and spat over the side. "Shit! The bloody swell's huge!" he said, to no one in particular. Landing the boat intact and the implications of a mishap weighed heavily on his mind. The soldier sat stiffly, clutching his musket with both eyes closed, as the Uppersteersman skilfully manoeuvred the small craft through several patches of reef. The sail was struck and the prow grounded onto white sand. When Abel yelled, they all jumped with alacrity into the surf to haul the boat beyond the high tide mark. Too late Dirk realised he was still wearing his fine leather boots. Damn!

The men paused to catch their breath and orientate themselves. The immediate vegetation was low, the grey-green spinifex and succulents clinging precariously to the loose sand. Further inland, a cluster of eucalypt trees swayed in the breeze and brightly-coloured green and yellow parrots screeched noisily to signal the trespassers.

"That could be our water hole," Abel pointed. "Bring the barrels and whichever weapons you want and let's get going. The sooner this is over the better. We'll search the hollows for water. And stay together!"

Suddenly, as they trudged through the sand hills following Abel, six of the most amazing-looking creatures burst from a thicket. As if on signal, the four men halted in astonishment. The brown furry animals were large and hopped on well developed hind legs, their huge tails brushing the ground behind. They bounded towards a slight rise, then stopped. Standing on hind legs like begging dogs, they examined the intruders, their ears twitching forwards and sideways, their uplifted noses sniffing.

The soldier kneeled, loaded his musket with powder and shot and tamped the ball down the barrel with the ramrod. He shaded his eyes to judge the distance and then taking calculated aim, squeezed the trigger. A small puff of smoke curled upward as one of the creatures fell, kicking its legs in pain. The remaining animals vanished over the hill.

"Good shot," grunted Abel. The soldier's eyes blinked and he looked inordinately pleased with himself. There had been precious little to be pleased about on this accursed voyage to date.

Abel paused, biting his lip thoughtfully. "Claas, could we stalk the animals to kill more?"

"Hmm. I'm not sure how timid they are. If we fan out and approach with care, it might be possible." A check of arms revealed that pistols, shot and powder were carried by Abel and Dirk. Claas had shot for nineteen firings of the musket, depending on how long the powder lasted.

"It's decided then. But first we look for water."

Following Abel, the men pushed their way through the prickly vegetation to the depression and began digging with their hands. Soon they had dug a hole large enough to draw on with a cask. The water was brackish and muddy but the sediment would likely settle and could always be strained through charcoal onboard ship.

"That'll do," puffed Abel. The four were a sorry sight, covered in mud, their hands and forearms scratched by the prickly vegetation and all panting for breath from the effort. "Let's fill these barrels and get them to the boat. It will take two trips. Then we'll plan the hunt."

After fastening the barrels in the boat, they returned to the sand dunes to eat their repast. "Now Claas, what do you suggest?" Abel asked.

Claas frowned, biting his lip. Then he lifted a finger wetted with spittle above his head to ascertain the direction of the wind and proceeded to draw in the sand, giving instructions as he did so.

When he had finished, Abel said "Right men, follow Claas."

Two hours passed. The hunt was successful with four animals killed. They had stood no chance against the firearms. The carcasses were gutted to lighten the load before making the final trudge over the sand hills. Abel noticed nervously that the wind now blew from the north-west. Grey clouds, moving with increasing speed, covered the sun.

The outgoing tide had left the dinghy stranded from the water's edge, requiring much pulling and pushing to launch. Abel was becoming alarmed. He looked at the *Delft* in the distance, bobbing at anchor in the strengthening wind. It was mid-afternoon with deteriorating weather and a rising sea.

"Come on, hurry up and load the animals. Looks like a change in the weather."

The carcasses and barrels were secured with their weight distributed along the bottom of the dinghy. The weary men pushed the boat through an increasing surf and hurriedly took their places at the oars. Water splashed over the gunwale as each wave hit the starboard side.

Then the rain came in sheets across the water and drenched the frantic rowers in seconds. It added to the water rising in the bilge, which slowly turned red, mingling with the blood oozing from the carcasses.

The squall was sudden and fierce and the use of sail impossible. The men rowed and bailed with increasing desperation, while Abel coaxed, shouted and swore as yard by precious yard they managed to increase their distance from the shore.

Over an hour passed and the sky darkened. They tried to set the sail but the onshore wind continued howling and it was an impossible task. The sun was setting in an inky black sea and Abel was panicking. "Where's the bloody ship?" Everybody turned and looked. The ship had disappeared. Nobody answered. Dirk began to quietly sob to himself, the tears joining the rivulets of water dripping from his hair.

* * * * *

On 13th May at the dawn espied the South Land. South-westerly wind. Topsails breeze. Cast the lead at 40 fathoms. Anchored 1 mijlen from shore in 30 fathoms. Landing party sent to seek survivors of Vergulde Draeck and fresh provisions. Understeersman Abel Jonas, sailor Hans Pietersz, soldier Claas Willemsz, passenger Dirk Witsen went in ship's boat. At noon observed latitude 32 degrees 35 minutes longitude 115 degrees 35 minutes. Strong squall from north-west mid-afternoon. Shore party not returned. Lifted anchors and beat to windward for safety. 10 mijlen off coast at start of dog watch. Anchored in 60 fathoms. Wind blowing hard. May the Lord watch over the men ashore.

* * * * *

As the men hung exhausted over the oars, Abel continued to scour the horizon. Nothing! What to do? What to do?

Then, as if an angry Neptune himself had decided to join in the disastrous turn of events, a king wave arising seemingly from nowhere like a demon from the deep, slammed the starboard beam. hurling the boat over. Being at the stern, Abel and Dirk were tossed clear and came to the surface floundering. In increasing darkness, Abel reached for a struggling Dirk and hauled him towards the boat. Spitting, coughing and gasping for breath, they dragged themselves onto the upturned hull. Dirk clung to the keel and the remains of the smashed rudder. Abel spread-eagled himself across the bow section and hung on for grim death.

The other two were nowhere to be seen. "Ahoy. Ahoy." For some minutes Abel continued to call in vain but then decided to save his breath.

As hard as Abel and Dirk tried, there was no way they could right the boat. The sail was caught around the mast, perpendicular below them. Together with the tangle of ropes, stays and tied barrels and animal carcasses, it proved a remarkably effective sea anchor.

The distraught Uppersteersman tried desperately to gather his thoughts. He swore and slapped the sobbing Dirk, realising their only chance of survival was to remain clinging to the upturned boat until morning and praying that Captain Phillipsz would send a search party for them.

It was the longest night of mental and physical anguish either of the men had ever endured. They were cold, shocked and terrified. Not daring to sleep in case they slipped from the hull, they continued a muddled conversation, droning on about anything and everything. When one didn't answer, the other kicked, hit or prodded. Their minds numbed and their muscles cramped. The hours crept by.

Came the dawn! Grey, windy, raining. They had made it to the dawn!

* * * * *

Abel saw it first. A single, grey, triangular-shaped fin and tail cutting through the black water as the shark approached the drifting boat.

Carcharodon carcharias, the Great White Shark. The largest predator in the world. It was a tribute to the perfection of the creature that it had changed little since its appearance in the Devonian period 400 million years before.

The mature female was a massive twenty-four feet in length and weighed two tons. She was longer than the boat. The two young she carried were all that remained of the original sixteen fertilised ova. They had fed on the yolks of weaker surrounding eggs, after devouring their own. It was a case of survival of the fittest in the womb.

The shark had not eaten for some time and was ravenous. Sensing the blood from the animal carcasses, she had changed direction and her pace quickened as the streak led her towards the upturned dinghy. The female was wary, worried by the movement of the mast and sail in the water, so she swam slowly in a large circle around the boat and commenced her reconnaissance.

Slumped over the stern section of the keel, Dirk's white fingers gripped the remains of the rudder. Abel knew he was conscious, because he could hear him muttering. He had obviously not seen the monster, so he slapped him on the shoulder. "Wake up, Dirk," he whispered. "We have an unwelcome visitor."

Dirk lifted his head and followed Abel's gaze. Eyes opening wide, he screamed. A long, loud scream. Pumping adrenaline brought him to full sensibility.

"Lord have mercy upon us. Christ have mercy upon us." He shivered and shook spasmodically, forcing himself to look again and began thumping and kicking the wooden planks and shouting to frighten the leviathan. Abel joined in. The shark ignored them and began a tighter circle.

For an hour, the two men followed the slow, almost lazy, circles with horror-filled eyes. Each had come to the same realisation of his plight. The first to weaken would be eaten alive. Languidly, the shark lifted its head to gain a better perspective on the situation. An unblinking eye, a solid black disc, fixed on Abel, mesmerising him, willing him to slide from his precarious position. Abel dragged his eyes away. The shark resumed its circling.

Then, with a sudden decisive movement, the monster charged. She came in hard, just below the surface and the surge of power initiated so much momentum that she slid up the side of the boat, splintering the wooden hull. Time stood still while Abel watched the shark, poised motionless, before she flicked her huge tail and heaved herself a further two feet. Raising her head, she rolled her eyes back in their sockets and jutted the protruding upper jaw beyond the lips. Abel saw hundreds of symmetrical, triangular, razor-sharp, serrated teeth bite his foot off cleanly above the ankle. A jet of blood spurted from his lower leg as the shark slid back below the surface.

Screaming in agony and terror, Abel saw the blood pouring from the stump of his leg. He could not relinquish his grip on the boat to staunch the flow. "Help me, help me," he pleaded.

Dirk was frozen with fear and utterly incapable of helping anyone. Several minutes passed as Abel alternately sobbed and prayed. His blood ran down the splintered wood, causing a spreading crimson stain in the water.

Without warning it was back. Excited by the first mouthful of flesh, it attacked from the other side. Abel threw himself away from the gaping jaws, lost his balance and toppled into the water. In a frenzy the shark followed the splash and chopped him in half as his head reached the surface. Dirk's last glimpse of Abel was a white upturned face with terrified, staring eyes disappearing into swirling, bloody water and a hand reaching upwards in vain.

Tossing her head, the shark swallowed the body chunks. She swam towards an offshore reef a mile away, where she gave birth to her two young, each about three feet long. They swam around tentatively in the new and colder environment before shedding their umbilical cords and placenta. The shark waited before disgorging a portion of Abel's torso as a welcoming feast for her offspring and then headed leisurely out to sea.

* * * * *

On 14th d° in the morning returned to area of landing party. Weather gloomy. Winds blowing strongly from north-west. With small sail only searched for signs of landing party. Fired cannon for attention. At noon observed latitude 32 degrees 40 minutes longitude 115 degrees 40 minutes. Waited until four glasses out in the afternoon watch. Consulted with Commandeur Purmer. Decision made to continue to Batavia. May the Lord show mercy upon the men. May the Lord keep them.

* * * * *

Dark eyes watched patiently from behind the first line of sand hills. A group of natives had followed the movements of the shore party the previous day and now watched the lone survivor, as he was cast ashore with the remains of the boat.

Tribal lore told of white-skinned persons arriving in the past and as these djanga were the spirits of their dead ancestors, they must be treated with

9

respect. However, this family of the Bindjareb tribe of the Nyoongar had not seen such white apparitions before. They were intrigued by their antics until they saw the killing of the kangaroos and then they became frightened. This remaining one certainly did not appear to be a threat. Still, one should always be wary of the unknown, so the group waited patiently, crouched on their heels among the spinifex.

Time passed. The elderly man rose to a standing position, juggling his spear into a balanced position, before cautiously approaching the inert figure. His two wives, one grey and wrinkled, the other young and smooth-skinned, followed apprehensively. Two children remained hidden in the bushes with their grandmother.

When Dirk eventually came to his senses, he stared wide-eyed at three naked black figures peering down at him. On seeing him awake, they stepped backwards, hesitating for a moment as they weighed up the danger. The man held his spear in readiness, motioning the women to move behind him with the other arm.

The Dutchman's mind was in turmoil as he tried to bring himself back to some sort of reality. He felt nauseous and had a raging thirst. "Help me," he whispered hoarsely and stretched out his upturned palms towards the natives. "Water. I need water," he said, licking his dry lips.

"Kypbi," the man said. The young woman hastened to the hiding place, returning with an animal skin full of water. Kneeling in front of Dirk, she offered him the dripping bag. He grabbed it and gulped the water noisily.

Bruised and battered, Dirk pushed himself to his feet and shivering gazed back at the remains of the boat being pounded by waves in the shallows. There was no sign of the *Delft*.

"Fire," he shouted. "I must have smoke." There was no response. Dirk fell to his knees and desperately scraped together a few sticks, holding his hands over the pile and pretending to warm his hands.

"Kalla!" The natives were astonished. Why would anyone want a fire? There was nothing to cook and it was not cold. The elder's eyes narrowed. The djanga wanted to attract attention. Perhaps there were more of his people nearby. He shook his head and began walking quickly away with the women following.

Dirk was distraught. He had no means of lighting a fire to signal the ship. He was bareheaded, barefooted and clad in wet, ragged clothes. His weapons were lost and the fortune around his waist was worthless in his present situation. He was alone, defenceless and without food. His eyes widened, as he came to the terrible realisation that he was marooned on Terra Australis!

"Wait!" he called at the departing group. Pausing, they looked back, before continuing their way south through the low scrub. Dirk frantically set out after them. The natives ignored him and kept moving quickly and effortlessly through a lightly-wooded valley. Dirk stumbled along behind.

The Dutchman trailed the natives for about an hour. The male led with the females and children following. Periodically, the group stopped and scouted for food, the women chatting as they placed various items into plaited bags tied around their waists. By this time Dirk was tired and hungry and glad when the group stopped near a thicket of tall trees. The women and children busied themselves collecting wood and bark, while the elder disappeared for a short while and returned with a small furry animal slung over his shoulder. Dirk watched as the older wife fired some gathered grass, to which were added twigs and wood until it burned brightly. When the fire died to embers, the dead animal was tossed on whole and soon a delicious aroma arose. The meat was chopped into pieces with a vicious-looking hand axe and the available food spread on the bark. The elder took his portion first, followed by the children and then the wives and grandmother. Dirk was offered the remains, which he ravenously wolfed down.

The women fed the glowing coals with sticks and then constructed a shelter of branches. Darkness descended on the camp site and the family sat in relaxed fashion around the fire, the women singing lullabies to the children. When they became sleepy, they were gently laid inside the shelter. The adults curled up in animal skins close to the fire, while Dirk shivered on the outskirts until, on a signal from the man, the young woman made a space for him. The fire soon warmed him and very soon he fell into a deep sleep.

The elder lay awake pondering the events of the day. He did not want the stranger tagging along because he was an extra mouth to feed but the stranger would not survive long without their help. Geran brought a change in the weather and it was time to head inland for the seasonal fishing. With the rains, the fish in the rivers swam downstream ahead of the fresh water. Happy family groups congregated and brush barriers diverted masses of mullet into races from which they were scooped. The mandjar of the Bindjareb people was an annual event of tribal significance when friendships and kinship ties were strengthened, betrothals arranged and trading undertaken. The elder knew they should leave soon, as before long the coastal area would become wet and windy and the game would move further inland.

The man gazed thoughtfully at Dirk who was sleeping peacefully alongside his younger wife. She had borne him no children. He had been unable to perform the sexual act for many moons before she came to his side and felt guilty about his inadequacy. Perhaps he could offer her to the stranger. He would think further about the idea.

While the women rekindled the fire next morning, Dirk climbed a nearby hill. The storm had passed and the day was fine. He scanned the horizon.

Nothing! He wandered disconsolately down the hill. What to do? He knew nothing of this land and wouldn't be able to provide for himself. The natives seemed friendly enough. He decided to trail behind for as long as they allowed him. Meanwhile he would build up his strength and keep a look out for the *Delft*.

The following days were as perplexing as they were pleasant. Dirk was treated as a member of the group, supplied with adequate, if unusual, sustenance and at night provided with a lovely young woman who clearly wanted to please him. At first he had been appalled by the thought but desire quickly overcame differences in skin colour and he eagerly looked forward to the nightly coupling. Meanwhile the natives busied themselves collecting the fruit of shrubs and drying the meat of animals speared by the man or clubbed by the women.

At regular intervals, Dirk climbed the hill and peered at the horizon. He stacked a large amount of firewood on the eastern side of the hill in the lee of the prevailing westerlies. The young woman showed him how to make fire, rotating a stick between the palms of the hands, until the friction on another stick produced sufficient heat to ignite dry grass. She shyly presented him with two fire sticks with which he practised daily until he was successful in lighting a fire by himself.

At dawn on the fifth day following the catastrophe with the ship's boat, the family arose earlier than usual and began preparations for their journey. When Dirk realised what was happening, he became frantic with worry. The family could not understand why the white man was so agitated, until they began to walk away from the camp site. He did not walk with them. Rather, he ran towards the ocean stabbing his finger in its direction and yelling to them in his incomprehensible language. The elder shrugged his shoulders. They were already well behind schedule and must leave now. Dirk chased them and grabbed the young woman's arm, pulling her back towards the camp site. The elder stepped forward placing himself between them. He held up his hand with the palm towards Dirk, who could not mistake the gesture. The man said something to the grandmother who knelt and took food from her bundle, wrapping it in a small skin before passing it to the stranger. The family turned and walked away until they were lost from sight among the trees.

A forlorn Dirk watched them go, as he had no alternative but to remain close to the ocean in case there was a rescue attempt. Clutching his package, he wandered to the top of his lookout and sat down, remaining there all day, staring out to sea. Towards sunset, with heavy step, he returned to the camp site by way of the waterhole and made a fire, not without some difficulty. After eating a portion of the food, he fell into a restless sleep wishing his companion of the previous nights was with him. He awoke cold, stiff and lonely with the dawn.

The Dutchman began a systematic reconnoitre of the surrounding bushland. An outcrop of limestone extended for miles both north and south. He discovered many caves and noted the position of a large cavern, which led back into an inner cave. A freshwater spring ran down the rock close by. The cave would be his protection from winter storms. The ocean could be seen from the top of the rise and his pile of wood was ready a short way down the hill.

Dirk prepared his shelter. He swept the area with leafy branches and carried in wood and grass, stacking it in piles along the walls of the cave. A path was cleared to the spring by removing debris and fallen boughs and inside the cave a hearth of stones was arranged and wood set for a fire. Finally he fashioned a bed of small branches and leaves. Then he sat on a rock at the entrance and in total despair sobbed until he had cried himself out.

In the afternoon, he lit the fire and ate some food.

* * * * *

The next morning Dirk found a piece of wood for a cudgel, gathered some small, round rocks for throwing and resolutely set off to hunt for food. He had limited success, killing a lizard which he roasted for dinner. The following day it poured with rain and, catching nothing, he was forced to eat the last of the food provided by the natives. The smell was bad and he gagged as he swallowed. On the third day, he killed and cooked a small furry creature, which looked suspiciously like a kind of rat. Then the storm struck with a howling wind and teeming rain. The thunder and lightning were awesome. It lasted all the next day. By this time, Dirk was frantic and when he eventually risked going outside, nothing could be seen beyond a few feet. He was so hungry, he could think of nothing but food. In desperation, he tried some leaves from a nearby tree but regurgitated the lot immediately.

Hunger finally compelled him to venture outside again. In heavy rain, he slid in the mud, caught his foot under a fallen branch and plunged headlong over the edge of the pathway knocking himself out. On regaining consciousness, it was almost dark. Grimacing and crying out with the pain, he crawled towards the back of the cave, dragging a badly broken right leg with portions of white bone protruding from the bleeding flesh.

"Dear Lord, blessed is your name. Help your servant. Help me please," he whispered as he manoeuvred himself into a sitting position.

After Dirk had bandaged his swollen bloody leg with his shirt, he leaned back, despairingly assessing his situation. His hunger and thirst were joined by the overwhelming agony of his tortured leg. Together they spelled disaster.

After a terrible night of hunger cramps and racking pain, broken occasionally by short periods of semi-consciousness, Dirk roused himself to a fine dawn. The storm had abated. His lower leg was now so swollen that his skin was stretched taut. He was desperately hungry and thirsty and there was absolutely nothing he could do about it.

13

As dusk closed in, the waves of excruciating pain increased in intensity. Dirk reviewed his life and thought about the future he had envisaged for himself. A happy marriage and a highly successful career, initiating opportunities for wealth when he returned to Amsterdam. Opening his money belt, he took out the rings and examined them. They had been chosen for a bride he would now never see. He replaced them carefully in the belt as the tears of sorrow and pain ran down his cheeks.

It wasn't the lack of water and food that caused the hallucinations three days later, although this contributed to the general malaise. It was the systematic and assiduous attention of increasing numbers of bacteria. Multiplying without opposition in the dead tissue of the lower leg, they inexorably attacked adjacent healthy flesh, which decomposed. The gangrenous tissue turned black. The putrefying cells stank. The body, unable to combat the infection, lapsed into unconsciousness.

Morning. Dirk was dead.

* * * * *

Nearly nine months later, a joyous event occurred for an Aboriginal family camped near a stand of eucalypts not far from the ocean. It was burnoru, the height of the hot season and in the late afternoon, following a scorching day, a young woman gave birth to a healthy boy. The elderly male of the family named the baby Mogang, meaning stranger, after a djanga with whom the family had made a brief connection. The child was light brown in colour and all judged him perfect, except the first wife, who considered his jaw and lower lip far too prominent.

CHAPTER 1
Beginnings

It was a gloomy winter's day in November 1823. Continuous rain hammered the library windows of an impressive mansion in an affluent suburb of Manchester. Thomas Peel Senior faced Thomas Peel Junior across a large oak desk. Thomas Senior held the dominant position by virtue of paternity and size. He could also shout the loudest.

"Damn you, Thomas!" he yelled, thumping his fist on the desk. "Don't you ever think of anyone but yourself? Your mother lies ill upstairs, I need assistance with the firm and you're talking about marrying some unknown, tawdry actress and moving to Scotland. You've done nothing since finishing Harrow except laze around the clubs of London. Now you have the temerity to front up and ask for an increase in your already substantial allowance. I won't have it! I just won't have it!"

Before his father was able to regain his breath, Thomas Junior interjected, addressing his father in an unusually controlled manner. "Sir, I am also concerned about Mother's illness. I know how much it worries you. It also worries me. However, as you have said on many occasions, unless Mother is removed to a warmer, drier climate her health is unlikely to improve." His large bulk shuffled to a more comfortable position. Although not as broad-shouldered as his father, he was nevertheless an impressive size.

"Well then, what about the business?" Thomas Senior asked. "If I relocate the family in the south, I'll not be able to continue the necessary day-to-day management. You know how the firm has grown in the past few years."

He continued, seemingly having to get it off his chest. "Five sons. One a reverend with a chronic illness, one a gentleman who sees no necessity nor inclination to work for the money he receives and three sons running their own businesses, two who choose to remain in a foreign country rather than assist their father." Almost as an afterthought, he added "And four daughters, who think money grows on trees. God, give me strength! For the last time, for the sake of the family, I am urging you to take over the control of the firm."

"No!" Thomas Junior replied, surprised at his own boldness. "Sir, we've been through this over and over again. I will not be tied to Manchester and the business. I have no interest in the business and find the constant concern about money distasteful to say the least."

Thomas Senior leapt to his feet in a towering rage. "Yes, but you're happy to siphon off money in large amounts to keep your gentlemanly habits fuelled!"

he spluttered. "Well, that's it then. All will be sold. Your mother, sisters and I will take up residence in the south of England. I'll see my lawyer in due course and you may expect to receive a final settlement from me. That will be it, Thomas. Don't expect any more. Ever! Ever! Do you hear? Go!" His father was shaking as he gestured towards the door.

Thomas Junior beat a hasty retreat. This certainly wasn't the response he had anticipated. Damn! What now? Tawdry actress indeed. Mary Ayrton was a lady. She had been on the stage but as a singer and accomplished musician. She was mature and loving and filled him with a sense of purpose. Any which way, he was determined to marry her and the sooner the better.

However, to be fair to Thomas Senior, he had tried everything within his power to provide for his second son. At Harrow, Thomas Junior was a good student and excelled in the manly sports of riding, shooting and hunting. Yet he did not get on with his fellows. In fact he was downright unpopular. Following school, he received a regular and generous allowance which allowed him to live an independent life. However, he had no close friends and no one in the family understood him or felt any affection towards him. He was a nonconformist and a show-off. At the age of twenty-four, he fathered an illegitimate son who was flaunted in front of the family and for whom he insisted on taking responsibility. He was puffed-up with his own self-importance and carried unrealistic ambitions about his future, because, as ambitious as he was, the ambition was not focused.

If one cared to look a little deeper, one would see a family jealousy that obsessed Thomas Junior. Although he hardly knew his cousin Robert Peel, he was continually reminded of his successes. Having secured double first class honours in classics and mathematics at Oxford, he entered Parliament at the age of twenty-one, became Chief Secretary for Ireland and in 1822 accepted a place in the Cabinet as Home Secretary. Now thirty-five, he was assured of an illustrious future. At thirty years of age, Thomas, with a huge ego and lofty ambition, was working as a clerk in a lawyer's office.

* * * * *

Four days after the confrontation with his father, Thomas' older brother Robert died from galloping consumption.

Six weeks later, Thomas married Mary Charlotte Charité Dorking Ayrton in a private ceremony with two members of his club as witnesses.

Five months later, Thomas Peel Senior placed his house and business on the market for sale.

Fourteen months later, Thomas Peel Senior, his wife Dorothy and their four daughters moved to Penzance in Cornwall.

* * * * *

16

Thomas Peel received no word from the family solicitor. The allowance continued but at a reduced rate. He rightly assumed that the property and business had not yet been sold and in 1825 moved to Scotland with his wife, their first born, Julia and his illegitimate son Frederick. Thomas was to manage the estate of Carnousie and act as Master of the Hunt for Lord Kennedy. It was the first time he had been financially embarrassed and therefore the first time he had been forced to apply for a position. He was not a happy man and the situation was not improved by constant nagging from Mary, who demanded that he ask his father for assistance. Thomas refused to do so.

* * * * *

On 28th November 1826, Captain James Stirling R.N. completed berthing arrangements for HMS *Success* at the Port Jackson docks in the colony of New South Wales. As a visiting Captain of the Royal Navy, he had received a formal invitation to attend Governor Ralph Darling in the early evening and then join the Darling family for dinner.

It was a glorious, balmy evening as Stirling was transported by hansom to the Governor's residence. Smoothing the front of his naval frockcoat, he contemplated his present situation. At thirty-five, he should be consolidating his career rather than starting over again. All had progressed well until 1814, when Rear-Admiral Sir Charles Stirling was relieved of duty following a court martial on charges of corruption. His uncle had sponsored his naval career and some even inferred that his nephew had received preferential treatment. In any event, during 1819, James Stirling was taken off the active list, and placed on half pay, along with 200,000 other sailors and soldiers being demobilised following the Napoleonic Wars.

Business concerns, travel in Europe and marriage to Ellen, daughter of James Mangles, a wealthy director of the East India Company and High Sheriff of Surrey, had all been pleasant diversions. However, financial upheavals of the mid-1820s, which caused the collapse of the family business, had forced James to seek a return to active service. He frowned as he reflected on the events of the past decade. Things were certainly not looking prosperous on the home front and this was the reason he was particularly interested in opportunities which might offer themselves in the colonies. His personal motto was 'Make every post a winner'.

Stirling was ushered into the Governor's library, a comfortable, airy room bordered with shelves of well worn books. French windows led to a luxuriant garden. As the aide-de-camp announced him, Stirling clicked his heels and gave a short bow from the waist. Governor Darling met him with a vigorous handshake and friendly smile. He had an open face, with high eyebrows that gave him a slightly surprised look.

"Captain Stirling, welcome to Sydney. I trust matters concerning your ship are in order and you will enjoy a relaxed evening." In turn he appraised Stirling, who came so strongly recommended. He saw a slim man of medium height with a long straight nose and brown eyes. His dark hair was combed forward and bushy sideburns continued below his ears. He seemed of serious intent.

"Thank you, Your Excellency. All is in order and with your encouragement I shall be delighted to enjoy such an evening," Stirling replied with a pronounced Scottish accent.

The Governor motioned his guest to a sofa and seated himself on a leather chair nearby. "Before we commence the pleasantries, I would appreciate you providing me with some background information on your business in the colony. I will then bring you up to date on some strategic activities I have recently authorised."

"Of course, sir." Stirling inclined his head and stretched his lean body into a comfortable position. It was wonderful not to be on a rolling ship for a change.

"Please start by informing me of your brief. I have some knowledge from the dispatches delivered this afternoon but dispatches of necessity are short. You are probably aware that I have little faith in the settlement of northern Australia. I believe it to be a combination of business knavery and official folly. However, for reasons beyond my understanding, the Colonial Office continues to pursue same. Now it appears you're being sent to the rescue of another failure."

"That may well be so sir, as the *Success* has been commissioned to transfer the present settlement of Fort Dundas on Melville Island to another site, I believe closer to the fishing grounds further to the east."

"It is my belief that it's all trial and error," the Governor retorted impatiently. If it doesn't work here, we'll try again elsewhere. All a waste of time, money and lives. We'd be much better served establishing a permanent settlement on the west coast. I'm doing my bit for that cause at the moment." He proceeded with great satisfaction to relate to Stirling how he had anticipated orders from Lord Bathurst, the Colonial Secretary and already dispatched Major Edmund Lockyer in charge of a detachment from the 39th Regiment in the brig *Amity* to King George Sound. "I sincerely hope I'm right or there'll be trouble," he added more seriously.

Darling leaned forward. "Stirling, do you know how many damned Frenchies have been sneaking around our coast?" He did not wait for a reply. "Since late last century, we've had evidence of the comings and goings of Vancouver, d'Entrecasteaux, Baudin, Hamelin, Freycinet, du Camper and de Bougainville. That we know about! Rumour has it that d'Urville is on our southern shores at present. Heaven knows how many ships are lurking around our coastline without our knowledge. They make no secret that they are making extensive surveys, penetrating miles inland in some places. What a cheek!" The Governor was becoming excited. "What we need is a drink," he said, ringing the bell.

After brandies were served, Darling resumed. "Major Lockyer has been given instructions to be firm with any Frenchies that show up. It should be signified to them that the whole of New Holland is subject to His Britannic Majesty's Government and that orders have been given for the establishment of King George Sound as a settlement for the reception of criminals. And if they don't like it, we'll arrange another Waterloo. Eh? Another brandy before dinner?" he asked, still chuckling at his own joke. But Stirling knew he was in earnest and judged it to be a favourite theme.

Eventually, the butler interrupted them to remind the Governor that his family awaited them in the ante-room and they joined them for introductions. Mrs Elizabeth Darling was short and dark, with a pleasant, happy disposition and Cornelia about eight years old and Frederick about five were on their best behaviour to meet the distinguished guest. It was explained there was a baby, Sydney, an obvious name choice for their first born in the colony, already asleep. The children were then bundled off to bed by the nurse. Mrs Darling was young, much younger than her husband and again with child. She chatted on, making easy conversation, mainly related to recent happenings in the colony. Stirling found her captivating. In spite of constantly deferring to her husband, she was obviously an extremely astute woman. He learned of the success of the Australian Agricultural Company chartered in 1824 and of the sheep and cattle mania seizing all classes of people. Interesting, Stirling mused. He was surprised to find that the population of New South Wales had reached 30,000 persons.

After shipboard fare, dinner at Government House was an epicurean delight. Tomato soup, roast lamb with mint sauce and fresh vegetables, followed by apple pie with fresh whipped cream. Stirling attacked his food with relish.

A fine claret was served with the meal and they stood as the Governor made the toast to the King. "One of our earliest and finest wines," he commented, holding the glass up to the light from the chandelier. "Gregory Blaxland, a successful explorer of the Blue Mountains, had the foresight to establish a vineyard at Parramatta. Brought the vines from the Cape. Some of his prime clarets have won medals in London."

Polite conversation and the intimacy of the family group caused Stirling to long for Ellen his young wife, barely nineteen years herself and Andrew their baby son, born only months before he sailed for the colony. The greatest disadvantage of service in the navy was being away for such long stints. He shook himself back to the present. All in all, it had been a most convivial and informative evening. The Governor and his Lady had given him much to think about.

As a result of the previous night's conversation, Stirling decided to spend two days exploring Sydney Town and its outskirts. He dressed in one of his few civilian outfits; double-breasted frockcoat, strapped pantaloons, fine linen shirt and the fashionable mailcoach neckcloth, topped with a tall beaver hat. The driver of the hired hansom, an ex-convict, was an asset as a guide. He knew a great deal about Sydney and its environs and seemed pleased to be able to impart his knowledge. Within the hour, the early morning heat of the antipodean summer had Stirling stripped to shirt and trousers. Wearing a plaited straw hat purchased from a street vendor, he felt cooler and more comfortable and, judging by the clothing of the locals, was now far more appropriately dressed.

Sydney was a bustling town. 'On the move' was the way Stirling would describe it. There were many new buildings in different stages of construction and convicts in grey and yellow jackets and duck overalls were laying old dirt roads with limestone slabs. Abundant fresh farm produce was available from stalls and drays. Stirling selected some oranges and found them delicious. There was an air of optimism and anticipation, refreshing after the poverty and social unrest of England, where the post-war period had resulted in massive unemployment and thousands starving to death.

As the hansom progressed west, buildings became sparse and farms increased in number. The homesteads were much larger than English holdings and looked prosperous. Stirling asked the driver about the breed of sheep. "Merinos they be, sir. Capt'n Macarthur had them brought here at first and crossed them with a Cape breed. You'll find them everywhere in the colony now."

Stirling stayed overnight at a comfortable inn and again enjoyed roast lamb. He gleaned a great deal of information about sheep farming and wool production from three prosperous-looking gentlemen present in the dining room. They boasted about expanding their holdings and indicated a strong confidence in the future of the colony. Wine from Blaxland's vineyard was available and two dozen bottles of the finest claret were purchased.

The drive back to Sydneytown the following morning was leisurely and enjoyable and at dinner aboard ship that evening Stirling finished a bottle of Blaxland's claret and thought it an excellent vintage.

* * * * *

The First Lieutenant roused Stirling soon after dawn. "Excuse me, sir. Sorry to wake you but I wish to report that the watch has espied a French man-of-war sailing into Sydney Cove."

20

"Thank you, Jefferies." Stirling dressed hurriedly and strode out on deck. Adjusting his telescope, he peered at the approaching ship. It flew the French tricolour and Stirling reckoned it was bound to be d'Urville. His face broke into a delighted grin. This will raise the Governor's hackles!

Late morning, Stirling received a sealed message, delivered personally by the Governor's aide-de-camp. It read:

> *Captain James Stirling, HMS Success*
> *Would you be so good as to be in attendance at Government*
> *House at 3 o'clock this afternoon of 2nd December.*
> *In haste,*
> *Governor Ralph Darling*

Stirling arrived at Government House at ten minutes to the hour.

"Good afternoon, Captain Stirling," the aide-de-camp greeted him. Two other naval officers of Captain's rank were already waiting, somewhat impatiently it appeared, in the ante-room.

"I have pleasure in introducing Captain George Scott of HMS *Warspite* and Captain William Fawkner of HMS *Volaze*. Gentlemen, may I present Captain Stirling of HMS *Success*." The captains clicked heels and nodded.

"Would you follow me, sirs." The aide-de-camp led them into a study cum office. Stirling noticed that the wood-panelled room had no windows.

"Gentlemen, please join me. Thompson, remain and take notes as necessary." As the men seated themselves at a large table, the Governor rose and began pacing around the room. The men followed him with their eyes. Eventually he cleared his throat. "Thank you for coming at short notice. I have asked you to attend this meeting to discuss a matter of importance. As you would be aware, the *Astrolabe* arrived this morning. I have already met with Captain Dumont d'Urville, who would lead me to believe that the object of his expedition is solely for the purpose of general science. However, I am not convinced, since he admitted to spending eighteen days exploring King George Sound. A devilish long time for general observations and even the collection of scientific samples. It is my opinion that he was assessing the Sound as a porting facility." He thumped the table. "d'Urville must think us simpletons. I consider it fortunate that he found three of His Majesty's ships here. He may in consequence be more circumspect in his proceedings than he otherwise might have been."

The Governor returned to his chair. "I have had Thompson take down some orders, which I will now put to you." He placed his hands flat on the table and leaned forward conspiratorially. "There will be no written copy but by the time you leave Government House today you will understand the meaning and intent of the orders perfectly." He paused for the significance of this statement to penetrate. "First, I am requiring that at least two of our ships remain in Port Jackson at all times until d'Urville departs. You will need to liaise on this to ensure that this occurs. Secondly, I am demanding that there be no loose talk, particularly in relation to sailing schedules, while crew members are in the company of the French. This will necessitate a modicum of secrecy. Thirdly, I am asking you, whenever possible in appropriate gatherings, especially those where any French officers may be assembled, to stress that the settlement at King George Sound will be permanent and that all of New Holland is now held to be under the jurisdiction of His Majesty King George IV. Gentlemen, let us now discuss these issues."

The discussion continued for over an hour. After Darling stressed that confidentiality must be maintained, he asked Stirling to remain behind. Thompson was dismissed.

"Well, Stirling. What did you make of all that?" Darling looked very pleased with himself as he motioned Stirling to be reseated.

Stirling suspected he was about to undergo some sort of test and quickly gathered his thoughts. "Sir, under the circumstances, I am of the opinion your orders are timely. In spite of d'Urville's remonstrations about a scientific expedition, he has sailed a man-of-war into our waters, without obtaining permission. In my judgment, he has cannon of size enough to fire on us where we sit right this minute. Highly unlikely, I am sure, sir," he added quickly as Darling started, "but I would class his behaviour to be disrespectful, as well as being downright impudent. The precautions you have taken are entirely appropriate."

The Governor leaned back in his chair looking pleased with himself.

"However, may I make a suggestion, sir?"

"Please do, Stirling."

"Perhaps you might consider dispatching a communique to the *Astrolabe* forthwith, ordering d'Urville to raise anchors and remove his ship to a new anchorage, at least one mile from the Cove. It is what he would expect."

Governor Darling paused and tugged on his beard thoughtfully before answering. "Yes," he said. "A sound suggestion, if only to assert authority." He smiled. "Even an army man should have considered that."

"Further, I have a favour to ask, sir," Stirling continued. "I would seek your permission to approach d'Urville socially, with the view of seeking out further information. It may not be helpful, but on the other hand it might provide another side to his story. In any event, I would be interested in hearing of his adventures."

"You don't need my permission, Stirling. However, under the circumstances I am pleased that you asked and pleased to accede. A bit of espionage in the colony. Eh! Let me know the results of your discussions. I'll await them impatiently."

* * * * *

Early the next morning, Stirling sent a message to d'Urville requesting permission to call upon him. The fresh-faced young midshipman acting as courier arrived back on board and, barely able to curtail his excitement, stiff-backed and standing to attention reported. "Captain Stirling, I have pleasure in informing you that Captain d'Urville would welcome you on board the *Astrolabe* at six bells in the forenoon."

"Thank you, Marshall. Then I'd better get a move on. Have the ship's boat stand by."

Captain d'Urville greeted Stirling on deck and the two men moved to the captain's cabin, which Stirling noted, with some annoyance, was much larger and more expensively outfitted than his own.

Fine French brandies were consumed while the captains discussed personal backgrounds and experiences. The subject of the Napoleonic Wars was mentioned, then politely discarded. Stirling found the Frenchman well read, enthusiastic about his adventures and an extremely good conversationalist. Dumont spoke fluent English, his description and explanation superb, much to Stirling's relief as his French was only passable. He found himself admiring d'Urville and appreciating his company.

Just after noon their conversation was interrupted when the French Captain received a communique. "Damned official games," he said impatiently. "Your Governor has ordered me to take the ship a mile further away from Sydney Cove. Does he think I would start another war by firing on a British settlement? I'm sorry Stirling but I must comply immediately."

Stirling took his leave, after inviting d'Urville to join him for dinner, while the *Astrolabe* was being provisioned. The Frenchman accepted the invitation for the following night. He muttered that he would now need more time to undertake preparations for sea, being required to anchor so much further out.

The evening aboard HMS *Success* was most agreeable. Conversation flowed easily, fostered by several bottles of Brush Farm's fine claret. The only communication Stirling judged to be of any strategic importance came after he commented on the continued attention the French had paid New Holland over such a long period of time.

d'Urville had downed his glass in a gulp and made an exasperated gesture. "I am of the opinion that our government has been greatly interested in the Southland since the 17th century, when French ships were sent to explore the southern seas. More so, after Cook mapped the east coast in 1770 precipitating the establishment of this colony. Since the Dutch lost any interest in New

23

Holland, only the French and the British have remained active with regard to commissioning exploratory expeditions. The British were decisive, while the French prevaricated and procrastinated and continue to do so. How do you think I feel about it? How do you think French explorers over the years have felt about it? I tell you, Stirling, we have felt both frustrated and stymied. And still they procrastinate. If the decision rested with me, I'd establish a settlement on the west coast immediately. Such a settlement would be extremely important in terms of trade and communication with Asian ports."

After d'Urville's departure, Stirling sat pondering over his final glass of wine. He allowed his mind to run over the events of the past few days. On analysis, the series of conversations seemed to add up to the greatest opportunity ever offered him. He yawned. Time enough on the morrow to begin formulating a plan. A plan for the future. He felt more optimistic and excited about the future than he had in a long time.

In the morning, Stirling awoke refreshed and with a remarkably clear mind. He washed and shaved, dressed, ate a light breakfast and compiled a short letter to Darling requesting an audience at the Governor's earliest pleasure. A midshipman was dispatched to deliver the missive immediately and ordered to await an answer. Stirling was not surprised to receive a reply in just under two hours, inviting him to wait upon the Governor at 4 o'clock that afternoon. He selected a quill, dipped it in ink and began making copious notes.

At the appointed hour, Stirling presented himself at Government House. He was taken to the windowless room, where Darling awaited. For the next hour, Stirling detailed his meetings with d'Urville during the previous two days and his interpretations of the sum total of the conversations. The explanation was systematic and thorough and he did not refer to his notes, which lay unopened on the table. Occasionally, Darling interrupted and asked a question.

"That's the sum total of my observations, sir," he said, when he had finished. "To me, it all points to a single conclusion."

The Governor's eyes lit up in anticipation. "Captain Stirling," he said. "I am of the firm conviction that we must expedite events. What do you suggest?"

"Sir, *Success* will not be able to undertake her prescribed mission to Melville Island until the monsoon season is over. It is the time of devastating cyclones. Therefore, it seems that I will be confined to Sydneytown for the next five months at least, unless you deem it appropriate to assign me to special duties in the meantime. Perhaps these special duties could involve the Swan River area?"

Darling fell back in his chair, slapping his knees and roaring with laughter. "Stirling," he said, "you're as cunning as a fox. I like it. Special duties, eh? If I deem it appropriate to assign them, eh? You'll have them, I promise, when I have a proposal in writing detailing why I should commission you to explore the Swan River area. It must be a reasoned argument, not too long and not too short and be totally convincing. You have a week to produce such a proposal. The best of luck, my good man." The Governor began laughing again, as Stirling strode down the hallway. "I like it, I like it," he repeated again, in farewell.

Stirling was an intelligent, well educated man, who read widely. He had an excellent memory, which he could draw on like an encyclopaedia. During the first four years of marriage, they had lived near Ellen's family. James Mangles directed a company involved in extensive trade in the Indian Ocean. Countless hours had been spent poring over charts and books related to the region. Stirling was always interested in the discussions, mainly because of the implications for defence but also because he hoped that at some stage in the future he would be offered a position in the company. Such genuine and shared interest had fostered the gathering and storage of a great deal of information.

A week to the day, Stirling presented Governor Darling with a detailed proposal and justification of the potential and need for the settlement of the west coast of New Holland, specifically the Swan River region. Stirling argued cogently on the basis of his professional observation. He emphasised that the Swan River would be of agricultural, commercial and strategic importance and urged that immediate action be taken in this regard to prevent any foreign power from occupying such a position. Mention was made of the many recent French expeditions in the area.

Darling was convinced. He wanted to be convinced, as he had long held the view that all New Holland should be under the British flag. Here was a reputable captain, with no assigned responsibilities for five months, who was eager to be involved with the future settlement of the Swan River. Stirling's credentials were impeccable. He was a knowledgeable and experienced naval officer and in addition well connected, having married into a family that was influential both in Westminster and the East India Company. It was also obvious that he was extremely ambitious and possessed of a thoroughly ruthless energy.

Summoning Stirling to his residence, the Governor congratulated him on his proposal, which in his opinion would stand up to any scrutiny. He then gave Stirling orders to prepare HMS *Success* for an exploratory expedition to the Swan River and adjacent areas of the west coast of Australia. The expedition was to leave as soon as possible. Darling would have given almost anything to be going with him.

With Charles Fraser, the New South Wales government botanist aboard, HMS *Success* sailed from Port Jackson on 17th January 1827, arriving off the Swan River on 5th March. Sixteen days were spent exploring the adjacent area and a further seven the coastline between Rottnest Island and Cape Leeuwin.

Fraser echoed Stirling in compiling a glowing report regarding all aspects of the area. By their very quality of description, any reader would be convinced of the possibilities for successful settlement. The report was punctuated with superlatives, high expectations and almost excessive enthusiasm. Stirling concluded by saying: 'Swan River appears to hold out every attraction that a country in a state of nature can possess. I am therefore of the opinion that it ought to be immediately retained'.

On his arrival back in Sydney Cove, Stirling submitted his report to Darling, who enthusiastically endorsed the findings. A copy was dispatched to Lord Bathurst, along with a recommendation from Darling, that a settlement be established at Swan River, on the first ship departing for England.

While Stirling waited for *Success* to be provisioned, he spent some days gathering information regarding the availability of suitable land for sheep farming. He frequented the lounge of the Pastoralists Hotel in King Street, made contacts at the Navy Club in the Rocks and by appointment met the Chief Clerk in the Lands Department. Asking questions, listening carefully and studying maps, he learned a great deal. By the time a grateful Darling had rewarded him with 2560 acres for services to the colony, Stirling had purchased an additional 9600 acres of prime land to the south-west of Parramatta.

On Darling's advice, four days prior to sailing north, Stirling submitted a formal request asking to be considered for the superintendency of any colony established at Swan River. This was subsequently supported by Darling who wrote that Stirling's 'conduct and character made him well qualified for the situation he was so desirous of obtaining'.

HMS *Success* reached Melville Island in June and the settlement was relocated to Raffles Bay on mainland Australia. Stirling named the place Fort Wellington to mark the twentieth anniversary of the Battle of Waterloo, raised the British ensign, fired a salute and was glad to leave the mangrove swamps and myriads of insects behind.

When Stirling arrived at the East India station in Penang to report on his action, he was struck down with a severe fever. He was also homesick and missing his beautiful young wife Ellen, whom he had met when she was thirteen years of age, courted when she was fifteen and married the day she turned sixteen. He had spent precious little time with her to date. In addition, he was especially eager to ascertain the results of his and Darling's dispatches to the Colonial Office, which he was sure would be facilitated by his presence in London. After much reflection on his future, Stirling made a difficult decision. He put all his eggs in one basket, an unusual step for him and requested that he be invalided home on half pay.

Awaiting him in London on his arrival in April 1828 was a six month old dispatch informing him that it was not the intention of His Majesty's

Government to form a settlement at Swan River and accordingly his request for a superintendency could not be granted.

A dejected James Stirling returned to Woodbridge in Guildford and the love and devotion of Ellen. He rejoiced in finding his sturdy son walking and talking, even if the chatter was largely unintelligible. It was happiness greater than he could remember or had thought possible. Yet, in the background a burning ambition fermented. His family and especially his father-in-law pledged their full support in every effort to bring about the establishment of a settlement at Swan River.

CHAPTER 2

Swan River Mania

Thomas Peel hated fuss. From the day he made the decision to return to London, there was nothing but fuss. Mary was alternately excited and depressed. She had loathed her enforced exile in Scotland and longed for the music halls and theatres of London. Even the weather of London was appealing after the freezing winds of the north. On the other hand, two more children had been born. Thomas was now three and Dorothy just twelve months. Mary hoped that naming the first son and second daughter after their paternal grandfather and grandmother might lead to a reconciliation between Thomas and his parents but Thomas declined to even inform them. This brought on periods of hysteria, when Mary berated Thomas for days on end. On these occasions Thomas would ignore his wife and spend more time than usual fraternising with male acquaintances on adjacent estates. The idea of returning to London accompanied by four children and not having the opportunity to return to her previous lifestyle sent Mary into fits of depression. However, the attraction of London under any circumstances far outweighed Scotland's isolation and she therefore became excited and then fussed. Thomas couldn't wait to return to the peace and quiet of familiar all-male clubs.

Eventually, all was ready and on 3rd May 1828, they took the coach, arriving in London six days later. It was a most uncomfortable and unpleasant experience. The children cried from Carnousie to London, non-stop and in unison. Thomas escorted Mary and the children to their accommodation in Osnaburgh Street near Regent's Park, gave the newly recruited servants their orders and escaped to the Windham Club forthwith.

During the following weeks, Thomas spent a great deal of time at the Club. He had enjoyed the outdoor environment in Scotland but now back in London was in his element. Cousin Robert, after resigning from his Cabinet post the previous year over the issue of Catholic emancipation, had been returned as Home Secretary and Leader of the House of Commons. Thomas bathed in reflected glory and, while his relative retained such a position of power, was determined to make the most of it.

Colonel Thomas Potter Macqueen, a member of the House of Commons, who owned extensive grants of land in New South Wales, became acquainted with Thomas Peel. Assessing him as an easy target and perhaps a useful political ally in the future, Macqueen struck up a friendship with the younger man. He judged him to be a strange combination of intelligence, cunning, naivety and gullibility.

Thomas became enamoured of the idea of becoming a landowner of substance in the colonies. He avidly read all the literature he could lay his hands on and barraged Macqueen with questions, absorbing the answers like a sponge. He discussed the great southern continent with anyone who would give him the time. Peel became an instant expert on the antipodes and a huge bore to boot.

* * * * *

At the first opportunity, Stirling set about reversing the British Government's decision with regard to the settlement of the Swan River. In his usual methodical manner, he prepared a careful plan of attack. Returning to London, he lobbied individuals in positions of authority and forwarded a letter to the Under Secretary for the Colonies reiterating the salient points from his original report on the suitability of the Swan River for settlement. Fortuitously, Sir George Murray and his assistant Horace Twiss, who had recently received political appointments associated with the Colonial Office, were friends of James Mangles, Stirling's father-in-law.

It was made known to Stirling that the only impediment to the settlement proceeding was the question of expense. Accordingly, he changed his emphasis and pressed for private settlement, as this would reduce the financial commitment of the government.

Such a scheme would require demonstrated support from financial backers and the public, so Stirling launched an immediate publicity campaign through English newspapers. Provided with a copy of Stirling's original report to the Colonial Office, the *Hampshire Telegraph* initiated the action in Portsmouth, highlighting the positive features of the Swan River and its environs. London newspapers, including *The Times* and *Sun*, reprinted the article. Although there was a positive response from the public, no major backers came forward. Stirling was still optimistic but it was evident that the government must indicate its intention and willingness to back the proposed settlement before individuals would commit themselves. It was a dilemma.

* * * * *

Macqueen, hearing from his parliamentary colleague Sir George Murray about Captain James Stirling's exploration of the Swan River area and his interest in the establishment of a colony for free settlers, decided to take a bold step. Although the details were still sketchy, he arranged for James Stirling and Thomas Peel to be present at the Windham Club at the same time and then took the opportunity of introducing them and initiating a conversation about the colony of New South Wales. In no time at all, Stirling and Peel were engrossed in discussion.

It was inevitable that Stirling and Peel would meet. Both were from wealthy backgrounds, both had connections with important and influential men, both were ambitious and both had an avowed interest in the colonies. It was only a matter of time before an astute observer would see potential benefit in bringing them together. Macqueen was a great believer in building bridges between individuals for their mutual advantage and, of course, his own.

* * * * *

On the first floor of the Windham Club, Macqueen and Peel sat smoking their pipes and reading the latest edition of *The Times*. Macqueen dropped his paper to the floor and stretched his legs. He peered out of the window at the early evening activity in Pall Mall before turning to Peel.

"So, Peel, where is all this enthusiasm leading, eh? Do you intend pursuing your interest in the colonies?" Macqueen asked casually. He didn't give Peel time to answer before adding, "That Stirling fellow has the right idea. He's not worrying about a colony where all the best land has been allocated. By hook or by crook, he's intending to be a prime mover in establishing a new colony. It's a shame really that we can't get in on the deal. We could make a fortune." He paused to let the final comment sink in. Peel's eyes were wide open.

Pursing his lips and drawing on his pipe, Macqueen continued. "Schenley and Vincent could be interested in investing in a scheme. Only to do with the Swan River, I would suspect. Of course, with my experience in negotiating land grants and your connections, we would form a rather impressive syndicate. What are your thoughts about such an association, Peel?" Needless to say Peel indicated more than a little eagerness to proceed immediately.

* * * * *

Thomas Peel, Thomas Macqueen, Sir Francis Vincent and Edward Schenley met in a private room at the Club and began exploring possibilities. Very soon they were absorbed in earnest deliberations.

Two hours later, Macqueen called for attention. "Well gentlemen, it appears there is agreement. We will make an immediate approach to the Colonial Office. Peel, I suggest you take the front running with this since your connections are the strongest. Twiss will be obliged to take seriously any proposal you put forward. Our combined weight should at least guarantee us a reasonable hearing." Schenley and Vincent nodded, accepting the suggestion as though it was the first time they had heard it.

"Gentlemen, it will be my pleasure and privilege to do so," Peel responded in pompous fashion.

* * * * *

Returning from parliamentary business in the north, Sir George Murray found the usually sedate Colonial Office in an uproar. The publicity campaign initiated through the English newspapers had stirred just the reaction Stirling had anticipated. They were calling it 'Swan River mania'. The Office was inundated with inquiries. Sir George had been informed that it was the brainchild of the ambitious Captain Stirling, who was determined to be involved in the establishment of such a colony. Murray was not surprised. He knew and respected the family and had heard the whispers. No turning back now! He issued instructions to the Admiralty to carry out all necessary preparations for taking possession of the western coast of New Holland. Captain Charles Howe Fremantle was to be commissioned to sail immediately in HMS *Challenger* to annex the area.

Stirling had won. He was jubilant. All his careful plans had come to fruition, with a bonus. There would be a colony at Swan River and it would comprise free settlers. A great victory! Yet it was only the beginning. Now the negotiations would begin in earnest.

* * * * *

Thomas Peel had a problem. He had led the other members of the Association to believe he had the financial resources required for involvement in the venture. He did not. A runner was sent to the family lawyer demanding an urgent meeting. Contact was also made with the Colonial Office, requesting that Horace Twiss see him as soon as possible. It was a tribute to the Peel name that appointments were arranged by both parties for Peel's preferred day and time.

When Peel first became interested in New South Wales, he took certain steps regarding the possibility of receiving an advance share of his final inheritance as suggested by his father at the conclusion of their last and stormy meeting. This was left with the lawyer to finalise. On the death of his older brother Robert, Thomas became the eldest son. The lawyer was confident he could arrange a suitable settlement and so it eventuated. On the sale of his Manchester assets, his father authorised the deposit of £30,000 into his son's account at the Bank of England. However, there were two provisos.

The lawyer coughed nervously. "The first stipulation, Mr Peel, is that you will never request money from any member of your immediate family." As Peel had no intention of ever deigning to request money from his family, he nodded. "The second stipulation is that you will leave England within twelve months and not return until after the death of your father. You are to sign a contract to that effect before arrangements will proceed. If you refuse, you will lose your right to any share of the inheritance." Rather severe the lawyer thought but then, in discussions with Thomas Peel Senior, the depth of feeling underlying the animosity between father and son was evident.

Although greatly pleased to be in receipt of the legacy, Thomas was astounded by the second condition. If he accepted the deal and then the syndicate's proposal was not negotiated satisfactorily, he would have no choice but to travel overseas. If he didn't accept, he would lose his share of the inheritance anyway. It was Hobson's choice. Thomas signed the contract. He did not tell Mary.

His meeting with Horace Twiss was rather more propitious. The Parliamentary Under-Secretary for Colonies seemed genuinely pleased to hear of the Association's intentions. Peel was surprised to find that the Admiralty had been advised by Sir George Murray only the previous day to annex the western coast of New Holland. What an amazing coincidence! He sent runners to call the syndicate to an immediate meeting.

Next morning, the four members of the Association, each with his own lawyer, together with an independent accountant, met at the Club to draw up a proposal for submission to Sir George Murray. Thomas informed the members that the Admiralty had commissioned Captain Fremantle only two days before to claim the western coast of New Holland but none seemed overly surprised. The meeting continued all day. The lawyers wrote ceaselessly and the accountant covered page after page with figures. Eventually there was consensus and the lawyers withdrew to finalise the documentation. After becoming signatories to the proposal, the men toasted the Association with numerous brandies as they brashly discussed the future.

When Peel was invited to meet with Twiss to discuss the proposal, he received an encouraging response. However, Twiss should never have been placed in the position of negotiating such a proposition. He owed his appointment to the patronage of Robert Peel and was consequently at a disadvantage when dealing with his cousin.

Twiss also had connections with Stirling's in-laws and, not knowing who else to turn to for counsel, invited Stirling to the Colonial Office to assist in evaluating the Association's submission. After they had perused the proposal and discussed it in general terms, Stirling made some calculations. "You will need to have these figures verified Horace but I estimate that the gentlemen concerned are proposing to invest £300,000, for which they will receive the right to select four million acres of land."

Embarrassed because he had not calculated the figures himself, Twiss muttered angrily about being in such a difficult position. Stirling silently agreed. He could appreciate the situation, as he was about to exert some pressure on Twiss himself.

"Horace, I think a combined approach to the negotiation of the Association's proposal is necessary. As you would be aware, preliminary approaches have been made to me by Sir George regarding the stewardship of the colony. I am reasonably confident as to the outcome of these discussions. Although there has been no public announcement, there is an expectation in government circles and on Fleet Street that I will be offered the position. A further meeting with Sir George has been arranged for this evening and I hope it will bring some finality to the matter. I would be pleased to meet with the gentlemen in your company to put forward some appropriate conditions and perhaps restrictions. I cannot believe that they would expect to have their proposal accepted carte blanche."

Stirling could hear Twiss' sigh of relief. He could see the man visibly relax.

"Thank you for your support, James. I think it an excellent suggestion. Could we discuss the restrictions you would impose?"

A clerk was called to act as scribe. When Stirling finished outlining his recommendations, he said, "Horace, I suggest you arrange for the meeting to be held in your office and don't inform the others you have invited me to be present. Strategically, it may be useful." Twiss hastened to agree.

* * * * *

Peel and Macqueen were nominated to represent the Association. When they arrived at the office of the Colonial Under Secretary, they were surprised to find Stirling there. The men nodded to one another. Twiss welcomed them.

"Gentlemen, there have been further developments concerning the establishment of a colony at Swan River. Captain Stirling, would you please update the Association members with regard to the administration of the settlement."

Macqueen smelled a rat. Stirling appeared too relaxed and confident.

"At a meeting last night, Sir George Murray asked that I assume responsibility for the establishment of the Swan River settlement. Further, I am to be appointed the administrator with the status of Lieutenant-Governor. I am pleased to say that the colony is expected to be self-sufficient and will not be connected to the eastern colonies. It will answer directly to this Office. I will receive no monetary remuneration for my services. However, I have been offered the priority right to select grants totalling 100,000 acres. This, of course, impacts on the requests made in your proposal."

Macqueen's face reddened and he looked decidedly angry.

Twiss intervened at this point with a deliberate cough. "Gentlemen, there are further amendments I should bring to your notice." He proceeded to read out the list of changes and restrictions.

Macqueen was now furious. "This is totally unfair and improper," he protested. "You gave Peel a verbal assurance." Peel nodded vigorously. "We have committed money, made undertakings, given our word to potential clients.

How can you face us and tell us we now have amendments to our proposal? Twiss, this is outrageous!" Macqueen shook with anger.

Knowing that Stirling was now the key player in the affair and would back him to the hilt, Twiss was unperturbed by the outburst. He spoke slowly as if to allow time for his comments to be absorbed. "The verbal endorsement was approval in principle only and was never any more than that. I have decided to recommend these amendments and am confident they will be accepted by Sir George. Every step will be taken to ensure they are vigorously enforced." Twiss concluded, "It is immaterial to the government whether you proceed or not but if you choose to go you will be treated as individuals and not as patrons of the settlement."

Macqueen stood. "Mr Twiss, be assured that I shall be in touch with Sir George immediately! Peel, I can see no reason to continue this meeting. I am leaving." He stormed from the room.

Peel started to follow, then turned to Twiss. "Mr Twiss, I accept the offer. Regardless of the Association's actions and decisions, I intend going with Captain Stirling under any circumstances." He nodded to the seated men, who looked decidedly surprised and departed.

"That's done it," Macqueen said, as they reached the footpath and he signalled his hansom. "Peel, contact the others and let them know the results of our meeting and Stirling's amendments."

"Stirling's?" Peel queried.

"Of course," Macqueen replied, impatient with the man for being so easily duped. "They were Stirling's all right. Twiss wouldn't have concocted them on his own. I'm going to call on Sir George now to put our case. Wish me luck. We're going to need it."

All the protestations and appeals to Sir George Murray were dismissed. However, Twiss eventually compromised and the amendments were softened to allow each Association member up to 250,000 acres. Macqueen, Schenley and Vincent withdrew from the Association. Peel couldn't withdraw. He had no choice, because he had signed a contract to leave the country. The problem was that he barely had sufficient money to go it alone. Some of his inheritance had already been spent in keeping up appearances. Day-to-day expenses in London were costly, especially those associated with the Club.

After lengthy negotiations with the Colonial Office, Peel signed the final papers on 29th January. By the agreement, he was given priority of choice, after Stirling, of 250,000 acres, which he chose on the southern banks of the Swan and Canning Rivers and, since the other Association members had withdrawn, a further 250,000 acres would be allotted when he had landed four hundred settlers. A final stipulation, inserted just before he signed, made it an imperative that the first shipload of emigrants be landed before 1 November 1829, if the priority choice of land was to be settled.

Stirling had played a brilliant hand with his cards held close to his chest. Having seen the Association as a potential monopoly and therefore dangerous to his plans, he had broken it. When Twiss told him the Colonial Office had received over a hundred requests for information from prospective settlers in just over a month, he knew there would be no shortage of emigrants. His key strategy of carefully fostering the spread of Swan River mania had certainly worked and worked well. At the moment the newspapers were describing it as the promised land!

* * * * *

On 9th February 1829, the *Parmelia*, a vessel of 449 tonnes, commanded by Captain Luscombe, sailed from Plymouth on the tide. Hundreds saw the ship on its way. Sir George Murray arrived by coach to personally farewell Stirling and publicly acknowledge the approval of the British Government. Families and friends gave the *Parmelia* a send-off to remember with flags, streamers and bunting. The band played 'God save the King' and 'Abide with me' and there was much weeping and wailing on the wharf and the ship. The passengers comprised the first seventy emigrants to the western coast of Australia. Some were enthusiastic, some apprehensive, some downright frightened. However, all were optimistic. Through the early morning mist, HMS *Sulphur* could be seen ploughing along in the wake behind. Besides provisions, it transported a detachment of soldiers from the 63rd Regiment of Foot under the command of Captain Frederick Chidley Irwin, whose responsibility was the security and protection of the colonists.

Lieutenant-Governor-elect James Stirling stood on the aft deck with his arm around Ellen who was with child. He whispered in her ear and she responded by looking up at him and smiling. "Yes, James," she replied. "Yes."

CHAPTER 3
Point of No Return

On occasions, Thomas Peel could be an extremely impetuous man and yesterday had been one of those occasions. On impulse Thomas had gone to the races. He lost. In fact he did not pick a single winner. Returning to the Windham Club, he tried to recoup his losses by playing cards but Lady Luck had deserted him. He doubled his bets and his IOUs mounted. In one disastrous day he lost almost £9,000! He was beside himself in frustration and exasperation. How could he have been so reckless, so downright stupid? It wasn't the first time. He remained at the Club overnight and drowned his sorrows in port. Now he had a mammoth hangover and felt ten times worse.

Just before noon, he was approached by a stranger who introduced himself as John Harrison, a new member of the Club. Thomas put aside his newspaper and invited Harrison to join him. From the conversation that ensued Thomas learned that the newcomer was a London merchant of means.

"I ship goods to New South Wales for Mr Solomon Levey. He's done very well buying and selling land in the colony and has recently arrived in England to seek new investment opportunities. He is particularly interested in the Swan River area. I've heard around the Club that you might be looking for another partner, now the Association has disbanded."

Thomas sat bolt upright. "I would be delighted to meet with the gentleman," he said, breathing a sigh of relief. Perhaps his luck was changing at last.

The meeting with Solomon Levey at his business premises in Tokenhouse Yard was extremely fruitful. Peel found him to be a serious, rather dour man but straightforward and to the point. He was dressed immaculately in clothes of expensive cut. Levey made it obvious that he wanted to obtain access into the Swan River scheme and that he saw a business arrangement, with himself as the silent partner and Peel continuing to give his name to the scheme, as the best way to facilitate this entry. Peel was exuberant and agreed to meet with Levey after their lawyers had drawn up a draft contract for negotiation. Peel also agreed to provide £20,000 for the partnership. However, at this stage he no longer had £20,000.

The contract was signed in March and torn up in April, when Peel reluctantly admitted to Levey that he did not have the requisite money. In the same month, the Bill relating to the government of the Swan River Colony was presented to the English parliament. By strange coincidence, an article appeared in an official publication strongly emphasising the advantages of investing in the colony and giving the impression that it was to be founded by the government, or at the very least with the approbation and co-operation of the government. Consequently, public attention was drawn to the proposed settlement and specifically to the tentative grant of land made to Thomas Peel. The article further intimated that there was little incentive for any settler who did not procure land through Peel.

Peel was ecstatic, Levey surprised and encouraged. Another more complicated ten year partnership was drawn up. The agreement placed Levey in control of all the money and Peel in control of all the land under the title of Peel and Company. Peel did not deem it prudent to inform the Colonial Office of the arrangement, in view of his partner being both Jewish and an emancipist, preferring to maintain the public perception that he was the sole investor and promoter of the scheme.

After bolstering his failing courage with two double brandies, Peel caught a hansom cab home and relayed the news. There was an almighty row. The children were bundled off to their bedrooms by scurrying servants, leaving Thomas and Mary facing one another across the living room. Mary had never been the submissive wife. When she lost her temper, it was terrible to behold. With fists clenched at her sides and face contorted in anger, she shouted at Thomas. "How could you do such a thing? A new colony with nothing there. It could be a wilderness."

Thomas managed two words. "Stirling said---"

Mary interrupted. "You're a fool, Thomas! Anyone could see what Stirling has been up to, just by reading the newspapers."

Thomas acted quickly. He walked across the room with his arms outstretched and clasped his wife to his chest. This usually calmed her. She clung to him and began sobbing. "What about the children? There are wild black natives. What about the children's safety? You only think of yourself." Mary was blubbering into his shoulder.

"My dear, calm yourself. I am thinking of us all. It is a wonderful opportunity. It will make us our fortune in a few years and then we will return to England. You will have the house of your dreams, with all the servants you require. We will attend the theatre whenever you wish. The finest, most expensive fashions you desire will be yours and you'll be the toast of London. I will give you anything but this venture is essential for all this to take place. As you well know our allowance is barely adequate for us to pursue our present lifestyle."

Mary stopped weeping. She looked up, fluttered her eyes and said, "Could I really have anything I wanted, my dear?"

Thomas pulled her close and looked over her shoulder at his reflection in the wall mirror. He saw a liar. A total fraud. He said, "Of course, my darling, I promise."

Mary was excessively attentive to her husband for the remainder of the evening and particularly so after they retired to bed. She placed only one condition on the Swan River scheme about which she remained adamant. She, Julia, Thomas Junior and Dorothy would not travel to the colony until Thomas had provided appropriate accommodation and guaranteed safety for herself and the children. Frederick, who was now eleven years old, was to go with his father.

* * * * *

A large, make-shift office was opened in Piccadilly and staff employed. Peel placed Adam Armstrong, his newly-hired land surveyor, in charge of the clerks. With enormous energy, Peel set about the task of preparing for the venture of his life. Time was of the essence, as the first shipload of emigrants must be landed before 1st November and the voyage to the Swan River would take at least a hundred days. It was now the end of April, which meant the ship must sail by mid-July at the latest.

A handbill was issued outlining the conditions under which individuals could join the Association in order to avail themselves of land grants. Indenture contracts were drawn up, agents authorised, the *Gilmore* purchased, additional ships chartered and emigrants selected. The office was in a condition of continual chaos and the paperwork totally out of hand, so additional clerks were hired. There were lists, lists and more lists. The situation could only be described as pandemonium, with a mass of impatient individuals pushing and shouting for attention in Eagle Place. On one occasion, Peel lost his temper and, shoving through the crowd, flattened a particularly obstreperous individual. This resulted in some order for a short period of time. At the very least it made Peel feel better.

The weeks sped by and, realising the hopelessness of the time line, Peel made a final appeal to Twiss, asking for an extension of the arrival date for his first ship to the colony. The request was refused but Peel was informed he would be allowed to extend the landing of the remainder of his four hundred emigrants until the last day of April 1830. However, this concession did not solve the immediate problem and the schedule was becoming increasingly impossible to meet.

Thomas Peel and son Frederick took a coach to Plymouth and waited impatiently for the arrival of the *Gilmore* from London. Peel knew time was running out and this caused increasing frustration and anger. Day after day, the two of them prowled the wharves watching out for the ship. At night, a despondent Peel sat in the hotel's lounge, alternating between bursts of optimism and fits of depression. He was even missing Mary and the children. Where was that wretched Captain Geary?

* * * * *

Late on the first day of June, the *Parmelia* arrived at the Swan River and was sighted standing off Rottnest Island by the lookout at Arthur Head. Captain Charles Fremantle called for his telescope and as expected it was the *Parmelia*. The following morning, he was rowed across from HMS *Challenger* and introduced himself to Stirling.

"Join me in a light repast, Fremantle, as I have not as yet eaten." Fremantle accompanied Stirling to a cuddy off the main cabin and brought him up to date with developments on shore.

Stirling was delighted by the briefing. "You have achieved more than I had expected or hoped for in the time available, Fremantle. I commend you. It will give the colony a head start. Now, I would like to find passage into Cockburn Sound and anchor immediately. After nearly four months at sea, I am naturally eager to land the colonists and their gear as soon as possible."

Against Fremantle's advice, Stirling insisted on attempting to find a passage into Cockburn Sound. Within hours a storm blew up from the north-west and the *Parmelia* ran aground on a sandbank. To lighten the ship, the women and children were offloaded to either Carnac Island or HMS *Challenger* amidst much panic and confusion. All the boats from the *Parmelia* and HMS *Challenger* were used in an attempt to pull the ship from the sandbank. It took eighteen hours to free her but, on inspection, Stirling was greatly relieved to find that no serious damage had been incurred. Nevertheless, the final assessment indicated she had lost her foreyards, rudder, windlass, spare spars, longboat and skiff and was taking four inches of water an hour, which required continuous pumping. It had been touch and go.

HMS *Sulphur* arrived a week later, having been held up effecting repairs at Cape Town and joined the *Parmelia* at anchor in Cockburn Sound. That night Stirling gave a thanksgiving party aboard the *Parmelia* for the officers from the three ships and their wives. And thankful Stirling was, realising how close he had come to total disaster and the loss of his ship.

Over the next two weeks, crew from the HMS *Challenger* assisted with the disembarkation of emigrants and the establishment of the settlement. Because of continuing squally, wintry weather, the storehouses and huts were erected on the leeward side of Garden Island, fronting Careening Bay and the settlers were able to land their livestock and goods safely in calm, shallow water. Besides, the damaged *Parmelia* needed a safe anchorage for repairs, the colonists would be more comfortable and John Septimus Roe was given the chance to commence the necessary surveying on the mainland without hindrance and interference from impatient settlers. It was a typically well considered move by Stirling, especially since Garden Island was part of his own grant and the buildings could be useful in the future.

On 17th June, when the weather had moderated somewhat, the settlers on Garden Island assembled to hear Captain Irwin read the proclamation officially inaugurating the colony and appointing Captain James Stirling as Lieutenant-Governor. Stirling offered silent and heartfelt prayers at the conclusion of the reading. The following day, the ceremony was repeated for government officials at Rous Head on the northern bank of the Swan River.

Stirling chose a site twelve miles upstream for the capital of the new colony, which he named Perth in honour of Sir George Murray's electorate in Scotland. It was on a sloping hill facing south behind which lakes and swamps abounded. Strategically, it was a sound choice, being inaccessible to naval attack, yet the waterways were of sufficient depth for the transport of passengers and goods from the coast. A high hill a mile or so to the west provided a magnificent view across the wide expanse of river.

Two months later, the formal procedures followed when naval captains Stirling, Fremantle, Currie and Dance, in full naval uniform, were joined at the site of the capital by Captain Irwin and soldiers of the 63rd Regiment of Foot, resplendent in their uniforms of red, white and blue. Noteworthy civilian representatives were Peter Broun, the Colonial Secretary and John Septimus Roe, the Surveyor General. The assembled dignitaries were watched from a distance by a flock of brilliant green parrots, patched with several colours, that perched high in a eucalypt tree. Mrs Dance chopped down a sapling to commemorate the occasion, speeches were made, volleys were fired and cheers were raised. Disturbed by the rifle shots, the birds fled, their heads raised, emitting strident alarm calls.

A grateful Stirling rewarded Captain Fremantle with a land grant and officially named the settlement at Arthur Head in his honour, before HMS *Challenger* sailed for England.

As the weeks progressed and the weather moderated, the settlers were transported from Garden Island and relocated on the mainland south of the river mouth. They found low scrub, white sand hills and sand, sand and more sand. By the 5th September, town blocks in Perth and Fremantle had been surveyed by the industrious Roe and his team. Blocks on the river east of Perth were made available a month later. The settlement of the Swan River Colony had begun!

CHAPTER 4
Delays, Delays, Delays

Ex-Royal Navy lieutenant, William Geary, Captain of the *Gilmore*, had a fearful temper, which exploded almost spontaneously when he was placed under excessive pressure. He was not a capable man, particularly when dealing with people and consequently often found himself at boiling point with crew, passengers and especially owners or individuals to whom he was beholden. He was exasperated with Peel. The man brought out the worst in him, being rude, arrogant and patronising and harping continuously about the necessity for haste. Geary couldn't stand the sight of him. The feeling was mutual but Peel was of the opinion that the Captain should at least demonstrate a level of servility to his employer. This, Geary refused to contemplate.

The first of the indentured servants boarded the *Gilmore* at the London docks, as soon as permission was granted. Samuel and Annie Andrews, carrying their meagre possessions and leading two small children, boarded in mid-July. Samuel had explained that being early gave them the advantage of selecting a corner position in their allocated area before the arrival of the rest of the passengers and this would allow them to huddle better for warmth with their few belongings protected behind them. On their arrival Samuel had approached Tim Norton, the ship's carpenter, who persuaded the harassed Captain that an extra pair of hands skilled in woodwork would be very useful and the only cost would be a portion of ship's rations.

Samuel Andrews was a determined, honest and God-fearing man who committed himself totally to anything he wanted or believed in. He was devoted to his wife Annie, William their son of three years and Sara Jane just two years old. Three older children had died in the diphtheria epidemic of 1825, each choking to death in front of their sorrowful parents, as the symptomatic false membrane grew across their windpipes. Samuel was extremely grateful to have been offered a position as an indentured servant with Thomas Peel. The contract was for five years, for which Samuel would receive four shillings a day for labour and after three years would be allotted fifty acres of land, a huge grant in his eyes. With unemployment at its highest level since the Napoleonic wars, the family had been on the borderline of starvation the previous winter. They had lived in appalling conditions in a dilapidated, leaking shed at the rear of a run-down inn, where Samuel received a few pence a week as a yardman, not being able to find employment in his trade of carpentry. Only handouts of food from the parish church, of which they were regular communicants, had seen them through. Now, they had been offered a new beginning in a new country and eagerly, albeit apprehensively, looked forward to it.

As Annie fed the children gruel, she lovingly regarded her offspring. William was a beautiful child, far too beautiful for a boy. Sara Jane was also beautiful and possessed an inner serenity and contentment that was unusual in a child so young. Both had taken their mother's colouring and were fair in complexion, with snowy white hair and startling blue eyes. Each was possessed of an adventurous and curious nature and Annie found that keeping watch over them was a full-time job.

Over the past week there had been continual hustle and bustle, shouting, frequent swearing, banging, bumping and much confusion. Annie, in her quietly competent way and with her newly acquired knowledge of shipboard procedures, assisted the new arrivals as much as possible. It was clear that many of the emigrants were not as confident about the future as the Andrews were.

With days to go, their compartment in steerage was already overcrowded and being below the water line, there was little light or fresh air. Thirty adults and children scrambled for sleeping and eating space in an area 22 feet by 25 feet with headroom of only four feet to the beams. The holds were full and deck space limited with goods and animals crammed together. Horses, cattle, sheep, goats, geese and ducks would be transported on the upper deck in boxes made to size and bundles of hay for feeding were lashed to the bulwarks.

Late afternoon, Samuel arrived for his supper. "Things are happening, lass. I hear we are fully laden and the Captain wants to leave the day after tomorrow. It seems everybody is aboard, except those joining us in Plymouth including the Master. Tim says there have been some almighty rows between the Master and the Captain. He says it doesn't bode well for the voyage." Samuel spooned gruel into his mouth and followed it with a crust of bread, looking thoughtful as he chewed. "The Lord was watching over us when the agreement was made for me to help Tim with the carpentry," he said. "It's to continue. They've not been able to find another carpenter. And I'm to get some payment, Annie."

Annie looked relieved. "The extra money will be welcome. I was worried we wouldn't be able to afford fresh fruit at our first stop after Plymouth. Where will we be stopping?"

"Cape Town will be our only port of call. Mr Peel is trying to make up time. Something about priority grants, Tim says. Yes, Annie, I'm glad about the extra money too, especially for the sake of the babes." He put a reassuring arm around his wife. "All will work out, lass. Just wait and see. The Lord has been guiding us in our new venture, I feel sure."

Sara Jane's little arms were waving for attention. "Da," she said, falling into Samuel's lap. Her father stroked her head and held her affectionately, responding to his children's questions until it was time to return to work.

Samuel's information was correct and two days later in the early morning, amidst much noise, hymn singing, waving and weeping from the assembled crowd, the *Gilmore* was pulled from the docks by the ship's longboats, the crews rowing hard to join the outgoing tide. The Andrews' family had no one to see them off. Samuel stood quietly at the starboard rail watching the emotional scene. Down below, Annie cuddled her two children and comforted frightened women who knew they would never see England again.

Immediately following the docking of the *Gilmore* at Plymouth, Captain Geary met with Thomas Peel at the Royal Hotel, reporting that he had been delayed by unfavourable winds and a disputation with the crew. Almost a mutiny, he hastened to explain. Peel was not surprised. The crew probably found the Captain as thoroughly unpleasant and objectionable as he did. The interview ended on an acrimonious note. Peel gave Geary a tongue lashing, which didn't improve matters and ordered him to make ready to sail immediately.

The *Gilmore* departed Plymouth on 10th August. Peel was past the point of no return and knew it. He had no choice but to go on.

* * * * *

For the first part of the journey, from Plymouth to Cape Town, the ship rolled and pitched continuously and monotonously but they were free of storms and the seas were not rough. After a few weeks, most of the 169 passengers, of whom 79 were children, found their sea legs and conquered their initial nausea and squeamishness. However, at least half the children contracted measles, which made life miserable for everyone concerned for some weeks.

For those of curious nature, the time allowed on deck provided much of interest and entertainment. There were birds and flying fish to be seen, dolphins to be shot at and fish and sharks to be caught on strong cord lines. Samuel was adjudged by all as the best fisherman after landing a succession of sharks about five feet in length. The latter brought a welcome change to the diet. Their white flesh, which the sailors called flake, was delicious.

King Neptune and entourage were hoisted over the rails in the longboat on the morning the ship crossed the equator, fortuitously on a fine and calm day. The sea god was attended by Queen Amphitrite and both were surrounded by Tritons, their bodies draped with smelly fish skin mantles. Samuel grinned as he recognised the skins of the sharks he had caught weeks before. Neptune sported a huge seaweed beard and all wore paper crowns and brandished pitch forks, their three prongs menacing the nearest passengers. To the children's delight, the Tritons drenched them with buckets of water and they were ordered to sing 'God save the King' before the visitors were lowered over the side in the ship's boat. William tried to join them but was pulled back by Annie amidst much laughter from King Neptune and his followers who beckoned him on. The windless days continued and the *Gilmore* was becalmed off the African coast for nearly a week.

Every Sunday, the Andrews' family joined over a hundred others crowded on the quarter deck for the Church of England service. If the weather was fair, prayers and hymns were followed by a sermon from the Reverend Marcus Williams, otherwise only prayers were said, the congregation dispersing hurriedly below for shelter. Services were also held to commit the dead to the deep, the Reverend conducting five such services for victims of accident, dysentery and childbirth before the ship arrived at Cape Town.

Samuel and Annie had decided to abstain from sexual intercourse from the day Samuel signed his mark to the indenture. On her calculation, this would prevent a child being born during the voyage. By mutual consent they continued their abstinence aboard the *Gilmore*, mainly because of Annie's modesty but also because they did not know what faced them in their early days at the Swan River Colony. However, the lack of privacy or fear of the unknown did not deter others in the crowded quarters. There was much panting, bumping and humping in the darkness of the night.

When it rained, providing the ship was not rolling too much, Annie placed containers on the deck to collect fresh water, which was hoarded for the children. The ship's water smelled and tasted vile and caused intestinal pain and diarrhoea in many of the passengers. In the rain, Annie spread their clothes on the deck and scrubbed and stamped on them to eradicate the dirt, lice and fleas.

Thomas Peel was seen on deck infrequently, although his son mixed readily with the other youths. Peel refused to acknowledge the lower classes and restricted his socialising to the company of those he considered to be his peers. This left him George Dunnage, Captain Richard Meares, John Lyttleton, Jack Devenish and their families. He would not associate with Geary. Peel was not lonely, regularly joining male company for cards and a few rounds of drinks. Otherwise, he kept to himself.

At Cape Town, there was another yelling match between Peel and Geary. The Captain married Susan Smythe, a young female passenger, of whom he had become enamoured during the voyage. Naturally, he wanted to spend some time in comfort and privacy ashore to consummate the union. Peel refused the request. Geary went anyway and a further five days were lost.

The expression 'being lulled into a false sense of security' could not have described a situation more perfectly than that pertaining to the *Gilmore*. The first two months of the voyage would have been passable, if not agreeable, to most of the passengers. However, the remaining months were a nightmare and for many the worst experience of their lives. The storms came and went one after another with hardly a break between them. The ship rolled, lurched and plunged. Captain Geary would not allow passengers on deck, because he considered it too dangerous and so, in cramped quarters, they ate reduced rations, endured their waking hours and slept. Most of the adults managed to conduct their ablutions and pass their waste in prescribed areas outside the compartment. However, the sick and the young could not. By the time the roughest section of the voyage, that through the southern Indian Ocean, was upon them, the cabin was awash with urine, faeces and vomit. It was a continuous and never ceasing chore for those women capable and well enough to face the mess and stench. Annie led the band of individuals willing to attempt the daily clean-up. When the weather was fine and the sea calm enough, bedding and clothes were washed and hung to dry on improvised lines on deck with the older children standing guard to prevent items blowing overboard. Passengers washed themselves and their children in tubs of salt water behind the drying bedding. When the storms returned, so did the mess and stench. It was exhausting work and Annie was a tower of strength to her companions. One after another the groups of passengers in other compartments followed their example.

During the first of the storms, Samuel motioned Annie to the side and whispered that she should follow him. She asked Elizabeth Smith, a woman slightly older than herself, with whom she had become friendly, to keep an eye on the children. Unsteadily, Annie followed Samuel up the ladder, across the deck and into the entrance to the cabin area at the rear of the ship. The *Gilmore* was bucking in an alarming fashion.

"Samuel, what's happening? What's the matter?"

Samuel had his serious face on. "We have been asked to perform a special and personal task for the Master. He has a bad bout of sea sickness along with the dysentery, as has young Master Frederick. They've both been ill for some days and Mr Peel won't let the surgeon assist until the cabin has been cleaned up. I offered to help, knowing you could cope."

Samuel took her into the large and well appointed cabin. Father and son were both of grey-green complexion and lying in clothing and bedding stained with vomit and bodily wastes. The stink was abominable. She felt their brows and found them burning with fever.

Annie turned to Samuel. "You'll have to help me." She proceeded to outline what needed to be done and what materials were necessary. Samuel followed orders and they set about together to complete the tasks as soon as possible, not without difficulty in the constant rolling motion of the ship.

Several hours later, Annie's new patients rested comfortably in clean clothing and fresh bedding. Washing was draped around the walls of the cabin to dry. Peel and Frederick had been given large draughts of boiled water but no food, as Annie continued to alternately sponge their foreheads. Dr Lyttleton was summoned and he administered a potion to reduce the debilitating effects of the diarrhoea. A slightly built man, he did not appear too healthy himself. Annie thought the surgeon and his wife Sarah were two of the most caring and compassionate persons she had ever met and Annie and Sarah frequently made small talk while strolling on deck in fair weather. Mrs Lyttleton did not hold with the inherent English class system and did not care who knew it.

Peel gruffly thanked Annie and Samuel and asked whether they would continue to minister to his and Fred's needs as long as was necessary. Naturally, they agreed to do so, as they really had no choice, being Peel's servants. After five days the Peels were almost back to normal and from that moment on the Master acknowledged Annie and Samuel with an almost imperceptible nod whenever he saw them.

During those terrible months of abnormally bad storms, Annie assisted in the birth of Elizabeth's fourth son, pulled a rotten tooth with a pair of Samuel's pliers, treated four children for conjunctivitis, released the pressure on a badly bruised toenail, bandaged numerous cuts and lacerations and calmed hysterical women sure they were to end their lives at the bottom of the ocean. Meanwhile her own family remained happy and healthy.

On 15th December, the *Gilmore* dropped her anchors in the dark blue waters of Gage Roads off the mouth of the Swan River and swung into a light south-east breeze. Gulls and terns wheeled and banked around the ship, anticipating food scraps. In a blazing sun, with a temperature of 88° Centigrade, the passengers lined the rails. There was much laughter and joking. They were pleased, ever so pleased and relieved, to have finally arrived at their destination. However, some were happier than others. Two crew members and twelve passengers had died in transit. Three boys and two girls had been born and survived. Two boys were not so fortunate. Most of the animals had died or been washed overboard during the storms and much of the cargo in the hold had been damaged by salt water.

Thomas Peel stood on the poop deck fuming in frustration. He was six weeks too late to claim his preselected grant of 250,000 acres abutting the Swan and Canning Rivers.

Chapter 5

Clarence

Excited passengers scanned the shoreline, shading their eyes from the morning sun as they watched the activity. At the highest point of land adjacent to the river mouth the Union Jack fluttered in the easterly wind. Stranded on the white sand, just to the south, lay a hulk. The brigs *Amity* and *Thomson* were anchored not far from the *Gilmore* and tenders plied their way backwards and forwards from the beach below the flag.

Samuel kept a tight grip on William, who sat on his shoulders. Annie held Sara Jane's hand as she peeped through the railing. "Where are the buildings?" she whispered to her husband.

Samuel pointed to the flag. "They will be behind the flag pole hill, I would reckon. Between the river and the ocean. At least that's where I would build. Can you see the mouth of the river?"

Annie nodded. "The beach is beautiful and so white and the sea so blue. I know what it is! Everything seems clean."

"Aye, Annie. That it does. And we have a brand new life ahead of us."

Sara Jane began their usual game of pointing at objects and asking names. Elizabeth, who was standing nearby, holding her new baby, said, "bird, sky, William, bird, another bird." Everybody laughed. It was a time for laughter. They had made it safely to their new country, half a world away from home.

Shouted orders from the Boatswain caused heads to turn. Crew members moved the settlers back to allow the lowering of the longboat and sailors slid down ropes to hold the craft steady while Thomas Peel seated himself. "Three cheers for Mr Peel," called one of the more excited settlers and this received an exuberant response from the crowd. Peel waved in imperious manner as the boat was rowed away towards the river mouth. Personally, he wished he could be meeting Stirling under more auspicious circumstances.

The journey by lighter to Perth took four hours. When Peel protested, he was told it was a faster trip than usual due to the early strong onshore wind. He was not impressed and continued to complain. Mid-afternoon, he arrived hot, tired and frustrated at a makeshift jetty and was pointed in the direction of the headquarters of government. This turned out to be a collection of assorted tents, two storage sheds and a fenced area for animals. A wooden house was under construction.

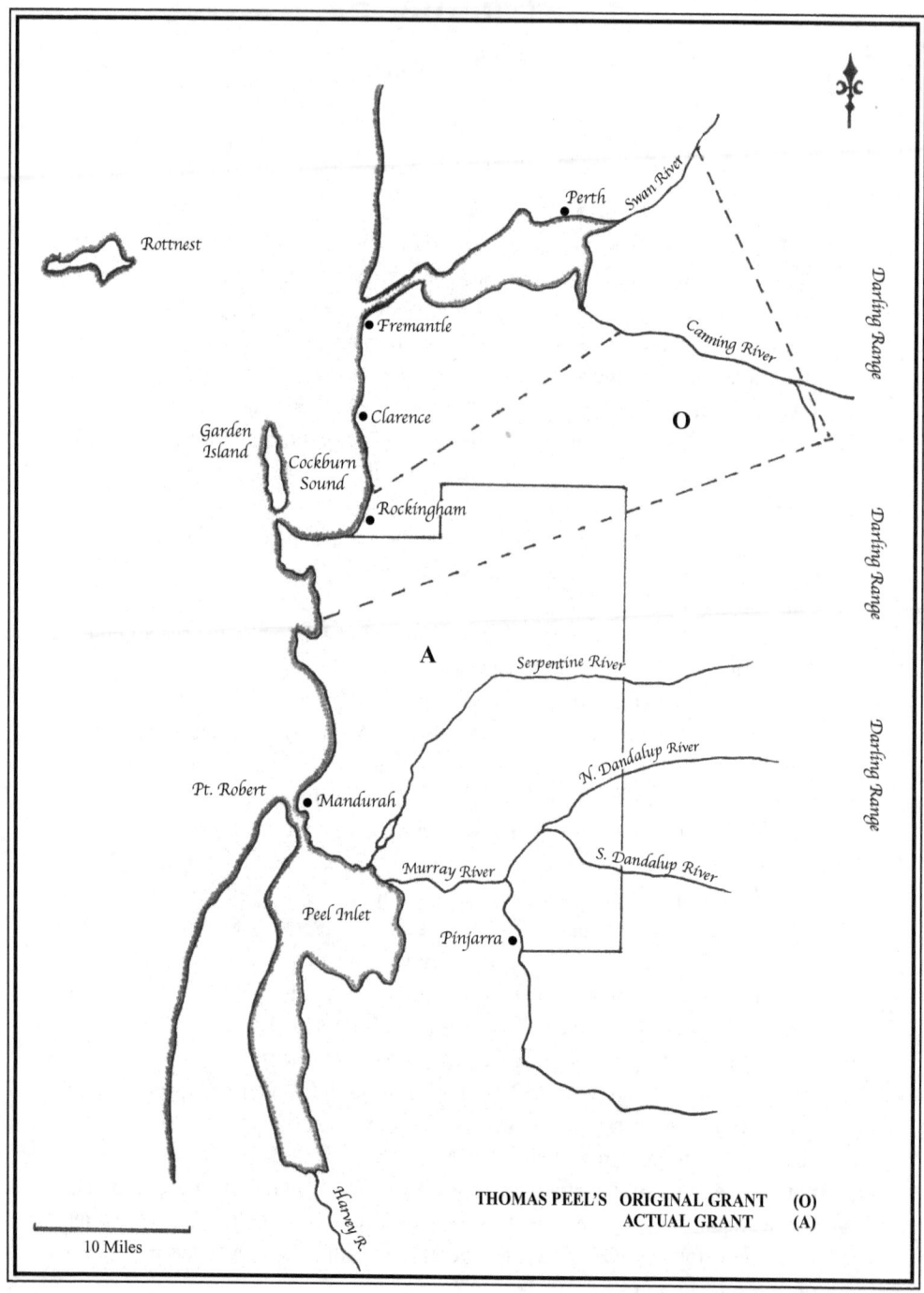

Rottnest

Perth

Swan River

Darling Range

Fremantle

Canning River

Clarence

Garden
Island

O

Cockburn
Sound

Rockingham

Darling Range

A

Serpentine River

Pt. Robert

Mandurah

N. Dandalup River

Darling Range

Murray River

S. Dandalup River

Peel Inlet

Pinjarra

Harvey R.

THOMAS PEEL'S ORIGINAL GRANT   (O)
ACTUAL GRANT   (A)

10 Miles

Lieutenant-Governor James Stirling met Mr Thomas Peel Esquire in the reception tent. The two men shook hands formally. "How are you, Mr Peel?" inquired Stirling. "I hope your voyage was without misfortune. The lateness of your arrival had us worried."

In a most discourteous manner, Peel burst into an explanation of the unnecessarily late departure from England, the becalming off Africa, the wait in Cape Town while Captain Geary honeymooned, honeymooned do you mind and the sequence of violent storms which hammered the ship across the Indian Ocean.

Stirling waited patiently for him to finish. "Sit down, Mr Peel," he said. "Pour yourself a wine or water. I'm afraid, as yet, we don't stand much on ceremony here."

Motioning Peel to a sofa, Stirling seated himself. A bottle of water and carafe of wine with glasses had been placed on a side table between them. Apart from a few scattered couches and a map table, the tent was bare. There was no flooring. Peel walked through raked sand.

"We waited until November 2nd," Stirling began deliberately. "When you had not arrived by the stipulated date, I had no alternative but to reallocate your preselected grant immediately. Those were my orders and everyone at Swan River knew it to be so. Many settlers awaited that date, because their eyes were firmly fixed on your allotted land, especially the prime areas adjacent to the Swan and Canning Rivers. Mr Peel, I must say that I am sorry for the situation in which you find yourself. A most unfortunate outcome."

"Well, what's to be done?" A miserable Peel slumped in the couch. "I'm here with a hundred and sixty settlers, all raring to go. Some aboard are expecting to choose their grants immediately. The indentured men are looking forward to regular work and pay. Nearly half are children." He poured himself a glass of wine and gulped it down.

The Governor leaned forward, a sympathetic expression on his face. "I have mulled over your position and what I could offer you in compensation for the loss of your preferred land. I am prepared to negotiate an alternative grant. Would you care to examine our map? Mr Roe has been extremely busy surveying over the past months. I'm sure that with my knowledge of the area, I could assist you in making a selection of some suitable land."

Peel joined Stirling at the table on which a map was spread. Stirling began by pointing out the geographical features and the location of previously allotted land.

"Now, what I propose is that we objectively assess the alternatives." He placed his right hand over the section north of Perth. "This area is barren compared with the land south of the Swan River. Further, there are no safe anchorages." He shifted his hand to the east. "The land beyond the Darling

Range is as yet unexplored and therefore of unknown quality. Besides it would be too remote for your needs. As you can see, the land around the Swan and Canning Rivers is all taken. However, I hope to interest you in a grant to the south of Cockburn Sound. I am prepared to allot 250,000 acres in a block. You would obtain a grant of equal size to your original allocation but further south.

With increasing interest, Peel watched and listened carefully as Stirling pointed to a lightly pencilled line enclosing an area level with Garden Island and extending south to a river named the Murray. "The advantages of this particular grant include frontages to the safe anchorage of Cockburn Sound, to the Murray River and to a large inlet into which the Murray and Harvey Rivers flow. The inlet is only a day's sail from Fremantle, through comparatively calm waters sheltered by islands and reef. I would propose that the inlet be named Peel Inlet." When Stirling concluded, Peel asked a number of questions which were answered to his satisfaction.

An expression of total relief spread across Peel's face. There was a hint of a smile as his finger traced the area. "Done. In for a penny, in for a pound."

The two men shook hands and toasted the agreement with the contents of the carafe. Peel was brought up to date with developments in the colony and invited to share the evening meal and stay over in an adjoining tent provided for visitors. Stirling apologised for the absence of his wife who was indisposed. Lamb stew and suet pudding were served with a red wine. Stirling personally thought he had handled a potentially difficult situation remarkably well.

Next day, Peel returned to the *Gilmore* and enthusiastically addressed the assembled passengers from the half-deck. He gave a glowing account of the alternative grant, insinuating that he had selected it himself.

"The *Gilmore* will sail tomorrow for the protected waters of Cockburn Sound and anchor off Woodman's Point. Christmas will be spent aboard ship to allow time for the construction of storage sheds. You will all be disembarked in time to celebrate the New Year on land." The address was followed by cheering, laughter and clapping. Peel felt very pleased with himself.

Christmas is really for children. The boys and girls on the *Gilmore* experienced a Christmas they would never forget. The adults did everything they could to make it a joyful occasion. William received a horse and Sara Jane a doll, both carved from off-cuts of wood used in maintenance work aboard ship. Carols were sung heartily, games played vigorously and the ship's bell rung to herald Father Christmas who arrived dressed in a red hunting coat tied with a rope belt and "Ho Hoed" around the deck before disappearing into a rear cabin. Christmas dinner was fried snapper with slices of freshly made bread and there was plenty of it. Annie decided that it was one of the best meals she had ever eaten. The strangest part of the total proceedings was the weather. It was hot, oh so hot! However, all agreed that, although Christmas 1829 was very different, it was a wonderful experience and one they would all remember. After the sunburnt children had been put to bed, the adults sang hymns, many in thanksgiving.

On 28th December, commencing as soon as it was light, the ship's boats began ferrying passengers and their goods to the beach. The few surviving animals were lowered into the boats in crates or directly into the water to swim ashore.

The Andrews' family was one of the first to reach land. They carried most of their belongings and sufficient rations for a week. Samuel helped Annie from the boat with some of the gear and then returned for the children. A third trip completed the transfer. The adults, laden down with their belongings, trudged barefoot through the fine white sand with William and Sara Jane happily chasing each other alongside.

Above the high tide mark, sand hill followed sand hill for several hundred yards before they came upon some trees and open grassland. Most of the grasses seemed to be dead but the trees were green and shady, although very different from home.

"You wait here for me, lass," said Samuel. "And keep a close eye on the children. There might be snakes or other nasties." Annie shivered. "I'm going to look for a likely spot to build a camp. And I'll find the whereabouts of the storehouse. When you see Elizabeth and Edward tell them what I'm doing. I reckon his idea of our families staying close together for company and protection was a good one." Samuel took an axe and strode into the bush.

Annie passed the time observing the antics of a great variety of birds. Apart from the all too obvious ravens and some that looked like swallows, none was recognisable. Her favourites were the many large black and white birds that cawed frantically in chorus and fussed as they pecked titbits from the ground.

When Samuel returned, the Smith family had joined Annie and the children under the trees.

"I've found a place to set up camp," he called. "There's water, shade and some protection from the wind. It's a little way south of here."

Excitedly shouldering their belongings, the group followed Samuel to his chosen site. They saw a shallow swamp of fresh water surrounded by trees with large strips of white peeling bark. There was a flat open area, slightly uphill and it was there they shed their packs. Several large trees with masses of bright orange flowers were named Christmas trees because of the season. The most amazing of the unfamiliar plants had a round, dark brown trunk of six feet or more topped with hundreds of green spikes, from which long green stalks protruded.

"The scenery is a tad different from home," grinned Edward, as he dropped his load. "Still, it looks as though this should suit."

"Right," said Samuel. "We've got two days to settle in before we meet with Mr Peel. Let's discuss what we need to do to make ourselves as comfortable as possible." While the adults talked, the seven older children played hide and seek. Elizabeth nursed the baby. After agreement had been reached, Annie, Samuel and Edward set about their assigned tasks while Elizabeth cared for the children. Two rough frames of tree trunks were erected and covered with canvas from the storehouse. These would act as sleeping areas and family shelters. Edward dug a well, deep enough to allow the settlement of sediment to occur and for a bucket to be filled. Samuel prepared a deep hole to the north of the camp site and away from the swamp and over it constructed a crude privy seat. He surrounded the structure with tree branches to give some privacy. Annie helped the children to collect wood and this became their daily chore. Within a few hours, the tasks were completed and the families shared a meal of rice and sweet tea. After months aboard ship, it was bliss to eat from a stable plate.

* * * * *

Two days later, Thomas Peel stood on the top of a small sand hill and addressed a worried group of over fifty men. All were sunburnt and bearded. Peel wore a full suit, his only concession to the heat being a straw hat that he had commandeered from a servant.

He began. "I have decided to name this proposed township Clarence, after the Duke of Clarence, who, as you would be aware, is the heir to the British throne." Most of the men looked at him blankly. Ignorant bastards, he thought. "It is my intention to devote the month of January to formalising the deeding of this grant, to supervising the surveying of the town site and to erecting the necessary buildings for the security and protection of the food and provisions soon to arrive from London on my following two ships. In February, I will travel south to explore the Murray River and Peel Inlet area." He paused for the name to sink in. "Tomorrow, an hour after dawn, all servants will report to the store building to begin work. When not required for prescribed duties, you may attend to your family needs in terms of providing food, water and shelter. The recently erected sheds hold little food. Most stores were consumed during the voyage. You will be largely fending for yourselves until a ship arrives."

There were murmurs of disapproval and anger at the last statement but no one was prepared to challenge Peel on the issue. Some hands went up to indicate questions. They were ignored. Peel strode away in the direction of his temporary shelter, a wooden structure which had been used to transport horses aboard the *Gilmore*.

Samuel and Edward walked back to their camp site, discussing Peel's comments. They had been fortunate with food so far. Edward had packed a rabbit trap unaware that rabbits were not native to Australia. However, it proved effective and caught an unknown furry creature the first night and a small kangaroo on the second. The main problem was the flies that were attracted to the meat in hundreds. It became rotten in a day or so because of the heat and was soon flyblown.

The families ate kangaroo stew for dinner. Edward had proposed they share their food supplies and Samuel gratefully accepted the offer, having much to gain. As the adults sat and the children slept around the fire, the smoke of which acted as a deterrent to the mosquitoes and midges, Samuel concluded that closeness to water definitely had disadvantages as well as advantages. He broached the subject of the exploratory party going to the Murray River. "I would like to go, Edward. It would be a chance to see some of the country and learn more about the plants and animals. I could also find out about the different soils and the kind of crops we might be able to grow."

Edward caught the drift. "I could provide for both families while you're gone. It probably won't be more than a couple of weeks. And then you could share the information with us. We would all be better off that way. In three years, we'll be working our own land."

"It's decided then. I'll see the Master tomorrow."

Peel accepted Samuel's offer to travel as his servant on the expedition to the Murray. Meanwhile, the indentured men gathered each day for work duties. There was little to do, so the men formed groups and rostered the jobs to allow themselves more time to provide for their families. Samuel and Edward assisted in the construction of the storage sheds and yards for the few remaining animals, then took turns in netting fish, digging wells and collecting firewood. There were too few tasks and many of the men ceased reporting in the mornings. Why bother? No one supervised them anyway. Peel was away most of the time, firstly in Perth completing details of the land grant and later observing Sutherland, the Assistant Surveyor, as he surveyed the site for Clarence. Adam Elmslie, Peel's general manager, sometimes remunerated the workers with promissory notes and sometimes not. There was little in the store in the way of food and redemption of the notes was hardly worthwhile. Therefore, the men reasoned, working was not worthwhile.

Natives were seen in groups and some approached the men as they worked, although not the women and children at the camp site. An adult always remained to keep an eye on their possessions, as the natives were rapidly gaining a reputation for helping themselves to the settlers' belongings. Samuel was courteous in his manner but would not accept gifts or exchange items with the black men. He was adamant about this and insisted they all follow these procedures. Under no circumstances were any of the children to approach or even acknowledge the presence of natives. Samuel wanted to watch and learn more about their habits first.

Annie and Elizabeth had their hands full with the children, who wandered around in the nearby bush and shallow swamp area, made cubbies, climbed trees and generally flourished in their new environment. They eagerly greeted each new day and fell into their bedding exhausted at night. All were continually hungry and usually dirty. From the beginning, both mothers insisted that all members of their families scrubbed regularly. Their clothing was kept clean and their bedding washed weekly. All drinking water was boiled. It was a matter of common sense to Annie. If one kept oneself clean, one was less likely to become sick. She followed the dictum of cleanliness being next to godliness. While the summer heat continued, there was no need for persuasion. Everyone was happy to bathe in the swamp or in the ocean. Apart from sunburn, bites and the occasional scratch or bruise, all were a picture of health.

On the 21st January, the *Industry*, one of Levey's ships, arrived from London bringing equipment, livestock and provisions for Peel's settlers. Those servants with promissory notes were able to supplement their supplies and the Andrews and Smiths enjoyed sugar in their tea for the first time in weeks.

Peel's second passenger ship, the *Hooghly*, sailed into Cockburn Sound in mid-February unloading a further one hundred and seventy-three settlers. Clarence was becoming crowded and the settlers impatient. Those waiting to receive grants were the most impatient but until the land was surveyed, there was nothing they could do. Peel knew that some were interested in land to the south and it was therefore now imperative that he explore the extent and boundaries of his grant.

Taking the opportunity to utilise the services of the *Industry* before she departed for Sydney, Peel ordered Captain Young to sail to the mouth of the Murray and wait while he and his party explored the area. Samuel and Ken Jones, another indentured servant, accompanied him. In typical fashion, Peel left without informing anyone else.

* * * * *

The exploratory voyage to the Murray was a wonderful experience for Samuel. Returning three weeks later, he described his adventures to the adults after the children were asleep.

"Everything is so clean. The water is so blue and the beaches so white all the way down the coast. We stayed well out to sea because of the reefs and islands and there are plenty of them. The journey only took half a day each way. We sailed down on the land breeze and coming home in the afternoon we used the sea breeze. Fairly flew home we did! The river mouth was silted up and the sand bar was hundreds of yards across at low tide but I suppose it flushes out with the winter rains, as we were told happens with the Swan. Hot! I've never been so hot, wandering around in the bush, dripping with sweat and covered in flies. I wish you could have seen the birds. In the estuary, thousands of birds were eating thousands of fish. Huge schools of silver fish. They seemed to be never ending. Would feed an army. And crabs galore. You would never starve in the Peel Inlet. That's what it's now called. We hauled the dinghy over the bar at high tide and sailed for miles up the estuary, until we found where the rivers entered on the eastern side. There are two rivers. The Murray we already knew about. The other one, Mr Peel named the Serpentine because its course wound along like a snake. The waterways are huge and go miles to the south. I've found where I'd like to settle, Annie. On the Serpentine. I've found our place," he said, putting his arm around her and pulling her close. The four friends continued to talk on excitedly for an hour or so, their happy faces reflecting the glow of the dying fire.

That night, Samuel and Annie slipped away and made love beneath a tall eucalypt tree. Afterwards, they lay together contentedly discussing their future under a clear, starlit sky.

"I love you so much lass," Samuel said, kissing Annie gently on the cheek. "We'll make a wonderful new life together in this strange land. I can't wait for you to see the Serpentine. It's so untouched, so quiet and so beautiful." Annie murmured something incoherent and Samuel, smiling, realised she had already drifted into sleep.

CHAPTER 6
The Duel

If there was one human trait that pervaded the settlement at Clarence, it was laziness. There was little to do once the essential tasks were completed. The storage sheds had been erected and supplies of wood, water and food were available. There was no work, therefore there was no pay. In early 1830, some of the settlers, including George Dunnage, Jack Devenish and Richard Meares, took up sizeable grants just outside the area surveyed for the Clarence town site. All three had houses in various stages of construction and wanted to prepare the land for the first winter rains and seeding. However, their diligence only made the behaviour of many of the immigrants indolent in comparison.

A few indentured servants used their savings to refund Peel their transport costs and, in return, received small holdings commensurate with their remaining resources. Others repaid Peel and took up positions as servants, or labourers with settlers who had been allotted grants on the Swan or Canning Rivers. The poorest indentured men, with the exception of some stronger characters like Samuel and Edward, having no alternative, idled the hours away and spent their remaining money gambling and drinking.

As a consequence of inadequate provision of fresh food and little attention to hygiene practices, sickness became endemic. Frustration led to brawling and in the following months, twenty-one men were transported to Fremantle and imprisoned in the hulk of the *Marquis of Anglesea*, a fortnight at a time, for unruly behaviour. When Peel was resident in Clarence, which wasn't often, he ignored the obvious problems. He spent a great deal of his time on Garden Island, where Samuel had constructed a small shed and cooking lean-to for him. There, in solitude, he could watch through his spy-glass for his last transport. He refused to listen to the complaints of common servants and could not be bothered doing anything to improve the situation at Clarence. When the *Rockingham* arrived, he would decide on appropriate action.

On 30th April 1830, the stipulated deadline for the arrival of the remainder of the four hundred settlers passed and that part of the contract to obtain a further 250,000 acres was broken. Peel simmered in frustration, anger and anguish. Once again the tardiness of one of his captains had cost him dearly. Would nothing go right for him?

On a stormy morning in mid-May, Peel awoke to find the barque in question already anchored off Garden Island, obviously intending to ride out a north-easterly squall. It was less than a mile from his hide-out. He hastened to the Pilot's house, yelling for attention as he approached. A dishevelled figure appeared yawning in the doorway. "My ship's here," Peel shouted. "Hurry up! I want you to take me out to her immediately."

"And who would you be?" the startled Pilot asked. He knew there were settlers on the island but lived a hermit's life by preference, choosing not to communicate with the others.

"I am Thomas Peel and that is the *Rockingham.*" Peel jabbed his finger towards the ship. "I demand you take me aboard immediately."

The Pilot acknowledged the authority inherent in the command. The crew were rounded up and rowed Peel out to the *Rockingham*, not without difficulty in the strong offshore wind.

By the time Peel climbed aboard, he was frantic with worry about the safety of his ship, the provisions and the passengers.

"I am Thomas Peel. Where is the Captain?"

A tall man with a face full of whiskers stepped forward. "I am Captain Halliburton."

"This is my ship and I insist you allow me to take command. I am familiar with Cockburn Sound and can make safe anchorage. I want the ship unloaded as quickly as possible."

The astonished Halliburton thought he must be facing a madman. He was the Captain and held total responsibility for the ship. "I will do nothing of the sort, sir."

Pushing Peel aside, he leaned over the railing. "Come aboard Pilot and guide us into the Sound."

Shouting "Bloody hell!" Peel charged the Captain. A single mighty blow knocked Halliburton to the deck where he lay stunned. The passengers were aghast and the ship's crew froze. The Pilot helped him to his feet.

Never in his life had Halliburton been so humiliated and so furious. Keeping his calm before the watching crowd, he strode towards Peel.

"Get off my ship. Now! Leave in the pilot boat immediately!"

When Peel yelled "Damned upstart!" the Captain let fly with a punch that sent him reeling.

"That's it," a furious Peel whispered. "You will hear from my second."

The man really is crazy. Halliburton held his temper while Peel, holding a handkerchief to his bloody nose, lurched across the rolling deck and departed with the pilot boat crew.

With all but the royal sails furled, the Pilot demonstrated great skill in directing the helmsman through the reefs and sandbanks by a series of intricate tacking manoeuvres. The anchors were dropped and the ship swung to face the north-east. The whole exercise had only been possible because the breeze was blowing offshore. Not even a fool would anchor this close to the coast with an onshore breeze.

The Captain ordered the longboats lowered and unloading to begin. By the time two trips had been made to shore and back, the wind had swung to the north-west and now blew across Cockburn Sound and onshore. Halliburton gave the command to veer cable, thereby extending the length of anchor line for safety. As the crew moved to obey, the capstan broke, the cable snapped and the *Rockingham* was adrift.

Pandemonium reigned. Captain Halliburton had few choices. He gave directions that single male passengers were to leave in the longboats immediately, thereby lightening the load. Within minutes, all four boats had overturned throwing the passengers and crew into the surf. Men could be seen floundering in the foam and staggering to shore. The remaining passengers were sent below. The Boatswain ordered the topsails set. There was no alternative but to run with the wind and hope to make it through the southern passage, out to the relative safety of the open sea. All to no avail. The *Rockingham* could not respond quickly enough against the strengthening north-west wind and ran aground broadside in Mangles Bay several miles to the south. The shock was violent, echoed by splintering timbers. Although listing badly, with rigging churning in the surf, it was quickly ascertained that miraculously, there were no casualties aboard ship. A call from shore gave the all-clear there.

"Thank the Lord for that," Halliburton said under his breath. "Boatswain, everyone is to remain on board until morning. Those on shore will have to do the best they can."

In teeming rain, Thomas Peel stood on the top of the highest hill on Garden Island cursing at the top of his voice, his fists pumping the air above him.

* * * * *

The following morning, with winds abating and seas settling far more than his own temper, Peel sailed his dinghy to Clarence, sent for Samuel, chose horses for both of them and gave Samuel a riding lesson while they rode towards the *Rockingham*. He briefed Samuel about his duties as a second for the duel. As usual, Samuel didn't question Mr Peel but the question crossed his mind as to what would happen to them all if the Master was killed. He wondered how Peel had obtained his black eye.

The *Rockingham* lay on its side about a hundred yards from shore. Most of the passengers sat forlornly on the beach, waiting impatiently for the remaining passengers and their goods to be unloaded. Some straggled through the water with bags on their shoulders. Peel called them together. They were hesitant at first, remembering his display of temper the previous day.

58

"Welcome to the Swan River Colony," Peel began in a loud voice. He remained astride his horse, which shied away nervously from the crowd. "I am sorry your arrival was so inglorious. Due to the incompetence of your Captain, you are ten miles too far south and I have a wrecked ship. As a consequence, you must find your own way to the settlement at Clarence. Tomorrow, I will send a wagon for your heavy equipment. Otherwise you must use your own animals and carts to transfer gear. You will be met in Clarence and allotted some unoccupied land as a temporary measure. I do not anticipate that you will remain there for long. Most of the settlers are moving on as soon as possible." He concluded with a nod and without another glance at the assembled group, rode north along the beach.

Samuel waded through the waves to the *Rockingham*, gave his name and requested to see Captain Halliburton. On receiving permission, he climbed the rope ladder to the precariously angled deck and waited. Halliburton arrived sporting a black eye and Samuel guessed the perpetrator. Following preliminaries, Samuel asked for Mr Peel's mail. When the canvas bag was brought from the Captain's cabin, Samuel handed over a sealed letter.

"I am to await a reply, sir."

Halliburton broke the seal and scanned the letter. A look of surprise came over his face.

"Well! I'll be damned! A duel." Halliburton burst into laughter. His prowess with a pistol was legendary in Sheffield. He tore the letter to pieces and threw it overboard. "Tell your Master my choice is pistols at twenty paces. His will suffice since I do not carry duelling pistols aboard ship. I accept his reasons for the meeting taking place on the island and will land on the beach below the highest point of the island, mid-morning three days hence. You'd better bring someone to render medical assistance. Your Master will most certainly need it." The Captain laughed again as he walked away.

Samuel rode back to Clarence to report to Peel. He had memorised the conversation as best he could and repeated it carefully. When he reached the final sentence his Master frowned. Peel had not seriously considered the possibility of being wounded. He chose to ignore the warning. "Tell someone else to rub the horses down. I want you to come with me while I have some shooting practice."

The hour before dark was spent teaching Samuel how to load powder and shot into the elegant brace of duelling pistols. When Samuel asked about the engravings, Peel read out the words engraved on the barrel 'Mortimer. Gun maker to His Majesty'. "Best pistols made in London," he said proudly, polishing the saw handle butt with his sleeve.

Samuel placed canvas targets on a tree twenty paces away and watched nervously as Mr Peel practised his aim. The exercise was repeated during the following two days and Samuel assessed his Master to be a fine shot. If only he would take aim and fire more rapidly!

While walking back from their makeshift firing range on the second day, Samuel's curiosity finally overcame his manners and he asked Mr Peel how he knew so much about duelling.

"It's against the law you know. That's why we must meet in secret. All will be sworn to secrecy. As to how I am aware of such an activity if it is illegal, it is not because I am an experienced dueller. On the contrary, I have never taken part in a duel. The reason I have an understanding of procedures and protocol is because every boy in the great public schools dreams of being victorious in a duel of honour. Duels are the most practised events at school, albeit with toy pistols. Everyone learns and plays at duelling from an early age. The Masters encourage it knowing many of their charges will find themselves challenged or issuing a challenge at some time in their lives."

This wasn't at all reassuring to Samuel, who asked no more questions. Privately, he considered it a foolish act. No issue of pride should result in injury or death.

On the fateful morning, Samuel arrived at his Master's shelter early. Within a short time, they were sailing Peel's dinghy to Garden Island. It was one of those warm and sunny autumn days with a gentle breeze and light seas. Peel sailed expertly and they landed on the island in just over an hour.

Carrying the pistol case, Samuel followed Peel along the usual path to an open area at the foot of the highest hill. Not far away the Master's lean-to nestled in the trees to the south and Peel wandered off in that direction. He felt an urgent need to relieve himself.

The two seconds met in the centre of the open space and introduced themselves. Samuel found himself stammering with nervousness. Halliburton's second was Francis Robertson, the Boatswain from the *Rockingham*. They were accompanied by Lieutenant Wilson, the assistant surgeon from HMS *Sulphur*, who had arrived separately. Samuel explained that Mr Peel had decided against bringing a surgeon. Robertson thought Peel rather optimistic under the circumstances.

The seconds began the formal preliminaries. Distances were paced out, checked and rechecked. A line was drawn in the sand. Samuel presented the wooden box containing the loaded pistols to Robertson for inspection which he concluded meticulously before nodding his approval. Meanwhile the two opponents waited on opposite sides of the open area, Halliburton leaning casually against the trunk of a wattle tree watching the proceedings, while Peel paced up and down on the edge of the open area. He was shaking and hoped it was not visible to his adversary.

All agreed that Robertson should give the commands since he had acted as a second in a duel some years before. He called the duellists to select their pistols. Being the challenged, Halliburton had first choice. Peel picked up the remaining pistol and glared at his opponent. Halliburton had a smirk on his face which infuriated Peel. Robertson explained the procedure and asked whether either man had any questions. Both shook their heads.

"Right," he directed. "Hold your pistol by your side with the barrel facing downward and follow me." He led the two men to the marked line.

"Back to back," he ordered. The opponents turned together and stood back to back. Both were hefty men.

"Pistols up." Pistols were raised to the ready position.

"March ten paces on the count and then stop. Do not turn until the command." Robertson counted slowly to ten as the men took exaggerated and stiff-legged steps away from one another. Samuel thought it resembled the dead march at a funeral and hoped that wasn't an omen.

"Turn," came the order. Both men turned simultaneously and assumed a sideways stance.

"Fire!" yelled Robertson.

Samuel froze. It was as though all the action slowed down. He saw Halliburton extend his pistol arm first, Peel a fraction later. Both took aim but Peel took longer. The ball from Halliburton's pistol hit Peel's right hand as he squeezed the trigger. The pistol flew from his hand and the shot hit the trunk of a tree to his right. Peel shrieked and fell to the ground, blood spurting out of a gaping wound, from which the thumb and two fingers hung shattered.

Samuel and Wilson sprinted towards Peel who lay screaming and writhing in agony. Halliburton dropped his pistol and walked away, disappearing through the trees in the direction of his boat. Robertson picked up their belongings and hurried after his Captain.

The lead had pierced the webbing between thumb and forefinger. Wilson opened his black bag and applied a tourniquet to the upper arm. He quickly administered a strong dose of laudanum. Peel swallowed it between cries of pain. The surgeon selected a piece of clean lint, soaked it with a solution of chloride of lime and wrapped it around Peel's hand, asking Samuel to hold it firmly in place. Peel screamed. Wilson threaded a ligature of waxed silk through a curved needle and waited for the opium to take effect. Before it did, Peel fainted with the pain. On instruction, Samuel sat behind Peel with his left leg straddling Peel's chest and held his Master's forearm tightly between his hands. With meticulous detail and considerable dexterity, Wilson pulled the ragged edges of skin together and began stitching, first the thumb and then the two fingers, to the palm of the hand. As each digit was sutured to his satisfaction, it was wrapped in lint that had been soaked in water. Finally, he bandaged the whole hand. The tourniquet was then removed and the right arm placed in a sling. Peel remained unconscious while he was carried to nearby shade.

"Well! This is a nice to-do!" Wilson exclaimed, looking at Samuel. "Peel will need constant attention for some weeks. If we take him back to Fremantle, there would be hell to pay if it became known that the wound was the result of a duel. Halliburton would likely be charged. The rest of us could be charged as accomplices." He paused in thought. "We could say he shot himself while hunting kangaroos on the island and could not be shifted. No. How could he manage to shoot himself in the right hand? Nobody would believe us." Wilson continued to ponder. "I know. You're his servant, I presume?"

"Yes, sir. Samuel Andrews." His mouth was dry and he was feeling decidedly squeamish.

"Well Andrews, we'll say you went with Peel to the island on an overnight hunting trip and he contracted a fever. You sailed to my ship, which by chance is anchored close to the island, to ask for assistance. If necessary, I will verify your action and explain that as Peel could not be moved, I remained with him, while on my orders you returned to Clarence for provisions. No one from *Sulphur* will contradict my story. How does that sound?" He pursed his lips together. "Best we can do, I reckon. Mr Thomas Peel wouldn't want anyone to know he'd lost a duel anyway."

It was all arranged. Samuel waited with Peel while Wilson informed Halliburton of the plan and then they carried Peel to his hut. The surgeon remained on the island to tend Peel while Samuel sailed to Clarence. Halliburton and Robertson returned to Mangles Bay, where repairs were to begin on the beached *Rockingham* within a day or so. Halliburton had told his crew they were going hunting for fresh meat on Garden Island, so that part of the story was already in place.

Samuel hurried to his camp site at Clarence. Because he had given his word not to discuss the duel, he told none of the others what had happened. "Annie," he called, beckoning her. "Mr Peel has become feverish and needs attention. He's on the island."

Elizabeth came out of the Smith's hut. "What's the matter, Samuel?" she asked. When Samuel explained, she immediately offered to mind William and Sara Jane. Edward was off in the bush hunting kangaroos. Samuel packed food and bedding and quietly told Annie that she would need clean cloth for bandages, as well as any necessary cooking implements. She did not ask the obvious question when she handed him her best petticoat worn on Sundays. She only had two but it was all she could offer.

As Samuel reckoned the Master's son should know about his father, they stopped at Peel's shed to pick up Frederick. "Fred, your father's feverish and needs to remain on the island." The concerned boy bundled up some warm clothing and bedding, including additional clothing for his father and followed Samuel. Although the sea breeze was fresh and some tacking was required, they were unloading the dinghy before dark.

The next month was critical for Peel. It was cold and wet and winter storms blew up regularly. Annie was assiduous in her attention but Peel's condition fluctuated from fair to seriously ill. She bathed him and changed the bandages regularly in the way Wilson had directed and fed Peel whenever he called for food or water. The surgeon visited his patient weekly and Samuel took these opportunities to sail Annie back to Clarence to see the children. They both missed them dreadfully. Fred remained on the island with his father.

At first, although weak from loss of blood and in considerable pain, Peel appeared to be improving. However, within two weeks the wound was oozing pus and he developed a high fever. Wilson explained that this was the crucial period. Annie sponged Peel continuously until exhausted and then Samuel took over. Fred was helpful and clearly very worried about his father. For the fever, Wilson mixed a concoction of powdered nitre, carbonate of potash, antimonial wine and sweet spirits of nitre with water. Peel said it was abominable to taste but obediently swallowed his dose three times a day. He was terrified of dying. Wilson left a supply of laudanum but Peel preferred brandy, which Samuel obtained from Elmslie at Clarence when he collected Peel's mail and necessary provisions. The manager was persistent in his questioning but Samuel just repeated the story as decided and was mostly noncommittal.

When Peel was well enough to read his correspondence, he was alarmed to learn that Levey's Sydney firm Cooper and Levey had publicly stated in *The Sydney Gazette* that they had relinquished any connection with Peel and Company. Peel's promissory notes were redeemable through Cooper and Levey and Peel rightly assumed he was heading for a further financial crisis.

Nearly two months passed before Wilson cleared Peel to return to the mainland. During that period, while Annie, Samuel and Fred stoically attended him, Peel remained in a state of semi-drunkenness. Annie did not approve of strong drink but under these circumstances the effect of the brandy made her task easier. After a few drinks, Mr Peel was more complaisant, less surly and more amenable to suggestion. Otherwise, he was irascible, cantankerous and altogether thoroughly objectionable. However, Annie being a caring woman saw her role as supporting her husband and therefore his master. She would never think of complaining and was gratified by the occasional mumbled thanks from Peel.

On their return to Clarence, Peel was not wearing a bandage. Wilson's surgery had produced superb results and the wound had healed cleanly. Nevertheless, Peel never regained his fine motor control and would spend hours painstakingly practising writing with his left hand.

* * * * *

There were still four hundred persons living at Clarence and Mangles Bay. Following reports of deaths and sickness, Stirling dispatched Dr Alexander Collie, Chief Surgeon on HMS *Sulphur,* to investigate the situation. On his arrival in July, Collie could find no one who would take responsibility for the settlement.

The next day, Peel returned from his enforced sojourn on Garden Island.

Dr Collie read from his report. "Mr Peel, from the time of your settlement here, twenty-nine persons have died, which includes several stillborn babies and two young children. Two women have died in childbirth. Dr Lyttleton is currently treating patients with dysentery and scurvy and many others are sick with nonspecific illnesses." Peel expressed genuine dismay at the extent of the dissipation, disease and death.

It was an indictment on the health standards and practices of the time that when Collie reported to Stirling, his submission inferred that the situation was not out of hand and he was not unduly perturbed about the conditions. He suggested that much of the sickness and many of the injuries were due to excessive alcohol consumption. Besides, he had been led to believe it would be indiscreet to blame Peel and any repercussions might affect his own future.

Soon after his return, Peel was petitioned by a group of his indentured servants who wanted release from their contracts. They had received no pay for nearly two months and had received little food from the dwindling supply of stores. A miserable crowd they were, dirty, gaunt with hunger and clothed in tattered canvas. Peel had no ready cash and no one would redeem his promissory notes.

"I will speak to you all tomorrow," he said and dismissed them.

Peel was now fed up with Clarence. It was nothing but trouble and he had endured enough. The depression following his wounding and illness still lingered. The word was passed around that Peel wanted to speak to the settlers at noon the following day. Over one hundred men and some women attended in drizzling rain and assembled as close to Peel as possible to hear the address.

Standing on a box, Peel raised his right arm for silence. In the other he held a battered umbrella. "I have decided to leave Clarence and settle on the Murray River," he began. More like abandoning Clarence and escaping to the Murray, he thought. There were mutterings in the crowd. What would this mean for them? What would they do? Where could they go?

"As you would know, Adam Armstrong and three other families have been at the Peel Inlet for some months now. Armstrong sent a message yesterday that he has located fertile soil in a large depression a mile north of the inlet and is already having success in growing vegetables." This painted a rather more rosy picture than Armstrong had described but Peel wanted to attract some volunteers to go with him. There was safety in numbers. Peel had been informed on his return that George Mackenzie, a nineteen year old labourer, who had travelled out on the *Gilmore*, had been speared through the heart by natives the previous month while building a house on the Murray. With a young man's courage, he ventured too far away from the protection of Armstrong's group and paid the ultimate price. It was alleged that the murder was a payback killing because settlers at Clarence had fired on some natives a few days before.

Peel continued. "Any man will be released from his contract on the proviso that all my transporting expenses are repaid within two years. I will lodge details with the Chief Magistrate in Fremantle. You will be expected to make contact with him to ascertain your commitments, then you will be free to take up employment with other settlers seeking labourers. The store is nearly empty. I will take what I need to establish myself on the Murray. Some of the remaining provisions will be distributed to you in an equitable manner depending on the size of your family. The rest will be sold. My equipment will be placed under guard until such time as I require it. It is my intention to set out for the Peel Inlet within the month and men wanting to accompany me should report to Mr Elmslie tomorrow morning. All such requests will be assessed individually, taking into account the capabilities of the applicant." Peel climbed down from his box and walked towards his store, leaving a stunned and thoroughly wet crowd.

Later, the *Swan River Guardian* was to report: 'It is well known that Mr Peel has sold more nails, iron, pans, two legged pots, three legged pots and pots without any legs, than all the Colony put together'.

CHAPTER 7

Perth

S amuel and Edward discussed their options as they hurried back to the camp site.

Ignoring the rain, Annie and Elizabeth ran to meet them. "What happened?" asked Elizabeth. "Tell us! Quickly! What did Mr Peel say?"

Samuel laughed. "Whoa! Give us a chance. I'm not sure it's good news anyway."

Edward butted in. "Peel is abandoning Clarence. He is moving to the Murray as soon as he can organise it. We're to be given some food and have the choice of being released from our indentures or going with him to the Murray."

The two women looked with dismay at their husbands, waiting for a lead as to their decision.

"Is either shelter empty?" asked Samuel.

"This one." Annie pointed to the brush and canvas shelter on the left. "The children are in the other hut eating their lunch."

All the possibilities were considered at length but in the end the two men reluctantly agreed they must go their own ways. Annie and Elizabeth were noticeably upset at the prospect of being parted. The deciding factors were that Elizabeth was again pregnant and, in spite of her vigorous protests, Edward decided the journey south would be too difficult with six children under ten years and another on the way. The Smiths would make their way to Fremantle and hope that Edward could find work. Samuel, of course, knew where he and his family would head. South to the Serpentine. They would take their chances with Mr Peel. Samuel had only a few shillings left and certainly not enough to branch out on his own. Better the devil you know than the devil you don't, as the saying goes.

When Peel examined the names of the volunteers to accompany him to the Murray, he found the list to be very short. It comprised John Tuckey, forty-two, widower, with children Charlotte and James, both twelve; Thomas Eacott, whose wife Elizabeth had died in childbirth at Clarence and his daughter Ann, six; Thomas Watson, twenty-five, agriculturalist; Daniel Myerick, nineteen, carpenter; and Samuel Andrews, thirty-five, his wife Annie, thirty and their children William, four and Sara Jane, three. Five able bodied men! Hell's bells! What could he hope to achieve with five workers? At least the Andrews were among them. Damned fine woman that. Never complained about anything. "Inform them I'll take them all," Peel said angrily to Elmslie. "Tell them we'll leave on the full moon in September." He turned on his heel and left.

"Good riddance!" hissed the manager at the departing figure. "You'll have my resignation the day before you leave. That will create more problems for you." Elmslie could take no more. He had accepted his position on the assumption that the appointment would lead to land and wealth. It had led to nothing, except a small and irregular pay, much trouble and a great deal of rudeness.

* * * * *

Thomas Peel was worried. All his plans were collapsing. He had no ready cash, few provisions and little hope of any further assistance from Levey. The Association was finished. On the positive side, he was still young at thirty-seven, again healthy, had the rights to 250,000 acres of land in the newest British colony and his cousin was Home Secretary and Leader of the House of Commons for Great Britain. Peel decided it was time to pay another visit to Governor Stirling and perhaps make the acquaintance of some of the colonial dignitaries. He had buried himself, almost literally he thought wryly, at Garden Island and Clarence for too long.

"May I come with you, Father," pleaded Fred.

"No son, not this trip. I intend seeing the Governor and my time will be occupied with business." Peel remembered his last visit and was determined to enjoy himself. He did not want a twelve year old hanging around.

"Will you look out for a dog?" Fred had been begging for a puppy since their arrival in the colony.

"All right. I'll see what I can do." Peel had already decided it would be sensible to train a watchdog for the Murray. He certainly did not want natives approaching them unseen and unheard. The murder of Mackenzie had alarmed him somewhat.

Peel waited for fine weather before setting out for Perth on horseback. He wore his best riding gear, a black coat, grey corduroy breeches, jockey boots and a dark green broad-brimmed hat with the low crown favoured for riding. He carried a crop across his legs, although he seldom used it on his favourite horse, Goldie, a handsome chestnut filly. In the saddle bags were a set of clothes suitable for evening wear. Peel hoped to be given the chance to wear them in appropriate company. He was looking forward to mixing with persons of birth and social standing after enduring the dregs of society at Clarence.

This line of reflection took Peel back to England and the social whirl of the summer season. And, of course, his family. Mary wrote regularly and every ship arriving from London had a bundle of letters and newspapers. Before leaving for the Swan River, Peel had set up a trust account from which the lawyer paid the family bills and arranged a monthly allowance for Mary. He had to admit that he missed his wife and children but there was no way he would contemplate their presence in the colony until he was firmly established. In any case, that had been Mary's stipulation. Guiltily he realised that the last time he had written was before the duel. That was months ago!

Jogging along the sandy track to Fremantle, Peel relaxed and enjoyed the scenery. The Australian bush grew on one. The naturalness was refreshing after the English countryside with its neat and tidy, cleared and fenced fields. And such wide expanses of water and land with no one for miles. Except natives, he thought suddenly, spurring Goldie into a canter. Wretched injury and it still pained so. He changed the reins to his left hand.

On the outskirts of the port, Peel passed through the slums of South Fremantle. The area was even worse than Clarence because more individuals were crowded into a smaller space. He looked with distaste at the amazing collection of shelters surrounded by the usual debris of humans living in close quarters. Empty bottles and pieces of packing cases and casks were strewn everywhere. Old papers blew about in the wind. Peel counted three drunks staggering along the track and several men sleeping it off on the ground.

He headed straight for Samson's store in Cliff Street for an ale. Besides holding a spirit licence, Lionel Samson had been appointed one of two postmasters at Fremantle. He had selected an excellent position located centrally between Bathers Bay, where the ships unloaded and the Swan River. Peel was surprised to see the amount of development that had taken place in the three months since his last visit. Several limestone houses were under construction in Phillimore Street. The buildings extended right to the street line of the allotments. Sand was heaped against stone walls. A witty naval officer, visiting the colony, had been reported as saying that one could run Fremantle through an hour glass in a day!

Peel was welcomed by Lionel Samson and consumed a pint of locally brewed beer, which he found to be a splendid thirst quencher. He was informed that George Leake, John Bateman and William Shenton had all indicated an intention to establish businesses in the immediate vicinity. Samson proudly informed his visitor that it looked as though development in Fremantle would exceed that in Perth, at least in the early stages. Borrowing pen and ink, Peel took the opportunity to write a note to Mary, which took an inordinate amount of time as he painstakingly tried to co-ordinate his left hand. He sealed it with wax and left it with Samson to be forwarded to England on the first available ship.

At Preston Point, the river was traversed in a flat-bottomed ferry punted by two men, who sang bawdy songs as they worked. The crossing took only fifteen minutes, yet cost two shillings. Daylight robbery, Peel thought, galloping along a well defined sandy track, which ran close to limestone outcrops on the northern bank of the river. Arriving at Freshwater Bay, he again stopped for refreshments, this time at Halfway House. While he consumed freshly-baked bread with tasty cheese and a tankard of ale, the genial host described the recent disastrous floods, when the river had covered the flats for twelve days before subsiding. Peel didn't remember much of July. He continued on his way, finding the riding easy until he reached Point Resolution, where he came across more rocky outcrops. The final section was beautiful, with Mount Eliza on his left and a broad expanse of water leading to the Canning River on his right. He had to admit that Stirling had chosen a magnificent site for the capital.

Perth was also growing. Peel turned onto the track leading away from the river and headed north. At last he was out of the mud! Lofty trees grew in large numbers on the sandy rise. At the crest of the sloping hill, limestone paths had been laid and several stone houses were under construction. There was a crude sign nailed to a stately eucalypt tree, on which was painted the name 'St George's Terrace'. Papers were tacked to the tree and Peel stopped to read a handwritten news sheet and several public notices signed by the Governor which gave permission for individuals to practise variously as a surgeon, an auctioneer and a lawyer. Peel reckoned it had to be the most primitive government notice board in the Empire.

Following the road to his right, he stopped at the most substantial building in an unimpressive row of wattle and daub huts. It had an outside chimney and adjacent horse railings and troughs. Above the door a notice displayed the words 'Perth Arms'.

"This'll do," Peel said aloud to himself. He hadn't ridden for any distance since the accident and it had been a long day and would soon be dark. His muscles were stiffening and he needed a good bath, warm fire and hot toddy, not necessarily in that order.

Peel threw the yard boy a penny to rub down and feed Goldie and shouldering his saddle bags, entered the inn. It had a main drinking and eating area and doorways with canvas drops led to rooms beyond. There was a good-sized fire burning in the stone fireplace and Peel flopped into a wooden chair to absorb the warmth. When the serving girl approached, he said "My name is Thomas Peel and I need a room for the night. I require a rum toddy immediately, hot water for a bath as soon as possible and a large meal to follow."

Catching the name, the innkeeper scurried out from behind the bar. With a pronounced bow he said, "Welcome, Mr Peel. You will be attended to immediately." He waved the girl away. "Come from Clarence today, sir?" he inquired politely as he wiped the table.

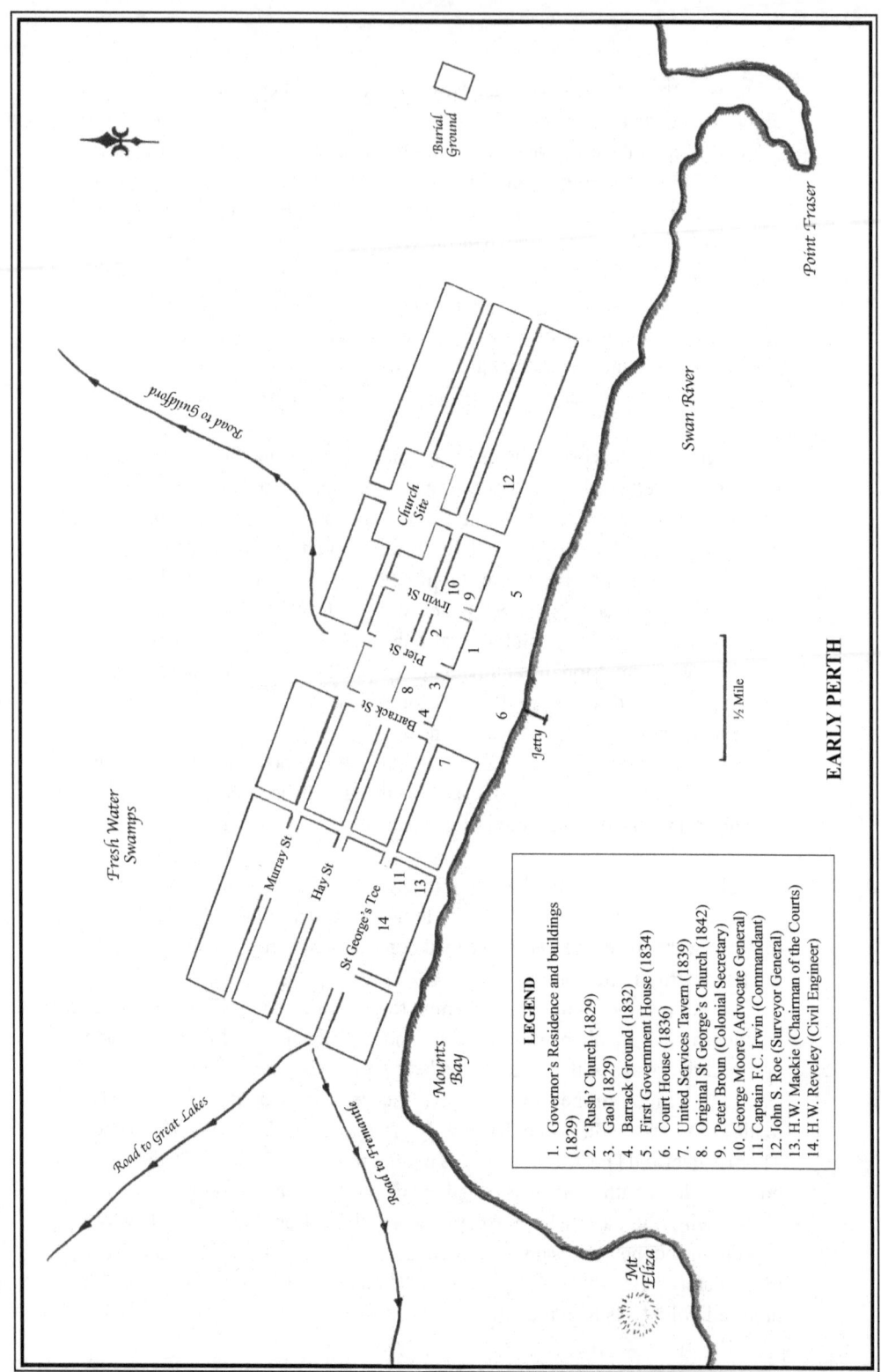

EARLY PERTH

LEGEND

1. Governor's Residence and buildings (1829)
2. 'Rush' Church (1829)
3. Gaol (1829)
4. Barrack Ground (1832)
5. First Government House (1834)
6. Court House (1836)
7. United Services Tavern (1839)
8. Original St George's Church (1842)
9. Peter Broun (Colonial Secretary)
10. George Moore (Advocate General)
11. Captain F.C. Irwin (Commandant)
12. John S. Roe (Surveyor General)
13. H.W. Mackie (Chairman of the Courts)
14. H.W. Reveley (Civil Engineer)

½ Mile

Road to Guildford

Fresh Water Swamps

Road to Great Lakes

Road to Fremantle

Mt Eliza

Mounts Bay

Swan River

Point Fraser

Burial Ground

Church Site

Murray St
Hay St
St George's Tce
Barrack St
Pier St
Irwin St

Jetty

Peel grunted assent. He couldn't stand obsequious men. "What's the girl's name?" he said, nodding in the direction of the cooking area.

The innkeeper smirked. She always did the trick. Best decoy one could hope for in a colony where men greatly outnumbered women and most females were attached. "Her name's Mary. Nice piece, ain't she? Would you like her to join you for a chat when her chores are over, sir?"

Peel nodded, trying to look uninterested. When the rum was brought, he gulped it down and ordered another. The girl's name had thrown him somewhat.

Two hours later Peel was clean, warm and replete. The stewed meat and potatoes were delicious, even if it was swan. After taking off her apron, Mary came to sit with Peel. The girl wasn't pretty but she had a lovely smile and her eyes lit up as she answered Peel's questions. By now there were no other customers in the inn.

At 10 o'clock, Mary accompanied Peel to his sleeping area behind the canvas screen. Her father had explained that Mr Peel was a very important figure in the colony and she was to do all she could to please him. The price was set at one shilling. Mary hated having to act like a whore but her father insisted the extra money was needed. Some men were all right. Others roughed and hurt her and she remained upset and withdrawn for days, feeling soiled and worthless. She worried constantly about becoming pregnant.

As Peel prepared for bed, Mary undressed and climbed into the cot. She shivered with cold and apprehension. A naked Peel followed her to bed. He fondled her gently for a minute and the girl began to relax. Then with a loud "Oh hell!" he threw himself upon her and was immediately thrusting. He ejaculated shouting "Mary!" and then promptly fell asleep. The girl spent an uncomfortable and sleepless night with the heavy body half covering her. His snoring was incessant. With the dawn, Peel took Mary again, then pushed her from the bed, demanding breakfast. He hadn't felt so good in months.

Peel paid the innkeeper his dues and sent the yard boy with a message to Governor Stirling saying he would pay a call late morning. Mounted on Goldie, he filled in time exploring the environs of the capital. Firstly, he cantered to the top of Mount Eliza. The soil was sandy and the trees sparse enough for easy travel by horseback. The view was spectacular. To the east the bush was burning in the Darling Range, which extended from north to south as far as he could see. Damned blacks, always firing the bush! He tipped there would be a spate of bushfires this summer after such heavy winter rains. The many branches of the Swan River meandered through the flats before opening out into the impressive waterway. He could see the small cluster of buildings that was Perth. A series of lakes marked its northern boundary and to the south a headland jutted towards Mount Eliza marking the confluence of the Swan and

Canning Rivers. "If only--" Peel started to say out loud. "Damn, damn, damn!" he yelled as he galloped back down the hill.

He rode down a track leading to St George's Terrace. As he passed the Perth Arms, Mary, who was sweeping the front step of the inn, gave a friendly wave. Peel ignored her and continued on until he reached Barrack Square, where he reined in and looked with interest at the large number of tents arranged in orderly rows, obviously for use by the 63rd Regiment. He saw Captain Irwin striding across the parade ground. Commandant Frederick Chidley Irwin was a career soldier. However, in addition to receiving an annual government stipend, Peel knew him to be a man of independent means, holding sound investments in commercial concerns in England. He was well built and wore small wire-rimmed spectacles. Peel waved and gave him a hoy. Irwin turned and recognising the rider, smiled and saluted.

Dismounting, Peel shook the Captain's hand, gritting his teeth with the pain from his recently healed wound. Greetings were exchanged.

"Where are you staying, Peel?"

"The Perth Arms."

"Well, you must join me for dinner this evening."

"Thank you, Irwin. I will look forward to it."

Peel explained he was meeting Governor Stirling later in the morning, so Irwin offered to show him around Perth in the meantime. He called for his horse and the two men spent the next hour inspecting the progress made in the capital.

They visited the surprisingly spacious church with a vestry on one end. "It was built by my men in a few months," Irwin said proudly. "Seats the whole of Perth. During the week it is used as a school, as you can see at the moment." He gestured to a serious young man conducting a lesson with a group of boys. "On Saturdays it converts to the Court House." Peel saw a wooden frame, with wattle and mud plastered walls and a roof thatched with rushes from the river flats. The Church of England had certainly come down a notch or two from St Paul's Cathedral in London, he thought wryly.

South of Barrack Square was a much smaller but rather more substantial building that served as the gaol. "It's the grog that does it," Irwin explained. "Almost every prisoner has committed a felony under the influence of alcohol. The majority of crimes comprise theft, brawling or the careless use of firearms, sometimes at the natives, unfortunately. The Governor has been severe in sentencing individuals taking unlawful or arbitrary action against the natives but he can only act on reported offences and I suspect they are the minority."

Irwin guided Peel to Government House, showing him the hospital marquee on the way. "Here we are Peel. That's the Governor's house on the brow of the hill. The others are temporary accommodation for government officials, such as Roe, Broun and Reveley. You would have passed my cottage in the Terrace. It's not far from the Arms. Has a new brick house under construction behind it. I'll see you at sunset." Captain Irwin turned and cantered north along the track to the Barracks.

Peel dismounted and tethered Goldie to a railing. There was a horse trough nearby and she drank noisily. Straightening his clothing, he walked towards the wooden building. Against protocol he kept his gloves on.

The aide-de-camp led him to a comfortable sitting room where the Governor and Mrs Stirling were drinking tea. This time there were floorboards. Peel saw a composed and beautiful young woman, dressed in a long, dark blue frock and grey cape, appraising him with deep brown eyes. He nodded when Stirling stood and greeted him. Peel refused to bow. Stirling introduced him to his wife, who offered her hand. Peel took it gingerly, muttering something she could not hear as he bent over. What an awkward man, Ellen thought as she excused herself and left the room. A servant poured tea and handed it to Peel. Smiling at his guest, Stirling inquired, "Is this a social visit or are you here on business, Peel?"

Peel sat uncomfortably on the edge of his chair juggling his cup and saucer in his left hand. Stirling judged the rumour about Peel being wounded in a duel to be true.

"I am here because I feel entitled to request assistance from the Government under my present circumstances," Peel began forthrightly, without formally addressing the Governor. "As you would be aware Stirling, I was ill on Garden Island with a fever for nearly two months and unable to conduct my business at Clarence. Most of the indentured men have already left my service or intend leaving shortly. Few have repaid my expenses and I suspect I shall not see many returns under two years. My store is practically empty and I am informed that further supplies will not be forthcoming from Sydney in the near future." More likely never, Peel assumed. "The *Rockingham* has been refloated with difficulty and until trials prove her to be seaworthy, there is no guarantee she'll be of any further use to me. As a consequence of these misfortunes, my promissory notes are not being honoured, thereby creating further difficulty. I intend travelling to the Murray River next month. There is some evidence that the growing of crops will be successful near the mouth. In any case, animals, birds and fish are plentiful and will provide sustenance for my party. However, as you well know, the natives in the area are becoming troublesome. Only a month has passed since the murder of Mackenzie and it is my belief that military protection is a necessity." Peel fixed his eyes on Stirling. "How can the Government provide me with some assistance?"

Stirling already knew all the details of Peel's problems. The colonial intelligence system, consisting of gossip, rumour and innuendo, was remarkably effective.

"Peel, I am truly sorry about your ill health and the beaching of the *Rockingham*. We can do nothing about such personal misfortunes. However, I feel sure that we can be of assistance in other ways. Hmm," he paused in thought. "Firstly, we could provide you with necessary stores and some cash to wind up Clarence, if that is your wish and to outfit your new venture. As you know there is little available cash in the colony and that is one of our major problems. Naturally, you will be billed for these special allowances and we would expect repayment when you receive reimbursement from your indenture contracts. Further, your commitment to the Colonial Office was to land four hundred settlers before the 1st of May, in order to receive your second land entitlement of 250,000 acres. Because the *Rockingham* was late, you will be forced to relinquish this additional grant."

Peel began mumbling.

Stirling ignored the distraction. "There is absolutely nothing that can be done about that Peel. The stipulation was in writing and unequivocal. However, although I would not acknowledge it publicly, the original impositions were severe, allowing little leeway for any unfortunate occurrences over which you had no control. My personal view is that your decision to move to the Murray River is to be commended. It will allow experimentation in crops and grazing in a new region. I will offer you official protection by allocating a detachment of soldiers to the area. Irwin will be asked to make such arrangements. Further, I would be pleased to travel with you to the Murray River to gain first hand knowledge and experience of the new settlement. We could well spread the load of your relocation by commissioning *Sulphur* to assist."

Peel's eyebrows lifted. Again, Stirling had taken the wind out of his sails by providing an immediate solution to his problems. It was almost as if he had been expected. He agreed to be ready to board HMS *Sulphur* off Woodman's Point on the fourth day following the full moon in September. The servants and their families would leave on the land trek on the day of the full moon and await at a predetermined rendezvous near the mouth of the river.

Peel was enthused. After taking his leave he rode for several hours exploring the river track to Guildford, before returning to the Perth Arms to change for dinner with Irwin. The future was still not bright but it was a damned sight brighter than it had been yesterday.

His clothing pressed by Mary, a resplendent Peel strolled down St George's Terrace at dusk, pretentiously prodding the sand with his cane. Dressed to the nines he is, Mary thought admiringly, as she peeped through a window. He wore grey corduroy trousers, white shirt with blue scarf, black leather shoes, gloves and a dark grey frock coat with velvet collar. He eschewed the wearing of hats at night.

Peel found Irwin's wattle and mud house to be rather disappointing and no better in standard than any of the others. The new brick building being erected at the back of the block appeared much more substantial in size and construction, as befitted a man of Irwin's position.

A servant opened the front door and, taking Peel's cane, led him through the foyer to a large dining room, which obviously also served as study and library. Irwin and another man were seated at an oak table. The six chairs and table legs were beautifully carved and clearly the work of a master craftsman. Peel was irritated to find the men casually dressed in open-necked shirts and cotton trousers.

Irwin rose and welcomed Peel. He introduced his other guest, George Fletcher Moore, a lawyer and agriculturalist, who had settled on his Millendon grant at Upper Swan. Moore was a man of large frame in his early thirties, with an attentive and intelligent face and broad smile. Peel knew of him and his prowess as a lawyer but they had not previously met.

The group laughed their way through vegetable soup, stewed parakeets, baked apples and two bottles of claret. All born into wealthy families, all well connected, all well educated, all of Tory persuasion and all members of the Church of England, the three epitomised the social fabric and upper class structure of Great Britain. It had just all been reassembled at the Swan River.

At 11 o'clock, Peel returned to the Perth Arms and again nodded at the innkeeper. There were other customers sitting at tables. When they left, Mary followed Peel to the bedroom. To the second, she reckoned it to be an exact repeat of the first session and spent another sleepless night pinned to the mattress. On reflection, after Thomas Peel left for Clarence, Mary was sure she must have pleased him, because on each occasion, as he ejaculated, he had shouted her name.

CHAPTER 8
To the Murray

Clarence was dubbed the deserted village. Families and individuals began drifting away, a few to Mangles Bay but most heading in a northerly direction to Fremantle and some on to Perth and the Upper Swan area. The Andrews' family farewelled the Smith family. There were many tears, Annie and Elizabeth being particularly upset. Only the two women were really aware of the extent of the support system they had built and shared and now were losing. The camp site seemed a forlorn and lonelier place after their departure.

Samuel comforted Annie as best he could but for once felt he was not enough. "I'll be all right love," she said. "Just give me a little time. I miss Elizabeth a great deal. You'll never know how much. But God's will be done. We must now go our own way and that way is with Mr Peel."

Samuel noticed Annie's eyes misted with tears on occasions but made no mention of it. He continued to be as supportive as possible and within the week, at least on the surface, Annie was back to her own contented self.

It was a glorious spring morning when Peel arrived at the Andrews' camp site. A small red kelpie cross bitch ran along behind Goldie, wary of the flying hooves. William and Sara Jane were apprehensive at first but soon patted the playful puppy, receiving affectionate licks in return. Peel dismounted and attempted to discipline the dog with little effect. "I bartered some stores for her. Her name's Smiley but I don't think she knows that yet." The puppy barked happily at her master's comment.

"She really does smile, Mr Peel," Annie said. "Look at her! She's lovely!"

"Well, so she does," Peel acknowledged, while pulling two wrapped parcels from his saddle bags. He had stopped at Samson's store in Fremantle to make the purchases. The long thin one he gave to Samuel. "It's on loan as long as you stay with me."

The larger more bulky item he passed to Annie. "In appreciation of your assistance during my illness," he said almost shyly. Then embarrassed, he abruptly remounted and rode off through the eucalypts.

Annie's surprise and delight showed in her eyes, as she opened the parcel to find rolls of white calico and serviceable grey drill. "How wonderful! There's enough cloth here for petticoats and skirts for me and shirts and trousers for you, Samuel. The offcuts will probably clothe the children. It's very generous of Mr Peel."

She turned to Samuel. Eyes open wide, he was staring at a musket, complete with powder horn and bag of shot. "It's a Brown Bess, Annie! An India Pattern Brown Bess, the same as the soldiers use. We have protection at last. Our safety has been my greatest worry. God bless him!" Clutching their gifts, Samuel and Annie walked back to their shelter. "I'm glad we're going with Mr Peel," Samuel said. "It's a whole new adventure." Annie couldn't help but think there could be more to the gift of the musket than met the eye.

Early next morning, with a chill still hanging in the air, Fred Peel rode into the camp site. "Morning Andrews. Father asked me to summon you to him as soon as possible. You are to travel to Fremantle with Tuckey, Eacott and Watson to fetch a bullock team. The servants and their families will use them to transport themselves and their goods to the Murray. Oh and some of our equipment and animals as well. Captain Meares, Mr Devenish, Father and I will sail on the *Sulphur* with Governor Stirling and a detachment of soldiers to guard us at the Murray. It's all so exciting! We're on our way at last," he added, spurring his horse and galloping away.

Annie reassured Samuel she would be all right alone with the children overnight and he hurried away to report to Peel. It was a long day and night for Annie. While it was light, she kept herself busy with the children and sewing a skirt for herself from the cloth delivered by Mr Peel. After dark, she watched imaginary figures darting in the shadows made by the fire. This was the first night Annie had spent in the bush without adult company and she was nervous. Of what she wasn't sure. She did know she wasn't enjoying the experience at all.

With the sunrise, Annie saw natives behind the trees near the swamp. They were often there in the mornings and it had not worried her before but on previous occasions there had been other adults present. She had never felt threatened before but recently there had been stories of the settlers mistreating them. Some had retaliated and been shot. There had been woundings and killings of settlers in return. She remained in the shelter and tried to ignore them but they came closer and stood watching from about a hundred yards away. Four naked men carrying spears and throwers. Each had a vicious looking stone-headed axe tucked into his woven grass belt. Annie became worried. Very worried. She called the children, settled them in the shelter and told them to be quiet. William thought it was a game and tried to scramble outside. Annie slapped him on the leg and repeated her instructions. The boy sat perfectly still. Only his father hit him. His mother had never lifted a hand to either of the children. Annie pulled on an old pair of Samuel's working trousers before taking off her skirt and jamming his largest hat on her head. She nervously picked up the musket in both hands from where it was leaning against the back of the shelter, squared her shoulders, took a deep breath and strode purposefully through the doorway taking several steps towards the natives. She slowly raised the musket to her shoulder and took up a firing stance. The gun was nearly four feet long and very heavy and she knew she wouldn't be able to hold it up for long. However, the effect was instantaneous. With nervous chattering and signs of consternation the natives turned and scattered for the protection of the trees. They had gone! Annie felt it. She lowered the barrel of the gun and, shaking all over, hurried back to the children. Samuel arrived back mid-morning to find his wife and children crouched in the shelter and Annie still dressed in his clothes.

* * * * *

The incident with the natives upset Samuel greatly. He wanted to get away as soon as possible. Mr Peel had placed him in charge of the expedition and it was a matter of organising the other settlers in their preparation for the trip south and then moving them on their way. Annie and the children were ready within the hour. The other families seemed to dither. Samuel put it down to the unknown, Annie put it down to the absence of a mother and they were both right. After explaining the need to be on their way as soon as possible because of the rendezvous date with HMS *Sulphur*, Samuel began to gain some co-operation and soon had the volunteers assembled near the bullock team harnessed to the four wheeled wagon.

Two hours later they had loaded Peel's heavy equipment and their own few belongings. Pigs and poultry were packed in sturdy crates to prevent their escape. Goldie, two breeding mares and Fred's young stallion were tethered to the wagon. A bull, three cows and a small flock of sheep followed, the cattle wearing loose hobbles to restrict their progress. Annie and the children took turns at walking and riding in the wagon. Samuel rode the horses in rotation and, being an inexperienced horseman, initially had some difficulty, especially with the young stallion. The other four men either drove the bullock team forward with whips or attended the animals.

It was beautiful spring weather, the like of which none of the newly arrived settlers could have possibly imagined. Everything was green and bursting with growth, vitality and colour. The wild flowers were exquisite. The travellers variously called them unbelievable, beautiful and wonderful. The children collected armfuls of the magnificent blooms, remarking on their pleasant fragrance. They called each other when a new species was found. There were hundreds of different blossoming trees, bushes and flowers. The south-west of Australia, the oldest part of the continent, was unique. Nowhere else in the world would these children have been able to view plant life of such ancient origins. The flora of the eucalypt woodlands had survived unchanged through aeons of time.

Assisted by Annie, who had been accepted as a foster mother by the other children, a competition was organised to choose a favourite flower. The brightly-coloured green and yellow cones, like large candles, on the trees with irregular leaves were chosen by everyone except Thomas Watson. Being an agriculturalist, he ruled them out as being trees rather than flowers. He insisted this also ruled out the flowering eucalypts. They all liked the wattle bushes with their masses of yellow flowers, except Charlotte, who said they made her sneeze. Annie didn't like the dark green bushes with the bright red flowers, because she said they looked like chickens' tongues poking out at her. The others all hooted at this. None of the children liked the 'ouch bush', as they named it, because of its spiked tubular leaves, although they agreed that its small brown-centred yellow flowers were pretty. Annie and the girls favoured the delicate orchid type flowers. The men and boys didn't. However, consensus was reached on one wildflower. It had tall deep red stems and long individual green flowers with a red base. Both the stems and flowers were densely coated with a red furry covering. William said the flowers looked like the paws of a kangaroo. Everyone laughingly agreed and the Kangaroo Paw won.

No one had travelled to the Murray River by land except Adam Armstrong and his band. Armstrong's report to Peel regarding the way south was not very helpful and by the time Peel had repeated the directions to Samuel it was a case of the blind leading the blind. However, on the basis of several known geographical features, the most logical route was determined. They should remain reasonably close to the sea but inland of the line of sand hills, so as to stay out of the sandiest areas. They should travel on the western side of the string of lakes located generally on a north-south axis down the coast. They would know they were at the Peel Inlet when they arrived at it! The journey should take about three days.

On the first day, the track was easily discernible and they passed Mt Broun on their left and the turn-off to the Mangles Bay settlement, now known as Rockingham, on their right. From then on there was no track, so they forged their own. Samuel scouted ahead on horseback and then returned to the party to guide them through the least dense scrub. This worked reasonably well. Occasionally, however, when there just didn't seem to be a way through the more heavily treed areas, the men had to wield axes to clear a path and then their progress was very slow. They stopped every few hours to rest, until late afternoon, when they would make camp. Locating the nearest water was easy, they just followed the animals. Samuel found his newly acquired musket a boon for providing fresh meat daily and after early failures was now a reasonable marksman. He tried to convince Annie that she should learn to use the gun but she refused to have anything to do with it.

The estimate of three days for the journey proved to be overly optimistic. It took four and a half days, because the animals were so much trouble, having a tendency to wander off to graze in different directions at every opportunity. It was exasperating but nothing could be done. Samuel realised how much they needed a dog. After finding Annie so terrified at the camp site, he had vowed to obtain one for guard purposes as soon as possible. Now he was doubly determined.

* * * * *

Two days after the full moon, HMS *Sulphur* anchored off Woodman's Point. The ship carried passengers and provisions from the government storehouse in Fremantle. The loading of perishable seeds and fodder from Peel's store began. The following morning, on a light south-east breeze, the *Sulphur* raised anchors and set sail for the Peel Inlet. On board were Governor Stirling, Thomas Peel, his son Frederick with puppy Smiley and John Septimus Roe. Joining them by their own request were Richard Goldsmith Meares and Jack Devenish who, having experimented with the limestone rock area of Clarence and finding it wanting for any serious agricultural pursuits, were taking the opportunity to assess the Murray River area. Also aboard was a detachment of soldiers, comprising Lieutenant Erskine, Sergeant Smallman and twelve privates of the 63rd Regiment.

When Samuel and his weary travellers appeared at the mouth of the Murray River late morning on the first day of October 1830, they found HMS *Sulphur* riding at anchor in the small bay to the west. Peel had been delighted when Stirling had judiciously named it Robert Point after Cousin Robert Peel on their arrival.

CHAPTER 9
The Andrews' Place

After lunch aboard ship, Stirling, Peel, his son Fred, Roe, Meares, Devenish and Erskine were rowed ashore. Held securely in Fred's arms, Smiley barked continuously with excitement and there was laughter and a sense of anticipation among the settlers. The Lieutenant's horse was lowered by cradle into the water and left to swim ashore, spooked all the way by playful dolphins. Following trips ferried ashore the soldiers and the personal belongings of the visitors. Peel's stores and equipment would be unloaded the following morning.

Having seen the arrival of HMS *Sulphur*, Adam Armstrong was there to meet the longboat as it beached. A tall handsome man in his mid-forties, widowed in Scotland, he had been determined to make a new start in the colonies and had been the only employee in Peel's London office to add a degree of sanity to the chaotic proceedings prior to the departure of the *Gilmore*. Since their arrival in the colony, Armstrong had been Peel's most dedicated and hard-working servant. With his five sons, the eldest a strapping twenty year old, the youngest just seven and one daughter aged nine, he had led the first settlers to the Murray area to establish a farm on the Serpentine River about ten miles upstream to the north-east. The abnormally wet winter of 1830 and the subsequent floods had forced the group to withdraw to the mouth of the estuary and await Peel's instructions.

"Welcome, Your Excellency. Welcome, Mr Peel." Armstrong was acknowledged with nods.

By now both land and sea travellers had gathered on the beach, with the exception of Tuckey and Myerick who waited with the wagon and animals. Peel didn't bother to introduce the servants but Annie was honoured when the Governor presented himself to the lone woman.

"I commend you on your courage in joining the new settlement Mrs---," he paused. "Mrs Andrews," Peel butted in. "An honest and faithful servant. Wish I had more like her." Annie, flattered by the attention, curtsied, Sara Jane and William hiding behind her skirts. "A complimentary introduction, Mrs Andrews," Stirling said, as he acknowledged Annie. He was surprised at the comments, as he had never heard Peel say anything positive about anyone before.

After horses were brought for Peel and the Governor, Armstrong led the waiting group along the beach over the sand hills and up a slight hill to the east. From the top of the rise the sea was visible to the west and north and the inlet to the south. It was an impressive view. On the slope protected from the westerlies by the hill, Armstrong's group had erected tents and the beginning of a vegetable garden could be seen in the depression below. Fruit trees were planted in lines, a few sheep were tethered to stakes and a corral contained four milking cows. Several dogs of assorted mixed breeds raced towards them barking and Smiley joined them. About twenty men and women and numerous children stood watching Peel's group approach and then assisted the new arrivals to unload the cart and secure the animals. Samuel chose a piece of dry land on the northern edge of the settlement to set up a temporary camp for his family.

Peel commandeered the largest tent for himself and, after ordering his belongings placed inside, took Stirling on a tour of the area. Certainly the immediate vicinity looked fertile enough, the soil a rich black colour for some hundreds of yards to the east of the declivity. It had obviously been a swamp in some previous era and in the lowest sections was very damp, the horses' hooves leaving deep prints in the mud. Turning to the south, the riders travelled to the inlet through a stand of paper bark trees shedding huge sheets of white bark. Here the water was still muddy after the winter rains. As they walked the horses through salt marsh along the edge of the estuary, the two men discussed progress in the colony.

Peel reined in his horse when they reached the point where the river narrowed. "Let me show you something interesting, Governor. Something I discovered on my last visit to the Murray."

Peel delved into his pocket and pulled out a handkerchief, which he opened to reveal the remnants of lunch. He scattered the bread and pork pieces out across the water as far as he could. The result was instantaneous. The water boiled with activity as hundreds of fish of all sizes leapt and fought for the titbits. Stirling stared in astonishment at the incredible display, holding the reins firmly, as the horses backed away from the water's edge, their eyes rolling in fright.

"Good grief, Peel!" exclaimed Stirling. "I've never seen anything like it. What are they?"

Peel laughed. "A mixture of fish. We caught mainly whiting and mullet when we netted on our last visit and could hardly drag in the net. The settlers here call the really big ones kingfish, probably because they grow to such an exceptionally large size. The estuary is an enormous nursery. The fish feed on one another of course but the waterways supply a never-ending food chain. An ecological Eden, one would suppose."

Stirling was impressed by the demonstration. "We're not short of fish in the Swan but this is quite amazing. I'll wager there'll be a fishery in the Peel Inlet in the future." They chatted on companionably as they rode back to the camp.

The Governor stayed for three days. He and his group slept aboard HMS *Sulphur* and spent the days exploring the area on foot and by sail in the ship's dinghy. Needless to say, fish was the staple diet. Meares and Devenish were pleased with what they saw and expressed a wish to negotiate a land grant further up the Murray where the water would be fresh. Peel said he was amenable to the idea and would discuss such a deal when he next travelled north to civilisation. The men laughed politely at the joke.

Thomas Watson set to and in remarkably short time constructed himself a modest dwelling which Peel immediately appropriated. Watson was furious and an altercation with Peel ensued, resulting in the servant's dismissal. He knew he should not have lost his temper with the Master and that he was being used as an example to the other men but all the same felt hardly done by. With a bag containing his few belongings slung over his shoulder and unable to rid himself of some very disrespectful thoughts about Peel, he set out resolutely on the track leading back to Fremantle.

Peel negotiated verbal contracts with his newly-arrived servants. The married men were each allotted fifty acres, to which they were not legally entitled until the completion of three years of service. For this concession, they agreed to give the Master one quarter of their produce for two years. Peel would provide them with initial seed and cuttings and some farm implements. In addition, supplies such as sugar, tea and vinegar would be made available from Peel's store on a barter basis. Tuckey and Eacott received adjacent blocks of land to the north-east of Peel's farm and Mandurah House as it became known. Myerick, being single, was ordered to stay in the village and work Peel's land, for which he would receive a labourer's wage.

The contract settled between Peel and the Andrews was different and in many ways a generous one. They were allocated the land on the Serpentine River that Samuel had coveted on his previous journey to the area but in addition to a portion of seeds and cuttings and basic farm implements, Peel provided Samuel with a mare in foal and riding accoutrements, a cow in calf, two ewes and two nannies with young at foot, eight piglets and six hens accompanied by a possessive, strutting cock. However, the trade-off for such an open-handed gesture was two fold. The animals remained Peel's possessions and every second offspring was to be handed over to him when mature enough to be weaned. Such an arrangement had obvious benefits for both parties but for the Andrews' family it was a dream come true. The further condition was ill-defined and rather nebulous in nature and extent. Peel could call on Annie or Samuel for assistance at any time, the only proviso being that the care and safety of the children would never be compromised.

When Adam Armstrong made the suggestion that Samuel take his two oldest sons, Adam Junior and Francis, with him to his selected land, the offer was accepted with alacrity. Adam wanted his sons to receive instruction in carpentry and to attain a degree of independence. Samuel needed as much help as he could get and two well built young men also added to the security of his family.

Privately, Armstrong approached Annie. "Mrs Andrews, I have a special request to make of you." Armstrong was fiddling with the rim of his straw hat and showing outward signs of embarrassment. He cleared his throat. "Mrs Andrews, my wife died seven years ago and although I have tried hard to be both mother and father to my children, there are occasions when I know I have not been able to provide adequately for the instruction of my sons with regard to etiquette and dealings with women. Could I prevail upon you to take every opportunity to tutor Adam and Francis in this regard? I would be appreciative of any advice you saw fit to give them."

Annie replied with inward amusement but outward solemnity. "Mr Armstrong, thank you for placing your trust in me regarding such an important matter. I would be pleased to do so and will take the responsibility very seriously."

Peel supplied the bullock cart and, with Eacott as the driver, the Andrews' gear and those animals which could be caged were transported up the estuary. The children rode on the flat-top. Everybody else, including the larger animals, walked.

* * * * *

The Andrews' family had been at their place on the Serpentine River for several weeks and, together with Adam and Francis, had worked with enormous energy to establish some of the necessary structures for the farm. Their selected land was located on the northern side of the major channel of the Serpentine River where it branched as it entered the inlet, close to the delta of the Murray and about seven miles from Peel's village. Because of the windings of the Serpentine, a tail of land about one mile in length surrounded on three sides by water was created. This meant that only a few hundred yards of brush fence needed to be constructed to keep the animals confined. With the key animals tethered securely and canvas and brush shelters for themselves, this had been the first task completed. It took two weeks and resulted in aching backs, scratched limbs and blisters upon blisters.

The proximity to the river and inlet caused Annie great anxiety. As much as she tried to keep an eye on them, there were times when Sara Jane or William or both just seemed to vanish. On these occasions, everyone would down tools and there would be a frantic search. Eventually, Samuel forbade them going

84

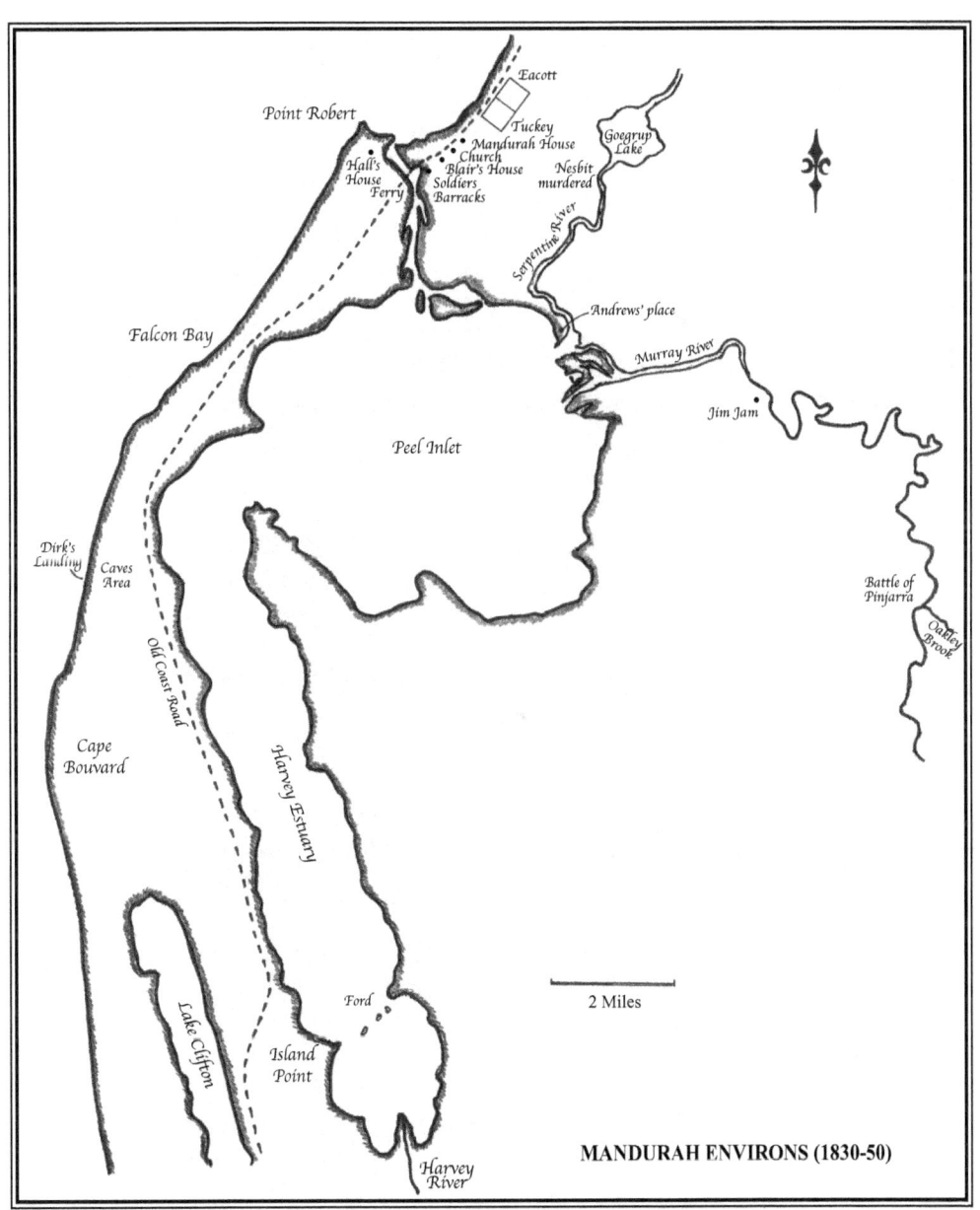

Point Robert

Eacott

Tuckey
Mandurah House
Church
Blair's House
Soldiers
Barracks

Hall's
House
Ferry

Nesbit
murdered

Goegrup
Lake

Serpentine River

Falcon Bay

Andrews' place

Murray River

Jim Jam

Peel Inlet

Dirk's
Landing

Caves
Area

Battle of
Pinjarra

Oakley
Brook

Old Coast Road

Cape
Bouvard

Harvey Estuary

Lake Clifton

Ford

2 Miles

Island
Point

Harvey
River

MANDURAH ENVIRONS (1830-50)

near the water. Slaps and cross words followed but the attraction was too great. Finally, Francis politely intervened. He was a caring and likeable seventeen year old, who adored Sara Jane and William and spent much of his free time entertaining them. Eventually, after a particularly exasperating day, when the children wandered away several times to paddle, Francis asked whether he could try an experiment. At the end of their tether, Annie and Samuel agreed.

"Right," said Francis. "Work's over for today. We're going to the sandy beach over there. I'm in charge and everyone must call me 'Sir' and follow all my orders. Anyone who doesn't must spend time collecting firewood."

There were groans from the waiting group. "Anything but that," Adam said. "Sir!"

Sara Jane and William could sense a game coming up and had silly grins on their faces. Like the Pied Piper, Francis led them to the river.

"Mrs Andrews. You are excused because you are on watch." Francis winked at the woman he now saw as his surrogate mother and whom he respected enormously. "You may sit on that log." He pointed to a dead tree trunk washed up on the river's edge and pulled a serious face, frowning and pursing his lips.

"There will be no laughing, William."

Holding both hands over his mouth the boy tried desperately not to laugh.

"You will all strip to your trousers, except Sara Jane who has special permission to keep her dress on." Everyone kept a straight face.

"All make a line facing the water. Space out!" Francis ordered. "On my command slowly march into the river. Do not stop and do not turn around. March!"

With exaggerated and stiff movements, Samuel and Adam commenced a slow march into the water.

William and Sara Jane hesitated for a moment, then followed tentatively. As the water reached their chest, they both glanced back at their mother who pretended to be watching a noisy flock of gulls disputing ownership of a dead fish.

The children took further steps. Sara Jane being the shortest, began to panic as the water level reached her chin. "I can't go any further," she called.

"Keep marching," came from Francis.

"Stop. I have to stop," cried the little girl, gasping to take a breath.

"Everybody stop," shouted Francis. "The game is over."

He rushed into the water and scooped Sara Jane up with one arm and William with the other. Both children looked frightened as he gently lowered them to the dry sand.

"It's all right my little ones. The serious part of the game is over. The fun is now about to begin."

The adults crowded around the children patting, laughing, hugging and reassuring. Annie explained the danger and how they should be afraid of the water until they had learned to float and swim. Then the lesson started. Everybody had so much to say that the children were totally confused.

"Quiet!" Francis frowned at Samuel and Adam. "No one gave you permission to talk. Go and collect firewood. Mrs Andrews and I will instruct the children in safety in the water."

Looking absurdly abject, the two men shuffled off slowly with shoulders hunched. The children looked to their mother and Francis and then heard gales of laughter from the direction of the house. Everyone joined in.

From then on, until the children could demonstrate confidence and competence in the water, a time was set aside for daily lessons. Annie followed Francis' lead and together they patiently taught the eager children to float, then kick, then dog paddle. Sara Jane was much more co-ordinated and learned faster than William who splashed a great deal for little forward progress. However, within a few weeks, both children could stay afloat and tread water. It wasn't long before they could dog paddle. Samuel and Annie felt indebted to Francis. They just wouldn't have known where to begin and praised him as a born teacher.

The praise was not lightly given. Both Adam Junior and Francis were well educated in English expression, reading and writing. They spoke the King's English, as the saying went. Annie saw another opportunity and that night, after an early evening meal, broached the subject. "Adam and Francis, I have a favour to ask."

The Armstrong brothers looked up from their final chores for the day, polishing the leather gear of the farm horse. "Yes, Mrs Andrews," said Francis. "What can we do for you?"

"Well, you both speak so well. Although I received some instruction from the local vicar and have always tried to improve my speech, I know I am limited. Would you please correct the children whenever they use wrong words?"

Francis smiled but seeing Annie looking embarrassed, he stopped instantly. "I'm sorry ma'am. I wasn't laughing at you but our father was always correcting us and now you are asking us to be the tutors. It is surely poetic justice. Of course, we will. Won't we Adam?"

Adam nodded but without enthusiasm. "Not all the time," he said. "It was the bane of my life as a child and I would not inflict such constant correction on anyone. However, if the error is blatant, I will suggest an alternative."

It was settled and the children rather enjoyed the attention. Their pronunciation and grammar improved and Francis began to entertain the possibility of becoming a teacher.

Following their exhausting introduction to fencing, a corral was built of tree trunks to house the larger animals at night and an extensive vegetable garden prepared. Cuttings of citrus, apple and fig trees and grape vines were planted. Oats were experimentally seeded in a small plot. Samuel had been told by Adam Armstrong Senior that it was a crop better able to stand a potentially salty soil than wheat. Francis constructed a lifelike scarecrow to frighten the birds from the vegetables as fragile leaves broke the earth's surface but the two rowdy children were far more effective.

Food was not a problem for the Serpentine group because birds, fish, crabs and kangaroos were plentiful. The Brown Bess was only used to shoot the occasional pelican or kangaroo. Adam had created a fishing net of sorts out of string begged from his father and became adroit in casting it from boughs overhanging the river.

Meanwhile, the Andrews and Armstrongs lived in separate tents, with Annie preparing all the food at a common fireplace. Two wells, although not deeply dug, supplied fresh water with a brackish taste, which Annie insisted on boiling for drinking purposes. A privy had been built fifty yards from the site of the house. Now all their efforts were concentrated on house building and Annie was grateful that summer was approaching with the weather mainly fine and warm.

* * * * *

"Samuel, I can't do any more for the moment." Annie was helping to plaster mud from the river onto the walls of the house. "I'll have to rest." She put down her bucket and slowly straightened her back, hands on hips. The baby was not showing yet but was making its presence felt.

"Sit down, lass. You've done enough for one day anyway." Samuel led Annie to their outside seating area. It comprised three large logs lying in a triangular formation about ten yards from the partly-built house. It also acted as a play pit for the children. "That's enough boys," Samuel called to Adam and Francis. "We'll pack it in for the day. Go for a swim and catch some fish and crabs for supper."

A wattle and daub house was exactly that. First a solid framework was constructed from the branches of eucalypts. The corner posts were thick and set deeply into the ground. The cross bars needed to be reasonably straight and long and thick enough to bear the roof. Additional cross bars were used as a base for the walls. Samuel showed the young men how to chop and chisel sections from the wood so they fitted snugly where they came together in the structure. Strong cord was used to hold the struts in place until holes were bored with brace and bit to take precious nails or screws. Next, branches from the wattle tree were collected and tied vertically, layer upon layer, to the cross bars, leaving strategically placed spaces for doors and window frames. Finally, the brushwood walls were plastered with mud. This needed to be done in thin layers and left to dry before the next layer was applied. It was a back-breaking task. The roof was simply sheets of paperbark laid on canvas spread over thin beams. The canvas acted as a ceiling and prevented insects falling into the house. Further beams were placed over the bark covering to prevent the roof being carried away in the wind. Canvas doors and windows were a temporary measure and the sand floor was coated with mud and compacted to reduce the incidence of fleas.

The house slowly took shape. It faced east for the morning sun and had a verandah at the rear where the cooking was done in an open fireplace. Samuel's attention to detail was evident and the structure was sturdy and symmetrically pleasing to the eye. With the addition of canvas partitions and a lean-to for Adam and Francis, the basic construction was completed and belongings moved inside.

Weeks passed and the new settlers gradually established the Andrews' Place, as it became known. Each evening after supper a roster of chores was prepared for the following day. Everyone was involved in the discussion and in the decision-making, as far as was practicable. The knowledge of the Armstrong boys, gained from their previous experience farming up-river, was invaluable. It was a pleasant and co-operative working environment, satisfying and productive for all. Annie included the Armstrongs as part of her family and the young men received the loving and demonstrative care they had missed for so many years.

By early summer, the mare and cow had given birth to their young, most of the fruit trees were progressing well and the vegetable patch was producing a varied and continuous supply of fresh vegetables. Carrots, lettuce, peas, beans, beetroot, tomatoes and pumpkin flourished in the rich soil. However, there were some disappointments. The apple trees found the temperatures too high and the potatoes found the soil too wet. The vegetables attracted snails like magnets and the only solution was to pick them individually from the plants by hand. The children became adept at de-snailing the vegetable patch each morning with quite remarkable speed and thoroughness. All in all, Samuel could not have asked for more.

He often pondered about the natives. Why were they never seen on his land? They were certainly becoming a nuisance at the Village, hanging around waiting for handouts of flour, stealing anything not returned to store sheds and scaring the settlers when they approached silently through the bush. They had an uncanny ability to appear suddenly as if they had just materialised from nowhere. In the same way they seemed to be able to melt into the bush, becoming invisible when it suited them. Samuel was constantly on the alert but had not seen one native in the area.

* * * * *

As often seems to happen when everything is going well, almost too well, fate took a hand. It was nearly time for lunch and Annie was stirring a large pot of kangaroo stew. The men were working some distance away and the children had gone with them to give their mother a break while she prepared the main meal of the day. She idly watched the fowl. Walk, scratch, peck. Walk, scratch, peck.

Then suddenly, without warning, Annie was struck by an excruciating pain. A pain so severe that she fell to her knees, gasping for breath and doubled over in agony. She knew instinctively that it was the baby coming ahead of time. There had been spots of blood over the past few weeks which had not occurred in any previous pregnancies. She had prayed to God for help and being a very pragmatic person accepted there was little else she could do.

The pain continued mercilessly and felt like a burning knife turning in her abdomen. Annie tried to call Samuel but no sound came. She could not move. Then she felt the first dribble of hot liquid running down her leg and saw the stain spreading through the cloth of her dress, followed by a sudden rush of fluid. She tried to hold the flow as she felt the thicker mucous membrane and tissue being passed. Annie knew her baby was flowing into the earth and there was nothing she could do. She began sobbing.

The men and children found her half an hour later when hunger drove them to the house. Samuel started running when he saw Annie on the ground. "Annie. Annie. Oh, my God! Annie." He gently picked up his semi-conscious wife and carried her into the house, placing her on the main bed that he had only recently and so proudly completed. Francis took the children on a walk. Adam brought water and left Samuel to attend to Annie. When she came around, she had been washed and clothed in a nightdress. Samuel sat beside her, unashamedly crying.

The pain subsided somewhat but the bleeding continued for days. Annie was too weak to get up and Samuel ministered to her needs. The children and Adam and Francis made short visits behind the canvas curtain but Annie spent most of her time sleeping and trying to regain her strength. Samuel stayed by her side, Francis looked after the children and Adam did the cooking and essential chores. It had been a severe shock for everyone.

Several weeks passed before Annie was able to take tentative steps and assume control of the running of the house. An infection was responsible for a slower than expected recovery and this caused her further worry but eventually her body returned to health. She knew her inner self would require far more time to mend, as she grieved silently for the lost baby.

* * * * *

Just before Christmas, Samuel constructed a wooden contraption to trail behind the mare. The stimulus for invention arose from the need to carry produce to and from Peeltown. Samuel had discovered that the easiest way to travel to the river mouth was to skirt the estuary shore where the sand was firm. The Trail consisted of two long light branches connected by cross arms, all with the bark scraped from them and fastened together with rope and strips of hide. The middle segment was covered with kangaroo skins sewn to the cross struts. It was tied to the horse's saddle and, at its widest part at the base, its two long legs ran across the sand. Thus goods could be strapped to the Trail for transportation.

Adam and Francis set out on Christmas Eve with the farm's produce for Mr Peel and additional vegetables for barter. Twelve chickens were packed into a crate and made a huge fuss about their captivity as they were strapped to the Trail. The cooking essentials needed were flour, tea, salt and sugar but in addition they all craved fresh fruit and dripping or lard. Kangaroos had such lean meat that little fat could be obtained from their flesh. The Armstrongs were also to ask if any cloth and sewing necessities were available, because they all needed a new set of clothing. The young men would spend the festive season with their father, sister and brothers before returning.

It was a quiet Christmas for Annie, Samuel and the children. There was a wattle Christmas tree with the star woven from swamp spinifex and the decorations a variety of bird feathers. One of the roosters was pot-roasted in the Dutch oven and served with fresh vegetables and gravy made from the juice. The meal was special because it was their first home-grown Christmas dinner. The children were taught some of the easier hymns and carols and told stories, remembered from church services. They had a Bible but Annie could only read the simple words and Samuel none at all. Only the children received gifts and William was presented with a rudimentary fishing pole and Sara Jane a faceless rag doll.

The afternoon was spent on the estuary's edge building sand castles and trying out the fishing rod. William caught four crabs, several snags and no fish. After much persuasion, even though it was Christmas Day, William and Sara Jane were allowed to play in the shallows to cool off. It was still very hot. Samuel and Annie held hands and watched contentedly from the shade of a large paperbark tree.

Several days later, when the wishbone had dried out somewhat, Samuel and Annie hooked their little fingers and pulled but weren't sure what to make of it when both sides snapped so neither could make a wish. Annie hoped it was not an omen.

* * * * *

91

Peel invited himself and Fred to Christmas dinner with the Armstrongs, taking two bottles of claret as his contribution to the fare. He had assumed the role of the benevolent dictator of Peeltown and was rather enjoying the experience. It intensely annoyed everyone else and he knew it but didn't care one iota.

By the time lunch was over, it was mid-afternoon and Peel had drunk both bottles of claret. Fred helped him home but Peel just picked up another bottle and insisted on being accompanied to the recently constructed army barracks in Soldier's Cove a mile south of his house. He lasted another two hours in the company of the soldiers and passed out just before dusk, propped up by the trunk of a gum tree. Fred finally fell asleep on the sand next to his father, who snored his way through the night.

CHAPTER 10

Western Australia for Me

The afternoon sun beat down on black-haired, black-bearded, black-skinned men, who crouched on haunches, loudly discussing a matter of importance to the tribe. Their long beards partially covered the rows of cicatrices across their chests. They were Bindjareb men, renowned as the fiercest fighters of the Nyoongar people. More mesomorphic in build than most western Aborigines, they were tall and had strong physiques. There was much gesticulation. A wrong must be redressed. Four days before, a brother of one of the men had been killed near the large white man's settlement two day's walk away. He was returning after visiting a relative to deliver a letter stick on behalf of the tribe and news had travelled back that he was shot when he wandered into an area in which white men were hunting kangaroos. Now a decision must be made about avenging his death.

The oldest man spoke. "Geeyar is too young to travel alone. He has just entered manhood and should not bear such responsibility."

A hot head burst in. "I will avenge!" The name of the dead man could not be spoken or his soul would not rest in peace.

Another shook his head and his fist. "I am more closely related. I will do it." They were getting nowhere.

The old man sighed audibly. "The matter has been discussed at length and the sun will soon set. I suggest that a group of men escort Geeyar and assist him in avenging his brother." He paused. "Is there a better idea?"

There was silence. The suggestion had merit. All close relatives who so desired could be involved and receive acknowledgment from the family. The elder rose, leaving Geeyar to choose who would accompany him and which white men were to be attacked.

* * * * *

Sergeant John Smallman was off-duty and dozing in the early morning sun. A cord fishing line dangled from his hand as he leaned against an empty cask at the river's edge. The cheekiest of the gulls roused him periodically as they ran up the sand to steal the scraps of pickled pork he was using for bait.

He awoke with a start, warned by his soldier's sixth sense that something was wrong. The gulls were squawking as they now floated together in safety on the water. Shading his eyes, Smallman quickly looked around. At first he saw nothing out of order but then to the south noticed a group of natives approaching through the samphire marsh. The sergeant scrambled to his feet and ran up the beach shouting loudly to warn Lieutenant Erskine and the privates cooking their breakfast over open fires. There was a rush for guns, powder and shot and bayonets were hurriedly fitted. The Lieutenant ordered the soldiers to remain at arms and the two women and their children to hide in the huts. Smallman was to await the blacks unarmed on the beach to ascertain their intentions.

Their intentions became obvious all too quickly. The moment they judged themselves within range, the natives launched a volley of spears which hummed towards Smallman. Weaving and ducking he sprinted to the safety of the barracks and grabbed his gun. Approaching at a run, the attackers threw another barrage of spears.

"Take aim! Fire!" shouted Lieutenant Erskine.

Corporal Barron lined up the young man leading the attackers and fired. Geeyar screamed in pain as he took the ball in his right forearm, which now hung uselessly at a grotesque angle.

The natives stopped in their tracks, turned and fled the way they had come.

In a matter of minutes, things returned to normal, although some of the younger men were clearly shaken by their first encounter with natives. The women and children crept from the shelter of the huts. From that day on, guards were always on duty.

* * * * *

During the first few months of 1831, a number of settlers left the Murray, Armstrong and his children among them. Although there were no further attacks, the constant sighting of natives was unnerving and some of the men wanted better guarantees of safety for their families. Adam Junior and Francis departed with their father for Perth leaving a saddened Andrews' family. The young men were just as upset. There was much hugging, many goodbyes and occasional surreptitious dashing of tears from the corners of eyes.

As the sorrow following the departure of Adam Junior and Francis slowly subsided, Samuel and Annie settled into their new lifestyle and delighted in their existence on the farm. They harvested their crops and, with meat and fish in abundance, there was always plenty to eat. The cow provided milk and the fowl eggs. Annie made bread in the Dutch oven and butter in a small box-churn. As the female animals came into season, they were taken to Peeltown and serviced and duly produced young. The Master's entitlements were delivered regularly. After one such visit to Peeltown, Samuel returned with one of Smiley's pups, a black kelpie cross, which not surprisingly was immediately dubbed Blackie by William. "Blackie. Blackie. He's black all over," the boy shouted.

"The dog answers to Happy," Samuel said quietly. "He's already been named by Master Frederick and I see no reason to change it." Seeing the crestfallen look on his son's face, he followed up by saying "Come on son, call Happy. He needs lots of love now he's left the litter."

William called the puppy, who took an exuberant leap at the boy accompanied by much barking and tail wagging. So Happy he became and Happy he was.

Annie's only sadness was brought about by Samuel's decision not to risk her health again through another pregnancy. He had been shocked far more than he would admit by the miscarriage and her subsequent illness and refused to tempt fate by engaging in sexual intercourse. Because of their total and consuming love for one another, it was a huge sacrifice for both of them.

"I could not live with myself Annie. Don't you understand? If anything happened to you I would totally blame myself."

Annie argued back. "I want more children. God will protect us, I'm sure. Please Samuel. It's not right. We are man and wife." Samuel tried to make light of the situation by saying they would just have to save and store their love and feelings until Annie ceased her monthly courses. Annie insisted she would take the risk. Samuel would not allow her to do so.

* * * * *

It was now nearly a year since Peel had arrived at the Murray. On occasions, he travelled by horseback to Clarence to finalise the sale of items from his store or to Perth for a break from Peeltown but it was a long, lonely ride.

Mail and supplies from the Government Store at Fremantle were delivered every three months aboard HMS *Sulphur*. The regular order comprised barrels of pickled pork, flour, sugar, tea, suet, tobacco and vinegar, together with lamp oil, candles and cloth. The goods were then issued from Peel's store. Rum was provided initially but discontinued after several alcohol-induced fights were broken up, with some of the men nursing black eyes and bruises for days afterwards.

Mary wrote regularly asking about her husband's house and establishment. Where was he? What did the house look like? How many rooms did it have? What sort of carriage did he have? Had he purchased a pianoforte for her yet? Was there a problem with the natives? When Peel did reply, it was in vague terms. He always ended on an optimistic note, promising that everything would be in place in about twelve months' time. The end of the twelve months never came.

Peel continued to write long epistles to Governor Stirling about difficulties on the Murray and in his boredom became more and more insistent. Stirling would sigh in exasperation when another bundle of mail arrived via the *Sulphur*. Peel received polite responses that rarely acceded to any of his requests. Nevertheless, because of the very nature of the man, constantly demanding attention somehow made him feel better.

When HMS *Sulphur* arrived at the Murray in late August, it brought three letters for Mr Thomas Peel Esq. One bore the Royal Coat of Arms seal, one the Agricultural Society seal and the third, a personal seal. Peel tore open the official letter to find an invitation to the inaugural Governor's Ball to be held in Perth on September 2nd. Thinking about it, he became quite excited. Back to civilisation! Back to the Perth Arms and Mary! The second letter gave notice of a special meeting of the Agricultural Society to be held at noon on the same day. The third letter was an offer by Peter Broun for Peel to join his party for the Ball. Mr Broun was inviting guests from outlying places to stay at his Perth residence before and after the event.

Just what I've needed, thought Peel. Everyone who's anyone will be there. I'll be able to negotiate those land grants with Meares and Devenish and catch up with the latest news and gossip. Peel could hardly wait and began preparations the following day. At dawn on the morning of the last day of August, he set off north on Goldie.

After a tiring, full day's ride, Peel spent the night at Collins Hotel in Fremantle. The following morning, he purchased a new dark grey suit, silk shirt and tie and dancing pumps and caught the ferry to Perth, leaving Goldie stabled at the hotel. Arriving at the Barrack Street landing mid-afternoon, he lugged his gear up the hill to the Perth Arms where he bluntly asked the innkeeper whether Mary was available. He was told that she had been unwell and was staying in Guildford with friends. Cursing, Peel paid the yard boy to carry his gear to Broun's house on the corner of Hay and Irwin Streets. There he was met by a gracious Caroline Broun and made to feel welcome with wine, sandwiches and cake, before falling satiated onto a mattress in the single men's dormitory, a large tent erected in the backyard. He did not stir as newcomers made their way to palliasses with the aid of lamps.

On the day of the Ball, the remaining guests, those who lived in reasonable proximity to Perth, arrived at Broun's house. Peel was flattered to find that the man second in status to the Governor had invited only those persons who in Peel's opinion were suitable and commensurate with his own class. Colonel Hanson, Quartermaster-General, stationed in Madras and a young naval lieutenant, Lord Frederick Beauclerk, were invalids from the Indian wars; Captain Thomas Bannister had led the first overland expedition between Fremantle and King George Sound; Mr George Leake, a well known merchant and landowner at Upper Swan, with his daughter Ann; and Captain William Dance of HMS *Sulphur* with his wife Helena.

Peel attended the meeting and luncheon of the Agricultural Society at noon, during which over fifty men of agricultural, horticultural and pastoral interests approved a petition to the Home Government asking that the Colonial Treasury be authorised to make advances for the purchase of stock. An injection of money and stock was considered essential to boost colonial resources. The afternoon was spent walking around Perth with Captain Bannister, who provided Peel with much valuable information about the country between the Swan River and Albany. Together with three other men, Bannister had blazed a trail to the south-east to meet the Canning River at Kelmscott and then travelled south and east to King George Sound. Peel was interested to hear as much as possible about the hinterland, because in the back of his mind was the germ of an idea of making Peeltown one of the stopovers for travellers making their way south and south-east.

Soon after 7 o'clock, Mr and Mrs Broun and their guests began assembling in the drawing room. As the appointed hour approached, excitement and anticipation filled the air. George Leake, a charming and cultured widower, had privately asked Thomas whether he would jointly escort his daughter Ann to the Ball and Thomas had felt honoured, knowing that women would be in the minority that night. Strains of 'Greensleeves', played by the military band, could be heard drifting through the trees. The sky was clear and stars twinkled above. Led by the Broun's, the way lit by lanterns held by servants, the group set off along a path just wide enough for two. Thomas was proud, thoroughly enjoying the experience of having a sophisticated young woman on his arm. Ann was equally proud at being escorted by the largest landowner in the colony and a cousin of Robert Peel. The company chattered and laughed as it moved along the path.

For the first time since the settlers had arrived at the Swan, protocol prevailed. The Ball was an obvious attempt by Stirling, prompted by his wife, to raise morale and remind those of appropriate class and status that wherever possible the colony should hold to the traditions and elegance of the Old Country.

The Governor, in full dress uniform, accompanied by Mrs Stirling, wearing a low cut gown and sparkling jewels, waited to formally receive their guests as they were introduced by the aide-de-camp. Ann felt as though dozens of butterflies were flying around inside her and only kept her calm by quietly taking deep breaths.

"Ah, Mr Peel. Good evening. We are glad you could make it up from the Murray. Miss Leake you look a picture this evening."

"Good evening, your Excellency, Mrs Stirling," they said, bowing and curtsying respectively and moving on as the next introductions were made. With a hundred and eighty guests to introduce, the aide-de-camp could not allow tarrying.

Four rooms of the Governor's house with connecting arcade and verandah were provided for the visitors. A large supper marquee had been erected with openings onto a common space to extend the area for dancing. It was splendidly fitted, decorated and festooned with naval flags and bunting. Facing the entertainment area, the regimental band sat stiffly on a raised platform awaiting the end of formalities. White river sand had been spread to hide the black dirt and a dance floor constructed. Guests, gathering in groups, were offered either a fruit or rum punch by uniformed waiters. Mr and Mrs William Brockman conversed with Captain and Mrs Richard Goldsmith Meares and Mr and Mrs James Drummond, doubtless about agriculture and the Leakes, Shentons, Samsons and Batemans, were almost certainly discussing commercial interests. That is, at least the husbands were. The wives were comparing finery behind fluttering fans. There was a hum of excited conversation.

Ann and Peel joined her family group. She accepted a glass of non-alcoholic punch and viewed the scene while talking politely. The ladies wore an impressive array of dresses and stoles in every shade of every colour with all the family jewels on display. Ann felt sorry for the large number of men restricted in their formal attire as always. Medical men, lawyers and clergymen wore black suits and naval and military officers and appointed government officials were dressed in blue frockcoats with gilt crown buttons and white duck trousers. Those from the land were free to dress more flamboyantly and did so. Mr Peel looked impeccable in his fine new clothes. Without exception, both men and women wore gloves.

Many gentlemen stopped and bowed to Ann. Some made small talk, others intimated they would return to claim a dance later in the evening. Being the only child of George Leake had its advantages. Peel became quite proprietorial, taking her arm and following the Governor and Mrs Stirling to the centre of the large open verandah for the first dance. Luckily it was the customary waltz with which they were both familiar.

Hours passed and the dancing continued. Peel was glad to be interrupted occasionally by one of the younger men in order to give himself a break and time for a drink. Besides, he didn't know many of the steps and preferred to sit out the gallopades and Spanish dances. He was relieved when two sets of old fashioned dances were laughingly called for by those who did not dance the modern steps and particularly pleased when Caroline Broun approached him for the Ladies' Choice.

At midnight, there was a pause in proceedings as glasses were filled with champagne. Governor Stirling proposed the Royal Toast to His Majesty, King William IV and everyone lifted their glasses as the band played 'God save the King'.

The Governor then proposed a second toast. Holding his glass high and turning to face his wife, he said, "To the Ladies of the Colony, who have so nobly and cheerfully borne fatigues and hardships with their husbands in the settlement of this new land." Murmurs of surprise and nods of agreement followed as the males of the company lifted their glasses. "To the Ladies!" came the loud assent in unison.

Within minutes, the trestles in the marquee were covered with a delicious and abundant supper. There were ample supplies of fresh bread, salads and vegetables, curried eggs, poultry, roasted and pickled meat and veal and ham pies. Apple pies, trifles, cakes and jellies with jugs of custard and cream were provided for the sweet tooths. It was the largest banquet held in the colony to that date and the guests showed their appreciation by leaving little food on the tables.

As the last supper plates were removed, the bandmaster signalled and a long chord was played. The aide-de-camp took up a position in view of all the guests and waited for silence. Excited chatter was hushed as Governor Stirling stepped forward.

"Ladies and gentlemen, this evening we have a pleasant surprise for you." Heads turned to one another and everyone began talking again. Stirling smiled and waited patiently for attention. There weren't too many pleasant surprises in a new settlement.

"I'm sure you'll concur that Mr George Moore is recognised as the foremost bard of the colony." There was an immediate murmur of agreement and acknowledgment from the assembled guests.

"I am pleased to announce that this evening Mr Moore is to entertain us. He will perform his latest verse to music." There was polite applause but as Moore walked to stand in front of the band the clapping increased in anticipation. Lawyer, settler and explorer, he was a respected and admired member of the community.

The band played the chorus of the popular Irish ballad 'Ballinamona Oro' as Moore straightened his back and threw back his head to better project his voice to the large crowd. He burst into song with feeling, carefully enunciating the words and adding gestures wherever possible. His smiling face and obvious enjoyment in his own performance delighted the crowd. He sang:

From the old Western world we have come to explore
The wilds of this Western Australian shore;
In search of a country, we've ventured to roam,
And now that we've found it, let's make it our home.

And what though the colony's new, Sirs,
And inhabitants yet may be few, Sirs,
They'll soon be increasing here too, Sirs,
So Western Australia for me.

With care and experience, I'm sure 'twill be found
Two crops in the year we may get from the ground;
Good wood and good water, good flesh and good fish,
Good soil and good clime and what more could you wish.

Then let every one earnestly strive, Sirs,
Do his best, be alert and alive, Sirs,
We'll soon see our colony thrive, Sirs,
So Western Australia for me.

No furious south-easterns, no burning simoon
Our harvests to blight and our fruits to consume,
No terrible plague, nor no pestilent air
Our livers to waste, though our lives they may spare.

Our skies are all cloudless and bright, Sirs,
And sweet is our lovely moonlight, Sirs,
Oh this is the clime of delight, Sirs,
So Western Australia for me.

No lions or tigers we here dread to meet,
Our innocent quadrupeds hop on two feet;
No tithes and no taxes we here have to pay,
And our geese are all swans, as some witty folks say.

Here we live without trouble or stealth, Sirs,
Our currency's all sterling wealth, Sirs,
So here's to our Governor's health, Sirs,
And Western Australia for me.

George Fletcher Moore raised both hands in the air as he concluded, then gave the Governor a slight bow from the waist. The guests had not missed his pun and nod to Stirling as he sang 'Our currency's all sterling wealth, Sirs' and now with much laughter the crowd joined in exuberant applause. Take that Stirling, thought Moore with a great deal of glee at his ingenuity. See if you can call our new colony anything else except Western Australia now! Everyone in the colony was aware of Stirling's preference for the poetic name used by the Greeks and Romans. Hesperia! Land looking west! Country looking towards the setting sun indeed! Moore bowed facetiously to the crowd to acknowledge the prolonged clapping.

"Encore! Encore!" At first, the call came from a few but was quickly picked up by all. The Governor himself continued to applaud. Moore bowed again in response to the acclamation and turned to the band. The introductory chords over, he began singing again but this time he was joined by those with a good memory. 'Western Australia for me' was echoed loudly at the end of each stanza and Moore was convinced it was having the desired effect. He made sure that special emphasis was placed on the first syllable of the word 'Western'.

Dancing resumed and a second supper, much lighter than the first, was served at 4 o'clock. As the sun rose over the Darling Range, the band members packed away their instruments. Weary guests wandered back to their homes, or the homes of their hosts, singing the song that was to name the colony.

* * * * *

On a fine day in July 1832, George Fletcher Moore, newly appointed Civil Commissioner and Member of the Legislative Council, set out to ride to Perth from his property on the upper Swan. He was pleased with events of the last six months and saw his elevation in the colonial government as a reward for public service. Captain James Stirling's commission as Governor and Commander-in-Chief, as well as his appointment to Vice-Admiral of the colony, had arrived in December and was well received by the settlers, who accepted it as a sign of the increasing development and status of the colony. The first sitting of the Legislative Council had been held in February and its principal business was to establish the Civil Court. Moore's appointment as Civil Commissioner had followed.

Today's meeting would be interesting. It had all been set up so very well. Certain influential citizens of the colony had collaborated to make sure that the land-holding settlers were fully informed on certain facts about the present state of the colony and the need for representation to His Majesty's government for assistance. With his improved status, Stirling would be in a better position to negotiate on behalf of the colony. Letters to the Colonial Office had achieved little, so a personal approach was deemed necessary. Stirling must travel back to London and intercede on their behalf.

Moore patted his pocket. He had prepared the petition to the Secretary of State for the Colonies after a great deal of discussion with the Governor and members of the Legislative Council. It laid out the problems facing the colony, which in a nutshell were the scarcity of provisions, the want of cash, the need for more livestock and the fear of the natives. With signatures from all the eminent citizens adjoined this day, the petition would be a document of importance and hopefully initiate positive action in the Colonial Office. Moore whistled as his horse trotted along the path beside the Swan River. He kept a close lookout and observed the precaution of wearing a brace of pistols in his belt.

* * * * *

101

Following his arrival in London in December 1832, Stirling immediately called upon Under-Secretary Hay at the Colonial Office. He presented the petition and requested that an increased annual vote be considered by the Parliament. Hay was unsympathetic.

"Public and parliamentary attitudes towards the colonies have changed over the past few years sir," Hay explained. "Colonies are now expected to be largely self-sufficient, at least in terms of the cost of their civil establishments." He concluded by saying, "In my view, it would be unlikely that the Parliament would favourably consider a grant for the Swan River but Parliament will of course make its own decision." Privately he thought how dare Stirling leave his post in the colony without permission. The impertinence of the man appointing Captain Irwin as Acting Governor and just sailing away!

Stirling retaliated with a long missive defending the colony and his actions and in his usual methodical way proceeded to deal with each issue in detail. Almost every day, Stirling made contact with the Colonial Office, always following a verbal communication with a memorandum or formal letter. The barrage of dispatches were well written, cogently argued and utterly rational. Hay sighed. He wished that Stirling would accept the current policies and procedures and return forthwith to his isolated Swan River Colony.

Stirling had no intention of returning to the Swan River Colony without a guarantee of resources to solve at least some of the problems he had enunciated. Knowing that Robert Peel had refused the Office of Prime Minister during the year and that the Government was unstable after a general election in 1831, he shrewdly used Thomas Peel's difficulties in the colony to exemplify the difficulties of all the settlers. Although not currently holding a position in government, Robert Peel was an extremely influential and respected member of Parliament. It was a common expectation, that he would be invited to assume the Prime Minister's Office again in the near future. At the same time, Stirling painted a rosy future for the colony. A colony with great possibilities. A colony of which Great Britain should be proud.

When the Governor's return to England was reported in the newspapers, as the astute Stirling made sure it was, he received much popular attention. Fleet Street was entranced and the press followed Stirling from London to his home at Woodbridge in Guildford and back again. He allowed each reporter an extensive interview and made it clear that he would be pleased to provide comment on the Swan River settlement at any time.

Certain personages did not take long to realise how to make capital of the popular figure and his stories of the antipodes. The following month Stirling was summoned to Buckingham Palace and with much pomp and ceremony was knighted by His Majesty, King William IV. When the King said "Arise, Sir James," Ellen was sure her heart would burst with pride. As Stirling took her arm to lead her from the throne room, he whispered "You've always been a lady even when you were thirteen but now you've the title to go with it, Lady Stirling." Ellen gave her husband's arm a short tug and smiled graciously as they received congratulations from the assembled dignitaries.

To indicate support for Stirling and the Swan River Colony and to provide further impetus for the requests on the petition, a public dinner was held and the presentation of an embossed silver urn made to Stirling. The Swan Cup was inscribed 'Presented to Captain James Stirling R.N. Governor of Western Australia by the relatives and friends of the settlers at Swan River in testimony of their admiration of the wisdom, decision and kindness uniformly displayed by him and of their gratitude for his strenuous exertions with the Colonial Department for the benefit of that settlement. May 1833'. Stirling's portrait, holding the cup, was subsequently painted by the renowned artist Sir William Beechey. The publicity was all grist for the mill and Stirling revelled in it.

While in London, Stirling received two visitors in his rooms at Lincoln's Inn. Both were directly concerned with and held a strong interest in, the affairs of Thomas Peel of the Swan River Colony.

The first was Solomon Levey, who wanted his partnership with Peel recognised, having received no satisfaction from his negotiations with either Lord Goderich or the Colonial Office. Stirling knew that the man was ill as soon as he saw him and assumed rightly that Levey wanted to put his affairs in order before he died.

Stirling informed him fully of the situation in the colony. "Mr Peel was extremely disappointed that the goods expected from Sydney did not arrive, Mr Levey. He was left in a parlous position and was forced to borrow funds from government. I was pleased to assist because of the contribution Mr Peel had already made to the development of the colony."

Levey appeared genuinely surprised. "I knew nothing of this, Governor Stirling and can only apologise for what I hope will be a temporary problem. The situation will be expedited as soon as possible."

"With regard to your partnership arrangements Mr Levey, they are a matter between Mr Peel and yourself. As you would understand, government would be loath to interfere, unless it became a circumstance requiring litigation and you proceeded through the judiciary."

Levey was obviously frustrated with this advice, although he clearly knew there was no alternative. It was exactly the same advice he had received from the Colonial Office. The problem was that he was running out of time.

"Governor Stirling, I assure you that I have no intention of taking Mr Peel to court. I just need clarification on some issues and do not have the time to travel to the Swan River."

Levey then thanked Stirling and left the room in obvious pain, his right arm clutching the left side of his chest. Stirling heard of his death soon after and felt sorry for the man. He was only thirty-nine when he died. Stirling admitted to himself he would feel sorry for anyone who was involved in business with Thomas Peel. Levey's death also explained why the promised supplies had never arrived at Swan River and why Peel's crippling debts continued to rise. He already owed more than £2000 for stores and services provided from government resources.

Stirling's second visitor was Mrs Mary Peel and Lady Stirling remained with her husband as decorum dictated. A fine looking woman, Stirling thought. Dressed in fashionable clothes and adorned with hat, scarf and gloves, she flounced into the room and seated herself elegantly in a chintz-covered chair. She was impatient for news of her wayward husband.

Within minutes, it became abundantly clear to the Stirlings that Peel had not been honest with his wife in regard to his activities in the colony.

"Yes, Mrs Peel," Stirling said carefully. "There have been unfortunate incidents with the natives. Several deaths have resulted and I can fully understand why Thomas would not wish to risk the lives of his family. He is more vulnerable than most, being so far from the major settlements. I am sure your husband will contact you as soon as he feels the situation is sufficiently safe. He must surely miss his family, as much as you miss him."

Mary was reassured by Stirling but still worried about her position. Nearly all the money lodged in the bank had been spent and although she had asked her husband for supplementary funds, they were not forthcoming. She could not wait very much longer. Besides, she did miss Thomas, as did the children. Why hadn't she married an ordinary man with no adventurous inclinations? She knew the answer. To her, marriage was a business arrangement, an arrangement to benefit her financially and this had always been her intention. That she loved her husband as well was a bonus. Mary determined that it was time to make some serious resolutions about her future and the future of her family.

During his final months in England, Stirling won a number of major concessions. He would have appreciated more but admitted to himself that the approvals granted by Parliament were more than reasonable given the times. There was to be an annual grant of £10,000, an increase of four members in the Legislative Council, a liberalisation of land laws to enable occupants to dispose of holdings without the previous requisite improvements and an increase in the civil and military establishments. Revenue was to be raised from a duty on spirits and the sale of crown land.

It was a satisfied Stirling, who set sail with his family for Fremantle aboard the *James Pattison* on 9th February, 1834.

CHAPTER 11
The Aborigines

In the Pleistocene epoch, over 40,000 years ago, groups of people roamed from Asia to the north-west shores of the continent of Australia. During oscillations of climate, huge ice sheets, emanating from the poles, formed around the globe and, as the water froze into glaciers and ice caps, sea levels dropped exposing wide expanses of land. Explorers, traders and adventurers journeyed around the shores of a larger South-East Asia, along the chains of islands and then to Australia, using canoes and rafts to cross short stretches of water. With the extended coastal plains, such stretches were fewer and narrower. Movement in Australia was also facilitated by lower sea levels and settlement was initially coastal and then riverine. Until the ice caps melted and sea levels rose again, bands of people arrived in Australia and progressed south and east.

Over time, the Australian Aborigines, as they came to be called much later, moved across the continent. Each large group developed a special affinity with a tract of land that they accepted as their responsibility and that other groups recognised as theirs by right of occupation. The mythological past, or Dreaming, connected the people to their land and stories were passed from generation to generation to explain and substantiate the inextricable links between the land and the people and the relationship of the 'being' of the people, within space and time and through space and time.

Each large grouping had a broadly-based linguistic, social and cultural identity. They acknowledged common ties and gave themselves a name. The Aboriginal people of the south-west region of Western Australia were such a group and called themselves variations of the word Nyoongar, which translated meant 'man' or 'person' or 'people'.

The Nyoongar were of medium height, when compared with Europeans at the time of their arrival at the Swan River. Long-limbed and hard-muscled, they moved with a remarkable suppleness and fluidity. The bones of their faces were prominent, the mouth large with thick and protruding lips. When smiling, they displayed strong, white teeth, which contrasted with the blackness of their skin and hair. Apart from an identifiable dialect, the major difference between the Nyoongar and surrounding Aborigines to the north and east was that circumcision was not carried out during initiation ceremonies.

Within the Nyoongar were smaller groups of people, or tribes, who could trace their relationship by actual or implied genealogy and who had strong kinship links. The Bindjareb of the Murray River and the Whadjug of the Perth area were two such tribes. They were the land-occupying groups and the inhabitants claimed religious, hunting and food gathering rights because of custodianship vested in them by supernatural sanction. The designated land did not have firm boundaries but was discernible to all because it contained natural features significant to the protectors of that land. Because the occupation of the land was based on such strong environmental and spiritual ties and because tribal law dictated that one group did not have rights to land inhabited by another group, there were few disputes with an underlying territorial motive.

Since large groups of people rapidly denuded the land of food resources, tribes travelled in smaller family groups, especially during winter when the rivers flooded and few fish could be caught. Families usually comprised a man and his wife or wives and children and sometimes included several generations.

Tracks criss-crossed the land joining sites of significance and tribal meetings were usually held where a number of pads intersected. Messengers and traders were permitted to travel across tribal boundaries but were expected to declare their presence and identify themselves in kinship terms.

Because of Aboriginal societal connections and kinship structures, chiefs or leaders were neither appointed nor elected. Older males made the decisions for the family, although women were consulted on some issues. However, woman's business was the sole prerogative of the female members of a group. It was accepted that decisions about certain subjects would be made by women with little or no interference from men. Solutions to tribal problems were arrived at after discussion by male elders but matters were usually referred to female elders for their consideration. On occasions, a particular man could receive an enhanced status because of bravery or charisma, or perhaps the ability to plan ahead for the perceived good of the group. There were no political alliances between neighbouring tribes and differences were usually resolved by appropriate payback action at family level. This was then considered to be the end of the matter, unless that payback was deemed to require further payback.

Anthropologists have estimated that when the British arrived to colonise the Swan River area, the Nyoongar of South-Western Australia comprised thirteen tribes with a population of about six thousand persons.

From the 1820s, for the first time, Aborigines were confronted by invaders. Not just shipwrecked sailors, fishermen or explorers from South-East Asia or Europe but immigrants with the might of the British Empire backing their decision to colonise a land considered empty, because the inhabitants did not fit their definition of a civilised people.

106

Initially, the Aborigines welcomed the settlers, thinking them to be djanga, the spirits of their ancestral beings but it soon became apparent that the influx of white people did not treat them as kin. In fact many treated them very badly. On the land that they had inherited from the Dreamtime they were shouted and sworn at, treated with derision, chased away and savaged by dogs, whipped, shot at, poisoned and murdered. Their animals and birds were hunted incessantly to supplement the food supplies of the new settlers and consequently the Aborigines found their previously adequate resources depleted to the point that it became necessary to beg food from the colonists. They reasoned that if their food was taken they should receive food in return. Some settlers gave them food, others did not. When stomachs growled in hunger, the Aborigines began to steal from the whites and spear their animals to provide for their own families, since tribal law restricted them from hunting or gathering food on land occupied by other tribes. By tribal custom, they were permitted only to take food from their own land and there were now insufficient natural resources on that land. The settlers could not understand why the Aborigines did not move away when the land was claimed as a government grant, then occupied and farmed. They did not understand that the Aborigines could not leave. They were bound to their land by the Dreamtime. There was nowhere else they wanted to go, or could go.

As dissent and disputation increased, government officials tried to communicate and negotiate with members of the displaced tribes. But to whom should they speak? With whom could they negotiate? The natives had no chiefs. No individual could speak for anyone except the members of his own family. It was a hopeless situation. The Aboriginal cultural and societal relationships were as incomprehensible to the settlers, as the invade-and-conquer mentality of imperial Great Britain was incomprehensible to the original inhabitants of the land.

The combination of ignorance and misunderstanding of one another's cultures and the arrogance of the British settlers, based on perceptions of a right to colonise, led to situations that were largely unavoidable and that became increasingly inevitable.

* * * * *

Attempts at a colonial press spawned newspapers such as *The Fremantle Journal, Perth Gazette, The Fremantle Observer, Swan River Guardian* and *West Australian Journal*. The following serious incidents involving natives were reported through official communiques or the newspapers between May 1830 and April 1834.

May 1830	A native is killed in an assault on a Perth house and Ensign Dale and Major Smallman are wounded in the skirmish.
July 1830	George Mackenzie is speared through the heart near Peeltown.
May 1831	Natives besiege a house in Perth, resulting in a settler killing a native. Troops follow the attackers to Lake Monger and natives withdraw following a skirmish. George Kedger is killed and a boy wounded on the Canning.
December 1831	Thomas Smedley, servant of Archibald Butler, a farmer with a Canning River holding, kills a native caught stealing potatoes. The native is kin of Midgegooroo who returns and fatally spears another servant, Enion Entwhistle.
February 1832	Private George Budge of the 63rd Regiment is speared to death at Murray River. Reuben Beecham is killed and John Chipper wounded at Greenmount.
June 1832	Natives led by Yagan, son of Midgegooroo, ambush William Gaze and John Thomas, servants of Archibald Butler. Thomas escapes but Gaze is fatally speared in the back. Yagan is declared an outlaw with a bounty of £20 on his head.
September 1832	Yagan is captured while fishing in the Swan River with Donmera and Ningina and is imprisoned in the Round House at Fremantle before being sentenced to exile on Carnac Island.
November 1832	Yagan and others escape from Carnac Island by stealing a boat.
January 1833	Several natives are killed at York.
April 1833	Peter Chidlow mortally wounds Domjum, brother of Yagan, when he attempts to steal food from a Fremantle store. Domjum's head is hacked off by a settler. (It re-appears in 1837 displayed on a shelf in the office of William Clark, publisher of the *Swan River Guardian*.) In retaliation, Yagan, Midgegooroo and others ambush and murder Tom and John Velvick

	who are transporting stores by cart from Fremantle to Bull Creek. A reward of £30 dead or alive is placed on Yagan and £20 on Midgegooroo and Munday.
May 1833	Captain Ellis captures Midgegooroo who is sentenced to death and executed by firing squad. His body is left hanging from a tree in St George's Terrace as a warning to natives.
July 1833	William Keats, a shepherd, shoots and kills Yagan. His brother James kills another native. William is speared to death. James escapes to claim the reward. Yagan's head is chopped off and smoked in a hollow tree for three months to preserve it. The head is taken to England and exhibited in sideshows.
March 1834	The Murray River store is ransacked by natives. Peel's house is attacked and Fred Peel and two guards are threatened. More arms and ammunition are sent to Peeltown.
April 1834	Yeedamira, detained for raiding farm houses, is shot dead by Private Dennis Larkin while trying to escape from the Kelmscott military barracks. Weeip murders Larkin, impaling him to a wooden doorpost with his spear. A reward of £20 is offered for the capture of Weeip dead or alive.

* * * * *

And so the cycle of events continued. Theft of food and spearing of animals by natives precipitated retaliation by settlers, which necessitated revenge by natives, which resulted in retribution from settlers, which required payback by natives.

By June 1834, there were about six hundred natives in contact with the settlements at Fremantle, Peeltown, Perth, Guildford and Kelmscott, while the colonists now exceeded eighteen hundred persons. As more immigrants arrived and settled further afield, so the skirmishes increased in both number and severity.

CHAPTER 12
The Family

The attack on Peel's house in March frightened and unsettled everyone. When Fred was menaced by the young black, he received an ugly gash on the chest from the spear point. It left the youth in terror of the natives. Never an adventurous child, he was now in constant dread of further attacks. Gibbering, stuttering and stammering became part of his expression. For weeks, Peel could get no sense from his son who spent the days huddled in a chair in the living room and the nights curled in his bed in the foetal position. Smiley, responsive to the fear exuding from her master, was never far away.

What had prompted the attack Peel wondered? Relations between the Murray tribe and the settlers had been amicable enough over the past twelve months. Two young women from a local native family now lived in a nearby bark hut and prepared his food, collected firewood and carried water from the well. They were friendly and seemed happy enough to receive flour and sugar in return for their efforts, which although spasmodic, were welcomed. There were no ties and they came and went as they pleased. Several men from the tribe occasionally fronted to assist with farming chores in exchange for food and at no stage had they given any indication of malevolence or animosity. So why the attack? What made some of the natives so troublesome and belligerent all of a sudden, seemingly without provocation?

Peel felt sympathy for his sensitive and introverted son who had just turned sixteen. The safety of his establishment was a constant worry. He was also becoming tired of the isolation and lack of any sophisticated company. The journey by horseback to Fremantle or Perth was long and tiring and therefore only undertaken for special occasions. It was a primitive existence, particularly so, as before his arrival in the colony, Peel had always enjoyed the good life. Clarence to the Murray River might have been out of the frying pan and into the fire! Peeltown would never amount to anything. It was just a large farming property supporting its master and labourers well enough but not producing sufficient cash crops for profit.

Enough was enough. Peel was becoming increasingly mortified by the lifestyle he was now leading. There were regular passers-by on their way south to explore farming opportunities at Port Leschenault and the Vasse River. Here was Peel, of impeccable family and political ties, living at least one day's ride from civilisation in a hovel at Peeltown. It was all too embarrassing. He decided on a name change. The Peel family name would not be given to a lowly farm. Henceforth the settlement would be known as Mandurah, derived from the native word mandjar. It was the name given to the area by the local tribe and translated as a meeting and trading place. Once again Peel was ready to move on.

Two servants were dispatched in different directions to deliver messages. One headed east to the Andrews' Place to summon Samuel to report to his Master and the other trotted north to lodge an advertisement with Charles Macfaull, the publisher of the *Perth Gazette*. The carefully worded and rather optimistic public announcement offered Mandurah House to let for a period of seven, fourteen or twenty-one years, either furnished or unfurnished. Peel painted a rather exaggerated and rosy picture of both the farm and the dwelling and gave the reason for the vacancy as the proposed relocation of the establishment to Pinjarra.

As usual there was no planning. However, in the back of his mind, Peel still held the view that Pinjarra could become a staging station between the Swan River Colony and the southern outposts. It seemed more likely now than the Mandurah route. If so, he might be able to attract settlers to the area and sell or lease his land. To ever succeed in Western Australia he would need capital and the only option open to him was to sell some of his land. The major problem was that most of the settlers were landowners and like himself had no ready cash. It was a dilemma he had to face and solve.

The following day, Samuel arrived at Peel's house with his Trail overflowing with farm produce. Only the chickens really interested Peel, because they could be sold in Fremantle or exchanged for other necessities, such as wine of which he was running short again. Samuel was invited into the kitchen, seated at the table and offered a mug of water. In a lean-to outside, the northerly wind blew warmly and a native woman alternately stirred a pot of stew suspended over the fire and turned the handle of a butter churn.

"I've called her Dukun. It means to cook," Peel responded to Samuel's curious glance. "Her sister is Kypbi, meaning water. I've learned enough to make myself understood. Well, I think they understand me, although mostly they just grin and nod. They seem to find most things amusing which is a change around here. Fred, say 'Hello' to Andrews."

There was no response from Fred. The youth's eyes continued to dart around the room and through the unshuttered windows.

"The boy is still upset about the attack on the house. You heard about the skirmish, I suppose?"

"Yes, sir. Could you please tell me, Mr Peel, what causes them to suddenly attack the settlers? Why do the men attack out of the blue so to speak? We have not seen one native on our place. They don't approach or request food. Yet here at the mouth of the river there seems to be a problem. Why?"

"I don't understand what causes the sudden anger," Peel replied, looking perplexed. "I really don't know for sure, although they have a very straight-forward system of retaliation. It seems that if a native is hurt, there must be revenge. Not necessarily on the perpetrator of the act but on anyone associated with that person, whether it be a family member or servant. In the case of the recent attack, there didn't appear to be a motive. None of the settlers here can give a reason as to what prompted the action. Or if they know, they won't admit to it. You can see how it's scared the wits out of my son." He waved his hand in Fred's direction.

"As to your place, Dukun told me a long and involved story about a native family becoming very ill and dying on your land soon after the arrival of the first settlers down here. When Armstrong and company were washed out upstream of your place and came down to the inlet, someone must have passed on influenza or measles or both and all the family died in a very short time. The whole area is now forbidden land to the blacks, which is why you haven't been troubled. You've been damned lucky. I'd thank my lucky stars if I were you."

As was his wont, Peel abruptly changed the subject. "Andrews, I've called you here to inform you of my intention to let Mandurah House, in order to re-establish myself near the ford at Pinjarra. The water is fresh there. I have land to lease and am negotiating an arrangement with Meares and Devenish. I hope eventually to found a township. The land is much more fertile upstream and is sure to be suitable for wheat and sheep farming." Peel was enjoying listening to his own voice and called for a rum before continuing. Dukun hurried to fulfil the order.

"I'd like you to remain at your place as a back-up for me. All this is going to take some time to set in place." As he paused to take a mouthful of rum, Samuel quietly expired the drawn breath he was holding. The last thing he wanted was to leave the Serpentine.

"You'll keep the animals you already have. We'll continue our present arrangement for the moment. I'll take some of the animals from the Murray and sell them off in Mangles Bay or Fremantle. The rest can remain at the inlet with a few labourers to mind the farm and equipment until I call for everyone to join me at Pinjarra." Samuel was dumbstruck. "Do you understand, man?"

Samuel nodded. He didn't dare ask the obvious question. "Yes, sir," he answered.

"Well, that's all Andrews."

Samuel hastily stumbled to his feet. He was about to say his farewell but Peel had already picked up a newspaper from the table and was scanning the pages. Samuel had been dismissed.

Thomas Peel was very pleased with his decision. In pompous fashion, he informed his labourers of the plans and if they indicated dismay or displeasure it was ignored. He had made up his mind and that was that. It was hoped that some fool would see prospects in the Murray region and negotiate the lease. Henry Edward Hall, a wealthy gentleman from Leicestershire, had recently taken up a government grant and settled on the other side of the river mouth with his wife Sarah, five children and ten servants. He was a man of substance and standing and if he could be fooled by the possibilities of the district, so others might be fooled. Peel optimistically waited for a communication from Perth.

* * * * *

Call it coincidence. Call it careful planning. Call it bad luck. It really depended on one's viewpoint but in April when Peel's advertisement appeared in the *Perth Gazette* another notice informed the colony of the arrival of the barque *Quebec Trader* from London. The only passengers of importance were Mrs Thomas Peel, her children Julia, Thomas and Dorothy, thirteen, nine and seven respectively and Mrs Bridget Ayrton, her mother, a reluctant traveller of seventy-five. Sarah Scott, the family servant accompanied them. After a rough voyage, poor food and suspect water, all were exhausted, ill and cranky. There was no one to meet them. Mary had decided to surprise her husband and surprise him and everyone else in the colony she certainly did.

On Thomas Peel's departure for the Swan River, Mary had arranged for all the reputable newspapers to be delivered to her home. She scrutinised every issue and when there was mention of the colony she carefully cut out the section and pasted it into a writing book. She absorbed every detail. Any gossip overheard at soirees she filed away in her mind for later examination and interpretation. All in all, there was precious little information. She looked in vain for mention of Thomas. When his name did appear it was often in derogatory or pejorative terms. The writings of Edward Gibbon Wakefield, particularly *England and America 1833* had become fashionable and Mary was furious to read the criticisms of the colonies, especially the Swan River Colony. Wakefield openly censured Peel's scheme. He exaggerated the size of Peel's grant, overlooked the fact that he had not received his original allocation and gloatingly inferred that the Peel family had formed some sort of less than ethical alliance to promote the scheme. His information was often incorrect, which wasn't surprising as he had never been to the Swan River. It was all so unfair.

When Stirling arrived in London and the Swan River Colony was reported on so favourably by Fleet Street, Mary was reassured. By the time Stirling was feted and knighted, Mary became quite excited. After her audience with Sir James, Mary began wishing she had travelled with her husband. Thomas needed her support. He always lived for the day, the moment. He would benefit from her practical point of view and support for the future. She would go to him.

Once Mary made up her mind, that was the end of it. She would not be deterred. The bank manager was summoned and ordered to withdraw sufficient money for the journey. He hummed and hawed and eventually admitted that the Peel family was already living on an overdraft. Mary refused to accept this. The bank manager delivered cash the following day. The family lawyer was summoned and ordered to lease the Regent Park house and book passage on the first available ship sailing to the Swan River Colony. All travel arrangements were completed within the month. Mary's aged mother resisted for a few days but under pressure from her daughter eventually gave in. She really had no choice, as it was go with the family or remain in London alone and without means.

So here they were at Fremantle. On being ferried ashore, Mary demanded to be taken to the best hotel. The horse and cart took four trips to deliver the mountain of luggage to the Stirling Arms in High Street. Mary had refused to leave any of her clothes or favourite possessions behind. She was here for good. Less than impressed with the hotel, Mary ordered that her husband be informed immediately of the arrival of his family. The manager sent a servant posthaste to inform Peel of the good news.

When he arrived, Peel, who was just settling down to a few late afternoon clarets, nearly had a seizure. "Christ Almighty, man! Is this some sort of a bloody stupid joke?" he spluttered leaping to his feet. "My family is in England."

"Your family is in Fremantle, sir. They arrived yesterday aboard the *Quebec Trader*. Mrs Peel sends her kindest regards and asks that you meet her and the children at the Stirling Arms as soon as possible."

They left with the dawn. Fred was instructed to supervise a clean-up of the house and environs. The native women were to receive special rations on completion of all the chores. Peel had no choice but to bring his family back to Mandurah House. He certainly couldn't afford to put the family up at a hotel for any length of time. Hell's bells! What a mess! He wondered why Mary had changed her mind. She'd have a fit when she saw the Mandurah establishment. Oh God, save me from her disappointment and anger. He trotted on. An awful headache, the result of his binge the previous night, was exacerbated by every stride of his horse.

Late afternoon, a dusty, dishevelled and unshaven Peel pulled up outside the Stirling Arms and tied Goldie to the railing next to the water trough.

His family were taking tea in the lounge. Mary arose and dramatically held out her arms. She ignored her husband's appearance and the stale stink of alcohol, sweat and dirt.

"Mr Peel, my dear. I am so pleased to be with you again."

Trying desperately to gauge the situation, Peel stepped hesitantly towards Mary. She really did seem pleased to see him. He took her in his arms and embraced her.

"Mrs Peel. What a surprise!" Her response was eager. He held her at arms length. "You look wonderful. A sight for sore eyes." And she did!

Peel turned. "Mrs Ayrton. Welcome to the Swan River Colony." The old woman sat fidgeting in her chair. She nodded, keeping her eyes down.

"Children, greet your father," Mary said. The children looked nonplussed. They hadn't seen their father for five years. Was this dirty, untidy, unshaven, sunburnt man really their father?

Thomas Junior walked tentatively forward, his hand held out. His mother had instructed the children to say nothing about the scars their father had written he had received in the hunting accident. Looking keenly into Thomas' face the boy said "Hello sir," as he shook his father's hand. The nine year old was a small replica of his father, who observed him proudly. Fine looking lad.

His daughters rushed him, then stopped and curtsied. In unison they chorused "Hello Father."

Gallantly, Peel took each small hand in turn and raised it to his lips. "Welcome, Julia. Welcome, Dorothy."

The youngest daughter butted in. "Dora. My name is Dora, Father."

Peel looked to Mary, who smiled. "Yes, my dear. The child insists."

"Then welcome, Dora," Peel said, raising her hand to his lips again.

The remainder of the day was spent catching up. Peel answered hundreds of questions. Some he answered truthfully. Most responses however were evasive. No need to paint the total picture all at once. Mary had intimated that they were here to stay and he wasn't sure whether to encourage that line or not. Better to wait and see how the land lies, he decided.

After a night of fierce lovemaking, during which Mary subtly and not so subtly alternatively enticed and urged her husband to heights of sexual endurance he had all but forgotten, Thomas changed his mind and hoped the family would stay.

Mary was surprisingly tolerant and cheerful about the situation in which she found herself and the conditions she was forced to endure. There was little that could be done about it and she knew she only had herself to blame. A schooner was hired to transport the family, their servant, Sarah Scott and the mass of luggage to the Murray River. Additional provisions and furniture were purchased from Samson's and stored in the vessel's hold, Goldie being harnessed on deck and blindfolded to curb her nervousness. Peel found himself actually enjoying the children's company as he pointed out the landmarks on the voyage south.

It was when they approached Mandurah House that Peel held his breath. The family walked ahead of several farm labourers staggering under their loads. It was hot for April and the flies were bad, so each of the family members had been given plaited straw hats to protect their pale skin from the sun's rays. Peel knew they would all turn brown soon enough but hoped it would be gradual and not painful. He had adopted a paternal manner with the children but after a few days his patience was rapidly wearing thin. The constant attention-seeking was intrusive and distracting. However, for the moment, he was determined to be on his best behaviour. He was pleasantly pleased to see that the animals had been penned and the yard cleaned and raked.

Fred was at the front door. He had watched the sailing vessel anchor two hours before. Almost at attention, he stood fearfully awaiting his stepmother, half-brother and half-sisters. Since his father had left for Fremantle, he had worried continually about how he would be received on the family's arrival.

He need not have worried, as Mary was also playing her part to perfection.

"Frederick," she said. "It is good to see you again. You have grown so. Almost a man. Thomas you must be proud." She put her arm around the boy's shoulders and hugged him to her. Tears came to Fred's eyes but he managed to blink them away.

"Welcome, Mrs Peel. Welcome, Mrs Ayrton," he muttered formally. "And welcome brother and sisters." Following their mother's example, the children ran forward and took Fred's hands pumping them up and down. The atmosphere relaxed markedly.

Mary marched into the house, followed reluctantly by her husband. The curious children followed.

At first there was a speechless silence, then Mary said "This place needs a woman's touch. It's clean enough but it requires furnishings for comfort and decorative purposes. And no glass in the windows! Mr Peel, I insist on help to make this house an abode befitting our family."

Peel was astonished. At least the house was clean and tidy, the sparse furniture rearranged to best advantage. Bless you, Fred!

Four black faces appeared at the open window. "Abba," Dukun and Kypbi chorused, smiling and waving small branches from eucalypt trees in friendly greeting. From behind them, two fierce-looking men stared at the women and children and pointed, making unintelligible noises. They had bones through their nasal septa and bird feathers stuck in fur bands around their heads. Their faces bore ceremonial scars.

All the females screamed. Long and loud it continued. Mrs Ayrton dropped to her knees in a praying position, Julia and Dora hid under the table, Sarah Scott swooned and fell to the floor and Mary threw herself into her husband's arms. Frederick and Thomas Junior froze in terror. All continued to scream, as Peel, extricating himself from Mary's clutches, gestured the natives away from the house.

"It's all right," he said over and over again reassuringly. "They're friendly." It was to no avail. No one was reassured and the screaming continued.

"Silence!" Peel boomed.

He waited, then yelled again. "I said silence and I mean silence." The screaming receded to a whimper and then stopped. Everyone looked to him.

"Would you listen. Listen to me carefully. The two women work for me as house servants. The men are members of their family and sometimes help in the fields. They are friendly. Friendly, I tell you. They were merely greeting you."

He turned to his eldest son. "Fred, ask Dukun and Kypbi to prepare tea. Tell them to send the men away. I shall see them tomorrow. Now would you all sit down and try to relax. Thomas, help your grandmother to her feet."

Bit by bit they settled down. After numerous cups of tea, some laced with brandy to soothe nerves, Mary ordered Sarah to organise beds for the adults and mattresses on the floor for the children. Except for personal bags, the luggage stacked outside the house could wait until tomorrow. Bread was served with a variety of jams for supper, the children were dossed down and Mrs Ayrton helped Sarah clean up while Mary sat with Thomas on a couch on the verandah.

Plans for the future were discussed and for the first time Thomas was honest with his wife about their situation. After a particularly searching question from Mary he replied, "Mary, you must accept the position here. Everyone has access to land. Most have more land than they will ever be able to develop. However, the problem is that few of the settlers, including myself, have ready cash. Not many exports have been developed and land may not be sold unless it has certain improvements. I have no money to improve my grant further. In fact I owe over £2000 to the Government for stores and equipment. There is money owed to me from indentured servants who have gone it alone. Gone with my permission because there was insufficient work for them and I could not afford to continue feeding families for nothing. It could be years before I receive reimbursement, if at all. I am stuck here at the moment. That is why I chose not to bring you and the children out here. I could not provide for you in a fitting manner." Peel sighed. "Please understand. Eventually my grant will be valuable and then I will be able to sell or lease portions of it. At the moment it is worth nothing, because nobody wants to buy it."

Mary did understand. It had become abundantly clear when they arrived in Fremantle that the Swan River Colony was no more than the beginnings of a permanent settlement. The Murray River was just an outpost with even fewer of the niceties to which she was accustomed. She opened her mouth to ask a question but it was anticipated.

"And at present I do not have the funds to allow you the choice of returning home. So here you will have to remain until Stirling returns. Rumour has it that there will be a loosening of the regulations regarding the sale of land. The Colonial Office has apparently acknowledged at long last that the current situation is crippling further development. There you have it. You're here to stay. At least for a while. I would sincerely ask that you accept your lot for the moment. We must all make the best of it. And my dear, I'm afraid that Sarah Scott will have to go. We just can't afford her. I'll write to Peter Broun and ask him to arrange alternative service for her in Perth. She can travel back on the supply ship on its next visit."

Bringing out a beautifully embroidered white handkerchief, Mary forcibly blew her nose and then dabbed the corners of her eyes. Peel thought she almost looked contrite.

"Thomas dear, I'm so sorry. I should have waited as you wished. It was foolish of me to be so impetuous." Then she burst into sobs in a suitably subdued fashion.

Peel placed his arm around his wife's shoulders, gently pulling her towards him and kissing her forehead. "Hush, my dear. Everything will be all right in the end." It was a turning point in their relationship as both realised the extent of their problems. There would have to be compromises, many compromises.

CHAPTER 13
Ambush

Several days later at dusk, as the finishing touches were being made by two farm labourers to additional rooms for the new arrivals, a rider furtively reined in his horse at the rear of Mandurah House. Peel was called and hushed a snarling Smiley. The weary horseman was Captain Ellis, the Superintendent of Native Tribes.

"Good evening Mr Peel. I'm sorry to interrupt but I am the bearer of news which may impact on your safety."

"Come in, Ellis." Peel led the way into the front room of the house and, motioning Ellis to a chair, poured them both a glass of brandy. "Now, relate your news."

"I have travelled from Perth with a detachment of soldiers from the 21st Regiment of Foot. As you would know they recently arrived from Van Diemen's Land to replace the 63rd Regiment on their transfer to India. We are here to apprehend the natives responsible for a brazen daylight robbery of flour from George Shenton's mill at South Perth five days ago. The soldiers are presently in hiding at the barracks."

The Superintendent took a sip of his brandy. "A group of over thirty Murray River tribesmen forced the door of the mill and carried off every bit of flour in the storeroom. About 980 pounds of flour was stolen, sir. Shenton was thrust outside and forced to lie on the ground, while the flour was apportioned. He was spared on the intervention of a Perth native who feared retribution on his own tribe."

"The bastards," Peel interrupted. "They get more and more aggressive."

"Yes, sir. Well, after the Murray River tribesmen had gone, Perth natives identified some of the thieves from their footprints in the spilt flour and informed me and my assistant Francis Armstrong when we arrived to investigate the robbery. Young Armstrong has developed an unusual capacity to understand and speak the native dialects. The leaders of the attack on the mill were identified as Yedong, Calyute and his son Monang."

"I know them well, Ellis."

"I wanted to apprise you of the plan in case anything goes wrong, Mr Peel. We intend to set a trap at the barracks. An ambush is always dicey but I feel a more sensible strategy than trying to locate the natives in their own habitat." He hesitated. "I'm also worried about the 21st Regiment. They might be a regiment of the Royal North British Fusiliers but I consider their general attitude towards the natives leaves a lot to be desired. The native problem in Van Diemen's land was not handled well."

"Each to their own opinion Ellis but thanks for the warning," Peel said, as he showed Ellis the door.

* * * * *

The following morning Yedong strolled casually up to the barracks. Ellis and his men remained hidden inside the huts. The youth, satisfied that the coast was clear, wandered off and returned shortly afterwards with Calyute and Monang to receive their weekly flour supplies. They were the very picture of innocence. What a cheek, thought Ellis peeping from behind a shutter. As if they haven't received enough flour for this week!

Ellis' men split into two groups and crept through the open door at the rear of the hut with loaded rifles at the ready. When the three natives approached from the front to receive their rations, four soldiers ran around each side of the building shouting at the top of their voices attempting to hustle them towards the troops pouring from the barracks door. Monang broke loose and sprinted for the trees.

"Fire!" ordered the Lieutenant.

Shots were fired, one hitting the fleeing native in the thigh. Monang fell heavily but quickly rose and ran limping into the brush.

Meanwhile there was bedlam in the hut. Yedong made a dive for a window but was felled when a rifle ball grazed his skull.

"Shit!" yelled the Corporal. "Grab the bastard, for Christ's sake."

Two soldiers immediately seized the stunned native and bound him by the wrists and ankles. Meanwhile, it took four men, a kick to the groin and a bayonet wound in the arm to subdue Calyute.

A search for Monang revealed no trace of the escapee beyond bloodstains leading into a swamp. Ellis wasn't prepared to leave the soldiers open to a hail of spears from hidden adversaries and called the hunt off.

"Back to the barracks, men. And make the prisoners so secure that there's no chance of them running for it. We'll be on our way as soon as possible."

The two bloodied captives, wrists firmly trussed behind their backs and tied together by neck ropes, remained under close guard. A farm cart was borrowed from Peel and the defiant natives pushed on board. As the detachment was about to leave, two other natives, seen hovering by the side of the track, were recognised as Wamba and Gummol, both also suspected of being involved in the attack on Shenton's Mill. They were seized without further bloodshed, bound and heaved onto the cart, which set off immediately towards Fremantle. Ellis did not want to be fending off any rescue attempts.

Only the barest details of the retaliatory events were passed on to his family by Peel. No one had been permitted to leave the house during the morning except to visit the privy and Peel maintained a close lookout at all times, his rifle at the ready. After the shots were heard, he said that Ellis and some soldiers were rounding up natives who had stolen flour rations from the mill south of Perth and would not elaborate further. When a soldier came to borrow the cart, he informed his family that the miscreants had been caught and were being taken to Perth where they would be punished for their crime.

What Peel did not consider however, was that by providing his cart to transport the prisoners to their judgment, he was implicating himself in the whole venture. At least that was the way the Murray tribesmen perceived it, as they remained hidden behind trees, watching their friends and family members being taken away by the soldiers in Peel's cart.

* * * * *

Peel's family remained upset and scared. The conditions were primitive and the insects were unrelenting in their attention. It was flies all day and mosquitoes all night. Everyone began to grumble and the complaints were endless. It went on and on. Peel could not tolerate any more and sent for Annie Andrews, who arrived fresh and smiling.

Within three days she had everyone fresh and smiling. It was a miracle. A schedule of events for each day was planned. With soldiers always present, family members were involved in as many activities as possible. Games were taught. Animals, birds and insects were identified. Regular walks were undertaken. Wildflowers and the prettiest natural bushes were picked to decorate the house. Hats were plaited from the reeds found in the swamp and gum nuts were tied from the brim to keep flies out of the eyes. Annie's own precious supply of citronella oil was shared and the Peels warned that dawn and dusk were the danger times for mosquitoes and that a smoking fire would help keep them away most of the time. Lists were prepared of necessities to be requested from Fremantle for delivery on the next supply ship. One special item was allowed each family member. Peel shuddered when he reckoned up the cost but said nothing. Annie cleaned and cooked and sewed and, because everyone had fallen under her spell, they all started lending a hand to get things done rather than sitting around sulking and bored. Annie's optimistic and caring attitude and cheerful approach to everything she did was infectious. After three days the Peels began to feel guilty that their family could not take responsibility for their own lives and were keeping Annie away from her husband and children. They reluctantly waved her goodbye when Samuel, William, Sara Jane and Happy arrived to take her back to the Serpentine. Things settled down after that and Peel breathed a sigh of relief.

In Perth, the four natives faced sentencing. Wamba was released with a warning because of previous good behaviour and assistance provided to Peel and Hall on their Mandurah farms. Gummol, Yedong and Calyute received a public flogging and a month's imprisonment at the Fremantle Round House. Calyute received a second sixty lashes before being released. By the time he returned to the Murray River in mid-June, he was bitter, angry and hungry for reprisal. With his tribesmen, he began plotting revenge. The payback needed to be seen by all to be worthy of the punishment meted out to Calyute, Gummol and Yedong and the wounding of Monang. Added to that, the humiliation of a tribal elder of Calyute's status required a special level of retribution. There was much discussion among the elders of the tribe over the next few weeks. Slowly, a plan was devised.

Fine weather was required for their ruse to succeed, so the avenging group waited. After a particularly windy and wet week, the sun rose on early morning fog promising a clear, crisp winter's day. On signal, Calyute and eighteen men, selected for their spear-throwing skills, gathered their weapons and leftover meat from the previous evening's meal and moved silently from the awakening camp at Bindjareb. All wore kangaroo skin cloaks, for it was the cold season.

They crossed the Murray and Serpentine Rivers at the fordable section near their entrance into the Peel Inlet, scouted the forbidden area of the Andrews' Place and by the middle of the day had arrived at Barragup. This was the site where stick traps were built for the yearly feast when the fish moved down the river. The mandjar held three moons ago had been a great success, as the fish had been more plentiful than usual and Calyute's position as a revered elder had been enhanced when he had taken another young wife. Yornup was truly beautiful with a shyness he found appealing. And then he had been captured and flogged many, many times. Twice! He angrily tossed his mane of long grey hair at the shame he felt in falling for the white man's trick at the barracks. The scars on his back were still excruciatingly painful, although of course he did not acknowledge the discomfort. He had allowed his first wife to apply poultices of red gum softened with emu oil to the welts, all the time however evincing the appropriate amount of impatience and indifference to the proceedings.

"Calyute! Calyute!" The leader of the expedition turned to face his eldest son Monang. His thigh wound had healed well and there was no sign of a limp. Always impatient! Why were young men so impatient?

"Who will hunt food?"

"You go, Monang. Take four others. Stay well away from the white men."

The rest of the men reluctantly gathered firewood and set up camp, chores normally reserved for the women. When the hunters returned with two kangaroos, a small party of the most experienced trackers, led by Calyute, slipped through the trees in a westerly direction towards Peel's house.

It was late afternoon, as the natives approached the farm with extreme caution and remained hidden in the trees. Two horses, including Peel's, were close to the barn but three others were spotted grazing well away from the house on the edge of the cleared area and as yet had not been tethered for the night.

"Good," Calyute whispered. He motioned the other men behind him and, like shadows, they flitted through the trees until they were as close to the three horses as they dared without frightening them. The planned strategy was carefully followed. Each of the men positioned himself and crawled on his belly towards the horses through the tall winter grass. They made barely heard hissing and clicking noises as they approached the animals. Slowly the mare and two geldings backed away until they were in the trees, whereupon the natives rose slowly to their feet and drove them several miles eastwards towards Big Lake. When the reedy water's edge was reached, Calyute speared the black mare and Yedong and Monang the two geldings. Satisfaction gleamed in their eyes as they retrieved their spears. That was the first level payback. The men then returned quickly and quietly to their camp and evening meal.

When Fred Peel could not find the valuable horses to tether them in the stable, he reported back to his father, who wasn't too concerned and certainly didn't intend to search the bush after dark.

"Let them be until morning," he said. "We'll look for them then." Peel returned to his letter writing.

Next day, before the Peel household had breakfasted, a rider pulled up in the yard and asked to see Mr Peel. He introduced himself as Edward Barron, a former sergeant major of the 63rd Regiment.

Barron explained his mission. "When I received my discharge last month Mr Peel, I took over the management of the United Services Tavern in Perth. I need a quality mare and have received advice that you had one for sale, so decided to ride south in the hope of negotiating a sale before other bids were made. As you would know sir, good horses are few and far between in the colony at the moment."

Peel invited the visitor to join his family for breakfast. "It's true I advertised a mare for sale and a fine specimen she is but the horses wandered off into the bush last night. We'll have to round them up this morning." He hesitated and then said "Weren't you stationed at the barracks here at some stage, Barron?"

"You've a good memory, sir. I was here in '31. In fact I was the soldier who winged the young fellow when the blacks attacked the barracks. A good shot if I do say so myself. Smashed the bone. I'd bet he's not thrown a spear with his right arm since." He was grinning widely.

After breakfasting on boiled eggs, toast and tea, Peel was contemplating where to begin the search for his horses.

"Damned nuisance," he said to Barron. "I can't understand it. They've never wandered away like this before. Still, I can't afford to lose them. If it takes all day, the search will go on. Who's this now?"

Barron followed Peel's gaze through the doorway to see two natives sidling up to the house.

"It's Monang and Unah," said Peel. "Wonder what they're up to? Nothing good, that'll be for sure."

As Peel and Barron walked onto the verandah, Monang began gesticulating and pointing towards the morning sun. Barron picked up the word 'horses' in a string of unintelligible sentences. Peel translated to the visitor. "They say they know where the horses are. What a stroke of luck! They want me to go with them but I'll ask for a volunteer from the barracks to accompany you. It will give me time to write some letters that you can carry to Perth for me on your return."

There were further protestations from one of the blacks.

"No, Unah. I have said that I will not go in search of the horses and that is that! Fred, take yourself off to the barracks and ask for a volunteer to go with Mr Barron."

Fred ran off down the track with Smiley barking at his heels. He refused to leave the house without the protection of his dog. Monang and Unah strolled to the edge of the trees and squatted, waiting with rather disconsolate expressions on their faces. There would be trouble later when the others found out they had been unable to lure Peel into the bush.

The search party left midmorning moving in a north-easterly direction. It comprised Edward Barron, Private Hugh Nesbit, servant to Lieutenant Armstrong, the commander of the detachment of the 21st Fusiliers, Nesbit's ginger and white terrier dog Spot and Monang and Unah.

The two natives scouted ahead, stopping every few minutes in an elaborate display of examining tracks and discussing their meaning. The whites followed on horseback. Barron reckoned the tracks were more than twelve hours old but did not pursue the issue.

Before long, cooeeing and shouting were heard from a distance and Barron realised that groups of natives were keeping pace with them in the bush, while remaining hidden.

He called to Nesbit, who reassured him that everything was all right. "I know most of the Murray natives well. They'll do us no harm. Don't worry, Mr Barron."

Nevertheless Barron was worried and his concern heightened as the natives emerged from the bush a few at a time and formed what could only be construed as an escort on either side of the two white men. Barron counted nineteen armed men shouting, gesturing and laughing. They pointed to the ground, then ahead, then at the two riders. Barron recognised Calyute and Yedong, whom he had watched receiving their floggings in Perth in May. Calyute would not meet his eye and stayed well away from him. Barron began to feel decidedly uncomfortable. Trapped would be a better word. The ex-sergeant major had a soldier's sense about such things and again called to Nesbit and again received a wave and another reassurance.

After travelling about three miles, Goegrup Lake became visible through the trees. At the same time, Barron looked back and saw a youth who had closed in and was only a few yards behind him. The young native had a strangely misshapen right arm and a look of intense hatred on his face. He carried his spear like a lance in his left hand. As their eyes met, Calyute shouted a command from his position halfway between the horsemen. Several natives shipped spears into throwing sticks with a clacking noise. Barron's eyes widened in terror. He'd been right all the time. Ambush! Shouting, "Save yourself Nesbit!" he spurred his horse.

Too late! From close range, the youth with the disfigured arm thrust a spear upwards into the small of his back. Flinching in agony, Barron fell forward over his horse's neck and galloped in a wide circle away from the natives. He was followed by a barrage of spears. One pierced his left side and one his right arm. From behind him, he heard Nesbit shriek. A terrible shriek! He could not stop or they'd both be goners.

Several natives were in pursuit and they ran easily and quickly through the light undergrowth behind him for a short distance before calling off the chase. Barron managed to knock off the shafts of two spears but the quartz heads remained embedded. He could not dislodge the spear in his back, which bounced up and down with the horse's movements causing agonising pain. He hung on, desperately urging his horse to keep going, while praying and thanking God he was still alive. It was impossible to erase the image of loathing exuding from the native who had lunged at him. The utter, total, all consuming look of hatred on his face.

As Barron galloped off, the natives converged on Nesbit, who had fallen from his horse on the impact of spear thrusts from Calyute, Nunar and Woodan. The gelding was speared as he staggered towards it to remount. Terrified, it took off, chasing after Barron's horse at full gallop with the spear protruding from its flank. Spot received a vicious kick from one of the men and fled yelping into the rushes near the lake, his ears flat with fear, his tail between his legs.

With almost sacrificial ceremony, first Yedong and next Monang thrust at Nesbit. Then, amidst much shouting, each of the others stepped forward and jabbed at the screaming young man as he rolled on his back, vainly trying to avoid the spear thrusts. He was near death when Woodan finally clubbed him with a kodjah and cut his throat with the sharp teeth of a tabba.

* * * * *

125

It was near noon and the Peel household was the very picture of domesticity. Mary and the girls sewed, Mrs Ayrton and Sarah prepared food for lunch and Peel and his two sons, after overseeing some labouring in the orchard, were playing cribbage. The barking of the dogs brought Peel to his feet and he wandered outside.

The horse pulled up at the verandah steps and Barron, mercifully falling into unconsciousness, rolled off to land at Peel's feet. He remained inert, blood pouring from his wounds.

"Hell's teeth!" shouted Peel. "Children will all remain inside. Fred, fetch me my rifle, powder horn and shot, then take the horse and inform Lieutenant Armstrong that Barron has been attacked. And ask that Eacott, Tuckey and the others be alerted. Heaven knows what's happened to Nesbit! Mary, fetch hot water. I will need your assistance. Bring a sheet, scissors and the sharpest knife."

In the end, it was old Mrs Ayrton who was the most help. Mary swooned at the sight of so much blood and was sent back inside to mind the children. Sarah couldn't face the task and vomited noisily behind the kitchen lean-to. Peel dragged Barron, now semiconscious and groaning with pain, to a couch on the verandah and stripped him to his underwear. He then threw a blanket over the bloody body and left his mother-in-law to her ministrations.

Slowly, carefully, with much patience Mrs Ayrton excised the quartz fragments from the lacerated flesh. She alternately poured whisky over wounds as they were cleansed and into Barron's mouth each time he regained consciousness. Flaps of skin were cut away or sewn together with catgut she found in the medicine chest. The ghastly cuts were finally covered with bandages cut from sheets. By the time she had turned him on his stomach to reduce body weight on his wounds, he was breathing stertorously.

Armstrong arrived with eight of his men. Peel outlined what he knew of the happenings of the day and two privates were dispatched immediately to Fremantle to report events and escort medical assistance to Mandurah. The rest of the detachment marched off in the direction of Lake Goegrup. They found the carcasses of the horses first, signalled by the squawking and squabbling of a collection of predatory birds.

Then they heard the mournful howling of a dog. Spot had returned to his dead master's side and sat waiting next to Nesbit's body, uttering regular, long, loud, doleful cries.

The bloody corpse was tied to two thin branches for transport back to the barracks and immediate burial. The soldiers were grim-faced as they took turns in carrying the makeshift stretcher. Of all the members of the military stationed at Mandurah, Nesbit had made the greatest effort to communicate with the natives.

The confused terrier ran loyally behind.

* * * * *

Five days later, Captain Ellis arrived with Mr Thomas Harrison, a surgeon from Fremantle and an escort of soldiers from the 21st Regiment. After Harrison examined and rebandaged the wounds, he commended Mrs Ayrton for her medical prowess. By this time, Barron was lying comfortably on his side on a couch near the fire and on Harrison's assessment would be well enough to travel north by cart within a few weeks.

Ellis and his command spent a month searching the bush for the murderers, all to no avail. Not one male was sighted, although two old women were captured and subsequently released. The detachment returned to Perth, providing company for Barron. Governor Stirling was due back in the colony in mid-August and Ellis considered it essential that he receive an early audience to report on the deteriorating situation with regard to the natives. Peel gave him a letter to deliver to the Governor, urging immediate retaliatory action and reinforcements for the Mandurah barracks. In case Stirling had not yet returned, a duplicate letter was prepared for Captain Irwin, the Acting Lieutenant-Governor.

The colonists had borne enough and called for blood. The *Perth Gazette* took up the call and on 26th July, the editor made his strongest statement to date.

> *We earnestly and bitterly lament that another is added to the list of the murdered at the hands of the natives and, although we have ever been the advocates of a humane and conciliatory line of procedure, this unprovoked attack must not be allowed to pass over without the severest chastisement; and we cordially join our brother Colonists in the one universal call for summary and fearful example. We feel and know from experience, that to punish with severity the perpetrators of these atrocities will be found in the end an act of the greatest kindness and humanity.*

Sir James Stirling and his family arrived back in Fremantle per *James Pattison* in August 1834.

CHAPTER 14
Stirling Returns

Captain Theophilus Tighe Ellis waited impatiently in the reception room to be called into the Governor's office. Government House had been extended over the previous two years and was now a substantial wooden building, more befitting the King's representative. Stirling, on his arrival in Perth, was eager for information. It seemed that half the colony had been summoned to report and bring him up to date on events pertinent to their responsibilities. Now it was the turn of the Superintendent of Native Tribes and for the umpteenth time Ellis read through the account of events and follow-up action since his appointment as Constable in 1833.

The title of Captain was one of courtesy. Like most officers of his Majesty's forces, Ellis had retained his rank after being stood down on half pay from the First Royal Infantry Regiment based in Kingstown, Ireland at the end of the Peninsular Wars. His modest salary and the earnings from a small holding were sufficient to provide a comfortable income but as the years progressed he became more and more bored.

Following the death of her husband the previous year, his sister, Mrs Mary Bolger, had begged "my big brother Theo," as she called him, to escort her and his six nieces and three nephews to a new start in life at the Swan River colony. He sold up readily enough to accompany her. As a bachelor of forty-eight, with no other living relatives, there was nothing to keep him in Ireland. After a dreadful voyage out on the *James*, during which he and other passengers had numerous altercations about the quality of the food and their quarters with the obdurate Master, Mr Edward Goldsmith, they arrived in Fremantle in May 1830.

Within a year Ellis was appointed Government Resident of Kelmscott and had received a grant of over two thousand acres in the Avon Valley, whereupon his sister stated that the settlement was too primitive and the summer too hot and prevailed on him to relocate to the cooler climate of Van Diemen's Land. This he was not prepared to do. He felt, quite justifiably so in his opinion, that he had fulfilled his family responsibilities and he did not wish to uproot again, especially as he was now receiving an allowance and developing useful connections. So his sister packed her things again and set sail for Hobart Town with eight of her children. The second eldest niece couldn't face another sea voyage and, with her mother's permission, remained in Perth to keep house for her uncle, of whom she was very fond.

However, Ellis missed his military style life and when the new Superintendent's position was advertised he applied and was appointed soon after. He relished the close association and camaraderie with the soldiers and his appointment was the nearest he could get to the career he had enjoyed so much.

"Captain Ellis," the aide-de-camp greeted him. "The Governor will see you now."

Ellis was ushered into a large office, cum study, cum library. Stirling met him with outstretched hand. "Seat yourself, Captain Ellis. I was pleased to see that you accepted the Superintendent's position. My sources inform me that you, Norcott and Armstrong, the interpreter, make a fine team and are performing admirably in a difficult job. Bring me up to date."

The hour passed quickly. The Governor listened carefully, interjecting when he required elaboration. A secretary took notes. Stirling knew a great deal about Ellis. He was well educated, dependable and respected by the colonists for his studious approach in all business and professional matters. He also managed to hold the respect of the natives and was clearly the right man for the position.

"Tell me, Ellis. What would be your opinion about the formation of a permanent Mounted Police Corps? A special group to deal with native problems. An autonomous group not connected with the Regiment so that it has more flexibility in determining its own movements and schedules. The Metropolitan Police, now established in London, have been very successful in combating crime. It seems to me that at the moment you are constrained or at least restricted to an extent by having to clear all initiatives with Captain Irwin when you require support troops. And I suspect that on occasions there would be competing demands or even conflicting interests. Such a policing force would not necessarily be required to follow the strict dictates of the Colonial Office as demanded of the military with regard to the treatment of natives."

"What would be the primary objective of such a force, sir and to whom would it be responsible?"

"Well, I'm still thinking the whole idea through but my initial proposal to Captain Irwin was that the Corps would be a strategic attack group ready to deal with any conflict with recalcitrant natives efficiently and at short notice. It is clear that such problems have increased in my absence, both in number and severity. I cannot allow the settlers to go unprotected and the Regiment's resources are being stretched to the limit as the colony expands. My discussions with the Colonial Office made it quite clear that requests for additional British troops would not be considered. In answer to your second question, the Mounted Police Corps would be responsible to me through their appointed commander, to whom I would delegate authority."

Stirling looked pointedly at Ellis. "If you were offered the position Captain, would you take it?"

Ellis pondered for a moment, a concerned look on his face. "Yes, Your Excellency. I would." He leaned forward in his chair. Stirling noticed the way he was wringing his hands. "The escalation of conflict and the increasing number of woundings and deaths of both settlers and natives have been a real worry to me. I would be pleased to participate in any plan to settle relations between the two races. Something must be done and the sooner the better."

"It might involve some unpleasant duties, Captain."

"I would have expected unpleasant duties, Your Excellency."

"Yes but of the type of those presently involving Devenish? I have heard rumours. No, more than rumours. Confirmations of Devenish's dealings with the native women. Do you know of similar cases?"

"Well, Your Excellency one hears stories about settlers and the native women. As I understand the situation, they are mostly transitory relations and involve bargaining. Services for handouts you might say. Many of the natives don't seem to have a problem with such arrangements. More's the pity, Sir James." The Captain was squirming in his seat, clearly embarrassed at having to admit the occurrence of such liaisons.

Stirling continued." Jack Devenish however is a different kettle of fish. He takes a woman in until she is noticeably with child and then discards her. What's more he mistreats them. I'm told they often show signs of violence. Would you be prepared to take a man to task over such an issue?"

"Of course. As required, Your Excellency."

The Governor rose and shook Ellis' hand. "Thank you, Captain. We will be in contact with you. Needless to say our conversation should remain confidential for the present. I will make a public statement through the *Gazette* in due course."

Following his meeting with Ellis, Stirling consulted with the members of his Executive Council. Moore, Irwin, Roe and Broun were of the opinion that the situation required stern measures and that the colony would not develop and prosper unless the ever present threat of native attacks was removed. Settlers were not inclined to venture onto new grants or those located at any distance from military protection. The Council endorsed Stirling's proposal to establish a Mounted Police Corps.

On the 30th August, the *Perth Gazette* announced the increased Civil Establishment of Western Australia and the regulations for the management of public business. Included in the list was the appointment of Captain T. T. Ellis as the Principal Superintendent of Mounted Police. The primary aims of the Corps were to protect the settlers and ensure the safety of the mail carriers. Further duties included provisions to protect the natives from injury and to ensure that the settlers observed due legal process in this regard.

In a conciliatory gesture, the Governor met and pardoned Weeip of the Perth tribe for the spearing of Larkin in April and ordered the release of his son Billyoomerri, who had been held hostage against further violence. Part of Stirling's bargain, translated to Weeip by Ellis and reported in the *Gazette*, stated 'That a great number of men would be mounted on horses, whose business it would be to ride through the Country punishing with severity, any of the blacks who molest white people'. It was further explained, that if the black men committed any violence or robbery, the Governor would not leave one of their men on the coastal side of the Hills. Of course, in spite of Ellis' and Armstrong's genuine attempt to translate the intentions of the Governor, the content of the message was largely incomprehensible to the frightened native.

Stirling then dispatched a small detachment of experienced troops to Mandurah by schooner. They were to ascertain as much as possible about the location and movements of the Murray tribe and to act as a visible deterrent to further attacks.

Meanwhile, the schooner was to transport Thomas Peel to Fremantle and arrange his immediate river passage to Perth to meet privately with the Governor on 26th September. The glimmering of a plan was taking form in Stirling's ingenious mind.

* * * * *

Stirling rose from his desk as Peel entered the library at Government House. "Welcome, Thomas," he said, shaking his guest's hand. Peel noted the use of his given name.

Stirling continued. "My apologies for a summons at such short notice but I received your letter about the severity of the native attacks, which we need to discuss. Ellis has provided me with a full report."

Peel nodded. "That's all right, James." Two could play this game. "I was glad for the excuse to travel to Perth. I'll be able to catch up with the changes you appear to be implementing with such speed. Thanks for providing the schooner for my use and the additional troops in the area in my absence. I must say my family are not appreciating their stay in Mandurah. They prefer to see it as a sojourn to be concluded as soon as possible. Everyone has been terrified since the attack on Barron and Nesbit, which is not at all surprising."

Stirling motioned Peel to a chair at the end of the table.

As he took his seat, Peel said, "And sincere congratulations on your elevation to the knighthood. Well deserved, of course and hopefully also a recognition of the colony's progress. Cousin Robert was very pleased at the developments. As you probably know he is presently touring the continent but is expecting to be recalled to take Office in the near future."

Stirling was careful not to show his surprise. He knew all the particulars but had not reckoned on Peel having been informed of the situation so quickly.

"Sir Robert has been a supporter of the colony from the beginning and that has always been appreciated," was his only acknowledgment of Peel's comments. The man had such a damnable smug look on his face.

"Now Thomas, to business. I'd like to bring you up to date on some proposed changes to regulations regarding land. Further, I have some plans for the Pinjarra area that I am sure will interest you. The developments taken together could affect your future prospects here quite handsomely."

Stirling leaned back in his chair and explained succinctly the soon to be gazetted changes in regulations for the sale of land in the colony. "First Thomas, land laws will be liberalised so that owners can dispose of a portion of their holdings, even though the previous conditions of improvement have not been fulfilled. This will allow present owners to divest themselves of partially improved property to newcomers or more wealthy settlers and use the capital to improve or provide stock for other holdings. You might consider assigning some of your land to former indentured servants, both those who have submitted claims against you or those who owe you money. Their improvements could then be cited and could also attract other settlers to your land."

"Hmm. An interesting possibility."

"Yes, especially for someone in your position," Stirling commented. "Secondly, town allotments can be assigned, providing that a right of occupation is secured at a price of from £2 to £5 and this right would merge into a title of fee simple when stipulated improvements are effected. Such action will facilitate the purchase of town lots and consequently lead to a demand for more town sites to be gazetted with the spread of the settlement. Finally, forthwith crown land will not be allocated in grants but will be sold at a minimum of five shillings per acre."

Peel contained himself until Stirling had finished and then launched into a series of questions. The only answer he objected to was that the Secretary of State had categorically asserted no further grants of land were to be made to Thomas Peel. In view of the fact that no further grants of land would be made to anyone, his arguments slowly subsided.

Stirling then brought Peel around to his line of thinking.

"What the colony needs is a line of garrisons located appropriate distances apart between Perth and Albany, say one day's ride. Such fortifications would ensure the safety of settlers, travellers and the consignment of goods and mail between the two centres. As you would know Thomas, Albany is already acknowledged as a better porting facility than Fremantle for many wares and it could be developed as an all-weather port in the future. Eventually the garrisons would be gazetted as towns and joined by formed roads."

Stirling pointed out that Pinjarra was the logical site for the first garrison and township. What he didn't point out was that he was banking on the success of the scheme to the extent that it would affect his own grant entitlements, which included large tracts of land along the route proposed.

Peel saw pound signs beginning to emerge from every suggestion. The liberalisation of the land rules combined with the idea of a garrison and township at Pinjarra could open exciting possibilities. In fact, it was the shift he had planned before the family arrived. The soil was so much better upstream and the river was fresh. A huge grin spread across his face, then as quickly turned into a grimace.

"It wouldn't be possible, James. Not without ridding the area of the Murray tribe. They are just too warlike, too unpredictable, too hostile. They've murdered four settlers and wounded two since our arrival. They're ten times as hostile as the Perth tribe and greater in number. Unless their numbers are reduced significantly, there would be little chance that the plan would succeed." Peel looked quite glum.

"Thomas, the native problem was discussed at length last week by the Executive Council. The decisions are still classified information but there was unanimous support for the formation of a Mounted Police Corps with Ellis in charge. Their brief would be flexible but their primary concern is to provide protection for the settlers. Have you caught up with the *Gazette* yet?"

Peel shook his head. "No but if I'm following the gist of the conversation, we will soon have a force that doesn't have to answer to Irwin because they'll be paid from your coffers. A force that answers to you and therefore is not directly responsible to the Colonial Office. Am I right?"

"Yes, you're exactly right. Due to the present unrest, it should be assumed that we have the support of the Swan River settlers to proceed to move on the establishment of the first of the planned outposts on the road to Albany and that will be Pinjarra. When we tell them, that is. The Mounted Police Corps will provide necessary protection while a township is surveyed."

The next hour was spent devising a plan. A plausible scheme. Logical reasons. Defensible arguments. A time schedule. Newspaper releases. The two men didn't see it as a conspiracy but a necessity for both their own futures and the future of the colony and the solution to several major problems in a single action.

The first steps were taken over the next few days, when both Peel and Stirling became involved in a burst of activity and letter writing.

Peel wrote that very day to the Governor formally requesting that he have made to him the grant in fee simple of 'the tract of 250,000 acres between Clarence and the Murray River now in my possession under a Licence of Occupation from the local Government'. He further pointed out that he saw this grant as being only a 'partial performance of a conditional engagement to confer on me a much more extensive grant'. Peel already knew that his second request would be rejected but with his usual obstinacy included it anyway. An addendum listed and described the improvements to his property in terms of buildings, fencing, animals, crops and gardens.

The next letter was to the *Perth Gazette* and included a notice to the indentured servants of Thomas Peel Esquire to be published in the following day's edition, 27th September. This notice informed previous employees of Mr Peel's willingness to negotiate with them in settling any claims or counterclaims that might be brought by either party in order to save the expense and delay of proceedings in a Court of Justice. Meeting places would be set up in Perth, Guildford and Fremantle and Mr Peel would be in attendance.

Past servants were further advised that the Governor had reserved a site for a township in the Pinjarra district adjoining Peel's land and intended clearing a road from Perth through Pinjarra to King George Sound commencing this summer. Protection and assistance in the formation of Mr Peel's settlement would be afforded by the Governor. Fifty acres of land and rations would be provided to selected servants to enable them to cultivate the land and maintain themselves till the next harvest. The only condition was that they repay their debts by moderate instalments at which time the allotments would be 'conveyed to them respectively as their absolute property for ever'.

Of course, it was a blatant bribe to entice past servants to enter into repayment arrangements with the hope of being selected to receive land holdings. Peel would benefit on both accounts. The notice would also inform the colony of the intentions of both the Governor and Peel with regard to the Pinjarra district and provide impeccable reasons for the actions planned to follow.

To add a government assurance, Stirling placed a notice in the same edition of the *Perth Gazette,* to the effect that road clearing would begin in the Murray River area of the proposed township that summer and that he would extend protection and assistance during the establishment of Mr Peel's settlement on the banks of the Murray. The proposed road would cross the ford at Pinjarra. Few settlers would know that the ford was the location of the meeting place of the Murray tribe and that fact was not disclosed.

For the records, Peel then wrote officially to Stirling confirming that his offer to his indentured servants was now public and reminding the Governor that a settlement at Pinjarra would be unlikely to succeed without military protection. Stirling responded to Peel, acknowledging that the improvements to his property were adequate to provide the basis for an application for grant in fee simple. Peel subsequently forwarded his application to the Executive Council on 1st October.

* * * * *

When the schooner returned from Mandurah, the troops were debriefed and a report on their findings personally handed to Stirling. The only item of interest was the confirmed location of the main camping ground of the Murray tribe on the northern side of the confluence of the Murray River and a small tributary some distance upstream from the land set aside for the Pinjarra town site. Several native tracks crossed there and intelligence suggested that the natives were likely to congregate there within the month as small family groups returned to the area at the end of the rainy season, as October was a traditional meeting time.

Governor Stirling was eager to proceed. Captain Ellis was ordered to assemble the Mounted Police Corps immediately, so they could be outfitted and undergo any necessary training. By mid October, the Corps was formed. The men were carefully selected and included three experienced officers and seven privates. The privates were chosen from soldiers late of the 63rd Regiment, who had claimed their discharge in the colony when the regiment was transferred to India and most of the men had some knowledge of local dialects. They were supplied with new green uniforms to distinguish them from resident soldiers and to provide a level of camouflage when patrolling in the bush. Finally, the police were each allocated a Baker double-barrelled percussion carbine and three hundred rounds of ball cartridges. Like the Brown Bess, the Baker was a military rifle but considered a far superior weapon. The Corps began intensive training.

CHAPTER 15
The Battle of Pinjarra

The Governor summoned Ellis to Government House and on arrival he was led by the aide-de-camp into the map room and seated opposite Stirling at a large table.

"Captain Ellis," Stirling began without the usual introductory pleasantries. "How is the preparation of the Mounted Police Corps progressing?"

"Extremely well, Your Excellency. As you are aware, they have all had previous military experience. We have just completed two weeks' intensive training and I can vouch for their readiness for any required duties."

"Good." Stirling cleared his throat. All this conniving made him feel uncomfortable, even if it was essential for his personal and professional future and indeed the future of the colony.

"I would like to confirm a strategy for our expedition to the Murray. You need to know exactly what I have planned, so that a comprehensive and concerted approach can be made. Let me give you some preliminary information."

Ellis thought he appeared agitated, which was unusual for the Governor.

"Both you and I have accepted our positions with an expectation that we will assume responsibility for the protection of all the inhabitants of this colony. All. White and black. However, it is now clear to the Legislative Council that we have reached a time in our development when the settlers are more in need of protection than the natives. Indeed, if the activities of the Murray tribe are not curtailed, the settlement is in danger of collapsing. No one is prepared to venture far from the major centres. And rightly so. They cannot be expected to place their own lives or the lives of their families in jeopardy. My worst fear is that there could be a coming together of the native tribes. A uniting of forces. If this ever occurred they could annihilate us by stealth by picking off small settlements one at a time. Our military numbers are small and spread too thinly and that is why it was necessary to constitute the Corps."

Stirling motioned Ellis to a map of the colony pinned to the wall. "You can see Ellis, that the surveyed sections of settlement south of Perth have been extended by Mr Roe from all the available information. Scale cannot be guaranteed but would be reasonably accurate. George Smythe has added the grants along the Murray River and the site of the proposed Pinjarra town site." His forefinger traced the river and hesitated on the location of the proposed town site. He turned to Ellis. "As you know, none of the grants have been taken up apart from Peel's and Meares' because of the native problem. Have you any questions?"

Ellis scanned the map. "No sir," he replied.

"Captain Ellis. Disregard anything you hear or read. I speak to you in confidence, as an officer and a gentleman. This is not a journey solely for exploratory purposes. What I am also proposing is a retaliatory expedition to arrest the ringleaders of the ambush by the Murray tribe. It is my intention to incarcerate them, possibly on one of the islands, for a considerable length of time. When the murderers of Nesbit have been taken away, hopefully the other members of the tribe will disperse. They will certainly be strongly advised to shift their main camp to another section of their tribal territory. While we are in the area, Mr Roe and Mr Smythe will survey the town site. A suitable location for the establishment of a garrison will be determined and a detachment from the 21st Regiment will remain at that site. They will meet us in Mandurah and travel with us to the Pinjarra area. I think perhaps you, Norcott and five of your troopers should accompany the party. That will leave a corporal and two policemen in the Perth area in case of any trouble, although I doubt they will be needed. The Perth tribe have been very quiet lately from all accounts. The trouble arises in the south."

Stirling paused in consideration. "I believe Peel and Meares should also join us, since they are the major land owners in the Pinjarra district and Meares has just been appointed District Superintendent for the area. That should do it."

"What about a surgeon, Your Excellency, in case someone is wounded in making the arrests?"

"Not necessary, Ellis. In any case we don't want anyone to surmise that this will be a punitive expedition. The public will be notified that it is an exploratory excursion." Both men, particularly Ellis, would later regret this decision.

On the following Saturday, *The Western Australian Journal* announced that the Governor, accompanied by the Surveyor General and an escort of mounted police, would proceed to the Murray and Mount William and return by way of Kelmscott, thus passing through country affording extensive pasture. The purpose of the excursion of an estimated fourteen days was 'to explore the country in the neighbourhood of Mount William, with a view to form an establishment on that line of road to King George Sound - a project of the first importance to the colony'.

As it turned out, the departure of the expedition was postponed several days when George Moore informed Ellis that Guerip was in the upper Swan district. Stirling wanted all the perpetrators of Nesbit's murder together at the Murray camp site.

And so the elaborate deception was put into place. Sir James Stirling and Mr John Roe left Perth openly on horseback on Saturday 25th October. Their departure was reported in that morning's newspaper. They crossed the Swan River by ferry at Preston Point, several miles upstream from Fremantle and met George Smythe and Corporal Delmidge, who had travelled by boat from Perth. Supplies were unloaded and packed onto horses left near the ferry by prearrangement. The four men travelled leisurely through Fremantle. Several miles to the south they stopped for the midday meal at a hut provided by Mr George Robb, for the convenience of the Governor's party. Here they were joined by Captain Richard Meares and his son Seymour, who had journeyed across country from Guildford and Captain Ellis and his deputy Charles Norcott leading five mounted police.

The party travelled at a comfortable pace, reaching Peel's establishment in Mandurah just before dark the next day. Ellis directed his troopers to continue to the barracks. The Governor and his entourage were greeted by Thomas and Mary Peel.

"Welcome, Your Excellency. You made good time." Peel nodded to Meares, Roe and Smythe. Welcome, gentlemen." The men shook hands. "My wife, Mrs Peel and our children Fred, Julia, Dora and Thomas." The visitors were presented in turn. The females curtsied and the boys bowed. With a twinkle in his eye, the Governor bowed to Mrs Peel and acknowledged each of the children, as did the other visitors. It was clear the children had been primed for this important occasion. Introductions completed, the younger children were packed off to bed and the men seated themselves at the table. Lamps and pipes were lit. Wines were served. Seymour and Fred were sent to attend to the unsaddling and hobbling of the horses. The women served cold meats, cheese and bread, followed by jellies and fruit and then retired to their bedrooms. An animated conversation began and the underlying excitement was clearly evident as aspects of the impending foray were discussed. The map was brought out and studied at length. The plan was deliberated again and again.

At dawn, as the visitors rolled out of their bedrolls in the main room, there were some obvious groans and holding of heads. Peel grinned. He had not overindulged the previous night knowing how green the wine was. However by mid morning, after a walk to the estuary, a wash and a feed of freshly netted fish compliments of Fred and Seymour, everyone was ready to push on. Horses were saddled, pack horses loaded and the party farewelled by the Peel family. Two corporals and eight soldiers of the 21st Regiment joined them as they passed the barracks. Soon after one o'clock, on a glorious spring day, twenty-four men set off around the Peel Inlet foreshore with two of Peel's dogs running alongside, snuffling for quarry on the samphire flats.

Samuel Andrews was waiting for the group at the ford, where the Serpentine entered the estuary, having been alerted by a trooper sent on in advance of the main party. He rode up on horseback, with the Brown Bess snug in a possum skin wrapper tied to the saddle bag. Peel made brief introductions and Samuel dropped back and followed several paces behind his master. He was both pleased and excited about being included in the exploratory party.

When the horsemen crossed the delta of the Murray River, many signs of natives were observed. Several families had crossed the sand bars since the tide had receded that morning, as evidenced by the large, medium and small footprints and dog tracks. The drag marks of spears and digging sticks could also be seen. Ellis carefully examined the marks in the sand and estimated the natives were about two hours ahead. He spoke briefly to Stirling, who then gave the order to slow down their progress, as he did not want to overtake the natives, who were almost certainly heading for Pinjarra. Roe took some compass readings and the group set off on a south-easterly bearing. By 5 o'clock they came across a broad stretch of the Murray River and twenty minutes later bivouacked about ten miles from the Murray mouth at a place the natives called Jim Jam. They were now about halfway between the Murray-Serpentine delta and the major camp site of the Murray tribe.

* * * * *

It was late afternoon and there was much excitement at Bindjareb. Another four family groups had just arrived and everyone hustled and bustled to assist them in the preparation of shelters. The nights were still cold and the dew near the river could be heavy. Greetings were shouted, laughter abounded and expectation hung in the air. Dogs ran about barking at anything and everything. After the rigours of the wet season, everyone looked forward eagerly to the kambarang meeting. Their people were coming from every direction, following the pads that converged on the main dry weather camp site at Bindjareb.

Later, there would be dancing. That morning, there had been much discussion between the elders about a suitable location for the entertainment. Eventually, agreement had been reached and an area on the edge of the camp site was cleared of shrubs, grass and debris by the women and children and the topsoil softened with digging sticks for the stamping feet of the dancers. A tall stand of eucalypts acted as a backdrop to the stage and beneath the largest tree a short divider fence of leafy boughs was erected by the men. On the other side of the cleared area, wood had been stacked in piles in readiness for firing.

Warranang called to her husband. "Budulu. There is my brother Katta and Nangatta. She has a baby at last. I must go and welcome them." She took the hand of her daughter, Binda, a beautiful child and hurried away.

Budulu followed her admiringly with his eyes and was delighted to see his young brother-in-law, with his wife cradling the new baby, walking through the trees from the direction of the hills. He hoped he had brought some rock chips for spear heads, as he was down to his last few flakes.

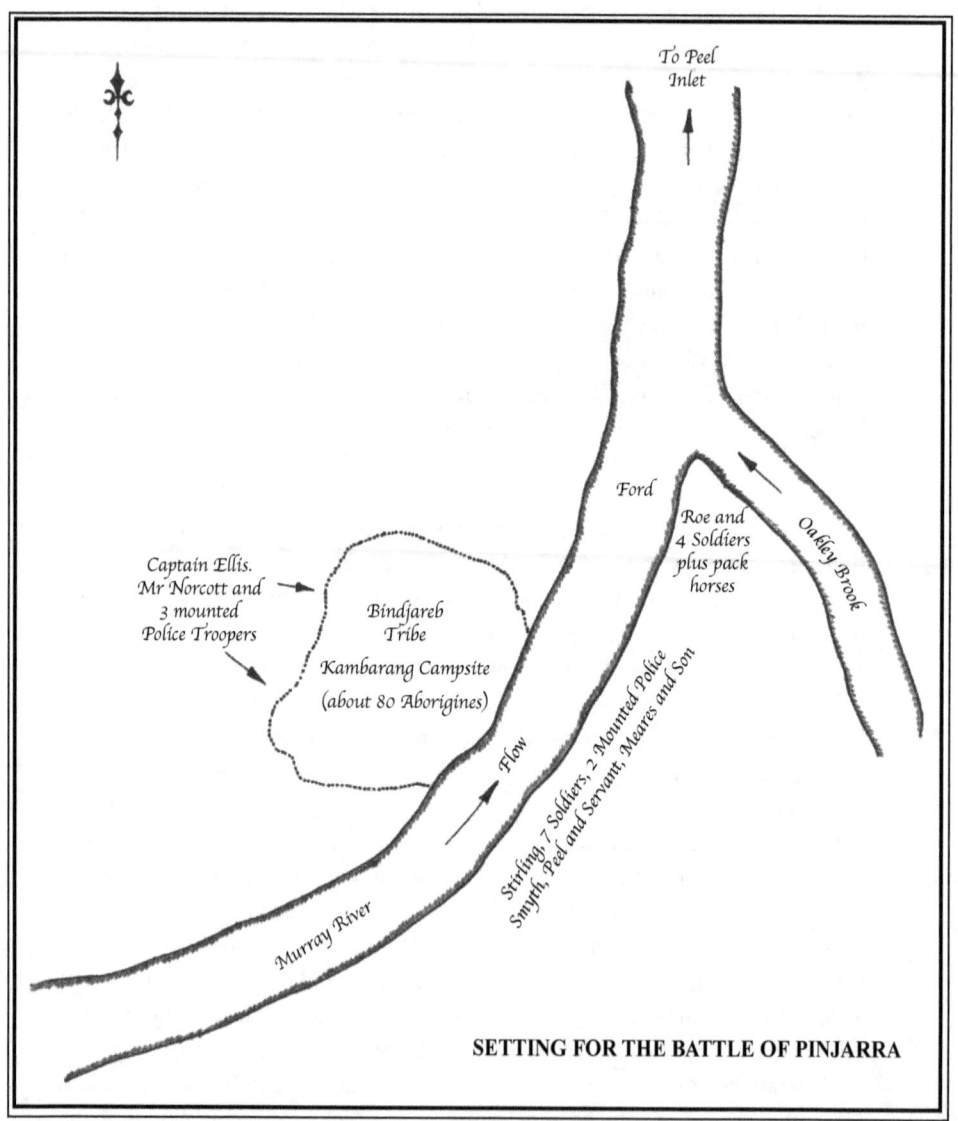

To Peel
Inlet

Ford

Oakley Brook

Roe and
4 Soldiers
plus pack
horses

Captain Ellis.
Mr Norcott and
3 mounted
Police Troopers

Bindjareb
Tribe

Kambarang Campsite
(about 80 Aborigines)

Flow

Stirling, 7 Soldiers, 2 Mounted Police
Smyth, Peel and Servant, Meares and Son

Murray River

SETTING FOR THE BATTLE OF PINJARRA

He beckoned to their only son Yeddi, who was playing a game with some smooth river stones. "Come with me, my son and we will greet our kin." Yeddi dropped the stones and followed his father, walking with a graceful rhythmic movement. He was a handsome child of nine summers, two summers older than Binda. Secretly, Budulu thought his son the best looking child in the tribe but of course did not say so. Warranang had no such modesty and took great delight when other mothers looked admiringly at Yeddi.

Budulu approached Nangatta who was talking excitedly with Warranang. "Greetings sister. I hope you are all well."

Nangatta nodded shyly, the baby gurgling contentedly in its mother's arms.

Warranang butted in. "My husband, it is a boy. We have a beautiful nephew and he is named Jandu."

"Welcome to our family, Jandu," Budulu said, stroking the baby's head. "May you grow tall and strong like your uncle."

Grinning, he turned to his brother and welcomed Katta warmly, with an affectionate slap on the shoulder.

"Welcome, little brother," he said. Katta was a hand taller than Budulu. "I hope you have brought me some borryl flakes. I have some very straight spear wood to exchange."

Katta held Budulu at arms length and gave him a happy smile. Large white teeth gleamed. "Of course, my littlest brother," he said pointedly. "I have brought you the finest borryl. Strong and sharp and we have lizard with us to share. Tomorrow, we will make spears."

The brothers-in law conversed contentedly, glad to be together again. They were the only two men of their generation on both sides of the family. Budulu led Katta and his family to his shelter near the river where they greeted grandmother, Mandu and grandfather, Yabbal. The women quickly constructed another conical brush shelter with its entrance facing north away from the wind. A fire was lit, fish and lizards cooked and as the families shared the food, there was much laughter and chatter. Reunions were always such happy occasions.

Later, as the purple dusk gathered and the granite outcrops of the scarp turned golden with the rays of the dying sun, Budulu and Katta strolled over to pay their respects to Calyute, who now had two wives as befitted a respected elder. Budulu saw that his newest and youngest wife Yornup was a beauty and was with child. Three other children born to his first wife played close to the shelter.

The men crouched a short distance from Calyute's fire and Nunar and Winjan joined them. The brothers felt honoured to be in such company. The elders brought the younger men up to date with the latest events, as Budulu had spent the winter to the south of the large inland waters and Katta had foraged in the hills. Neither knew the details of the recent encounters with the whites. Calyute did not mention the origin of his scars and was not asked. Clearly though, the Bindjareb men had not remained unscathed. Budulu was pleased for the status of the tribe that the floggings and imprisonment of his kin had been avenged but wondered whether that was the end of it. Surely the whites would not let the Big Lake ambush go unavenged. A payback killing would almost certainly follow.

Budulu shivered involuntarily as they returned to their shelters. He wished that his wife's uncle Odern, who was renowned among the Nyoongar as a boylya gadak, was with them, as he possessed special powers and was highly revered by the Bindjareb people. Sometimes he would read the future through the flames. Although now past middle age, he had chosen not to take a wife and resented intrusions into his solitary existence preferring to travel alone. No one had sighted him for many moons.

As darkness fell and the moon appeared in the east, a dozen men, including Budulu and Katta, gathered their belongings, moved quietly into the trees beyond the cleared area and disappeared behind the brush fence. It was time for dressing.

Meanwhile the stacks of wood were lit and tended by several men who took great care and pride in their allotted task. When the kindling had caught, large logs were dragged over to the fires to provide continued light for the night's show.

Suddenly, came the signal that everyone was anticipating.

"Youaal." The welcoming call from the Master of Ceremonies was accompanied by a single beckoning gesture, yet no one missed it.

The tall elder now stood motionless in front of the row of fires. He was painted with white pipeclay and red ochre and wore a headband and armbands decorated with an impressive array of tail feathers from the pink and grey cockatoo.

The audience assembled quickly, all knowing their respective places, though there were some disputes over positions at the ends of rows, supposedly offering the best vantage points. Because it was a family night, men, women and children could sit together except where members held a special role in the proceedings. Binda kept looking and calling for her father.

"Hush, Binda," said Yeddi. "You will see Father soon when he will come out from the trees. Don't you remember last year?" The little girl shook her head. Yeddi put his arm around her reassuringly and she settled down. The three generations of the family sat waiting impatiently.

With an exaggerated arm movement, the Master of Ceremonies indicated two men, who had appeared from the bushes and were standing to the side of the stage. The performance was about to begin! An immediate hush descended on the gathering, as the musicians began clacking the ends of a matched pair of kylies held loosely in the middle, their right wrists flexing and extending in unison near their thighs. When the rhythm was established, a select group of women seated in the front row began beating their folded skin cloaks with open palms. The overture continued for some minutes and the audience began to sway in time to the music. Soft clapping of hands and cupped hands on thighs provided increased depth to the sounds.

On a cue from the dignified elder, eight men emerged from behind the brush shelter and followed their leader, dancing in measured movements with a high knee action into the full light of the fire. Gasps of appreciation came from the audience. The men were covered from head to toe with painted dots and perpendicular, horizontal and zigzag lines all in white. All wore a headband of human hair from which protruded white cockatoo crest plumes and they carried decorated sticks in their right hands.

The dancers, in perfect unison, stepped slowly around the stage several times, swaying their bodies from right to left, their movements in exact time to the beat of the music, their feet stomping with the pulse. At precisely the same time, they began chanting a song as they took up their positions, four on each side of the flattened earth stage. When the song ended, they stood motionless, waiting expectantly.

Binda cried out in fright as a grey-haired elder with a full beard, ran from behind the shelter. He leapt high in the air and landed lithely in the centre of the stage holding a balanced and dramatic pose. Stretching slowly upwards to an upright position, he stood quivering, his body, arms and legs vibrating unceasingly. The movements continued for several minutes during which time he remained silent. Then he led the men into their assigned positions around the stage with the same high stepping rhythmic action.

The assembled crowd of about eighty applauded vigorously.

Slowly the Master of Ceremonies raised his arms. There was immediate quiet as he turned and again pointed to the hide.

From behind the shelter strutted an emu. Well, it certainly looked like an emu! Budulu had been heavily greased all over and Katta had painstakingly pressed emu feathers over his body and down to his knees. Long pieces of bark were fastened to his feet. His left arm and hand were bent and raised above his head, the hand wrapped in possum skin with a large black eye drawn in charcoal on each side. The audience froze in case it might take fright and run, however it just kept strutting, carefully placing its feet on the ground and then rolling its body forward, taking large steps as it walked in stately fashion around the stage.

A hissing came from the crowd as breaths were drawn in through clenched teeth. A hunter had appeared from the darkness behind the hide and commenced a slow circling movement around the outside of the motionless dancers. He held his spear at the ready in its thrower. The emu had not seen the hunter and continued its sedate walk, occasionally pausing to fastidiously peck at the ground.

Binda began to giggle and had to place both hands over her mouth. She knew the hunter was Uncle Katta and had suddenly realised that the emu had long shapely legs which looked very much like her father's.

The audience loved it and was clearly divided as to whose side to take. Every time the hunter stalked the emu to within a few strides, the stupid bird would nonchalantly turn and strut the other way. A soft sigh of relief could be heard together with sounds of exasperation. In the end the emu won, when it darted between the stationary players and disappeared into the trees with the hunter in determined pursuit. The exit of the actors followed by the dancers was greeted by hoots and loud applause. The Master of Ceremonies signalled the end of the evening's proceedings and amid much chatter and laughter the crowd dispersed to their family fires.

* * * * *

Odern awoke with a start and reached to touch his magic stick, secure in his waistband. The noise of horses' hooves and gunshots were so deafening that he was forced to place his hands over his ears until the sounds subsided. Hurriedly pulling some dry grass, he sparked the embers of the dying fire and within minutes it was blazing. As the flames grew and his gaze intensified, he firstly became entranced, then mesmerised. Slowly, the picture formed and the sounds returned.

He saw family groups slowly awakening with the dawn. His brother Yabbal and sister-in-law Mandu had joined their sons and families for the morning meal and people huddled around fires as it was chilly and a dew covered the ground. Everyone was excitedly relating last night's events and the emu stalk was discussed step by step. Budulu was persuaded to demonstrate the emu walk again and again, while adjacent family groups chided Katta. Fancy letting the emu escape! The hunters always killed their prey in the stories. It was agreed that it had been one of the best performances anyone could remember and of course Budulu and Katta received much praise. Their individual contribution had been lauded by all and it would go down in song and story for many rotations of the seasons.

Some of the dogs began to bark but no one took much notice. They were engrossed in conversation. Blasts from a whistle and warning shouts from the men camped on the area farthest from the river eventually penetrated the noise of chatter.

"Arm yourselves. Prepare to fight. Beware, white men approach."

For a moment no one moved. Impossible! The whites had never invaded their camp site, nor had ever been near their camp site. What could this mean?

"Hurray, Katta. Now! They must be approaching from the south. Gather your spears."

Budulu and Katta hurriedly picked up their weapons and stationed themselves between their families and the increasing shouts of warning. The thud of hooves could now be heard clearly. There were many horses.

The picture faded and the sounds drifted away.

Odern shook his head to clear the vision and then kicked sand over the fire. Gathering his few possessions, he headed away from the ocean and walked hurriedly towards Bindjareb.

* * * * *

Stirling's party began to stir at 5 o'clock to a frosty morning, with a heavy dew and fog. As they arose from bed rolls and pulled on boots, they stamped and rubbed hands together to gain warmth. Dawn was just approaching, when Ellis ordered the hobbled horses to be rounded up and saddled and any metal accoutrements bound with cloth strips to muffle the sounds of their advance. Breakfast consisted of hardtack and smoked fish with a swig of water and Samuel served Peel, the Governor and Meares in that order. As the sun rose over the Darling Range, the bed rolls and eating utensils were fastened to the pack horses and a final check made of the camping area. Roe took a bearing for the Pinjarra area and the group turned south-east away from the river. The ground was swampy and the going heavy.

Peel brought up the rear because he had insisted on bringing his dogs. They were now tethered to Samuel's saddle and not enjoying the experience. Smiley in particular was impatient with the slow progress and the fact that she was unable to chase the wildlife. Total silence being ordered, the men moved in almost funereal procession.

It was about 8 o'clock, when Stirling and Roe led the party back towards the Murray River with Roe estimating that they were approximately half a mile south of the proposed town site and about double that distance from the native camp. The river was narrow, only about thirty yards across and flowing quickly, the water still high from the winter run-off. Here the banks were high, comprising slippery red loam covered with light shrubs and saplings down to the water's edge. Tall tuarts and red gums grew along the crest of the banks. Stirling gave the signal to stop and rode back to confer with Peel and Ellis.

"Any final thoughts, gentlemen?" Heads shook. The consensus was that the plan for engagement should proceed.

Within half an hour, they had traversed the ford over the brook and assembled with minimum noise in the trees on the eastern side of the Murray

River. They could now hear the occasional native shouts and cooees drifting across on the westerly wind. Once again they stopped and the three leaders deliberated, resulting in Peel leaving his dogs with Samuel, recrossing the river on horseback and reconnoitring on foot. He didn't like what he saw, quickly estimating the native numbers to be anything up to a hundred, far more than expected. Peel had offered to establish the whereabouts of the ringleaders of the attack on Nesbit and Barron. There was no way he was going to go any closer. Hell's bells! He had expected a group of about thirty. He hurried back to Stirling and called him away from the waiting men. Samuel was close enough to overhear the conversation.

"James," Peel whispered excitedly. "This is much too dangerous. There are over a hundred blacks that I can see. There might be more. I'd be a fool to go any closer alone. The Mounted Police should just chase the natives towards the river. As we originally planned, that won't initially implicate the soldiers. Hopefully, Calyute and the other miscreants will be captured on the way, as they are likely to be the ones that hold their ground."

Stirling had never seen any previous evidence of cowardice in the man. Perhaps he was just being cautious and Stirling should heed the advice. Good God! How would it look if there were casualties among the British! And if Thomas Peel was one of them!

Ellis and Roe were called up to be apprised of the amended strategy. Ellis wondered why Peel had backed down from being part of the attacking group, particularly since he was the one who best knew the Murray tribesmen and could identify most of them. Then he was informed of the estimated number of natives. Peel might be able to get away with it but there could be no backing down for the Principal Superintendent of the Mounted Police.

Rain began to fall.

Accompanied by three troopers, Ellis and Norcott crossed the river at the ford and took up a position to the west of the native camp site, which was situated between Ellis' group and the river. Saddles were checked and rifles, swords and pistols were at the ready. Norcott took a surreptitious swig of brandy.

Roe, who had refused to carry any weapons, was to take charge of the baggage, including the wagon and packhorses. He reckoned he had done his share of killing when serving in the Royal Navy under Captain Phillip King and afterwards vowed never to carry arms as a civilian. Four soldiers with loaded rifles were to remain with him and guard the ford from the easterly aspect.

Stirling, Peel and Andrews, Meares and son Seymour, Smythe, two mounted policemen and seven soldiers remained concealed in a line on the high ground on the opposite side of the river from the native camp site, which could just be seen through the trees from their vantage point. It was certainly a much larger gathering than had been anticipated.

All was in readiness. The rain stopped and the sun came out.

Northcott blew a series of sharp blasts on a whistle tied around his neck. He heard loud shouts from the camp. Ellis led the charge. Norcott seeing Nunar with spear poised in a throwing stick shot him in the left shoulder and saw him fall. He took aim again and fired. Another native fell. Ellis and a trooper galloped past him. Norcott counted eight natives on the ground. Constable Heffron held his right arm which had a spear through it. He had dropped his rifle and nearly swooning from pain had reined in his mount with his left hand and sat dazed on his horse which turned in small circles.

At first the native men held their ground but as they saw the disastrous effects of the rapid fire carbines on their fellows they began retreating. Within a few minutes most of the natives were fleeing in disarray towards the river. Several shelters were burning, knocked over into fires in the rushed retreat. Mothers gathered children and babies. The old and infirm were run down and killed by horses' hooves. Mandu saw her husband's head sliced off and the headless body fall under a galloping horse. She ran back to him and was chopped in the thigh by a slashing sword. Mandu fell sobbing to the ground next to her man of thirty summers.

Ellis spotted Calyute and swung his horse in that direction, not seeing the wounded Nunar, who threw the spear that pierced his left temple. He dropped heavily to the ground and felt himself drifting into unconsciousness. There was nothing he could do about it, as none of his body parts would move. Blackness followed.

Norcott saw Ellis fall. He reined in his horse and galloped to attend his leader. Noting Ellis' condition, he gave the signal to regroup. At the one long whistle blast, the three troopers returned, one leading Heffron's horse.

"Captain Ellis is badly injured. We've done enough damage," Norcott shouted. "Let's clear out of here. Did anyone see who got the Captain?" Two policemen shook their heads. Heffron did not answer. "Smith, go and fetch Constable Heffron's rifle. It's on the ground over there. Johnson, help me get Captain Ellis onto his horse. Take care of his gun."

On the far bank, Stirling stood up in the stirrups. He turned to Peel who was next to him.

"I can't see what's going on? Who's that on the ground? It looks as though Ellis is down." Then the whistle blast was heard.

"Damn! That's regroup or retreat. Something's wrong. Men, prepare to fire and defend yourselves." Dozens of men, women and children could be seen scrambling down the opposite bank and leaping into the narrow stream.

The Governor distinctly heard the words "Shoot the bastards!" from beside him.

"Form lines and fire at will," ordered Stirling. Immediately taking up their prescribed standing or kneeling positions, the soldiers commenced firing.

"It's like target practice," one young private remarked above the noise of rifle fire.

"Yes. Just like in Van Diemen's Land. Got him. That's three so far."

Budulu toppled to the ground. Warranang screamed, dropped Binda and turned to help her husband. Blood was gushing from his neck. His eyes rolled back. He was dead. She could not stop screaming. Yeddi stood transfixed and terrified next to her, the whites of his eyes huge. His mother shoved him towards the river.

"Hide. Hide and wait for Great Uncle Odern" were the last words he heard as she pushed him hard. Yeddi toppled over the edge of the bank, sliding down the slippery slope into the river. He hit his head on a partially submerged log and in a dazed state, pulled himself under a large tree trunk on the water's edge. Frozen with fear he remained in his hiding place.

Warranang lifted Binda into her arms again and paused. She didn't know which way to run. In that moment of indecision she presented herself as a perfect target. The rifle ball passed through Binda's abdomen and lodged in Warranang's heart. They fell together.

Katta and Nangatta were picked off by rifle fire as they tried to swim to safety across the stream. The crying baby floated out of her mother's arms and slowly drifted downstream.

Samuel Andrews quietly arose from the grass in which he was lying to view the attack, quietly walked away from the river towards the trees and as quietly as possible vomited up his breakfast. Flushed with anger at what he had witnessed and with a depth of sorrow and shame he had never felt before, he stumbled on. He could watch no longer.

When Calyute realised they were caught in a crossfire, he called his family to follow him. His youngest son Unia they left bleeding to death, the back of his head shot away. Mindup, his first wife, was wounded in the arm, although fortunately it was only a graze. They ran bent over along the top of the bank downstream towards the ford. The trees gave them protection. Calyute stopped suddenly and threw himself to the ground. His family did the same. Someone had sneezed. He lifted his head slowly and saw Roe and four soldiers crouched in a stand of wattles. They were not looking in Calyute's direction. The soldiers were firing at natives wading or swimming downstream, or running along the bank of the river to escape.

Calyute motioned his wives and children to follow him. The family made their way down the steep bank and ran into the water as far as possible before wading to the other side. Winmar, Nunar and some others were just to their right. They were equidistant from both Stirling's and Roe's groups and were not seen. Reaching the other side they quietly climbed the steep bank and disappeared into the safety of the trees. However, it was all too much for

Yornup, Calyute's youngest wife who tripped and fell a few hundred yards from the river. Without lessening his stride, Calyute scooped her from the ground with strong arms and ran to safety into a copse of wattles. As the group burst through the brush on the other side they were momentarily in the open. A shot rang out and the ball blasted through Yornup's foot. Calyute ran on into the trees, the blood spraying his legs.

After about an hour from the initial charge led by Ellis, Stirling called the bugler to sound the cease-fire and led a contingent across the ford to the camp site to survey the scene. Several more males were shot as they were flushed out by Peel's dogs. Bodies were scattered everywhere. Stirling found Norcott looking totally inadequate with the unconscious Ellis. His head had been bound but blood seeped through the bandage. Ellis was semi-conscious and muttering incoherently. All bad signs Stirling knew from experience. Heffron sat propped up against a tree, his arm bandaged with the sleeve of his shirt. He was drunk on the only medicine available - Norcott's precious brandy. Guiltily, Stirling remembered telling Ellis why a surgeon was not to accompany the party.

"Peel. We must remove Ellis and the corporal to your Mandurah house immediately. They both need care and rest. No doubt you have laudanum and medical supplies at your place?"

"Yes, Stirling. Of course. Straight away."

"Lieutenant Armstrong, call Mr Roe."

With Peel, Roe and Armstrong in attendance, Stirling gave his final orders for the day.

"Right men, these are the procedures to be followed. Peel, Norcott and I will depart with the wounded and an escort of the Mounted Police for Mandurah with all urgency. The wounded will receive attention at Peel's house and a doctor called from Fremantle post-haste."

"Lieutenant Armstrong, you will remain here as long as you feel it is necessary to ensure there is no chase or reprisal by the natives. Although under the circumstances I think that unlikely, it is better to be sure. You will then lead your men and the remaining settlers back to Mandurah. I want no more casualties and now consider it would be ill-advised to leave a military detachment in the area as I had planned. It is more appropriate that the detachment is stationed in Mandurah."

"Mr Roe, you will assess the situation, prepare an official report of the incident and then return to Mandurah. Naturally no surveying will be undertaken at present."

"Gentlemen, I expect you all to keep confidential the events leading up to and including today's skirmish until the official report is tabled in the Legislative Council. Are there any questions?" There was no response. "Thank you all for your support. I will leave immediately."

Peel looked for Samuel and not seeing him assumed he would follow later when he had rounded up the dogs.

The group led by Stirling and Peel departed for Mandurah immediately. Two of the mounted policemen were given the task of riding on either side of Captain Ellis' horse to support him. Heffron rode behind, talking to himself.

Lieutenant Armstrong assembled his men and rode in a loose formation across the ford to the southern bank of the Murray. Samuel felt forced to follow, as he felt he just had to know the worst. Soldiers were sent out to count the dead and Samuel heard a corporal reporting fifteen dead natives in the camp site area and five more bodies at the bottom of the bank. They were only counting the adults. The river and surrounding bush were not searched. No sense in inviting a spear from a hidden survivor.

Because the dogs had not been fed since the previous night, Samuel tied them securely to a tree branch trying not to think what might happen otherwise. The blowflies were at their worst in October and were already buzzing around in large numbers. He began to feel squeamish again and took some deep breaths to gain some control, surmising correctly that the official report would give a much lower number of natives killed than in fact was the case.

Following a keening noise, Richard Meares and Seymour found eight women with more than a dozen children crouched in the scrub behind a brush shelter. All were terrified and crying. They were herded out by the riders. One woman could understand some English and Armstrong told her to pass on the word that if any white men were injured in retaliation, the soldiers would be sent to kill all the natives. They were then released to pass on the message but remained huddled together in fear in the area of the previous night's performance for several minutes before rising and running back into the shelter of the trees.

Samuel wandered off alone in the direction of the river. He did not feel proud of the morning's events. In fact, he felt downright disgusted. Because he had never had any dealings with natives, he felt no anger or bitterness towards them. Suddenly he stopped motionless in his tracks. Was that a flutter of an eyelid? A woman lay against an older man who seemingly had no head. Then he saw it several yards away, with eyes and mouth open and buzzing with flies. Samuel glanced back at the woman. Yes, she was alive but feigning death. Middle-aged, with a horrible slash to the thigh. The blood had already congealed and was turning black in the warmth of the morning sun. It was also covered with flies. He continued his walk.

When Roe called the group together to report on their findings, Samuel bent to untie his horse and then exclaimed loudly to no one in particular that his horse had a swollen fetlock and he would walk it down to the river to bathe the injury.

"If it's all right with you, Mr Roe, I'll take off this afternoon, as soon as possible, sir," he said. "I've got the dogs to protect me. I'll go directly to the Serpentine, taking it slowly. Need to get some salve on it. Belongs to Mr Peel. A damned nuisance, wouldn't you agree?"

Roe nodded absently, not being able to rid the scenes of carnage from his mind. Peel's servant could make his own way back. He had enough to worry about.

Samuel led the horse down to the river. While he made splashing noises and waded through the shallows two small black unblinking eyes watched his every move through the fork of a fallen tree, willing him not to come closer. Yeddi did not move a fraction of an inch and had not done so for hours. On either side of him floated two bodies. One was his Uncle Katta.

Samuel heard Armstrong, Roe and the others ride back over the ford to the supply wagon presumably for their midday meal. He didn't know how he would ever eat again.

Dragging his gelding back up the steep bank to the native camp site, he strode quickly towards the woman. She must have passed out from pain or loss of blood, for when Samuel bent over and dripped some water onto her mouth, she came to with a start and a frightened look on her face. Then thirst overcame her and she quickly opened her mouth for the liquid. She continued to stare at him with wide eyes.

"It's all right," he said quietly and soothingly. "If you don't let me help, you'll be dead by nightfall." She didn't understand the words but his voice and actions were reassuring.

Samuel returned the water flask to his saddle bag and bent to lift the woman. She was lighter than he had reckoned but all the same it was no easy matter to place her on the saddle. She did not struggle but with the saddest expression Samuel had ever seen, just stared down at the man without a head.

With the movement, the gash began bleeding again. Samuel pulled his knife and, quickly cutting a strip from his sleeping blanket, wrapped it tightly around the wound. The woman did not utter a sound although the pain must have been agonising. The dogs' leads were untied from the tree and fastened to his right stirrup. He swung up behind her and perching on the rear of the saddle set off slowly to the south-west. Not comfortable for either of them but they would manage. When well away from the scene of what he concluded could only be described as a massacre, he released the dogs to forage for food. The Brown Bess had remained untouched, securely wrapped in its possum skin.

CHAPTER 16

Twists of Fate

Samuel arrived at the farm after dark and had never been so glad to be home in all his four years on the Serpentine. Happy raced out, barking a greeting to the other dogs and Annie ran smiling from the kitchen verandah wiping her hands on her apron. A surprised look crossed her face as she saw the semi-naked black woman swaying with fatigue and pain on the saddle in front of her husband.

"Samuel. What has happened? Who is this woman?"

"Help me lass. I'll explain everything later. Be very careful. She has a bad wound on her thigh."

Carefully, Annie and Samuel lifted the near senseless woman from the horse and carried her to the house. Samuel was going to place her on the side verandah where the Armstrong boys used to sleep but his wife insisted on placing her on the couch in the main room near the fire.

Annie took control. The bloody strip of blanket was carefully removed with warm water and the wound cleansed with a splash of brandy. The injury was assessed with many 'tches' and 'tuts'. Needle and catgut from the medicine chest were washed in hot water and the edges of the wound sewn together. Bandages, torn from an old shirt of Samuel's, were wrapped around the thigh. Throughout the whole process the black woman did not move, nor did she make a sound but her eyes watched Annie throughout.

"Now Samuel, it's your turn. Stable the horse and then wash yourself. There's fresh water in the basin. You're filthy! I don't care how tired you are, you're not getting into bed like that."

When Samuel returned, the woman was sitting up with a cushion behind her back, being fed by Annie. It was kangaroo stew and obviously to her liking but after a few mouthfuls she shook her head to indicate she had eaten enough. Annie covered her with a light blanket before turning to her husband.

"Now my husband," Annie demanded, "I want to know every detail of what happened since you left home the day before yesterday."

Samuel told the story from start to finish and Annie was horrified.

"Why the women and children?"

"I don't know. Things just seemed to get out of hand. It was terrible, Annie. Just terrible. I was ashamed of being a white man. Heaven only knows how many were killed."

Next morning, Annie and Samuel were woken by the children, who wanted to know about the naked woman bathing in the river. Annie hastily pulled on a dress and rushed to the water's edge. Her patient was sitting on a log and had removed the bandage and was treating the wound with a handful of fresh tree gum. She had washed both herself and her scanty pubic covering of kangaroo skin and she was dripping water. As Annie drew near, she covered the gum salve on her thigh with a piece of paper bark from a nearby tree and bound it to her leg with reeds. The white woman had just received her first lesson in native medicine.

Annie supported her as she hopped back to the kitchen lean-to. The woman indicated she did not want to re-enter the house and sat on a log in the sun to dry. Samuel took an axe to a nearby tree and returned with a sapling from which the bark had been shaved. Its fork fitted neatly at the height of the women's armpit and had been padded with the remainder of his shirt. She knew immediately what it was for and nodded to Samuel. After moving around outside using her new crutch, she turned and gave a fleeting glance of gratitude for the freedom it offered.

The children were bursting with curiosity. Where had the woman come from? Why was she staying at their farm? Why didn't she wear clothes? How had she hurt herself? Why didn't she speak? How long would she stay? And much, much more. Annie and Samuel, as always, were as truthful as possible. Where they knew the answers, they explained things as best they could. The woman spent much of her time sleeping, dozing or just resting. She consumed everything given her to eat and drink. However, no word was spoken, no emotion shown - until the fourth day.

The woman was sitting under a tree, looking across the river at a bevy of pelicans, her leg stretched out, the crutch beside her. She was weaving a bag out of rushes from the water's edge. Sara Jane thought she looked much too sad and sidling up to her put an arm around her shoulder. The woman pulled the little girl to her and began to sob.

"Don't cry," said Sara Jane. "It's all right to stay with us. Do you talk? What's your name? Would you like to cuddle my doll?" She thrust her rag doll towards the woman.

Half an hour later when Annie wandered out of the house to check on her daughter, she found the two chatting away, albeit without much understanding.

"Mum," called Sara Jane. "Her name's Mandu. That's a nice name, isn't it?"

Annie sat down in the sand beside them. "Mandu," she said pointing at the woman. The woman nodded shyly.

"Sarjan," she said pulling Sara Jane close.

The girl shook her head. "Sara", she paused, "Jane".

"Sarjan" the woman said. "Doll." She held the doll up with her other hand.

"Annie."

"Annie."

"Mandu."

"Mandu."

"Doll."

"Doll."

"Sara Jane."

"Sarjan."

The little girl laughed and for the first time a flicker of a smile passed across Mandu's face.

* * * * *

It took Odern nearly two days to reach Bindjareb. He hurried as quickly as he could but his rheumatism was bad at present, even though he rubbed emu fat onto his joints every morning.

When he arrived at the camp site, his worst fears were realised. The place was deserted. Abandoned shelters, fires and implements told their story. Debris was scattered everywhere. He leaned on his stick as he walked eastwards along the high banks of his favourite river. Instinct led him. Then he saw them - freshly dug common burial mounds. There were three family mounds and that meant many dead. Nearby were thirteen separate graves, indicating the burial places of significant Binjareb men.

Odern felt an overwhelming sorrow. Grief for his people, grief for his family, grief for himself. An almost tangible loneliness surrounded him and he slumped to the ground. What to do? For once in his life, he felt so helpless.

Then he heard the sobbing. It wasn't real sobbing but an inner crying for help. He didn't hear it with his ears but with his heart. It was emanating from somewhere down stream and it was a powerful message, refusing to be ignored, insisting on action.

Using his stick, Odern stood. He moved his head from side to side, breathing in, his mouth open to better focus his senses. The power drew him and he followed. It led him back past the camp site, down the bank to the river. A large log lay to his left on the water's edge. He walked along it and squatted to peer behind it. He saw a small black head protruding from the brown water.

"Yeddi," he whispered. Two eyes opened and there was a sigh of relief.

"Great Uncle Odern. Oh, I'm so glad you're here." Tears welled in the boy's eyes as his Grandfather's brother gently assisted him from his hiding place and gathered him into his arms. Odern thought the boy must possess a great deal of potential to have exerted such a force in his weakened state.

"Now, now," he said, pulling him to his chest. "Tell me all about it."

The boy sobbed for some time and Odern held and comforted him. He must be about ten summers old and was a well proportioned child with a long straight nose and prominent jaw and lower lip. Altogether a fine-looking boy.

"When Mother pushed me, she said to hide and wait until you came for me. I've been so frightened. White men came. What happened? Where's Mother and Father and Binda? And Grandfather and Grandmother?"

Odern sighed. "I don't know Yeddi. I don't know. We'll find out in time. Come with me. Away from here. This is now a place to be left in peace." With great sadness but grateful at finding his kin, he helped the boy back up the river bank.

* * * * *

Later that week Samuel rode to Mandurah to return Peel's dogs. Surgeon Nicholas Langley was in attendance, having been summoned from Perth. Samuel heard that in spite of cuppings, bleedings, medicine and dressings, Captain Ellis was not responding. He was in great pain and delirious most of the time. A schooner was on its way to transport him back to Fremantle. Stirling and most of his entourage had left for Perth the morning following the battle, as it was now being called. Samuel reckoned that was stretching the facts. More like a massacre, he thought. He did not mention Mandu.

* * * * *

The Andrews' family were very determined. It became almost a competition to make Mandu happy. To make her talk and smile. Bit by bit she seemed to respond, to come out of her inner self, to demonstrate some of her inherent warmth. As their communication improved, it became possible for Mandu to express her feelings through words and some of the hurt and anguish was released. Slowly her mind, as well as her body, was healing.

What was most amazing was the children's ability to pick up the native dialect. Within a few weeks, they were conversing with Mandu about day-to-day activities and could readily translate to their parents the intent of the dialogue.

The wound healed well, but because the muscle group had been damaged so badly, walking was still painful and so Mandu continued to use her crutch. She was not unhappy being with the Andrews' and decided to remain until she was more mobile, since it appeared they would not send her away until she was ready. In any case she was not sure where she would go.

* * * * *

Over two weeks had elapsed since they had left the camp site at Bindjareb. Odern had taken his great nephew south-west past the inland water and across the island ford to the caves area. He knew they would be left alone, because only a boylya gadak would dare to enter such a secret place. However, his power would protect those he favoured.

As they travelled, Odern was surprised to see the moojarr bursting into its yearly masses of orange blooms. It was flowering exceptionally early this year. Earlier than he could ever remember. The moojarr was a tree that had an acknowledged association with the dead. Its wood was sacred and never used for any purpose by the Binjareb people. Then he realised the significance of the phenomenon. It was flowering early to commemorate the recent dead and he bowed his head in respect.

Yeddi soon regained the weight he had lost while hiding in the river. He now accepted that his family must have gone to the home of the dead beyond the sea to the west since they had not returned for him. Sometimes fathers returned from the spirit world for sons but it had not happened this time. He mourned alone, because the names of the dead could not be mentioned for some time after their death. Feeling great pity for the boy, Odern reassuringly told the story of how the spirits of the dead lived in much the same way as they had lived in the flesh and that animals, fish, bulbs and fruit were plentiful in the country across the sea.

It was the end of the kambarang and the hot season would soon be upon them. The many caves provided shelter from weather coming from any direction and there was a spring nearby, which emerged from the hillside and flowed into the huge inland waterway. Game was plentiful. They were not far from the coast and Odern was looking forward to being warm again. His joints were not nearly so troublesome in the summer.

However, no sooner had they settled, than Odern became aware of a nagging call. It had no substance but there was clearly a message trying to get through. He groaned. Here we go again!

Odern ordered the boy to stay where he was and walked south until he was well away from the cave area. He climbed the highest hill from where he could see the waterway to the east and the ocean to the west.

"Now," he called loudly, raising his arms in the air. "I am ready. What do you wish to tell me?" He waited and waited and began to call again with rather more impatience. "I am here. What do you want of me?"

Slowly Odern felt a presence. It was palpable. He covered his eyes with his hands and saw a vision of the river that provided the fish for the geran mandjar, near to its entry into the large waterway. He hissed to himself. That was forbidden land, where some of his people had died of an unknown sickness six winters before. Then the vision showed his sister-in-law Mandu standing with the aid of a crutch. She had been injured. In the fight with the white men? But she was alive. He breathed a sigh of relief. Then he saw a white woman beckoning Mandu, who turned and with a nod hobbled towards a hut. The vision faded.

On the death of a brother, a man must assume responsibility for his sister-in-law. Normally he would be expected to take her as a wife but Mandu had been through the Monyo ceremony and, having the status of a Moyran or Grandmother conferred by Calyute, would be unlikely to marry again. However, Odern was still beholden to care for her if necessary.

"You could have let me know earlier," Odern grumbled. "Now I have to travel all that way back."

Leaving Yeddi hidden in the cave with a supply of food and without informing him of the vision, the boylya gadak crossed the ford and again made his way north.

* * * * *

Mandu sat under her favourite tree near the river watching the pelicans as they glided in to land on the water. So graceful for such large birds. She was drowsy in the warm sun and had already dozed off several times. Her leg was healing well and she could now walk short distances without the crutch. Her mind was still dull with the pain of the loss of her husband and presumably her son and his family but the memory was not as acute.

Something made her look up. She blinked the sleep from her eyes and peered across the river. On the other side, a spear throw away, stood a grey-haired elder wearing a kangaroo skin cloak and leaning on a walking stick. It was Odern, her brother-in-law. He made a single motioning gesture with his arm, turned and walked into the bush.

The time had come to leave. Mandu stood, picked up her crutch and woven bag and made her way through the shallows towards the river mouth, following Odern into the trees on the other bank.

When the children ran down to the river to call Mandu to the midday meal, all they found were the prints of her left foot and the holes made by the crutch disappearing into the water.

* * * * *

Soon after the beginning of the new year, Annie accepted the fact that she was again pregnant. She had missed two menses and often felt sick in the morning. Her Christmas dinner was even left unfinished.

It would have been just after Samuel returned from Pinjarra. He had woken Annie shouting out "Stop shooting! Stop shooting!" After she calmed him down, they made love for the first time since her miscarriage and obviously were not careful enough. Still, Annie had always wanted more children and was secretly pleased. She desperately hoped and prayed that this time there would be no complications, otherwise Samuel would never forgive himself.

Annie's prayers were not answered. Within days she started to bleed. It was irregular and in small amounts but it was clearly a danger signal. She waited a week before she told Samuel, who became alternately worried, angry and guilt-ridden. He had set the rules and he had not kept them. If anything happened, he would be to blame. Annie tried to talk sense to him but he would not listen.

In her heart, Annie knew the baby was dead. She was saddened, because she realised this was her last chance. God had decided there were to be no more children and she must accept it. She waited stoically until the pain began. Stabbing pain coming in spasms. It was excruciating. Worse than anything she could remember. The foetus was eventually aborted but not all the placenta. The bleeding continued.

Work on the farm ceased. Samuel took over the household chores as Annie needed frequent rests and became easily distressed, which was an unusual state for her.

After a few days, Annie was so weak from loss of blood that she was forced to stay in bed. The blood and fluids passed began to smell putrid and she knew she had contracted an infection. She became feverish, her speech incoherent and she could eat nothing, taking only water. Samuel bathed her and washed the bedding and nightdresses as necessary. He prayed constantly but saw his wife slipping away.

The children became very upset that their mother would not talk to them and this saddened Samuel further. He cooked damper and a vegetable soup and told them to make up their beds on the side verandah and remain outside. Another day passed and Annie's temperature rose still higher. Samuel was now bathing his wife continuously. He was both exhausted and distraught. Finally, Annie's breathing became quick and difficult and she died just before dawn.

* * * * *

In early January, a small low pressure system had developed in the intertropic convergence zone over the sea off the north-west coast of Australia. Within a few days, the pressure at the centre decreased dramatically and an anticyclone, four hundred miles in diameter, formed at forty thousand feet. Steered firstly by north-easterly and then by north-westerly winds, it inexorably began its gradual curving path southwards, following the western coastline.

Although the course of the cyclone was relatively slow, the system generated winds of a hundred and fifty miles an hour and created havoc on flora and fauna even while the eye was hundreds of miles offshore. By the time it crossed the coast at Cape Leeuwin five days later, the dry topsoil of the coastal plain was being sucked upwards for miles, visibility on the ground was reduced to less than a hundred yards and debris was flying through the air.

As the sun rose over the Andrews' Place, a devastated Samuel knelt beside the bed praying, his elbows resting on the bedspread and streams of tears running down his cheeks. Hours passed. He could not take his eyes from Annie's face. It was as though she was in a peaceful sleep. She was the only woman he had ever loved and because he had loved her so much, she was now dead. He held himself responsible and prayed for forgiveness.

Samuel returned to reality. The frightened cries of his two children, huddling on the verandah, penetrated his thoughts and memories. The house was beginning to sway wildly and pieces of the roof were lifting in the gale force wind. He rushed outside and took Sara Jane and William by the hands. The safest place? Where should they shelter? The wind was clutching at the children as he tried to think.

One of the children's favourite play spots was in two huge tree trunks at the river's edge. Surely they would be safe there. Samuel ran towards the river dragging the children behind him and tucked them in the water between the logs.

"Don't leave your hidey hole," he said. "You must not climb out from this spot. You must not leave. William, hold Happy. Do you understand?" The children continued to cry but both nodded.

Samuel raced back to the house to retrieve the body of his wife. As he bent over to lift her from the bed, the central roof beam cracked and fell directly onto his lower back pinning him to the bedside. His lumbar vertebrae were crushed. There was no feeling and no pain but no matter how hard he tried, he found himself unable to move his legs.

He attempted to call the children but the strengthening winds caught his voice and carried it away. Smoke now filled the cottage and the heat grew in its intensity.

The conflagration that destroyed the Andrews' Place had its beginning in a small brush fire lit by a native family to flush out game. Fanned by the hot cyclonic winds, it gathered energy as it moved through a thick patch of dry scrub and, roaring forward with increased force, quickly devoured a huge area of bush as it swung down from the north. It raced to the western bank of the Serpentine following the river's edge for miles until it burned itself out when it reached the inlet just past the farm.

Enveloped in flames, Samuel died thanking God for Annie in his life and praying for the safety of his children.

CHAPTER 17
Two Cultures

Yeddi was overjoyed when Great Uncle Odern returned with his Grandmother. She limped badly but the boy asked no questions about the injury or about his family. He knew the law. Mandu gathered him towards her and hugged him, held him away to examine him and, satisfied that he was unharmed, hugged him again.

"You are a fine looking boy Yeddi and I am proud that you are my grandson. Ten summers now?" she questioned.

Yeddi nodded. "And I am proud to be your grandson. And I am so glad you are safe and here with us," he rushed on, blinking back tears.

"Now, now. We are together again. Everything will be all right. Great Uncle Odern will look after us." She sat down and held Yeddi tightly, as if to protect him and rocked him backwards and forwards, making crooning noises.

Odern gruffly interjected, finding the reunion and all that it embodied very upsetting. "We will wait here over the hot season and in geran, with the first rains, we will join the others at Barragup for the mandjar." Those that remain of the Bindjareb tribe, he thought.

* * * * *

Well, that was the plan but like many a plan, it did not eventuate.

After the passing of one full moon, Odern began to have visions again. "Give me some rest," he grumbled. "Sometimes I tire of your messages. And this vision should be directed elsewhere, I'm sure." But the visions persisted and leapt into movement each dusk as the evening fire was lit.

Finally Odern addressed Mandu. "This is your fault, sister. It's that woman who helped you. She is very ill and could soon leave this earth. Wherever whites go after they leave the present," he added testily.

"Annie is her name. What about her husband? And the children, Sarjan and Willum. What about them?"

Although Odern knew that the white man had rescued Mandu and that the family had cared for her, he was becoming impatient with all the questions.

"I don't know, woman. I will watch the flames tonight." Being asked questions he could not answer exasperated him.

Mandu held her tongue. Her brother-in-law was becoming more and more irascible as the years passed. It was all this living alone, she was sure, and he hadn't been looking after himself. At least his aches and pains were lessening with her treatments. She had collected the leaves of the bush bearing the small mauve bell-like flowers and burnt them. Odern was willing to try anything and would crouch by the morning fire to inhale the smoke.

That night, Mandu fed her grandson and Odern some of the red roots she had roasted that morning and cakes made from pounded yanjidi roots mixed with water. She kindled the leaves and grass and tended the fire until it was blazing in front of the cave entrance. Then she and Yeddi waited expectantly for Odern to receive a message.

He sat with his back to the setting sun and stared into the flames. Mandu watched him as he slowly passed into a trance-like state. Then he began mumbling, the words difficult to understand. Yeddi sat bolt upright, his eyes wide, as he also stared into the fire.

"The woman is sick, very sick. The white man looks after her but life is slowly leaving her body. There is nothing he can do." Odern paused for several minutes.

"A storm is coming and a fire fanned by the wind follows. The father hides the children in logs near the river." There was another pause.

"Both the father and mother are gone in the fire. The winds and flames have passed on. The children are safe."

No one moved. It took some minutes before Odern returned to the present. Grey-faced, he looked worn out with emotion and fatigue. It was becoming more difficult as he grew older. He had been aware for some time that he was slowly losing the power and that made him irritable. In fact, everything seemed to make him irritable lately.

Yeddi spoke in a whisper. "Great Uncle, I could see people in the fire. As you spoke, I could see. It wasn't clear but I could see things." He stopped, unsure whether he should have admitted to what he had seen. It was all very frightening.

Odern spoke gently to the boy. "Do not worry, my nephew. That the spirits wish to enrich your powers is a favourable sign. We will spend some time and find out the extent of your strength. It is not unusual that the power resides in family members."

A cough interrupted the dialogue. Mandu stood up. "What are we going to do?" she said. "I must go to the children. They are so young. Younger than Yeddi. They need help, the way I was given help. We can't just leave them to fend for themselves."

Her brother's eyes rolled and he sighed audibly, looking as though he was about to lose his temper. Then he stopped and looked at Yeddi thoughtfully. "All right," he said. "We will travel back. All of us. Yeddi will observe the white children and tell me whether they were in his vision. We will leave at first light in the morning."

However, the next morning, the winds grew in strength and soon the cyclone in all its fury traversed the coastal area. It was the most violent storm that either Odern or Mandu could remember. The three Aborigines huddled in the cave in the darkness. It was futile trying to keep a fire burning and the sparks were a danger flying everywhere, so Odern threw sand over the coals. When the wind abated and they crept outside to see the damage, a huge pall of smoke was hanging in the sky to the north. Trees were ripped out of the ground and debris was everywhere. Odern said they were favoured by the spirits and were fortunate to have the shelter of the cave.

And so it was the following day that they crossed the southern estuary at the island ford and walked north-east, skirting the boggy areas close to the waterways. Being the dry season, they made good progress along the traditional pad, wading the deltas of the Murray and Serpentine Rivers in the late afternoon.

One glance in the direction of the farmhouse showed only the limestone chimney remaining. The trees and vegetables were gone and the corral and shed had burned to the ground. The animals had disappeared, either burnt or escaped to safety across the river. Some large logs still smouldered.

They found the two children with Happy, the only other remaining survivor, sitting at the water's edge on top of the logs that had saved their lives. Mandu hurried to them. They burst into tears but just sat where they were. Mandu looked and knew why. Their feet were badly burnt, the skin blistered and peeling off in large flakes. William held out his arms and sobbed "Mandu. Mandu. Mummy and Daddy have gone in the fire. We tried to find them. The ground was too hot."

"Hush, my babies," said Mandu. "Grandmother is with you. Put your feet back into the water, while I prepare a soothing mixture." She spoke slowly in her dialect, which Odern was surprised to find they seemed to largely understand. He noted their scorched upper clothing and their spasmodic coughing from the inhalation of smoke.

"Yeddi. Collect leaves from the red gum tree. There is one untouched by the flames over on the far bank."

The boy ran to the river mouth and across the sand bar and returned in a few minutes holding some small branches. He handed them to his grandmother who stripped the leaves, placed them in her mouth and began chewing vigorously. From the string bag tied around her waist, she drew a sharp quartz chip, some pieces of possum skin, a bone needle and some kangaroo sinew and sitting on the log quickly fashioned four small slippers with the fur on the inside. Carefully she lined the base of each slipper with a mash of chewed leaves and tied them to the children's ankles.

"Now my babies, you must sit still for a while and not put your feet to the ground."

When William and Sara Jane began to ask questions, Mandu nodded to Odern who put on a stern expression and frowned at the children. He was holding his magic stick. Small down feathers from the pink and grey cockatoo were attached to each end of the stick by tree gum and intricate designs had been burnt into the wood. There was immediate silence. Yeddi knew exactly how they felt. No one spoke when Great Uncle held the magic stick. To do so could invite intervention by the spirits. He shivered.

The children were piggybacked. Odern, to his distaste, found himself having to hold William when the boy needed to relieve himself. The great boylya gadak of the Bindjareb people doing women's work! But Mandu could be such a harridan in order to get her own way. He had seen her in action before. It was just as well there were no other men to watch him behaving in such an unseemly fashion.

Within the hour, the group had crossed the rivers at the sand bar, built a fire for light and to keep away the mosquitoes and night spirits and eaten some roots and quandongs collected on the way north. Happy was not hungry. There had been plenty of burnt carcasses left after the fire.

Mandu sang softly to the children as she prepared another dressing to place in the now soft wet slippers. Odern held out his hands for them, walked out of range of the fire light, urinated in each and returned them to his sister-in-law, who placed them on the children's feet. That should do the trick, Mandu thought. A boylya gadak's urine had curative properties.

It took three days to travel back to their cave. William, nine and Sara Jane, eight were carried all the way on the backs of the two adults. Yeddi carried the weapons belonging to his great uncle and his grandmother's woven bag. With Mandu's recently healed wound and Odern's rheumatism, although now less painful, many rests were needed. The dog scoured the bush, kept itself in food and came back with a range of snakes, lizards and small marsupials, which provided for the group. Whenever he became excited and barked, Odern would smack him lightly on the snout with the magic stick. The dog learned quickly.

The first night was the hardest. What did one say or do with three recently orphaned children? Mandu said and did what came naturally to a gentle and caring person. She spoke comforting words, she gave lots of hugs and cuddles and she crooned songs until they fell asleep. Odern was surprised by his feelings. He found that he didn't even mind helping with the chores and was actually enjoying the company. And of course the respect accorded him as an elder. For this reason he remained aloof.

Following Yeddi's lead, Sara Jane and William stopped talking and asking questions about their parents. Everyone had lost loved ones. Everyone was sad. Yeddi explained to them that to talk about the dead prevented their spirits resting in peace. Sara Jane asked whether that had something to do with going to heaven but Yeddi didn't know.

With Mandu's constant attention to the children's feet and Odern's regular urine contribution, the healing process was fast. New pink skin appeared in just over a week. After another week, their possum skin slippers were discarded and slowly the soles of their feet hardened.

Getting used to wearing so little clothing was more difficult, especially for Sarjan who felt embarrassed when her cotton dress disintegrated from a combination of the scorching from the fire, soaking in the river and harsh treatment from brushing past spiny shrubs. Mandu sewed a skirt of soft skin from a female kangaroo for the child and one for herself and because the February weather was so warm, that was all they needed. In deference to the little girl, Odern and the two boys wore a small apron of kangaroo skin, which hung from a plaited fur belt. They all rubbed animal fat and mud over their bare skin and sat close to the smoke of the fire at dawn and dusk to keep the mosquitoes away. The fair skin and snowy hair of the white children rapidly took on a decidedly dark appearance.

Day by day, the white children picked up more and more of the Aboriginal dialect. Some of the sounds were a little difficult at first but they soon mastered them. It was easier to talk in the new tongue most of the time than to have to translate what they were saying. However, Yeddi picked up English soon enough and then they spoke a curious mixture of languages which didn't worry them but frustrated the elders. So when Mandu or Odern were present, everyone spoke the language of the Bindjareb. The Andrews' children became Sarjan and Willum. The dog became Habbi.

"What does Yeddi mean?" Sarjan looked inquiringly at the boy.

"A song."

"Why are you called a song?"

"Because my mother heard a song soon after I was born."

"And Mandu?"

"Sunbeams."

"That's a lovely name. And Odern?"

"The sea."

"I like that idea. I'll do the same when I have a baby."

Odern avoided initiating conversation regarding what to do with the children. Mandu accepted that this was his prerogative and waited for his decision. She was as happy as could be expected under the circumstances and genuinely loved the extroverted white children, as she loved her reserved grandson. She realised that she had entered a new phase of her life and assuming some responsibility for her newly-acquired family gave her a purpose.

Leftover lizards had been eaten for breakfast. The children were playing hide and seek in the trees.

Odern turned to Mandu. "The children must learn how to provide for themselves. We begin the lessons today. They will follow and watch us. You

164

take the girl and I'll take boys." The elder rose and moved to gather his spears and axe.

"No," Mandu said. "As far as possible, we should stay together."

Odern stopped in his tracks. Had he heard correctly? "What did you say, woman?" he said sternly.

"I said we will all learn together. What happens if you have an accident? I need to know more about hunting. And the boys may need to know more about food gathering. Or what if Nyoongar other than Bindjareb come upon a little girl and a woman as we gather. We would be defenceless. You know what the Whadjug men from the north are like. They're probably sneaking around right now looking for Bindjareb women without a husband or brother-in-law to protect them. Don't give me that fierce look, because it will make no difference. We will talk tonight after the children are asleep. You seem to have made some decisions that I need to know about. I have always been consulted about children in the family before. In any case, I am a Moyran."

Odern looked decidedly sulky, but Mandu ignored him and called the children. They came scampering out of the bush. She could hardly tell white from black!

"Great Uncle has decided that you need to be shown ways to hunt and gather food and we begin today. Yeddi, you know much about this already but will now also learn how women go about collecting food." Yeddi started to say something but on receiving a stern look from his great uncle stopped. "And you'll help the two younger children whenever you can. We'll all travel together. We will follow Odern." At least that should make Odern feel more in command. Within a few minutes, the fire was put out with sand, goods were collected from the cave and the group moved off in a southerly direction trailing behind Odern.

Suddenly Odern halted, motionless in his tracks. Everyone stopped, watching him and waiting. Odern was sniffing the air.

"A white man on a horse passed by this morning." He moved a few yards towards the water and pointed out hoof prints in the soft sand and splashes of horse dung on the ground. "See the shape of the horse's hoof with the special shoe the white man places on the foot? See its dung? The white man is riding north." He walked a little further. "This is where he stopped. The horse has made many prints in the one place." They all followed Odern. "The man has taken his shoes off. He has walked the horse to the water for a drink. How are his prints different from mine?"

The three children looked at him blankly. Yeddi glanced again at the prints and said "His toes all turn towards the middle of his foot, especially his big toe."

"Yes," prompted Odern. "Why is that?"

There was another pause. "Because his boots press in on his toes," replied Sarjan.

"Good girl," said Odern. "Now listen to me very carefully. From now on we must listen, look and smell. We must be alert at all times. We need lessons on how to hear, how to see and how to smell."

The ford was crossed at the island and the followers stopped when Odern stopped.

"Keep very quiet," he whispered. "If the spirits are disturbed, they will make the wood crooked. I must approach very quietly with my shadow behind me."

Everyone remained motionless as Odern carefully approached a dense thicket of trees. He gave an audible sigh of relief. "It's all right, they've gone," he said and began chopping down some tall and very thin saplings with his kodjah.

Odern motioned them forward and explained. "This is the best wood for spears within our tribe's boundaries. Come and hold it. All of you." He looked pointedly at Mandu, who returned the look with a serious and subservient expression. They each picked up a sapling. "Notice how straight and light they are. The wood is also much easier to work. Remember what the trees look like." Odern discarded some saplings as not being suitable. The remaining twelve were stripped of their small branches and carried back to the cave.

Several hours were spent meticulously scraping the bark from the saplings with sharp stones and remnants of bones or shells.

"The spears must be as round as possible and tapering to the rear end to keep the weight towards the point," Odern explained. "The point needs to be heavier if the spear is to travel truly." When he was satisfied, the sticks were placed over coals in the fire and the straightening process began. As the wood became flexible, each stick was bent into shape using the feet and arms to push and pull. Yeddi was the only one strong enough to help. Animal fat was rubbed into the wood and the spear blanks were placed on flat ground to cool. The three shortest and most irregular were nominated as digging sticks and one that had broken, when Odern had tried to straighten a slight bend, was made into four throwing sticks.

"Right," said Odern. "Let's have a seafood dinner. Mandu bring a carrying bag. Yeddi, bring the cleft stick. Willum fetch the club." Odern picked up two of his spears, each with one hardened, barbed wooden prong.

"What do I carry?" asked Sarjan.

"Hmm," said the elder, his brows furrowing and his lips pursing, as if considering the question carefully. "You can carry one of my spears."

Mandu couldn't believe her ears. Yeddi felt a moment's jealousy but it quickly passed. Sarjan was everyone's favourite. Such a lovely nature, if not sometimes a little stubborn and demanding.

The group assembled at the water's edge. They had about two hours till sunset. It was a glorious, warm afternoon.

Odern gave the instructions, repeated them and took up his position standing on a log at the water's edge holding a spear in each hand. He had dropped the inedible remains of the lizards they had eaten for lunch into the water in front of him. Already small fish darted around the bottom. Odern lifted one spear as a signal for quiet and then placed the points of both spears below the surface and stood perfectly motionless. Odern saw dark shapes moving towards him. Two large mullet of at least half an arm's length. He waited until they were below his spears and then thrust hard, so that the barbed prongs went through their heads to the sand. Everyone crowded around as he carefully lifted the points of the prongs to the surface in a circular motion, turned and shook the fish till they fell onto dry land. The children cheered.

"Kalkada," Odern said, pointing at the flapping fish.

"Kalkada," repeated Sarjan and Willum.

"Good. Now watch carefully." Odern sawed off the heads of the fish with his tabba and threw them into the water close to the log. Almost immediately several large blue crabs sidled up to the bloody bait. Sarjan jumped up and down on the spot and the crabs scuttled away.

"Quiet!" Odern whispered. "Stand still. All of you."

After a few minutes the crabs came back. Some were swimming, some walking carefully to sense any possible danger. Odern stabbed with his cleft stick and pinned a crab down by the legs.

"Show them, Yeddi," he called. Yeddi leapt into the water and approaching from behind, gripped the large male firmly between the thumb and other fingers in a scooping action. He climbed out onto the log and dropped it into the woven bag held out by Mandu.

"Father used to do that," Willum said excitedly, then paused. Tears came to his eyes and he brushed them away. "Could I try to catch a crab?" he asked.

"Karri," said Odern. "It is called a karri."

"Karri," echoed the children.

"Crab," said Yeddi. And so the language lessons were expanded with each new experience.

Yeddi took his turn with the forked stick and Willum retrieved the next crab.

With dusk and their return to the cave, Mandu and Sarjan carried two large mullet and six crabs, five blue and one brown in the string bag. Odern showed the children the round under-flap of the brown female compared with the triangular-shaped flaps of the blue males.

The fish and crabs were cooked in the coals of the fire. Mullet were oily fish, Mandu explained and therefore did not dry out in the heat. After a short time, the scaly skin of the fish was lifted off and the backbones removed. The shells of the crabs were peeled off and the legs cracked between two rocks to extract the fleshy portions. The resulting meal was delicious.

That night, after the exhausted children had fallen asleep, Mandu turned to Odern. "My brother, what have you decided to do about the white children?"

A long silence followed, as if Odern was thinking through a whole range of issues. His deliberations were always protracted. Eventually he began. At first, he did not look at his sister-in-law as if pondering as he spoke.

"It is a difficult decision to make. The children should be taken to the whites in the settlement at the mouth of the estuary. But I don't trust that Peel fellow. He has betrayed our people too often. The children have no kin in the colony. Yeddi has asked. Who would look after them? However, I know that whatever happens, sooner or later they must be returned to their own people." He looked up. "At the moment I am being selfish." Mandu managed to keep a perfectly straight face. "I never wanted to marry. Now the spirits have given me a family. Since I found you and the children, I have been happier than I can remember for many, many seasons. I want to keep this happiness for a while. I am laughing again. Even my rheumatism is better."

Mandu's eyes misted. She did not want the children to go either. "Then let us continue as we are for a while. The children need time to heal their grief. At the moment they seem to be getting along well." She leaned forward and put her arm around Odern's shoulder. "Perhaps I am selfish as well."

"However, something else is worrying me," Odern said. His voice assumed a serious tone and Mandu promptly resumed her sitting position. "Yeddi is entering that period of his life when he would normally be adopted by his mothers brother's people."

Mandu knew of the process if not the detail. Her son had been taken away by her older brother soon after he was ten summers old. He had spent time with many families of her kin. Remembering Katta, tears sprang to her eyes. She blinked them away.

Odern continued. "During a period of time of up to three rotations of the seasons, the men will teach and care for the boy. He will learn all the skills of hunting and fighting and learn about men's business and become familiar with the laws and customs of our people. In the evenings, stories and legends would be told and explained to him by the older men. Animals would sing for him in dreams and he would learn their songs and sing his special versions around the camp fire."

"Odern, there is no one left to take Yeddi and teach him the skills and customs of his people. They have all gone to Kurannup. You are the elder of the family. You have special powers. You must take that responsibility. There is no one else to do it."

The elder sighed and leaned back on his rock. "It is a big responsibility, usually shared by many. And I am of your husband's kin, who are White Cockatoo, not of your kin, who are Crow. I have been worrying about that. And my bones are getting old."

"Let me worry about your bones. You just said they're feeling better. Odern, you are the very best person to prepare Yeddi for his initiation." Mandu paused. "I beseech you."

"Well, as you say, there is no one else. Yet, if we are to stay together, the white children will incidentally learn many of the skills and customs. Except for men's business. Sometimes I will need time with Yeddi by myself. And I will have to explain to him that it is acceptable to share some of the knowledge with a girl, since she is not of our people. I will talk with him tomorrow."

The next day was one of those wonderful end of summer days, with a light offshore breeze and cloudless sky.

"Odern, can we go to the beach? I can see the ocean but I can't remember ever swimming in it," Willum asked. "Only the river."

Odern reluctantly agreed. Like many Aborigines, he was not a water person at all. The family walked over the sand hills. There was a white beach to the right and reef and rocks to the left. While the Aborigines went to the left to hunt for shellfish, Willum and Sarjan plunged into the calm blue water and began to swim. Since Francis' lessons, their skills had improved enormously and they now skimmed through the water with strong strokes, sometimes a type of crawl and sometimes a type of sidestroke. When Mandu realised what was happening, she panicked and ran back, shouting to the children to come out of the water but they just waved and dived and splashed.

When they did run from the water, they each grabbed Yeddi by an arm and dragged him in. He was terrified but trusting them, went in up to his chest. After that they all walked to the reef which was exposed on the low tide. Odern and Mandu prised flat shells from the rocks with sharp stones and Willum dived over the side and came gasping to the surface with a lobster held firmly in two hands. He recognised it as a sea animal that his father had sometimes brought home from the village near the sea. The excited response from Mandu was so positive that he repeated the feat several times. She had eaten these creatures on occasions and found them delicious.

Yeddi insisted he be given a swimming lesson but with much spluttering kept sinking. Sarjan showed him how to float first and then kick his legs. When the wind turned and the waves came up, they happily wandered back over the dunes. It had been a wonderful morning and fruitful and Willum was pleased that he and Sarjan had shown that they had something worth teaching Yeddi. However, it was made abundantly clear that Mandu and Odern would never be tempted to enter the ocean.

As they climbed the hill to their cave, Yeddi pointed to a column of smoke rising some several hundred feet into the air. Odern hurried his brood into the cave and crept back outside to assess the situation. There were actually several fires burning beyond the other side of the estuary. He strode inside holding the magic stick. Everyone froze waiting for Odern to speak.

"The survivors of the Bindjareb people are returning to their camp site and they are signalling one another. It would be dangerous for us to be seen together, for as yet they might be vengeful on whites. Everyone must be on the look out. No one should stray too far from the caves area, as we are safe here. This whole area is forbidden to the Bindjareb, since a death here a long, long time ago."

Sarjan stood. "Speak," ordered Odern.

"Are you going to send us away?"

"No. Not until you are ready to go or circumstances force us to do so. There will come a time when it will be right that you return to your own people but until that time you can stay with us."

"Thank you." Sarjan sat down, looking pleased.

"However, you must all realise that we must keep our distance from both our peoples if we want to avoid trouble. We must stay by ourselves and not allow others to get close. Do you understand?"

Mandu and the children nodded.

"Just for tonight, we will cook after dark," Odern said. "We don't want our people thinking we are a stray family signalling our presence. And you two whities had better replace the dirt you usually wear as it all washed off today. Otherwise the insects will eat you alive tonight." He put away the magic stick and sat down. Sarjan ran to sit in his lap. Odern held her and said "How about a Dreamtime story while we wait for dark?" The nods were unanimous.

Odern cleared his throat as he chose his words. "You have all seen the moojarr tree. The one with the masses of orange flowers that blooms in the hot season." There was a chorus of yeses.

"We call it the Christmas tree," Willum added.

"Well," continued Odern, "the moojarr is known to our people as the Kaanya tree, which means the tree of the souls of the newly dead." There was now complete silence. They all leaned forward. "Since the Dreaming the soul of every one of our people has rested in the branches of a Kaanya tree after leaving its mortal body on the way to our spiritual home named Kurannup, which lies beyond the sea. Sometimes mothers or fathers will call a child to join them while they rest in a Kaanya tree and then the child will leave the earth and join the parent. Sometimes parents do not call at all and then a child will know that the parent wishes the son or daughter to remain in the present life. This is often a sad time for the child but it must always be remembered that the

170

parent knows best. The Kaanya tree is a special tree and because of this none of our people ever shelter or rest beneath the shade of the tree of souls, no flower or bud or leaf of the tree is ever touched by anyone and no animal seeking shelter beneath the tree is ever disturbed. However, our people do not fear the tree. They respect and revere it. It is held sacred for its special memories."

Odern paused before continuing. "Did you know that there is a winding road from our land to the sea's edge? It then travels along the bottom of the sea to the shores of Kurannup where the spirits of our people live and dwell in the same way as they lived on earth, except that all the Kurannup people are white. Every soul has its black skin removed as it sleeps and when it wakens it is white like all its other Kurannup relations."

The story made everyone feel sad and yet made everyone feel better. Sarjan and Willum now knew that their parents and Yeddi's parents were together across the sea and that Kurannup was another name for heaven. However, the little girl wondered why she had always been led to believe that heaven was in the sky. Then she decided that perhaps it really didn't matter where it was.

The following morning, Odern called Yeddi to walk with him. The elder explained the situation to the boy, who was pleased that he was about to enter his pre-initiation period. He nodded as his great uncle concluded with "Is that all clear?"

"I am honoured, Great Uncle."

CHAPTER 18
An Aboriginal Education

The moons pass and there is so much to learn.

They began with listening, looking and smelling lessons. At any time of the day, Odern would say "What can I hear?" or "What can I see?" or "What can I smell?" Sometimes he would make everyone sit down and just listen, or just look, or just smell. At other times they would stand, crouch, or lie on the ground and after a few minutes one would be asked to describe what he or she had heard, or seen, or smelled. The white children took weeks before they managed to get many right answers but slowly it seemed that their ears, eyes and noses were opened and it was a whole new world. A wonderful new world. A world that lived with them.

Many early lessons were about plants and in these Mandu took the lead. "You must never pick the flower of a plant that bears edible food, as it is the mother of the seed or fruit. Such plants must not be interfered with or damaged out of season, because they need to be protected to bear food in later months."

And so the children began to identify plants and their potential as a food supply. The flower stem from the balga and a type of wattle yielded an edible gum. Flour was produced after pounding wattle seeds and this made a bread when mixed with gum and water and cooked on stones in the fire. The yellow banksia cone contained a sweet honey-like substance, which could be sucked from the flower and the children relished it. Mandu also showed them how to dig a small hole, line it with bark and fill it with water. The cones were steeped in the water to extract the honey and when the resulting infusion was drunk it was delicious. A palm-like tree produced a poisonous fruit but the children were taught how to soak the fruit in water for several days, bury them in sand until they had dried out and then roast them in the fire. Then they were edible.

There were fire-making classes also conducted by Mandu and they continued every morning until the three children could each skilfully and quickly start a fire. The long sticks protruding from the balga trees were broken off. One piece was placed vertically in a hole carved from another piece, held in position on the ground by the feet. When quickly twirled between the fleshy part of the palms, the heat generated would eventually ignite dried material placed around the hole. The children considered it a wearisome business but persevered. Sarjan, being more dexterous and patient than the boys, was the first to succeed.

One morning, the children were ordered to each pick up a spear blank and carry it to the beach. A spinifex bush at the edge of the sand hills was selected as the target and throwing lessons began. Odern demonstrated how to hold the spear poised and balanced above the shoulder, with the elbow up and the chest forward. He then took a step onto the left foot to throw hard, so that the spear travelled in a straight line to hit the target. They also had to allow for the wind. It was all very bewildering and tiring but eventually Yeddi hit the bush twice in a row and was declared the day's champion. While the others collected shellfish for the evening meal, Willum continued to practise until he also managed to hit the bush in consecutive throws. From then on, whenever the children had time, they practised throwing their spear blanks at targets.

Then it was spear-making. Four pieces of hardened spearwood were oiled again with animal fat and trimmed to a fine point. Odern had some chips of quartz, some animal teeth, pieces of bones and sharp shell fragments. Gum from the balga tree was collected, ground with charcoal, heated slowly on a fire stick and roughly coated along two sides of the spear head for about a finger length. The tiny scraps of stone, shell, bone or teeth were placed in the warm gum in two lines and the fire stick used to adjust their positioning. When the gum had cooled, the children could not budge the flakes and Sarjan squealed when she nicked her thumb on a sharp scrap of stone. After Yeddi was reassured that Sarjan was not badly injured, he turned to Odern.

"What about the miro, Great Uncle?"

Odern smiled. "All in good time, Yeddi. You must learn more about the flight of the spear and get your eye in before you learn to use the thrower."

That night, Willum and Sarjan learned about the Waugal.

"The Waugal is the great magic snake," explained Odern. "It is a spirit that lives everywhere. In the air, in the sea, in the sky, in rivers and lakes, in hills and in caves." Sarjan surreptitiously looked behind her. "But mostly it lives in deep water holes. It made all the big rivers as it travelled over the land. Where it camped on its travels are sacred sites. When a person passes one of the forbidden places, he must strew rushes on the ground, or he will become ill and will die very soon. Only elders and boylya gadak are safe. The Waugal keeps law and order throughout our people. It watches over the Nyoongar and keeps them healthy as long as they obey the laws. If they break any of the laws, it will afflict them with sickness or punish them in some way. It is unwise to cook food too close to some water holes or the Waugal might come out and eat the food and the people."

Yeddi looked to his great uncle. "Why must rushes be strewn on the ground near sacred places?"

"One does not question the law, Nephew. It has always been so and you would be very unwise to tempt the Waugal. Some say it is to make a comfortable resting place for the serpent."

Odern took charge for the next few days and after breakfast it was tracking. The group of four followed him through the bush, making frequent stops. The elder would patiently explain the difference between the age and location of bird and animal droppings, point out their tracks, their likely hiding places, identify their characteristic noises and calls and show where larger animals had broken small branches or left tufts of fur on the bark of trees as they passed. The white children were amazed. Even Mandu and Yeddi were impressed. Great Uncle knew so much! That afternoon, Odern picked up his spears and thrower and they all followed him down to the bushland near the estuary.

When they had settled on some rocks Odern spoke. "The first thing to remember is that the kangaroo hears, sees and smells better than we do. That means we must be downwind and out of sight for as long as possible. It also means that Habbi must remain still and quiet." On hearing his name the dog's tail began wagging. "Good dog! At least he doesn't bark all the time now. So Willum and Sarjan, you are in charge of Habbi. Mandu will show you how to weave a band for the dog's neck and then you will be able to hold him if necessary. Today, I will take you all with me. Firstly, you must learn the ways to approach a kangaroo."

The four followed Odern as he headed into the breeze, his spear notched into the miro. Without weapons, they copied his every move exactly. The search for sandy patches between bushes. The exaggerated placing of the feet to the ground, so that twigs were not snapped, nor leaves rustled. The creeping around shrubs and trees after using them for cover. The holding of small leafy branches as camouflage. The constant pausing and sniffing of the wind.

All at once Odern stopped and with his left hand made a pawing movement and then scratched his ribs. Willum mimicked the movement and not being able to contain himself, laughed out loud. A large kangaroo leapt from the scrub ahead and bounded away. "Oh, no!" said the boy covering his face with his hands. "I'm sorry Odern. I'm so sorry. I didn't know it was there."

Odern shrugged his shoulders. "Back to the rocks and let's learn a few more signs."

After the children were sitting contritely on the limestone rocks, they watched Odern and listened carefully as he explained. Then they copied the signals to be given with their non-throwing arm. Female kangaroo - lean back, then scratch breast. Male kangaroo - pawing motion with hand and arm, then scratch ribs. Emu - hand and arm bent above head. Duck - hand and arm bent from forehead. Keep down - patting movement to the side. Listen - place the fingers behind an ear lobe, then turn the head. Look - hand shading eyes. Stop - hand up to shoulder, palm forward. This was serious business and also a great deal of fun, as each took turn in leading and giving the signals.

It was all repeated the next morning and the next and the next. On the fourth morning the children and Mandu followed every signal perfectly. After several hours on the hunt, Odern speared a female kangaroo through the hip. The trail of blood was followed for several hundred yards before they caught up with the wounded animal and Odern clubbed it to death. With its two front and two back feet tied together and a branch placed beneath the pairs of feet, the two boys proudly carried the carcass back to the cave.

Using Odern's tabba, Mandu carefully skinned the kangaroo. When winter came they would need cloaks for warmth and many skins would be needed to clothe the family. The skin was pegged fur down in the sun to dry and the children assisted in scraping off the adhering flesh and grease with pieces of bone and fragments of shells. Mandu explained that when it was nearly dried out, they could help her rub it with grease and work it again with scrapers, until it was soft enough for sewing.

The kangaroo carcass was chopped into quarters and the tail removed for the extraction of sinews. Long strips of flesh were sliced from the haunches for drying out and the remainder was cut into smaller pieces for cooking. The entrails were thrown to Habbi. It was now midafternoon and everyone being hungry, a fire was lit and heaped with branches. As the flames burned down, the pieces were placed on the coals and were soon cooked, the juices oozing from the meat. It was a mouth-watering meal. The children helped store the leftover meat in the cool of the cave for breakfast and hung the strips of meat to dry by plaited string from an exposed tree root hanging from the roof. They watched carefully while Mandu showed them how to extract the sinews from the tail of the kangaroo. Firstly, she bit off the flesh around the tip of the tail. Then the end joints of bone were twisted and turned until they separated from the other joints, whereupon with a strong pull, over a dozen sinews the length of the tail were pulled out. These were wound around a stick diagonally and left to dry.

One morning, Odern sat the children down outside the cave and brought out his kylie to show them. It was a curved throwing weapon with one side flat and the other slightly rounded. One handle was longer than the other. "The kylie is a very special weapon because it can be made to do many different things depending on how it is thrown. It must be looked after carefully, because each kylie takes a long time to make. One must learn what makes it lift into the air and what makes it come back to the thrower. It requires much practice to master the throwing of a kylie." The children each inspected the weapon.

"Can you throw one of these, Yeddi?" Sarjan said as she turned the implement over, examining it carefully.

Yeddi laughed. "Yes and no, Sarjan. I can throw one but I never manage to hit anything much and it sometimes won't come back."

"I'm going to learn how to throw the kylie to hit things and to make it come back," Sarjan said seriously.

The boys were much more interested in spear throwing and wanted to perfect the art so they could use the miro. Sara Jane begged Odern to help her make her own kylie and after a week of whittling and scraping a specially shaped piece of wood selected with Odern's help, she disappeared down to the beach to try it out. She returned exhausted. "All I do is chase it," she complained to Yeddi.

"Bring your scraper and come with me, Sarjan. I'll help you."

When they reached the beach, Yeddi took the kylie and after scrutinising it, scraped several shavings from the flat side and made the short handle more pointed. "Now, Sarjan, you must throw it holding the shortest end with the round side down if you are aiming at birds. Pretend there is a bird flying just above that tree on the far sandhill."

Sarjan threw the kylie with an overarm throw and it flew through the air clipping the top branch of the tree before falling to the ground.

"That was a good throw. You might have hit the bird but remember the kylie won't return if it hits something."

"Show me how to make it come back, Yeddi."

He retrieved the kylie and said, "Watch carefully, Sarjan." Holding it now by the longest end and with the flat side down Yeddi threw the weapon. This time it spun up into the air, arced, swung, hit the hard wet beach sand with one end about ten yards from them, rebounded into the air with a rapid rotary motion and spun in a circle to land at their feet.

"Your try Sarjan."

Sarjan thought carefully before throwing the kylie to match Yeddi's action. It performed exactly as his throw had and returned to land almost on her foot.

"Hooray," she said, picking it up and throwing it again and again.

"Some throwers can catch the kylie on its final lift, Sarjan."

"Then I will practise until I can, Yeddi."

Odern refused to be involved in women's work, as he called it, but encouraged the children to accompany Mandu when she went food collecting. There were so many different types of bulbs, roots and tubers, ranging in colour from white, to fawn, to yellow, to pink, to red. Some were only a few inches below the surface, others were deep and needed strong digging sticks. One root looked like a new potato, one like a bulb and some of the tubers sprouted protuberances like small potatoes. Mandu taught the children to look for the right types of soils to gauge whether the roots might be present, as digging several feet for nothing wasn't much fun and certainly didn't fill empty stomachs. Most of the roots were eaten raw but some tasted better roasted. For reserve stocks, especially for the wet season, roots and tubers were pounded between stones, mixed with a little water and made into cakes. Gum from the wattles was also pounded, moistened and made into flat cakes. The cakes were broken into pieces and eaten as snacks, while the group walked.

When the swamps began drying up, frogs were prised from the mud in the shallows with digging sticks and freshwater tortoises located on the bottom using the feet to feel for their shells. They were delicious when wrapped in bark and cooked in the embers of the fire. Ducks were caught occasionally by swimming under water, grabbing them by the legs and quickly wringing their necks. Willum was the most successful duck hunter, because he could hold his breath and swim underwater the longest but it was both difficult and exhausting and they mostly arrived back at the cave empty-handed.

Snakes and lizards were plentiful. The children were shown the two snakes they were to avoid and leave for Mandu to club. One was about as long as Yeddi was tall, with a broad head and narrow neck. Its upper surface was black and its lower surface bright yellow. The other was longer, a dull greenish-brown on the top and greyish-white underneath. When the first snake was found sunning itself on a log in early summer, Mandu killed it instantly by hitting it sharply with a stick. Once again the white children were pleasantly surprised when coaxed to sample the cooked meat.

Mandu seemed to be able to find grubs everywhere and when the white children got over their initial aversion to the idea, they voted the bardies from the wattle trees to be the best, although the balga tree and various gum trees also provided a tasty snack. The children didn't think this fair as the wattle produced only a couple of grubs a tree, although each was as long as an adult's finger, while the balga could produce hundreds. All one had to do was to find a balga with a withered top, give it a good kick or push and when the tree fell over, the bardies were clustered in the roots and trunk. The boys nipped off the fleshy part with their teeth and ate them raw and squirming but it was a long time before Sarjan could eat them uncooked.

With the colder weather approaching, it was time to fashion kangaroo cloaks. Odern already had his well worn buka but the others all needed clothing for winter. Mandu brought a number of skins from the cave. All had been regularly rubbed with grease and scraped and were now quite flexible. Two skins were placed side by side and trimmed with a tabba. The edges were then sewn together with sinews threaded through holes made by a sharp pointed stick. The holes were placed every half finger length or so. When she had finished stitching, Mandu said, "Yeddi, stand up and let me try on your buka." With the fur on the inside, she shaped a collar and hung the cloak from the boy's shoulders. Yeddi held it in place. "Now, I expect you want your spear arm bare?" The boy nodded emphatically and the buka was rearranged. Mandu fastened it at the right shoulder with a bone. "Next!"

"Can I help?" said Sarjan.

"Of course," replied Mandu with a smile. "After I've sewn a buka for you."

At first light, Odern and Yeddi disappeared. The others assumed that this was part of the teaching of men's business as explained to them by Odern and did not follow. On their return at noon, Yeddi excitedly described some new tracks he had found and led the younger children and Habbi off to investigate. Odern winked at Mandu as she plaited fur headbands for the children and a reed collar for the dog.

The children returned tired and hungry late in the afternoon. Willum and Sarjan had followed numerous tracks pointed out by Yeddi, to no avail. They all ended at a rock face, or water, or the foot of a tree but no animals were found. In the end Yeddi could contain himself no longer and with a grin admitted having set the trail while Odern was resting in the sun. He took them back over the tracks he had formed with fingers, thumb and heel of hand showing them how to identify the false footprints and tail tracings. Didn't they notice the lack of fresh droppings, the absence of any scent, the unevenness of the spoor?

"No," said Willum with a rueful smile. "But I did think it odd that the tracks ended at a tree, water, or rock outcrop. Sarjan, we've been fooled. We still have a lot to learn."

Sarjan looked so crestfallen that Yeddi picked her up and swung her around. "Don't be upset my little one. It was just a joke. I've had much more teaching than you and I'm nowhere near Great Uncle's knowledge. Tomorrow you can give me another swimming lesson. I still can't float."

* * * * *

And so the six seasons recognised by the Nyoongar people passed and summer was with them again. The family remained a happy unit, well fed, cohesive and caring. The children were skilful in tracking, hunting and gathering food and weapon-making, although Sarjan's small hand prevented her using the miro to throw a spear and Willum also found it difficult. They could recite dozens of Dreamtime stories and legends. They knew the steps pertaining to male and female dances respectively. All could prepare food and cook and all could make garments and bands for arms, legs and head.

However, sometimes differences in aptitude emerged and these were fostered and developed by the adults. Yeddi obviously had an ability with regard to the supernatural, inherited through his Grandfather Yabbal, Odern's brother. He seemed to have a sixth sense about things and continued to strengthen his powers of communing with spirits and seeing into the future through the medium of fire, although he only discussed such matters with Odern. Sarjan also seemed to have heightened senses and utilised these in experiments with plant leaves, flowers and barks for healing purposes. The boys were better spear throwers but Sarjan could follow tracks that were almost invisible to everyone else. She could also throw the kylie with great accuracy and was able to bring down a bird in flight. They could all swim well and run with great agility through the bush. At the same time all could freeze motionless and melt into the vegetation, indiscernible to the adults. In fact,

Mandu eventually scolded the children for frightening her by jumping out from hiding places as she walked by.

The children developed a sign language that enabled a form of conversation without talking. Little gestures, facial and eye signals, motions of hands and fingers and an overall body language allowed each to understand the others' messages. It became a game and as the signals were refined, talking was hardly required, their rapport and empathy were so acute. The secret language was particularly useful when hunting animals.

The family changed their abode every few weeks. All that was needed was to shift into another cave and there were plenty in the vicinity. When they had completed the circuit, they would shift back into the first cave. Animals, birds and insects cleaned the surfaces in their absence. Because the region was forbidden to the Bindjareb tribe, there was always plenty of game.

* * * * *

By February 1837, Sarjan and Willum had been part of the Aboriginal family for two years. They had grown inches in height and enormously in physical ability and self-assurance. But in particular, they had gained an understanding of the environment and their place in it. They were one with nature. They could mimic the sounds of birds and animals and swim with schools of fish and dolphins. The dolphins were particularly friendly and seemed to welcome contact with the children. Sarjan developed a special rapport with a young female in the estuary who often appeared when the girl was collecting food. When Sarjan ventured into the water, the dolphin would nudge her until she stroked it gently on the back.

Odern spoke with Yeddi. "It is time my great nephew. Time to be initiated into the tribe. You have learned your lessons well and are ready for the rites of manhood. We will travel to Barragup, when the Bindjareb people assemble for the fishing mandjar. We must trace relatives on your mother's side of the family, no matter how distant, so that your initiation can take place. You must prepare yourself mentally both for the initiation and for the fact that I must therefore return Sarjan and Willum to their own people in the near future."

Yeddi bit his lip. He had always known that the parting must take place one day but he loved the two white children as he would love his own kin.

"Yes Great Uncle. I understand but it will not be easy. And I will worry about them, especially Sarjan."

"Yeddi, I think Sarjan will be able to look after herself," Odern said drily. "I have never known a female of her calibre in my life. She is a remarkable young woman. We will all miss both Willum and Sarjan. They have enriched our lives. Fate has been both harsh and kind to us all over the past three summers."

The next morning, when Yeddi and Willum went hunting, scratch marks and grains of sand were discovered on the bark of a red gum tree. A possum had been foraging on the damp ground during the night. Willum used his kodjah to chop toe holes into the trunk and climbed to its hiding place in a hollow branch. He turned the axe handle in the hole, catching the animal by its fur and threw it down to Yeddi who caught it deftly avoiding angry teeth. "That's the other half of tonight's dinner," he said as he jumped down. "We have enough with the yellow-bellied snake you killed earlier." Yeddi had snapped the possum's neck and was pulling its entrails through a small hole he had cut in its abdomen. He wiped his hand on the animal's fur. "I need to talk to you Willum. Wait here a moment while I get rid of the possum." He ran back to the cave and hung the carcass in a nearby tree.

The boys walked towards the beach and sat on a sand hill overlooking the water. "Willum, Great Uncle spoke with me yesterday. He said I am ready for my initiation. It is burnoru and within two moons it will be time for the meeting of my tribe at Barragup for the fishing mandjar. Message sticks must be sent out. Great Uncle will search for any of my mother's male relatives. If none can be found, others of my mother's generation will be asked to take their place. A date and time must be arranged for the ceremony."

Willum's expression said it all. A look of great sadness, almost of grieving, spread across his face. In a moment it was gone. "Yeddi. How wonderful for you." He held his friend by the arms. "I know how important this is to you, even if I don't understand it." He paused considering. "I suppose this will mean that we must return to our people soon."

Yeddi nodded. "We will always be friends." He stopped to think, his brow furrowed. Then the solution became evident. "You will be my babbingur, Willum. You will not be able to attend my initiation but there is no reason why you still cannot be my babbingur."

Willum looked at Yeddi questioningly.

Yeddi laughed. "It's a word we haven't used before. It means friends for life. Soul mates. A merging of our inner selves. Will you be my babbingur? It is my greatest wish."

Willum nodded.

The boys stood up. Yeddi took Willum's right hand in a double wrist grip. "Babbingur, Willum," he said.

"Babbingur, Yeddi," Willum responded.

The hardest part was telling Sarjan. She burst into tears and ran off into the bush. The girl's mind was in turmoil. She didn't want to leave Yeddi, or Mandu, or Odern. She worshipped the ground Yeddi walked on. Where would they go? Who would look after them? She was frightened and felt deprived of her security, of her happiness, of her family for a second time.

Everyone wanted to follow her. Yeddi interrupted. "It is my duty and I will go." He knew where she would be. Down near the estuary, where the dolphins and pelicans fed. Sometimes the children remained there for hours watching the passing parade of nature from the fork of an overhanging tree.

Yeddi saw Sarjan and quickened his step. He cooeed but she didn't respond. He clambered up the tree and sat next to her. She looked at him with the most disconsolate of expressions and then looked away. Yeddi took her hand.

"Sarjan, I am so sorry to cause you to be unhappy. It is the last thing I would wish. You know that to be true." She sniffed and wiped her eyes. "I must find my people so that I can take my place as a man in the Bindjareb tribe. You must find your people and grow to womanhood understanding their customs. As must Willum grow to manhood with your people. The past two rotations of the seasons, while we have been a family, have been wonderful but now it is time to part. You must be brave. We will all be unhappy for a time, believe me. Come back to the cave. Everyone is worried about you."

Sarjan nodded and the tears flowed again. "I understand everything you say, Yeddi but I am just so sad. I will miss you so much. I will never see you again."

"Of course you will, Sarjan. I will find out where you are and will keep in contact when I can. That is my word. I just hope that our peoples are now at peace. Come with me. The old ones worry." She followed him down the tree and up the hill to the cave.

For the next hour, the children were thoroughly miserable. No one said anything. Eventually, with tears in her eyes, Mandu said "Yeddi, take Willum and Sarjan and find me bardi from the balga to roast on the fire."

Yeddi fetched a kodjah and tabba from the cave and set off down the track. Willum and Sarjan followed him dejectedly.

The three stopped beside a likely balga. Yeddi placed his weapons on the ground and said, "Sarjan, this afternoon Willum and I sealed a special friendship. It is called babbingur. It means that we have a bond between us forever. Do you understand?"

The girl nodded, her eyes to the ground.

"I have decided that you should also be my babbingur." Sarjan's head jerked upwards and her eyes widened. She ran to Yeddi and he lifted her into the air and swung her around. Lowering her to the ground, he took hold of her right arm in the double wrist grip. "My babbingur," he said.

"My babbingur," Sarjan repeated.

"Now Willum and Sarjan, you must allow me to strengthen the ties. Since you cannot be at my initiation, I will mark you and you will mark me." Yeddi fetched the tabba. "Hold out your right arms."

The sharp tabba slid across Sarjan's upper arm and a trail of blood followed as the skin was cut. It ran down the arm and dripped from the elbow. The girl grimaced but made no sound.

"Willum." The boy stepped forward and the act of bonding was repeated. "Each of you must now mark me."

Willum and Sarjan each drew the edge of the sharp stone over Yeddi's upper arm. Two parallel lines of blood appeared. Yeddi smeared his blood with his finger and mixed it with Willum's blood and then smeared his blood again and mixed it with Sarjan's. He then picked up a limestone rock from the ground and crumbling it with his fingers sprinkled the fine dust over Willum's and Sarjan's wound. In turn, they did the same to the welling blood on Yeddi's arm.

"Right, my babbingurs. Now we will collect bardi." There were tentative smiles all round when they returned to the cave with handfuls of the writhing grubs. If Mandu and Odern noticed the cuts they gave no acknowledgment.

That night, Odern told the children that he would take Willum and Sarjan to the white people living where the waters entered the sea. They would travel north after the next full moon. Mandu and Yeddi were to remain in the cave area and on Odern's return, preparations would be made for the journey to Barragup.

"Now listen carefully," said Odern. "I have a special story to tell this evening." Everyone moved closer to the fire at the mouth of the cave in eager anticipation. Odern's stories were always enjoyable and usually carried a message of importance.

Odern began. "Once, a long, long time ago in the Dreaming, there was a tribe of grey kangaroos and a tribe of emus, who lived on land next to one another. The tribe of grey kangaroos lived near a large waterway, where the bush was always green and the food was plentiful and the emus lived to the north, where the land was poor and food scarce. One hot season, the land to the north was so dry and the food in such short supply that the emus travelled to the land of the kangaroos and ate their food. When the kangaroos found out, they fought the emus and told them to return to their own land. The kangaroos were strong and could scratch with their fore paws and bite with their strong teeth, whereas the emus could only peck. Many emus were killed but because they could run fast some escaped. After the emus had gone, an old male kangaroo and old female kangaroo who had been badly pecked in the leg and her grandson, found two eggs in a nest. The grandmother realised that the eggs must be kept warm and protected and placed them in her pouch for safety. When the eggs hatched, the chicks, one female and one male, jumped from the pouch and as they had no parents they were looked after by the kangaroos. It took the kangaroos some time to find out what to give the emu chicks to eat but bardi grubs and insects seemed to satisfy them and they quickly grew. So this strange group of three kangaroos and two emus stayed together in the south and taught one another about their habits and customs and lived happily as a family."

The corner of Mandu's mouth was twitching and she pursed her lips to avoid smiling. The children were engrossed, their eyes fixed on Odern.

"But eventually the older kangaroos realised that the young kangaroo must join other young kangaroos and that the young emus must travel north to the land of the emus. Everyone was sad because no one wanted to part but the wise old male kangaroo said that this was the way of life and just because they had been so happy together didn't mean that they would not be happy in the future with their own tribe. Although very sad, the young kangaroo and the young emus accepted the advice of the old grey kangaroo. The emus were returned to their tribe in the north and then the kangaroos sought out the rest of the kangaroo tribe. And everyone lived happily ever after."

When the children were asleep, Mandu's eyes twinkled as she remarked, "That was a wonderful story Odern. It's amazing really but I've never heard it before."

Odern muttered something to himself, as he curled up in readiness for sleep.

"Good night, old grey kangaroo," Mandu whispered.

CHAPTER 19
An English Education

It was a Sunday afternoon in late March 1837 and very hot. Still dressed in their finery following the church service held in the specially-built back room of Mandurah House, the assembled guests sweated uncomfortably, trying to digest a huge meal of lamb and vegetables followed by apple tarts and cream. Mrs Ayrton was serving cups of tea and Thomas Peel was topping up glasses of port.

"Outside now, children." Julia, Thomas Junior and Dorothy disappeared through the front door to the verandah. Peel missed his eldest son, Fred. He'd been unable to put up with his stepmother's nagging any longer and had taken a position on the *Dart*, a brigantine plying between Fremantle and the eastern seaboard. Fred hadn't been seen for the past two years, nor had he written.

Mrs Peel and Mrs Ayrton took the hint and left the room when all requests for tea had been poured.

Henry Edward Hall lifted his glass. "Thank you Peel for your invitation to this morning's service. It was appreciated, as was the meal. And Reverend Blair, your sermon was thought-provoking. It is time that we buried the hatchet, so to speak, with regard to the natives."

Peel butted in pugnaciously. "You can say that, now you live in Perth, Henry but it remains a serious issue in the outposts. I constantly worry about the safety of my family. It's just as well that we still have a detachment of the 21st Regiment at Mandurah." He turned to a uniformed officer. "I welcomed the appointment of Lieutenant Bunbury to Pinjarra. How many men do you have on the Murray now, Lieutenant?"

"Eight, Mr Peel. Two more than you have here. However, I should say that during the past twelve months there have been no signs of trouble. The Pinjarra incident certainly quietened things down. There was only one English death, wasn't there?"

"Yes," answered Peel. "Captain Ellis. He didn't recover from a spear wound to the head. Died in Perth. Shame really. He was a first class officer and policeman and actually sympathetic to the natives. So was Nesbit. It just shows they can't be trusted. Francis Armstrong took over Ellis' position as Superintendent and Interpreter of Native Tribes. Fine young man. His father used to be in my employ here at Mandurah and Francis actually worked for another servant of mine, who had a farm on the Serpentine. The family all died in a bushfire a couple of years back."

Peel paused and then continued. "I was sorry to hear that your father had passed on, Bunbury. Commendable career. My cousin Robert held him in high esteem."

Bunbury was heartily sick and tired of hearing about Cousin Robert Peel since his brief stint as Prime Minister in '34 and '35, but he had learned over time that one must play the game.

"Thank you for your condolences, Mr Peel. I respected my father a great deal, as of course I respect Sir Robert Peel, especially his reforms and innovations."

Peel looked smug. He thought that Bunbury showed all the signs of good breeding and the best connections. His father was Lieutenant-General Sir Henry Bunbury, a Baronet, who had served as a Member of Parliament and the Under Secretary of War. Because of this, Bunbury received regular invitations to Mandurah House and then stayed the night at the barracks in Soldiers Cove.

Reverend Blair spoke. "Mr Peel, I would like to thank you again for your generous hospitality and the use of your premises for services in honour of the Lord. Governor Stirling's support in allowing me to travel down and back on the supply ship is also acknowledged. Sir James recognises the need to bring the word of God to all parts of the colony."

Peel nodded genially, as he savoured being the centre of attention.

Blair then turned to Hall. "I'm told you are travelling back on the *Sulphur* tomorrow, Mr Hall."

"Yes, Reverend. I have finalised my packing and need to return to Perth as soon as possible. Thomas Watson, the ferry-keeper, is now occupying Dedallah and my old cottage. It was sad to have to leave Mandurah. My family and I enjoyed our years here since 1831 and did not want to leave, especially under the given circumstances." Hall's eyes dropped.

Those present were sympathetic towards Hall. He had lost almost everything when taken to court by the merchants Jones and Carter, as a result of not being able to meet his repayments as a commission agent. The Hall family was now living at the Perth Hotel and Henry was eking out a living brewing beer and practising medicine.

There was a lull in the conversation. Lieutenant Bunbury lit a pipe and Peel poured himself another port.

"Father! Father!" The silence was broken by a rush of footsteps and loud cries. The Peel children bounded into the room.

"Quiet!" thundered Peel. The children stopped in their tracks and stood to attention. Their mother and grandmother hurried into the room on the commotion. "Speak, Thomas," Peel addressed his son.

"Father, there are two native children by the gate. You have always said that we should inform you immediately if natives approach the house."

"Yes, that is so but such rowdy behaviour is indecorous, especially when we have guests. I will investigate." Everyone followed him onto the verandah.

"What have we here? Two lost native children?" Peel exclaimed.

The group on the verandah saw two frightened, half-naked native children standing at the gate. The boy held a black dog by the collar. They were watching an old white-haired man, carrying spears, walking towards the south. He turned once lifting his left hand in farewell before disappearing into the trees.

Willum and Sarjan turned to look at the reception on the verandah and saw three children, two women and four men staring at them. Several dogs were barking.

Peel beckoned them. They stood rooted to the spot. He called "Open the gate and come here." They did not move. They were terrified by this fierce-looking man.

"I will go to them," said Reverend Blair and he walked down the steps and slowly approached the children. The children saw a balding, elderly man in a black suit with a white shirt and collar. He had a pleasant smile on his ruddy face.

"Hello," he said, holding out his hands. "I am Reverend Blair. Who might you be? What are your names?" He enunciated his words carefully.

Blair didn't really expect them to understand and was surprised when the boy said "Willum," and then "Sarjan." He pointed first to himself and then at the girl.

Blair looked more closely and couldn't believe his eyes. These were not the features of the indigenous people. And the children's hair was streaked as if fair but darkened with dirt, clay and fat. There were also white blotches on their skin where part of the dirt had washed off. Excitedly he came to the realisation that the children were white.

Not to frighten them. Take it gently. One step at a time.

Blair waved to the assembled group on the verandah as if to dismiss them and slowly opened the gate, stepping through and closing it behind him. He sat down on a dead tree trunk lying near the fence and motioned the children to sit next to him. They looked at each other, clearly using a form of body language to pass on a message and then, as if satisfied, sat down together on his right.

In a facetious tone Peel said, "Suffer little children to come unto me," and laughing derisively returned to the house, followed by the adults. The Peel children remained on the verandah eagerly watching events. Nothing exciting happened at Mandurah these days.

"William and Sarjan. Sara?" Blair questioned the children. Back came the firm reply "Willum" and then "Sarjan."

"Where do you come from Willum and Sarjan?" he asked slowly. They both pointed to the south.

"Do you have a mother?" Two heads shook. "Do you have a father?" Two heads shook again.

"Where do you live?" The children remained motionless. "They don't know or won't tell me," Blair thought. Probably the latter, he surmised.

Slowly Willum said "Mr Peel".

Blair was surprised. "You want Mr Peel?" he asked. The boy nodded.

Not wanting to leave the children in case they ran off, Blair shouted to Thomas Junior to call his father. Looking disgruntled, Peel walked from the house and stood by the fence.

"Well, Blair. What is it?"

"Mr Peel, the boy asks for you."

"Don't be ridiculous Blair. Why would a native boy ask for me?"

Blair was used to Peel's manners, or lack of them and just smiled. "What about a white boy asking for you?" he rejoined.

"Well, I'll be damned!" Peel said. "It is a white boy covered in dirt. Who are you boy?"

"Their names are William and Sarjan or Sara Jane I suspect," said Blair.

"The Andrews' children? Impossible! They're the family that died in the fire over two years ago."

William said stiltedly, "Mother and Father were in the fire. We were saved."

"Obviously by natives. Phew, what a stink." Peel drew a white handkerchief and fluttered it about in front of his face. "First things first. I think a bath would be in order." Peel looked at the children with distaste. "Blair, see what you can find out. I'll tell the women to prepare a bath. Hot with plenty of soap. I'll have you called when it's ready." Peel marched back to the house.

By the time Thomas Junior came running down the hill to call the Andrews' children for a bath, Reverend Blair had a measure of their trust and confidence. The conversation was restricted but the intent of the communication was evident. He held two small hands as he walked them around the house to the washroom at the back.

Mrs Ayrton took control as usual and within half an hour had both children washed and dressed in spare clothes belonging to Thomas Junior and Julia. The transformation was nothing short of amazing. Still brown all over, their hair was now a silver blonde. They were well built and extremely handsome children and their borrowed clothes were stretched to the limit. Now that their fear and anxiety had largely gone, they exuded a self-assurance beyond their years when ushered into the main room.

"Children," said Peel. "You are safe here. This evening Reverend Blair and I will discuss your future and in the morning we will inform you of our decision." The intensity of the looks Peel received made him feel uncomfortable. "Now off you go and have something to eat in the kitchen. Julia, you will assist in spreading two palliasses on the floor in the south room." The children were dismissed. William and Sara Jane hesitantly followed the others.

After Hall and Bunbury had departed, Blair and the Peels discussed the future of the Andrews' children. Peel made it clear that three children at Mandurah House were quite enough and that his elder son Fred might still return. Just because Samuel Andrews had been one of his indentured servants, didn't mean that he should have to take responsibility for the children. There was no orphanage in the colony. They must be taken to Perth and fostered out. They could be made wards of the Governor. And so it went on and on.

Reverend Blair had other ideas and after waiting for Peel to exhaust the options said "I will take them."

"What! You would take on two orphaned children who have spent years with the blacks? Are you mad, Blair?"

"Perhaps, Mr Peel. But I see the children as a gift from God to my wife and also to me. We will welcome them into our Fremantle house and it will become a home. And I hope we will become a family. The Lord works in mysterious ways. Blessed is the name of the Lord."

"Amen," said Mrs Ayrton from the corner, without looking up from her knitting.

* * * * *

Yeddi had rebuilt the fire at the entrance of the cave for the third time and leaned forward to recommence his vigil. He knew that the message via the spirits would come because Great Uncle had said so but staring continuously into the fire and concentrating to his utmost was both difficult and tiring. The faculty of seeing through space had increased in strength with Odern's tuition and Yeddi was now confident of being able to receive mind pictures but sometimes they didn't visualise when he was ready. He must ask Great Uncle about this problem on his return.

Mandu waited impatiently close by. She was as anxious as Yeddi to know what was happening to Sarjan and Willum. She saw Yeddi stiffen.

"At last," he murmured. His eyes opened wide as he stared into the fire. The flames merged together and were a single entity. Dark figures begin to take shape. He sees Sarjan and Willum being approached by a white man, dressed in black. He is smiling and has a kind face. He talks to the children. The man calls and another man approaches, talks and then walks away. The three sit on a log and talk. The man in black is friendly. He takes the children by the hand and leads them to a house. The picture faded.

"Grandmother! Sarjan and Willum are in safe hands." A relieved Mandu gave Yeddi a hug.

* * * * *

After HMS *Supply* had anchored off Bathers Bay and the passengers had been rowed ashore in the longboat, Blair led William and Sara Jane around the base of Arthur Head, on which the Round House prison stood, along High Street and into Henry Street. He carried his leather valise. The children carried nothing, still wearing their second-hand clothing. A sailor had given them both a haircut as they sailed up the coast and Blair assessed them quite presentable.

Fremantle was a hive of activity, mainly related to sailing craft and the interests and needs of sailors and travellers. The majority of buildings, especially those established near Bathers Bay, were stores, hotels and inns, laundries, ships' chandleries and boat-repairing facilities. Further east, residences were being built and tracks cleared for the passage of wagons. Although the permanent population was only three hundred and sixty-four at the census conducted in 1837, the transient population often reached the same figure.

On the knock, Mrs Blair opened the front door and formally welcomed her husband home, without removing her attention for a moment from the two bare-footed children standing one on each side of him. The boy held a black dog on a rope leash.

"Mr Blair! What have we here? Two handsome children. And where did we find these handsome children?"

"Well, my dear Mrs Blair, this is William and Sara Jane Andrews and Habbi and they are here to stay with us. It's a long story but I fancy that the immediate need is probably a bite to eat and after that a bath."

"Of course, Mr Blair. At once. Come with me little ones and we will see what we can find in the larder."

A warm smile and welcoming hands were offered by a plump, elderly woman dressed in a long, black skirt and white blouse. The children felt immediately at ease. She ushered them through the hall and chattered away as she led them to the kitchen.

Blair smiled. At last his wonderful wife would have not one but three persons on whom to heap affection. Later, when he described the situation as best he understood it, they agreed to wait for the children to explain things in their own time. Little by little, the Blairs pieced together their story, all except the origin of the recent scars on their shoulders, which they steadfastly refused to discuss, saying that this would remain a secret until the time was right.

However, the most disconcerting mannerism, as far as the Blairs were concerned, was the unspoken language constantly in use between the children. Slight movements of the eyes or hands, a particular tilt of the head. Almost imperceptible gestures sent continuous messages between Sara Jane and William. When questioned, the children appeared puzzled. "It's just a way of talking," said the little girl. "We learned it when we were taught how to track and hunt animals. Otherwise they would hear us and run away or hide."

"I see," said Blair slowly. "You speak well, children. I've been meaning to ask you about that."

"Oh," replied William. "It was Francis. Francis Armstrong worked for Father and he taught us. When he left he said he might become a teacher because he enjoyed teaching us."

"And so he did, my child. So he did. He is now the Superintendent of Native Tribes and Native Interpreter and teaches at the school for native children. It is a very responsible position."

The children looked nonplussed.

"We have a lot to learn, my dear," said Blair that evening, as he closed his Bible. Earlier, they had discussed their prospects for the future which were now very different and in spite of his search in the holy book for direction, it was clearly still on his mind.

Mrs Blair looked up from mending her husband's socks. "That we have, my husband. That we have. And I'm going to enjoy every minute of it."

And so the children became William and Sara Jane Andrews again and lived with the Reverend Edmund Blair and his beloved wife Margaret in a small stone house in Henry Street, Fremantle, only two hundred yards from the vine-covered cottage, owned by John Bateman, which served as the Post Office. The roof was thatched and the floors compressed limestone but it had two bedrooms, a sleepout and separate kitchen and bathing room and was comfortably furnished with solid wooden furniture. The rather large sitting room had an extension used as a study for the Reverend. This was called his 'contemplating cuddy' and he looked forward to the times when he read from his extensive library and prepared for his twice-monthly services in the local hall.

The Reverend Edmund Blair, late of Swindon and London, had always sought a mission in life. His father inherited a valuable property from a bachelor uncle and insisted that his three sons receive a classical education by the best tutors before going up to Trinity College at Oxford. Edmund's passions ranged from Shakespeare's historical plays and the poetry of Walter Scott, to Euclid, to botany. His copy of Herschel's 'Introduction to the Study of Natural Philosophy' was well worn and he had an obsession about collecting plant specimens, birds' eggs, rocks and insects. When he turned to theology, he familiarised himself with Paley's 'Evidences of Christianity' and 'Moral Philosophy' and other books on divinity. On graduating a Bachelor of Arts, he was ordained a priest in the Church of England. Blair was a natural evangelist and enjoyed the furthering of God's work more than anything. He and his wife Margaret revelled in the challenge and, unable to have children, had time to commit to the responsibilities of the church. In the Swan River Colony, Blair was in his element. Since his arrival two years ago there had been much to accommodate his missionary zeal.

The day after Blair's return with the children, there was a visit to L. Samson and Son in Cliff Street. Mrs Blair chose two beds and bedding, two sets of drawers, two complete sets of clothing for ordinary day wear, sleeping attire and a set of clothes for Sunday best. All were removed to Henry Street and set up in the back bedroom for Sara Jane and in the sleep-out for William. It took weeks before the children would sleep on beds for a whole night. The shoes hurt their feet so much that at first they wore them only on Sundays. Meals were a difficulty because knives and forks had to be mastered. Habbi was ordered to sleep outside in the backyard but mysteriously appeared at the foot of Sara Jane's bed each morning. It wasn't that the children were being wantonly disobedient or troublesome and the Blairs knew this. What was necessary was understanding, patience, readjustment and compromise.

"And time," said Mrs Blair to her husband. "Are you praying enough, my dear? This is a trying period for all of us, especially the children."

"Mrs Blair, I have been especially attentive to my prayers of late, I assure you. Time is of the essence, as you have said."

* * * * *

Letters were dispatched to Governor Stirling and Mr Peter Broun, the Colonial Secretary, informing them of the situation regarding the children and on a visit to Fremantle on official business, Sir James and Lady Stirling called on Reverend Edmund Blair and Mrs Blair.

As cups of tea and scones were served in the sitting room, the future of the children was discussed. Following niceties, the Governor said, "So Reverend, you wish to adopt the children?"

"Yes, Your Excellency. It is the fervent wish of both Mrs Blair and myself that we are permitted to legally adopt William and Sara Jane."

"Have the children been informed of your wish?"

"Yes, Your Excellency. The matter has been explained fully to them and I am pleased to say they are in agreement with the proposal."

"Well, Reverend Blair, Mr Broun does not see any impediment to such a request but there are necessary procedures, as you would understand. Inquiries will need to be made in England as to any documents, such as wills and the like, that may have been lodged by Samuel Andrews prior to their departure. The Father was an indentured servant to Peel, I believe." Blair nodded. "I will propose to Peel that no claim be made under the circumstances. When the paperwork is complete, we will see about the drawing up of adoption papers. The children will indeed be fortunate to find a place in your family."

"Thank you, Your Excellency. We sincerely appreciate your interest and kindness."

At that moment there was shouting and laughter from the back garden. "Ah, the children are back from their fishing expedition," said Mrs Blair. "Excuse me, Lady Stirling, while I quieten their enthusiasm."

"May I attend, Mrs Blair?" and without waiting for an answer Lady Stirling followed her from the room.

Mrs Blair clapped her hands for quiet as she walked from the kitchen. The children were cleaning their catch and leapt to their feet as Mrs Blair introduced Lady Stirling. Sara Jane curtsied and William bowed. The girl was tongue-tied for a minute or two.

"Come, Sara Jane," said Mrs Blair. "You are usually not at a loss for words."

"But she, I mean Lady Stirling, is so beautiful."

"Thank you, my child but I suspect that it will not be long before you are classed a beauty and will have no peer in this colony. I wish you both well. You are favoured in sharing this home. Thank you, Mrs Blair. The children are both handsome, lively and well-mannered. An admirable combination of traits." Sara Jane and William repeated their curtsy and bow respectively, as Mrs Blair proudly followed Lady Stirling back to the sitting room.

* * * * *

The children continued their independent ways. From the moment Mrs Blair had set eyes upon them, they were loved and cherished to the point of being smothered. William felt confined and escaped as often as he could to roam the river flats and the ocean beaches. Most of the time Sara Jane went with him and although at first the Blairs were concerned for her safety, they soon realised how sensible and capable she was and tried to stop worrying. In any case there didn't seem to be much they could do about it. One moment the children were there and the next they were gone. Mrs Blair was comforted by the fact that the dog always trailed them and was particularly protective of Sara Jane.

The *Fremantle Observer* included an article about the arrival of the children but in deference to Reverend and Mrs Edmund Blair, who were well liked and respected citizens of Fremantle, the comment was merely a brief statement of fact. As the word passed around town, people nodded and spoke to the children. Most were understanding when they received little response and accepted that the children still found themselves in strange surroundings. So many people in such a small area was the most off-putting aspect of their new experience. The majority of contacts were friendly, although some individuals remained aloof. A group of boys, who followed them one day shouting derisive remarks, from what they considered was a safe distance, found themselves ducking and running for cover when William retaliated with a few skilfully thrown rocks. After that the boys kept well away, until one day William waved to them and with relief they waved back.

Blair forbad the children from swimming in the sea, because of the prevalence of sharks. Both the offal from the whaling activity and the rubbish from the anchored ships were an obvious attraction to the predators and the small cove at the foot of Arthur Head was facetiously named Bathers Bay. So William and Sara Jane spent a lot of time in the shallows of the river, upstream from the rocky bar at the entrance and after fashioning spears provided welcome and frequent fish and crabs for the meal table. Blair was fascinated when he first watched them fish. Their surreptitious signalling, patient and motionless waiting and deadly accurate throwing were incredible. On one occasion, Blair tried himself, bare foot, trousers rolled up, splashing through the shallows but gave up after an hour, having nothing to show for his efforts. Mrs Blair politely refused William's offers of snake or lizard but when her husband proudly returned from one of the children's hunting expeditions with a kangaroo in the buggy, she allowed William to use her best kitchen knife to skin and divide the carcass. She was intrigued when William pulled the sinews from the tail and wrapped them around a stick, explaining how he would use them to strap on the point of his new spear. For the next few days, they ate kangaroo tail soup and kangaroo stew and Habbi didn't have to hunt food that week.

Not to be outdone, Sara Jane used Blair's whittling knife to fashion a kylie. It took several days to prepare and trial but on her first hunting excursion she brought home a fat swan. Mrs Blair was not sure how to react, so thanked her and cooked it in the Dutch oven for the following day's Sunday lunch. The guests, Mr and Mrs Antony Smith and their three children were profuse in their compliments. Mrs Blair was just grateful that she wasn't asked where or how she had procured the bird! William and Sara Jane came through their first test of manners and the Blairs were pleased and proud.

Of great interest to the children was the newly-established Fremantle Whaling Company, whose storehouses were carved out of the rock cliffs south of the Round House. On the adjacent beach, furnaces and try-pots were erected and the beginnings of a jetty were evident. When a whale was sighted, the rival crews of John Bateman and Joshua Harwood could be seen launching their whaleboats and skimming to sea, gunwales with little freeboard, backs straining at oars with rowlocks muffled, each laden with harpoons, baskets of coiled line and lances. A crowd always gathered quickly, cheering the race. During the season, many natives congregated in Fremantle waiting for the scraps of meat left over after the oil had been boiled from the blubber. Sara Jane always looked for Yeddi but he was never there.

Eventually, after a month, Blair felt that the time had arrived for a more formal education. The children, having been given their heads, had settled down reasonably well, were polite and caring but had a limited vocabulary, no writing skills, no reading ability and absolutely no comprehension of the level of behaviour expected of well brought-up children of the upper classes. Reverend Blair did not blame anyone. That was not his way. However, with God's assistance, he certainly intended to rectify the situation.

So that morning, the children attended their first religious service. As yet a church had not been built, although such a venture was high on the priority list of members of the Church of England congregation. Communion and evening services were held on the second and fourth Sundays of the month in the local hall, a wooden building that served as a meeting place during the week. There was some agitation by the more devout parishioners for Reverend Blair to conduct weekly services but so far he had resisted, arguing that taking the word of the Lord to outlying communities was necessary and indeed expected of him for his small stipend.

William and Sara Jane watched the service with interest. They had to sit quietly while members of the congregation took communion which was boring but they were fascinated at the way Reverend Blair conducted proceedings. He really was important, especially when he held up the shining mug in front of him and everyone looked so serious.

"Sort of like Odern with his magic stick," Sara Jane whispered. William nodded sagely. He had entertained the same idea.

After the midday meal, the children sat waiting to be excused. Mrs Blair gave a small nod and Reverend Blair cleared his throat. Neither William nor Sara Jane missed the exchange.

"Children," he began. "It is timely, that we look to your education in terms of a preparation for your future. You can neither read, nor write, nor have an understanding of numbers and this is a sorry state of affairs. It is now June in the year 1837. How many years of age have you reached?"

Sara Jane looked to William, who said "I turned nine years just before the fire. We stayed with Mandu, Odern and Yeddi for two rotations of the seasons." He stopped and corrected himself. "For two years, before Odern brought us to Mr Peel's house. That makes me eleven years and about five months old.

"Then I must be ten years and five months old," said Sara Jane. "My birthday is in the same month as William's."

The Blairs looked at one another in astonishment.

"You both have very good memories children," said Blair. "Do you know the dates of your birth?"

William reflected for a moment. "The 6th of January. Yes, I'm sure that is right."

Sara Jane piped in. "And mine is the 7th of January." She looked at her brother for confirmation.

"Yes," answered William.

"How are you so sure?" asked Blair. "It's years since you would have talked about birthdays."

"Some things you just remember," said William. "I am one year older than Sara Jane and her birthday is one day later than mine in January."

The Blairs looked bemused.

"And we can count. Odern taught us," explained William.

"Show me how you count then," said Blair.

Without words both children touched their left thumbs with their right index finger and then the fingers of the left hand one by one and then held up their left hand. "Five," they said in unison. They repeated the process using their left index finger on their right hand and then held up both hands. "Ten," they said.

Blair turned to his wife and smiled. "There appear to be some things that cross the bounds of culture, my dear."

The rules were set. Lessons each morning, Monday to Friday, would be conducted by Reverend Blair at the kitchen table, unless he was called away on religious duties. Any additional individual work as necessary would be supervised in the afternoons by Mrs Blair.

At first the children found the imposed discipline onerous. They fidgeted, day dreamed and found any excuse to distract Blair from his intended lesson and escape from the house. Mrs Blair came to their rescue.

"My dear husband," she said one evening after the children had gone to bed and Blair was expressing his frustration at the slow progress he was making. "Do you think that you might be pushing the children too hard? Perhaps, if you made the lessons more practical and of shorter duration they might be able to concentrate better."

"Humph" was the reply but as Blair blew out the lamp and climbed into bed that night, he said, "I think your ideas about the children's lessons have merit, my dear."

Botany lessons were shifted to the bush alongside the track to the Canning district. After the first few minutes, Blair had the feeling that he was learning more than he was teaching. He was naming and explaining the function of the parts of plants and trees and Sara Jane was telling him which parts were edible and useful for healing purposes. He accepted there was a certain reciprocity of knowledge inherent in the morning's lesson.

Walking home they counted the number of steps out loud until they reached one hundred and then Blair explained the action of the joints of the body. That night they stargazed. The following morning it was back to the alphabet and writing. Mrs Blair showed the children how to make quills from the wing feathers she had kept from Sara Jane's swan. Then it was a geography lesson using the globe from the study and in the afternoon a biology lesson as they cleaned their catch of bream. Everything became a lesson about something, William decided.

Learning to read was hard work, because Blair's library comprised only adult books and so they had to make do with Mitford's 'History of Greece', Scott's 'Ivanhoe', 'The Works of William Shakespeare' and Hume's 'History of England' and of course the Holy Bible. He did have a copy of 'Webster's Dictionary' for reference purposes. They were introduced to poetry through Alfred Tennyson's book of poems. Sara Jane especially liked 'The Lady of Shalott'. Comprehension was taught largely through the use of two books, published in London in 1834 and 1835, describing life in the Swan River Colony. They were written by George Fletcher Moore and Captain Frederick Chidley Irwin. Blair read to them and then asked questions. The children noted the sections relating to the natives and argued that they could not have been guilty of the violent acts described by Moore. Blair did not pursue the issue, assuming that there were faults and exaggerations on both sides.

The carrot offered for all this intensive education was riding lessons. Blair reckoned that the dark brown gelding called Ascot, after the famous English race meeting town, belied the possibilities suggested by his name. However, he was well trained and enjoyed being ridden rather than pulling Blair around the parish in the buggy. Lessons took place in the late afternoons before Mrs Blair called the family to the evening meal. It wasn't long before the children took it in turns to gallop down the Canning track. On occasions when John Bateman was busy with his whaling or mail businesses, he lent the children his horse to give it a run and then the children would race. With dogs barking and chickens squawking as they scattered in the laneway, the children would pull up puffing and laughing at the back door. At first William was mortified when Sara Jane consistently beat him, regardless of the distance he chose. However, he took it in good grace. When on Mrs Blair's insistence, Blair bought a ladies' side saddle, Sara Jane was restricted and did not win again but she always had a grin on her face and a twinkle in her eye when she congratulated William after the race.

As the months passed, so the children's education progressed in leaps and bounds. Blair realised that he had two very clever children on his hands and delighted in the chance he had been given to impart knowledge. They stored facts easily, yet not mindlessly. They comprehended given information, so that they could explain, analyse and interpret details. They grasped concepts that he was sure were beyond most children of their age. And questions! He was forever answering or trying to answer questions.

"Mrs Blair," he said after one demanding morning. "The children are like sponges soaking up water. I'm having difficulty keeping up with them. They absorb everything I say and then ask why? or how? or when? or where? Sara Jane wants to know more and more about biology, botany and mathematics. I can understand her interest in the natural sciences but mathematics! William wants to know everything about mechanical principles, navigation, cartography and history."

"Then you must prepare yourself better. Do some more reading, my dear," said Mrs Blair, the corner of her mouth twitching.

And so he did. When he had finished re-reading his own library, he borrowed books. Letters were forwarded to his brothers in England requesting works on navigation and sailing. Nine months later he received copies of 'Midshipman Easy' and 'Pickwick Papers', a bundle of maps, a compass and books on navigation. He read voraciously, taking copious notes, finding the advanced mathematics required for navigation a challenge.

Meanwhile, the children received an excellent education. Creative activities were included and art and flute playing became Sara Jane's favourite sessions. William considered art a chore because it took so long to sketch a piece and hated the time required to practice on the flute. Nevertheless, he was proud when he completed a life-like drawing and could play a tune to his satisfaction.

Blair was surprised to find how much he enjoyed teaching and, because of his own intellect and enthusiasm, the children enjoyed learning, which has to be an admirable combination in the process of imparting knowledge.

He came to almost resent the time needed to attend to his parishioners.

CHAPTER 20
Growing Up

In the spring of 1837, a group of Bindjareb men gather on the banks of the Murray River several miles south of the camp site of Lieutenant Bunbury and his detachment stationed at the proposed site for the town of Pinjarra.

Yeddi stands tall, a serious yet proud expression on his face. He is surrounded by the closest surviving male relatives on his mother's side of the family. There are no uncles as would have been customary, but some more distant males of his mother's moiety, the Crow, had been located. The past moon had been spent in their camp in final preparations for the initiation ceremony. All had been impressed by the tuition Yeddi had received from his great uncle, who now stood proudly behind his great nephew. It was acceptable under the circumstances, although unusual. Odern was the most powerful boylya gadak in living memory and no one was going to suggest that the procedure followed was incorrect in any way. The past two years had seen many necessary changes to traditional practices due to the decimation of the Bindjareb people by the whites.

The ceremony is due to begin and once again Yeddi wishes that his babbingurs could be with him on such an important occasion. But that could not be.

One of his distant cousins steps forward and there is immediate silence. A piece of the small leg bone of a kangaroo is held in his right hand and Yeddi is glad to see that it has been sharpened to a point. His nose is grasped firmly from above and his head tipped back, stretching the cartilage. For an instant he cannot breathe. He feels pain as the bone pierces his septum but does not flinch. His nose is released and the bone is turned. He ignores the blood dripping onto his chin and chest. It is over and he is being congratulated. Smiling faces surround him and Yeddi is filled with pride.

* * * * *

It is two years before Yeddi sees Sarjan and Willum again. He too has been continuing his education and has connected with his remaining kin over several mandjars. After travelling the boundaries of the Nyoongar land, he now had a mind map of the natural features and the pads linking the different tribes and, being a fast runner, is often chosen to relay messages. Mandu has remained with Odern and they spend most of their time in the cave area, especially during the winter seasons. Yeddi keeps in touch, frequently visiting them and bringing gifts of food hunted on the way and chips of the hard stone found in the ranges to the east, requested by his great uncle for his spearheads.

Odern gives Yeddi secret and specialised instruction on how to punish individuals who break tribal lore or harm kin and how to heal the sick. After each visit Yeddi feels stronger and is aware of increasing powers. He realises how privileged he is in this regard and takes the instruction very seriously. In fact, he is growing into a responsible and extremely handsome youth in Mandu's opinion. He has a well developed physique with wide shoulders and long, finely muscled legs. His movements are lithe, almost graceful, yet he can run further and faster than any man in his tribe and can hunt to kill with more success than most. Importantly, as far as Odern and Mandu are concerned, Yeddi is held in high esteem by all members of the Bindjareb tribe.

When he stays with his grandmother and great uncle, he receives encouragement to further his communication skills with the spirits through the medium of fire. Several times he conjures up a vision of Sarjan. How different she looks in whites' clothing. Each time he feels both exquisite joy and great sadness. A very strange feeling, one he has not experienced with anyone else. The longing grows stronger and stronger. Yet, when he sees Willum in the flames, he just feels a close bond of friendship.

* * * * *

Habbi barked.

Blair, William and Sara Jane were categorising species of flora in their favourite area of bush south of the Canning track, when Yeddi stepped into the clearing.

"Yeddi! Yeddi!" Sara Jane dropped her notebook and pencil and threw herself at him. Yeddi could not keep a huge grin from spreading across his face. He placed his weapons on the ground and held her at arms length to better look into her eyes. Then he embraced her.

"My babbingur, you look well."

Reverend Blair saw a fine looking, well built but almost naked black youth with rows of cicatrices on his chest and a bone through the nasal septum taking hold of his daughter. A disconcerted look crossed his face and not knowing what to do he coughed. No one took any notice and William joined the other two in a sort of jig on the spot. Habbi ran around delightedly in circles.

"Yeddi. You have been through your initiation," said Sara Jane using Nyoongar words. She gently touched the bone. "You look ferocious." She drew her brows together and pushed her lips forward in an attempt to look fierce.

The young people, as Blair now called the children, were totally oblivious of him, yet only a moment ago they had been absorbed in the examination of a species of banksia tree, not previously recorded in their journal.

Blair coughed again and Sara Jane swung around.

"This is Yeddi, our babbingur. See his scars. He has two. We each gave him one. Remember you asked us about ours and we said it was a secret until the right time. Well, Yeddi gave us our scars." With that, she threw herself back at Yeddi, who this time momentarily held her at arms length and then stepped back, dropping his arms.

He spoke in his dialect. "Who is this man? I saw him in the flames but then he looked friendly. Now he looks angry."

Sara Jane purposely answered in English. "Yeddi, this is our father, Reverend Blair. He is sort of like Odern in our religion. We have been adopted by Reverend Blair and Mrs Blair. They are wonderful parents."

"And we are very happy," added William.

"I am now Sara Jane Andrews-Blair and Willum is William Blair. He didn't like the extra name. Thought it sounded a bit sissy."

Blair looked relieved but the stern expression remained. "This is all most unseemly behaviour Sara Jane and William. Most unseemly behaviour." However, he stepped forward and extended his hand to Yeddi. "How do you do, young man. I have heard a great deal about you."

"How do you do ," responded Yeddi shaking hands.

He turned to his two friends. "I am glad you are well and happy. I will keep in touch with you when I can," he said in good English. "Reverend," he stammered over the new word, "Blair, I am pleased to meet you." Yeddi picked up his weapons and walked off into the trees.

"Well I'll be---" Blair paused. "Well, I'll be a monkey's uncle."

* * * * *

The years passed. William retained his interest, almost an obsession, with everything connected with boats, sailing and the sea. With his excellent education and keen mind, Blair had been hopeful of William aspiring to greater things but this was not to be. When he turned fourteen years old he signed on as a junior crew member on a whaleboat plying between Fremantle, Perth and Guildford and occasionally travelled by cutter on special contract to Mandurah, Augusta, or King George Sound.

At first, sailing was hard work, especially when the boat had to be pulled across sand bars and flats, and loading and unloading the produce could be exhausting. but as William grew and developed body mass and strength, he found that by the time he turned fifteen in January 1841, he could put in a better day's work than many of the men. He received six shillings a week at first, of which Blair placed four shillings in an account for him in the Fremantle Agency of the newly established Western Australian Bank, at 5% interest. William kept one shilling for himself and gave the same amount to Mrs Blair.

Being well off financially, the Blairs did not need the contribution towards household costs but wanted William to be independent and responsible. His dream was to command his own vessel.

Sara Jane assisted her mother with household chores, occasionally helped her father prepare a sermon and continued her studies. Her particular interest remained the study of the native plants and she kept meticulous records of the different species, complete with samples of leaves, flowers and seeds, which she pressed between sheets of paper. By constant practice, she developed an ability to draw and produced a good likeness. Blair encouraged her talent by providing a set of water colours and different sized brushes. Her black and white sketches were transformed into wonderful coloured paintings. At fourteen years Sara Jane had the mind and body of a woman. A beautiful young woman.

However, in spite of all her activities, Sara Jane was restless. She needed a new challenge and found it in the nearby Green Post Office, as it was known, because it was almost completely covered in several varieties of green vines. On busy occasions, especially when ships berthed at the new jetty, Sara Jane helped John Bateman in keeping the records. The date of receipt and subsequent retrieval by the addressee were all entered in the official book and the young woman's immaculate handwriting and meticulous attention to detail were appreciated and indeed admired by the Postmaster. Little by little, Sara Jane took over more of the business, which freed Bateman to spend additional time with his commercial and whaling enterprises.

After one busy morning, during which Sara Jane sorted the mail and entered one hundred and twenty-five entries in the record book, Bateman came through the door with an excited grin on his face.

"Sara Jane. We've caught a whale off Carnac Island. And there are other humpbacks travelling south. Would you mind the Post Office for me for the rest of the week?"

It took Sara Jane only a second to reply. "Yes, Mr Bateman. What payment would you be making?"

Bateman looked surprised. "Payment? Oh, of course. Would four shillings a week be acceptable?"

"Four shillings and six pence," Sara Jane rejoined.

"Done," Bateman said. "You deserve it."

Sara Jane's bank account was opened the following week. Being under age and a female, her account was named Edmund Blair, No 2.

CHAPTER 21
Planned Departures

In October 1837, Sir James Stirling dispatched his resignation as Governor of Western Australia to Lord Glenelg, the Secretary of State for the Colonies. He had worried for some years about his future prospects if he remained in the colony. Development continued to be slow, due to lack of capital and a near stagnant population of just over two thousand persons. The settlers were demanding increased expenditure and decreased taxation, to which of course the Government could not accede and it was clear that funds and resources for expansion in Western Australia would not be forthcoming, at least in the short term. Stirling's annual salary of £800 was barely adequate as his family increased in number and his two oldest sons were approaching the age when they should be receiving a better education than that available in Perth.

Soon after, the Reverend John Wittenoom proposed the opening of two schools, a Classical School for the higher orders and an English School for the lower orders, both to be supervised by him and housed in the elegant Court House when it was not in use. Stirling's second son, Frederick Henry Stirling was enrolled in Class 3 at the Classical School when it opened in August but despite the efforts of Henry Spencer, the schoolmaster, it was clear that small numbers and lack of funding would cause its demise and it failed soon after. Too little, too late for the Stirling boys.

Stirling was convinced that it was time to leave the colony and seek new opportunities. Rumour abounded about the possibility of a renewed war with France. Perhaps he should return to the sea. The idea rather excited Stirling. He had been beholden to too many others for too long and looked forward to the idea of freedom from the pressures of government.

When Stirling received the official acceptance of his resignation on the 5th December 1838, he promptly took action to clear the administrative decks, so to speak and prepare for his departure. He set New Years Eve as his date of retirement from official duties.

There was an immediate flurry of activity as the matriarchs of Western Australian society began to organise a programme to farewell such a respected Governor and his Lady. By virtue of her husband's position and her consequent status in the colony, Mrs Caroline Broun assumed the role of co-ordinator of events. One woman was heard to say that it was just as well, because such a time frame needed a calm and resolute demeanour.

* * * * *

Mrs Mary Charlotte Dorking Peel, her mother and three children had now lived in Mandurah for nearly five years. Apart from a few visits for formal occasions, such as the annual Foundation Day Ball held at Government House, Peel refused to take his wife to Perth, in spite of her protestations and tantrums. He had little cash and simply could not or rather would not afford it. Besides, it would restrict his opportunities with likely young women in Perth and Fremantle. Along with other gentlemen in the colony, discrete dalliances were part and parcel of Peel's lifestyle. Liaisons with native women had not been possible since Mary's arrival because, justifiably, she saw the young black women as a temptation and had sent them away when her husband left on his next visit to Perth. Mrs Ayrton assumed responsibility for the cooking and cleaning with Mary occasionally lending a hand when she felt guilty, which wasn't very often and usually as a gesture when they received guests.

However, the resignation of Stirling, although not publicly announced, was well known throughout the colony. Mary waited in anticipation.

The invitations were delivered by the Reverend Blair on 12th December and were accompanied by an offer from Peter Broun for Mr and Mrs Peel to be his guests during the festivities. This time Peel knew full well that he could not avoid taking Mary to Perth for the round of farewell parties and to Fremantle for the departure of the Governor and his family. He reluctantly agreed when she began a campaign to wear him down. It began with frantic alterations to dresses for both day and evening occasions and continued with millinery. There were dresses and hats suitably displayed all around the sitting room for days and 'oohs' and 'aahs' from her daughters as Mary modelled the outfits. Peel just couldn't put up with the pressure and really had no excuse, because he certainly wasn't going to miss out himself. The children were upset about their Christmas being disrupted but were mollified somewhat when promised a second and special Christmas dinner on the return of their parents in January. Passage was arranged on the supply schooner and Thomas and Mary Peel left Mandurah on 18th December complete with numerous cases and hat boxes. Mrs Ayrton was left in charge and Private Peter Hammond, a likely looking lad, was stationed at Mandurah House as guard. He was in seventh heaven with two adolescent girls, nay young women, trying to catch his eye and a foster grandmother who prepared him delicious food.

For Mr and Mrs Thomas Peel, the following week was hectic. It began with the Farewell Ball held at Government House on 20th December. The Governor and Lady Stirling welcomed their guests in the reception area for the last time and spent most of the evening personally thanking them. Following the abundant supper, the aide-de-camp called for attention. The Governor stepped onto the podium and the assembled crowd fell silent.

With undisguised emotion, Sir James began. "Distinguished guests and I deem you all to be my distinguished guests, I welcome you on this special occasion to join me and my wife in our goodbyes. Some of you have travelled long distances and for that we thank you. Tonight, as Catullus, the esteemed Roman poet said, and I now repeat to you all, I say 'Hail and farewell'."

By now, many of the distinguished guests were blinking and white handkerchiefs were dabbing furtively.

"It has been nearly a decade since the *Parmelia* brought the first settlers to the Swan River and although we have all experienced difficulties and indeed hard times the colony is now established. As I am, you all should be proud to have been a part of history and an extension of our glorious empire. My wife and I thank you for the support that has always been forthcoming and wish you well for the future. I am sure your heirs will take great satisfaction in being able to say 'Our forebears founded Western Australia'. We sincerely thank you all."

Introductory chords heralded the national anthem and the colonists stood to attention as they solemnly sang 'God save the Queen' for the young Victoria crowned earlier that year.

Then somebody at the back called "What about 'Western Australia for me'?"

The call was repeated with many "Yeses" and "Where's George Fletcher Moore?"

A grinning and delighted George Fletcher Moore stepped forward and, after bowing to the Governor, took his place on the dais in front of the band. He gave a signal to the conductor and turned to face the crowd. "It is my pleasure, my friends."

As the band played, the crowd roared out the now well known words of 'Western Australia for me'.

George Moore called three cheers for Sir James and Lady Stirling and the response was deafening.

Then it was back to the dancing, which continued until breakfast was served next morning. It was a night to record in diaries and write home about.

A round of parties and dances followed. There was a function every night hosted by the elite of the colony and of course Mr and Mrs Thomas Peel received invitations. Mary had a wonderful time. She was attentive to the gentlemen, who responded graciously, and agreeable to the ladies, who would hopefully extend invitations for her to call when next in Perth.

On the last day of the year and his last day in office, a deputation waited on Stirling to present him with an address from all the colonists. It expressed their sadness on his leaving and their best wishes for his future. When the time came to part, many of the settlers acknowledged the difficulties the Governor had faced in the administration of the colony and were genuinely sorry to lose him.

Thomas Peel knew only too well how much he owed to Stirling's patronage. The Governor's final gesture was to formally recommend him to Mr John Hutt, who arrived at Fremantle on board the *Brothers* the following day and assumed his duties immediately.

Sir James Stirling and his family sailed for England on the afternoon of 5th January 1839. The largest crowd ever assembled in the colony gathered on the jetty, on the white beach at Bathers Bay, along the steep cliffs on each side of the Round House and in boats bobbing on the blue water. The Blairs received priority treatment and were standing in the front row of the crowd on the jetty.

Sara Jane looked everywhere but could not see Yeddi. He knew exactly where she stood and was more interested in watching her than the proceedings.

Dignitaries and gentry joined with servants and natives in giving a rousing three cheers as the Stirlings were ferried out to Gage Roads. Anchors were raised and sails set. The *Champion* disappeared past Rottnest on a fresh southerly wind.

However, the consequence of the continued contact with the highest level of society in the colony over the previous ten days was to cause Mary to yearn for London. She remembered what she was missing and the idea of returning to Mandurah became abhorrent. When Governor Hutt announced the appointment of Messrs Peel, Brockman, Leake and Tanner to the Legislative Council on 3rd January, it was the last straw. Her husband was now the Honourable Thomas Peel Esquire, Member of the Legislative Council, Justice of the Peace and Director of the Road District of Pinjarra. It looked as though the family was here to stay. She would never see her beloved London again, unless she could persuade Thomas to give up this miserable life in this miserable colony and return to England and the lifestyle that they and their children deserved. Mary began to plan.

On their return to Mandurah, the crusade of love was launched.

Thomas and Mary had always enjoyed a robust sex life but all at once the bedroom became the focus of their life. Thomas found himself thinking of nothing else and it was a case of early to bed and late to rise. Mary was insatiable and Thomas became her knight in shining armour.

Daily routines involved walking on the beach in the morning holding hands, sipping fine French wine in the afternoon with dappled sunlight filtering through the trees onto a soft rug and watching the sunset in the early evening from the lounge on the verandah.

The children were mystified. What on earth was going on? Their parents weren't acting like grown-ups at all!

Then the crusade of education was launched.

"Thomas, my dear," Mary murmured as they lay satiated under a stand of eucalypts after a picnic lunch and a bottle of Thomas' best wine. "I worry about the children's future."

"What about their future?" Thomas was drifting into sleep.

"Well darling, this year Julia will be fifteen, Dorothy twelve and Thomas fourteen years."

"So?" Thomas queried.

"What were you doing at fourteen years of age, my husband?"

"I was at Harrow receiving an education and an introduction to the manly sports."

"Then," Mary pleaded, "does not your son deserve the same? Is it not reasonable to expect that a blood relative of a past Prime Minister of Great Britain, the mightiest nation in the world, would receive the very best education available? Meet with and rub shoulders with the upper echelons of British society? Grow to maturity with the world at his feet? If we were at home, Julia would soon be preparing for her debut and the London season. Dorothy would be learning the niceties of social intercourse."

There was no answer.

"Thomas! I know you are awake. Answer me!"

"I'm thinking."

"Aren't you worried about the children's future? What can they achieve without an adequate education?"

"Of course, I'm worried about the children's future. I just haven't thought about it much. You know how busy I've been lately."

"Well, you must think about it, my dear. You must. How can they marry well? They are largely illiterate, ill-informed in the classical subjects and woefully inadequate where etiquette is concerned."

"Hmm." There was actually concern on his face. "Yes, I suppose you're right." Peel saw an instant solution. He sat up. "I will arrange for a tutor."

This was the last thing on Mary's mind. "Thomas, I was rather hoping that we could all return home to England." She took his hand and elaborated for several minutes.

"Mary, you know as well as I, that our financial situation will not allow it. I've persevered in my efforts to reclaim the money I'm owed by the indentured servants for their passage to the colony. Solicitors! Graham has been a hindrance and Clark positively dishonest. And you know how long the legal process takes. A ridiculous situation. The cash from whaling has helped but it is a pittance. All my land is mortgaged as security for my debt. Settlers are leaving the colony, not arriving. There are tens of thousands of acres available for private sale and the same available for purchase from the crown. Nobody wants to buy." Peel's temper was rising at the unfairness of the situation.

"When you put your mind to something, my dear, you can be very determined. Perhaps the solution is for me to take the children home to London while you resolve things here."

Thomas' immediate thought was what he would miss if Mary left. Lately he could think of little else.

"No, Mary. You are right. We should travel home as a family. I will investigate the situation fully as soon as possible."

Peel convinced himself that, since his promises in the contract signed to receive his inheritance had been kept for ten years, it would be reasonable to expect a change of heart after all this time. He had not asked for money from any kin and he had not returned to England. He occasionally heard from his brother William and knew his father was still very much alive. A healthy seventy-one years old. Surely his father would have forgiven him by now. After all, he was the eldest son. He would take the chance. In any case what could his father do to him on his return without creating a public scandal? Out of curiosity, Peel wrote to William and asked him to assess his father's feelings on the matter.

Meanwhile, within two months, for once it seemed as if Peel's fortunes were changing. He sold 10,000 acres of prime land on the Murray River to Captain Francis Singleton, a recent arrival from Ireland and received £1,250. It was some of Peel's best land and he was selling it at half the crown price but it was too good an opportunity to miss. £340 was paid off his debt to the crown and Peel was informed that accordingly the mortgage would be lifted from the 10,000 acres. With £910 cash, he was off to a good start. He could settle his accounts, pay passage to England and have sufficient funds to keep the family in appropriate circumstances for at least two years. After that he would appraise the situation.

As a consequence, Peel wrote to Governor Hutt formally requesting that he be allowed to extend the period of repayment of his crown debt of £2823 by two years so that he could return to England to put his affairs in order.

When the reply was received, Peel informed Mary.

"Some good news. Hutt has approved my request for an extension of time." He didn't point out that non-payment by that date meant foreclosure on the mortgage to the value of the debt.

Mary smiled. "Well done, my dear." Step one concluded.

The following month, a further 2000 acres on the Murray were purchased by Messrs Creery, Tate and Montgomery for £95. Peel paid the whole amount to the Colonial Secretary.

"Thomas. Are you going to let the farm while we are away?" Mary had absolutely no intention of ever returning to Western Australia.

"Yes, of course. I am forwarding a notice to be advertised in the *Gazette* with the next available mail. The lease will be offered from the first of January."

Mary smiled at her husband to indicate agreement. Step two concluded.

However, a difficulty arose when Captain Singleton requested clarification on the boundaries of his newly acquired land. Peel himself wanted an updated description of his own grant before he left the colony, as the original title deeds were vague, so he wrote to the Surveyor-General. Approval was given in June but the survey still had not been completed and it was now October.

Peel fumed in frustration. Damned public servants were anything but servants to the government! He wished Stirling was still Governor, as he would not have tolerated such delays.

"Thomas, if a booking is not made for our departure soon, we may not be able to leave in January when we had planned."

"Don't go on so, Mary! I will attend to it as soon as possible."

Two weeks later Peel received notification of their booking on the barque *Shepherd* leaving Fremantle in early January.

"We are on our way, Mary." Peel was actually looking forward to life in London again.

"Yes, my husband and I thank you for your consideration." Plan concluded.

But the plan, like so many of Peel's previous plans, was destined to fail. Again Lady Luck was looking the other way or perhaps Peel always left so many loose ends that time and events caught up with him.

In early November, Peel received a letter from the Colonial Secretary informing him that procedures for the drawing up of a new title to his land would not proceed until outstanding private debts were paid. The thirteen creditors were mostly former indentured servants but Graham, his lawyer and merchants Leake, Solomon and Pratt were also determined that moneys would be paid before Peel departed the colony. They knew he would not leave before the new title was signed, sealed and in his hands. The total amount owed was £671 14s 1d.

Peel was devastated. For once he felt like letting go and running away to England. Mary put him right with a few home truths about financial implications and the future.

"It is not the end of the earth, Thomas. Pay the debts, gain the title, sell some more land and then follow us to London. You'll probably only be six months behind us. There is enough money to send us home, I presume?"

After financial calculations and a full family discussion, unusual in the

Peel family, it was decided that Mary and the girls would leave as planned, Thomas Junior would remain to assist his father on the farm. He wasn't at all enamoured of the idea of a formal schooling in England and made a great fuss about the possibilities of farming upstream on the Serpentine. Mrs Ayrton offered to stay on and care for the men of the family. She could not face the thought of the voyage home and anyway preferred Mandurah to London.

So eventually, Mrs Mary Peel and Misses Julia and Dora Peel sailed for England on the *Shepherd* on 2nd January 1840. Many tears were shed as Peel farewelled them at the jetty.

"Goodbye, Thomas. I will miss you, my husband. Please make every effort to sell some land. I look forward to your early arrival in London."

"I assure you that I will follow as soon as I am able, my dear," he said, as he gave his wife a final embrace.

Peel felt very alone when he returned to Mandurah. He found himself wandering around the house, down to the estuary and along the beach. Even the incessant chatter and giggling of the girls was preferable to this silence. Yet in typical fashion, it only took a week or so before he hardly thought about them at all.

In February, Peel travelled to Perth and signed for the title to his land. He was to pay an annual rental of one peppercorn for Location 16 Cockburn Sound.

Two weeks later he received a brief message from his brother William. It concluded:

> Under no circumstances should you consider returning to England while Father lives. I am certain that he will carry out his threat and you would sooner or later find yourself incarcerated in Newgate Prison.

CHAPTER 22
Religious Matters

Reverend George King LLD arrived in Fremantle in 1841, following his appointment to lead the growing parish and oversee the building of Fremantle's first church. Being young and enthusiastic, he looked forward to his first major challenge since ordination.

Blair had anticipated such an appointment and was not surprised when he was informed of King's impending arrival. The fact of the matter was that he was actually relieved at not having to continue the full responsibility for the parish. On meeting with King, it was agreed that he would assist in providing services for the settlements as far south as Mandurah.

The following year, a special commemoration service was held in the local hall after the laying of the foundation stone for St John's Church of England by Governor John Hutt. The parishioners gathered for the event and jokingly agreed that it was entirely appropriate that High Street should have a gaol at its western end and a church at its eastern end.

Peel was in Fremantle on his way home from the April meeting of the Road Trust in Perth and decided to attend the ceremony. He had been sorry to see Stirling go but got on tolerably well with Hutt. That is, apart from the Governor's intervention in a dispute between Peel and Francis Singleton the previous year. In a fit of pique, Peel had resigned from both the Legislative Council and the Bench of Magistrates.

He strolled up to the Governor. "Good afternoon, Your Excellency. How are you this fine day?" he said, interrupting Hutt's conversation with the Reverend Edmund Blair.

The Governor turned. "Ah! Mr Peel." Everyone had been extremely solicitous to Peel since Robert Peel had been reappointed Prime Minister the previous year. Peel did not answer. He was staring at the girl. Next to Blair was the most beautiful young woman he had ever seen. She was tall, with fair, almost white hair, curling around her face and the nape of her neck. Her eyes were a piercing blue. Her figure was stunning. Dammit! She was staring right back at him. Unflinchingly!

"You would know the Blairs, Mr Peel," Governor Hutt continued.

"I know Reverend and Mrs Blair," Peel said hesitating.

The Reverend Blair proudly took the lead. "May I present my daughter Sara Jane Andrews-Blair. Mr Thomas Peel, my dear."

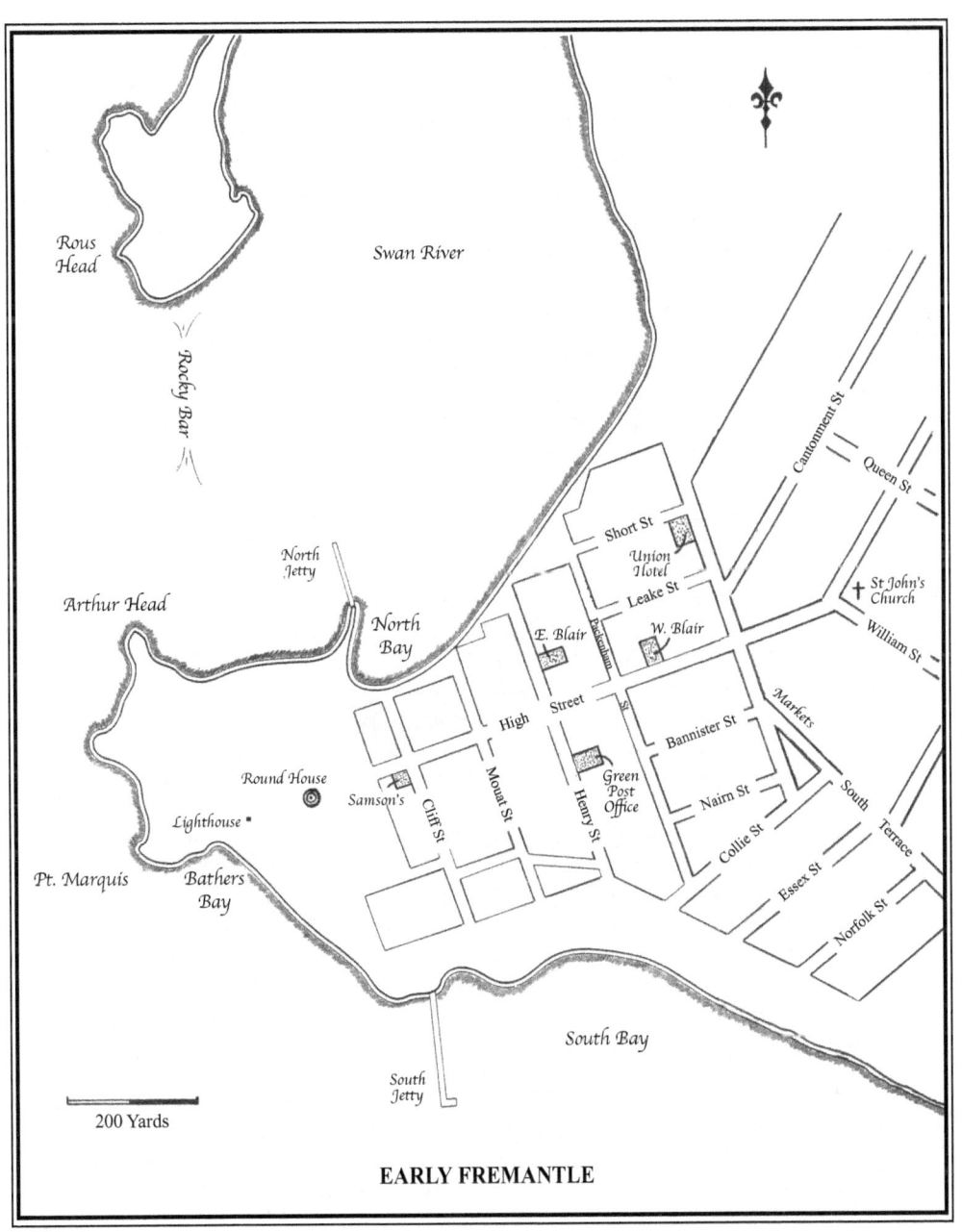

Rous
Head

Swan River

Rocky Bar

North
Jetty

Arthur Head

North
Bay

Short St

Union
Hotel

Leake St

E. Blair

W. Blair

St John's
Church

William St

Cantonment St

Queen St

High   Street

Round House

Samson's

Cliff St

Moat St

Henry St

Green
Post
Office

Bannister St

Markets

Nairn St

South

Collie St

Terrace

Essex St

Norfolk St

Lighthouse

Pt. Marquis

Bathers
Bay

South Bay

South
Jetty

200 Yards

EARLY FREMANTLE

Sara Jane extended her hand. "How do you do, Mr Peel. We have met previously. At your home in Mandurah, some years ago."

She was so graceful, so absolutely perfect, that he could hardly get the words out. "Er, yes, I remember now," Peel stammered, suddenly short of breath. He took her hand and bowed, holding it an unnecessarily long time. How could that filthy child have grown into such an elegant young woman?

As the group moved to the hall for afternoon tea, the Governor ushering the two ladies, Peel had one of his rash ideas.

"Blair, now that there are more permanent residents on the Murray, twenty-nine at last count, I am considering building a church near my home in Mandurah and requesting Reverend King to arrange for a minister. You presently visit us monthly. Do you enjoy the country experience?"

Blair knew exactly what was coming. "Yes, Mr Peel, indeed I do. Why do you ask?"

"Well, it would be my intention to provide a home for the minister and his family and of course an appropriate stipend. Would you be interested in such a position, Blair?"

"I find the proposition most interesting, Mr Peel, but I would need to discuss the matter with my family."

"Naturally. Perhaps we could explore the idea further on your next visit?" Peel pointedly strode off towards Reverend King.

William arrived home the following weekend and the question of relocation was discussed at length by the family.

"Mr Peel has promised a limestone building with a shingle roof for the church and a similarly constructed residence nearby. We would be provided with fresh produce from the farm and a buggy or cart placed at our disposal. I would receive a stipend and time off for a visit to Fremantle each month. Reverend King is of favourable disposition and would seek to contribute financially to the venture. I will be expected to conduct Divine Services each Sunday and attend to the spiritual needs of the settlers on the Murray as necessary."

"What do you want to do, my husband? I will always be content if you are happy."

Blair cleared his throat and looked serious.

"Thank you, my dear and I have always appreciated your commitment. However, we now have two children, almost adults and they also must be consulted."

No one spoke. The silence continued. William looked to Sara Jane and then back at his father.

"I'm away most of the time, so my opinion shouldn't count as much as Sara Jane's," he responded.

The young woman drew a deep breath. "I look forward to our new adventure, Father." And being closer to Yeddi, she thought.

So the decision was made. Reverend King and Mr Peel were informed, digs in a boarding house in Fremantle found for William, the house in Henry Street leased, the buggy sold but the horse kept, their furniture put into storage for transport on the supply boat and their belongings and provisions for the trip packed. Within the week, one of Peel's servants arrived with the bullock cart to transport the Blairs south.

That night, a most amazing celestial event occurred and continued throughout the journey south and while the family settled into their new home. Immediately after dark on 5th March, a strange light appeared in the west, slanting up from the horizon, like a tail emerging from an invisible core. It was very bright, large in size and grew larger each night for ten nights as it rose further above the horizon. Blair noted that it spread itself over a third of the firmament, its tail reaching to the belt of Orion. Sara Jane considered it quite awesome in its dimensions and intensity and hoped it to be a propitious sign for their relocation in Mandurah.

Their journey took four days. They followed the easily discernible track and found the regular signs for water where a large 'W' had been cut into the bark of a tree. Blair and Sara Jane took turns at riding Ascot which was a blessed relief from the cart. Because no outsiders were watching, Sara Jane was allowed to use 'a real saddle' as she called it and revelled in the opportunity. While poor Mrs Blair found the journey extremely uncomfortable bouncing around on the seat of the cart, Sara Jane enjoyed the freedom and took delight in bringing in a kangaroo on the last night, run down with Habbi's assistance and cooking it native style on the fire.

When they arrived in Mandurah, Peel showed them their new home. It was several hundred yards down the track towards the barracks and their furniture was already stacked on the front verandah. They all noticed that it was of wattle and daub construction with a bark roof held down with rough hewn beams but no one made comment.

"The church will be built between your house and mine," Peel said. "On the rise." He couldn't keep his eyes off Sara Jane and the young woman was fully aware of it.

"Thank you very much, Mr Peel," she said dismissing him, as she walked towards the house. "Follow me, Mother, as it appears we have much to do."

Mrs Blair and Sara Jane were instantly busy. The furniture was arranged in the rooms and the trunks and boxes unpacked. Curtains were hung and beds made. Blair drew water from the well and collected firewood. He then spent hours arranging his new 'contemplating cuddy' in the back room. Many of his books had been left for safe keeping with Reverend Wittenoom, who kept an extensive library in his Perth house.

Blair rummaged through a crate and came out to the kitchen beaming, waving a book excitedly. "I knew it to be no ordinary comet. It was Halley's Comet. It returns to earth's orbit for a short stay every seventy-six years. We have all been privileged to observe such a significant heavenly phenomenon. I will say a special prayer this evening before dinner."

* * * * *

Slowly the family settled into their new home. There was much to do but Peel occasionally sent a labourer to assist with the heavy work, such as fencing, a stable for the horse and shelving in the house. Meanwhile the building of the church commenced.

Sara Jane did the sensible thing and crafted hunting and fishing spears and a trap for crabs which were plentiful. Providing fresh seafood and kangaroo meat for the table was never a problem. The Blairs privately despaired when Sara Jane 'went native' as they called it and she was seen running barefoot along the shore, or swimming, albeit secretly, in her petticoat, or carrying the results of a successful hunt home over her shoulder.

However, she patiently explained that she did not want to discard the skills learned from her second family and in any case they needed the food. Blair had fostered independence and a strong will while educating both William and Sara Jane and really couldn't argue. In any case he adored his daughter and could refuse her nothing.

In the hope of seeing the young woman, Peel made it a point to ride more often but, apart from answering politely, Sara Jane made no attempt to foster conversation. On one occasion, when she was exercising Ascot in the shallows of the estuary and saw him approaching, she burst into a gallop and in spite of Peel's best efforts increased her lead as they raced home.

Peel became frustrated and invited Kypbi and Dukun to return as servants.

Eventually, on 1st June, while Perth celebrated Foundation Day, the Reverend King opened the newly completed church at Mandurah and after conducting the Divine Service, delivered an emotive address to the congregation. Personally, King considered it a shame that the church could not be consecrated but Peel refused to grant the land. However, a silver-plated chalice and paten donated by Peel's parish in England for use in Communion were blessed and placed on the altar. Peel was clearly proud of this touch. Along with everyone else in the colony, King found Peel an enigma, bordering on an eccentric. The only consistent behaviour he evinced was his irascibility.

* * * * *

Under pressure from the Colonial Secretary, Peel paid a further £375 off his debt to the Crown in late 1842 and again advertised in the *Perth Gazette* that Mandurah House was to be let for two years.

He was now determined to return to London and Mary. His brother William had written to inform him that their father was ill and Peel was prepared to take the chance that his father would die before he reached England.

Meanwhile, Thomas Junior regularly travelled to Serpentine Farm, which was leased by George and John Armstrong, brothers of Adam Junior and Francis. The lease would fall due shortly and Thomas Junior, now eighteen years of age, was eager to live there permanently.

"Father, you know it is my ambition to take on the overall responsibility for the property. That's why I didn't want to go with Mother. I didn't need that sort of education to do what I want to do. Just give me the chance."

Peel agreed to his son's request, subdivided an area of five thousand acres and deeded it to him. Mrs Ayrton offered to move to Serpentine Farm and housekeep for her grandson. She really had no choice, if her son-in-law was returning to England for good.

However, just when Peel needed to sell some land to pay for his expenses, Western Australia, along with the rest of the colonies in Australia, was plunged into a depression. It was a case of surviving not expanding and government and settlers alike were feeling the pinch. Peel's debt ballooned to £3,125, over one third of the total amount owed to the Crown by all the settlers. In fact, Peel's debt was increasing by an average of £156 per annum. Hutt received a stern reprimand from Lord Stanley, the Secretary of State, for his management of the colony's finances. Consequently, when Peel requested permission to sell some of his land, he received an affirmative answer but was told there could be no guarantee that a title would be issued, because unless the total debt was repaid, foreclosure of the mortgage, which fell due towards the end of the year, might be the only option remaining to the government.

Peel's hopes were dashed again. What buyer in his right mind would pay for land without the guarantee of a title? The answer was obvious. He returned to the house at Mandurah and lived alone, playing host to travellers and riding to Serpentine Farm, when he felt the need for company.

Two months later, Peel received a letter from his brother informing him of the death of their father.

* * * * *

The tide was out and on the turn. Ascot galloped along the foreshore, Sara Jane leaning over his neck and whispering encouragement. She headed for her favourite bay, where small islands dotted the water, just before the river expanded into the Peel Inlet. Here the dolphins fed. It wasn't as though they didn't feed everywhere in the enormous river system but Sara Jane knew their preferred area where the channel was deep and swept close to shore. Here they could dive and frolic to their hearts content, throwing mullet high into the air with their snouts and then leaping from the water in chase.

The dolphins knew her scent and trusted her. They allowed Sara Jane to swim and dive with them and she was never frightened. One particular dolphin with a white scar on his back would toss large fish onto the shore where they flapped until she collected them in her plaited bag. Mrs Blair was always mystified when presented with fish unmarked by spear barbs. Sara Jane said they were manna from heaven.

On this beach, Sara Jane waited for Yeddi on the morning of each full moon. If her father did not require the horse for church business she rode, otherwise she walked. Rain, hail or shine, she would wait for Yeddi. He couldn't always be there. Sometimes, he apologised for his absence the previous month, because he was carrying a message to another tribe or had been called to assist in a healing. Sara Jane understood, although his absence always saddened her, because it meant another month without his company.

Their empathy had developed as they matured but was based on a difference in communication ability. Because of Yeddi's special powers and training, he could receive signals emanating from Sarjan. He knew when she was happy, or sad, or wasn't feeling well. Her image could be sought in the flames when he wanted to see her. He worked hard at developing his powers, but sometimes the reverse did not occur. Sarjan could not always receive messages from him.

This morning, he was waiting. Sara Jane leapt from the horse and gave him a hug.

"Yeddi, you've trimmed your hair. I like it short."

He grinned. "How is my babbingur? You look wonderful. I think you've grown taller since I saw you two moons ago."

"I'd better put a stone on my head. I'm already up to your shoulder. Want a swim?"

There was no embarrassment, no coyness between them. There never had been. Yeddi dropped his loin cloth and woven headband and armbands. Sarjan, as she always became, pulled off her clothing. One black male, one white female dived together and came up laughing.

"Which island?" Yeddi asked.

"Pelican Island," she called. With strong overarm strokes she skimmed through the water and reached the beach first.

"You win as usual," said Yeddi panting, as he stood up behind her in the shallows. "I can run all day but I puff after a short swim. Race you round the island."

They took off together on a four hundred yard dash.

"You win as usual," Sarjan said, beaten by twenty yards. "Let's talk."

They always spent an hour or so catching up with the month's happenings. William was an atrocious correspondent and his activities sometimes remained a mystery, although infrequently Sara Jane saw him on their irregular journeys to Fremantle. Both were concerned about their 'other families', as they called them.

"Odern's joints continue to worsen and I don't seem to be able to do anything much about it. Grandmother Mandu and I have tried all the usual remedies. They just don't help as much any more. She says he grumbles all the time, except when I'm there."

"Father Blair lost another tooth last month. He eats only soft food, because his gums are sore. I dread growing old Yeddi, don't you?"

"Yes, of course. It seems such a long time away but I suppose it creeps up on you."

When the horse was available last summer, Sara Jane had made brief visits to see Mandu and Odern. On each occasion, she was dismayed to see the toll that time was taking on the elders.

"Anyway this is the way of things, Sarjan. Our elders have lived long and useful lives and will be remembered with reverence when they travel from this world. Race you back!"

* * * * *

Mrs Sarah Lyttleton arrived in Mandurah in 1843 to set up a boarding house. It was the same Sarah Lyttleton who had sailed on the *Gilmore* with Peel and the Andrews'. She was older and wiser, a widow, tired of the constant pressure of work in running her popular boarding house in Perth and yearning for the peace and quiet of a rural community.

When her husband died in 1835, Peel granted Mrs Lyttleton an acre of land in the centre of Peeltown near the ferry crossing and 400 acres on the Serpentine, in recompense for medical services rendered by the surgeon at Clarence but she had not taken up the grants. Now was the time! With the Australind scheme and the Vasse settlement to the south receiving publicity, more and more travellers were using the coastal track through Mandurah. She sold up, paid ten shillings in the pound to her creditors and left Perth.

Ever the independent woman, Sarah Lyttleton journeyed south alone, driving her own horse and cart. In usual style, she hadn't waited to communicate with anyone and therefore nobody knew she was coming. A labourer had been hired to build accommodation for her but he had further work in Fremantle and had not yet arrived. She set up her tent near the ferry on land she presumed was hers and was boiling a billy when Sara Jane rode past along the water's edge.

"Hello," called Mrs Lyttleton. "Would you like a cuppa?"

"Thank you. A cup of tea would be very much appreciated."

A bit well spoken for this neck of the woods mused the older woman as Sara Jane dismounted and tied the horse to a tree. Very pretty, with a natural, almost wild look about her. Bare-footed and sitting astride her horse too. There's an anomaly here. I'm going to like this girl.

The two women introduced one another. "Hmm. Sara Jane Andrews-Blair. You must be Annie Andrews' daughter." Sara Lyttleton had a twinkle in her eye and a broad friendly smile on her face. Her grey hair was drawn back into a long plait and a large straw hat sat perched on her head.

"Yes I am, Mrs Lyttleton," Sara Jane said with a puzzled expression on her face, "but you have me at a disadvantage."

The older woman roared with laughter, rose to her feet and gave Sara Jane a huge hug.

"I was on the *Gilmore* from England with my husband, John, the surgeon. Your mother and I were friends and spent many hours talking as we walked the deck together. A fine woman. You were only a tot. My daughter was also a Sarah Jane but spelt with an 'h'. She was seven and our son Edward three years old when we sailed. Edward returned to England on the *Champion* with Sir James Stirling in order to receive a grammar school education. My daughter lives in Perth and I'm due to become a grandmother later this year. Phew! I've told you the family history in a minute!" She paused. "Sara Jane, what happened to your parents? I seem to remember there was some sort of tragedy. It was about the time John died of consumption, when we were living in Albany."

Sara Jane told the story while they drank tea. She concluded, "So, the way I have chosen to see it is that, although I am sad at not growing up to know my real mother as any daughter would wish, I did gain an Aboriginal family and wonderful new English parents."

"You are wise beyond your years, my girl. Like another cuppa?"

Now Sara Jane was smiling. She didn't remember this woman but was glad their paths had crossed again. She was a real character. The younger woman insisted on taking Mrs Lyttleton home for the evening meal.

* * * * *

Mrs Lyttleton and the Blairs found the kind of friendship essential in a small settlement. They assisted one another when help was needed and provided the companionship of a like class from England. All were well educated and of the Anglican faith. Yet importantly they gave one another space when space was needed. It was a happy and productive relationship and one appreciated by all.

When the builder arrived from Fremantle, a wattle and daub residence was constructed on the very spot Mrs Lyttleton had pitched her tent. It consisted of three bedrooms, a parlour and kitchen. A stable and a large store were erected at the rear. Application was made for a publican's licence and when this was granted the Marine Hotel opened. At the same time, Mrs Lyttleton took over the running of the ferry and when the mail was re-routed from Pinjarra to

Mandurah, she became the postmistress, having experience in this business in Albany. She was determined to discharge her debts as soon as possible.

However, the ferry became a continual problem. The large boat often needed repairs and eventually had to be replaced by a smaller boat, requiring that any horses swim behind. Thomas Watson, who had been running the ferry service for her on Mrs Lyttleton's invitation, took it over on a lease arrangement in the second year.

At fifty-seven, Mrs Lyttleton's enthusiasm and ability to work long hours appeared to be waning. Sara Jane noticed that she moved more slowly and had lost some of her initial vitality, as though the two years in Mandurah had slowly drained the older woman's energy. Before long the Marine Hotel was leased to Watson, who moved from the Hall's cottage to the hotel to live and Sara Jane took over most of the mail business. It wasn't onerous and she enjoyed accepting some community responsibility. After a while the locals assumed that Sara Jane was the official postmistress.

* * * * *

The *Red Rover* arrived in Fremantle from Hong Kong in early May, 1845. While being unloaded at the jetty, a sick sailor, who should have remained in his hammock along with the other sick on board, slipped from the barque and joined the Friday evening crowd in the tavern on Mouat Street. He coughed, spluttered and rid himself of spittle onto the floor and nasal mucus onto his sleeve. He drank too much and spewed vomit onto bystanders. Then he passed out in a corner. The following morning, he crawled out onto the street and died. Within forty-eight hours, seventeen others who had been drinking at the tavern had developed the symptoms of the most deadly strain of influenza virus ever brought to Australia.

When a thirsty native stopped at the well outside Fremantle and drank from the bucket he fell ill and in terror of the white man's disease fled to his family in Barragup. Within the week, many of the Bindjareb tribe who had gathered for the fish mandjar were ill.

As soon as Odern realised what was happening he took Mandu and Yeddi to the side. "We must hasten away from this place. There is a sickness spreading. Gather your things together. We leave immediately for our cave."

Odern awoke two days later feeling dreadful. His body ached all over, his nose ran with thick yellow mucus, he sneezed continually and had a terrible headache and a wracking cough. Mandu and Yeddi did what they could, bathing Odern's body to cool the fever, forcing him to eat soft foods and to drink much water and giving him infusions of crushed eucalypt leaves, but they soon realised that the sickness would have to run its course.

Then the virus spread to Mandu and Yeddi and they became ill just as Odern began recovering. Odern did what he could but he was very weak and knew they would all die without someone to fetch food and water and administer the infusions. In his feverish condition, Yeddi kept calling for Sarjan. After carefully considering the alternatives and there certainly weren't many, Odern came to the conclusion that she was their only hope.

That night he peered into the fire and conjured up a picture of Sarjan, but in his weakened state, the image was not as clear as usual and he began to despair. There was one possibility. Odern concentrated all his efforts to entice the spirits to enter Yeddi's body. Working from within, they imparted strength and Yeddi raised himself to his elbows.

"What is happening, Great Uncle?"

"Yeddi, listen to me carefully. We are all very sick and need help urgently. I know you keep contact with Sarjan and that she is your babbingur. We are going to call her to come to us. It will be difficult, since she is not receptive as we are, but perhaps if we both try to communicate with her we might succeed. Are you ready?"

Yeddi felt terrible but put all his inner resources to work as he spoke through the flames to Sarjan.

"Sarjan. We see you. Mandu and Odern and I are sick. We need your help. Come to the cave."

With their combined powers the picture was well defined.

"There is hope," Odern said.

On the third time the message was repeated, the two men saw Sarjan put down her paint brush and rise from the table, a bewildered expression on her face. She looked around her, then stood riveted to the spot. "Yeddi," she said. "Yeddi."

The Blairs were in Fremantle on their monthly shopping trip, so the horse was available. Sara Jane stuffed the saddle bags, usually reserved for prayer books, with bread, biscuits, ham, cheese, pork pies and apples. As she passed, she called to Mrs Lyttleton, who was preparing a garden in front of the hotel.

"I'm going to my other family. They are sick. I might be away for days. Please let Mother and Father know."

Mrs Lyttleton nodded and waved as Sara Jane took off at a gallop.

By the time she arrived at the cave area, Ascot was covered in sweat and dirt. Leaving him unsaddled near the spring at the bottom of the hill to drink and graze, Sara Jane rushed up the hill and into the cave.

The three occupants opened their eyes. They looked ghastly. All were coughing and sputtering and having difficulty breathing. With horror, Sara Jane knew they were very ill indeed and possibly near death.

Yeddi gave a weak smile. "Sarjan," he whispered. "Sarjan, my babbingur."

"Oh, dear God! Please help me. I pray you, please help me." She prayed a great deal over the following days.

Sara Jane ministered to the sick family indefatigably. Each was sponged, fed and provided with eucalypt infusions at regular intervals daily. Sara Jane prepared some of her own concoctions, soaking the bark of the wattle tree in water to produce a liquid for drinking and crushing the leaves of what she called the weeping willow tree in hot water to provide an inhalant.

Odern continued to improve and within a few days, although weak, could help Sara Jane. Mandu still had a hacking cough but was now eating and on the mend. It was the strong young man, now emaciated and debilitated, who still remained seriously ill. He just kept regurgitating his food when he coughed. Sara Jane kept a constant vigil.

It was another two days before Yeddi started to mumble and managed to keep down his food.

Odern was fishing in the estuary, Sara Jane was grinding seeds for a gruel and Mandu was plaiting a possum fur headband for Yeddi when she heard a snuffling noise.

"Sarjan can you hear something at the back of the cave? A rat could be dangerous to Yeddi, if it comes looking for a feed during the night. He's on that side and we don't want to have to shift him."

"I'll have a look. We've never gone far into the caves. It gives me the creeps but we'll worry about Yeddi, if I don't."

Picking up a spear in her right hand and a burning banksia branch from the fire in her left, she cautiously made her way back into the cave.

Mandu waited nervously. The caves were never explored. They only used the entrance area as shelter. She shuddered. What if there is a rockfall, while Sarjan is hunting the rat? She could be trapped. What if she is bitten by a snake? She should never have suggested it.

Sara Jane appeared from behind the rock face with a large rat skewered on her spear. She swung it against the wall and it shrieked once before going limp. With a shake of the spear the carcass fell onto the coals and the fur flamed.

"There's a big cavern behind there," she said. "I'm going back again. I thought I saw something shining on the floor. It's not as scary as I expected." Picking up another torch from the fire, she disappeared behind the rock.

It was a few minutes before Sara Jane returned. "Look what I found, Mandu," she said holding out a handful of coins. "They were spread in a row on the ground. Probably in some sort of pouch or belt but the rats would have eaten it. There's a skeleton scattered around the back of the cave. Hope the poor man was dead before the rats attacked."

Mandu shuddered as she raked the cooked rat from the ashes.

Carrying firebrands, Sara Jane returned three more times before she was satisfied that she had found everything of value. "That's the lot," she said.

When Odern returned from fishing, Sara Jane was arranging the treasure into piles on a flat rock as she counted.

"Ten silver pieces, thirty-two gold pieces and all very old. I can see a 1650's date on some of them. And four beautiful rings. The skeleton must belong to a shipwrecked sailor. What an awful way to die, alone in a foreign land."

At that moment, Yeddi opened his eyes and said, "Water."

Sara Jane whooped, fell to her knees next to him, lifted his head and dripped water into his mouth from a wooden bowl. "Yeddi! Yeddi!" She kissed his forehead. "You're going to get better. Thank the Lord."

"Thank the spirits," added Odern.

The next morning Yeddi began to talk and managed to keep down his food and two days later, although still weak, was recovering well.

Sara Jane arrived back in Mandurah tired but happy. She explained what had happened in detail and showed her parents the treasure, as she called it. They were so pleased to see her that nothing was said about their worrying over her extended absence. Blair wrapped the treasure in oilskin and hid it behind a loose brick in the chimney. "I will make an appointment with Mr Broun and seek his advice about the matter on my next visit to Perth."

Meanwhile, after an itinerant labourer stopped for some work at Serpentine Farm, Mrs Ayrton had fallen ill. Thomas Junior, not knowing what to do, made his grandmother as comfortable as possible in the wagon and rushed her to his father's home. Within forty-eight hours Peel, Dukun and Kypbi were infected. The two native women returned to their families and passed on the virus.

When informed of their sickness, Mrs Lyttleton hurried to help the Peels. She managed to nurse them through the worst stage of the influenza bout before succumbing herself. Peel lived. Mrs Bridget Ayrton aged eighty-six years had a relapse and died. Sarah Lyttleton passed away four days later.

Miraculously, the Blairs did not fall prey to the virus and were a tower of strength in the small community. Mrs Blair cooked the results of Sara Jane's hunting expeditions, baked bread and made endless supplies of soup, which Sara Jane delivered to the ailing when she ministered to their needs. The Reverend Blair prayed for the sick, administered the last rights and conducted the funeral services.

"It is providence, my dear Mrs Blair," he said after a particularly exhausting day, when they were discussing the selective way the disease spread.

"All that matters is that our family has been spared. Blessed is the name of the Lord," his wife rejoined.

Within three months all but the most isolated settlements in the colony had cases of the virus. Not all succumbed but the very young and very old appeared particularly vulnerable. Unlike the whites, who had lived through epidemics of influenza since intercontinental travel had begun, the natives had no immunity. In hundreds they were infected and in hundreds they died.

* * * * *

In January 1846, on Reverend Blair's first trip to Perth after the epidemic, he made an appointment to take Sara Jane with him to meet Governor John Hutt and the Governor-elect Lieutenant-Colonel Andrew Clarke, who had recently arrived in the colony with his wife and family. They were residing at Government House as guests of Hutt until Clarke took over the administrator's position in several months time. Blair had been concerned about the cache of coins and rings that Sara Jane had found and wanted to know the procedural requirements for divulging the details and making an official claim on the find. In any event it was certainly a valuable discovery and would need to be lodged at the Western Australian Bank for safe-keeping.

They had booked into the United Services Tavern in St George's Terrace, a day earlier to spend time in outfitting Sara Jane, now nineteen, in the most fashionable clothing available. It really didn't worry Sara Jane very much but Mrs Blair could be very insistent on occasions, as her husband well knew.

"Just because we live at Mandurah doesn't mean that our standards should drop in any regard, my husband. I'm sure you will find the funds necessary for a complete wardrobe for our daughter. You know I would travel with you if it were not for my arthritis."

Money was available and the orders had been given, so to Shenton's store they went. The Reverend Blair handed over his beloved daughter to Mrs Guthrie, a stout matronly widow, who came strongly recommended to advise on suitable attire for every occasion.

"Now, my dear, the early Victorian look tends to be modest and somewhat sombre in colouring. Skirts now reach the ground and are swathed over many petticoats and a crinoline. This is a corsage, which fits tightly to give the body more shape." Mrs Guthrie paused looking down her nose through her spectacles at Sara Jane. "Although I must say that you do not seem to require much assistance in that direction." She smiled at the young woman, who was looking at her with a quizzical expression on her face. "Don't worry my dear. This introduction is usual and expected of me but I can shorten it, if you wish."

Sara Jane laughed. "Oh no, madam. I have a great deal to learn and will appreciate your tuition in these matters. Please proceed."

Thank goodness! This one has manners. Mrs Guthrie rustled around on a clothes rack and lifted several hangers onto a display hook. "Here we have a promenade dress of medium green silk and cotton with a dark green printed pattern. Note the general sentimentality in the style conveyed by the drooping of the shoulder-line. Accessories include this deep lavender silk mantelet with fringed edges, a lavender silk bonnet of the coal scuttle shape, white ribbons and white silk parasol. Of course, the hair would be parted in the middle with ringlets around the face." On each description a hand delicately indicated the item.

Another rustle and an afternoon dress of blue and white-striped silk with embroidered cambric collar and cuffs appeared. Then the evening dress indicating the growing popularity of the bertha. "Notice the broad horizontal draping of the bust, flounced with a fall of lace and complete with fan." Then the ball gown and so it went on.

When Mrs Guthrie finally asked whether she had any questions, Sara Jane inquired about riding gear. After a few minutes, the older woman emerged from a back room. "Here we have a habit of dark waterproof zephyr cloth, corsage decorated with buttons, gigot sleeves, petticoat, collar and cuffs of cambric trimmed with lace and a black beaver hat decorated with ostrich feathers and gauze veil."

"Mrs Guthrie, I ride astride."

"Oh! Well then, Miss Andrews-Blair, I suspect this outfit will not be appropriate." There was a twinkle in her eyes. "I shall find something more suitable."

Mrs Guthrie returned with several hangers of clothes and two boxes. "Such an outfit has been worn by the more daring," she said.

"Could I try it on, Mrs Guthrie?"

"Of course, my dear." As Sara Jane shed her clothing, the older woman wondered about the scar across her upper arm, the only blemish on a beautiful body but no explanation was forthcoming and she was never one to pry.

A few minutes later Sara Jane looked at herself in the mirror and nodded. So did Mrs Guthrie. The young woman was dressed in white doeskin trousers, a full sleeved white shirt ruffed at the throat and a plum-coloured Newmarket riding coat. Calf length boots of soft black leather and a black beaver hat added the final touches.

"The hat is called the Turf style and is quite the latest fashion."

"Rather looks like an upturned flower pot," remarked Sara Jane and they both burst into laughter.

"I love the outfit, Mrs Guthrie," she said, giving her a hug. "Thank you for your advice. Can we return to the dresses for size and I will need a long cape for winter and some night attire."

* * * * *

At 10 o'clock, the Reverend Blair and Sara Jane met Governor Hutt and Lieutenant-Colonel Andrew Clarke. The young woman looked fetching in one of her new outfits of navy blue and white.

After the Governor-elect had been introduced, Blair suggested that Sara Jane tell her story.

"Your Excellency, have you made Lieutenant-Colonel Clarke aware of my background in regard to being rescued by the natives on the death of my parents?"

"Er, yes, Miss Andrews-Blair. The situation has been explained."

Clarke nodded. "A most unusual story. I believe that you and your brother lived with the natives for two years."

Sara Jane waited for the Colonel to cease coughing into his handkerchief. He didn't seem very well at all. "Yes sir, I feel privileged to have had the experience. I will always recall those years with fond memories and be grateful for the lessons I learned and the love and care I received."

A remarkable story and a remarkable woman, Clarke decided.

Sara Jane continued. "During the influenza epidemic, I was called by Odern, the boylya gadak, a sort of medicine man, to assist the family, who had fallen prey to the influenza sweeping the colony. I was there for over a week ministering to their needs and am pleased to say they all recovered. While spearing a rat in the cave, I used burning torches for light and saw the glint of coins."

Blair was watching the facial expressions of Hutt and Clarke. He could barely contain himself. Here was this beautiful, young, obviously well educated woman relating an unlikely story to the two most highly-ranked men in the colony.

"Going back I found a total of forty-two gold and silver coins and two pairs of matched rings. Oh! And the scattered remains of a single skeleton. Since none of the coins were dated later than 1658 and allowing at least six months for a voyage to Batavia in the East Indies, the nearest outpost for European trade at that time, a ship from the Netherlands was probably wrecked on our coast, or a sailor for whatever reason was marooned. In any case, it could only be construed as an act of God. I therefore wish to lay claim to the items found."

Blair was now desperately trying to keep a straight face. There was a stunned silence for a moment and then Governor Hutt said, "Thank you, Miss Andrews-Blair. Could we see the items in question?"

Sara Jane produced a pouch and emptied the coins and rings onto the table.

"The coins seem to be from several different countries and the rings were probably destined for a husband and wife, as they are matching with one pair much smaller than the other. Engagement and wedding rings, I would think."

"Hmm," said Hutt. "You could very well be right." What deduction, what knowledge! In his estimation, she had just been upgraded from a remarkable to an exceptional young woman.

"Would you mind relating your observations to my aide-de-camp? He is of course entirely trustworthy. This whole matter will be recorded by Mr Broun and you will need to sign the declaration as a true statement. As guardian, your father will be required to verify the statement as far as he is aware of the facts and witness your signature, as will I. Meanwhile, I suggest my aide-de-camp seals the pouch with wax and places it in a safety deposit box at the bank. Because correspondence with the Colonial Office will also be required, you must understand that a decision is unlikely before the end of 1846."

The Governor turned to Blair. "Reverend, have you anything to add?"

"No, Your Excellency. I think my daughter put the matter quite succinctly."

CHAPTER 23

The American

Patrick Shaun Donovan O'Riley was an American of Irish extraction, who had lived his whole life in Boston. As was the custom, he married late, when his savings were sufficient to build a modest cottage not too far from the wharves where he worked as a longshoreman. Archina, a widow with three small children, had changed overnight from an obliging, happy woman eager to please him in every way to a nagging, unhappy harridan, who more often than not was too busy, too ill, or too tired to fulfil her wifely duties. The children, not having had the discipline of a father for some time, were ill-behaved and noisy. Two years later, he rued the day he had married. Gone was his debonair lifestyle and independence. He hadn't had marital sex for months and objected having to pay for it at the waterfront brothels.

Increasingly, O'Riley spent more time at the Seafarers Tavern and less time at home.

Sitting morosely in a corner of the bar, his huge muscular bulk overflowing the chair, he was lost in reflection about more carefree times. A soft voice broke through his reverie. "Could I fetch you another ale, Mr O'Riley?"

He looked up into soft brown eyes, a pretty face and long, black hair tied back with a yellow bow. "Thank you, Eliza. I'll go another." He should have married an attractive young thing like that, he brooded. Too late now. At thirty-nine and in the prime of my life, I'm trapped. What a miserable prospect!

As Eliza delivered his drink, a rowdy group of sailors poured through the swinging doors and positioned themselves along the bar. The spillover seated themselves at a table adjacent to O'Riley. Whalemen they'd be. Always seemed a jovial lot. Better paid than other seamen for their longer trips and more dangerous work. He'd been loading the *Jolly Rambler* with provisions this morning.

Before long O'Riley found himself included in their easy conversation. They had been in port for four weeks and were sailing on the evening tide. Off to Australia. They explained that the pods of humpback and southern right whales with their latest calves travelled slowly down the western coast between September and November on the way to their summer feeding grounds in Antarctic waters. The whalers followed them down as far as a settlement in King George Sound on the south coast.

"We're looking for crew," the bosun said. "Still short a few. We'd rather recruit from English-speaking countries because accidents always happen if there's a misunderstanding when you're in the whale boats. Too many lives at stake if orders aren't followed straight away when you're chasing." He eyed O'Riley's powerful shoulders. "You'd be a good'un at the oars or harpoon. Want a job?"

O'Riley was about to say "No", when he hesitated and replied, "Well actually, I would be interested in getting away and seeing more of the world. What does it pay?" And soon "How do I sign on?" and then "What do I need to take?"

Two hours later, with clothes in a canvas bag and his life savings of a few dollars in a leather purse, O'Riley boarded the *Jolly Rambler* and signed on for the round trip of about a year. There had been screaming and crying and begging from his wife, who cursed him for deserting the family but he didn't care. He'd never considered them his family anyway and was glad to be rid of them.

The whaler weighed anchor and sailed with the tide. Watching from the deck, O'Riley saw Boston fade into the twilight. He suddenly felt wonderfully free.

On the way to Australia, the *Jolly Rambler* called at Rio de Janeiro and Cape Town. O'Riley followed the lead of the other crew and traded with his few dollars for goods in one port to trade at the next to increase his wealth. He had a head for heights, didn't mind the difficult tasks aloft, enjoyed the rough all-male company and could hold his own in any brawl. While in Cape Town, he won a sizeable sum as the ship's champion for an arranged fight, knocking the other whaleman to the ground in the first round.

On their arrival at Fremantle, the men received portion of their pay and five days leave while the carpenters completed maintenance to the ship and provisions were loaded.

O'Riley went straight to the nearest tavern in Mouat Street and drank himself into oblivion. He woke up the following morning cold and wet-through on the sand at Bathers Bay with empty pockets, alongside several other crew members in exactly the same state. After returning to the ship for food and money, he repeated the previous day's activities, except that his headache was worse the second morning. He still hadn't had a woman and sex was now paramount in his mind.

On the third day, O'Riley played a different game. Alone, bathed and dressed in his cleanest clothes he entered a more up-market hotel in High Street called the Stag's Head. Sipping an ale slowly, he assessed the serving girls. One returned his glances and was certainly interested. In his best voice, he ordered food.

"Here you are, sir. Some nice ham, cheese and bread." She fluttered her eyelashes and gave an inviting smile. "You're an American, ain't you sir?" O'Riley carelessly threw an excessive amount of money onto the table.

"Yes and what would your name be?"

"I'm Matilda," she said giggling behind her left hand as she scooped most of the money into her apron pocket. Late teens, he reckoned and very pretty with flowing black hair and dark brown, almost black eyes.

"What time do you finish today, Matilda? I'd like to walk and talk with a pretty girl like you." And perform a few other tricks. He was becoming aroused. A quick glance told Matilda all she needed to know.

"I'll be finished at ten, Mr---," she paused.

"O'Riley. Patrick O'Riley. Then I shall wait for you, girlie." Just in case another randy sailor comes in the meantime, he thought.

The moon was nearly full and very bright as O'Riley and Matilda walked along the track by the Swan River. He towered over the slight girl. They made small talk to gauge the situation, as if they didn't already know it. O'Riley slipped his arm through hers and guided her to a white sandy beach The wind blew softly from the south-west.

"Ah, Matilda. I have some coins in my pocket. How much would you require to remain with me for the next hour?"

"Mr O'Riley, I would expect to be in bed in the next ten minutes." He started. "Calm yourself, sir. I would expect that you would join me." She laughed and kissed him, her tongue flickering around his lips before pushing its way into his mouth.

They were naked in bed in exactly ten minutes. The other woman had left the brush hovel at the back of the hotel on a nod from Matilda. There was no need for words. Matilda serviced O'Riley in the way barmaids had always serviced sailors. She gave him a double helping and because O'Riley wanted more of the same the next night, he promised to pay her double. It would nearly exhaust his money supply but would be worth it. As he left, he saw the other woman creep out of a shed and return inside.

On his last night in port, Matilda suggested that O'Riley remain with her till the morning. There was a price of course but the American was delighted with the arrangement and gave her the last of his coins. They enjoyed a gin before and after several vigorous bouts of sex and fell asleep in the early hours of the morning.

A bucket of cold water thrown over his head roused him. "Get up man, it's late. You'll miss your ship. Wake up! Wake up!" An older woman was shaking him.

O'Riley sat up to broad daylight. His head ached and he kept blinking his eyes to adjust to the light. "Oh, shit!" he roared, as he dragged on his canvas pants, hopping about on the hessian bag floor. "I didn't tell anyone where I was."

He ran from the hovel, sprinting down High Street and through the tunnel to Bathers Bay. His ship was not anchored in the bay! Panting, he peered towards Rottnest Island and could just make out sails on the horizon. With a fresh northerly wind filling her sails, the *Jolly Rambler* was on her way south without him.

Having no money or belongings and not knowing anyone in the town except Matilda, he headed back to the Stag's Head. The girl, looking a little the worse for wear, was serving drinks at the bar. O'Riley tried to muscle his way in but a new bunch of sailors held their positions.

"Push off sailor! Wait your turn!"

When O'Riley in desperation said "Matilda, I must speak with you. My ship has sailed and I need money." He received a blank look.

"Sir, we have not met. My name is Ester." He persisted with his pleas until a burly well dressed man emerged from behind the bar, thrust O'Riley's arm up behind his back, marched him to the door and shoved him onto the street where he lay sprawled on the sand. As he rose to protest, he was met by three angry sailors spoiling for a fight. One growled, "I said before to push off and I meant it. Leave Ester alone."

The American knew he was beaten but swore that next time he was in Fremantle, Matilda, or Ester, or whatever her name was, would suffer for his predicament. She should have woken him up. It was all her fault he had missed his ship. What was he to do?

O'Riley was in real trouble and knew it. He remembered the whalers talking about the Vasse or a name like it. He made some inquiries and found that whalers often took on supplies at the Vasse River. It was more than a hundred miles south, someone reckoned.

Wandering up and down the streets, he looked for a horse. A horse already saddled and unattended. He must steal a horse and make his way south as quickly as possible. If the *Jolly Rambler* stopped to do some whaling on the way, he might still have a chance to catch it at the Vasse.

It was nearly noon before he saw his chance. A dappled grey tied to a tree was grazing behind a large store. The horse whinnied softly as the man approached but was not afraid. O'Riley untied the reins, leapt onto the horse and kicking it into a gallop headed south.

By dusk, he was well on his way but took the precaution of turning east off the track to rest for the night. He found some flour, tea, sugar, cooking utensils and a tinderbox in the saddle bags and cooked a scone mixture which he ate with a mug of tea. Feeling much happier about his situation, he fell asleep.

The horse woke him at dawn, snickering for attention. It was thirsty, so he led it to a nearby lake to drink, filling the water bottle at the same time. Then he was on his way.

Several ramshackle buildings could be seen among the trees. They appeared deserted but he gave them a wide berth to be on the safe side. Eventually, the track meandered towards the coast and he came upon some more substantial buildings and what looked like a church. There didn't seem to be anyone around, so he left the horse at the back and slipped inside. On the altar were a plate and goblet made of sterling silver. He cursed silently when he saw the inscription 'Presented by W.A.H. Arundel to the Protestant Establishment at Swan River Western Australia'. Still, someone would take them off his hands, or they could always be melted down. In the corner he found a bottle of red wine, probably left over from the last service, he presumed.

He dropped his loot down the front of his shirt and sauntered from the church. Not being sure of the way, the American remained on the eastern side of the estuary as he rode south.

* * * * *

It was early June and the day of the full moon, so as arranged, Sara Jane waited for Yeddi at their secret waiting place. The trouble was that she never knew what time he would arrive or whether he would arrive at all. She sighed. She'd wait forever for Yeddi but each time she became more and more impatient. Because of religious duties, her father had needed Ascot and so she had walked. The sun was warm and so after a while she spread her cape on the ground, leaned against a paperbark tree and fell into a light sleep.

The sound of horse's hooves awoke her. It would be Mr Peel, she thought. Couldn't be anyone else as no one travelled on this side of the river. They all crossed over at the ferry site. What a nuisance he had become. She decided to pretend she was still asleep. Habbi was growling. "Hush, Habbi," she whispered and the dog fell silent.

O'Riley had consumed the bottle of wine and was both tipsy and thirsty. All his water was gone and he was hot. His face and neck were sunburnt and he wished he had a hat. He stood up in his stirrups. What was that up ahead underneath a tree?

Riding closer, he realised it was a person asleep. It was a girl! As he reined in, she opened her eyes and like a startled animal leapt to her feet and, backing away, slid around behind the tree, holding the trunk as a barrier between them.

He looked down at the most beautiful woman he had ever seen in his life. Wearing a long white dress with a wide-brimmed straw hat. Tall, lithe and healthy-looking. Huge blue eyes. Young, no rings, probably a virgin. His pulse quickened and he was overwhelmed by lust. He desperately wanted her.

Slowly she walked from behind the tree and stood staring at him. "Hello. Who are you?" she asked hesitantly.

"A visitor from over the sea." He shouldn't give too much away. The penalty for stealing a horse at home was hanging.

Sara Jane continued her appraisal making him feel uncomfortable. He was tall and powerfully built, his long, fair hair tied back with a piece of string. He was licking his lips as though thirsty and even though it was June was sunburnt. There was a twang in his voice and he was guarded, as if hiding something. He was unkempt, poorly dressed and barefoot. The horse must be borrowed or stolen. She decided she did not like this man but should remain polite and calm until Yeddi arrived.

"You must be thirsty." He nodded. "I can show you where to dig for water," she said in a quiet voice. "It's only a foot below the surface and is drinkable although a little brackish."

He dismounted and followed her. What a body! She walked like a cat. Educated too. A lady. Would make it all the better. He was going to enjoy the next hour.

"Thanks." O'Riley knelt and commenced digging, scooping the sand out in huge handfuls. He reached water in minutes.

"Let the water settle for a while before you drink." Instinctively, she thought she should distract him. For a few minutes, he impatiently waited, before slurping water from his cupped hands, watching her all the time. As the hole filled again, he dunked his water bag and then the horse took its turn.

"What's your name, girlie?" He had the most peculiar look on his face. Like the look that sometimes appeared on Mr Peel's face but much more pronounced. She didn't like it at all and for the first time in her life, she felt frightened, really frightened. It was an extremely uncomfortable feeling. Worst of all, she was trapped, unless she could reach the horse. Her only hope was the horse.

Although terrified, Sara Jane forced herself to assume a relaxed stance and began to stroke the horse. "Sara Jane," she answered. "What's the horse's name?"

"I don't know," he said and then realised he had given the game away.

He rose to a standing position. Sara Jane made a grab for the saddle pommel, but a long arm beat her to it and another gripped her wrist tightly.

"You're not going anywhere, girlie. Let's be friendly," and he put his arm around her and began pulling her close. Sara Jane screamed. Her hat fell to the ground. Habbi charged at the man barking and snapping but he was a very old dog now and slow. O'Riley produced a flick knife and slit the dog's throat. Habbi fell to the ground making peculiar slurping noises.

Sara Jane fought as hard as she could but the man was far too strong. He just held her at arm's length while she screamed and kicked and tried desperately to escape. All to no avail. Meanwhile, to her fury, he laughed uproariously.

Then the man stopped laughing and bent down to slobber all over her face. The stench of stale wine, rotten teeth and bad breath was overpowering. She bit his lip. He retaliated with a slap across the face, which made her nose bleed. She kicked his shin and received a harder kick in return. He then lost his temper and began to give her back handers to the face.

"You bitch," he yelled. "You're just like all women. Look as though you want it. Lead a man on with your pretty looks and then reject him. Well, I'll show you what a real man can do. Like it or not, I'll show you a thing or two." Out of control, O'Riley was shaking her backwards and forwards.

Petrified, Sara Jane gave up fighting. She bled from her nose and mouth and cuts and scratches from his nails. Red marks were appearing on her neck and arms and one eye was closing. She stood still.

Foam specks appeared at the corners of his mouth and his eyes glazed with desire as he ripped her dress from neck to hem. He released his rope belt and she looked at him in horror, as she realised what was going to happen.

Growling and muttering, he shoved her to the sand, placed his left arm across her neck to hold her down and forced her thighs apart with strong legs. He tore her pantalets to pieces and began pushing. Sara Jane screamed in pain, but he just kept thrusting and the scream sounded like a gurgle. Then she could not breathe. His arm was choking her. I am going to die, she thought. Then, please let me die, she whispered soundlessly.

As Sara Jane passed into a semiconscious state, O'Riley's body was pulled roughly from her. Yeddi knelt beside the person he loved more than anybody in his world, tears running down his cheeks. "Oh Sarjan, please be alive," he whispered. "Spirits hear me," he pleaded. She was breathing. There was hope.

Carefully Yeddi lifted Sara Jane and laid her on her cape in the shade of the paper bark tree. Wetting a piece of her petticoat, he gently bathed her face. She was bleeding from the groin area. He covered her with the torn dress.

Yeddi sat and waited. It was both an impatient and patient wait. Sarjan's body needed time.

Ten minutes passed and Sara Jane remained unconscious. Yeddi sat holding her hand, willing her to accept his strength of body and feeling. Ten yards away, shining black and green flies clustered on the huge wound made by the kodjah on the side of the dead man's head and drank from the blood that dripped onto the sand. Yeddi, usually so temperate, hated this man with a ferocity he had never experienced before. The intensity of his loathing was frightening. As reality returned, he knew that he must dispose of the body, for Sarjan's sake as well as his own. She had been violated but he had killed a white man.

Yeddi tied Sarjan's hat by its bow to a branch over her head and it swung in the wind, keeping away the persistent flies. He dragged the corpse to the water's edge and waded through the shallows to the deep channel. Small fish attracted by the blood followed him. There was a strong incoming tide, which by Yeddi's estimation would continue to flow for several hours. He let the corpse go and it was swept away slowly up river. To make sure, several dolphins appeared to assist it on its way by nudging it along. Yeddi shook his head in disbelief but then knowing how the dolphins felt about Sarjan, anything was possible. He gave a malevolent smirk, an unusual expression for him. By dawn tomorrow, there would be little left of the man's body. The fish, crabs and marine birds would make sure of that and the high tide would wash away the signs of the struggle and the blood on the sand.

Habbi was buried in the shade of a eucalypt tree and thanked for the happiness he had brought to three children.

Yeddi resumed his vigil sitting next to his babbingur. Time passed before he sensed rather than saw a change. Then she opened her eyes and seeing Yeddi whispered his name.

He cradled her head with his arm. "Sarjan, don't try to get up yet. Listen, while I tell you what has happened." He related his story from when he arrived until the disposal of the body.

"Habbi?"

"I'm sorry, my babbingur. Habbi was dead. I buried him under the gum tree behind you."

Tears came to her eyes and ran down her cheeks. "Yeddi, I was so frightened and he hurt me badly. No one has ever hurt me before. And he knifed Habbi." Her swollen lips and tongue slurred the words.

"He won't hurt anyone again, my Sarjan. If only I had been earlier, all this wouldn't have happened." He bent down and kissed her forehead.

"Don't blame yourself, Yeddi. I should have been more careful and not so trusting."

"Sarjan, that is your nature." Then his soft expression changed and he looked at her seriously. "I must take you away from here. What will we do with the horse? We can't take it back. Can we let it loose up here so that you can find it another time?"

"Yes. Hide the saddle and gear in the bush."

When Yeddi returned, he dropped to his knees beside Sara Jane. "Sarjan, can you stand?"

"I'll see soon enough." He helped her as she slowly rose to her feet, grimacing at the pain.

"I'm so sore all over and feel horrible. I must cleanse myself of this shame" and she walked slowly to the water's edge, knelt and washed herself all over several times.

"Yeddi," she said as she pulled on the torn dress, picked up what was left of her underclothing and untied her hat from the tree. "Please take me home."

Yeddi lifted Sara Jane with strong, yet so gentle, arms and carried her the two miles to the Blair's cottage.

* * * * *

Sara Jane refused to talk about her injuries, nor offered an explanation for her torn clothes or the disappearance of Habbi. There was no need to concern her mother and father. It was over and she had learned a lesson she would never forget. Part of the lesson was not to be so trusting. When she pondered over this, she decided that she would never again put her trust in a stranger, especially a white male stranger.

Reverend Blair spoke quietly to his worried wife about the American, who had missed his ship and caused trouble in Fremantle. The settlers at Rockingham had told the story of a missing horse and the likelihood of the sailor travelling south to catch his ship in Geographe Bay. They had been asked to apprehend the man if possible. "It all fits together, my dear. It appears our Sara Jane had a lucky escape, thanks to Yeddi. She does not wish to discuss the matter and that is really her prerogative. She is twenty years of age and we should allow her that discretion."

It took a long time before Sara Jane found herself able to relax. She was nervous and jumped at the slightest sound or sudden movement. Her body healed much sooner than her mind.

A month after the incident, she arrived back at the cottage with a horse and told the story that she had found it wandering free further up the estuary. She had also found the horse's saddle and the chalice and paten stolen from the church. The horse was returned to its owner via an officer of the 51st Regiment on the next supply ship returning to Fremantle and the silverware was returned to Peel. When thanked, Blair said "God's will be done," which was a little too cryptic for Peel. Blair declined to accept any rewards saying it was his duty to return stolen property. People wondered what had happened to the American.

CHAPTER 24
A Coming Together

From the time of the attack, by mutual agreement, Sara Jane met Yeddi weekly. Her babbingur was now more important to her than ever before. She counted the days until they met and prayed that nothing would keep him away. Nothing would. Yeddi had resolved that he would always be at their bay, now cleansed by many tides, every Monday morning. However, on Sarjan's request, they now met on a small, lightly wooded island about a hundred yards from the river bank. At low tide, it was a walk through puddles but when the tide was at its highest it was necessary to wade through thigh deep water. Somehow, it made Sara Jane feel safer. The episode with the American was never mentioned.

The Blairs did not interfere nor pass judgment. Rightly so, Blair acknowledged the possibility of his daughter choosing Yeddi, if a choice was forced.

Meetings were magic moments. They chased and swam and played with the dolphins. If the water was cold, they didn't notice it. They talked and laughed and teased one another. They speared fish, dived for crabs, caught birds and reptiles and lunched on nature's bounty. They were in love and did not know it. Neither had recognised the extent or significance of this wild happiness when they were together and sad yearning when they were apart.

Yeddi was asleep in the shade of a tree after their midday meal. Wet black hair shone and curled tightly. The straight nose, flared nostrils and prominent chin depicted a certain determination and yet long eyelashes, high cheek bones and full lips gave his face a sensuous appearance. His beard was wispy and like his hair kept short. From being of light frame some years ago, he was now muscled and his shoulders were broad. Long legs stretched out into the sun and his abdomen was flat, bound by sheets of muscle and tendinous fibres. Slender fingers indicated his creative and healing inclinations.

Sara Jane leaned over and tickled his foot with a leaf. Reflex drew it away and he awoke. With a wicked grin, Yeddi made a grab for Sarjan but she was too quick. The chase was on but he caught her in a matter of yards. Laughing, they tumbled to the sand together.

All at once everything was different. They felt the difference together. It was as though the playful children were instantly transformed into loving adults. They looked at one another and saw a new person. Someone each had not seen before and yet had known for years.

"Sarjan," Yeddi said in a husky voice that he did not recognise as his own. "My babbingur, my loved one."

She pulled his head to hers. Their lips brushed and then she kissed him gently, savouring the moment. "Yeddi, I have always loved you."

Slowly they began to explore one another's body. Tenderly and wondrously their fingers set their love on fire. They stroked and kissed and nudged, until aroused by passion Yeddi gently guided himself into her welcoming flesh. Sarjan cried out once, as Yeddi plunged deeper but then the pain turned to a new and exquisite feeling and she was lifted to a height of excitement and pleasure she had never experienced. Gasping with surprise and delight, they stayed clasped tightly together. Yeddi bent down and kissed her lovingly.

For the first time, Sarjan and Yeddi remained on their island overnight.

* * * * *

In May 1847, Blair received a letter from Governor Clarke enclosing a document stating in part that forty-two coins, as designated and four rings, as described, found by Miss Sara Jane Andrews-Blair in a cave south of Mandurah had been officially recognised as his property forthwith. In the meantime, they would remain in the Western Australian Bank for safekeeping. It had taken sixteen months for official approval to be given!

Sara Jane gave a series of whoops. "William will have his boat," she said clasping her hands together with a smile. "Father, we must write to William and tell him the good news."

It was two months before William answered the letter. He had been on a voyage to King George Sound and during strong winds had split the mast and he had been forced to wait for a replacement to be transported from Fremantle. He would now remain in Fremantle until his sister and father arrived and would seek information and prices of suitable vessels for sale. William was clearly excited.

And so in early August, Blair and Sara Jane sailed to Fremantle on the supply vessel to meet with William. He waited on the lower landing of the jetty. Sara Jane ran across the gangway and was gathered up in strong arms and swung around. She loved her brother dearly but was lucky to see him several times a year. After seven years a sailor, he was tall with a well proportioned physique. From loading and unloading cargo and pulling on sails and tiller, he had developed a powerful chest and his arms rippled with muscles. Hair and beard were bleached by the salt water and sun and he was tanned a deep brown.

"Well! Aren't we the clever one, finding a treasure trove. I hope it's a secret. It's much easier to deal and make a good purchase if people think you're scratching for the money."

"As far as I am aware, my brother, no one knows except the Governor, the aide-de camp and Mr Broun and they would be required to remain silent on the matter. What have you found? Are there any suitable boats for sale?"

A huge grin spread across his face. "There just happens to be a beauty advertised in the *Fremantle Observer* this week. We'll have a look at it after you're settled."

Blair joined them and received a firm hand shake. "Hello, Father."

"Hello, Son. You're looking well. Your mother sends her love and best wishes. The arthritis is worrying her lately but apart from that everything is fine."

William picked up their bags as they were unloaded. "I've booked you into the Royal Hotel in Henry Street. It's the best in town at present." The threesome chatted happily while they strolled to the hotel and dropped the luggage. They passed the Blair's house on the way and were pleased to see that the tenants were keeping it in good order.

As they approached the Fremantle agency of the Western Australian Bank, Sara Jane turned to her brother. "I ask one boon, my lord."

William stopped and bowed. "Of course, my lady. Your wish is my command."

"Then, my lord, I ask to retain one coin of the treasure cache. One 1657 gold unite. It was minted when Oliver Cromwell was the Lord Protector of the Commonwealth of England after they beheaded Charles 1."

Blair joined in. "Ah! Your favourite period of history, my dear."

"Yes and something to remember the past in many ways."

* * * * *

The bank manager, Mr W. D. Moore Esquire welcomed them into his office. Seated behind his large desk, his thumbs in the pockets of his waistcoat, he leaned back and assumed a look he considered appropriate for his position.

Introductions completed, Moore said "Ah, I believe you have accounts at the Bank." They all nodded. "What exactly can I do for you?"

Sara Jane answered. "Sir, I will need you to fetch an article from your safe, deposited by Mr Francis Lochee of your Perth Office on his last visit to Fremantle. It will be sealed and labelled with my name. Then I hope we can do business."

"Humph, yes, of course." He rang a bell and a young man hurried in. "Taggart, fetch the article for Miss Andrews-Blair from the safe." Moore was surprised to see the two men defer to the young woman. Most unusual.

Taggart returned with a battered pouch, handed it to the young woman and left the room. Sara Jane drew a sheaf of papers from her handbag and chose one to pass to the manager. He scanned it quickly and turned to Blair. "Sir, this document is addressed to you and signed by the Governor."

"That is so, Mr Moore. However, the contents of the pouch belong to my daughter. Therefore she will negotiate."

"Highly irregular to do business with a woman. Is she of age?"

"Mr Moore, please direct your questions to my daughter. She is quite capable of answering them herself."

Sara Jane smiled sweetly, as she watched Mr Moore frown and pull on his chin.

"Miss Andrews-Blair. Are you of age?"

"No, Mr Moore but would you please peruse this letter." A second letter was handed over.

Mr Moore's frown deepened and he turned to Blair. "As guardian, Reverend Blair you have a right by law to control your daughter's finances."

"You are quite correct sir, but I have chosen not to observe that prerogative. As you can see from the letter, I have legally nullified that right. Any money in my daughter's account is henceforth hers. My statement has received the sanction of the colony's leading lawyer, Mr George Stone. One of your bank's directors, I believe." He paused. "I sense you have a problem, Mr Moore?"

"No, no. Not at all, sir. All is in order. Let us proceed," he stammered.

The sweet smile and look of innocence lingered on Sara Jane's face. William felt sorry for Moore. His position of authority was quickly being eroded.

Sara Jane emptied the contents of the pouch onto the edge of the desk. One coin kept spinning and seemed to mesmerise the manager. When it settled, Sara Jane saw it was a gold unite dated 1657. She picked the coin up and placed it in her purse.

"Mr Moore, on the table are thirty-one gold coins and ten silver coins, together with four gold rings, two of which are encrusted with small rubies and emeralds. We would like three confidential and independent written valuations of the worth of each item in three days' time. The items are not to be taken out of your sight, except to be placed in the safe. We will then be pleased to sell the coins and perhaps the rings through an agent appointed by the Western Australian Bank, allowing of course a reasonable commission for services rendered. Would that be acceptable, sir?"

Moore looked stunned. "Er, quite so Miss Andrews-Blair. A satisfactory arrangement, I'm sure. Could I ask what security you have in terms of the items."

"Why, Mr Moore, we will have your supervision and my paintings." She stood and placed several sheets of paper in front of him. Meticulous representations of each coin and ring had been painted. "Both recto and verso sides have been drawn, with annotations, so there can be no confusion."

Three days later, at exactly the same time, the Blairs arrived back at the bank and were ushered into the manager's office. This time Mr Moore stood and welcomed his clients. "Please be seated," he said. A nervous cough followed. "I have here three itemised valuations for your consideration. When you have concluded your deliberations, please ring the bell and I shall return to be apprised of your decision and directions."

On the bell, Mr Moore returned to his seat. Sara Jane began. "Thank you, Mr Moore. We believe the assessments to be thorough and professional. They are likely to be fair, because the local experts have placed similar values on all the individual items, except the rings with the precious stones. I expect that is partly due to each individual's artistic leanings."

Moore blinked and then nodded. "I concur with your conclusions, Miss Andrews-Blair. Exactly the same supposition entered my mind."

"So," Sara Jane continued, "we accept the valuation of £596. Will the Bank buy the goods at that price and what commission would you expect for its services to date?"

Moore cleared his throat. "Yes, that price is reasonable. Would ten per cent commission be acceptable?"

"We were rather expecting around eight per cent, Mr Moore," Sara Jane rejoined.

Moore sighed. "Very well, Miss Andrews-Blair, I will have the papers drawn up for your signature immediately. Meanwhile, £596 less eight per cent commission will be placed into your bank account today."

"Rounded that's hmm - £548. Wonderful, it's more than enough," William said and positively smirked.

Moore's eyes rolled. "I hope you will all continue to invest in the Western Australian Bank," he said as he rose to his feet. And to Blair, "Your daughter and son do you proud, Reverend Blair."

"Thank you, Mr Moore. I agree entirely with your sentiments."

The following day, the Blairs were taken for a sail around Carnac Island in the cutter *Gull* by its owner Captain Neil Stewart. William acted as the for'ard hand and found it a well balanced rig, combining speed with seaworthiness.

"I'm back to Scotland," Stewart said in a broad brogue. "My wife's parents are old and my father-in-law wants me to take over his shipping business. Rather larger concern than mine, I must say. I'm not looking forward to the weather in the North Sea. Sorry to go actually. I, for one, have done well in the colony."

Stewart offered to give the names and details of his clients to William. "Good luck to you, young fellow. May King Neptune favour you," and he smiled as they shook hands on the deal.

William was ecstatic. He examined every inch of the vessel and found the timbers and sails in good condition. The planks were of local jarrah which, although heavier than other timbers, was more resistant to wood rot and borers.

Apart from some cover over the forward section, it was largely open to provide maximum storage space.

So William Blair became the proud owner of a cutter of 25 tonnes which he renamed the *Sara Jane*. It was 36 feet long from stem to stern, 10 feet in beam and drew 6 feet of water. With a single mast rigged fore and aft, it carried a mainsail and two head sails. The cutter was normally anchored off Bathers Bay, although Stewart advised William to seek a safe anchorage off Parker Point on the south coast of Rottnest Island, if a storm threatened from the north-west.

The arrangement was that Sara Jane paid for the vessel, William sailed it and the profits were to be shared 60/40 in the skipper's favour and paid into their respective accounts at the Fremantle agency of the Western Australian Bank. The papers indicated William to be the owner. He considered this unfair to his sister but she insisted.

"It is right and proper, my brother. It was a chance discovery that provided us the capital. You will work hard and I will receive a share. In any case, who has ever heard of a woman owning a boat?"

Sara Jane and her father returned to Mandurah. It was now mid-August and cold and wet. Both the Serpentine and Murray Rivers had flooded that winter and water collected everywhere in the low lying areas. Sara Jane realised how much her parents' health was deteriorating. Her mother's arthritis was so bad that sometimes she could not walk. Her father coughed continually and his eyesight and hearing were failing. His commitment to the settlers was only a single service each Sunday and he was now too frightened to ride the horse. Sara Jane knew that if she did not encourage a decision about a return to England, they would end their days in a scarcely adequate cottage in Mandurah.

She met Yeddi the following Monday. "Yeddi, what am I going to do? My mother keeps talking about home and how she will never see her sisters and nieces and nephews again. As she becomes despondent, so my father becomes despondent."

"I worry too, Sarjan. Grandmother and Great Uncle are so frail. When you last visited you saw how resigned they had become to being old. Oh, I never want to grow old. I want to be with you, loving you as I do, forever."

That night they built a fire with spare wood to fuel it till dawn and, covered by Yeddi's buka, nestled warm and comfortable in each other's arms as only lovers can.

* * * * *

Sara Jane knocked on the door of Mandurah house and it was opened by Peel. "Mr Peel, may I talk to you about my parents?"

"Come in my dear and warm yourself at the fire. Of course we can talk. You know I am always available for you. Didn't you come to me when you needed to return to civilisation? Now, what can I do for you?" Sara Jane could not abide this unctuous attention but sat down and proceeded. If only he wasn't so changeable.

"Mr Peel, I worry about my parents. They are growing old. My father is now sixty-eight and my mother sixty-five years of age. They have given their all to the colony since they arrived but now miss the comforts of their home near Swindon in England. It slips out occasionally, especially more recently when they have begun reminiscing about family. I feel beholden to do something for them, because they have been so generous in their care of us. The solution is to ask them to take me to England to show me London and their home and to meet their families, who will become my families. I know if I take that approach they will pack up and return for what they think is my sake. What I need to know is whether my father is on contract to you?"

"No. There was never a contract. Your parents are free to go when they please." Peel gave a piteous sigh. "I also yearn for my family. But circumstances still prevent me from travelling home. I fear dying in this hovel, in this forgotten settlement."

"I'm sorry, Mr Peel. I was unaware of your situation."

"Not your fault, young woman. However, all the more reason why you should do what you have suggested. You're like your mother, unselfish and caring. Do what you feel you should. It will be right I'm sure."

* * * * *

Sara Jane dreaded the next meeting with Yeddi. Her emotions seemed to be tearing her apart as she rode Ascot along the edge of the estuary. She knew that what she had chosen to do was the best decision for her parents and the worst for Yeddi and herself.

"How can I go?" she asked herself. "How can you not go?" she answered.

Yeddi was at first shattered. "My Sarjan, my babbingur. What will I do without you?" Then, as he watched the tears running down her face and realised the sacrifice she was making, albeit on both their behalves, he said, "It is all right, Sarjan, I understand. You must do this for them. I am being selfish. Promise you'll return, my loved one?"

"I will, my babbingur. My heart rests with you and I must come back to reclaim it."

They rode together on Ascot to the caves area. Sara Jane was saddened to see how frail Odern and Mandu had become in the few months since she had seen them last. She explained the situation and received the understanding she knew would be forthcoming from them.

Odern took her hands and looked deep into bright blue eyes. "Sometimes, we must do things for others that cause us much anguish, because they are for the best, even though at the time one is unsure whether this is so. You must trust your judgment, Sarjan."

* * * * *

And so it was that Sara Jane asked to be taken to England. The Blairs accepted the request as genuine and became excited at the prospect of returning home. A letter was written to Brian Hutchison, a reputable shipping agent in Fremantle regarding suitable accommodation on the first available vessel leaving for London. On their arrival at the port, Blair informed William that the house in Henry Street would be transferred into his name and that he should continue the arrangements with the Western Australian Bank with regard to his sister's share of the profits from the business venture.

William accepted the proposed arrangements and saw through Sara Jane's feigned pleasure and anticipation at travelling to England.

"Sara Jane, it's a wonderful present you are giving our parents, although I suspect it is a pretence about desiring to go to England. You don't really want to leave the colony do you?"

"No, my brother but we owe them so much and this way, in an indirect fashion, I am able to repay them on behalf of both of us. However, William there is one special request I ask of you. I need you to remain in contact with Yeddi. It is very important to me that when you write you can let me know how he fares."

"Of course, Sara Jane. It's a bargain."

CHAPTER 25

Cape Town

On 27th September 1847, William Blair farewelled his family on South Jetty, as they prepared to board a lighter to be ferried out to Gage Roads. They were to share a comfortable cabin on the *Lady Ursula*, a first class vessel of 450 tonnes burden.

Besides the Blairs, a Mr and Mrs Ian Noack were returning to England after assisting their sons establish a farm in the York district. They were a quiet couple and apart from sharing the main salon for dining purposes and the occasional game of whist, largely kept to themselves. However, they appreciated Reverend Blair leading prayers and the singing of hymns on Sundays.

The Blairs packed little luggage and those that they did take were mainly personal items. Furniture, and all but the Reverend's most precious books, were placed in the Henry Street cottage for William. Mrs Blair said that new apparel could be purchased in London but Sara Jane insisted in taking all her recently acquired clothing. In addition, she packed a valise with books to read, writing paper to record interesting aspects of shipboard life and her painting materials for visual representations of her travels.

However, Sara Jane spent none of her time at her favourite pastimes. Within a day of leaving Fremantle she was sick and sick again and again. For days, she could keep nothing down, especially in the mornings. It was an awful experience for a young woman, who had always been blessed with excellent health. Mrs Blair tried everything she knew, to no avail. A light porridge, lots of fluids, castor oil and bromide of sodium and Epsom salts, courtesy of the Captain, were tried in turn. Sara Jane continued to vomit. She stopped eating and remained in bed but that didn't help, as she then had severe spasms of dry reaching.

"Pray, Mr Blair, pray with all your might," his wife pleaded, then demanded.

A regime of light porridge and copious amounts of fluids was resumed. Sara Jane had to have sustenance. It was now seven weeks and her daughter was wasting away.

As the ship ploughed through the westerly swells, Mrs Blair made a decision.

"Mr Blair, we must leave the ship at Cape Town. Sara Jane needs a complete rest away from the rolling of the ship and she must receive proper medical attention. Do you have any connections in the Cape Colony?"

Blair was worried. His daughter had not responded to any of the treatments or medicine and his wife's counsel was sensible. There really was no alternative.

"Hmm. There was a fellow who graduated from Oxford with a Master in Arts a long time after me and was ordained soon after. About twenty years behind me, I think. Was appointed to the parish at Purton. Do you remember that young chap? Cameron Roberts was his name. He always talked about Africa and I vaguely remember someone writing and telling me that he went to Cape Colony, on its ratification as a British possession after the Napoleonic Wars. I have no idea if he's still there but I suppose it's possible."

Two days later, the ship rounded the Cape of Good Hope, sailed up the west coast and into Table Bay, escorted by myriads of birds. Shrouded in mist and cloud from a sudden squall, a hazy mass of stark, scarred mountains crowded the skyline to the south. The ship hove to and waited for the weather to clear. The crew nervously spoke about the remains of two unlucky vessels that could be seen wrecked on the shore.

When the wind dropped and the sun came out, the view of the mountains was breathtaking and the Captain pointed out Devil's Peak, Table Mountain and Signal Hill to the Blairs and Noacks.

"The white cloud around the top of the mountain is called its table cloth and if you look carefully, or with a little imagination, you can see the Lion's Head and Lion's Rump. Local legend has it that Table Mountain draws people to Cape Town. It is supposed to have magnetic qualities." A cannon shot, signalling their entrance to the Bay, echoed from the lookout station.

When Reverend Blair and Mrs Blair had said their farewells, they assisted a pale and weak Sara Jane into the longboat. The luggage followed and the crew rowed them to the wharf. Blair waved down a coach and pair and they were taken to what their black driver described as the best hotel in Cape Town, the Cape Town Inn. After Sara Jane was put to bed, Blair set off for Government House to pay his respects to Sir Harry Smith and to ascertain whether Cameron Roberts was a resident of Cape Colony.

Cape Town nestled at the base of the mountains and faced the Bay. At first, Blair was surprised to see how clean the town was but he soon realised the extent of the black population and saw the menial tasks they were performing. The older buildings were of Dutch architecture indicating the influence of the previous colonists.

A sentry challenged Blair at the entrance to Government House, which he considered looked no better than a country gentleman's residence in England.

He handed over a card, only to be told that his Excellency was leading a detachment of soldiers to quell an uprising of Kaffirs in the Province of Albany. However, directions to St George's Church were forthcoming and he hurried off towards the centre of town.

The building had a temple-fronted entrance portico with six pillars and faced St George's Street. Blair introduced himself to George Hough, the Chaplain. After the mandatory tea and scones in the vestry, Blair inquired about a doctor and Cameron Roberts.

"There is a very fine surgeon, whose rooms are not far from your hotel in Strand Street. His name is John Williamson and he is held in high esteem in Cape Town. And yes, Cameron Roberts still resides in the colony but left the service of the church for the service of Bacchus."

When Blair looked puzzled, Hough smiled sardonically. "He inherited some money and purchased one of the finest vineyards and wineries in the Constantia District. He's made a fortune but has strange ways and does not leave his property much. In fact, he stays away from Cape Town social circles all together, which is probably not surprising. If you make contact, ask him to deliver my usual order. I'm almost out of Madeira."

Blair did not pursue the cryptic comments. He abhorred gossip and innuendo.

The next morning, Surgeon Williamson examined Sara Jane. He was noncommital to the young woman and waited to discuss his findings with Blair in the hotel foyer.

"Your daughter has been suffering from morning sickness. I have given her a dose of aromatic chalk powder which I consider will settle the condition, particularly since she is now on dry land. You will need to obtain further supplies from the apothecary and administer it with all meals."

The expression on Blair's face said it all.

"You did not know, sir? As far as I can judge, she is over four months pregnant. I am surprised that the morning sickness has continued for so long but it could well have been exacerbated by motion sickness. Good day to you, sir. My account will be delivered this afternoon."

Blair was flabbergasted, to say the least. He called his wife from Sara Jane's bedroom and in hushed tones explained the situation.

"It was the American," he said. "He must have raped her. I wish she had discussed the situation with us. It must have been a terrifying experience."

"She chose not to do so, my husband and I can empathise with that. I wonder whether I would have wanted to talk about it if the same thing had happened to me. I doubt it. We must pray for our daughter and be understanding in her torment. You must make arrangements for the birth, as it is clear we must remain here for at least the next five months. I shall discuss the matter with Sara Jane."

After her mother had stumbled through an explanation of the situation, Sara Jane cried softly into her pillow. She had guessed of course. Her menses had ceased months ago. It was not that she was frightened at the notion of giving birth to a child out of wedlock. She was not and under the circumstances, no one could have more understanding parents. Her main worry was whether the child would be white or black and what would happen to it in either eventuality.

Soon after daybreak, Blair hired a carriage waiting outside the hotel. By coincidence it was the same black driver.

"Good morning, sir. A beautiful day. Where can I take you, sir?"

"I need to meet with a Mr Cameron Roberts, who is the owner of a vineyard and winery in the Constantia District."

Blair caught a flash of surprise before the man answered. "Surely, sir. The very best grape-growing property in the Cape."

Madeira Estate was twelve miles out of Cape Town on the road round Devil's Peak. The track was in good condition at first but soon became soft and their pace slowed. Blair, ever interested in nature, kept up a barrage of questions, which the driver cheerfully answered. When asked, he was generous in his praise of Mr Roberts as a caring owner, who treated his workers with respect as one would expect from a godly man. Blair, still wearing his white collar, wondered whether he was receiving a 'to be expected' representation. In any case the description was hardly congruous with the rather mysterious man described the previous day.

The carriage drew up at an ornate gate in front of the best kept establishment passed all morning. The grille was opened by a servant dressed in livery and as the carriage approached the residence, Blair saw an impressive building of stone with wide terraces covered with a variety of creepers flowering in many colours. Hedges of myrtle and geranium enclosed gardens and lawns and orchards of orange, lemon and fig trees could be seen to the rear of the house. Every other piece of ground, as far as the eye could see, was covered in vines, sprouting embryonic bunches of grapes. On top of the hill, the house proudly surveyed the scene back towards the peak.

An immaculately-dressed rider, taking hedges at a gallop, reined his horse to a halt next to the carriage. "Good morning, Alexander. Bringing another visitor to purchase the best wine at the Cape, I see."

The driver lifted his hat and grinned. "Of course, sir."

After dismounting, the handsome middle-aged man turned to Blair. "Welcome to Madeira Estate, sir."

Blair introduced himself and an engaging smile of recognition spread across his face as they shook hands.

"It's been a long time, Edmund. Which way are you travelling?"

"It's a long story, Cameron."

"Then join me for refreshments and let us catch up on events. Alexander, you know where to find some sustenance."

Roberts led Blair into a casually furnished open entrance area, which was cooled by a breeze from the west. A beautiful woman entered the room and placed a tray of drinks and biscuits on a central table.

"Thank you, my dear. Will you join us for a drink? This is an old acquaintance of mine, from my church days. Reverend Blair, this is my wife, Jacinta."

The woman was ebony black, draped in a light green garment which hung to the floor. A golden girdle with tassels was tied at the waist and the whole effect was extremely attractive. She wore loose brown sandals and was adorned with gold jewellery.

Blair was assessed at a glance from deep brown eyes and found to be acceptable. She always found men of the church to be either bigots or humanitarians. This one was an humanitarian. Her judgments were always right.

"Thank you, darling. I would be pleased to hear some news of the outside world." She extended her hand and Blair was not surprised to receive a firm handshake.

Following pleasantries, Blair was eager to proceed with the reason for his visit but Mrs Roberts was clearly interested in the conversation and making sound observations on some of the issues discussed.

Eventually, he said. "I have a concern, Cameron. Well actually a serious problem and I need to explain the situation in the hope that you might be able to provide me with assistance or at least advice." He cleared his throat. Mrs Roberts made no move to leave the room on the cue.

"Edmund, my wife and I share everything. We have no secrets. Please explain your problem and I hope we will be able to help in some way."

Blair was hesitant at first as he explained the situation, but it quickly became clear there was no need for shame or embarrassment in this household.

"So you see I need accommodation in Cape Town for five months or thereabouts. At least until the baby is born. After that I just don't know. It will depend on my daughter." His face fell into his hands and he began to sob. "It's my daughter you see. I love her so much."

Jacinta Roberts crossed the room and sat down on the couch next to Blair. He felt a comforting arm around his waist as she spoke softly to him. "Do not despair, Reverend. I am sure our Lord has led you to us." Her eyes met her husband's and tacit agreement was reached.

Roberts rose to his feet and walked to Blair, placing his hand on his shoulder. "Of course you will stay with us for the lying-in and as long as you

you choose after the birth. There is a guest house, seldom used, which is comfortable and it has all amenities."

Blair's head lifted and saw that the offer was genuine. "Bless you Cameron. You are truly a man of God."

"That is a matter of contention. We need to discuss it at some time. Others do not as readily appreciate or condone my decisions," Roberts said with a wry smile.

So Sara Jane and her parents were transported to Madeira Estate in the Roberts' carriage. Servants helped with the unpacking and attended to the domestic chores. It wasn't long before the Blairs realised the staff of the establishment were treated very differently from the usual treatment meted out to servants. They were accorded consideration, perceived themselves as part of an extended family and responded accordingly.

Away from the sea, with magnificent views of the hinterland, country air and fresh food, Sara Jane recovered. The lost weight was regained, her colour returned and knowing that everyone knew about her condition and her situation allowed her to relax. She was very grateful and eagerly looked forward to her hostess' regular visits.

Jacinta Roberts was a remarkable woman. Extremely intelligent, well educated, beautiful with a gracefulness portrayed in every movement, she also displayed a level of determination and independence equal to Sara Jane's. An immediate friendship was established. She confided in Sara Jane how she had met Cameron when she attended a mission school supported by the church, how he had formally proposed to her after she took up a house servant's position at a colleague's house, the outrage that had followed and the pressure placed on Cameron to resign from the Anglican Church following their marriage.

"He refused to resign saying that he had done nothing to deserve such a radical step and instead requested an extended period of leave, which was granted. He has requested and been granted protractions ever since. Meanwhile, a large inheritance allowed him to buy and develop Madeira Estate, which is now the foremost winery in the colony." Jacinta smiled. "The men from all religious persuasions purchase our wine, because it's consistently judged the finest. I find this somewhat ironic. Cameron laughs and says it's particularly ironic, because their orders provide us with a tidy profit."

A look of sadness passed momentarily across her beautiful face. "Only one thing could make my happiness complete and that is to have a child. We have been married for over ten years now and I have not conceived. Still, I am eternally grateful for a wonderful husband."

The Blairs also responded to the kindness and assiduous attention of their hosts and their staff. Regular fresh food and exercise also improved their health and Mrs Blair found that her arthritis was less painful away from the waterlogged ground of Mandurah. She wrote to William saying that his father had made contact with an old acquaintance in Cape Town and that, as Sara Jane had been unwell during the voyage, they would enjoy his hospitality until she had returned to full health. Because they did not know their departure date, William should forward letters to Swindon. That night, in her prayers, she asked the Lord's forgiveness for her omission of the full details.

Christmas and New Year came, were celebrated and went. In some ways, the Blairs and Roberts' had much for which to be thankful and much to look forward to in the future. Paradoxically, however, Reverend and Mrs Blair were not looking forward to the birth of the baby, except to free their daughter from an immediate problem and yet Reverend and Mrs Roberts would have given their fortune for a child. Sara Jane must wait for the birth to make her decision on the importance of the occasion. Such are the anomalies of life, she thought.

On 7th January, a special party was held to celebrate Sara Jane's twenty-first birthday. Jacinta insisted on a formal dinner with special dishes. Cameron raided his cellar and the finest Cape wines were opened to make the toasts. Dressed in their finest apparel, they came to the table determined to make the most of what could have been an awkward situation. It wasn't. Sara Jane was so radiant in pregnancy, so expansive, so grateful to her parents and her new friends, that the evening could only be acknowledged as a dinner to be remembered with pleasure.

She insisted in responding to her father's toast and standing at the head of the table, spoke sincerely and confidently.

"Mother, Father, Jacinta and Cameron. Wherever I might have been on this earth, at the time of the twenty-first anniversary of my birth, I can truthfully say that under the present circumstances, I am privileged, proud and pleased to be sharing this celebratory dinner with you."

"My early life was happy until the tragic death of my parents," Mrs Blair dabbed her eyes with her handkerchief, "but such tragedy resulted in William and I being fortunate in finding, through the intervention of our Lord, an Aboriginal family who cared for us, loved us and taught us the ways of their culture. Those two years, I will always treasure in my heart."

"Then when the time came, our Lord intervened again and we were delivered to the Reverend Blair. Mother and Father have provided us with love and understanding, which must have been difficult on many occasions." Blair nodded sagely. "Our education was comprehensive and exemplary and for that I will always be grateful. That we were legally adopted and received the Blair name, so highly respected in Western Australian circles, I thank them. Two orphaned children with little prospects of any sort of a future were suddenly not only acceptable but respectable. I toast you with all my love and gratitude, Mother and Father." Sara Jane lifted her glass and sipped.

"To our new friends, Jacinta and Cameron, I say thank you for your compassion and kindliness in my time of need. Once again our Lord intervened and, in bringing us together, has enriched all our lives." Jacinta and Cameron murmured assent. Sara Jane looked to them, lifted her glass and again sipped.

Cameron received a nudge in the ribs and hastened to respond. "My friends, it gives me great pleasure to say, that it gives me great pleasure to be with such great friends. To us!" Amid laughter, they all stood and toasted one another.

* * * * *

Sara Jane, the baby visibly asserting its presence, sat at a small table doing a large jigsaw puzzle, Mrs Blair was contentedly knitting a matinee jacket for the baby and Jacinta was reading. Blair was out sampling the latest bottled wine with his host.

Sara Jane sighed. "I need inspiration. Read to me, Jacinta."

"I'll see if you like some excerpts from Browning's collection, 'Bells and Pomegranates'. Are you familiar with Robert Browning's work, Sara Jane?"

"No, I'm not, although I enjoyed reading about his elopement with Elizabeth Barrett last year. It all sounded very romantic to me."

Jacinta nodded, laughing. "Although what a controversy! There are distinct disadvantages about being famous. Now, this poem is called 'Soliloquy of the Spanish Cloister'." She began reading in a serious tone.

Gr r r-- there go, my heart's abhorrence!
Water your dammed flower-pots, do!
If hate killed men, Brother Lawrence,
God's blood, would not mine kill you!
What? your myrtle bush wants trimming?
Oh, that rose has prior claims--
Needs its leaden vase filled brimming?
Hell dry you up with its flames!

Sara Jane had started grinning and then giggling. Mrs Blair joined in.

"Another! Another!" cried Sara Jane, enjoying the recitation enormously.

"Well, how about this verse?" Jacinta looked up sternly. "Ladies! Please! I'm sure this is supposed to be a serious soliloquy as befits the cloistered life in a monastery." She waited for the jocularity to subside.

Oh, those melons? If he's able
We're to have a feast! so nice!
One goes to the Abbot's table,
All of us get each a slice.
How go on your flowers? None double?
Not one fruit-sort can you spy?
Strange!-- And I, too, at such trouble,
Keep them close-nipped on the sly!

With approaching darkness and the final stanza concluded, the three women were laughing loudly when the men arrived home, somewhat the worse for wear.

"Is that the tolerance of the Roman Catholic faith?" asked Jacinta. "My, my! Browning was extremely insightful of the foibles of man, don't you think?"

"Perspicacious, I would describe it," said Sara Jane and they all laughed again. The latest game was to use synonyms, the longer the better.

"What are you laughing about? The three of you are almost hysterical. Let us join in too." Blair, having enjoyed an afternoon learning about the intricacies of winemaking and far too much sampling of the goods, was trying hard to enunciate his words.

After Sara Jane took a turn in reading the poem, both men were smiling broadly. "I hope that's not what the world sees in the religious man," said Roberts. "Intolerance, impatience, jealousy and sarcasm! Would not relate to the ordained of the Anglican Church would it Blair?" When they left to dress for dinner, they were all chuckling.

On the 25th April 1848, Sara Jane gave birth to a son. He had black hair, deep brown eyes and a prominent lower lip and chin. His skin was a chocolate colour. The midwife was surprised but said nothing. Nor would she discuss anything she had seen or heard. Loyalty was paramount in this household. After sponging the baby, she wrapped it in a towel and placed it against the young woman's side. The baby's cries awoke Sara Jane who had dozed off. She looked down and gave a wistful smile. Thank God it was Yeddi's child! She had been sure in her heart that the baby would be his. How she missed Yeddi.

"You have a son, ma'am," the midwife said with a smile. "A beautiful baby boy."

Sitting up, Sara Jane cradled the baby to her breast to feed and a short time later, fell asleep with an arm protectively around her sleeping son.

Blair paced up and down the main sitting room. He was unsure what to do. The matter had been discussed with his wife but for once she told her husband that it was Sara Jane's baby and Sara Jane's decision and he should wait to discuss it with her. He continued pacing until he saw the midwife carrying a bundle of used bedding from his daughter's room.

"Mrs Blair," he called and they hurried into the bedroom. He stopped and stared at the baby. Finally, he spoke. "I never considered that the American could have been a Negro," he said, fixed to the spot. "I never even considered it."

"Well, don't ask Sara Jane about it, my husband," she whispered. "It's over and I expect she will not want to discuss it now, since she did not want to discuss it then. It's the future that is important."

Because Sara Jane had some difficulty in expressing milk, Jacinta called for a wet nurse. A large happy-faced, black woman arrived and fed the baby.

Jacinta insisted that Martha move into the room set aside for the infant so as to be available to provide for its every need. Martha returned shortly afterwards with her gear and own baby.

Sara Jane was out of bed within twenty-four hours, much to the disquiet of Mrs Blair and spent most of her time with the child. In actual fact, she was forced to share Gurdu, as she had named him, with Jacinta, who was besotted with the baby. Everyone was curious as to the name but no one asked the obvious question. There was no native word for love in Yeddi's dialect as far as Sara Jane knew. Gurdu was a word loosely meaning 'heart and feelings' and that was as close as she could get to the way she had felt when she first saw him.

On his wife's advice, Blair waited. Impatiently but he waited, while the whole household cooed and fussed over what Blair considered had been trouble from start to finish and he wasn't sure whether they had arrived at the finish. However, he gave thanks to God for Sara Jane's return to glowing health.

When Sara Jane had time to consider her alternatives for the future, she discussed them with Jacinta.

"My mother and father will want me to travel to England with them as planned and for their sake I would like to go. It was I who suggested the idea in the first place. However, explaining rape, an unmarried mother and a black child to new relatives could be a difficulty."

"Just a trifle," said Jacinta facetiously.

"I could return to Fremantle and claim that I took pity on an orphan child in Cape Town."

"Or," said Jacinta, "you could do both those things. Why not leave Gurdu with me and collect him on your return journey to Western Australia? I somehow assumed you were going back."

"Well, I think my parents would like me to stay on with them but it has always been my intention to go home. I know I could find work bookkeeping, or as a governess, or serving in a store. Remember, I already have a share in my brother's transport business."

"Then, as I said, there is an obvious solution. Leave Gurdu with me. I would be so happy to look after him. Go on to England and meet your new family and see the sights and then return via the Cape and collect Gurdu."

"Jacinta, would you? I will hate leaving my baby but in this case I feel it is the best thing to do. My mother and father have been so looking forward to introducing me to their families. And the sooner I leave, the sooner I'll return. If I don't have to wait too long for berths, I should be back in about five months."

"Sara Jane, there is nothing I would enjoy more than to look after Gurdu."

That evening, Sara Jane had a long and serious talk with her father. When they had finished, they both wore troubled expressions, Sara Jane because she did not want to worry her father and Blair because he wanted to ensure his daughter's happiness more than anything in the world.

"I understand, Sara Jane and I wish you well with all my love. If it is your choice to return to Fremantle when the time comes, then your choice will be respected."

Three weeks later the Blairs sailed on the *Neptune*, a large and comfortable barque. Apart from a brief stopover for fresh fruit and vegetables in Porto Praya in the Cape Verde Islands, the journey was uneventful. To her relief, Sara Jane was not seasick and found time to do some reading and sketching. She also did a lot of thinking and missed Gurdu every minute of every day. Even more than she missed Yeddi, if that were possible.

The *Neptune* arrived at Gravesend at the end of August 1848 and was towed by steamer to St Katharine's Docks under the lee of the Tower of London the following day. As they travelled up the Thames, Sara Jane remembered one of Browning's poems that Jacinta had read to her.

> Oh, to be in England
> Now that April's there,
> And whoever wakes in England
> Sees, some morning, unaware,
> That the lowest boughs and the brushwood sheaf
> Round the elm-tree bole are in tiny leaf,
> While the chaffinch sings on the orchard bough
> In England-now!

She laughed out loud.

"What is it my dear?" her mother asked.

"Well, you see it's August, not April and it's summer, not spring but I'm in England - now!"

CHAPTER 26

Nine Elms

London! London! Sara Jane couldn't believe her eyes. It was so big, so old and so elegant. It was also very dirty. After disembarking at the large and very busy London Docks, they took a carriage to the George Inn in High Street and booked rooms for a week. Blair went to the Bank of England and cashed in a bank draft drawn on the Western Australian Bank and then the family went shopping. They started and finished in Burlington Arcade. What a spree! It was a year since Sara Jane had shopped in Perth and all her clothing, except her riding gear, was worn in spite of careful attention from Mrs Blair, who was a meticulous seamstress. They all needed a new wardrobe and even Reverend Blair, who normally hated shopping, joined in amiably. He particularly enjoyed the changing expressions on his daughter's face as she was able to choose from such a wide range of goods. Tired but excited, they returned to the inn.

Sara Jane had never seen so many people. "Father, I had never thought about the people. About how many people lived in a big city. About the transport needed to shift them from place to place. It's so very crowded."

"London is the largest city in the world, my dear. Frankly, I feel sorry for those who are forced for whatever reason to reside here. Enjoy your visit. It's an experience you will never forget but be grateful it's not your home. The countryside is a much more attractive proposition."

Then they began sightseeing and it continued for five days. A coach was hired each day, in deference to Mrs Blair's arthritis.

To the Tower of London, with its concentric defences of eighteen towers and two bastions and fascinating, if grisly history. Wearing his collar had advantages, Blair thought, as they were escorted as privileged visitors by an ancient and sad-looking yeoman warder.

"Built by William the Conqueror it was, sir," the warder said. "Just within the old Roman walls." He addressed every comment to Blair.

After a while, with a twinkle in her eyes, Sara Jane asked "Weren't some of King Henry's wives beheaded here?"

"Er, yes, miss, so they were. His second wife Anne Boleyn and his fifth wife Catherine Howard were executed in Tower Green." He obviously considered such a subject inappropriate for young ladies.

When they arrived at the charred remains of a huge building, Sara Jane couldn't help herself. "This must be the Grand Storehouse burned down in 1841. When will they see fit to rebuild it do you think, Father?" Blair referred the question to the warder, who had to admit that he didn't know. He looked at the young woman with a new respect.

To Westminster Abbey, where nearly every British monarch since William the Conqueror had been crowned and many buried. Sara Jane looked with incredulous eyes at the Abbey's roof, soaring above its three tiers of arches and the magnificent Gothic nave, the tallest in England. She had never seen anything so impressive. "I think I need to do some reading about architecture," she said to her father. "I can't understand how the roof stays up."

To St Paul's Cathedral, where Blair took over the commentary. "The first cathedral was built in 604 AD. It was destroyed with so many other treasures in the great fire."

"1665 - Lucky to be alive. 1666 - London burnt like sticks," Sara Jane piped in, putting her arm through her father's. "You taught us our history well, Father."

As they wandered through the magnificent edifice, Sara Jane marvelled at the vision of Sir Christopher Wren, the architect of the new cathedral completed in the early 18th century. They stopped at his tomb and Sara Jane considered that the epitaph, written by his son, said it all. 'If you seek a monument, look around.'

To Regent Park and Hyde Park and Kensington Gardens with their impressive open meadows and groves of fine old trees. Coaching through such verdant growth after the native bush of home made Sara Jane homesick and she couldn't stop thinking about Yeddi and Gurdu for the rest of that day.

To Buckingham Palace, which had been chosen by Queen Victoria as her London residence and there they saw the changing of the guard in the palace forecourt. The Grenadier Guards accompanied by their band were a magnificent sight and sound. "See - Queen Victoria is in residence. Her royal standard flies." Blair pointed to the fluttering flag and then stood to attention. "God save the Queen!"

To Trafalgar Square and a statue of Admiral Lord Horatio Nelson, completed only six years before. The inscription informed them that the column was 167 feet and 6 inches high. "He certainly has enough pigeons and assorted military paraphernalia to keep him company," Mrs Blair observed derisively.

To the Houses of Parliament. The Union Jack flying over the Victoria Tower indicated that Parliament was sitting. From the observation gallery the threesome watched proceedings and Sara Jane wondered how men who held the reins of power and controlled government could behave in such an undignified fashion.

"William would have loved the historical sites," said Sara Jane on their final day of sightseeing. "I am going to make him promise to see them one day. Thank you, Mother and Father for such a wonderful experience."

"Your mother and I have been watching your eyes and expressions with great delight, my dear. It has always been our fondest hope to bring you home to England."

Mrs Blair nodded happily. "Yes and tomorrow we begin our journey to Nine Elms and you will meet the family. I am so looking forward to that."

The journey took two days. The first night was spent at an inn outside Reading, about fifty miles by road from London and midafternoon on the second day they arrived at Swindon. Blair's younger brother Henry met the coach. After the luggage was transferred, the driver skilfully turned the four-in-hand towards the family home.

Henry was charming, courteous and, like his elder brother, highly intelligent. His dry wit had Sara Jane entertained in no time at all. The usual description of tall, dark and handsome applied. Silver hair at the temples gave him a distinguished appearance and this was reinforced by his verbal expression. His speech was highbrow but not supercilious. The cut of his clothes emphasised his debonair manner. All-in-all Sara Jane was pleasantly impressed. She was surprised he was so young and, with typical frankness, said so.

"A very forward question, I must say but I suppose you're entitled to know all about your family. Our mother, God bless her, delivered Edmund at the age of seventeen years and was obviously so exhausted with the whole affair that it was twenty years before I was born and another two years before Edward arrived. She obviously believed in spacing her family. Unfortunately, it was all too much for her and she died giving birth to Edward. Sad really, as I have always regretted not knowing her longer. Everyone says she was a wonderful woman."

A look of deep sorrow spread across the young woman's face. "Oh, I'm so sorry Henry. I didn't know. I understand what it's like to lose one's mother. At least I had eight years. Forgive me."

Her father patted her hand. "It's all right my dear. Of course you didn't know. And Henry shouldn't be facetious about such things. It's one of his few failings." He looked sternly at his bother.

Henry pushed aside the criticism with a laugh and pointed proudly through the window. "See, here is Nine Elms."

In the distance, a large manor house nestled comfortably among lush green fields. Sara Jane counted the nine elms spaced along the driveway. Smoke rose from several chimneys and beaming servants were standing in their designated places on the entrance steps.

When the coach came to a halt, a butler signalled and two servants opened the doors to help the occupants down. A plump and smiling housekeeper, with hands clasped in an almost prayer-like position, stepped forward. She was trembling in eager anticipation.

"Welcome home to Nine Elms, Reverend and Mrs Blair."

"Thank you, Mrs Yates," Blair acknowledged her. "I am indeed glad to be home at last." He proudly took his daughter's arm. "May I introduce our daughter, Sara Jane Andrews-Blair." Mrs Yates bobbed and came up with a smile on her face, which could only be described as satisfied. "Mrs Yates has been with us longer than she would probably like to admit, Sara Jane."

"How do you do Mrs Yates. I am delighted to have the opportunity of visiting the family home and look forward to my sojourn." A genuine smile followed.

"Welcome, my dear. I hope your stay with us is enjoyable." Her heart was immediately drawn towards her new charge. Piercing eyes as blue as the summer sky. Shoulder length hair as light as sunbeams. There was something strong, yet soft, proud, yet empathetic, confident, yet caring. She was so pleased for the Reverend and Mrs Blair. Mrs Yates hurried away to her duties humming happily.

The butler organised their luggage and the new cases signalled their spending spree.

"A little shopping on the way I see," Henry remarked as the luggage was unloaded. "No stores in the colonies then? Or is it that by the time stocks reach the antipodes and you buy them and then travel home, they are unfashionable?"

"A little truth in both your proposals, Uncle," Sara Jane responded with an innocent smile.

Henry started, then relaxed and said, "There'll be none of that, my young woman. Being adopted, I will not permit you to claim me as an uncle. Perhaps in time I may permit you to lay claim in other directions. A friend perhaps," he added hastily.

Everyone laughed, except Henry, who kept a straight face. Good Lord, he thought, I'm captivated, activated, scintillated, animated. All in an hour! She is everything Edmund promised. I'll write some poetry. That will help me over her. We can't have this at my age. After forty-seven years, I refuse to be tempted by Cupid.

When the luggage had been placed in their rooms, and travelling clothing had been discarded for more suitable attire, the family settled in comfortable chairs in an airy room filled with potted flowers.

Henry pulled the bell cord for attention. "We will have tea now, Mrs Yates," he said when the housekeeper bustled into the room. Looking grateful at being asked, she hurried from the room.

"So, Edmund, what are your visiting plans? Edward, of course, expects a call as soon as you are settled."

"Hmm. To begin with, as well as brother Edward and his family, Mrs Blair's sisters and their families, there's cousin Jack and of course the Right Honourable Oswald and Lady Powell out of courtesy and for their patronage in the early years."

"Edmund, you know you are welcome here for as long as you require, or forever if you will. The estate was your bequest."

Henry turned to Sara Jane. "It should be explained to you Sara Jane that, with your father's customary kindness and generosity, Nine Elms was signed over to me when I came of age. He said the Lord's work should not be shared with the management of a large country estate. That's why I'm a county gentleman instead of an army officer." He shuddered. "Thank goodness!"

Over tea, served from an exquisite silver tea set and tiny scones with strawberry jam and cream, an order of visits was planned, beginning in a fortnight. This would allow time for contact to be made and invitations to be issued to the Blairs.

When they had concluded their discussion and the utensils were being cleared, Henry said "Mrs Yates, please ask Aubrey to bring the mail from Australia. I'm sure it will be welcome."

There were three letters from William, one before he was informed of their stopover in Cape Town and two written since. One of the letters was addressed to Sara Jane and was handed directly to her.

"I suppose three missives are reasonable from a young business man on the move," said Blair with some sarcasm, as he broke the wax seal on the first dated letter.

The two letters to the family were read aloud by Blair. They contained day-to-day information about the doings of Fremantle and its inhabitants, which seemed mundane and uneventful, how the sea transport business was faring, which was very encouraging and how William had survived a storm with gale force winds off Cape Naturaliste on a return voyage from King George Sound, which was worrying. Mrs Blair said she would write this very week on behalf of them all.

Sara Jane was bursting with curiosity by the time she reached her room. She hurriedly broke the seal and read:

Fremantle
26th April 1848

Dear Sara Jane,
Sorry to hear that sea voyages do not agree with you. Just as well I am not so afflicted or I would be a disastrous sea captain. I hope you are now in good health and enjoyed your stay over at the Cape.

I saw Yeddi yesterday for the first time. He called at Fremantle on the off-chance that I would be home and I was! It seems he had some premonition of good news about you. I don't know what all that was about. He has been travelling the south-west as a special envoy of sorts for the Nyoongar. Apparently, he is one of only a few trusted to carry the message stick and is now accepted as a fully fledged boylya gadak. Remarkable for such a young man but then you know Yeddi. That is the good news along with the fact that Odern and Mandu still maintain their independent lifestyle and for their ages are well.

The bad news, in so far as Yeddi perceives it, is that since so many natives have been killed in retaliation by either whites or other blacks, or have died of the diseases carried by the settlers into the colony, their critical mass for the maintenance of tribal lore, ceremonies and indeed kinship requirements for betrothals and marriage, become more difficult. The tribal structure seems to be breaking down. He estimates that the total number of his people between Perth, Mandurah and the hills would be about three hundred. It is indeed a tragic situation, although there would be many who would think otherwise.

The natives are feeling increasingly vulnerable as they are forced off their traditional hunting areas and camp sites. In many cases, they have no alternative but to move further afield and join with other decimated groups (often considered an unpopular decision by both groups), or stay in one place, work for the farmers and become dependent upon them.

Either way, they are losing the justification for their existence - their land - and are becoming lost souls. No longer have they access to many of their sacred sites and therefore their ancestry. Because of this, the Dreaming stories, traditionally passed down to the next generation, are becoming meaningless.

Yeddi does what he can to support and advise and keep kinship groups in touch with one another, but says it is becoming difficult because of the distances involved and the increasing apathy of his people.

Of course, he sends his best wishes to his favourite babbingur, as you are and looks forward to seeing you on your return.

Regarding our business, you'll be pleased to know that I am currently negotiating the purchase of another vessel of approximately the same size and tonnage as the Sara Jane and will need to hire a crew. Business is booming and our bank accounts reflect this. We are now regarded as both a safe and reliable sea transport firm and have contracts weeks in advance. The paperwork is the bane of my life!

Kindest brotherly regards,
William

Sara Jane wrote to William the same week.

Nine Elms
14 September 1848

My dearest William,

Thank you for the personalised news, especially the good news about our transport enterprise. I have made the decision to return to Fremantle and will sail in due course after I have met our English relatives. I feel my future is in Western Australia and actually miss the colonial lifestyle. I'll probably stop over in Cape Town on the way home and catch up with the Roberts. They are a wonderful couple.

Yeddi is now obviously a leader of his people which is not surprising. He had all the necessary qualities and a fine education from Odern. I worry that he will try to shoulder too much responsibility and am fearful that there is an inevitability of what the future might hold for his Nyoongar. However, he must do what he must do. It is destined to be. I miss him greatly.

I am returned to good health and look forward to meeting our relatives beginning next week. It will be a little daunting as I am also to meet Earl and Lady Powell, the sometime patrons of the Blair family.

We spent a week in London and it was an experience never to be forgotten. Its very size and population is awesome. With your love of history, it is a destination you must place on your future itinerary.

Our Uncle Henry, who flatly refuses to be acknowledged as such, is a dear and a younger, lonely version of our beloved father. He will relish the company of our parents in the future. I must admit

I never dreamed of the affluent surroundings they left behind in order to administer the Lord's service in the colony. They will certainly be more comfortable at Nine Elms as they grow older. I am glad under the circumstances that I decided to accompany them to England. It has all been for the best.

I promise to put my mind and energy to bringing the paperwork up to date on my return, as my penance for neglecting our partnership.

Your loving sister,
Sara Jane

When she could, Sara Jane escaped with her drawing pencils and water paints and spent many enjoyable hours producing credible water colours of flora she had never seen before. Between Nine Elms and Lydiard Mansion, the home of the Powells, was an extensive forest called Lydiard Park. Portions of it were suitable for riding but most was densely timbered. Sara Jane delighted in riding or taking long walks through the forest and was frequently accompanied by Henry, who obviously enjoyed his time with her. She also explored the library at Nine Elms and found it well stocked with books from Homer's *Odyssey* and other classics to the contemporary literature of Charles Dickens. She was ecstatic to find leather-bound copies of *Oliver Twist* and *A Christmas Carol* on the shelves. It became her favourite afternoon hide-out as she avidly devoured volume after volume.

When the round of visits commenced, Sara Jane found that she genuinely liked all the members of her new family. They were down to earth, no nonsense people of similar ilk to her adopted parents. She listened with great interest to the conversations of the men of the family but followed the women in not speaking unless asked to express an opinion. The family knew of the tragic deaths of her real parents and the children's rescue by the natives but obviously it was not considered an appropriate topic for discussion and was not raised.

The protocols and rather stiff behaviours were inhibiting at first but Sara Jane soon realised that they set the scene for what was considered to be appropriate conduct and actually assisted everyone in knowing what was expected of them. So, she began playing the part of the young lady, gracious, witty but not too witty, talented but not too talented, educated but not too educated, which pleased her mother and father immensely. They were so proud of her and she wanted to keep it that way, especially since she intended leaving for Fremantle before the winter storms of the northern hemisphere.

Henry was an enigma. He was the epitome of the English gentleman, reflected in his dress, conversation, behaviour and of course his manners.

His solicitous attention towards Sara Jane did not waver, yet he was never the sycophant. If she could describe it, she thought he treated her as an out-of-reach princess. She decided that she liked and respected him enormously.

"Have I told you the origins of our names?" he said, as they rode leisurely through Lydiard Park on a glorious autumn day.

"Whose names?" Sara Jane answered absently. She was thinking of spring, as it would be on the other side of the world with its myriads of beautiful wildflowers.

"Ours. My brothers and mine. Edmund, Edward and Henry."

"No. Sorry, Henry. My mind was in Western Australia. Tell me."

Henry's face fell momentarily. Then he smiled and began his obviously oft-repeated story. "Not surprisingly our father was a history buff, who was fascinated by the stories of our past kings. For some reason, he became particularly interested in three kings by the names of Edmund, Edward and Henry."

He paused and Sara Jane said "What's wrong with that? They are fine English names. Many kings were so named."

Keeping a straight face, Henry continued. "But you see the particular kings in question were Edmund the Magnificent, Edward the Martyr and Henry VIII."

"I know about Henry VIII," said Sara Jane wondering where all this was leading.

"Well, Edmund the Magnificent reigned from 940 to 946 AD and was murdered, Edward the Martyr reigned from 975 to 978 AD and was murdered and Henry VIII reigned for thirty-eight years, had six wives, divorced two and had two of them beheaded."

"Well then, Uncle," Sara Jane said. "You had best look to a preacher. If history repeats itself, you've a lot of marrying to do," and laughing she spurred her horse for home.

* * * * *

It was a cool dawn three mornings after the Blair's return from their final family visit. Sara Jane had remained on her best behaviour to the last, but was glad it was all over. Today was the special reception by the Right Honourable Oswald Richard Powell, Earl of Lydiard and Lady Eleanor Juliet Powell and their sons Viscount Charles Sebastian Powell and the Honourable Robert John Powell. It was to be afternoon tea at precisely 3 o'clock. The Blairs were in a state of nervous excitement and saw this as both the culmination and highlight of the round of visits for their daughter.

Sara Jane snuggled under the bedclothes as she mulled over the events of the last fifteen months. She decided she wouldn't have done anything differently if she could have lived it over again. She sighed. It was another week before she would catch the coach back to London and board the *Henrietta* en route to Cape Town and then Fremantle. Sara Jane was ready to return home.

Time to get up. A morning outing would put her in a better frame of mind for meeting the nobility. She arose, washed and dressed herself in her riding gear. The rest of the family had announced at supper the previous evening their intention to sleep in and partake of breakfast later than usual.

When she entered the large country kitchen, the fires were burning brightly and the kettle boiling. She sipped a steaming cup of tea and ate hot buttered toast with marmalade jam, prepared by a happily fussing Mrs Yates. The scullery maid was sent to alert the stable boy to saddle Miss Andrews-Blair's horse, Midnight, a black gelding lent felicitously by Henry for the duration of her stay.

Sara Jane decided to take the village road and then return to Nine Elms through Lydiard Park. She trotted in leisurely fashion beside the rutted road.

Time passed and Lydiard Village had been long left behind. Rain clouds were hanging low in the sky and she was going to get a drenching before she arrived back at the manor. Never mind, she had thoroughly enjoyed the morning's exercise. The sun was well hidden but it was at least noon. She'd better head back to Nine Elms and prepare for the special afternoon tea.

What on earth was happening up ahead? Sara Jane stood up in her stirrups to obtain a better view. About twenty villagers were walking in a line only a few yards apart and searching the undergrowth, some with the aid of staves. She rode up to the nearest person, a wizened old woman.

"Good morning, grandmother. What have you lost?"

The old woman's reply was incomprehensible and then Sara Jane saw that she had no teeth. A boy close by called out. "A girl from the village 'as gone missin'. Emma's 'er name. She's only four years old. Gone off lookin' for 'er brother this morn, ma'am." The boy rejoined the line.

It began drizzling and Sara Jane worried about the lost child as she reined to the left and headed up into Lydiard Park. Then the sky opened and it was teeming with rain. Sara Jane slowed Midnight to a walk until she found a huge oak tree under which to shelter. The rain continued for some time.

What was that on the bush ahead? A shred of cloth. Sara Jane dismounted and plucked the scrap of pink cotton from the branch on which it was caught. She fingered it and wondered whether it was connected to the lost girl. It did not appear faded. She'd better have a look, just in case.

With Midnight's reins in her left hand she began looking for signs. Nothing! Another thirty minutes. Nothing! It had been a long time since she had used her tracking skills and in poor light, after rain, in a forest, perhaps she was overestimating her capabilities. Perhaps it was a forlorn hope. Then, angrily, she remonstrated with herself. Be positive. A little girl's life could be at stake. She travelled back in time. "Open your eyes and see. Open your ears and hear. Open your nose and smell." How many times had she heard Odern say those words.

Sara Jane crouched as she had been taught to do in difficult terrain and carefully examined the ground. A broken twig to the right. She had gone that way. Muddied leaves where she had disturbed them. A faint toe print. Then nothing. She must be careful. If she treads on a clue unwittingly, she could obscure it. More disturbed leaves. A broken shoot on a branch. Footprints. Ahh! A soft section. More footprints. Easier than the sand at home. A slight track, probably made by animals. Yes. Scats on the ground. Could be deer. The small footprints were clearly visible now for a hundred yards or more as the girl followed the animal pad.

What is that smell? Sara Jane sniffed the air with her mouth open the way she had been taught. Urine. The girl had relieved herself at the side of the track. More footprints. Bruised leaves on a bush. She had picked up a stick and was dragging it behind her. Good girl! She had discarded the stick. Pity! The track divided. Which way? To the left. No clues. I've lost her. Back to the fork. Try the right. Forest floor debris disturbed. She's fallen over onto her hands. She's back on her feet. Another fifty yards of clear footprints.

The rain ceased. Another fifty yards or so and the prints were clearer. Made after the rain had stopped. She must be close.

"Emma. Emma." Sara Jane kept calling.

A faint cry? Sara Jane turned her head and called again. She was answered by sobs and hurried to the sound.

A small girl in a torn pink dress crawled out from a hollow log and between sobs said, "I'm Emma."

Sara Jane knelt down in the mud and gathered the little girl in her arms. "Hush, little one. It's all right now. You're safe. I will take you home."

When Sara Jane lifted her up and carried her towards Midnight, Emma grabbed her rescuer around the neck and held on tightly. The horse pawed the ground and the girl screamed to be put down. The compromise was that Sara Jane pig-a-backed Emma all the way back to the village and Midnight walked behind.

As they approached the first house, they were spotted and shouts brought the villagers running. A grateful mother took Emma into her arms and there were hugs and much excited chatter ensued. All's well that ends well, thought Sara Jane, as she accepted the villagers' thanks.

Except now there was no way she could make the afternoon tea engagement. She swung up into the saddle. "Midnight, I think I'm going to be in big trouble."

By the time Sara Jane arrived at Nine Elms it was late afternoon. An anxious Blair was waiting in the stable. "My dear, what happened? You're wet through and plastered in mud. Come inside and change. You'll catch pneumonia. We've had the servants out looking for you in the forest for the past hour. We thought you might have had a fall."

After a hot bath and a change of clothing, Sara Jane explained what had happened to her worried parents and Henry. Naturally, they approved of her course of action under the circumstances. She had no choice but to assist in the search for the little girl, but what a shame they had missed the afternoon tea.

"Perhaps there'll be another time," Sara Jane said and this seemed to comfort her mother.

The next morning, while the Blairs ate breakfast, a rider reined in at the Nine Elms stable. He handed a letter to the butler who entered the dining room and presented it on a silver tray. Henry broke the seal and read out loud:

> "The Right Honourable Oswald Powell, Earl of Lydiard and Lady Eleanor Powell request the pleasure of the company of the Reverend Edmund Blair and Mrs Blair, Miss Sara Jane Andrews-Blair and Mr Henry Blair to tea at 3 o'clock this afternoon."

"Sykes. Please inform the messenger that the Blairs would be delighted to accept the kind invitation to tea at Lydiard Mansion this afternoon."

Laughing, Henry turned to Sara Jane. "I suspect you are now a local celebrity my dear and as such must pay the price. I've never heard of two invitations to Lydiard Mansion in two days. Have you, Mrs Blair?"

"No, Mr Blair. That I have not," she answered contentedly.

After careful consideration, Sara Jane chose a soft wool afternoon dress of royal blue, which matched her eyes to perfection. A high neck indicated the propriety of the occasion and was trimmed by a delicately finished white lace collar. The bodice was fashionably tight and pointed to the front and rounded at the back. She refused to wear the ubiquitous corset. Because of her height, the long tight-fitting sleeves and long skirt with numerous petticoats gave her an almost regal look. A matching cape and bonnet completed the outfit.

The Blairs arrived by carriage at Lydiard Mansion, just before 3 o'clock. As they drove through the entrance gates and up the drive, Henry informed Sara Jane of some of the specifics of the building. It gave him the excuse to look directly into her eyes. He was finding it impossible to keep his own away from her face.

"This is an example of quite recent trends, my dear. It's known as Early Victorian Jacobean architecture. The eastern wing burned down a decade ago and the mansion was rebuilt after the original structure was considered unsafe. Only five years old and very modern in so far as it has central heating and even water closets attached to most bedrooms. Astronomically expensive, of course but then the Powells have enormous inherited wealth and a very healthy annual income from their estates and shipping business."

Peering through the window of the carriage, Sara Jane could not believe her eyes. The building was a huge three storey construction with dozens of turrets. It was built in a light cream stone and large windows gave it an open look. Decidedly nice. Elegant and tasteful. On a slight rise, it was surrounded by immaculate, almost manicured gardens clearly designed and established by a person of distinctive expertise in the field.

The carriage came to a standstill at a wide stair leading up to the northern aspect of the building. Liveried servants stood to attention at the base of the steps and moved forward as the vehicle stopped. The doors were opened in unison and the Blairs emerged, to be escorted into a large entrance hall complete with statuettes and tapestries. Servants hurried forward to take capes, bonnets, hats and gloves.

The butler, an elderly man with a dour expression, said "This way please ladies and gentlemen. The Earl of Lydiard and family await in the library." Sara Jane stood tall and took a deep breath.

Servants held the large double doors open and the Blairs entered the library. Henry had described it as a feature but Sara Jane was totally unprepared for its size and sumptuousness. There were tiers of shelves full of books, writing desks and writing chairs, reading tables and reading chairs, divans and ottomans, with large fireplaces set into each wall. It was like a huge communal sitting room and ten times as big as the Blair's library. How she'd like to be let loose in here!

Three men rose to their feet as the butler, standing to attention and with pronounced formality made the introductions. "Mr Henry Blair, Reverend Edmund and Mrs Blair and Miss Andrews-Blair."

Henry stepped forward and said "My Lords and Lady. We thank you for your invitation. May I especially present our new family member, Miss Sara Jane Andrews-Blair." Sara Jane curtsied and rose to look at the three men standing stiffly and clearly not at ease.

"And Sara Jane, this is the Right Honourable Oswald Richard Powell, Earl of Lydiard and Lady Eleanor Powell, Viscount Charles Sebastian Powell and the Honourable John Robert Powell. The men gave short bows and Lady Eleanor, a remarkably well preserved woman of middle age, nodded discerningly from her chaise longue, perusing the young woman she had heard so much about in the past twenty-four hours. She liked what she saw.

"Come over here my dear and sit next to me. I must hear all about what happened yesterday. Do seat yourself Mrs Blair. John call for the tea."

As soon as Sara Jane and Mrs Blair were seated, the men sat down and the tea trolley arrived.

Viscount Charles Sebastian Powell fixed his eyes on the most beautiful young woman he had ever seen in his life and he had seen many. It seemed that every mother in England contrived to arrange a meeting with her daughter. Sara Jane was laughing politely at a comment made by his mother. Tanned, not the pallid complexion of English women, with white even teeth and a healthy glow about her. Fair, almost white hair dropped to the shoulder and curled. And her eyes were as blue as her royal blue dress. Full of the zest for living, he assessed. Beautiful, just beautiful. Charles was entranced. Even his father was staring.

"Now young woman, you must tell us how you found the little girl." Lady Eleanor smiled, as she chose a tiny cucumber sandwich from the proffered silver plate.

When everyone had been served Sara Jane began. "I followed her tracks my Lady and found her taking shelter in a hollow log. Then I carried her to the village, as she was too frightened of my horse to ride with me. It was nothing really. The signs were quite clear, broken twigs, disturbed ground, footprints, bruised leaves."

John started snuffling behind his hand. He stopped when his mother looked down her nose at him.

"Is something wrong, John?" The young man hastily shook his head. "Well then, stop that ridiculous noise and listen," she said sternly to her younger son. "You might learn something useful. Spare me! One son says nothing and the other snuffles. Go on, my dear."

Sara Jane was beginning to feel uncomfortable. "There really was nothing else my Lady, except to request your pardon for our non-attendance yesterday and thereby putting you to the inconvenience of arranging another afternoon tea."

"It has been our pleasure, my dear. Oswald wanted to especially thank you on behalf of the villagers and the estate. Didn't you, dear husband?"

"Er. Yes, of course, my dear."

The Earl had sparse grey hair, a very red nose, bleary eyes and was sipping what looked like a sherry. He was old, much older than his wife. He stood and his hands shook as he moved towards her. Sara Jane rose from her couch. "We would like to make a small presentation to you Miss Andrews-Blair in gratitude for your assistance and success in the search for the little girl. Without your intervention there could have been tragic consequences. I hope you consider the offering appropriate under the circumstances. It was my wife's idea. She heard you needed one." The Earl handed Sara Jane a long thin parcel wrapped in a light green cloth.

Sara Jane carefully unwrapped the gift and her eyes gleamed with pleasure. It was a beautifully crafted leather crop. The card said 'In appreciation, Earl Lydiard'.

"Thank you, my Lord. I will treasure it always." She curtsied and then on impulse kissed the old man on the cheek.

Mrs Blair nearly swooned, but the Earl looked pleased and his wife nodded in approval.

On the way home in the coach, Sara Jane said. "I wonder how Lady Eleanor knew I had lost my crop in the search?"

Henry continued to look out the window, a look of total innocence on his face. "I expect a little bird from the forest must have told her," he eventually said, a pleased grin on his face.

Later, Sara Jane questioned her mother about the strange family. "Lady Eleanor is the Earl's second wife, my dear. He didn't remarry for a long time after his first wife, whom he worshipped, died giving birth to a stillborn child. He was heart-broken and found solace in the bottle, poor man. Then Eleanor came along and snared him and he pulled himself together. Well relatively, anyway. She gave him two sons but John is a simpleton and Charles, the heir, an introvert. Should have been sent away to boarding school. That would have fixed him but instead he was tutored at home. At twenty-five, I suspect he is yet to make a decision of his own. He's actually very talented in many directions. His prowess in the manly sports is legendary in these parts. He excels at horse-riding and bare knuckle boxing. A real enigma in many ways."

"But Mother, he didn't speak once."

"No, my dear. He has a speech impediment. He stammers very badly. It's probably part of the reason he's so shy and refuses to court. I assure you there is no shortage of young women who would wish it otherwise."

"In that case I feel sorry for the poor man. I've never met such a withdrawn person. Fancy his mother allowing him to dress in pale blue silk and look such a sissy. And that lank, fair hair hanging over his face. It's a shame."

"Sara Jane, I think it suits his mother that he remains unmarried," was the final, perceptive comment.

* * * * *

Hooray! Today's the day! I'll soon be on my way. Sara Jane laughed at her rhyme. Home to Western Australia. Home to Yeddi. Home with Gurdu.

The packing was completed and all Sara Jane needed to do was organise her hand luggage. She felt guilty because nobody wanted her to return to the colony. They had all felt quietly confident that when the time came she would stay. At least stay for Christmas. She countered that plea with a comment about the deteriorating weather. Her mother and father were keeping stiff upper lips but Henry's behaviour was positively embarrassing. He was acting as though the world was about to end, moping around the manor, snapping at the servants and muttering to himself. How could a grown man act in such a way?

Poor Henry was so lovesick he was incapable of controlling his feelings.

They drove into Swindon after breakfast. The farewells were long and emotional, because the Blairs all knew there was little chance they would ever see Sara Jane again.

Finally the coachman called "All aboard!" and the passengers took their seats. Sara Jane waved her white handkerchief from the window until the coach turned right at the sign 'To London'.

CHAPTER 27

Gurdu

Still October, not even winter as yet. The wind and rain lashed the *Henrietta* as she plunged and rolled and surged and rolled. Sara Jane in a single cabin, courtesy of the Blairs, relaxed and enjoyed her 'being time' as she called it. Time to be by oneself and think, read, reflect and sketch. It was bliss. And I'm on my way home to Gurdu and Yeddi. She wished the ship could fly.

The weather was atrocious until they passed the Canary Islands and then the winds moderated and passengers ventured out of their cabins and out on deck. Sara Jane was polite to the other travellers but made no effort to join in any of their social activities, such as playing whist or reading poetry. She ate her meals in the main dining area, politely making conversation when addressed and then returned to the seclusion of her cuddy. On fine days, when there was little wind and wave, she would take her sketch book and draw aspects of ship-life from the poop deck.

In just under seven weeks, the *Henrietta* hove to in Table Bay.

Sara Jane had written ahead weeks before her departure and, knowing that the Roberts would be expecting her, hired a carriage from the docks and journeyed directly to Madeira Estate.

As she paid the driver, she was beside herself with excitement. A servant took her bags and Sara Jane, in a most unladylike fashion, bounded up the steps. Jacinta stood at the entrance to the reception room holding Gurdu. Both were encircled by loving arms and a laughing, crying Sara Jane held them close.

"Oh, it's so good to be back. Can I hold him? He's heavy! Thank you, Jacinta. Thank you."

"He's heavy because he never stops feeding. I had to find another wet nurse. Together Gurdu and Martha's own baby drained the poor woman dry. He's not eight months old until Christmas Day and yet he's already sitting up and crawling."

Sara Jane took the bundle and looked at her son. Crisp black curly hair abounded and deep black eyes peered intently at her, as if she too was under scrutiny. Both liked what they saw and smiled. Gurdu gurgled as his mother kissed him on the forehead and whispered "You're as handsome as your father."

Jacinta's eyebrows lifted but she said nothing, for at that moment Cameron joined them. He welcomed Sara Jane and called for tea and they amiably discussed what she had seen and done while in England. At first Sara Jane held Gurdu, who was a wriggling, squirming mass but in the end, she put him onto the floor where he sat flinging his little arms around and making a great deal of noise.

"The week of shopping and sightseeing was a wonderful experience. Everyone born in the colonies should travel to London at some stage of their lives to realise how much one's forebears left behind when they journeyed to settle new lands."

Jacinta looked hopefully at Cameron. "I was born in the colonies, my dear but you haven't taken me to London to see the Queen."

"Then I shall, my pussy cat. Then I shall. Next year, in the English summer, we shall travel to London to see the Queen."

Jacinta shrieked and hugged Cameron. "Thank you, my love. Thank you, Sara Jane. What a good idea that was! I've been trying to get him out of the Cape for years but he won't leave his precious vines. Says we've the best place in the world in which to live and that I should be happy but of course I have nothing with which to compare it."

Asked about her relatives by adoption, Sara Jane answered frankly. "I liked them all. They were exactly as I had expected and warmly welcomed me to the family. However, I found the way in which women were expected to continually defer to their menfolk tiresome to say the least. Things seem to be much more relaxed at home and here. Perhaps people who travel far away to establish the colonies have the opportunity to discard some of the old conventions."

With a smile and pointed look at her husband, Jacinta said she would report her experiences to Sara Jane after her visit to England the following year.

Finally, Sara Jane related the episode of the lost child and the subsequent meeting with Earl Lydiard, Lady Eleanor and their two sons. "It made me think that perhaps the line of inheritance should be matriarchal," she concluded with a laugh.

"I concur with your thoughts, Sara Jane. I met the family many years ago when I was a young pastor in Purton. A rum lot to say the least. Still, many families of the English establishment are in fact controlled by the mother or grandmother. It's probably reality versus perception as to who continues to enforce the protocols of the upper class."

That afternoon, while Cameron did the rounds of the estate and Gurdu had his afternoon sleep, Sara Jane and Jacinta discussed the future. "I'll go back to our old home in Henry Street and keep house for William and do the paper work for the business. When Gurdu is older, I'll get a housekeeper and perhaps do some bookkeeping for other firms."

Jacinta was fidgeting and biting a nail, a sure sign that something was worrying her. Sara Jane waited. Eventually, Jacinta said, "Sara Jane, who is Gurdu's father? I couldn't help but overhear what you whispered to your son. You always led me to believe the father was the American."

"Oh! It just slipped out. I'm sorry Jacinta, I didn't want to deceive anyone. I just considered it best to maintain the facade, particularly if I was to take my baby to England." She hesitated. "Gurdu's father is my babbingur. The native boy, with whose family I spent the two years, except that now he's a handsome man and a respected boylya gadak of his people. I love him with all my heart and can't wait to show him his son."

"Does he know?" Jacinta whispered.

"No. I didn't know I was with child when I left the colony."

"Sara Jane, I am your friend and I will be honest. You are prepared to take Gurdu back to Western Australia as the half-caste bastard son of a native? Have you considered what the reaction would be? They would not permit you to marry a black man. The establishment would never allow it. No man of the cloth would dare conduct the ceremony. Sara Jane, look what our marriage did to Cameron. Think what will happen to you and Gurdu if you take him with you as your son. Not only will you be an outcast with your people but if Yeddi's people found out, he would be an outcast with his people. You would both be pariahs."

Sara Jane burst into tears. "I thought you would understand. Of all persons, I thought you would understand, Jacinta." Still crying, she hurried sobbing from the room.

Jacinta sighed in pain for what she had felt beholden to say. "But I do Sara Jane, I do. I understand only too well."

When Sara Jane could cry no longer and her despair seemed to be overwhelming, she sat on the edge of the bed, her head in her hands and prayed. She prayed to God and spoke to the spirits but received no response or counsel. She felt very alone and went to sit next to Gurdu's cot. The child slept peacefully and for the first time Sara Jane felt unsure of herself and her plans. In her heart, she knew Jacinta was right but she also thought that somehow with Yeddi's love and support they would find a way.

An hour passed and Sara Jane was no closer to a solution or peace of mind.

A knock on the door interrupted her thoughts and a servant asked whether she would like a cup of tea and her mail. Sara Jane thanked her and received both within a few minutes.

There was one letter from William. Sara Jane had asked that her parents send their mail to Fremantle.

My dearest sister,

I am forcibly detained at home because of the winter gales, which gives me a chance to write to my favourite sister. Only the larger ships dare to tempt fate in this weather and even though the new addition to our fleet is larger than the Sara Jane, I consider it too much of a risk to venture forth. I've named her Margaret after our mother. I hope you approve. Both presently lie at anchor, close to shore off Parker Point, Rottnest and are as adequately protected from the north-westerly storms as is possible. David Long, the new skipper and I sailed them over when the barometer plummeted and came back together in the dinghy. It took hours. Next time we'll stay over.

I have bad news. Mandu passed away last month after a series of severe attacks of influenza. It seems to strike at the change in the seasons. She had been unable to recover from one bout before she caught another and then another and finally succumbed on June 14th.

As you would understand, Mandu's dearest wish was to see Yeddi betrothed and married before she died and so Odern travelled to the Barragup mandjar in May to make the required arrangements. Yeddi was subsequently betrothed to a young woman from his father's moiety, the White Cockatoo and, because of his grandmother's poor health, they were married immediately, as it turned out just the week before her death. Jida, small bird, as she is called, had been previously betrothed to an elder, who had died and as he had no brothers and Yeddi was well respected and eligible by their kinship lore, it was considered an appropriate match. To that time he had indicated no interest in marriage but under the circumstances I suppose he saw it as a responsibility he could not evade.

I couldn't be there, of course but Yeddi brought Jida to meet me last week. She is a beautiful young woman and they seem contented enough. He asked that I inform you of the marriage when next I wrote and hoped that you would be happy for them both.

Yeddi says that Odern grows older and more grumpy but is still able to look after himself. He strenuously resists joining any of his kin and continues to prefer the solitary lifestyle.

I trust the remainder of your stay at Nine Elms was enjoyable and that you caught up with the Roberts as planned and therefore received this letter.

I look forward to your return,

Kindest regards,

Your loving brother,
William

Sara Jane sat staring at the letter. Finally, accepting that she was as composed as she was going to be after the news of Yeddi's marriage and Mandu's death, Sara Jane lifted Gurdu from the cot where he was babbling happily and re-entered the sitting room. Jacinta was reading a newspaper. Her face showed that she had also been crying.

"Jacinta, may we talk?"

"Of course, my dear. I was hoping that we could."

"Events have caught up with me through the mail. I have also considered your advice carefully. You are right, of course. My heart doesn't usually control my head but for once I couldn't or wouldn't see things clearly."

Jacinta motioned Sara Jane to sit next to her on the sofa and placed her arm around her shoulders. "Tell me, Sara Jane."

The contents of her brother's letter were explained as Sara Jane cuddled her baby in her lap. "In one way I am devastated and in another, I think I knew that my dearest wish could never be. I just refused to accept the inevitability of the situation. I am a romantic and I thought true love would find a way. In any case, it is now not possible. Yeddi was just following his destiny and as Odern would have said, 'It is the way of things'."

The ebony-coloured woman held the fair-skinned woman close as she discussed what she saw to be the only two obvious and reasonable alternatives. "As I see it Sara Jane, you can take the baby back to Fremantle as an orphaned child that you happened upon in Cape Town, or you can sign Gurdu over to us and we will legally adopt him. Naturally, I would give anything to keep Gurdu. Both of us love him with all our hearts and I told Cameron that I would pose the question to you on your return, not knowing at the time that you loved his father. Cameron wants as much as I to raise Gurdu as our son. To be brutal in presenting you with the alternatives, it comes down to an unmarried white woman bringing up a supposedly half-caste orphan in Fremantle, or a married white man and black woman bringing up an adopted half-caste son in Cape Town."

By the time Cameron galloped up to the house, it was decided. Sara Jane would leave Gurdu, to be renamed Gurdu Blair Roberts, with his parents-to-be for adoption. The proviso was that if the boy for any reason ever queried the identity of his natural mother or father, he would be informed and provided with the necessary means to meet with them if that were possible. Sara Jane's gold unite was left with Jacinta who promised to have a jeweller attach the coin to a gold chain. It would be presented to him on his twelfth birthday as an English substitute for the tribal initiation he would never undergo.

For Sara Jane, it was a distressing compromise, but one she knew in her heart would be best for her son. She insisted that Gurdu's cot be moved back into the main bedroom and that Gurdu's waking hours be shared with Jacinta. The Roberts were concerned for Sara Jane and by Christmas Day feelings and emotions had settled. After a huge Christmas lunch, Cameron brought out his best wine, an 1832 Madeira Estate Burgundy and the three friends, now inextricably bound together, toasted Gurdu Blair Roberts to be. Sara Jane slept fitfully until the early hours of the morning, when Yeddi entered her dreams. Holding her, he asked for her understanding regarding his marriage to Jida, which Sara Jane gave. At last, she fell into a deep sleep.

Chapter 28
Fremantle Homecoming

Rottnest slid past just before sunset and by the time the *Camelot* anchored in Gage Roads to await the dawn, the island was a silhouette against a red sky. It was 11th March 1849.

Sara Jane was tired of travelling. Living out of suitcases was a nuisance, and crushed and not very clean clothes were both abhorrent and embarrassing to her. She'd be glad to return to Henry Street, even if it was tiny compared with her recent residences and to be able to run her own house for the first time.

A lighter arrived alongside the *Camelot* just after dawn and unloading began. Sara Jane, being an early bird, was on the first trip to shore. The only significant change she observed, as they approached the jetty, was the increase in the number of ship yards scattered along the beach front in South Bay. She wondered whether such activity would affect their business.

When her luggage was unloaded, Sara Jane called a fellow with a barrow, obviously waiting around for work as a porter and within thirty minutes she stood, surrounded by her baggage, in the familiar ankle-deep sand outside the Henry Street stone cottage.

"Ho! Ho!" Sara Jane said aloud. The garden definitely required some tender, loving care and the stone walls were in desperate need of several coats of whitewash. However, thank goodness, the thatched roof had been replaced with shingles. You'd better be working very hard, brother William. No other excuse will be acceptable.

It was disappointing that William was not home but Sara Jane found the key to the door hidden in its usual place behind a loose stone under the step and let herself in.

The place was a shambles! The sitting room floor was covered with newspapers, books, charts and dirty cups and dishes. At least there were now floorboards she noticed and supposed that was something. The main bedroom had clothes scattered everywhere and the bed was unmade. There didn't seem to be a clean utensil in the kitchen and the bathroom was knee deep in discarded and dirty clothes and towels. Her room seemed to be the repository for stores, spare rope and sails and various miscellaneous items. A large anchor stood against the backyard wall.

The only room that looked the same as when they had left was her father's cuddy, with the exception of the wooden desk, which was covered to several inches with papers pertaining to the business. A quick look indicated contracts, sales receipts, bank statements, delivery slips, bills of lading. It went on and on. Some of the papers were over twelve months old, dating back to the receipt for the bank cheque for the purchase of the cutter. Sara Jane sighed as she retrieved her bags from the front step and placed them on the floor of the tiny office. Welcome home!

In view of what was awaiting her, Sara Jane decided to buy in some bread, butter, cheese, bacon, eggs and milk and then check whether any mail had arrived from England, before starting the clean-up. With a letter written very soon after her departure and forwarded on a fast ship, it was a possibility, albeit a slight possibility. She made her purchases and then called into the Post Office. Mr Bateman was not there and a rather flustered young clerk, who introduced himself as Matthew Cooke, eventually sorted the mail.

There was one letter from Nine Elms addressed in Henry's hand. It had been stamped and dated by Cooke only the week before. She opened it as soon as she arrived home.

Nine Elms
21st October 1848

My dearest Sara Jane,
You have been gone a day and it feels like an eternity. Nine Elms without you lacks youth and spirit, both of which I had learned to appreciate in your presence. I am forlorn and miss you far more than I had anticipated, if that is possible.

I now understand how your mother and father were so happy at the other end of the world when they had you. You ignite the light of life when you are near. Bless you for bringing them back to the comforts of the manor for their remaining years. I was not fooled in that regard from the beginning and, I suspect, neither were they.

My best wishes are with you as you return to carve out your life in the colony. I would give my all to have the wings and the stamina to fly to your side.

Meanwhile, since I have neither of those attributes, I have enclosed a verse composed during a fierce storm last evening.

My undying affection,
Henry

Sara Jane read the poem with an incredulous expression on her face.

AWAY FROM YOU
Desolate and despairing, time hangs heavy
And the day drags from hour to hour.
Missing you, unable to cast your image
From my mind and concentrate on now.
How thoughtless is time in intervening periods,
That it does not race ahead and find
The moment of our next meeting and quickly
Bring spaces together and mind to mind.

Slowly, she folded the two sheets of paper and replaced them in the envelope. "I am sorry, my Uncle," she whispered. "I was so engrossed in myself and my own concerns, that my eyes did not see. Odern would not be pleased with such regression."

Determined not to dwell on Henry's letter, Sara Jane changed into more suitable attire and launched herself into the tasks ahead. Three hours of washing dishes, clothes and bed linen, two hours of sweeping, scrubbing, cleaning and polishing, thirty minutes bathing herself, an hour of shopping and an hour of food preparation left her tired but satisfied. As she sipped another cup of tea, a list was drawn up for William's immediate attention when he arrived home, whenever that might be.

That night, sitting in William's leather chair, inherited from their father, Sara Jane tried to read a copy of the *Perth Gazette* purchased that morning. It was impossible. The words of Henry's poem kept repeating themselves and as hard as she tried she could not push them aside.

Only one way to deal with this, she thought and that was to write the letter she was avoiding. She placed the lamp, paper, ink and quills on the table and sat down. Nothing. What could she say without hurting Henry? She had considered him as an adopted uncle, which of course he was but that did not preclude marriage by law and that had obviously been a possibility in his eyes all the time. Her eyes had been blinded by her own love. Someone had said that in *The Merchant of Venice*. "Love is blind and lovers cannot see," she whispered. Blissfully she had been unaware. Finally, Sara Jane dipped the quill into the ink and began writing.

Dear Henry,

I arrived in Fremantle yesterday and found your letter waiting for me. Thank you for such lovely thoughts of which I must profess I was unaware during my stay. For that I apologise profusely, as I have never been one to trifle with another's affections and would not have entertained the notion with you, whom I hold in such high esteem. Forgive me Henry, if in any way I led you to presume that I was making myself available. It was never my intention.

The voyage home was pleasant and largely uneventful, except for our stopovers at ports to take on fresh provisions. Of course, my father had made sure I was in the best cabin, given the Captain's was already taken and so I was very comfortable. I passed the time reading and drawing and some of my sketches depict ship-board life quite well, if I do say so myself. However, it's a shame ships do not cater for bookworms, as I had read all the books I had packed by the time we reached Cape Town. It was just as well that I stopped over and was able to replenish my supply there.

The Roberts were very happy, as they were in the process of adopting a young half-caste boy, having given up the possibility of a child of their own. If you ever decide to travel Henry, you must take the opportunity of meeting Jacinta and Cameron, as they are a wonderful couple. Their home is comfortable and they enjoy having visitors and entertaining. Besides, the Madeira Estate wines are some of the best available anywhere, especially their reds. I can recommend them.

William was not at home when I arrived and the place was in a terrible state. It has taken me all day to clean up and the whole house is smaller than your library! I've decided to advertise for help as soon as I've caught up with the business records. In his letters, William assured me that we were doing very well, so we should be able to afford a servant.

I hope this letter finds you in good health.

Kindest regards,
Sara Jane

As she signed her name, Sara Jane sighed. "I'm afraid that's the best I can do, my Uncle. I'm sorry it is probably not what you are hoping for."

The next day, still no William, so the garden was tackled. It was one of those wonderful autumn days, with little wind and a gentle sun. Sara Jane put on an old long-sleeved shirt and a pair of white canvas trousers of William's and with a straw hat perched on her head, commenced the outside chores. While she worked, she thought of Yeddi and Gurdu. Should all be explained to Yeddi? If so, how and when? He had a right to know but would it only cause further worry for him and bring painful memories back for her? So far, she had managed to largely sublimate the decision-making period and the farewells. She thrust the concerns from her mind. All in the fullness of time, she thought, as she attacked the grape vine.

By mid-afternoon, the resultant pile of clippings had been stacked in the back laneway and 'Remove rubbish' added to William's list. With a stiffening back, she decided that a hot bath was in order and 'More exercise' the first item to place on her own list.

The third day, Sara Jane dressed in her best morning apparel, walked to the Fremantle Agency of the Western Australian Bank and requested an appointment with Mr Moore. When he appeared, he was frowning, until he realised who was asking for him. Knowing how much the bank accounts of Miss Sara Jane Andrews-Blair and Mr William Blair were worth, his manner became ingratiating, almost toadying. The touch of a smile spread across his client's face as she stepped forward to shake his hand, which always seemed to put him at a disadvantage.

"How do you do, Mr Moore?"

"My dear Miss Andrews-Blair. I am delighted to see you again. Please be seated. I trust your journey was without mishap and that you enjoyed a pleasant holiday."

"Yes, thank you. However, I must admit that I'm glad to be home. Travel does not seem to suit me." She paused for a moment and then asked, "Mr Moore, would you be so good as to provide me with a statement of the balance in my account?"

Moore bustled out and returned shortly to hand a sheet of paper to Sara Jane, who gave it a quick glance.

"Thank you, Mr Moore. I know this to be a highly irregular request but on the strength of my balance, could I withdraw say five pounds for my use? My brother William is away and as I do not know the details of his schedule and therefore the time of his home-coming, I need some money to see me through. He was unsure of my travel arrangements or I'm sure he would have made some financial provision for me in advance."

"It is quite acceptable, Miss Andrews-Blair. Although unusual, your custom is regarded so highly that I am sure we can waive the requirements for a male guarantor in your case. Tell me, have you yet come of age?"

"Why yes, Mr Moore. I turned twenty-one years, while I was overseas."

"Then from now on Miss Andrews-Blair, there will be no need to have your transaction forms countersigned by your brother." Moore pulled a form from his desk drawer and handed it to Sara Jane. "If you would be so kind as to write the amount you wish to withdraw and sign the form, I will authorise the cash withdrawal immediately."

Sara Jane smiled to herself as she walked to the local supplier of firewood. It was amazing the way a little economic independence opened doors for women.

With the firewood delivered and stacked in the back yard, Sara Jane turned her attention to the records of the business. Firstly, she made piles of papers by month across the sitting room floor, then she selected an unused exercise book from the shelf, mixed some ink powder with water for both red and black ink, sharpened some quills and with great care printed 'Blair Transport Enterprises' in black on the cover. She then ruled lines down the pages in pencil and, month by month, painstakingly entered the cash receipts and payments.

The cutter had been purchased, outfitted and provisioned in August 1847 and as there had been no other incomings, the expenditure was balanced against the original amount received from the sale of the treasure cache and William's personal contribution. Sara Jane marked that down as the Preparatory Month. In September, there were a few receipts for short trips while William trialled the vessel and some payments on operational debts had been made. As the months passed, the incomings improved and by February were in excess of outgoings, so more bills had been finalised. Custom steadily increased and by April, all the creditors had been paid with interest, including William who had reimbursed himself for his initial contribution. Sara Jane declared April to be their first month in the black and each successive month also showed a profit except June when the *Margaret* had been purchased. For all transactions to the end of June, she calculated average monthly revenue and expenditure and reconciled the monthly bank statements with her own calculations. She was out by an amount of £5 10s 6d in March but on a search found three receipts tucked away in what she presumed to be the petty cash tin on a shelf. When the receipts and petty cash were combined the totals matched. Thank goodness for that!

After some bread and cheese, Sara Jane worked with the papers relating to the period 1st July 1848 to the end of February 1849. When she had finished, she was well pleased with the final figures. It was all good news. I don't know how you did it William but you deserve a gold medal as big as a frying pan, as our mother used to say.

Time to light the lamps. Wearily, she closed the book. *Blair Transport Enterprises has done very well, my brother. It will take another few months of repayments on the* Margaret *and then it will be clear profit.* Sara Jane's eyes were thoughtful as she looked down at the book. *Perhaps Blair Transport Enterprises should be expanded.*

* * * * *

It was late morning when William arrived home. He saw the open door and whooped, dropping his bags and rushing through the house. Sara Jane was mending some clothing at the kitchen table and turned at the noise. She barely had time to rise before William had her in a bear hug and was swinging her around.

"Sara Jane! You're back! At last you're back!"

"William, I'm very glad to be back but would you please put me down immediately or you might be speared by a needle."

Her brother put her gently to the ground and kissed her on the forehead. "It's wonderful to see you and you look marvellous. I want to know everything. I'll fetch my things. I'm starving. Is there anything to eat?"

"Yes, as soon as you wash up. Phew, William, what have you been conveying?" She screwed up her nose.

"Pigs from the Vasse," he laughed. "All right, all right, I'll wash first." He picked up a bucket and walked out to the pump for water to fill the tub. "Hey, everything has been cleaned up. I have to admit I did neglect the house a little."

Sara Jane agreed in a sarcastic tone. "Just a little, my brother. Just a little."

When William re-entered the kitchen he looked very healthy, very virile and exuded confidence. A clean white shirt and navy blue trousers made all the difference. Her brother was burly, with broad shoulders, narrow hips and long legs. The muscles in his brown arms rippled. His snow white hair was pulled back and tied carelessly with a leather thong. Deep blue eyes flashed as he spoke. Sara Jane assessed him to be an extremely handsome man, even if she was perhaps just a trifle biased in that direction.

Leftover bacon and egg pie, bread and cheese and fresh fruit were served. William demolished the lot and asked for more. Excellent fruit and vegetables were being grown at Spearwood, several miles to the south-east where the natives cut their spears. Sara Jane had bought supplies at the Friday markets and made a mental note to triple her order, as she brought out a second helping of fruit.

"You've filled out, my brother," she said, when William pushed his chair back from the now bare plates. "Sea life must be good for you."

"It's because I enjoy it so much, Sis. It's all I've ever wanted to do. Must have been a few old salts scattered throughout our ancestors. The business is doing well financially. We'll talk about that later when I explain the paperwork to you. I feel a bit guilty really, because I've obtained contracts that used to be assigned to some of the other skippers but I guess that's competition. We've now a sound reputation based on reliability of schedules and careful handling of the goods, whatever they are."

Sara Jane rose and went into the cuddy, returning with her record book. She remained standing. "Hmm," she said for attention, as she opened it and read.

WILLIAM BLAIR AND SARA JANE ANDREWS-BLAIR TRADING AS 'BLAIR TRANSPORT ENTERPRISES'

She paused for effect, looking up to see a grin sliding across her brother's face, before continuing.

Report of business records from 1st August 1847 to 28th February 1849

Debtors: Matthew Smythe, Luke Collins and Robert Watson, for carriage. Total £59 12s 6d.

Creditor: Francis Abrahams, balance on purchase price of the *Margaret* £219.

Net profit: £431 8s 2d.

Business Proposals for Consideration

Proposal 1: A separate bank account be opened for 'Blair Transport Enterprises' to facilitate record keeping.

Proposal 2: The balance owing to Abrahams be paid in full forthwith.

Proposal 3: The feasibility of selling the *Margaret* within 12 months to purchase a boat of higher tonnage and greater potential speed be assessed.

Proposal 4: A discount of 2% for every £50 worth of carriage completed within 6 months be allowed.

Proposal 5: Special off-season rates determined on goods of a seasonal nature be provided

William shook his head.

Sara Jane continued: in order to shift market marginally to either end of the season.

William nodded.

Proposal 6: If spare storage space is available, regular clients be permitted to load goods, additional to those already contracted, at a discount of 20%.

William shook his head.
Sara Jane amended her statement: at a discount of 10%.
William nodded.

Proposal 7: If space permits, owners of goods be allowed to travel free with cargo.

"Already happens," William said.

Proposal 8: Sara Jane be authorised to employ help for upkeep of house in order to provide time for bookkeeping and development of business strategies.

William dissolved into howls of laughter, as he nodded vigorously. "If we've been doing well with only one head, what will we do with two?"

For the next few hours, as they sat at the table, Sara Jane told William about England, Cape Town and the journeys between. She left out nothing knowing that William would never betray her trust. Tears came to her eyes as she spoke of Gurdu.

William covered her hand with his and gave it a squeeze. "Sara Jane, as hard as it was, it had to be your choice. My feeling is that you made the right decision for everyone, although you have been left to bear the grief. I suppose it's a sign of my emotional naivety but I never envisaged the strength of feeling that existed between the two of you. With hindsight, I should have guessed."

That evening, William, looking decidedly uncomfortable in his best suit, which Sara Jane had already decided to relegate to second best when a new, more fashionable one could be tailored, escorted his sister to the Stirling Arms for a meal of roast beef, the usual fare on a Saturday night. He said it was the least he could do.

As they entered the dining room, a well dressed matron turned to her husband and in audible voice said, "What a handsome couple!" Sister and brother kept straight faces, as they followed the waiter to their table.

In celebration of Sara Jane's homecoming, William ordered two glasses of the hotel's best wine and the waiter served a Madeira Estate shiraz. When they toasted Blair Transport Enterprises, Sara Jane whispered, "It's a small world, my brother."

William nodded in agreement. "That it is. Glad you're home, Sis," and in concert Sara Jane joined him in the raising of their glasses for a second time.

CHAPTER 29
Yeddi

Yeddi despaired of ever convincing his people that, because so few of them were left in the region bounded by Perth, Mandurah and the hills, payback needed to be of a corporal rather than necessarily of a capital nature. By his calculations, as he visited the different groups, there were now less than three hundred Nyoongars remaining in the area. Tribal lore demanded revenge, if it was suspected that a member of another family group was responsible, either directly or vicariously, for the death of one of its own members. But did it mean to the death?

His discussion with tribal elders was not definitive. The important aspect of the payback was that justice was seen to be done. Yeddi had lengthy debates and deliberations with Odern and there were a number of interacting factors. Because there was an intent to injure, together with indignation to the point of rage exacerbated by clashes with whites, usually combined with peer group agitation, the injury, either by accident or design, was often more substantial than was warranted as the payback. Therefore each wounding was usually more severe than the previous wounding until a death occurred and this consequently required a death henceforth. Not only were the settlers decimating his people by murder, poisoning and the introduction of disease, his people were slowly annihilating themselves.

It was so frustrating and so difficult trying to talk to the scattered and diminishing groups. What to do? He had achieved little during the past twelve months and wondered whether his people would ever adapt to the changes occurring. Since Dreamtime they had lived in harmony with nature and been able to maintain a largely peaceful existence with neighbouring tribes. Now frustration and anger, brought on by the consequences of the coming of the whites and the loss of their land, threatened to do in a generation what nothing else had managed to do since the creation of his people in the Dreaming.

Yeddi was also worried about Sarjan. He knew she was back, since his last reading of the flames but something had changed and he wasn't sure what it was.

"My husband, your food is ready."

Yeddi came out of his reverie and nodded at his young wife, now with child. Jida beckoned and pointed at the cooked meat heaped on two pieces of bark. The third held a soft mashed mixture.

"I'm coming, Jida."

The sun was setting and presented its last display for the day. The sky glowed red and the evening star shone unblinking in the west.

Yeddi walked disconsolately back to the cave. Odern had not been well and they had been staying with him for the past moon. "I'll carry Great Uncle his food. Would you bring water?" Jida nodded.

The old man lay on skins on the floor of the cave with his buka covering him. The flesh had dropped from his frame and his face was gaunt, his beard sparse and grizzled. He looked tired and worn-out. The glow from a fire lit the cave and warmed the interior.

"Are you in pain my Great Uncle? Will I fetch more medicine?" Yeddi had prepared a concoction of bush herbs, which reduced pain and assisted in sleeping.

"No," Odern responded weakly. "The potion is still working. You have learned the way of the plants well, my Nephew."

Yeddi supported Odern's head and shoulders so that Jida could place the gruel of powdered wattle seeds and gum into the old man's mouth. He shook his head after only a few mouthfuls.

"Enough Jida. You are a good wife and Yeddi will be proud of you." After water, he closed his eyes.

They left him then and ate their meal near the fire outside the cave. As usual, Jida was attentive, offering her husband more meat and then water. Yeddi watched her as she wrapped the remaining meat in kangaroo skin kept for the purpose and hung the bundle from the branch of the nearest tree. The bark and bones were thrown into the fire.

Jida was a beautiful young woman and he had thanked the spirits for making her available for their marriage. He did not deserve such a gift, since he had ignored such things as family responsibilities, kin negotiations and betrothal and had gone his own way. The way of Sarjan. It had seemed so right at the time and his eyes had been closed to all but the woman he loved. He knew now in his heart that Great Uncle had been aware and understood their love and had made a decision not to interfere. For that time of total and complete happiness, Yeddi would be forever grateful.

A weak call came from the cave and Yeddi hurried to attend, signalling Jida to remain where she was. She busied herself stacking wood close by for the night's fire and tomorrow's cooking.

Yeddi squatted next to the man he respected more than any other in his world. "Yes, Great Uncle. I am here."

Odern spoke slowly and with effort. "Nephew, it will soon be time to travel across the sea and I need to talk with you before I leave."

Yeddi was about to remonstrate and then remembered to whom he was speaking. "Yes, Great Uncle, I am listening."

The conversation ranged widely, mainly reinforcing important lessons taught and points made before Yeddi had been accepted as a boylya gadak, firstly by some members of his tribe and then by all his people. One didn't go through a test, or stages of progress, or have to demonstrate competence. One was recognised as a boylya gadak and therefore one became a boylya gadak.

Odern's voice dropped to a whisper and he was breathing stertorously. "There is one thing I would ask of you, my Nephew."

"Of course, Great Uncle," Yeddi replied, his voice catching in his throat.

"I ask that you keep in touch with Sarjan, for both your sakes." Yeddi's face showed surprise. "You have a responsibility for one another and this should continue while you both live. I have been aware of the strength of feeling between you and I considered it a good thing. However, especially for a man, there is a time when one must assume responsibilities beyond oneself and take steps towards the future. This you have done. The right man, a white man, will come along and, relying on Sarjan's common sense, which I'm sure we can, she will marry and be happy as you are."

Odern paused to take breath and gather his strength. Yeddi remained perfectly still, waiting.

"You need more practice with the pictures in the flames, my Nephew. When did you last check on Sarjan?"

"Only three days ago."

"What did you see?"

"I saw that Sarjan was back in the stone house in Fremantle."

"And?"

"Sarjan was well, although I thought she had changed."

"Did you seek her in the flames, when she was over the sea?"

"Yes but the picture was too blurred. However, I did feel something strange, something that felt close to me. I could not identify it."

"I am sure that Sarjan will divulge the whole story in her own time and until that time you must be patient. It is enough to tell you that she has borne you a son, who for all the right reasons, has been left in the best of care in another country across the sea."

Yeddi leapt to his feet. A delighted expression spread across his face. "A son. That is truly wonderful news, Great Uncle. I must go to her."

"Yes, Yeddi, you must but not for bearing you a son. You will go to her to welcome her back. To welcome her home." Odern paused again, his breathing now rapid and shallow. "After you have buried me." He paused, gathering strength before handing Yeddi his magic stick. "I bequeath my magic stick to you. Use it wisely."

The look on Yeddi's face turned to anguish. "Not yet, Great Uncle! Not yet! I have so much more to learn."

"Perhaps but I have no more time, my Nephew." Odern's eyes closed, his body relaxed and a peaceful expression replaced the pain that had etched his face.

Yeddi sat watching the body of his Great Uncle until the fire burned itself out. There were no tears but the grief was spontaneous. Memories flooded back. Great Uncle as the frightening hermit boylya gadak when he was a child, as the rescuer after the massacre of his people, as the father figure, as the tutor for his initiation, as the guide and mentor during the steps towards becoming a boylya gadak himself.

"It is over," Yeddi said to Jida as he emerged from the cave's entrance.

Rocking backwards and forwards, Jida began an eerie, high-pitched wailing, which was continued throughout the night. Yeddi sat on the highest dune and looked out over the sea into the blackness until the sun rose above the hills and warmed him and he knew it was time to prepare for the burial.

For the grave site, Yeddi chose a gentle valley, where the balga grew in profusion. He scooped out the earth with his hands and made piles of sand at each end of a hole dug in the direction of the rising and setting of the sun. When the hole was of sufficient depth, Yeddi returned for Odern's body. Carefully, using a brand from the fire, he burned the nail from the little finger of his uncle's right hand, a symbolic gesture to remind him not to use his fingers to try to scrape his way from the grave. With care and reverence, he placed his great uncle's body, wrapped in his well worn buka, face up in the grave with his head looking to the east so he could watch the sunrise. Small leafy branches were laid over the body and the earth returned to the hole until the surface was level. A pile of sand remained at each end to mark the grave site and Yeddi carried limestone rocks and placed them over the grave to prevent the body leaving, or animals digging up the remains, before the spirit had left to travel to Kurannup. He called Jida to bring his great uncle's miro, which he partially buried so that it stood upright at Odern's head. Jida had whitened her face with ashes and continued to keen as she built and lit a fire nearby. Yeddi carefully marked the trees surrounding the burial site with his tabba.

"It is done, Great Uncle. May your spirit travel quickly and safely to its new home across the sea."

Yeddi idly watched the smoke from the fire. It was supposed to indicate the direction he should take to find the perpetrator of his great uncle's death. He had no intention of taking any such steps. There was no need for retribution. No human being had taken his great uncle's life. His body had just succumbed to old age. All the same, Yeddi sighed a breath of relief when the smoke rose vertically.

After transferring their gear to a new cave, Yeddi explained to Jida that he must inform his kin of the death and then would journey to Fremantle to carry out the last wishes of his great uncle. No further explanation was given or expected. As Jida was pregnant and unable to move quickly, she was to await his return, which would be within the week.

Next day, with an elaborately carved message stick in his hand, Yeddi ran south to the island crossing and then north-east. He travelled until he came across the first of his kin. After staying overnight and communicating the news of his great uncle's death, he handed over the letter stick for circulation and followed the pads north towards Fremantle.

As he ran, Yeddi had much on his mind. He presumed that Willum would have informed Sarjan that he had married but he didn't know whether Willum knew about their son and certainly Sarjan wouldn't know that he knew about his son. It was all very complicated. Yeddi desperately hoped that Sarjan would understand about his arranged marriage and why. He had tried to enter her dreams and on one occasion believed he had succeeded. If only things could be different but of course that was impossible. Pausing only for an occasional drink at one of the fresh water springs and a mouthful of dried possum meat, he hurried on his mission, arriving in Fremantle a short time after the sun had reached its zenith.

* * * * *

Sara Jane had been busy. After early morning shopping at the markets, she had baked bread, prepared soup, cooked a pot of beef and vegetable stew and was just putting the finishing touches to an apple pie. William was due back from King George Sound this evening, after doing the coastal tour as he called it and knowing how hungry he always was for home-cooked meals, it was worth the extra effort.

There was a knock on the back door and Sara Jane assumed that William must be playing a game, because he always burst through the front door. Perhaps it was a client arriving via the laneway.

"Coming," she called out, as she wiped her hands and took off her apron before opening the door.

Sara Jane and Yeddi faced each other across the limestone step.

Yeddi stood motionless, holding his spears and thrower. He was taller than Sara Jane remembered and his torso had filled out, although he was still lithe and long of limb. Black, curly hair touched his shoulders and was held from his face by a fur headband stained red with ochre. Thank goodness the bone had gone from his nose. His eyes flashed and a slow smile spread across his face.

Sara Jane's eyes closed to savour the occasion. She stepped forward to lean her head on his chest. The smell of him, the springy hair and the feel of the rows of rough cicatrices against her cheek. Then her eyes snapped open to make sure the moment was real.

"Oh, Yeddi. I have waited for you to come to me," she said softly. "I was certain you would know that I was back."

Yeddi, seeing the love of his life looking even more beautiful than he remembered and so pleased to see him, dropped his weapons and held her tightly to his chest.

"My babbingur, I am so glad you came back. I was never sure you would be able to return. I thought perhaps you would feel obliged to remain with your parents. If that happened, I knew I would never see you again. It was something I didn't want to think about." He stepped back holding her at arms length to better look into her eyes. "So, with all my heart Sarjan, I welcome you home."

Tears ran down her face but Sara Jane could not stop smiling. "I promised I would return. Remember? I had to come home to reclaim my heart."

The expression on Yeddi's face changed to sadness. Now he must tell Sarjan about his marriage to Jida.

"Sarjan. Events have occurred that I must inform you about."

She placed her hand across his mouth. "I know, my babbingur. I know about your betrothal and marriage. William wrote me about it. I am happy for you, because he told me you are a man respected by your tribe, a boylya gadak at such a young age. I was so proud when I heard. Of course you had to take a wife. I thought I told you that I understood when you visited me in my dreams."

Yeddi's eyebrows lifted. "I wasn't sure I had reached you across the sea." He took her hands as he sat Sara Jane down on the garden bench in the shade of the grape vine. "Thank you for understanding."

She said, "I have something to tell you, my babbingur."

This time he placed his hand gently over her mouth as he said, "I know Sarjan. Great Uncle," he paused, not being able to say the name. "Great Uncle told me before he died, two nights ago. It's all right," he said, as Sara Jane frowned with pain. "He was ready to leave his tribal grounds. His last words were of you." He stopped to remember the moment and then asked, "So tell me about our son."

The sequence of events were related and his face showed concern when the supposed sea sickness was mentioned and relief when she explained how her parents had assumed the American was a Negro when the baby was born. When Sara Jane had finished her story, Yeddi said what he knew he must say, even though his heart weighed heavily.

"You made the only decision possible under the circumstances, Sarjan. The Roberts sound like wonderful people." He had a dreamy expression on his face. "I hope that the spirits bring us together one day. Gurdu. It's appropriate, although how he'd ever explain his name, if he returned to his people, I don't know." He gave a sly grin. "I'm sure he will return and when he does, he will be the most handsome young man in the tribe."

Sara Jane took a deep breath. "Thank you, Yeddi. I also hope that I will have the chance to see Gurdu again. It is my most fervent wish. He was one year old last week, on 25th April. However, as Great Uncle always said, 'What will be, will be'."

Yeddi was about to say something, when there was yelling as the front door flew open and William charged through the sitting room into the kitchen. "Sara Jane, where are you?" Seeing the back door open, he dropped his bags and strode through. Yeddi stood.

"Yeddi! It's good to see you." He slapped his friend on the back. "I'm back early, Sara Jane. Is there anything to eat?" He stopped and looked sheepish. "Oops, sorry. Hardly an appropriate greeting to my two most favourite persons."

"No. That it was not. However, I now know what to expect on your return. You're starving, as usual." Sara Jane stood up. "Come Yeddi, it's time we all had something to eat." She offered her hand and led him inside. "Sit down at the table and I'll prepare some food. William, wash! Also, as usual, you stink! What was it this time?"

"Chooks and goats. The chooks literally shat themselves in fright. The goats were uncontrollable, ate their tethers through, ate half the rope on board and then shat themselves silly. Great trip! Sorry about the language Sara Jane but you did ask and I couldn't have explained it in polite terms. I'll wash for dinner, since we have a guest."

Sara Jane and Yeddi laughed at the explicit description, as William pulled a towel from the closet and, singing loudly, headed for the pump and then the bathroom. On his return, the old relaxed atmosphere, ever between them as children, returned.

When William was informed of Odern's death, the conversation revolved around memories of happy times together as children after their respective rescues.

"His bark was much worse than his bite," William summed up after each had given a personal epitaph. "Because of his influence, I suppose we will all carry certain aspects of his philosophy with us through life."

"That is the way of things," said Sara Jane, a pensive look on her face.

Hearty servings of steaming vegetable soup, fresh crusty bread and a strong cheese were served and eaten. The men agreed that Sara Jane was a fine cook and that they would keep her on.

"Thanks a lot you two but I intend to appoint a servant as soon as possible. I placed an advertisement in some of the store windows last week and passed the word around. Hopefully some applicants will present themselves tomorrow."

Sara Jane walked Yeddi to the back gate. "Keep in touch, my babbingur. I still miss you dreadfully and need to be reassured that you're safe and well. Time will help us both but I'm told one does not easily get over one's first love. That's certainly the way I feel at present."

"I feel the same, my Sarjan." He brushed her lips with his fingers, gave the gesture of farewell and with a heavy heart headed towards High Street and the track leading south.

CHAPTER 30
Expanding Horizons

Two girls presented themselves for interviews the next morning.

The first knocked at the front door at 9 o'clock, was about sixteen years old, well groomed and very conscious of her manners. She was dressed in a grey dress and white apron and wore button-up boots. Her black hair was neatly drawn back from her face in a plait, which was tied with a blue bow.

She bobbed when Sara Jane asked her name and responded, "Alice, ma'am. Alice Gardiner. I'm sixteen. My father is a sailor and we live in a cottage on the south side of town. My mother died of the flu' in the ep'demic of '45. She was with child." It all just poured out. She was invited inside and sat straight-backed at the kitchen table.

"Who looks after you, Alice?"

"Mrs Thomas, next door, keeps an eye on me, she does, when Dad is away. But I'm all right by myself, ma'am," she added hastily. "I can sew and clean and cook." Thinking that she was perhaps being too forward, Alice stopped abruptly. She had a hopeful expression on her face, anxiously wringing her hands in front of her apron.

"Well, in that case Alice, I think you and I shall get on very well." The girl looked up expectantly. "Shall we say one week's trial, with Sunday off and your pay to be five pence a day for a start? Today being Saturday, I'll expect you at 8 o'clock on Monday morning. Washing day." Sara Jane shook her hand formally, trying to look serious about this no doubt serious matter.

"Thank you, ma'am. Oh, thank you so much." The girl fairly danced out the door.

That had been rather easier than she had expected. Sara Jane was satisfied with Alice and would now not need to interview any more applicants. She settled down to prepare some invoices.

An hour later, there was a barely audible knock on the back door. Ready to dismiss any further job-seekers, Sara Jane opened the door to find the scrawniest, dirtiest girl standing bare-footed with hands clenched. Her torn dress was ill-fitting and too big and someone had made a poor attempt at sewing it to size. Huge brown eyes looked at Sara Jane with suspicion. Her black hair hung uncombed and had been carelessly cut at shoulder length.

"Come in," Sara Jane said and seated herself at the table. Here's a challenge, if ever I've seen one, she thought.

In ungainly fashion, the girl shuffled into the room and peered around as if expecting danger.

That's it! She's wary and on her guard. "Sit down, lass. What is your name?"

"Lizzie."

"Lizzie, what?'

"Lizzie Rothwell."

'Where do you live, Lizzie?"

"At the back of the Cliff Street Inn."

"Who looks after you?"

"My mum."

She's certainly a child of few words. "Is there any other family?"

"Sister and brother. Both older. Uncles visit when ships come in."

Ahh! I'm getting the picture now. "Why do you want to be a servant, Lizzie?"

"My Mum says I'm old enough and should be earning my keep elsewhere."

"You mean, you'd like to live in?"

"Yes."

"How old are you?"

"Sixteen."

"You're very small for sixteen, Lizzie."

"Well, not quite sixteen miss."

Sara Jane considered the inquisition had gone far enough. Alice was definitely the better prospect.

"Lizzie, I've already interviewed another girl this morning who is older and suitable," Sara Jane paused. The little girl was trying to sit tall and be brave but the tears were rolling down her grubby face.

"That's orlright. I'll try somewheres else. I'm not much good at aught anyways."

Sara Jane saw common sense disappearing out the window. She couldn't bear seeing such disappointment stamped on the girl's face.

She smiled and continued. "However, there's much to do and if you would like to try the position for a week, we could make a deal. Say five pence a day. You can stay in the sleep-out and start as soon as you like."

The transformation of facial expression dispersed any doubts in Sara Jane's mind. Pleasure, anticipation, excitement all flashed momentarily across Lizzie's face. A huge smile followed. "Much obliged, miss." She hurriedly let herself out the door, before her new mistress could change her mind.

Well, I think Alice and Lizzie need us more than we need them, Sara Jane reflected but we can afford two servants and it will certainly be an interesting experience.

Lizzie was back in ten minutes with a bundle of belongings and a grey and white tom-cat. Fred promptly climbed onto William's favourite chair and went to sleep.

Sara Jane served left-over steak and kidney pie and stewed fruit for lunch and assessed Lizzie's eating capacity to be superior to William's, relative to size.

The pair spent the remainder of Saturday washing Lizzie and her few clothes, trimming her hair, making up the bed in the sleep-out and sewing a dress from a bolt of cloth William had brought home as part payment by a client short of cash. Sara Jane gave Lizzie a hair brush and donated one of William's short-sleeved shirts as a temporary nightdress. Throughout, Fred assumed a supervisory role, occasionally lifting his head and stretching out a paw in proprietary fashion from his vantage point.

When Sara Jane woke the following morning, it was to a tray holding a steaming cup of tea and a slice of toast and marmalade served with the largest smile possible on the small face. Fred followed Lizzie into the room, leapt onto the bed and curled himself at Sara Jane's feet, purring with pleasure.

"Thank you, Lizzie. What a nice surprise."

"I give him a bit o' bacon, miss." Lizzie pointed at the cat.

And here beginneth the first lesson, Sara Jane thought. Of many, she suspected. "I gave Fred a piece of bacon," said Sara Jane placing the emphasis on 'gave'."

"No, miss. I give Fred 'is bacon," Lizzie said emphasising 'I'. She stopped. "I see. You are going to help me to talk proper." She struggled to remember. "I gave Fred a piece of bacon."

"Right! Good girl!"

Sara Jane was rewarded with another beaming smile from the now clean face.

* * * * *

While she prepared for her first church service since her return to Fremantle, Sara Jane could see Lizzie moving about the house orientating herself. She opened drawers and cupboards and trunks, nodding from time to time and humming a tune unfamiliar to Sara Jane. When she saw her mistress approaching the front door, she hastened to open it. "Goodbye, miss."

"Goodbye, Lizzie. I'll be about an hour and a half. I've some catching up to do."

On purpose, Sara Jane had missed two of the fortnightly Sabbath services, feeling that she needed some time to herself and not wanting to give people the opportunity to invite her to any welcoming activities until she had settled.

When she walked down the aisle of St John's, completed and consecrated only the previous year and took her seat in a vacant pew, there were many complimentary glances and nods of acknowledgment. She knelt to give a short prayer of thanks for a safe return home, a thriving business venture, her reunion with Yeddi and her new servants. An apology was given for partaking of food and drink before communion but she was sure she would be forgiven under the circumstances. She then took her prayer book from her drawstring bag and waited for the service to begin.

The Minister was young and serious and Sara Jane missed the rapport that was present in the past when her father conducted services. Nevertheless, she felt closer to God than she had for a long time. It was good to be home. She was charged up with energy and looking forward to new challenges.

On the steps of the church to greet his parishioners after the service, Reverend Jonathan Spencer introduced himself and held Sara Jane's hand overly long as he welcomed her back to the flock. He had found it difficult to take his eyes from the sophisticated newcomer during the service and had stumbled as he said the words of the Lord and passed her the wine goblet.

John Bateman eventually rescued her and, taking her arm, walked her around to greet the waiting groups. "Yes, I am glad to be home." "Yes, it was a wonderful trip." "Yes, I met many of my English family." "Yes, my mother and father are well and have taken up residence at the Nine Elms manor."

Strolling down High Street with John and Mary Bateman and five of their nine children, Sara Jane was surprised when Bateman made an impassioned plea, which was strongly endorsed by his wife. Would Sara Jane consider managing the Post Office again? At an appropriate remuneration, of course. As soon as possible. Bateman had recently been appointed to the Fremantle Town Trust and with his flourishing business interests needed competent managers to assume responsibilities in some of his ventures.

The decision was easy to make but Sara Jane displayed the slightest reticence, saying she would call at his office at 2 o'clock on Tuesday afternoon to discuss the proposition and it was left at that. She wanted to be taken seriously when any proposals for their future were negotiated. Besides, she had decided that she needed more information on which to base her arguments.

As she approached the Blair cottage, Sara Jane was pleasantly surprised to see that the front yard had been raked, the step polished and the mat shaken. "Hello," she called, as she opened the door. The front parlour had been tidied, the floors polished and the rugs swept and beaten. The coat and umbrella stand in the hallway shone with wax and Sara Jane's paintings had been dusted. It seemed Lizzie worked like lightning as she was now on her hands and knees scrubbing the kitchen floor.

"Hello, miss. Kettle's boiling. Like a cuppa?" She sat back on her heels looking pleased with herself.

"Whoa! Lizzie, there won't be anything to do for the rest of the week. Today is the Sabbath. A day of rest."

A crestfallen expression appeared on Lizzie's face. She looked so sad that Sara Jane wished she had bitten her tongue.

"Come here," she said. "I'm sorry. You take me so seriously. I'm pleased, Lizzie! Everything you have done is marvellous. Thank you." She led the girl by the hand and they sat down together on the kitchen bench. Now, tell me how you know so much about house cleaning?"

"My Mum had to do the cleaning for the Inn and when she was tired after working late, or wasn't feeling well, I would do it." Lizzie spoke slowly and carefully, choosing her words.

What a find! She's trying so hard. "Lizzie, whoever taught you, taught you very well indeed. How about that cuppa then?" Sara Jane gave the girl a quick hug and went to change. She did not see Lizzie clasping her arms where she had touched her, or the look of exquisite pleasure on her face.

Lizzie retired to bed early that night, leaving Sara Jane to bring the business records up to date. Normally, she wouldn't work on a Sunday but after the morning's conversation with Bateman, she felt she needed to know their exact financial position. Because the paperwork was now dealt with regularly, she found it a simple enough task and on this occasion it was completed in an hour.

William had implemented all her suggestions, except that of selling the *Margaret* and building or buying a larger, faster vessel and the business kept him so busy that the idea had received only cursory attention. She decided that she needed to pin him down on the issue and costs because if the boat was to be built, it could take months before it was handed over, fitted with rigging and trialled at sea. In any case, it would be sensible to use the winter period for the building, when William would have more time to oversee the finer points of the operation.

She yawned but felt she needed to conclude this Sunday with a reading from the Bible. The kettle from the wood stove was still hot, so the pot of tea was freshened and a cup poured. The large Bible was brought from the cuddy and opened reverently on the kitchen table.

A floor board creaked and Sara Jane swung around to see Lizzie with a shawl around her shoulders standing at the door holding Fred. "I woke up, miss and heard you still up. Thought you might like a cuppa but I see you have one." She continued to stand there.

"Would you like me to read to you from the Bible, Lizzie?"

"Yes please, miss," the girl nodded in eager agreement.

"Well then, come and sit down with me at the table. It's warm here. I'll read Psalm 121."

"What's a psalm?"

"Hmm. A psalm is a sacred song from the Book of Psalms from the Old Testament."

"What is the Old---?" Lizzie stopped.

"Testament. It's one of the two parts of the Holy Bible. There is the Old Testament and the New Testament." Sara Jane looked at Lizzie. "Lizzie do you want a lesson on the Bible or do you want to hear Psalm 121?"

"Both," came the answer without hesitation.

"Right. We'll begin with Psalm 121." Sara Jane returned to the Bible.

"I will lift up mine eyes unto the hills, from whence cometh my help.

My help cometh from the Lord, which made heaven and earth."

"It's sort of funny words, like cometh. And what hills are they talking about?"

"Liz-zie!" Sara Jane looked stern.

"Sorry, miss, Please go on."

Lizzie managed to make the lesson last an hour before Sara Jane bundled her off to bed.

Next morning, Sara Jane welcomed Alice and, after introductions, duties for the day were allocated. By 9 o'clock she was seated in the back office of Lionel Samson's store poring over the shipping news in past issues of the *Perth Gazette*. For two hours, she scanned every newspaper from 1845 to the current edition of May 1849. What she found was extremely interesting, by inference as well as by content. Shipping was only reported if it sailed to or from places outside the colony. Coastal travel within the colony was obviously not considered to be of sufficient importance and consequently the Blair's business was never recorded. She found spasmodic mentions in other sections of the papers when William felt the need or remembered to place an advertisement. The information given did not appear to be adequately detailed or forward-looking and would be unlikely to be helpful to their outlying clients by the time they received their papers. Neither did it highlight some of the features and special services they provided.

Sara Jane's first memorandum noted the need for a draft schedule to be prepared well in advance, taking into account seasonal factors affecting the transport of produce, as well as seasonal weather conditions. This would be updated on a monthly basis to allow accurate final schedules to be advertised in plenty of time and at regular intervals. Additional consignments would be transported by special arrangement between scheduled trips. This way, Sara

Jane believed they would have the best of both worlds. Clients wishing to make sure that their goods would be transported at a particular time could book in advance and periods of time between schedules would allow for maintenance and special contracts.

The second memorandum was about cargoes. The announcement of departures and arrivals generally gave details of destinations and last ports of call and listed the goods carried. John Bateman, who was fast becoming recognised as a leader in commerce and trade activities in Fremantle, had dispatched his first shipment of sandalwood to Singapore in December 1845 and since that time there were regular mentions of sandalwood being carried to Asian ports. Sara Jane made a note of the date of departure and destination and the date of return of each ship.

After lunch on Tuesday, Sara Jane changed into her favourite afternoon dress and cloak, purchased in London, to keep her appointment with John Bateman. He ushered her into his office and, showing just the right amount of deference, called for tea and served it himself. Sara Jane was very fond of Bateman and appreciated the almost avuncular attention he paid her. Of medium height, he had greying, unruly hair, white sideburns and a kindly mouth. Sara Jane judged him to be in his late-fifties.

Having spent the previous night again mulling over the business records, especially monthly profits, seasonal fluctuations and trends, Sara Jane opened the conversation.

"How is the sandalwood business, Mr Bateman? I believe you are shipping increasing amounts north to Asian destinations. Is it as lucrative as I have been led to believe?"

Bateman's head shot up from his preoccupation of passing the sugar. "Sara Jane." He stopped. "Can I still call you by your Christian name in informal situations?"

Sara Jane nodded.

"Then, you should address me accordingly."

"Yes, John."

A quizzical expression appeared on Bateman's face.

"Sara Jane, are you intending to use this information as part of your negotiating strategy with regard to the manager's position at the Post Office?"

"John, how could you suggest such a thing? I am just interested in keeping in touch with possible future opportunities. Since my return, many hours have been spent on analysing our business records and they have provided some interesting insights. Further, only this morning I have been perusing the back issues of the *Perth Gazette* in Mr Samson's office. Purely to bring me up to date, of course."

"Of course! And pray, what did you find?" Bateman's eyes twinkled.

"Well, it's rather an overview of our present situation. I need to spend some time thinking things through and discussing ideas with William." Sara Jane gave a sigh and a reflective look stole across her face.

"For one thing, Blair Transport Enterprises needs some on-shore management. William is a fine seaman and skipper but it's clear we require an office that is open on a regular basis to provide for communication with clients. We also should be doing more with regard to operational planning. Finally, we must be more forward-looking. Where should we go from here? That's why I asked about sandalwood trading. It seems to be a logical step for us when we purchase our new boat."

"Whoa! You've only been home a few weeks. Take time to think things through, as you have said." Bateman pursed his lips. "Tell you what. How about putting some ideas and questions down on paper. I promise I'll answer them to the best of my ability. When would you like to meet again? Don't forget we need to sort out the Post Office problem. It's the Post Office that I have to rush off to now. It's nearly time to open and the young fellow is unwell."

"Would tomorrow at 9 o'clock be suitable, John? Here in your office?" Sara Jane said, as she rose.

"Yes, that will be fine. I'll be waiting. Anything to persuade you to take charge and free me to expand my other business enterprises."

Sara Jane returned to her desk in the tiny study and jotted down some notes. At first she worried that John Bateman would find her presumptuous and reject her proposals out of hand but she knew him to be a man of sound reputation with recognised business acumen and reckoned it would be worth a try. Besides he seemed to have faith in her ability.

They met as planned the following morning.

John Bateman began. "Sara Jane I intend to be very frank and knowing you as I do, I'm sure you will appreciate such an approach in our negotiations." He waited for a response.

"Yes, John, that's the way I would prefer to proceed." She drew her notes, a notebook and a pencil from a leather writing case.

"Right then. I have two sons and seven daughters as you know and, as much as I love my daughters, I wish the situation could have been reversed. My business is thriving and like you I want to take the opportunities as they arise. I am sixty years old and would like to hand over the reins little by little during the next few years. John is now twenty-five and last year took over my whaling team. He is doing well and runs one of our small boats on the river in the off-season. Walter is obsessed by everything to do with the sea and at twenty-two years is a competent mariner but needs instruction in navigation, preferably not with one of my captains. He also leans towards the store and Post Office businesses but is not ready to settle down ashore as yet. Elizabeth has remarried, after her first husband, transported for stealing from the wreck of the *Cumberland*, died while serving his sentence. Unfortunate business all round. Her second husband, Ferres, is doing well as a stonemason and I am helping him in tendering for the provision of stone for public works. Mary Ann married Oliver Lodge last year and with some financial assistance from me took over the Crown and Thistle Hotel. My other daughters have not married as yet. Perhaps when they do, a husband or two might be interested in working in the family businesses, but until then I either stop expanding or recruit help. That's it in a nutshell."

In turn, Sara Jane was forthright about what she was prepared to do and what she wanted in return. She quickly churned over the information Bateman had just given her.

"John, I would like to put some propositions to you, which I would normally defer until William was able to be present but as you want early decisions they could be discussed and if agreeable wait for final ratification on his return."

"Yes. That would suit me. Please continue, Sara Jane."

"I will take over the management of the Post Office either until the end of this year or until you are satisfied that your clerk is capable of assuming that responsibility. If Mr Cooke does not prove suitable we could renegotiate a contract."

Bateman nodded. "Well, that's good news."

"I would like your permission to use the Post Office for communicating with our clients for an hour after the normal closing at 4 o'clock. This would not interfere with Post Office business and would provide me with an office. As you would realise, I cannot conduct business from our home down the street because, in William's absence, it would not appear proper for an unmarried woman to be seen to be having male visitors."

They both smiled, as she lowered their eyes with just the right amount of decorum.

"Finally, I would request that you assist William to enter the sandalwood trade. We propose building a new boat and with your guidance it could be built as a vessel suitable for Asian markets."

Bateman appeared momentarily disconcerted. "Rather a hard bargain Sara Jane, as I can't see what you could offer in return that would be a fair exchange, especially to a business competitor."

"Well, from my point of view, I would manage the Post Office each afternoon, say from 1 o'clock to 4 o'clock, Monday to Saturday. During that time I would train Mr Cooke in postal matters and social skills. The records of the Post Office would be my responsibility and completed on a monthly basis for your inspection. I am aware you have an accounting background but can assure you that the records will meet your requirements and be to your satisfaction. All matters pertaining to the Post Office would be completed free of charge until the end of 1849."

Bateman looked surprised but nodded.

"Further, with William's concurrence, Walter would be taught both the theory and practice of navigation, spending time on board our vessels as necessary. He would be paid for his work and receive the instruction gratis."

"Hmm," was all Bateman said, tugging on his beard as the worth of the proposals were assessed.

"Sara Jane, I would make one suggestion and one further request of the Post Office matters." He was staring straight ahead, his fingers steepled near his chin.

"Yes John. What would they be?"

Bateman's deep brown eyes met hers. "My suggestion is that you don't borrow to build a ship and that's what you would need for Asian markets but that you and William learn more about overseas trading and the consignment of goods from me in the first instance. Such an approach would be profitable, without the risk of losing your own vessel through shipwreck, piracy or typhoons."

"I'm sure your advice is sound in that regard, at least for the present. The borrowing of capital was a concern. It would be wiser to wait until our equity in the new venture was greater."

"I would definitely concur with your final statement. My additional condition regarding the Post Office is that you take my second daughter Maria under your wing, say one morning a week and instruct her in postal matters and record keeping." Bateman had a calculating smile on his face. "And pass on some of your good common sense, Sara Jane. That would be the bonus."

"Agreed. I will certainly try and I thank you for your trust and confidence in us."

"Shall we shake on it then, until William returns to endorse our proposals, as I'm sure he will." Bateman rose and extended his hand and Sara Jane gave it a strong shake. This must be a first in the colony, he thought.

By the time William arrived home from Augusta three days later, with a load of produce from James Turner's property, Blair Cottage, as named by the new servants, was spotless. Routines had been established for the girls to the satisfaction of each, which seemed to be that Alice took responsibility for the sewing and cooking and Lizzie did everything else. They complemented one another in every way and took a great deal of pride in their work. Sara Jane couldn't have asked for more in that regard. However, the best part about being relieved of the housework was the time she now had to explore future possibilities and opportunities for the business in terms of the suggestions put forward by Bateman.

William as usual was grateful that Sara Jane had acted so positively, in order to further the future of the business. The idea of improved scheduling and advertising he accepted, acknowledging that more planning would be beneficial to all concerned. He agreed with all the proposals negotiated with Bateman and was particularly excited about the sandalwood suggestion. Of course, listening to talk around Fremantle, he knew of the increased trade with Asian ports, especially Hong Kong, since its occupation by the British in 1841 during the Opium War.

On Sara Jane's insistence, Bateman had a contract drawn up by Alfred Stone, the colony's leading solicitor, during one of his fortnightly visits to the port. All three signed it and Sara Jane commenced work in the Post Office the following Monday.

The first meeting to inform the Blairs of the present situation in the sandalwood trade was held two days later in Bateman's office.

"Firstly, let me briefly describe what has been happening over the past few years," said Bateman. "And some of the background about sandalwood." He smiled as Sara Jane produced the inevitable graphite pencil and notepad.

"Sandalwood is a parasitic tree which takes its sustenance from the roots of other plants. Consequently, when the sandalwood, gum and jam woodlands in the York area are cleared, there are no hosts and the sandalwood cannot re-establish itself. That is the bad news and that is why we were paying more for the cut wood, as the collectors were forced to travel further afield. I say were, because in the recent depressed market for our normal agricultural products, more pastoralists have been cutting down more and more sandalwood and, as we all know, an oversupply leads to lower prices."

"So, until the species is wiped out, the good news is that sandalwood is in abundant supply at a reasonable price in the colony and in high demand in Asia where the oil extracted from the wood is used for the making of perfume and incense. The Chinese offer incense in their religious practices, so the demand is not going to go away." He sniffed a small wooden carving on his desk and handed it to Sara Jane. "Sandalwood," he said.

"There are some problems in coordinating the process of collection, storage and consignment, especially the latter but these are surmountable. My major profit comes from the sale of goods exchanged for the sandalwood through my stores and for this you would need to have a retail outlet."

Sara Jane looked up from her note-taking.

"Don't despair though, Sara Jane, because it is possible that your firm could act as an agent for me with the settlements around the coast and these are increasing in number and population, albeit slowly. Of course, if you entered the trade, you would need to be doing this in any case. Let me give you an example. Say in their off-season, July to September, Ray Simpson and his neighbours cut sandalwood to prescribed lengths of about six feet, which I would insist upon for ease of storage on the ships. He arranges the cartage with or without an agent in Guildford, from York to South Fremantle, where I store it. Depending on quality, he is paid from £5 to £7 a ton in cash or the equivalent in goods for his delivery. Being a wholesaler/retailer I can give them goods at a discount and unless they are desperate for cash they get a better deal that way. Sometimes one of my two vessels will be available, sometimes not. When appropriate alternative transport can be arranged, I negotiate with the Captain or a trusted passenger to act as my agent. After the cargo is landed in an Asian port, the wood is exchanged for goods to be brought back to Fremantle on the same ship or by another transport. It is more profitable to bring back cheap goods from other places, especially those which are in short supply in the colony and sell them here at a good price, than to take cash. If there is no available ship travelling to Fremantle, the money is deposited in the local branch of the Bank of England and a bank draft drawn on our local bank. For security reasons, I only trade in ports under the British flag and at no time do I take unnecessary risks."

Sara Jane was scribbling furiously.

"I began with a 4 ton shipment to Bombay in December 1845 and followed it with a similar shipment to Singapore in June 1846 to test the market. Bombay showed a small profit, while Singapore was excellent. Since then, I have traded with Hong Kong agencies and those have been better than Singapore but further to travel. Singapore pays a consistent price of £12 per ton for our sandalwood. As far as I can ascertain, the colony exported some 1335 tons of sandalwood to Asia last year. Some ships were wrecked or hijacked and some traders lost their money to unscrupulous individuals, who won't be seen in these parts again. I'm sure you heard about James Moulton from Guildford, who chartered a vessel to take his cargo of sandalwood to the Far East in '45. It was two years before his family learned that he had been murdered by the crew. To date, I have been lucky. Touch wood!" He touched the sandalwood carving on his desk. Sara Jane did the same.

"So it's not a bed of roses. The return trip to Singapore averages four months if nothing goes wrong. Hong Kong five months. The monsoon season can be a problem for obvious reasons. I don't worry about other ports. It's too difficult finding reputable agents. If the payment is in cash and goes into the bank, it has to be retrieved at a later date, or a bank draft authorised. If payment is in goods, they must be sold before you receive your profit in cash. So there can be a cash flow problem unless you have available funds set aside in case of need over that period of time. I exported about 500 tons last year and estimated I made about £2000 profit. A tidy sum, but I worry from the time the vessel leaves Fremantle till it, or the money, or bank draft arrives back. And the time will come one day, without any doubt, when it doesn't."

The discussion continued for an hour with William wanting to know about the size, tonnage and necessary specifications of vessels for the future and Sara Jane asking questions related to financial planning and profit margins. Bateman believed they had the potential to become a highly successful business team and was rather enjoying the patronage he was able to give.

Sara Jane left the men rather unwillingly when a bottle of brandy was opened.

* * * * *

Widji crouched beside her niece in a shelter some fifty paces from the main camp. The rain was heavy and periodically sheet lightning lit the sky, followed by rumbling thunder. The shelter had been prepared with care but continuous strong winds and rain had weakened the structure and now it leaked. Jida was racked with another fierce contraction. Would the baby never come? She had been in labour since midafternoon and was tired and distressed. What if there was something wrong? Her Aunt had tried to reassure her by saying that the first baby was always frightened of the new world it was being forced to enter and often resisted. One must be patient, because it was just making the way easier for later brothers and sisters.

Jida began pushing as the next contraction began and with a rush at the end, as if even the baby had had enough, the head emerged and the tiny form slithered into Widji's waiting hands. Widji wiped its face and placed the yelling baby onto the waiting kangaroo skin as she proceeded to cut the umbilical cord with a sharpened edge of quartz. Then she held the howling bundle, while waiting for the expulsion of the placenta. It was not long. The baby was passed to Jida while Widji wrapped the afterbirth in the piece of kangaroo skin and buried it behind a nearby tree, carefully placing a log on top of the disturbed soil to prevent animals from unearthing it. She did not want the baby's health to be placed in jeopardy.

She returned and squatted. "Jida. It is a boy. That will please Yeddi. How do you name him?"

"Malgar, after the thunder of the storm. Perhaps he will become as important a malgar gadak as his father is a boylya gadak."

"Good. It is a strong and powerful name. I will leave you now to report the birth and will return with food."

The next morning was cold but the rain had gone. A glowing banksia cone was used to light a fire and Yeddi came to the seclusion shelter for a few minutes to watch his son being purified. Widji held the baby cupped in her hands and waved him through the smoke before rubbing cold ash over his body. "Malgar," she said before handing him back to his mother.

"Thank you for a son, my wife," Yeddi said. He turned and walked back to the camp. Widji would not allow anyone to disturb Jida until she had rested for several days.

CHAPTER 31
Rottnest Island

The winter of 1849 was a succession of storms and wild weather. On two occasions in July, the *Sara Jane* and *Margaret* were hurriedly sailed to Rottnest and anchored off Parker Point, when the barometer plunged, heralding north-west gales. The dinghies were pulled well beyond the high water mark of the nearest beach in Porpoise Bay and William, David and the crews sat huddled in a limestone cave with limited provisions for two days until the storm abated and the boats could be sailed back to the mainland.

William was like a caged animal prowling around the house, when his activities were curtailed by the weather and this unsettled Sara Jane when she wasn't at the Post Office. Eventually she suggested that he visit Thomas Mews Junior and discuss plans for the building of a larger sailing vessel suitable for the transporting of goods to Asia. It would be a year or two before they could proceed with such a deal but to make a decision on the timing required an estimate of the costs involved, including fittings and rigging. William made regular visits to Mews' shipyard in Bathers Bay and borrowed and copied every chart of northern waters he could get his hands on. He also managed to inveigle invitations to inspect some of the vessels anchoring in Gage Roads or tying up at the jetty and spent hours drawing plans of sailing vessels of 200 to 300 tonnes. Both his passion for boats and his keen mind were appeased for the present.

Lizzie prayed for continuing bad weather. Captain Blair was her hero and when he was around the house the girl was in seventh heaven. Being totally focused on his project, William was completely oblivious of the girl's feelings.

In August, the *Sara Jane* was pulled up onto the Mews' slipway and labour hired to assist William in scraping the annual growth from below-water planks. She was then caulked and painted, fitted with a new boom and sails and made ready for sea. The *Margaret* being the more recent acquisition and requiring only a few minor repairs, sailed to King George Sound under Captain Long, returning ten days later laden with casks of whale oil. Everyone, especially Sara Jane, was glad they would soon be back to a regular transport schedule for both vessels.

One letter was received from their mother to say all was well at Nine Elms, except that Henry seemed to be uncharacteristically restless. She had packed

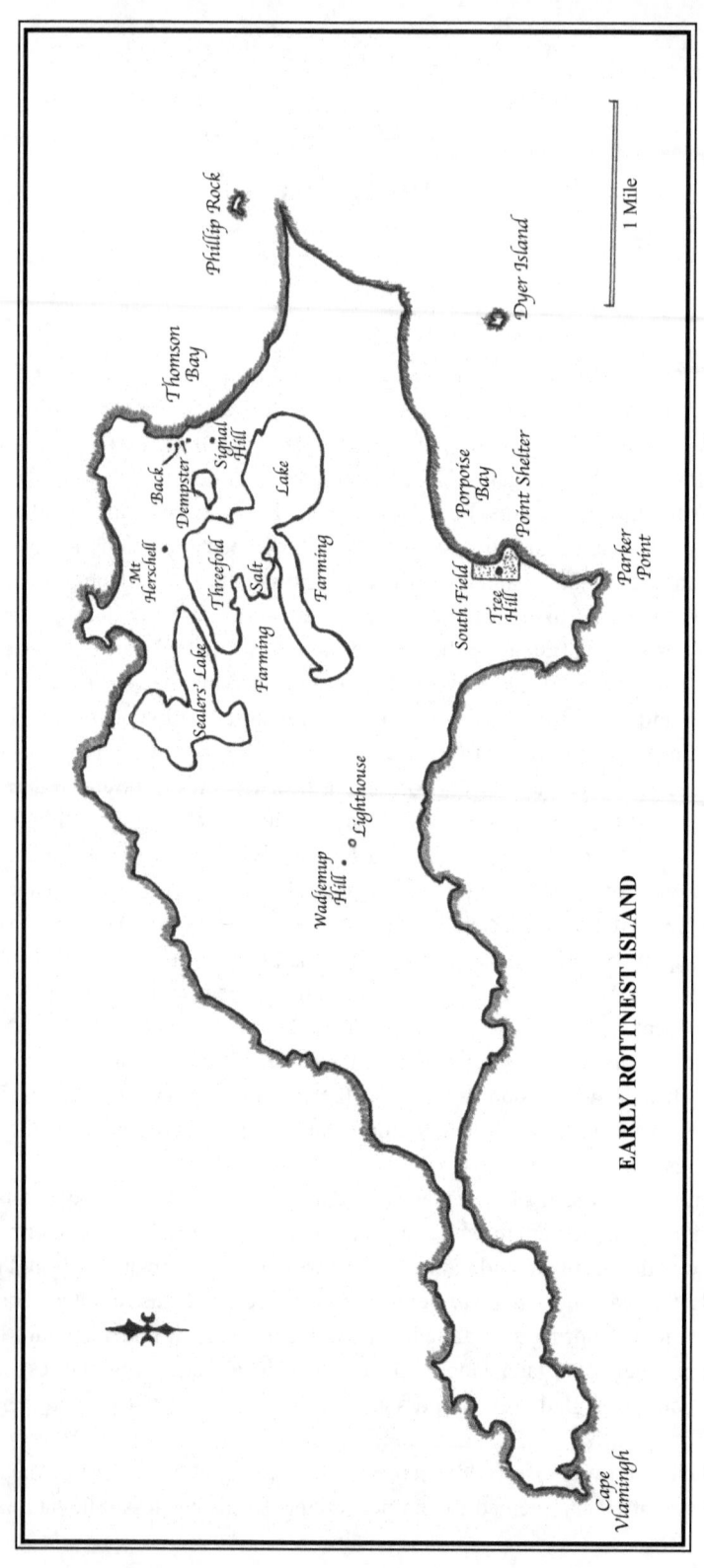

EARLY ROTTNEST ISLAND

1 Mile

Phillip Rock

Dyer Island

Thomson Bay

Porpoise Bay

Point Shelter

Back Dempster

Signal Hill

Lake

Mt Herschell

Threefold

Salt

Farming

Farming

Farming

Sealers' Lake

South Field

Tree Hill

Parker Point

Wadjemup Hill

Lighthouse

Cape Vlamingh

him off to visit a friend from his school days, who owned a large estate outside Hereford and was hoping that a change in scenery and some shooting would drive whatever was troubling him out of his system. Their father was having trouble with his joints and finding it difficult to write, which was frustrating him, because he had embarked on a rather ambitious genealogy of the family. She sent their love and hoped for a letter on the next available ship heading to England. Sara Jane wrote the next day.

Post Office responsibilities were challenging and rewarding. After the initial shock of having a young woman as his supervisor, Cooke settled down and found things much more relaxing. For one thing, he appreciated the amount of time Sara Jane spent in assisting him with his duties. Bateman was always so busy that he never seemed to be around when Cooke needed him. In addition, Sara Jane helped him in his all-consuming desire to learn to behave like a gentleman and his determination in this regard was admirable. By the time Bateman's daughter, Maria, arrived on the scene for her weekly half-day instruction, Cooke felt much more confident about all facets of postal business, was learning bookkeeping and had purchased some new clothing after seeking Sara Jane's advice.

Time to go home. Sara Jane packed up the business records on which she had been working and placed them in her leather carry-all. It was nearly 5 o'clock and she was looking forward to a cosy fire and the promised pot roast to be prepared by Alice. Lamb with mint sauce was her favourite and her mouth watered. A loud knock intruded upon her culinary thoughts. The door opened and James Dempster, whom she recognised from the church congregation, stepped inside.

"Hello there. I'm James Maclean Dempster. Am I too late to see someone about Blair Transport? He was of medium height, sported a full moustache and beard and had a cheeky smile on his face.

"Come in, sir." Sara Jane stepped out from behind her mail-sorting table to shake hands. "I am Sara Jane Andrews-Blair, a partner in Blair Transport Enterprises. William Blair, my brother, is at sea at the moment but you have come to the right place. I negotiate most of the preliminary arrangements. Would you take a seat."

Sara Jane lit the lamp, joined Dempster at the table and drew out her pencil and notepad.

"Now, sir, please explain how we can assist you."

"Certainly and thank you for extending your office hours Miss Andrews-Blair."

Sara Jane nodded and sat in readiness, straight-backed, business-like, yet clearly relaxed.

"I have been fortunate in being able to successfully negotiate a lease of Rottnest Island from the Government. The penal establishment is to be closed next month when Superintendent Vincent escorts the present native prisoners to Fremantle gaol. Of course, the legal documents are still to be drawn up and signed by all parties and that always takes an age but I have permission to begin moving stock to the island in the middle of September. That is why I need your services, which I might add come highly recommended. My first shipment will be about seventy sheep."

"Certainly, Mr Dempster. We have two vessels and would be pleased to assist your transfer to the island. You are indeed fortunate, as I believe it is a truly beautiful place."

The discussion took an hour and Dempster was more than satisfied. The young woman had certainly extended his planning. A preliminary schedule and tentative transport dates had been set, not only for the sheep but also for his family, their personal and household goods, farming equipment, building supplies, horses and more sheep. Dates and costs would be confirmed on William's return.

"Thank you, Miss Andrews-Blair. You have been extremely helpful. I wish you a good evening." Dempster departed, leaving Sara Jane very pleased with the deal.

"And now for my pot roast," she said in eager anticipation, as she blew out the lamp and locked up.

* * * * *

On William's return, Sara Jane briefed him on the conversation with Dempster and gave him her notes. William huffed and puffed all evening and had calculations on pieces of paper scattered over the table. He had run his fingers through his hair so many times, it hung in dishevelled fashion around his face. This was the only aspect of the business he disliked. In fact, he loathed and detested it but he couldn't expect his sister to know how many sheep, or horses, or sacks of grain he could carry on each of the vessels.

"Sara Jane, would you go through these figures with me please? You were always better at arithmetic than I was." He smiled at his sister sweetly.

"Of course, William dear. Flattery will get you everywhere." She winked at Lizzie who was looking up with a grin from a Standard 6 Reader that had been purchased for her. Lessons were proceeding at an admirable pace and the girl rivalled Sara Jane's own thirst for knowledge. It was disappointing that Alice displayed absolutely no interest in learning at all, considering it to be the preserve of the male of the species.

"It's all different because the distances are so short. We can't price on my usual daily rate and we'll have to return unladen, which is a waste. However, I don't want to lose a new customer, especially Dempster, because until he can afford his own vessel, he will need regular transport."

310

'William, why don't you offer Dempster some alternatives and see what he thinks? I would judge him to be a reputable man. You could also request a review of charges after the first three trips. You'll have a better idea by then. Or calculate costs on animal values. By the way, he mentioned something about salt being ready for conveyance to Fremantle in the short term."

More grunts and mumbles.

"That's enough you two! I can see the grins." William endeavoured to look fierce. "Try this. If one sheep is carried for a day, which includes loading and unloading, for threepence, how much does it cost to carry seventy sheep for half a day?"

Sara Jane deliberately paused.

A small voice from the mat in front of the fire said, "Eight shillings and seven and a half pence."

William looked surprised. "Then try this one Lizzie. If one sheep is worth four shillings and a sheep is to be transported at two per cent of its value per day, how much will it cost to transport seventy sheep for half a day?"

A slightly louder and more confident voice said, "Eight shillings and four pence."

Sara Jane could not control her mirth. "You are quite correct, Lizzie. William, your profit margin is too low. An unskilled labourer can earn four shillings a day at present. Even if Dempster helps with the unloading, you need at least four times that because it really is a day's work. You won't be able to do much else by the time you get back, clean the boat and so on. Perhaps all our prices are too low and that's why everyone is coming to us."

William sighed. "I think you two are both right. Come up here and sit at the table Lizzie and help me draw up the new scale of prices for Blair Transport Enterprises."

Lizzie floated to the table on cloud nine and sat next to William. She needed three tries at the first calculation before their answers were congruent. The physical proximity of her hero was very disconcerting.

William found out later from the port gossip that Dempster had also received quotes from Bateman and two other carriers. Bateman's quote was only slightly higher than their revised cost schedule. The other carriers used much smaller vessels and Dempster apparently judged a certain risk there. The feedback was that the lower rates, more flexible schedule and concern for the well-being of the family had won the day for Blair Transport Enterprises.

On the 19th and 20th September 1849, the *Sara Jane* and *Margaret* landed seventy-six sheep in Thomson Bay, Rottnest. Walter Bateman joined William for the first time as a crew member. He was a serious young man and, although the same age as his Captain, immature in outlook. William decided to take things slowly. He wanted to do the right thing by Bateman, whom he admired greatly and to whom he was now beholden.

Edward Back, the Pilot and several of his children were on the beach each day to greet the arrivals and they assisted in the unloading of the sheep. Dempster had been relieved to know that Back's wife and family were living permanently on the island, as they would provide company for his own family. The feeling was mutual.

The following week, James Dempster and his wife Ann, their seven children between two and twelve years and their personal belongings had a smooth trip to the island. Sara Jane took her first business trip and helped with the children. To pass the time, William kept up a commentary about weather, rocks and islands, wrecks, birds and everything else he observed to anyone who would listen. Experience had shown him that focusing the mind was a sound foil against sea sickness. Today, it certainly worked. The spring weather was perfect. The water was crystal clear and beautiful shades of blue and green in the shallows. White sand met the water and spinifex vied with species of succulents for the ground between the beach and the leaning melaleucas. Mauve daisies covered the slopes of hills further inland.

While the men unloaded the goods and transported them to Vincent's cottage, which was to be their temporary home until Dempster could renovate another cottage nearby, Mrs Dempster and Sara Jane walked the children to the ridge at the northern end of the bay. From the highest point, they could see the mainland and smoke from a fire in the Darling Range. The two women were conversing amicably when squeals of delight from the children had them racing down the hill, skirts and petticoats uplifted. The cause of the excitement became immediately apparent. Hopping away through the gully were several frightened wallabies. They could only be described as cute. About as cute as a possum, Sara Jane thought.

The lease was formally signed in October and soon after that William transported three labourers and six Aboriginal prisoners from the Round House to Rottnest to assist Dempster in his agricultural pursuits.

By the following trip, when additional farming equipment was carried to the island, Dempster had ensured that there was sufficient salt scraped from the salt lakes and stored in the building on Thomson's Bay to back-load five tons of superior quality salt to the mainland. It was sold at a good profit.

So Blair Transport Enterprises continued to receive contracts and made regular monthly runs in the *Margaret* at a special low rate, until Dempster purchased his own small sailing vessel.

Meanwhile, true to his word, John Bateman tutored William and Sara Jane in the intricacies of the sandalwood trade. It was agreed that they would commence their venture into overseas trade in 1850.

With their revised rates and the back-loading of salt to Fremantle warehouses, Sara Jane announced that monthly profits had significantly increased from September to November compared with the previous year.

* * * * *

Yeddi made two brief calls to Henry Street, one soon after the birth of Malgar and one towards the end of spring. He always visited on the day of a full moon and as close to midday as possible so that Sara Jane knew when to be home. Lizzie had been told the bare bones of the story about Sara Jane and William living with the natives and after the first call, when the appearance of Yeddi at the back door had sent her screaming for her mistress, she stayed out of the way and, as she had been taught, didn't ask any questions.

Sara Jane knew that she still loved Yeddi. Her heart always told her when he was coming and sorrowed for days after his departure. While she was with him, she was so filled with happiness and love, she felt that she would burst.

And Yeddi still loved Sara Jane, but because he had responsibilities and also loved his wife and child, the vacuum in his heart was partially filled. Nevertheless, whenever he approached the settlement at Fremantle, he was always eager with anticipation.

They were soul mates and although they each knew how the other felt, nothing was ever said. Silently, they each agreed that it had to be that way.

* * * * *

"Here's a letter for you, miss." The stern look caused Matt Cooke to immediately correct himself. "Er, Miss Andrews-Blair."

"Thank you, Mr Cooke." Sara Jane glanced at the writing, before placing the letter in her leather business folder.

When she arrived home at 5 o'clock, she placed her parasol in the stand in the hallway and removed her bonnet. She eagerly looked forward to letters from Nine Elms and this one was from Henry.

"Lizzie," she called.

The girl appeared at the kitchen door. "Yes, ma'am."

Sara Jane looked at her fondly. What a gem. In eight months she had blossomed with the nutritious and plentiful food and especially the attention. Her stitching skills were exemplified in the neat grey dress and white pinafore she had sewn for herself and her black hair was shining, pulled back from her face with a neat bow. Alice had accepted a position with Mrs Andrew Froude at an increased wage and Lizzie revelled at being in charge of the household. With adolescence and a developing persona, it was like the transformation of Cinderella. Since her mother's death two months ago, she had no ties. Her two older brothers had been placed in positions on a York property and, as both were illiterate, she could not correspond with them.

"Lizzie, would you wait ten minutes before serving dinner. I will retire to the sitting room to read my mail."

"Yes, ma'am."

Using a letter opener, Sara Jane carefully broke the seal.

Nine Elms
30th July 1849

My dearest Sara Jane,

Yesterday, I received your wonderful letter. I have been willing fair winds and good seamanship for nearly five months. Special entreaties were made regularly for the blessings of Neptune and Poseidon, in order to ensure that both Roman and Greek gods were appeased. They must have been listening. I shall not tell Edmund that I have extended my personal deities but will leave them on my list for prayers, as additional insurance for the future.

Your mother and father send endearments and beg your understanding of their tardy communication. Both are well and enjoying retirement but their arthritis is painful and restricts their writing. The cold weather here last winter seems to have affected their joints badly. In all honesty, it is now almost impossible for either of them to manipulate a pen with any certainty of legible results, which is an unfair twist of fate, considering how they both took such pride in their copperplate handwriting.

We are experiencing a glorious summer, with warm, sunny days and cool nights. It is always strange to realise the antipodes have their seasons reversed. I hope the winter weather in your part of the world is not inhibiting your commercial activities.

Your comments of March last gave me cause for contemplation. I travelled the continent as a young man. The Grand Tour as they call it. Such experiences were considered essential for the culmination of a gentleman's education! However, since then I have rather buried myself in Swindon and apart from the annual round of London theatre have really become a bit of a fuddy-duddy.

Thinking of you in a far flung outpost of the British Empire, fighting off the natives and establishing a colony, has fired my enthusiasm for adventure. Both your mention and my brother's description of the warm reception you all received from the

Roberts at their Madeira Estate, together with the opportunities
for imbibing exquisite wines is becoming increasingly attractive.
If I include the chance of seeing you, my dear and meeting
William, I am being drawn, nay impelled towards Western
Australia.

So what do you think of the idea that I turn an adventurous head
for far-off places, Sara Jane? Like Western Australia? Please
write and afford me your feelings on the matter.

My heart is yours,
Henry

Sara Jane was torn between laughter over the idea that Henry would hurry to her side to protect her from the natives and tears that he still felt such a strong affection for her, which she could not reciprocate.

There was another page.

WISHING AND DREAMING
I wish, I wish a thousand wishes
I dream, I dream a thousand dreams
I wish, I dream a thousand things
Each day, each night, no solace brings

Oh, my dear Henry, I must not write too soon this time. Did I encourage you? I thought not but who knows how the mind works when it is confounded by the machinations of the heart.

* * * * *

On a warm Christmas morning, Sara Jane and William exchanged presents.

Sara Jane received a small parcel. She carefully removed the wrapping to find a beautifully bound volume of a collection of poems by William Wordsworth. "William, what a thoughtful gift! How wonderful! Did you know he is called 'Nature's Priest' and is the Poet Laureate? An honour indeed." She clutched the book to her chest, as if to protect it.

William laughed with satisfaction. "Well, I'm glad it pleases you, my sister. I had Father make the purchase and Captain Joseph Carter of the *Bridget*, carried it personally. It arrived in the nick of time."

Then it was William's turn. Sara Jane handed him a huge parcel, which he placed on the table to open. As he unfolded the new clothes, he looked sheepish. "Sara Jane, whatever will I do with them?"

Now it was Sara Jane's turn to laugh. She looked almost smug. "You will wear them, my dear brother. They are the very latest style and cut and if you would like somewhere to parade, might I suggest that you escort me to church this morning? If I am ever to become an aunt, it will be necessary for you to take a wife, which is highly unlikely when you look a cross between a sailor and a pirate and are never seen in genteel company."

As William walked Sara Jane to her customary pew at St John's later that morning, John Bateman acknowledged the glowering William. In fact, the expression gave the young man a self-assured and confident, almost derisive look, which set tongues wagging around the Port of Fremantle and eager matrons reassessing William as a possible target. The dark grey serge frock coat hung from wide shoulders, the matching trousers emphasised narrow hips and muscular thighs and the crisp white shirt with striped satin waistcoat and matching neckcloth added a touch of hauteur.

"Phew, Sara Jane. It's hot in all this clobber. How can you put up with all the gear during the summer?"

"One becomes used to it, William. One must maintain standards."

"Well, I'm changing for Christmas lunch and that's that!"

"Permission granted but please dress again for dinner. Lizzie is having Christmas lunch with a friend but she has prepared a special meal for you this evening and I think you should show her due deference."

"Humph," said William but he grudgingly did as he was asked.

When Lizzie arrived at 5 o'clock, Sara Jane welcomed her formally as a visitor and then gave her a hug. She looked and acted like a young woman from the higher levels of society. Her speech was articulated with care, her dress was appropriately fashionable and her demeanour befitted the occasion.

She was presented with her first pair of gloves and reciprocated with a basket of home-made biscuits for their dessert. Her hero looked magnificent in his new clothing and she found it difficult to keep her doe eyes from him.

Her day was made when Sara Jane suggested that henceforth she should answer only to 'Elizabeth' and William agreed.

The following week, Sara Jane concluded her duties at the Post Office. Soon after, she met with John Bateman and presented him with a statement of the financial situation until the end of 1849, a report on the staff, namely Mr Matthew Cooke and Miss Maria Bateman and some recommendations to improve the efficiency of the business.

Bateman smiled as he thumbed through the papers. He now liked to think of Sara Jane as a protege. "Thank you, Sara Jane. I appreciate your efforts and would urge you to continue on a salary, if I thought it would do any good."

"No John, I'm not needed. Mr Cooke is ready to take charge and your daughter has adequately assumed the responsibilities as his assistant each morning. The Post Office is in good hands. However, I believe she is soon to marry Mr Lodge and if you need another part-time assistant, I could recommend a very capable and mature young woman. She'll is nearly seventeen, can read and write well and is unusually good at arithmetic."

"Well, I'll need someone within the next two months. Maria is already preparing for the wedding and the household is in the customary tizzy leading up to nuptials. Naturally, I would accept your recommendation, Sara Jane. Who is this young woman?"

"Her name is Elizabeth Rothwell. She resides at our home and assists with the management of the household. She recently began attending church services with me. I did introduce her to your family."

"Ah! That young woman. She is particularly pleasant of countenance, if I could phrase it that way. Speaks and dresses well too. With your endorsement Sara Jane, I'd be pleased to place Miss Rothwell at the Post Office, if she will accept the position."

"I have one final favour to ask of you, John."

"And what is that Sara Jane?"

"Would you allow me to still run our business from the Post Office after hours?"

"It would be my pleasure." Seeing Sara Jane about to speak, Bateman continued with a smile on his face. "And there will be no suggestion of payment."

Sara Jane put the proposition to Elizabeth that afternoon. "It would be a wonderful opportunity for you, Elizabeth. You would earn a salary and would learn about office procedures. Mr Bateman is as good an employer as you would find in the colony."

"Oh thank you, Sara Jane. You have been so kind to me in every way since I became part of your household." They were on a first name basis now and friends rather than mistress and servant. "Do you think I could do it?"

"I know you could do it, Elizabeth. I will employ someone else to help in the house."

Dismayed, tears appeared in Elizabeth's eyes. "No, Sara Jane. You said the position is part-time and I would prefer to still attend to the household. May I try to do both and see how everything works out?"

"Of course, my dear, if that is your wish." Sara Jane suddenly realised that unwittingly she had suggested discarding Elizabeth's security blanket. Her home because of her domestic position. She inwardly chastised herself.

CHAPTER 32
The Trial

D ubyt sat near a deep waterhole at the base of the high hills and gazed at the brightly-coloured stones he held in his right hand. What he desperately needed was some intervention by the sacred snake, some guidance in the problem that dominated his life and thoughts, some punishment befitting his adversary's contravention of his own rightful destiny. He shook the stones and looked again for an answer. There was none. No special prospect entered his mind. They could not override the hatred he felt in his whole being.

Dubyt hated Yeddi. He was obsessed with the idea that if Yeddi had not become the boylya gadak, he would have received the honour. It was totally unfair. Whoever heard of a boylya gadak of such a young age? He did not deserve it and if his great uncle had not shown favouritism to his kinsman, Dubyt would in time have become the one to carry the magic stick. The highest honour had been stolen from him. While Yeddi lived, he would never receive the respect or reverence that he deserved.

He stopped. His eyes darted and he looked around guiltily. Such thoughts were dangerous. It was said that Yeddi could see into the future, that visions appeared before him and that flames from the fire told him stories.

The stones were carefully replaced in their fur pouch and Dubyt walked back to the family camping place.

Several women whispered as the grey-haired elder passed. Most were frightened of him. He was cruel to animals and liked to see them in pain. He scolded children and found cause to exact punishment. He had three wives and none had borne him a child, although one, the widow of his deceased brother, had three children from that marriage.

Dubyt's opportunity came that very night and he judged it to be the intervention he had been beseeching from the sacred snake and which could change his life.

The final meal for the day had been eaten, the kangaroo skins spread and the fire stoked. Everyone settled down for the night and soon all was quiet, except for the usual snores and snuffles of a sleeping group. An hour later, his youngest stepchild, always restless in sleep, rolled into the fire. There were screams from the little boy, yells from the adults and frantic attempts to pull him from the embers but it was too late. By the time he was dragged from the coals, the blackened skin was peeling from his body, his eyes were blinded and little facial flesh remained. The wailing began.

Morning dawned fine and hot with a strong, blustery wind from the east. It was the typical summer pattern. Dubyt took charge of the proceedings as was expected of him. During the night, unable to sleep with the weeping and wailing of the women, he had devised an elaborate plan and it required the land breeze to be blowing.

By midmorning, the site had been prepared and a small hole dug. Dubyt carried the disfigured corpse, wrapped in kangaroo skin, to the grave site. Twenty-four sorrowful members of the Bindjareb tribe gathered around as the small parcel was covered with sand and eucalypt branches placed over the disturbed earth. Dubyt lit the prepared fire and all waited in fearful, yet fascinated, anticipation to discover who had been the perpetrator of such a horrible death. The flames from the fire grew higher and the smoke rose six feet before being caught by the wind and making its way towards the sea.

The group waited impatiently for the decision. Dubyt pointed in the direction the smoke was blowing and said one word. "Yeddi."

Gasps came from the family. How could this be so? Yeddi was revered as a boylya gadak. His reputation for fairness in advice and judgments was well known. Was he not travelling widely through the tribal lands to help the Bindjareb people displaced from their territory?

Dubyt lifted his hands. There was immediate silence. "The smoke travels directly to the cave of Yeddi, who talks with fires and sees in flames. He is the cause of my son's death."

The chatter recommenced.

"Does anyone doubt my word?" asked Dubyt sternly.

Silence again, followed by a shaking of heads, denials, then words of concurrence with Dubyt's decision.

"The men will come with me." The initiated males followed Dubyt. The wailing began again and the women threw handfuls of warm ash from the fire into the air above their heads.

* * * * *

Yeddi and Jida had returned to the cave area the previous month. They welcomed the quiet away from Jida's family camp. Not that they hadn't appreciated the assistance that the women had provided for Jida during the birthing, especially her aunt Widji but Yeddi found the intrusions of camp life interrupted his thinking. Remembering his great uncle's impatience with the close proximity of other families and his preference for an isolated existence, he accepted that it was possibly a family trait.

319

Jida was feeding Malgar, now six months old and was looking at her son with the loving eyes of a proud mother. He certainly had a healthy appetite. She changed him to her left breast and he resumed his noisy suckling.

Yeddi picked up his spears. "I'll fetch some meat for the evening meal," he said and disappeared down the track.

What he really needed was time to think. Something was niggling in the back of his mind. Some danger was in the offing but as he could not recollect any situation, or foresee any possible reason for his premonition, he was just left wondering. The hunt took longer than expected, probably because he was not giving it his full attention and it was midafternoon before he speared a kangaroo several miles down the estuary.

As he slung the carcass over his shoulder, he admonished himself. It all goes to show that one should concentrate on one thing at a time. Yeddi decided to explore the flames that night for an inkling to the problem.

He was not to be given that chance.

The smell preceded the avenging party and Yeddi knew he was in a perilous situation when four men stepped out from the trees some forty paces away. Their naked bodies were caked in wilgi and grease, giving the usual red colour to their skin and banksia branches were inserted in their headbands and armbands. They were men from the foothills and he did not recognise them.

One man stepped forward and uttered threats, shaking his spear at Yeddi and gesticulating wildly. Then the others joined him and so they advanced following the man in front. Yeddi dropped the carcass of the kangaroo and held his left hand up, palm towards them in the gesture of greeting but that seemed to infuriate them more. He called out, asking their names and what they wanted but to no avail. By this time they seemed to be almost trance-like in their anger.

With a dry mouth, a tingling up his spine and the hairs on his neck raised, Yeddi felt fear. It crowded in upon him. All the danger signs were present. He realised he should run but something held him back. Then he heard a terrified scream and saw Jida being dragged, clasping Malgar to her breast, behind another man. This man he did recognise. "Dubyt," he hissed. An evil man, despised by his great uncle, who had always said that the only status he held was by virtue of the trepidation he generated in his clan.

"Dubyt, release my wife. What is wrong? Talk to me."

Dubyt kept advancing and Jida kept screaming. Yeddi held his ground and then, as they drew closer, he saw the blood running from a flesh wound in her lower leg.

Yeddi's lips pursed, his pupils dilated and fury overwhelmed him. Uncontrollable anger took over the usually restrained and placid young man. An animal-like growl arose from the back of his throat and he roared in anger.

He threw his spear with all his strength and it flew true, entering Dubyt's right thigh and piercing the iliac artery in the groin region. On the way, it passed through the penis and testicles.

Dubyt fell to the ground screaming, Jida limped towards the cover of the trees clutching Malgar and the four men, having seen a demon throw a killing spear from an impossible distance, pushed the shaft of the spear right through the leg, picked up the writhing, shrieking Dubyt, his groin spurting blood and fled.

Yeddi ran to Jida and comforted her shaking body, before placing his armband over the bleeding wound. Lifting his wife and son together, he carried them back to the cave. Between gasps of pain she told him that she had decided to welcome Yeddi at the foot of the hill and had almost collided with the old man. She began shivering and sobbing again.

"Hush. It's all right Jida. They have gone. Dubyt will be dead within minutes. Now grit your teeth, while I attend to this gash. Luckily, it is not life threatening and should heal quickly."

Later, after Yeddi had administered a pain-killing potion and bound Jida's leg with a plaster of red gum covered with soft bark, he hurried back down the hill and along the estuary track to retrieve the carcass of the kangaroo and his weapons. There was a trail of blood leading to the south and Yeddi guessed the men were carrying Dubyt to their camp via the island ford.

On his return to the cave, Yeddi spoke of his suspicions. "I have an idea that I have been set up in some way for a payback attack. Dubyt has coveted my position as boylya gadak since great uncle prepared me before he entered the land of the spirits. He has always been an evil, cruel man and jealousy was probably one of his many failings. I would like to think that it is the end of the matter but I have a feeling there could be more to come."

* * * * *

The men from the foothills clan of the Bindjareb tribe had stopped to fashion a stretcher of branches fastened together with reeds and were carrying the corpse of Dubyt along the estuary track. They were too frightened to leave the body behind, because Dubyt had always bragged that he was able to talk with the sacred snake and although no one had ever seen any evidence of such communication, they were not prepared to take the risk. The body must be taken back to the family, so that it could be buried according to the law. Decisions about revenge could be made later. Their eyes were wide with terror and they did not speak as they headed for the ford at full speed.

* * * * *

Thomas Peel and the Governor rode their horses sociably, north along the estuary track towards Mandurah House. Captain Charles Fitzgerald R.N. had taken up his position the previous year and finding that he enjoyed Peel's company and could not overlook his connections, escaped on the occasional short exploratory survey when government responsibilities allowed. This brief tour had taken the Governor by cutter from Fremantle to Mandurah, where he had joined Peel, and on horseback they had travelled south along the coastal track leading to Australind and its junction with the track south from Pinjarra. They were now on their return journey. An escort of the 99th Regiment of Foot stationed at the barracks in Mandurah shuffled along behind.

Fitzgerald spoke. "So, in conclusion Thomas, I was sorry when informed about that unfortunate Rockingham land business but as you know, there was nothing that could be done while Pratt held a partial mortgage on your land. Without a clear title, the government could not facilitate your offer to surrender the ten thousand acres to pay off some of your debts to the Crown. What are your plans now?"

"Damned if I know, Charles. For a while it appeared as though I might be able to return to England to my family but it was not to be. It's been nine years now since my wife and daughters returned home. My son Thomas is a good lad and proving marginally successful in his agricultural pursuits at the Serpentine Farm. He recently turned twenty-one. I gave him the title to five thousand acres in '43. It may increase in value because the Canning-Pinjarra track passes through the farm and the Serpentine River provides a fresh water supply."

At that moment the four natives ran into view around a bend in the track and pulled up, startled by the unexpected entourage. The soldiers, led by Sergeant Watters, raced past the Governor down the path and took up protective positions. Determined not to relinquish the corpse, the natives stood their ground, not knowing what to do but very aware of the rifles pointed in their direction and the two dogs circling and snarling at them.

Peel spurred his horse forward and began questioning the natives. The Governor joined him and asked for a translation of the conversation.

"They are not locals. They're from the foothills area, adjacent to the Darling Range and were travelling to meet a relative. A medicine man, who lives nearby, attacked them and killed their leader and they are returning the body to his family for burial according to tribal law. He was an elder and they are clearly frightened at what has happened."

"Ask them why the other native killed their leader."

After an agitated exchange of words, Peel turned to Fitzgerald. "They say they don't know why Dubyt was killed, which I don't believe. It was likely a revenge foray. I believe it's the crux of the problem in the colony. Continual payback killings. That could explain why they are so far from home. They're all members of the Bindjareb tribe but there are factions and family squabbles, especially over their women."

"Ask them who was responsible for the death of their leader."

Peel spoke again with the natives.

"They say his name is Yeddi and he lives in a cave near here. He is a young man and a powerful boylya gadak, which translates loosely in our language to a wizard, magician or medicine man. I've heard of him and as far as I know he's not a troublemaker, although one can never be sure with these blighters."

"Let them go, Peel. They obviously want to be on their way. Would we be able to find them again if need be?"

Peel was surprised by the question and his brows lifted. "Yes, we can always trace one-eye there," and he nodded at a native with a scarred face and an empty eye socket. "But why would we want to find them again?"

"Oh, I was thinking I might make an example of this killing, in the hope that it would act as a deterrent on this payback business and we'd need witnesses. Indiscriminate injury and murder among the natives cannot be condoned by a colony governed under the auspices and therefore the judicial system of England. It is unworthy of us to allow it to continue without attempting to constrain it in some way." Fitzgerald paused. "Don't you think so, Peel?"

"Charles, my in-bones feeling is that it's so much a part of their culture, it would be well nigh impossible to change. Still, we are beholden to compel obedience to the law and to teach the natives to respect our God and King. Perhaps the enforcement of one of the Ten Commandments would indicate your intentions in this regard." Peel smiled and Fitzgerald did not pick up the sarcasm. Everyone in the colony knew how Fitzgerald felt about the natives since he had been speared in the thigh while exploring the Champion Bay area twelve months ago.

The Governor ordered the capture of the murderer and the dogs were sooled on their way back up the track. They found Yeddi and his family within ten minutes. Yeddi hid Jida and Malgar with their possessions in a dark recess of the cave and told her to wait until he came back or sent a message. He fended off the snapping dogs with a single spear as he led them away from the cave and then sat waiting at the foot of the hill, while the dogs continued their barking. He wore his red headband and nasal bone.

When the soldiers arrived, he pretended to be frightened and gabbled and gesticulated until the sergeant bound his hands and he was escorted back to the waiting group.

"You, Yeddi?" A man he did not recognise addressed him from horseback. He knew Peel by sight.

"Yeddi," he said and placed his fist on his chest.

"Do you speak English?"

Yeddi said nothing.

"It's no use Charles," said Peel. "Most of the outlying natives don't speak English, or if they do, it's an abominable pidgin."

Fitzgerald hesitated for a moment, then gave the order to resume their way north and to bring the native with them as a prisoner.

"Tie him to Hawthorn's belt," said Sergeant Watters, indicating a soldier at the rear of the group. "When you're ready, Your Excellency."

Fitzgerald nodded and the sergeant gave the order to march. The group moved off, with Yeddi being towed along by his bound hands.

What's all this about, he wondered. What have I done? Must have something to do with spearing Dubyt. The man with Peel must be the Governor. He kept wondering all the way to Peel's house, where he was chained to some equipment in the tool shed for the night. The following morning, he was transferred to the cutter.

It was the *Sara Jane*, hired by the Governor for the return voyage to Mandurah. When William saw Yeddi, he said nothing. In their silent sign language, his babbingur indicated that he should not be recognised. During the voyage back to Fremantle, the Governor joined him at the wheel for a chat and William elicited the information he was wanting about Yeddi's arrest.

"So what happens next, Your Excellency?" William was worried, very worried.

"He'll receive a fair trial and if found guilty at the very least will be imprisoned in the Round House for life. We can't have natives killing one another. It's a crime under English law and they must learn to abide by our laws. Thomas Peel said a native, Weewar by name, was found guilty in 1842 for killing another native and sentenced to death. This was commuted to transportation for life on Rottnest Island. Several others have received similar sentences and had them commuted since then. I would like to make an example of this Yeddi fellow, if he's guilty. Perhaps even hang him."

William's hands were gripping the wheel so hard his knuckles were white. His jaw was clenched in anger and he hoped the Governor wouldn't ask him a question.

He was saved when sharks were spotted chasing a school of fish and Fitzgerald hurried to the bow to watch the blood bath.

"You stupid bastard," William said under his breath. "We take their land, shoot and poison them, decimate them with our diseases, rape their women and you have the temerity to suggest they need more of our justice for conforming with their own tribal lore, which I suspect has been around for a lot longer than ours." He couldn't wait to rid himself of his passenger.

Later, on the pretext of needing to relieve himself, he gave the wheel to Walter who was crewing for him and engaged in the briefest of conversations with Yeddi. He agreed to find Jida and take her to her own family until the position had been clarified, one way or another.

When William arrived home and told Sara Jane the story, she was distraught. What could they do? Who could help Yeddi?

"We certainly can't appeal to the Governor. He wants to make an example of Yeddi to stop the payback cycle and to demonstrate that the natives must abide by the white law. What a pompous fool. Shouldn't have interfered in this one. Yeddi of all people. What I can't understand is why Yeddi killed the other native? It doesn't sound like Yeddi at all. Anyway, I've said that I'll go and inform Jida of Yeddi's wishes. I'll hire a horse today, sail to Mandurah with the horse on board first thing tomorrow, pick up Jida and take her to her family. That way, I'll be back the following day."

"How long before anything happens about Yeddi?"

"Several weeks or so, I expect. You know what government officials are like and there'll be paperwork galore."

"I'm coming with you, William."

"What? No, Sara Jane, it'll be a rush. We don't know Jida's people. There could be danger."

"William, I'm coming with you. I'm as concerned as you are about Yeddi's family and if I can't do anything here for Yeddi, I might as well crew for you. I just couldn't sit here waiting, while you're doing something useful. Besides Jida might not make her whereabouts known to a white man."

"Hmm. You've got a point there, Sis. Yes, I think it would be a good idea if you came."

At dawn, the blind-folded horses were led on board the *Sara Jane* by the reins from the lower level of the jetty and tied to forward thwarts. William had to admit that his sister was a competent hand. Having now crewed for him on several occasions, she was as capable, if not more so, than some of the casual hands he hired. Some of the mariners looked askance at her uniform of white duck shirt and trousers, a wide brimmed hat and canvas shoes but they were ignored. She quietly reassured the horses, as the wind filled the sails and they were on their way.

William sailed past Robert Point at the mouth of the Murray and anchored in a bay further south, which they had named Falcon Bay after the hunting birds seen in the area, when they were children.

There was some difficulty in deciding how to unload the horses but eventually William hove to against a reef exposed by the low tide and prodded the already saddled animals, who clambered hesitantly over the side. Sara Jane led the geldings slowly and carefully across the reef to the beach and waited, while William anchored the cutter in the bay and swam ashore.

They made their way as quickly as possible through the low brush and sparse trees, until they reached the area of the caves.

"William, Jida will be frightened. We'll have to give her time to identify us. She won't be far from the spring at Warrangup."

Brother and sister took different paths, close to the cave described by Yeddi in his hurriedly whispered instructions to William.

"Jida. Jida. We've come from Yeddi. We've come to help you," they each called in the native dialect, as they walked their horses slowly through the area.

It wasn't long before a sobbing young woman, carrying a baby, emerged from one of the caves. Sara Jane slipped from the saddle and hastened forward. She paused for a moment and then took Jida into her arms and whispered soothing words in her tongue. Her heart went out to the young woman and her baby, who looked remarkably like Gurdu. She bit her lip and blinked back tears of her own.

When Jida, who was much younger and more beautiful than Sara Jane had anticipated, was reassured as to the identity of her rescuers, William asked about the events leading up to Yeddi's arrest by the soldiers. Jida related what had happened and how Yeddi thought it might have been a revenge party but didn't know why that would be so. Then she was full of questions about Yeddi.

William told her what he knew, which wasn't much and informed her of Yeddi's message.

"Jida, Yeddi has asked us to take you to your family on the other side of the estuary. He is worried for your safety and wants you to remain with them. He said to inform you that he will come to you if it is possible. However, you must be brave and understand that the white man's law may never allow him his freedom again."

Jida nodded with downcast eyes. "I will collect my things." She limped slightly but Sara Jane saw that the wound was not bleeding and did not appear to be infected.

Riding on a horse was a new experience for Jida and clearly not a very enjoyable one. Clutching Malgar, she sat stiffly in the saddle, in front of William, who held her protectively with one arm. Sara Jane carried her few possessions. Yeddi's weapons were left in the cave.

They crossed the estuary at the island ford and reached Jida's family in the late afternoon. After accepting that these white strangers were friends of Yeddi's and could speak their language, there was much talking and few solutions. Although they did identify Dubyt and the one-eyed man as two of the culprits, they knew of no reason for the attack. The only resolutions from the discussions were the obvious ones. Jida and Malgar would remain with the family and William would inform Yeddi they were safe. Some of the men muttered about a possible payback from the foothills men over the death of

Dubyt and others argued they should seek revenge for the injury to Jida's leg. William said nothing. At this stage of the events, he thought the last thing needed was more bloodshed.

They were fed by Jida's relatives and stayed in their camp site overnight, leaving at dawn the next morning to arrive back at Fremantle in the late afternoon. Sara Jane helped to unload the horses and returned them to the stable in Cliff Street, while William was left to moor the cutter to their buoy in Bathers Bay. She was exhausted both mentally and physically as she headed home.

When her brother declared he would visit Yeddi in the Round House as soon as he could obtain permission, Sara Jane asked to go with him. For the first time in his life, William forbad Sara Jane permission to do something.

"It is inappropriate for a young woman to be visiting a native in gaol, especially one charged with murder. It will besmirch your name, cause gossip and be considered by all to be a scandalous act."

Sara Jane opened her mouth to object.

"Do not argue with me on this occasion, Sara Jane. I am the man of the house and therefore stand accountable and answerable for your welfare. I will not be accused of abrogating my responsibilities. You will listen and you will do as I say. I will report precisely on everything that is said."

"Yes, William," a subdued Sara Jane whispered.

* * * * *

An official-looking clerk hurried into the room. He stood with his hands clasped in front of him. "Would the Court rise," he called out loudly. The hum of conversation ceased as legal representatives, jury members, clerks, reporters for the press and spectators stood. With great decorum, Judge William Mackie entered the courtroom and took his seat, followed by the full Bench of Magistrates. Everyone then sat. There was not a spare seat in the Perth Court House on this hot February morning in 1850.

Introductory statements by Chairman Mackie concluded, the prisoner was called.

Sara Jane watched distressed and horrified to see the man she loved pushed forward roughly towards the bar by two guards. With hands tied and dressed in prison garb, he should have presented an abject figure. He did not. Yeddi stood tall and proud and wore his red wilgi-stained, fur headband and septum bone. His eyes viewed the judge unblinkingly and his jaw was set with determination. There was a murmur from the onlookers.

The Interpreter to Native Tribes was called and Francis Armstrong rose and took his place next to Yeddi. Sara Jane saw an older version of the young man who had taught her to swim in the Serpentine River so many years before.

After being sworn, Armstrong spoke quietly to Yeddi in his native tongue and explained the substance of the indictment. That he had killed a man of his tribe, which was against the law and consequently had been brought to court to stand trial on the charge of murder. Armstrong then asked whether Yeddi had any questions and Yeddi shook his head.

Mr Edward William Landor, a practising barrister of outstanding reputation stood up. He enjoyed and, in fact, openly used the courtroom as a stage for academic debate and had offered to be the Defence Counsel for the proceedings.

Judge Mackie gave an audible sigh. "Yes, Mr Landor?"

"Your Honour, on behalf of the prisoner, I plead the jurisdiction of the court and contend that it is not competent to try this case."

"You have permission to proceed, Mr Landor."

Landor entered into a series of elaborate arguments.

"First, it being declared that we acquired possession of this colony by occupancy and not by conquest, it follows that our laws would not apply to the Aborigines for offences committed among themselves, without some express assent on their part by which they agreed to acknowledge such laws."

He paused for effect.

"Secondly, even if the colony were acquired by conquest, it would still be necessary to show that our laws had been expressly imposed upon the natives and were to be henceforth received by them in lieu of their own."

Landor had his thumbs tucked into his waistcoat pockets and was clearly enjoying himself as he addressed the Bench.

"Thirdly, if they be subject to our laws, they must be subject to the whole machinery of the law and therefore ought to be punished for minor offences committed among themselves, such as slander, perjury, theft, indecent exposure of the person and so on."

Yeddi sent the occasional silent message to his babbingurs to cheer them up. The description of his Defence Counsel was very apt and had Sara Jane hiding behind her hands. He signalled that he was all right and was being treated well.

"Fourthly, the natives have laws of their own and stated punishments for particular crimes and therefore the prisoner would either have been punished already, or acquitted for the same offence, or would soon receive such judgment, by the only laws he is acquainted with or bound to obey. Therefore it is contrary to all justice that he should be tried and punished twice."

Landor was positively strutting across the floor. Sara Jane wondered how many individuals in the courtroom were appreciating his brilliant oratory. She was hanging on every word.

"Fifthly and finally, there is no act of Parliament which provides that the Aborigines shall be answerable to our laws. Therefore, as we choose to found our title on occupancy, no local proclamation is sufficient authority to make them so amenable." Landor bowed to the Bench, walked to his chair and sat down.

Richard Nash, the Acting Advocate-General, looking bemused, stood, paused, cleared his throat, paused again and then addressed the Bench, saying that he considered it unnecessary to reply to the arguments that had been addressed but would leave them to the decision of the Bench.

There was hurried consultation among the Bench members and, after further discussion, the learned Chairman announced that Mr Landor's objections were overruled by a majority of the magistrates.

Judge Mackie expounded. "There are three modes by which a nation may acquire foreign territory: treaty, conquest and occupancy. The first is out of the present question and although some of the measures of the British government may appear more easily justifiable, if referred to right of conquest than to that of occupancy, yet the theory of that government, as expounded by successive Secretaries of State, is that its possession of the territory is based on a right of occupancy."

"According to writers on the Law of Nations, there are two cases in which such a right may be exercised. First, in the case of an uninhabited country, which is not the present case. Secondly, when a large extent of country is roamed over by wandering savages, who make little use of the soil and subsist by the chase and spontaneous products of the earth. In such a case, those savage tribes have no right to exclude the rest of mankind from that of which they themselves make no proper use and of which the surplus population of other states wish to establish colonies, provided they leave the natives such a portion of the land that would be sufficient for their subsistence."

The Chairman paused and fluttered a white handkerchief, before dabbing his forehead.

"Those writers, however, do not prescribe by what common principles the interaction of the Aborigines and the newcomers is to be regulated. But as jurisdiction is clearly an inseparable incident of sovereignty, it follows that the British Nation having taken possession and assumed the sovereignty of a territory bounded by certain parallels and meridians, the law of that nation must be paramount. On the one hand there are those sacred rights of persons, which regard the safety of life and member and on the other, those offences against the Laws of God and the Law of Nature, which infringe those rights and among which offences, the vindictive spilling of blood is unquestionably one."

Judge Mackie took a long drink and then nodded at Armstrong, who rose and in the dialect of the Bindjareb tribe and in English, arraigned Yeddi.

"Yeddi, you are charged with the murder of the native Dubyt on the 28th December 1849 near the estuary track, south of Mandurah. This man was killed by a spear thrown by you, which caused extensive bleeding resulting in death."

Yeddi nodded and there was a murmur from the onlookers. He then spoke to Armstrong at length and after further questions from the interpreter, a plea of 'not guilty' was entered. The noon break was then called.

Sara Jane caught Yeddi's eye as he was led from the court room and signalled him to keep his head high to which he responded. He did not seem to be at all perturbed by the proceedings.

"Sanctimonious, condescending, patronising imperialists," Sara Jane said as she passed bread and cheese to William. They sat under a shady tree in the gardens surrounding the court house. "This is my first and I hope last exposure to the British justice system."

"Hush, Sara Jane. You censure Great Britain, the British Empire and Queen Victoria herself. You ought to be ashamed of yourself."

"I do and I mean it."

"In this instance, you have my full support," William said as he poured them both water.

Following the luncheon recess, Richard Nash rose and addressed the Bench.

"Your Honour. So much of the argument which has been presented by the Defence Counsel has been adduced with the view of influencing the feelings of the jury, though not directly addressed to them, that I feel it my duty, as ably as the subject has been treated from the Bench, to make a few remarks."

The Judge nodded his assent. "Proceed, Mr Nash."

Nash clasped his hands in front of him and strode to address the jury. His heavy boots squeaked in unison with the floor boards.

"Two laws govern mankind in their general relations: the Law of Nature where either of the parties is an uncivilised savage and the Law of Nations where complex aggregates of civilised men treat each other as individuals. The title of any nation to a savage territory, is that of occupancy where the savages do not resist and of conquest where they do. Does any man believe that if all the tribes had gone to the first party of settlers and informed them that they did not intend to allow them to reside here, that the British government would obligingly have abandoned the territory? In fact there never was a more unlucky case for such an argument than that of the prisoner at the bar, whose tribe had actually so resisted and been accordingly attacked and conquered in the fullest sense of the word. To assert that a savage rabble of wandering families has a right to say to the world, 'We will not use this land and we will not suffer anyone else to do so. We are resolved to continue as savages and the vast continent over which we wander shall continue a desert', would be at once to prohibit the civilisation of mankind and would be the greatest curse to the savages themselves."

The atmosphere in the courtroom was stifling and Sara Jane could see several heads nodding. She was particularly attentive to the erudite exposition but it was clearly too much for some. To her, the arguments being put forward by two pompous exponents of the British judiciary were a collective defence of colonialism and not necessarily either justifiable or logical. She thought they placed a large question mark over the principles underlying imperialism.

Richard Nash droned on.

"It is true that nations appropriating the territory occupied by savages incur duties but what are they? To substitute some sufficient means of sustenance for that of which they have deprived them; and to elevate their condition by instruction in the arts, duties and responsibilities of civilised life. Their native laws have been spoken of but I would like to know what they are. It is a burlesque upon all laws to call the few barbarous customs to which the respective families force each other to submit, whenever they are able, by the name of laws. I would like to know what code would acknowledge the law that any man may steal as many other men's wives or children as he is able; and that in return the other, or any other man may steal any other wives or children from the tribe of the former, if he is able; that any man may wound or kill any other man, if he is able; but that it is the duty of some other man to wound or kill some other man in return, if he is able. And to the benefit of such laws, humanity, forsooth, we are told, entitles the savage."

"If the savage is liable to any British law, he is liable to all. Undoubtedly, he is so liable and the only restriction upon the application of the law is that of time, for the duty of Great Britain is to teach all her laws to the savage as soon as he can be made to learn them and this case before us is an illustration. The savage has long since learned that to kill a white man will be avenged by death. Now it is necessary to advance his civilisation by teaching him that to kill his fellow savage is also a crime."

The learned gentleman then proceeded to call witnesses.

The first witness was Thomas Peel. After swearing on the Bible, he recounted the events of 28th December 1849 and his discussion with the four natives. Sara Jane thought he looked tired. Lines crisscrossed his face and his hair was unruly and almost completely grey.

Sergeant Watters was then called to the stand and sworn. He was very nervous and stammered.

"Last week, I visited the foothills men, who we met on the estuary track on 28th December. Mr Armstrong came with me. He told me what they said and it was that the dead native had been murdered by that Yeddi." He pointed at Yeddi.

The last witness was Francis Armstrong. He asked and was given permission to read his brief report.

331

9th February, 1850

Four men of the Bindjareb tribe were interviewed on the above date in regard to the death of one, Dubyt, who died of a spear wound to the leg on 28th December last. All four men stated that Yeddi threw the spear that killed him.

The men from Dubyt's clan claimed that they were on a peaceful mission to visit relatives when Yeddi attacked them without provocation.

Francis Armstrong
Interpreter to Native Tribes

He held out the piece of paper which was collected by a clerk and handed to Justice Mackie.

Sara Jane felt William stiffen and whisper "Liars".

Nash again rose to his feet. "On the evidence afore mentioned, I submit that the prisoner is guilty of murder and should be sentenced to death. That is the case for the prosecution."

Sara Jane froze in dread. She was aghast at the call for the death sentence. If it was British justice to be hung for protecting your wife, she wanted none of it. She watched Yeddi but he remained motionless, as if he had not heard or had not understood what was being said.

The Defence Counsel having been called, Landor began.

"I would like to remind the Court that the spirit of the British criminal law is not that of vengeance but of mercy. The spirit of that law is not so much to punish criminals as to deter crime. Among these poor savages, by whom our laws are neither recognised nor known, can they be supposed to operate in any degree as deterring men from crime? And, if they do not so operate, what are they but laws of vengeance and blood. They must be taught their value, for we must recollect that these savages have already laws of their own, which they are bound by imperious custom to obey. They, who consider the tenacity with which the human mind clings to received laws and customs and the prejudices of early years, must be conscious, that though we were to hang one half of the native population, for obeying their own laws, the remainder would still go on in the same practices, until all were exterminated, or confined in our gaols."

He then turned to address the jury.

"The habits of these natives are but the instincts of brutes; they know not the difference between right and wrong. It fills me with consternation and horror that one of them should be liable to receive a sentence of death, when guiltless of crime against any law with which he is acquainted. I am reassured however, that the severity of English law cannot be enforced without your sanction and

I look with confidence to you, who are alive to the rights of nature and the dictates of humanity. I implore you to be sympathetic towards this native in the pronouncement of your judgment and sentence."

The Chairman summed up. "I must remind all those present here today that the provinces of the Court and of the jury are distinct; the former is decided upon the law, the latter has only to consider the facts of the case. The Court has already decided that the prisoner is within its jurisdiction and therefore you the jury must not be misled by the arguments of the gentleman who has with so much zeal and ability conducted the defence of the prisoner."

The jury retired and, to Sara Jane's dismay, returned after a remarkably short deliberation.

Armstrong asked Yeddi to stand.

Judge Mackie then asked the foreman whether the jury had reached a verdict.

"Yes, milord. It is the unanimous decision of the jury that the prisoner Yeddi is guilty as charged."

In solemn voice, Judge Mackie made the pronouncement. "Yeddi of the Bindjareb tribe in Western Australia, this Court finds you guilty of the murder of Dubyt, also of the Bindjareb tribe, on 28th December 1849. You are hereby sentenced to death by hanging." He paused for the impact of the judgment to take effect. Sara Jane's head slumped forward and she covered her face with shaking hands. There was buzz of conversation. Judge Mackie used the gavel to bring the gathering to order. "However, in this case the Court has shown clemency. The sentence is commuted to life imprisonment."

CHAPTER 33
Transportation

Most native prisoners were now incarcerated in the Round House in Fremantle or the Perth Gaol. Only those who were considered to have perpetrated the most serious of crimes and were serving a life sentence were sent to Rottnest Island. They were assigned to either James Dempster or Edward Back, the first pilot appointed to Rottnest.

Berry, Blake and Brown, three Parkhurst boys transported for minor crimes in the slums of London, had been allocated to Dempster as labourers and Back's crew comprised himself, a coxswain and five other mariners. On occasions, natives were also utilised as crew but because attempts to escape by boat had been made when the opportunity had arisen, they were all locked up together in a common hut at night.

On the morning of 21st February 1850, with a gentle south-easterly blowing on his back, William Blair sailed the *Margaret* the twelve miles to Rottnest Island. On purpose, he had submitted a ridiculously low tender for the job and had won it. His crew was Walter Bateman and Sara Jane who had insisted on coming. The passengers were Sergeant Harris and three privates of the 99th Regiment of Foot who escorted the prisoner Yeddi of the Bindjareb tribe, assigned to the custody of James Maclean Dempster for an indefinite period.

Yeddi, bound with rope and wearing leg irons, was guarded on a side bench by two burly soldiers. He sat upright and held his head high as he fixed his eyes at first on the disappearing mainland and then on Wadjemup, the Nyoongar name for the island. Sara Jane passed surreptitious signals as she moved around the vessel and Yeddi answered them with minuscule movements of fingers and facial muscles. From his position holding the tiller, William could see it all and because he could understand the messages was devastated by the strength of emotion being expressed between the two.

"Don't worry so. I am alive."

"I will worry. I love you. I have always loved you."

"I may be released."

"I will pray it is so."

"It will be lonely."

"We will find a way to visit you."

"I worry about Jida's and Malgar's future."

"Jida's family will look after them."

William dashed tears from his eyes and gave his nose a loud blow. "Wretched cold," he said to the Sergeant standing near him.

With Walter at the prow guiding the way, William skilfully negotiated a passage through the treacherous reefs surrounding the entrance to Thomson Bay and pulled up beside the primitive jetty.

Dempster was waiting for his latest labourer and spoke loudly and inconsequentially with William and Sara Jane while Yeddi was bundled off the boat and left to crouch in the sand. Walter made the *Margaret* fast and would remain with the vessel for security purposes. Having turned over their prisoner to Dempster, Harris and his soldiers wandered off to eat some of their provisions before the return trip.

William apprised Dempster of the situation and some quick decisions were made, while Sara Jane hovered around Yeddi offering supportive words and promising they would arrange to meet him whenever possible.

With a nod to William, Dempster picked up some tools and struck the leg irons from Yeddi's ankles. "I know you can understand me, Yeddi. I do this because I don't believe in treating any man, regardless of race, as an animal. However, as the last native labourers ran off into the bush and had to be chased for hours, I ask you not to try the same. I will leave you to say your goodbyes, at least for the moment. You must be an exceptional man to have friends like William and Sara Jane." Dempster walked back up the path that led over the dune.

The babbingurs sat in the white sand overlooking a beautiful bay with clear water of every shade of blue and green. In the distance, the mainland could be seen and smudges of smoke arose from late summer fires. Try as she might, Sara Jane could not stop the gleam of tears from showing.

William reported on his conversation with Dempster. "Yeddi, Dempster is a good man and will treat you well. Bide your time and don't try to escape and perhaps we'll be able to seek your release on good behaviour in the future. No one has escaped from Rottnest to date. Dempster is willing to assign you to his southern field, which is the furthest from the settlement and has a hut and stable. You will care for the horses most of the time, although for the next few weeks until the rains, you'll work with the other natives scraping salt."

Yeddi nodded absently. "Thank you. Both of you."

"After you are stationed at South Field, weather permitting, Sara Jane and I will sail to Rottnest on each Sunday following the full moon and anchor in the small bay between Parker Point and Point Shelter. Point Shelter is the nearest point to Tree Hill which is in the middle of South Field. All labourers are given the Sabbath off. Yeddi, are you listening?"

Yeddi repeated William's message word for word.

"We will also report to Jida when we can."

Yeddi shook his head. "No. It will be better for Jida if she forgets me and takes another husband. She needs someone to look after her and provide for her and our son. It is the way of my people and very sensible. A woman with a young child should have someone who will take responsibility for her."

William bit his lip. "Yeddi, we do not want to interfere with the customs of your tribe. We will abide by your advice and wishes."

Laughter and loud voices were heard from behind the sand hills as the soldiers returned with Dempster. He'd kept them away for half an hour as promised.

"We must be on our way, Yeddi. Remember to look for us on the first Sunday after the second full moon from now."

"I will be waiting, my babbingurs and thank you for what you have done."

They stood. After ensuring the soldiers weren't looking, Sara Jane gave Yeddi a quick hug. William shook his hand.

Yeddi stood staring after them as they returned to the jetty. Dempster joined him. "Damned fine people those," he said, as William carefully negotiated the cutter through the patches of reef. They watched together until it became a speck against the backdrop of the mainland.

* * * * *

Sara Jane found it difficult to keep Yeddi out of her mind. He kept creeping into her thoughts and dreams. It could be at any time and the smallest thing seemed to trigger off memories. The smoke from a fire, the smell of banksia nuts, the sight of a native wandering the streets, pelicans flying overhead, swans drifting on the river.

After one particularly restless morning, pen and ink were placed studiously on the table next to a pad of paper and Henry's last letter re-read. She might as well be doing something constructive rather than just worrying about circumstances she could not change. Sara Jane sighed. If Henry wasn't family and I didn't love him in a kindly sort of way, I could ignore him but he is and I do, so I can't.

Sara Jane wrote:

Henry Street
Fremantle
1st March 1850

Dear Henry,

Thank you for your kind letter. I write to assure you that the natives are not overwhelming the colony, nor am I in any immediate danger. However, I thank you for your solicitude.

Please do not begin worrying when you read in the Times that Western Australia will become a penal settlement some time this year. It is certainly not the preferred choice but development has been inhibited by a labour shortage and expediency has won the day.

William is well and working hard. The business is progressing very satisfactorily and we now have two crew. David Long skippers the Margaret when William has a longer assignment on the Sara Jane and Walter Bateman, the son of a friend of ours, sails with William to learn navigational skills. We hire casual crew as necessary. I have even served as for'ard hand for William on occasions and thoroughly enjoyed it.

John Bateman and his family have been very supportive to both of us as our business ventures have expanded. We are meeting next week to explore possibilities in the sandalwood trade following John's success in exporting the wood to Asian ports.

As I mentioned in my previous letter, we have been employing help for ten months now. Elizabeth is seventeen and has grown into a caring and beautiful young woman. She is employed at the local Post Office each morning and keeps the house in order in the afternoons. She's more a member of the family now than a servant and I dread the day she meets a young man and leaves.

Please pass on my love and news to Mother and Father. I do write but know they relish any titbit of news from the colony. We miss them of course but acknowledge they are being much better cared for in the comfort of Nine Elms surrounded by servants and members of the family.

With regard to your visiting the Roberts and enjoying their excellent wines and wonderful hospitality, I can give you my promise that you will be welcomed with open arms. If you really do intend to travel on to Western Australia, I must hasten to inform you that even Fremantle and Perth are primitive when compared with any of the cities and towns that I saw in England. What did you call us? A far flung outpost. Well, that's certainly an appropriate description.

If I have not deterred you by now, you might like to obtain copies of five books written by gentlemen who have lived in Perth, except Ogle who compiled information from available sources. All were published in London. They are Extracts from the Letters and Journals of George Fletcher Moore, 1834; The State and Position of Western Australia by F.C. Irwin, 1835; The Colony of Western Australia by N. Ogle, 1839; Journals of two expeditions of discovery in North-west and Western Australia by G. Grey, 1841; and The Bushman by E. W. Landor, 1845. I have read them all and found them to be of great interest.

My kindest regards to you Henry and to all at Nine Elms,
Sara Jane

* * * * *

Elizabeth was now spending each morning, except Sunday, at Bateman's Post Office. She not only enjoyed the work but found it very challenging. In the afternoons she and Sara Jane attended to household chores until it was time for Sara Jane to await possible clients in her room at the Post Office. On this Tuesday, they were preparing to do the ironing. Fred supervised the making of starch, as he lay on the mat in front of the wood stove.

"Sara Jane, I can't thank you enough for your tutorship and encouragement. It has been less than a year since I came here to apply for a position and so many wonderful things have happened. I feel a different person. And it's all due to you. Even if you really didn't need my services, you took me in. I've always known that and will forever be grateful."

"Tush, Elizabeth. Your contribution to our household has been considerable. I should be thanking you. How was work this morning?"

"Matt - I mean Mr Cooke has been assisting me with the record keeping. Soon I should be able to assume that responsibility myself. With some checking by you, of course, to make sure that the books are in fact balanced."

"Hmm. Do you really need assistance from Mr Cooke, Elizabeth? I would have assumed that you would be quite capable of finalising the books yourself."

For the first time Sara Jane saw an almost coquettish look pass over Elizabeth's face.

"Oh, it's just that Mr Cooke likes to be seen to be in charge of everything. I don't mind. It doesn't really worry me."

"As long as you know who is really responsible and are not afraid to take credit where credit is due. Don't be subservient, Elizabeth. Always expect to be given and, where appropriate, indeed insist on your due. It is only right and proper."

Elizabeth's eyes sparkled. "And there endeth the two hundredth lesson."

Sara Jane's eyebrows lifted. "Is that the number? I would have deemed it closer to the thousandth."

338

"All right, I give in. You will help me to reconcile the bank statements though, won't you?"

"It will be a pleasure, my dear. Just make a booking when you require assistance."

Elizabeth picked up a flat iron, wiped it with beeswax, polished it with a flourish and walked in stately fashion to the table. "Thank you for your time, Miss Andrews-Blair. I must now attend to my household duties." She had the most supercilious expression on her face.

"Elizabeth!"

Laughing, the young woman placed the iron on its stand and gave Sara Jane an affectionate hug.

* * * * *

Later that week, John Bateman dropped into the Post Office to see Sara Jane while she was present at her 'Business hour'. She was preparing the monthly statement. "Hello John. What a pleasant surprise! Join me."

"Thank you." He sat down and placed his hat on the table. "Elizabeth is doing well, I hear. Young Cooke seems to be very pleased with her progress. It seems she has asked to learn to keep the books. You should have been a school teacher, Sara Jane."

"Spare me, John! Yes, she seems to have settled in and appears to have Matthew under the thumb." They both laughed. "What can I do for you, John?"

"Well, I thought it timely to commence our negotiations regarding sandalwood trading."

A flash of excitement appeared on Sara Jane's face. "Good. I'll look forward to that. William's due back any day from Augusta. Will you be available this week?"

"Yes, I'll be in town, Sara Jane. Give me a few hours notice." They agreed to meet in Bateman's office.

* * * * *

When Sara Jane and William arrived at the given time, Bateman had a file of papers on his desk. "I've been looking over my figures for the last sandalwood season and preparing forward estimates," he said, as they pulled up chairs and Sara Jane took out her notebook and pencil.

"We need to draw up some time schedules, which are pretty much dictated by the weather and seasonal work of the York farmers. Lambing will start soon and then after the first rains, the farmers will plough and sow their grain crops. That could be as soon as next month. Once the seed is in, it's usually maintenance time until spring, when shearing takes place. In the months between, sandalwood is cut and when the roads are dry enough, it is carted by wagon to Guildford. From there, the wood is usually carried by barges down the Swan River to Fremantle. Sometimes, it continues by wagon. Let's look at the best possible scenario. First rains, April. Ploughing and seeding, May. Sandalwood cutting, June. Delivery to Fremantle, July. In previous years it has arrived here between July and September."

Sara Jane looked thoughtful. "John, would you describe the northern weather patterns for me? I've been told they are very different from our south-west."

"Certainly. The north of Australia is subjected to heavy rain and cyclones in our summer. It's just called the wet, not summer. So December to February are the most dangerous months to sail from here to Asia. However, I hasten to add that typhoons could be at best described as capricious and once north of the equator, nothing can be guaranteed."

William grimaced. "Doesn't give us much time for a round trip to Singapore or Hong Kong during the most favourable months."

"Exactly. Unfortunately, as sandalwood dries out, so does its oil, or we could store it indefinitely. I have some left over from last season but the older wood seldom gets top price unless there's a shortage. So, that's that. It's sail north before December or take a chance with the weather. I took a chance with my first shipment but I wouldn't do it again."

Sara Jane looked up from her notebook. "What do you suggest then, John?"

"Ha! Straight to the point, eh? Well, for this season, I'm proposing that we form a proportional partnership. Say 20 per cent, 80 per cent in my favour. You can think that over. I'll arrange for you to buy a designated amount of sandalwood through agents at my purchase price and I will transport it equally in two of my ships to Singapore. William, you will sail as our agent on the first ship to be fully loaded and complete the transactions under my written instructions. That will give you some valuable experience and guarantee me that the deals are above board. You should be back in October. I will sail on the second ship. It's time I checked out the Singapore scene again. All going well, we'll both be back safe and sound before the end of November and each with a tidy profit. You can take your sales in cash or goods. If you decide on the latter, which I would advise you to do unless you're short of cash, you can back-load them to Fremantle, sell them through me on consignment or trade them as you visit coastal settlements. Things like tea, spices and cloth are cheap over there and expensive here."

"Aye, I can see the potential for profit in trading. What about Blair Transport during that time?"

"Well, I reckoned on that period being pretty much off-season for you and that probably one of your boats would be able to cope."

"Yes, that was certainly so last year, in our first full winter of business. David Long is a fine skipper. Could I count on Walter as crew? He's a good mariner. David could continue the instruction."

"I'm sure Walter would be agreeable. He seems happy with the arrangement and says his navigational skills are improving."

That night, William and Sara Jane sat at the kitchen table and discussed Bateman's proposal. They decided to accept it without amendment. Time to negotiate after they had gained some experience.

"It's too good to be true, Sara Jane. What an opportunity John's giving us. We're being taught the ropes by an expert. He's leading us into overseas trade. How fortunate we are. Our profit from the venture could be several hundred pounds."

"Well, he must trust us and think you are capable and responsible enough to close the deals in Singapore. That's a fine compliment, William. You must make sure you justify his confidence."

"I'll certainly be doing my best."

"However, there is one problem we haven't considered and that is our promised monthly visit to Yeddi. You will be away over four full moons."

"Sorry, Sis. I had forgotten in my excitement. Forgive me. Either David or Walter can ferry you over each month. It's an easy trip. The only tricky bit is navigating behind the reef into the bay to anchor. I'll arrange it for you within our business schedule and it will go ahead regardless of other commitments, unless of course bad weather blows up."

The contract, based on the deal that had been proposed by Bateman, was drawn up during Alfred Stone's next visit to Fremantle and signed by the partners in his presence. It was to remain in place until the financial position was finalised following the year's trading, when it would be reviewed.

* * * * *

For the first two weeks, Yeddi worked with the other six native prisoners on the salt lakes. The water had dried up around the edges during the summer months and this was therefore the best time of the year for the collection of salt residue. The natives used rakes, with wooden boards bolted onto the prongs, to scrape the crystals into mounds. The salt was then sifted, shovelled onto a dray and dragged by mules to the store in Thomson's Bay for later transport to the mainland. It was back-breaking work and continued from dawn to dusk. William Skinner, a brother-in-law to Dempster, was a hard task master.

With the first rains, the salt areas at the edges of the lakes became sodden and muddy and so Yeddi was taken to South Field and shown his duties. Because he was alone, he notched the bark of a tree to remember the Sundays when he would be free from work.

On the assigned day, the *Sara Jane* sailed into the bay and anchored. William rowed the dinghy to shore and Sara Jane's eyes searched the sand hills for Yeddi. He was nowhere to be seen.

"Yeddi," she called, cupping her hands. "Yeddi."

A black figure in grey shirt and trousers came running down the hill, waving his arms. He picked up Sara Jane and swung her around in delight. As William approached he slapped him on the shoulder. "I have never been so pleased to see anybody. Ever!" Yeddi said.

"What's this?" Sara Jane held up a metal disk hanging on a chain around Yeddi's neck.

"It's my number. We all have to wear them. The prisoners can be identified that way."

They ate a packed lunch in the shade of a tea-tree overlooking a beautiful blue bay and exchanged information.

"The business just gets better and better. Sara Jane is a whiz at snaring people. Once they've visited her at our office, she has them signed up by contract in no time at all."

"And we're going into the sandalwood trade later this year with John Bateman," Sara Jane added. "We'll consign our first cargo in the off-monsoon season. And I'm working on William to build a bigger house and he's slowly capitulating. How about you, Yeddi? Is it bearable?"

"I'm isolated here," answered Yeddi, "but I'd rather that than being in a group, as I was when we were scraping up the salt. That was hard work and we were locked up together every night. I didn't know any of the others. I've always been a bit of a loner, like Great Uncle and so kept to myself. Burning off has begun in preparation for ploughing and seeding but I've had plenty of practice at that." He grinned. "The food's adequate. We are given flour and salt meat. I've fashioned a spear which I keep hidden and have speared as many wallabies and fish as I need. Would be much worse in the gaol in Fremantle. There's lots of time to think and I find myself constantly worrying about my people."

William wandered off down the beach to give Yeddi and his sister time together.

Sara Jane sat close, as if to pass on additional strength. "Yeddi, you must aim to survive this punishment. I'm sure, when Governor Fitzgerald's term is completed, a new governor might be more amenable to the suggestion of reducing life sentences. They are far too severe. In your case especially."

"Sarjan, with your support, that is exactly what I intend to do. Survive."

CHAPTER 34

Twenty-one Years of Age

The convict question evolved over a period of time in the Swan River Colony and came to a head in November 1849.

In the year following the depression of 1843 and 1844, arrivals to Western Australia had fallen so much that for the first time since the original immigrants had disembarked from the *Parmelia*, there were no arrivals in the colony. In fact, it was even worse than that because one hundred and twenty-nine persons departed to either return to England or try their luck in other Australian colonies. This resulted in a severe shortage of labour, which gave the remaining workers better bargaining power and therefore better pay and conditions.

The Avon valley farmers, in particular, bitterly resented being forced to pay higher wages and found it demeaning to negotiate with servants. They began agitating for the introduction of convicts to provide labour, not only for the landowners but for public works, such as government buildings, roads, bridges and wharves. They argued that without either free or forced labour the economy would remain depressed. The suggestion was rebuffed by Governor Hutt but the mutterings continued.

Prior to this, sentiments in the colony had always reflected an aversion to the notion of a transformation to a penal establishment. Western Australians were proud that their colony was founded by free settlers. The idea of the integration of convicts with free settlers was abhorrent to the majority of the colonists and debated on ethical grounds. It was alleged that such an influence was bound to lower moral standards with devastating results.

However, when the wallets of the landowners were affected in a negative way it was considered a different state of affairs. Little by little, the whole issue became a matter of expediency.

Long letters were published in the *Inquirer*, petitions were circulated and the topic raised in the Legislative Council. By unanimous vote, the members decided that the need for such a move had not been substantiated. In 1847, the proponents went so far as to forward a long petition to the Secretary of State through Governor Clarke pleading their case for the introduction of convicts. In an enclosed dispatch, the Governor informed Lord Stanley that in his opinion the majority of colonists were not in favour of such an action.

Following Clarke's death, the matter was again brought up in the Legislative Council. Acting Governor Irwin cogently pointed out that transportation of convicts was being discontinued in other colonies for sound reasons and strongly urged all who were favourable to the measure 'to consider whether the injury likely to be entailed on the community and particularly on their own families, may not convince them, when too late, that they have obtained their object at a dreadful sacrifice'. And of course, no sensible Acting Governor would want to be seen encouraging such a radical change in the scheme of things.

With the arrival of Governor Fitzgerald, the issue was quickly back on the agenda. Earl Grey had asked Fitzgerald to put a proposal to the colonists that they accept ticket-of-leave men. Fitzgerald knew very well that the Secretary of State was a strong advocate for the transportation system. He also knew on which side his bread was buttered, as the saying goes. When the Fremantle merchants attended a public meeting held in the Perth Court House on 23rd February 1849, to oppose the suggestion of ticket-of-leave men and support a request that the colony become a penal settlement with all costs to be borne by the Home Government, the die was cast. The resolutions of the meeting were transmitted to Fitzgerald, who wrote to Grey suggesting that under the present depressed circumstances he was of the opinion that the majority of colonists would gladly learn that Western Australia had been chosen as a penal settlement. Within three months, an Order of Council was passed nominating Western Australia as a place to which convicts could be sent from Great Britain.

Several concessions were made. No convicts of a reckless or dangerous class were to be transported and female offenders were to be totally excluded. There would be at least an equal number of free settlers and all costs would be borne by the Home Government. The Secretary of State was prepared to bargain to achieve his objective.

* * * * *

James Dempster was repairing the roof, which had sprung a leak during a thunderstorm the previous night. He looked up to see a signal being hoisted to the top of the mast next to the Rottnest lighthouse. The lighthouse was not yet completed but a 40 foot mast and yardarm had been erected on both Wadjemup Hill and Signal Hill behind the stone cottages and signals were thus relayed by Samuel Thomas, the lighthouse keeper to the settlement and then to the mainland. Dempster called James, his eldest son, to fetch his telescope. The enlarged view showed the signal to comprise one flag and one ball, which indicated a single ship passing to the north of the island.

Dempster hurried on his way to Mount Herschell with James and Teddy running behind. Twenty minutes later, puffing his way to the top, he focused his telescope and sighted an unusually large vessel in the offing and rightly presumed it to be the ship transporting the first convicts to the colony.

When Edward Back returned from piloting the vessel into Gage Roads, he related all the details. "It was the *Scindian*. There were seventy-five convicts and fifty pensioner guards with their wives and children aboard. Oh and fourteen immigrant girls, who'll likely be snapped up by the matrons of Perth as servants. Captain Henderson of the Royal Engineers is the Comptroller-General of Convicts. He has brought a large staff including a Supervisor of the Convict Establishment and a Clerk of Works. They're all keen to get the scheme under way as soon as possible. They have to build their own prison and until that's finished are being quartered in Daniel Scott's premises. Bet he's getting a pretty penny for that. Do you reckon being the Chairman of the Fremantle Town Trust had anything to do with it?"

Dempster laughed. "Could be, Edward. Could be. Don't you find it ironic that our gift from England on the twenty-first anniversary of our foundation is a shipload of convicts for the establishment of a penal settlement?"

* * * * *

William and Sara Jane sailed to Rottnest to see Yeddi twice more before William left for Singapore. In July, heavy rain and gale force winds prevented the crossing. The same routine was followed on each visit. A picnic lunch with plenty of special goodies. Cornish pasties, apple pie and fresh fruit the first time and cold chicken, chocolate cake and fresh fruit the second. Yeddi gulped his share and all the extras and didn't want to talk till the food had been consumed.

"It's so wonderful to have a change, Sarjan." He sighed and fell back onto the sand holding his stomach, after devouring a huge lunch. "There's plenty of food here but nothing sweet. Not even flowering cones. That's what I miss. Thanks for the extra cake, my babbingur."

They talked about anything that came to mind. What was happening in the colony, what was happening with the business and what Yeddi had been assigned to do at South Field. William would wander off for the customary walk to let Sara Jane and Yeddi talk alone for a while and then it would be time to sail for home.

Sara Jane had received belated Christmas greetings from the Roberts'. The trip to London to see the Queen had been deferred until Gurdu was older. There was much news about Gurdu's incredible growth and development, in regard to his physical prowess and eating ability. After reading the letter out to Yeddi, she said, "I suspect this might be the exaggeration of proud parents."

"No, it sounds to me as though he's just taking after his father." Yeddi rolled away as Sara Jane lifted a hand menacingly.

The visits were heart-wrenching for Sara Jane and distressing for William but for Yeddi's sake they needed to be cheerful and optimistic. They considered themselves his lifeline to the future.

* * * * *

In mid-July, William left for Singapore. His head and heart struggled with such mixed feelings. There was apprehension at being away from the colony for the first time and yet this also evoked strong sensations of anticipation and adventure, disquiet at travelling on unknown waters under a Captain he knew only by sight, concern about his ability to transact the required deals to Bateman's satisfaction and a worry about leaving Sara Jane with the responsibility of the business. But excitement was the overriding sentiment. He was in a constant state of excitement. His horizons were being broadened and his inner self strengthened. It was as though he had been promoted and was taking a giant step into his future.

He felt totally beholden to John Bateman. What a chance! Not many individuals received such favours from someone outside their family. William was determined to justify Bateman's faith in him.

* * * * *

Walter Bateman held the tiller and Sara Jane was crewing as they sailed to Rottnest on a fine Sunday in August. The wind was a moderate westerly and the mainsail and headsails were set for a long reach to the south-west, before a final short tack and entry into the anchorage at Parker Point. The dinghy bobbed along behind.

Sara Jane had been mulling over an idea since they left Fremantle. The more she thought about it, the more she liked it. "Walter, can I take a turn at the tiller?"

"Er, I'm not sure William would approve, Miss Andrews-Blair."

Sara Jane had a stubborn look on her face. "Mr Bateman, are you aware that I am a partner in Blair Transport?"

"Yes, Miss Andrews-Blair. I had been so informed."

'Well, as a partner, I am asking you to allow me to take the tiller."

"It's against my better judgment miss, but I can't prevent you from doing so, if you insist."

Sara Jane, who had assiduously watched William at every opportunity whenever she was aboard, took the tiller and handled the vessel firstly with caution and then with confidence. Walter occasionally adjusted the set of the headsails.

"Ready about!"

"Miss! You can't!" Walter was scrambling and muttering as he readied himself, while Sara Jane brought the boat up nearer the wind.

"Hard alee!" Sara Jane called, as she pushed the tiller to leeward.

The cutter swung into the wind, the sails luffed and Sara Jane and Walter moved quickly to reposition themselves on the other side of the boat. The head of the vessel passed through the wind, the boom swung across and Walter automatically cast off the working foresail and jib sheets. As the mainsail began to fill, he hauled in the sheets and made adjustments as they settled into a beam reach on a port tack. The boat picked up speed.

Sara Jane grinned broadly at Walter. "Is everything in order up for'ard?"

Walter gave a tight-lipped smile. "Aye, aye, Skipper."

After anchoring, Walter rowed them to shore. He had his own lunch and some fishing tackle and was soon contentedly sitting on a rock a few hundred yards away.

For the first time, Sara Jane found Yeddi despondent.

"It's probably a time thing, Yeddi. You've been here for five months now and on your own during most of that period. Do you think you should ask to go back to the main settlement for a while?"

"No. I've thought it through and that would prevent us meeting and I couldn't bear that. Mr Dempster is doing us a favour allowing us to meet secretly and we can't let it become public knowledge." His head fell. "I think it's because Malgar reached his first complete rotation of the seasons last month. He's over twelve moons old now. I fear I will never see him again. I might never see either of my sons again."

"Yeddi, you must not dwell on such thoughts. If you do, it will eventually affect your mind and health. You must look forward to the time you will see Malgar again at least. Remember, Gurdu is my son too and it also distresses me that I might never see him again. We agreed it was best for him to remain with the Roberts, for his sake."

Deep in introspection, Yeddi remained quiet for while. "I'm sorry Sarjan. You are right. I will speak with the spirits and ask for strength."

* * * * *

In September, Elizabeth brought home a letter from the Post Office. It was from Henry. Sara Jane had to admit that she enjoyed receiving his letters after getting over the initial shock of his amorous feelings towards her. She pondered over the idea that it was always so reassuring to know that another person, particularly a worthwhile person, cared for you and how the feeling could often have the power to lead to reciprocation. She shook her head. No, not in this instance, she thought.

My dearest Sara Jane,

When your letters arrive, I am filled with love and good spirits. Each is read over and over again and when I can recite the contents by heart, I am ready to reply.

I lean more and more to the idea of visiting Western Australia and at this stage am considering leaving early in 1851. Everything is still very much up in the air but I have appointed a new steward, who is intelligent and hard-working and he should be on top of the activities and books pertaining to the estate by the end of this year. Then I will be confident in leaving Nine Elms for an extended period. I will write to the Roberts forthwith and beg their hospitality while I break my voyage in Cape Town.

The bookseller, with whom I deal in London, has managed to procure two of the books you recommended and is on the lookout for the others.

Moore's knowledgeable writings were both enjoyable and enlightening. Straight from the horse's mouth, so to speak. The final entry set me chuckling. 'By the way, my own letters are an odd medley; I hope that no stranger sees them.' And here is his journal being made available for all to see by the connivance of his brother and the publisher! Is he still living in the colony? If so, I would greatly appreciate the opportunity of meeting with him.

I found Ogle's work really just a compendium of facts and rather dry, being written with second-hand knowledge. It lacked the insight and inference of Moore's personal observations. Still, it certainly would have provided useful information for intending settlers in the earlier years of the colony.

Except for my journey across the Channel, I have no experience of sea voyages and look forward to sailing to Fremantle and hopefully joining William as he pursues his coastal trade. My only worry is seasickness and I would be mortified if I found I was prone to mal de mer. However, I am assured by my physician friends that it is often largely in the mind and that is what I'm banking on.

The Times reported the departure of the Scindian, with its cargo of convicts to solve the labour problems and reduce the depressed circumstances of Western Australia. I sincerely hope that the decision was the right one but only time will tell.

I pass on love and best wishes from your mother and father. They eagerly await your epistles, as I do. Both are happy and well within themselves and spend most of their days reading and trying to keep warm. They seek a sunny spot in the conservatory or a couch close to the fire. I wonder why old people are always cold and can only surmise it to be an affliction of the circulatory system.

I await our eventual reunion with all my heart and soul,

Henry

The inevitable rhyme was included.

WAITING
I send to you my love
To safeguard and to keep.
Mind it carefully and well
Till seeds of waiting we shall reap.

Sara Jane wrote to Henry the following day.

Henry Street
Fremantle
18 September 1850

Dear Henry,

Thank you for your news and especially the confirmation of your visit to Western Australia next year. It will give me great pleasure to return the hospitality you showered upon me at Nine Elms. I remember every detail of my stay with affection. I feel required to declare that our resources are severely limited compared with yours. There is a definite dearth of Earls in the colony!

Although I cringe with the comparison you will make between our abode and yours, I am sure your sojourn here will be of interest to your inquiring mind. Having the opportunity to travel with William on his coastal tours, as he calls them, will enable you to see the small settlements around our south-west coast. I have travelled with him on some trips and can now take control

349

of my namesake, which is the smaller vessel. It is an exhilarating experience.

George Fletcher Moore still resides in the colony and, although he holds high official functions, I feel certain that a meeting could be arranged. He serves on the Legislative Council and the Executive Council and farms a large property in the Upper Swan area. Several years ago, he married Fanny Jackson, the step-daughter of Andrew Clarke, a previous Governor of the colony, just when everybody assumed him to be a confirmed bachelor.

The arrival of the convicts has already boosted our flagging economy. Over two hundred persons were aboard the Scindian and when one thinks about the food and necessities required for that number of people, it makes a difference to a small port like ours. We expect increased business within a year as the positive effects of convict labour for agriculturalists are felt.

William left on his first overseas journey in July to transact business on behalf of our new partnership. We will be involved in sandalwood sales to Singapore in exchange for goods which are scarce in the colony. The venture promises to be quite lucrative, although there are many risks involved, including shipwreck, pirates and typhoons. I am saying additional prayers until his safe return. Psalms 23 and 27 are recited with great regularity.

Please pass on my love to Mother and Father.

Best wishes from all at Henry Street to all at Nine Elms for a Merry Christmas and Happy New Year.

Kindest regards,

Sara Jane

* * * * *

William arrived back in Fremantle in early October, brimming with self-confidence. Bateman's instructions had been followed to the letter and he had haggled long hours over the value of the sandalwood, especially the previous year's wood.

He explained everything to Sara Jane as they drank tea at the kitchen table. "Because my ship departed early and was blessed with fair winds, it was the first to reach Singapore this season. The merchants were eager to buy. There is always the chance that typhoons will sink the ships with the sandalwood cargoes and they'll run short of the wood. I took the money and then bartered for the goods that John suggested. If I do say so myself, I think my first trading venture was successful. However, we'll have to wait for John's assessment on that, after we sell the back-loaded goods."

"I'm proud of you, big brother."

"I heard you've been doing a little skippering on the side, Sara Jane."

"Just testing my namesake, William."

"I'm proud of you, little sister."

"Thank you. I'll demonstrate my ability when you give me the opportunity. Now William, please listen to me. I was serious when I suggested that we need a new house and I would appreciate you giving it some consideration. We can afford it, even if you are contemplating building a bigger boat in the future. The front rooms of Henry Street can be converted into our office and the back rooms and yard can be used for storage."

"Hmm," was all William said, a pensive expression on his face.

Sara Jane continued. "The lots in High Street, just east of Henry Street, are reasonably priced and away from the bustle of port activities associated with both the North and South Jetties. I would like to buy a lot immediately, have plans drawn up and move in before Christmas. Labour is not as scarce now that the convicts have arrived." Sara Jane gave a mischievous smile as she added, "I thought you might like to host a New Year's Eve party to mark your new status as an overseas trader."

William frowned and his eyes narrowed to slits. He pursed his lips and looked at his sister with an inscrutable expression on his face. "You do, do you? Do you think we are made of money? We will need a new and much larger boat, nay, ship, sooner rather than later, if we are to extend our business to overseas trading."

Sara Jane's disappointment was clear. "William, our rounded net profit for the first full year of operation of the business to the end of July 1848 was £292. It was a good result because the total outlay on the *Margaret* was repaid. Our net profit to the end of 1849 was £427. In your absence, I finalised the books for the last full year and our net profit was £507." Sara Jane stopped.

William was drumming his fingers on the table and looking out the window. He continued as though he had not heard a word his sister had said. Finally, he made comment. "Nevertheless, I think it to be an excellent idea and suggest that you move quickly, if we are to have Christmas lunch in our new house."

He ducked the well directed pot holder, just in time. A huge hug followed.

* * * * *

When John Bateman arrived home in November, the business partners met in his office to discuss events and bring one another up to date.

Bateman, being the senior partner, began. "Our only worry was being shadowed by pirates off Java, who were obviously rattled when we fired on them. The shot missed by a hundred yards but they didn't wait to see whether any more cannon balls would be forthcoming. The pirates hang around to pick off disabled vessels. Not the nicest of characters."

It was William's turn to report. "No adventures for us. We sprang a small leak on our return. Nothing serious. The carpenter had it repaired in a couple of hours."

"You did well scooping the best prices, William but I wasn't far behind. For some reason there was a feeling of doom and gloom about the typhoon season causing havoc this year. The locals can be very superstitious about such things. Anyway, it was all to our advantage, because they bought the whole shipment at near top price and averaging your price with mine makes for an excellent profit, potentially at least. We still have to sell the back-loaded goods here but should manage that before Christmas. If there's a problem, I can always tranship goods to Adelaide. We'll have to wait and see. I hope you were not relying on the money being available immediately."

"No but we were thinking of building a larger boat, ship really, over the summer months."

"But still only thinking, John," interjected Sara Jane softly. "William needs to produce some estimates of costings for the new vessel, sale of the *Margaret* and so on. And we have decided to build a new home in High Street, which is now under way. It has to be paid for and needs furnishing and all the expenditure must be taken into account. These are certainly very exciting times for the Musketeers, thanks to you, John."

"It's been a good business deal for me too. What did you call the partnership, Sara Jane?

"The Musketeers. I was reading Alexander Dumas' new book at the time. Their motto was 'All for one and one for all'."

"A sound motto for a business partnership, Sara Jane," said Bateman chuckling.

* * * * *

The house in High Street was not quite completed by Christmas Day 1850 but it was close. The plaster was dry and the floors had been sanded and polished but a final wipe over and clean-up was necessary before some of the old furniture and chattels could be transferred from Henry Street and the new furniture, mats, curtains and cushions delivered.

Sara Jane was delighted with the result. She had spent hours studying and amending the original plans and incorporating her personal touches to make the house more elegant and more comfortable for the inhabitants. Naturally, Elizabeth and Fred were moving with the Blairs.

352

The two-storey house was built of evenly-sized limestone blocks and fronted straight on to the proposed footpath. Currently, both the path and road were still white sand but Sara Jane was determined that their section of the foot path would be attended to as soon as possible. The architecture was of Georgian influence with its clean lines and the builder's proposal of verandahs or balconies declined in order to keep it that way, except for a ground-floor verandah at the back of the house for the drying of clothes. There were two bedrooms upstairs, each with its own dressing room and a joint sitting area between, which led into a small study cum library. Downstairs were two more bedrooms and a large sitting room with Sara Jane's new pride and joy, a square pianoforte, purchased for £65 from Scott's store. William was still groaning at the extravagance. The dining room, with a large jarrah table seating ten, was located down the hall from the kitchen. Access to a below-ground cool room and cellar was provided from a commodious pantry and the kitchen was a cook's dream with everything situated for convenience. A larger than usual bathroom was located behind the pantry. To date, Sara Jane had not been able to entertain because of the size of the small Henry Street cottage. Now she was looking forward with great pleasure to doing so.

In the end, because of the state of the cottage, with everything packed in anticipation of a shift before Christmas, William made a great show of taking Sara Jane and Elizabeth to the Union Hotel in Market Street for Christmas lunch. They tackled tomato soup, roast beef and Yorkshire pudding with vegetables and a rich fruit pudding with brandy sauce.

"Phew!" said William, placing his serviette on the table. "I need a walk to help lunch on its way. Who would like to join me?"

He paid the bill and with a flourish linked arms with Sara Jane and Elizabeth. They conversed affably as they walked back to Blair Cottage, stopping to admire their new house on the way. William took his role as the man of the family very seriously, doffing his hat to other strollers and joining Sara Jane and Elizabeth in exchanging Christmas wishes. Elizabeth was filled with pride, love and gratitude.

* * * * *

As things turned out, it wasn't a New Year's Eve party. Sara Jane wanted everything to be perfect for their first gathering and there were so many loose ends it just wasn't possible. So the party was held on the 5th January 1851 and became a Twelfth Night party.

Mr and Mrs John Bateman with their son Walter and David Long were met by their hosts and ushered to the sitting room. Sherries were served and hors d'oeuvres offered from platters bought for the occasion. There were salted almonds, savoury ham patties and Welsh rarebit or sardines on fingers of toast.

"Scrumptious," said Bateman after sampling the full range.

At 8 o'clock they were seated by place card at a meticulously arranged table in the dining room. A white starched damask table cloth and serviettes set off shining silverware and polished glassware and crockery. Vases of flowers adorned each end of the table. Everything was so obviously new.

Sara Jane and Elizabeth served dinner and William proudly opened Madeira Estate wines purchased from Samson's especially for the occasion. The menu had been carefully planned, so that minimum time was spent away from the guests. French vegetable soup was followed by jellied flounder and a lobster salad. The main course was roast turkey, cold sliced ham and boiled vegetables with white sauce. Fruit salad and whipped cream finished the meal.

"It is delicious, Sara Jane," said Mary, as William served her another slice of turkey. "John, I insist on an upgrade to our kitchen. Cooking is pure drudgery in mine."

The conversation flowed happily and even the reticent Walter and shy David voiced their opinions after a wine or two. Naturally the discussion kept returning to local topics, such as who was departing the colony and who were the new arrivals, who was gaining a benefit from the convict establishment and the present state of business. As the evening progressed, it became evident to Sara Jane that Walter only had eyes for her and Elizabeth was mesmerised by William. Sara Jane sighed. Should she let things be or intervene in this one-way attraction? She decided to let things be. Elizabeth was young and surely William would open his eyes sooner or later. For purely selfish reasons, Sara Jane considered it would be a fine match. As far as Walter's admiring glances were concerned, Sara Jane was flattered and as much for the father's sake as the son's managed the situation with aplomb.

Tea was served in the sitting room and was followed by glasses of port for the men. Mary helped Sara Jane and Elizabeth clear the table and stack the dishes.

"Thanks, Sara Jane. You've provided me with the best reason for renovating my kitchen. John's always after me to hold a dinner party but with my old stove and the arrangement of the appliances and furniture, it's just too much trouble."

"I'm glad to be of assistance, Mary. And I must say that John has been marvellous with us and we have really appreciated his counsel."

"I rather think he's enjoying it, Sara Jane. Helping individuals to reach their potential is one of his strong points. If John has chosen to provide assistance to you both, then you must deserve it. Besides," she said with a knowing smile on her face, "I've noticed that John usually gains from such arrangements as well."

Sara Jane looked to the others and then clicked her heels. "Mary and Elizabeth, I am now returning to the sitting room and requesting something I have never dared to request. Join me if you will."

"What is that, Sara Jane?"

"I am going to ask for a port." Closely followed by the other women she marched towards the sitting room.

John's voice was loud enough to be heard clearly. "Our superstitious northern agents were right after all, William. I received news only yesterday that the typhoons came and few buildings escaped damage. They wreaked havoc with the shipping and many lives were lost."

The women stopped dead. "I definitely need a port," said Sara Jane. The others swallowed and nodded as the implications became clear.

"William, I am now ready for a port," said Sara Jane sweetly as they entered the room. Mary and Elizabeth nodded nervously. David nearly choked.

"Have you a problem with that, David?" Sara Jane looked at him questioningly. "Do any of the gentlemen have a problem with that?" Her eyes swept the four men.

"Not at all. Not at all, Sara Jane. I think it entirely appropriate for a Musketeer," replied John.

"It's all right by me, partner," added William grinning.

"Aye, aye, skipper," said Walter.

David hastened to agree.

CHAPTER 35
The Shepherd

Thomas Chapman was a shepherd on McNeill's and Hall's Glen Mona Run, one hundred and twenty miles north-west of the town of Melbourne, in Australia Felix, that part of New South Wales south of the Murray River. The run was twenty miles long and half as wide in the Pyrenees area, so named because of its hilly nature. His employers were squatters and had several properties and so Tom was on his own, so to speak. He watched over the sheep and kept his own company, having no choice in the matter. Being illiterate, he was not able to communicate through letters, or keep a journal, or read books. It was a lonely life and apart from counting the sheep on each full moon, chasing off or trapping the occasional dingo and shooting kangaroos for meat, there was little to do and less to occupy his mind. He had been on the block for two years now and had saved only half of what he estimated he needed for his fare back to England and that was assuming the fares hadn't increased.

It had seemed such a good idea at the time. His bachelor uncle had died tragically when kicked in the head while shoeing a horse and Tom had inherited a small sum of money. On the spur of the moment, he made what he now considered to be a hasty decision. He would travel to the colonies, make money and return home to his village, worldly and wealthy enough to marry his girlhood sweetheart and provide for her in a way to make others envious. With permission from the village aldermen and the steward of the Manor, he had hitchhiked to London and booked a passage in steerage for Australia. Now he worried that Louise could grow tired of waiting and marry someone else.

Tom was both bored and homesick. Bill Hall had visited him in September to deliver his three monthly rations and take a tally of the sheep. As he left, he thoughtlessly said he would bring him something special for his Christmas lunch in the next quarterly parcel and this plunged Tom into a deep depression. Pondering about his future provided no solutions. He felt trapped.

Tom sighed in frustration. He whistled his dog, a speedy and hard-working sheep dog he had trained himself and signalled Blitzen to bring the sheep back to the brush pen for the night. After placing the makeshift gate into position, he opened one of the two bottles of rum allowed with each delivery of rations and proceeded to drink himself stupid. Two hours later, he needed to relieve himself. Singing happily, he staggered off into the darkness, tripped over a tree root, rolled down the hill, knocked himself unconscious on a boulder and came to rest with his nose inches from the edge of the creek.

"What the---?" Tom came back to the land of the living with Blitzen licking his face. He was cold, stiff and sore, with a terrible headache and a dreadful thirst. No more rum for a while, he promised himself. He cautiously touched the lump on his forehead. The morning sun shone into his eyes and with a groan, he rolled over to drink from the creek. As he cupped his hands, something glinted in the water beneath his fingers and he reached forward to grasp it. It was a gold nugget as big as a pigeon's egg. He yelled and Blitzen shied away in fright.

"It's all right, my boy." Tom patted the dog and stared long at the nugget, before walking back up the hill. He knew what it was by its weight and colour. "Everything's all right now."

Tom let the sheep out of their pen to graze, lit the fire and boiled some water for tea. He was thoughtful as he cooked and ate some damper. What to do? The nugget was withdrawn from its hiding place in the fork of a nearby tree and placed on the edge of the blanket on which he was sitting. Of one thing he was sure and certain. He was going home. But he couldn't just do a bunk. He owed something to Mr Hall and if he walked off the run and left the sheep, they would wander off and end up on someone else's land, or worse, be eaten by wild dogs or fall down gullies and injure themselves. They were such stupid animals. He would have to drive the sheep south to another of Hall's runs and make an excuse for returning home. His initial contract for two years' service had been fulfilled, so Hall could not hold him.

Meanwhile, one thing at a time. The fire kicked out and Blitzen ordered to mind the sheep, Tom walked down to the creek. Starting where he had found the gold, he systematically worked his way downstream, reasoning that the nugget could have been washed downstream not upstream. He found several smaller nuggets and became more and more excited. Then he foraged upstream for over a mile and, discovering more gold, realised it had all come from further up. Finally, fashioning a strong digging stick with his small axe, he turned over every rock from the small waterfall near the top of the hill for a mile or so downstream to where the creek became a lake. After the water had cleared, Tom pocketed another handful of small nuggets.

The next day, the nearest creeks were all carefully explored. Nothing. Not a single speck. At first Tom was puzzled but then surmised correctly that the lode must have surfaced only on the side of the hill nearest his hut and over time the gold had been flushed out by the running water.

That was that then. Tom packed his meagre belongings and tied the roll to his digging stick. Along with his shepherd's pay, the gold was bound securely by cloth to a piece of rope, which he tied around his waist under his shirt. He whistled Blitzen to round up the sheep, shouldered his load and set off to join the track south.

Two weeks later, he was on his way to Melbourne. Mr Hall had been sorry to see him go but accepted the young man's story about wanting to return home to England to marry Louise. He was grateful that Chapman had at least the decency to drive the sheep to him. Other shepherds had just walked off, leaving the sheep behind and he'd had the devil's own job rounding up the remains of the flock. Tom was paid out and given a little extra for his trouble.

On consideration, Tom decided to keep Blitzen with him as long as possible. Lone travellers were targets for thieves and now he had something worthwhile he wasn't going to give it up lightly. He reckoned he looked so down and out that thieves would hardly think him worth the effort but he wasn't going to take any chances.

Another week of walking and Tom found himself in Spencer Street, which was in dreadful condition from the heavy traffic of bullock trains. Sadly, he had said goodbye to Blitzen, giving him to a young man having difficulty shepherding a small flock of sheep just out of town. Blitzen was last seen expertly rounding them up and in his element. Tom wandered up and down the streets of Melbourne, marvelling at the number of people, until he found two prosperous-looking jewellery shops. He then returned to a boarding house he had passed on the way into town to make a booking and take a bath. Oh, to be clean again!

Two hours later, with his hair cut, his beard trimmed and wearing a new set of clothes and wide money belt, he chuckled as he looked at himself in the mirror. Wasn't a bad looking fellow really and scrubbed up well.

Back in Collins Street, he entered the premises of Charles Brentini, Jeweller. At first, Brentini believed he might be a well off immigrant but after a brief conversation guessed correctly that it was another lucky surveyor, squatter or shepherd. They were now appearing with greater frequency to off-load their illicit finds. The government laid claim to all gold found on crown land and consequently most dealings were underhand. Tom was as close-lipped as he could be without being rude, which wasn't in his nature.

"How much cash will you give me for these?" Tom tried to speak 'posh' as he called it, as he placed two small nuggets on the counter, leaving his hand close by.

Brentini pulled the scales towards him and weighed the nuggets noting their combined pennyweight. He pushed the calculations towards Chapman but the disconcerted expression told him the man couldn't read. "£18," he said.

"Not a penny less than £20," Tom responded.

"You drive a hard bargain, sir. £20 it is."

Tom insisted that payment be made in a range of coins and took his cash gladly in a donated leather drawstring purse.

He then walked down Collins Street to the jewellery shop of J. Forrest and Son and repeated the process with two more small nuggets he estimated to most closely resemble those he had sold to Brentini. He was offered exactly the same amount he had bargained for at the previous shop and took it, then produced two more slightly larger nuggets from a pocket and received a further £30. The £50 in cash disappeared into the leather purse.

Cole's Wharf was his final destination and he found the offices of several shipping agents in nearby streets. He chose the one that looked 'a cut above the rest' as his mother used to say and inquired about passage to London. He paid cash for a ticket and a cabin was booked for him on the *Georgiana*, leaving Melbourne the following Tuesday. Well satisfied with his day, he returned to the boarding house for dinner.

* * * * *

After a boring and uncomfortable voyage, Tom disembarked at the London Docks carrying a new leather bag purchased in Cape Town. Impatiently, he waited for a cab to the George Inn and next day, again impatiently, waited for the coach to Swindon.

On 8th January 1851, Thomas Chapman walked from Swindon to his village in new boots, giving himself blisters in the process. It was freezing cold and snowing but he whistled all the way. He was home, pleased with his colonial experience and the money he had made but, most of all, was so very happy to be home.

His arrival was greeted with disbelief. Who was this toff? It couldn't be Tom. But it was Tom, dressed to the nines. As soon as the villagers accepted that it was one of their very own, there was scurrying between houses, much shouting and a small crowd assembled.

Then Tom saw Louise in the throng. She was even more beautiful than he remembered. He dropped his bag and started towards her.

An unkempt man stepped forward and blocked his way. "Welcome back, Tom," he said. "Remember me? Ted Foster. You stayed away too long, Tom."

The villagers stepped away from Louise and Tom saw she was pregnant. She did not lift her head. He said "Hello, Louise," quietly, before being borne along by the crowd to the Chapman family's cottage in the centre of Lydiard Village.

* * * * *

Tom's youngest brother whispered to a friend in church that Sunday, who recounted the story to the blacksmith's assistant as they hunted bird's eggs, who communicated the news to the stableboy as he shod one of the Earl's horses, who informed the milkmaid for an exchange of favours, who told the scullery maid as she delivered the milk, who gossiped with the cook while peeling vegetables, who conversed with the butler over supper, who with great importance reported the matter to his Master, the Right Honourable Oswald Richard Powell, the Earl of Lydiard.

The story was out! Tom Chapman had found gold. He was worth £100!

"It sounds like village gossip to me, my dear," said Lady Powell, as she dabbed at her mouth with a damask serviette over dinner that night. "Surely, you are not going to take the story seriously. When did this fellow arrive home?"

"A few days ago. It appears he hasn't been sober since." He nodded at the servant to fill his glass.

"See! Why would a man drink so much if he had found gold? It makes no sense to me and confirms my suspicion that news-mongering is rife in the village. Oswald, you must demand that the aldermen take appropriate action."

"Ma-Ma-Mama," Charles stammered. "Perhaps To-To-Tom is ju-just cele-bra-a-ating. He-e-e is a-a-a goo-oo-ood man." In fact, Tom had been his closest companion as a child, when he was allowed out-of-doors unaccompanied.

"Men! You all stick together. There must be something more important to discuss. Which Shakespearian play is planned for the season? Find out for me, John. And we owe a dinner party for the Manion-Smiths. Perhaps we should hold that before we leave for London. I'll draw up a guest list." And so his mother continued on and on.

Charles sighed. He hated the annual pilgrimage to London. The theatre and musical evenings were agreeable, because he didn't need to converse continually but the constant chase by young women and the invitations to intimate dinner parties were endless. The latter were never fewer than twelve persons and invariably he was seated beside the next daughter in line to be married off. To have to listen to windy piffle all evening was so wearisome.

He excused himself from the table as soon as he thought it wouldn't incur his mother's wrath and wandered to the library. He had plans of his own for the visit to London and they included further coaching and some matched bouts to be arranged by his ex-tutor, Alfred Carson.

Carson had been instructed in his youth by the renowned pugilist Daniel Mendoza and was actually present at his idol's first loss and last fight, when he was knocked down by John Jackson. After that, Mendoza opened a school in London for noblemen and other talented young gentlemen and coached them in bare knuckle boxing techniques. His theory relied on good, quick footwork and a swift straight left jab and he constantly argued that superior agility would give an advantage over most opponents.

On arriving at Lydiard Mansion to tutor the introverted Viscount Charles Sebastian Powell, Carson saw the potential of using pugilism to lift the young man's confidence. Over time, Charles' prowess in boxing improved enormously and he remained unbeaten in all his contests but in spite of this his self-concept remained low. Carson tried everything he knew but Charles was unable to rid himself of the stammer and this seemed to be the crux of his image problem.

The prospect of boxing cheered Charles and he wrote to Carson asking him to schedule some fights for him during his stay in London. He also decided to see Tom the next day for a friendly bout to get back some form. Tom had been his sparring partner before he headed off to the colonies. The visit might also get to the bottom of the rumours about gold.

When Charles found Tom early the next morning in the back room of the family cottage, he was still inebriated from the previous night's binge.

Mrs Chapman bobbed to the Viscount and begged him to help Tom. "I don't know what to do, milord. He was never like this before. When he found out that Louise had married that oaf, Ted Foster, he drank himself silly and has been drunk for two days."

"I-I-I'll t-t-try Mrs Cha-a-apman." Tom's mother had always been the one to bathe their scratches, listen to their problems and feed their adolescent cravings for food, morning, noon and night. In many ways, she had been more of a mother to him than his own.

Charles slung the snoring man over his broad shoulders and carried him to the small lake near the village green. He was followed by a laughing group of boys who chanted:

'Tom went over the sea to see what he could see

When he came home, no more to roam

His pockets were bare and his girl was gone.'

Charles turned and glowered and the boys scattered. At least Tom left the village to seek the means for a better life. More than the rest of you are likely to do, he thought.

Tom was unceremoniously dropped into the icy water and came up gasping. "What the hell? Chas!" he said, using the nickname of their youth. He sat at the edge of the lake, the water dripping from him and looked so pitiful that Charles hauled him to his feet and gave him a hearty slap on the back. "C-C-Come on T-T-Tom, le-le-let's w-a-a-alk" and he dragged him off towards Lydiard Forest.

It was a very long walk and during the two hours Charles heard the whole story while Tom dried out and sobered up.

"It was a chance of a lifetime Chas but I lost Louise, so it was worth nothing. Nothing! I was a fool to think she'd wait." He looked so forlorn. "What will I do? I'm the laughing stock of the village. I've a small fortune stashed in the Bank of England and it can't help me. I must have said something about gold in my drunken state, which started the rumours but afterwards I said I'd made it up to get attention and they believed me. I can't stay here, that's for sure."

Charles had a frown on his face. His eyes were blinking in concentration. "Per-Perhaps n-n-n-not T-T-Tom. Y-Y-Y-You c-c-c-could t-t-t-take m-m-me, T-T-T-Tom. Take m-m-m-me to your g-g-gold. You ha-ha-ha-have gi-gi-given me a-a-an i-i-i-idea. M-M-My ch-ch-chance of a li-li-li-life ti-ti-ti-ti-time."

They talked through a few possibilities and arranged to meet the next day.

That night, Charles met with his father in an office off the library, considered to be the male sanctuary in the manor and put forward his proposition. They had always found strengths in one another that Lady Powell could not or would not recognise and were much closer than other fathers and sons of their ilk. Charles related the true story of Tom's travels and requested his father's permission to travel to Australia and search for gold with Tom.

"S-So y-you s-s-see Fa-ther, i-it was a-a-all tr-tr-true."

"Well, my boy, there's been a great deal of news about the Californian gold rushes reported in *The Times* over the past twelve months but as yet no word of gold being found in Australia. I can assure you of that. It sounds as though you could have the front running, if you're quick about it." He gave a wicked grin and poured two generous drinks. "I'd come myself if I were twenty years younger, just for some peace and quiet."

With a wistful look on his face, he lit his pipe and took a sip of port. "You are well prepared for your future, Charles. Your education has been excellent. Carson was a fine tutor in both the scholarly and athletic pursuits. Your ability in riding, shooting and bare-knuckle boxing is acknowledged throughout Wiltshire. There is really no reason for you to wait around here and it is bound to be an adventure and experience you will never forget."

He pulled on his pipe. "So go with my blessing Son and God be with you. I would have given anything to have travelled to far-off places but when your grandfather was killed at Waterloo, I became Lord and that was the end of my youth."

The Earl asked that his son return home immediately if necessary and they both knew what that meant. Regular correspondence from the antipodes was expected and promised. They agreed on an allowance of £5000.

Next morning, Charles requested an audience with his mother. They met in her sitting room and he put his case, being rather vague about the gold outlook and more positive about land prospects in the new Australian colonies. Lady Powell, puffing herself up in anger, launched an attack and as usual did all the talking with Charles standing and listening, with much foot shuffling. He was always at a disadvantage in such situations and had learned to accept the fact that sometimes a one-sided argument was actually preferable. It didn't seem to upset him as much.

When his mother realised that Charles was not going to either defend himself or retaliate, she resorted to tears. "You are an ungrateful son.

Everything possible has been given you all your life and yet you haven't taken a wife and settled down. I have no grandchildren, your father is old and you are leaving for the ends of the earth. Charles how could you? Tell me why? Why must you go?"

Viscount Charles Sebastian Powell took a deep breath. He was almost standing to attention. "Ma-Mama, to fi-fi find my-my myself."

CHAPTER 36
Kurannup

In late February 1851, Bateman called the Blairs to a meeting to discuss their financial position.

Looking very pleased with himself, he began. "I'd like to report that all the goods we back-loaded from Singapore have now been sold, either directly through my store, or by exchange for cash with the captains or agents of ships stopping at Fremantle. The arrival of the convicts and their guards and families has positively affected my sales already, I'm glad to say. The multiplier effect will ensure that a lot of the money keeps circulating around the community and gives a boost to business."

"Yes but those dismal-looking convicts in their gangs are an unfortunate addition to the local scene. I feel sorry for them."

"Ah well, Sara Jane, one must weigh up the advantages and disadvantages. When the convicts are assigned to the outlying settlements, Blair Transport will begin to receive further benefits. You must take the bad with the good. Now, back to our business and I have good news. Your profit from the partnership is £388. Here is written confirmation of the transactions and a bank draft. I trust you are both pleased with the result and that William will consider a further venture next year."

Brother and sister thanked John sincerely. It was an excellent profit for less than four months involvement in the sandalwood trade.

"Can you guarantee there will be no typhoons, John?" Sara Jane asked with an unusually serious expression on her face.

"You know I can't do that, Sara Jane."

"Then we must consider your offer carefully. Given the risks, it might be better to build our own vessel and use our own Captain, or to consign timber on a passing ship and hope for an honest agent and Captain. William is too precious to me and to Elizabeth. Personally, I feel the risk is too great. However, the final decision is William's, of course."

As they walked home, William asked why Sara Jane was so worried about typhoons.

"William, the three of us heard part of your conversation as we returned to the sitting room the night of the dinner party. I would bet on John not being directly involved again. Mary froze in the hallway. Let others take the risks. We are doing very well as it is."

"I'll think about it," William said gruffly. "Sometimes a man must do what he feels is necessary, regardless of the element of danger."

* * * * *

Still sulking at Sara Jane's outspoken comments the previous week, William refused to allow his sister to take the tiller on the way to Rottnest. She didn't argue. He would get over it soon enough, as he always did. Perhaps she had been too forward in front of John. A man's pride was indeed a fragile thing.

Yeddi had been back at the main settlement scraping salt for the past three months, so they hadn't been able to meet with him. As the dinghy approached the beach, Sara Jane looked over William's shoulder to see Yeddi sitting on the dune. He didn't run down the beach to greet them as he usually did or even stand as the dinghy grounded.

"Something's wrong with Yeddi," she whispered. "Bring the hamper for me please, William."

They sat down on either side of Yeddi and were shocked by his appearance. He had lost a lot of weight, his head hung forward and he showed no emotion at their presence.

"Yeddi, what is it? Are you ill? What has happened?"

"Hello, my babbingurs." He sounded detached and continued staring at the mainland.

"Yeddi." Sara Jane put her arm around his shoulders and held him close. Normally, William would leave them to themselves but he was so concerned that he stayed.

"Talk to me, Yeddi. What is the matter?"

"My heart sorrows. My spirit is unhappy. My body is unwell. Life has no meaning any more."

"Yeddi, we talked about this. You must not lose hope. While you live, there is hope for the future. If you despair, your soul will lose its way."

"The longer I am away from my land, the more I am losing all ties to my past and to my future. I am not connected to anything any more. I am adrift. Away from my sacred sites, I can no longer find my way to the Dreamtime, to my ancestors. I have been separated from my family, from my people, from my land and the animals and plants that belong to it."

"Yeddi, you must try harder. Talk to the spirits, look into the flames and ask for strength."

"I have tried, Sarjan. I have tried. The spirits no longer talk to me. They have left me. They have gone."

"Let's have some lunch and then we will talk about this some more," said William trying to be cheerful. He could not believe the deterioration in his friend over the past three months.

"Good idea." Sara Jane made a fuss about Yeddi's lunch but he only ate a few mouthfuls before saying he had eaten enough. She tried to tempt him but he was not interested.

When it was time to leave, the situation had not improved. It was as though Yeddi's soul was slowly leaving him. He was losing the will to live.

"Promise me, Yeddi. Promise me you will try, keep trying to talk to your spirits."

"Yes, Sarjan. I will try."

The figure on the shore grew smaller as they sailed past Dyer Island to open waters.

"Sara Jane, we'll have to come back soon to bolster Yeddi's strength. I don't think he will be able to hold on, without support. I never thought he would lose his way. He was such a strong boylya gadak."

"Perhaps that is the problem, my brother."

* * * * *

It was 9 o'clock on the following Sunday, when James Dempster knocked loudly on the front door of the Blair's new house. "I've been trying to find you, Sara Jane. I didn't know you had shifted."

"Welcome, James. Come in and see our new home."

Dempster was clearly agitated about something. "Sara Jane, I came to let you know that your native friend is languishing. I cannot ascertain any physical reason. It's as though he has a death wish. Edward Back says he's seen it before, when natives are left on Rottnest for long periods of time."

The news sent Sara Jane's mind into turmoil. She was trying to think what she could do. William was away with David but Walter should be around. Elizabeth was in the kitchen.

"James, I am about to ask you to be dishonest. Say 'no', if you must and I will understand."

Dempster nodded. "Go ahead."

"You called to bring me some fresh fish and told me nothing about Yeddi. I will sail to Rottnest immediately and take him off the island and away to a hiding place where I will care for him. If he recovers, I will deliver him to his kin or bring his wife and son to him, if I can. If not---" Sara Jane caught her breath and did not finish the sentence. "Under the circumstances, I have doubts about whether I can save him. He seemed to be drifting away from us at our last visit." Tears were running down her cheeks. "I will leave his identity disk and clothes in the hut as though he had discarded them and tried to swim to the mainland. 'What will be, will be', as Great Uncle always said."

"I beg your pardon?"

"Sorry, an old family saying. Will you help me, James?"

366

"Of course I will, Sara Jane."

Within a very short time, Sara Jane and Elizabeth had packed food, blankets and clothing into two of William's duffel bags, left a note and locked up the house. The note read:

3rd March 1851

Dear Willum,

Have taken Elizabeth south to the Warrangup spring in the babbingur cave area to see if it cures her poor health and recurring lack of spirits. Don't worry about us, we'll be fine. Join us if you will.

James Dempster called with some fish, he'd caught near your Rottnest anchorage this morning. I've taken it with me, because I didn't know when you'd be home.

Sisterly regards,

Sarjan

She didn't think it the cleverest message but was sure it would be intelligible to William.

While Elizabeth walked on, Sara Jane stopped at Bateman's and spoke with Walter who was about to follow the rest of the family to church.

"I'll sail with you, Sara Jane. I know you're capable but Elizabeth may not be able to manage." He was almost pleading.

"Thanks, Walter. I appreciate your concern but we will be away several days at least. I've promised Elizabeth a trip for some time to the curative spring. It's near where William and I lived as children. It might help her cough."

"What cough?"

"You didn't know Elizabeth has a persistent cough? It's particularly bad in the early mornings. Would you let Mr Cooke know that she will not be available for Post Office duties at least until next week? Thanks, Walter. You're very kind."

Sara Jane left Walter standing on the door step, a perplexed expression on his face.

With a ten knot north-easterly and under mainsail and jib, it was easy sailing to Rottnest, until the final tacking. By then Elizabeth had mastered the setting of the jib and was quite adequate as a for'ard hand, although she had sore hands from winching in the anchor and hoisting the sails and had needed assistance from Sara Jane.

The young woman had a look of exhilaration on her face as the wind swept through her hair. "This is wonderful, Sara Jane. Do you think William would take me with him on a short trip?"

"Why don't you ask him?"

"I will. I didn't realise what it would be like. It's like being in a different world."

"Are you ready, Elizabeth?" Sara Jane headed up into the wind and the sails began luffing.

"Drop anchor." Elizabeth sprang to the command and released the security pin. The anchor dropped with a splash. Within minutes the wind had taken the boat back and the cutter was swinging securely from the anchor line.

"Drop jib." The halyard was cast from the cleat and the sail ran down the stay. Hanks were unclipped. A stop was tied around the sail and it was stored under the forward decking.

"Drop mainsail." Elizabeth uncleated the main halyard and lowered and furled the sail with Sara Jane's help.

"Well done, for'ard hand. Looks as though you've had a tar or two in your ancestry."

The younger woman, who felt she had been through the most exacting trial of her life, smiled with relief.

"I'll go ashore alone, Elizabeth. Less weight to pull." She rowed the dinghy to shore and hurried up to the hut, fearful of what she would find.

Yeddi was lying inside, quite still, his eyes open. "I knew you would come, my babbingur."

Sara Jane knelt next to him and took his hand. It was cold, as if dead flesh. She rubbed his arm to warm it and bent to kiss his forehead. "What is wrong, Yeddi? What has happened, my babbingur?"

"My spirit has left me. I called it back but it was too late. I fear it might all be too late."

"Can you walk, Yeddi?"

"Yes, with your help, Sarjan."

"I'm taking you with me, Yeddi. Back to the mainland. Back to our cave. We will seek your spirit."

"Thank you, Sarjan." Sara Jane helped him to his feet. He was surprisingly shaky.

"Here are some of William's clothes. Leave your identity disk and gear in the hut. This has all been planned." She helped Yeddi out of his prisoner's garb and into clean clothes.

"Willum?"

"He is away. Elizabeth is with me. We will stay at the cave as long as it takes to get you well." Sara Jane asked that they use English so that Elizabeth was not excluded from any of the dialogue.

They sailed almost directly south, staying well outside all the islands as William always did and by late afternoon were moored in Falcon Bay. Yeddi's eyes did not shift from the shore all the way down the coast. Elizabeth helped Sara Jane drop both anchors for security and insisted in being instructed in rowing. She was reasonably competent by the time they had rowed the hundred yards to the sheltered beach.

Yeddi seemed to gather strength once away from his island prison and was able to walk to the dunes from the dinghy unaided. The women hauled the boat up the beach, unloaded their gear and provisions and the three set off south to the cave area. It took just over two hours to reach Warrangup Spring.

First things first. Sara Jane wrapped Yeddi in a blanket to keep him warm. Even after the walk, his skin was still cold. He seemed to have lost so much weight that he was shivering continually. When he was comfortable, the food was brought out and everyone ate some cold leftover pasties and jam tarts. The rest of the food was tied from tree roots in the roof of the cave or branches just outside. Blankets were spread and Sara Jane lit a fire at the cave entrance, using the traditional Aboriginal method, all the time giving a running commentary on what she was doing and why. Finally, Elizabeth was directed towards the spring and brought back a full canvas water bag and a billy of water.

Yeddi grinned slyly at the billy. "Great Uncle would not approve, Sarjan."

"Oh, I think he would. If I could ask him now, I bet he would."

At that moment a small willy willy blew past the cave entrance and scattered the fire.

Sara Jane looked pained. "You don't have to bring in supernatural reinforcements, Yeddi. That's not fair."

Elizabeth looked from one to the other, thinking that she must be missing something from the conversation. Sara Jane explained as best she could but Elizabeth didn't look convinced. "Don't worry, Elizabeth. All in good time." She was just so pleased that Yeddi was showing some interest in his surroundings.

Exhausted, all three were wrapped in their blankets soon after dark. Before she drifted off to sleep, Sara Jane prayed as she had never prayed before.

Yeddi was a little happier in himself the next day but still weak. He fell asleep again soon after breakfast. Sara Jane retrieved several of his weapons, that had been left in the cave when he was taken away by the soldiers. "Elizabeth, look after Yeddi till I get back. I won't be long but I'm craving for a native meal. It's something I've missed." She strode off carrying two spears and a vicious looking cutting implement.

By the time Yeddi awoke, Sara Jane was back with a small kangaroo. The fire was built up, allowed to die down to embers and the skinned and gutted carcass thrown on. Elizabeth pulled a face but the aroma brought her around and when Sara Jane chopped the kangaroo into portions and served it on a piece of bark, she accepted a piece, albeit tentatively.

"Could use some salt," she said, with a mouthful of haunch.

"Don't mention salt please, Elizabeth," said Yeddi as he picked up a second helping. "I've shifted far too much of it lately."

A shamefaced Elizabeth apologised.

"He's teasing, Elizabeth. He must be feeling a bit better."

During the first two days, Yeddi improved. Rest, loving attention and being on his own tribal lands were all having positive effects. The combined result was more like the old Yeddi and he talked happily about their childhood days. But then on the third day, to Sara Jane's distress, he suddenly seemed to regress. He did not want to talk, or eat, or drink and sat silently in the corner of the cave like a sick animal. No matter what Sara Jane said, she couldn't bring him out of it. He said he was not unhappy but wanted to explore his inner feelings and to find peace within himself.

Elizabeth stayed away for long periods but when she arrived back, nothing would have changed. Sara Jane was beginning to pine and Elizabeth had to speak firmly about the need for food to rouse her from her depressed state and get her out of the cave to hunt for game. Yeddi had started to talk to himself and rambled on in his own tongue. Sara Jane said he was talking with his Great Uncle and the spirits.

On the fourth night, Yeddi asked Sara Jane to build up the fire so that he might seek the truth through the medium of the flames. The two women watched as Yeddi assumed a trance-like state. Then his lips began to move and he rocked backwards and forwards in time to some inner rhythm until eventually, exhausted, he fell into a sleep, a sleep so deep that he did not move at all throughout the night.

A whisper woke Sara Jane at dawn. Yeddi leaned towards her. His eyes were open and his face alight with an inner glow. She sat up.

"Sarjan, I have communicated with Gurdu. He is a son of whom I am proud and I thank you for him. I have also seen Jida and Malgar and said my farewells. She is married to a fine man and understands that I can never be part of her life again. My guardian spirit says that it is time for me to leave for Kurannup."

"But---," Sara Jane's eyes filled with tears. "No, Yeddi. No."

"Don't cry, Sarjan. Please don't cry. What will be, will be. You always accepted that as a reason when Great Uncle said it. Please listen to me."

Sara Jane nodded. She was filled with sadness. A huge weight of sadness.

"I cannot return to Wadjemup. My guardian spirit will not allow it, nor would I want to do so. Many Nyoongar already lie buried there. It is a land of death and I would not live long if I returned. Nor can I return to Jida and Malgar, because they belong to another and I have no right to interfere now. I cannot stay here alone hiding for the rest of my life. It would be unbearable.

And I cannot live with you, my babbingur. We would be in danger from both your people and mine. As much as I love you, it would not be proper and would have no future. Therefore, I have no choice and have accepted what I must do. It is time and I will go. My spirit is ready."

Yeddi took Sara Jane's hands in his and looked into her eyes. "Sarjan, please accept the decision, as I do."

Sara Jane lifted his hands and kissed them. "I will do as you wish my babbingur."

"Then I am content. You must help me. I will prepare the site for my burial and you will complete the ritual. This must be according to the law or my soul will be forced to forever wander as a restless spirit. I will walk with you now and instruct you in what to do. I am already nearing my end. I know it and feel it. Don't worry about Elizabeth. She will not wake until you have finished. Explain to her what you think she should know. You are privileged to have such a friend. I can see her innermost feelings and she is a very worthy person."

Yeddi picked up the blanket and grimaced. "This will have to serve as my burial cloak. Come with me, my babbingur." He was unsteady on his feet, as he placed his arm around Sara Jane. They walked slowly down the hill towards the small valley where he had buried his great uncle.

* * * * *

They stayed another day at the cave. Sara Jane could not bring herself to leave Yeddi just yet. Although she had followed the procedures explicitly, as he had asked and he had held her hands and thanked her just before he died, she could not accept that it was over, that he had gone. Gone forever. The past few days now seemed unreal, as though they were part of some sort of nightmare and soon she would wake and he would be alive and with her.

Sara Jane wanted to explain everything to Elizabeth but found she could not. It was unfair on the young woman but every time she steeled herself to talk, she felt the need to be alone and would return to Yeddi's grave and sit on a nearby log and think and remember.

Elizabeth brought her servings of what was left of the food and water from the spring and Sara Jane ate and drank. Not a word was spoken. It was as though she had been struck dumb.

That night, Yeddi came to Sara Jane while she slept. He was his old self. He thanked her for her love and for assisting him at his death. His spirit had arrived at Kurannup and he had found his kin. He was now content and asked that Sara Jane cease her mourning for him. The time had come for her to return to her people.

Sara Jane woke. She blinked and looked around as though she expected Yeddi to be nearby. It was pitch black and she could see nothing. She was puzzled as to whether it had been a dream or not but it really didn't matter. Either way, she knew that Yeddi had come to reassure her and she must now accept the situation.

At dawn, Sara Jane rose and gently shook Elizabeth's shoulder. "Elizabeth," she said.

The young woman woke and sat up, blinking the sleep from her eyes. "Sara Jane, thank goodness you are all right." She hugged her. "I have been so worried."

"I am so sorry, Elizabeth but there was nothing I could do. My babbingur - I may not use his name - is now at rest with his kin across the sea and is content. I am ready to return home. One day I will explain everything to you."

"I would like that, Sara Jane. There is a lot I do not understand but I accept that this is not the time for explanations."

They were sailing north past Cape Peron when Elizabeth spotted the sail. She called to Sara Jane and pointed. "Is that William?"

Sara Jane focused the telescope and saw the *Margaret* about two miles to seaward and travelling in their direction. "Yes, it is. I think he's seen us."

Half an hour later, William edged up behind them. "Head into the wind, Sara Jane and give Elizabeth the tiller to hold." With all sails luffing, William slowly drew alongside the *Sara Jane*. "Jump aboard, Sis. I want to know what's happened while I've been away. Walter can sail the *Sara Jane* home, with our newest for'ard hand's help. Hope the spring water helped your bronchitis, Elizabeth."

Elizabeth nodded. "Yes, thank you, William."

With one arm holding the shroud for support, Sara Jane stepped up onto the gunwale, took Walter's arm in a double wrist grip and leapt across to the other vessel. Walter steadied her as she clambered inboard and then sprang lightly aboard the *Sara Jane*.

The two vessels sailed home in tandem.

William was naturally very upset, as Sara Jane related the events of the past few days. "The whites managed to get him in the end, that's what makes me so angry. All that nonsense at the trial about mercy. One way or another, the natives will succumb, as they fight for what they perceive are their rights or even try to live by their own laws and traditions. It is so bloody unfair. So bloody inevitable."

* * * * *

Sara Jane grieved. Her sorrow was inseparable. It clung to her and enveloped her and try as she might she could not drive it away. Every moment of the day, the memories flooded back. She could not dispel them and wasn't sure she wanted to as yet. They were such wonderful memories.

William also grieved but knew his grief was a minor consideration compared with Sara Jane's, so became the strength he considered she needed in looking to the future. He talked about the business and asked her opinions about issues that arose and tried to be the helpful and cheerful big brother. However, because of William's regular absences, it was Elizabeth who became the stalwart. She returned from her mornings at the Post Office with amusing stories about the clientele and busied herself around the house, all the time keeping an eye on Sara Jane as she had promised William.

James Dempster called one morning and Sara Jane thanked him for his thoughtfulness in informing her of the situation on the island.

"William told me about your friend's death and I feel for you both. He was a fine young man, Sara Jane but I fear he pined more than the others. He seemed to be a deep thinker and that would have been a distinct disadvantage in his circumstance. My story about his disappearance was accepted by the authorities. Apparently it's happened before. So that's the end of it, my dear and you should now try to get on with your own life. I've always thought that those who pass on from this world would not want to cause extended anguish for those who loved them and remain behind."

Sara Jane reflected carefully on what Yeddi had said to her and the advice given by Dempster. When Elizabeth arrived home, she sat her down and told her everything, except that Yeddi had been her lover and that she had borne his son. Only William and the Roberts should be privy to such information, she reasoned. The story of their rescue by the natives, the time spent with them and the lessons learned, she related. She explained that for the period of time spent with the natives they were family and how she and William had loved and respected them.

"So you see Elizabeth, it's a part of my life that I cherish as much as all the other important parts of my life. I thought I would be able to cope better than I have and I am sorry that indirectly you have had to share my grief."

"I feel privileged, Sara Jane and appreciate you sharing your confidences with me. You and William have now lost two families and that must be very difficult. But life goes on and I think it's time for you to face the world again. I'm sure that's what your babbingur would want."

"I know you are right but it's easier said than done."

Elizabeth put her arm around Sara Jane and held her. "Sara Jane, will you attend church with me tomorrow?"

"Yes." There was a pause. "I think that would be a sensible and beneficial way to face the world again and would certainly provide the right context." Sara Jane smiled. "Thank you, Elizabeth. You've been very understanding and a great support."

Things started to look up from the time of their attendance at the church service and when William arrived home, Sara Jane was almost back to her old self. There were lapses, of course and the improvement was gradual but there was now a cheerfulness and purpose evident in the High Street house and chores that had been ignored were undertaken with a new-found determination.

* * * * *

In early May, Elizabeth arrived home from the Post Office with a letter from Henry. Sara Jane looked pleased and excused herself to read it in private upstairs. She was more animated than Elizabeth had seen her look for some time. Thank goodness for that, she thought.

Sara Jane broke the seal, took out the pages and read:

Nine Elms
30th January 1851

My dearest Sara Jane,

I am so excited, that it makes a mockery of the decorum expected of middle-age. I haven't felt this way for years and am like a young boy going on his first hunting trip.

The Antoinette leaves Plymouth on the 7th of next month and I will be on my way to the antipodes at last! Everything is in order at Nine Elms and I can leave the management to the steward with a clear conscience. I don't know why I didn't do this a long time ago. Probably because I had no one special to visit anywhere in the world!

Following my communication to them, the Roberts forwarded me an invitation to stay over at Madeira Estate at my pleasure and, as you promised me, sounded sincere and enthusiastic at hosting another Blair. They certainly hold you and your mother and father in high esteem.

The worst of winter has passed and hopefully, as we move into spring, the weather will be favourable for the journey. Providing there are no mishaps, I'll be in Cape Town in early April, have a two week stopover there and, depending on the berths available on passing ships, will arrive in Fremantle in June some time.

Your prayers and the regular recitation of Psalms 23 and 27 must have had the required effect, because your mother told me of William's safe return when she received your last letter. Just to be on the safe side, would you follow the same procedure for me? I'll be safe then for the last part of my journey.

Viscount Charles Powell left for London last month on his way to the eastern states of Australia. Everyone was surprised, given he is the heir apparent to an earldom and his father's condition at best could be described as frail. Gossip has it that at last he stood up to his mother and decided to follow the rumours of gold being found in Australia. Rumours have been widespread around Lydiard recently.

I managed eventually to obtain a copy of Edward Landor's book The Bushman and found it very interesting and informative, albeit rather ebullient. He certainly has a way with words but pontificates excessively. I believe he is a barrister and can understand why he chose that profession. I found Chapter IX, 'The moral thermometer of colonies', especially elucidating, if I may be sarcastic. He says that 'The malleable intellect of our youth is annealed by the Demon of Gain upon the Anvil of Self-interest'. It seems all will be well in the colonies, if there is education, in particular religious education and if women inspire veneration and command respect. I'll be interested to obtain your views on that, my dear.

Your mother and father send their love and say they are pleased to have me as an envoy. At least they will gain first hand information on my return, regarding their daughter and son, the new home and the state of the business. That is, of course, if I can't persuade you to return with me to the old country with its comfort and safety <u>and</u> good morals!

When you receive this, I will be on my way.

I can't wait to be with you again, my dear,

My love,
Henry

Sara Jane's eyes moistened as she read the now expected addition. For the first time, it was prose rather than verse. It read:

.....and if our lives should never quite entwine,
our friendship lights my understanding of your world
and sheds a gentle lustre upon mine.....

"Elizabeth! Elizabeth! Henry will be here within weeks. There's so much to do. We must begin immediately."

It was just the impetus that Sara Jane needed. A room to be prepared, a welcoming party planned, a meeting with George Fletcher Moore organised, checks made on the coastal tour schedule so that Henry could be included. What should he see? What could be arranged for him? With whom should he meet?

CHAPTER 37
Australia Felix

C harles Earl and Thomas Goldman, as they were to be known, took the coach to London. Charles carried a letter from his father, giving the Bank of England instructions regarding financial transactions to be made for his son under his assumed name. Under no circumstances was the colonial bank to be informed of Charles' connection with the nobility.

In London, they went immediately to the shipping office of the Lydiard family and orders were given to make bookings on the first ship leaving for Melbourne, Australia. Charles explained that space should be set aside for the storage of mining equipment, which they were transporting with them, as they would be on-porting to San Francisco and the Californian goldfields after a brief stopover.

At Earl Lydiard's London house in Regent Street, the servants sprang into action when the young master arrived and announced that he and Tom would be staying until passage to Australia was arranged and that his mother would be travelling to London within the month to prepare for the season.

The Lydiard coach was brought from the stable and polished until it shone and the four matching greys looked splendid as they trotted down the Strand. They were driven with full regalia to King's College to see Alfred Carson, who was staying over for the summer break in readiness for Charles' visit. After a brief discussion of the major details of their proposed travels, Carson suddenly excused himself and returned forty-five minutes later, with a huge smile on his face.

"It's all arranged. I'm coming with you." He explained. "I was at Lydiard for ten years before I joined King's and have tutored here for eight years without taking any leave. I've accepted the responsibility for boys unable to travel home for term breaks on every occasion during that time and never shirked a duty. The Principal could do nothing but accede to my request for a year's absence without pay. You're not leaving me behind! I'm thirty-eight years old and haven't had an adventure in my life. Lead me to it, lads!"

With great excitement, boosted by the depletion of Carson's brandy supply, Tom told his story in full. They eventually left Carson to pack his books and belongings for storage and arranged to collect him the following morning.

A confirmation memorandum from the shipping office had arrived at Lydiard House. 'Cabin booked on the *Culloden* leaving from London

Docks the day after tomorrow.' The coachman was sent posthaste with the message 'Extend the booking. Now three passengers. Payment will be made tomorrow'.

Alfred Carson was waiting in the foyer with a welcoming smile. As always, his fair hair and beard were cut shorter than was considered fashionable. He appeared fit and well and extremely excited. Alfred always kept himself in shape being almost fanatical about the need to exercise one's body regularly. Such an amiable fellow and knew so much about everything. A veritable walking encyclopedia. Charles was delighted that he was joining them.

"Hu-hu-hurry a-a-along Car-ar-son. We ha-ha-have shop-shop-shop---thi-thi-things to-b-b-buy."

A detour to the Bank of England set their financial affairs in order. Apart from each man taking out cash for tickets and their own personal expenses, Charles set aside money for equipment in London and Melbourne and they agreed to divide these costs as necessary at a later time. The rest of their money was withdrawn as individual bank drafts on the Bank of Australasia.

The coachman then drove them to a store recommended by some of his cronies at the local inn. They received expert advice from Robert Heintz, a lucky miner, recently returned from California to persuade his wife not to leave him now he was rich enough to open a store. Two hours were spent choosing gear for the trip. Heavyweight wheelbarrows, picks, shovels, axes, tools, rope, tin dishes and pails. Two substantial cradles for washing sand and rocks. The mechanism for a small hand windlass. A tent, bed-rolls, camp oven, saucepans and other cooking utensils. The equipment was to be packed securely in crates and delivered to the *Culloden* lying at the London Docks. It was decided that suitable clothing and provisions would be purchased in Melbourne. Alfred spent a valuable thirty minutes in earnest conversation with Heintz, establishing what sort of terrain to seek and methods for extracting the precious ore.

On the 19th January 1851, the *Culloden*, A1, of 1000 tonnes burden, a fine frigate, commanded by Captain Harold Ferguson, was towed down the Thames to Gravesend, where she anchored for a further day to take on provisions.

Being of academic bent, Alfred Carson kept a journal.

21 January 1851

This morning, we raised the Blue Peter and took our pilot on board. To much singing by the crew, who were obviously glad to be on their way, the anchor was raised and the Culloden towed downstream by a powerful tug. Anchored at Deal for the night. Have decided to travel incognito as three gentlemen Alfred Castle, Charles Earl and Thomas Goldman exploring opportunities in land acquisition in the newest and most promising settlement in Australia.

22nd January

Away at last! The sails filled with a favourable breeze, we set sail this morning for Australia. We are all excited and looking forward to great adventures. I can see the change in Charles already, as he assumes some responsibility. His father showed great insight in giving his blessing to this opportunity.

25th January

Sunday service. The Union Jack was spread over the capstan and the bell tolled. The crew and passengers assembled to hear prayers read by the Captain. I received the distinct impression that it was a duty he did not much enjoy, because it was all over very quickly.

30th January

Much ado this morning when a stowaway was discovered hidden among stores on the lower deck. He was severely chastised by the Captain in front of the ship's company and then put to work with keep but without pay, for the remainder of the voyage. I suspect that he had been assisted by at least one crew member, so will be looked after.

22nd February

Becalmed off Africa! Last week, we made little progress. The sails flap to and fro but there is insufficient wind to fill them consistently and we seem to just drift about. We're lucky if we progress a few miles a day. Hot and humid and altogether unpleasant. Charles caught a huge shark today. It made good eating for the passengers, who toasted him at dinner for his efforts.

24th February

The Captain is concerned and suspicious about a vessel that has been following us for the past 24 hours. It is low-rigged and rakish-looking and appears to be of African origin. She will not answer our signals nor give her name.

25th February

Captain Ferguson has deemed it prudent to prepare all passengers for a possible encounter with the vessel following us. Today, muskets, cutlasses and boarding pikes were distributed. Companies were formed with a lieutenant in charge and each was stationed at a designated part of the ship by the Captain. We all watched at our appointed posts from 8 o'clock to first light.

26th February

The vessel still being in sight, the Captain ordered cannon to be prepared for firing tomorrow to indicate we are armed. A bit of excitement to break the monotony would be welcomed by all.

27th February

What a let down! Last night, the wind came up and the vessel slipped away in the darkness. I now think it was probably a slaver, as eager to get away from us when the wind came up, as we were to get away from her. At least we are on our way again.

3rd March

Wretched bill of fare and most of the food indigestible. Salt beef, we call it junk, salt pork, tinned soup and bouilli, rice, pease pudding, preserved potatoes, plum pudding, known in nautical terms as plum duff and ship's biscuits, very dry and hard and served with the inevitable weevils. Water foul and being strained before drinking. We're all very glad Tom suggested bringing casks of ale.

20th March

Cape Pigeons and Cape Hens skim the swelling waves. The pigeons settle in the water in the wake and devour the refuse thrown over the side, keeping a weather eye open for sharks. The predators follow us in large numbers, which doesn't bear thinking about in the middle of the ocean.

28th May

Southern coast of Australia now distinct. We're off Australia Felix at last! Rays from Cape Otway's lighthouse are visible.

29th May

The Souvenir, a small coasting schooner from Port Fairy, hove into sight this morning and the Captain gratefully followed the little colonial vessel towards the Heads. We were told that the gap between the two Capes through which we must traverse is very dangerous and has claimed many a ship. A pilot was signalled, who came aboard and took command. We were soon inside the Heads and the Union Jack could be seen fluttering in a gentle breeze from the flagstaff on Station Peak. All very reassuring. Today, we heard our first cooee, when saluted by a fisherman, indolently hanging a line over the side of his boat anchored in the roads.

30th May

We are all astounded at the extraordinary clearness of the atmosphere. Everything is so defined. The evergreen eucalypts look most singular.

31st May

Anchors dropped in Hobsons Bay. We've arrived! Spent several hours discussing plans for the next few weeks. Our equipment will be stored for the present, while we assess the situation. Have decided to continue to play the parts of two wealthy friends and servant travelling to the colonies. We've all had our hair cropped short. Chas looks a different person. Tom doesn't think he will be recognised by anyone. He's been practising talking like a toff and says he wants to get used to it for later, when he's allowed to be a wealthy friend! Chas and I agreed we'd like it to be sooner rather than later.

1st June

A small lighter came alongside our ship this morning to ferry us to Melbourne. We went together, of course and were impressed by the naturalness of the scenes on the banks of the Yarra River. Parrots perched in trees and storks stood unconcerned at the water's edge. We unloaded at a primitive little landing called Cole's Wharf, where our luggage was placed on a dray and we were transported to the centre of town. Found digs in Elizabeth Street on following the advice of the driver. This suited us, as we had decided to keep a low profile and didn't want the notice we could possibly attract at a hotel. Rich pasture and farming land is now attracting squatters in large numbers and clearly this has been the stimulus for the development of the necessary infrastructure for the export of wool and other agricultural products and the importing of building materials and goods for domestic use. The streets are wide and paved and generally in good condition. Most of the buildings are of rudimentary construction, the majority made of wood. Some more substantial administrative, commercial and church buildings are evident and many more have stone foundations laid. Prince's Bridge is still under construction. Melbourne is undergoing a period of growth and the population now exceeds 10,000 persons, our knowledgeable driver expounded. Everyone is agitating for separation from New South Wales but to no avail. Tom sat grinning throughout the conversation, pretending he had never visited Melbourne before.

The boarding house was built completely of wood and obviously very new. Mrs Simpson was plump, welcoming and glad to receive boarders. She winked at the driver of the dray, who blushed and hurriedly unloaded the luggage. As he turned the dray in the wide street, she smiled happily. "He brought you to the best boarding house in Elizabeth Street and will be back for a bite later as his reward. Worth his weight in gold," she said.

Tom started and then relaxed. "Pity there's not some of that about. Then you'd be in clover, ma'am."

"Aye," Mrs Simpson said, as she led them to their rooms, "They say there's gold been discovered but if so it's the best kept secret in Melbourne. In February, a fellow found gold only seventy miles from Sydney. That caused quite a stir. Lunch is at 1 o'clock, tea at 5 and supper at 9. If you're not on time, you miss out."

The next morning, their crates were delivered and with Mrs Simpson's permission and an agreed storage fee, they were locked securely in a shed in the back yard of the boarding house. "They'll be safe there," she said. "No one would dare steal from me." Alfred thanked her and paid an advance fee for three days. Mrs Simpson retorted, "It's a pleasure to deal with gentlemen." The three men later decided that perhaps they needed to adopt a more down-to-earth appearance and demeanour for their own safety.

Charles, considered by vote to be the best judge of horseflesh, selected three horses at a nearby stable and also purchased saddles and other required accoutrements. "W-W-We al-al-so n-n-need t-t-two m-m-mules a-a-and a-a-a f-f-f-four wh-wh-wheel d-d-dray a-a-and f-f-f-four b-b-b-bullocks."

Alfred added, "And two additional wheels and spare spokes and wood for repairs. The bullock team will need to be yoked and fully equipped. The horses and mules will be tied behind."

"Fine, sirs. I'll hold the horses, until I can find the mules, complete with the necessary leather work and panniers and a fully equipped bullock team. I'll let the widow Simpson know as soon as they're ready."

After lunch, the three men outfitted themselves with clothing. It was June and already cool. With winter ahead, Tom stressed the need for light, warm and strong clothing. They each chose three serge shirts, three pairs of moleskin trousers, two vests, two pairs of blucher boots and two loose neckties, all of assorted colours to their own taste. Coats and wet weather gear they had brought from England. The clothing was packed individually into three canvas bags. Broad-brimmed hats they wore, laughing at one another as they walked back to their digs, with their bags slung over their shoulders. "We'll at least look the part, lads," Alfred said. "I can't wait to do some exercise. I feel like a lump of lard."

"Well, let's leave as soon as possible then," said Tom.

Alfred agreed. "All we have to do is purchase provisions. That won't take long at all." Charles nodded assent. "Let's drop this gear off and get moving."

For the next three hours, they wandered the streets of Melbourne. Provisions for their trip were ordered at a store not far from their rooms. Tom knew the essentials and Alfred added a few niceties, as he called them. They could always shoot kangaroo for meat, if necessary. The goods were left to be suitably packed for travel and would be delivered immediately. Tom pointed out the jewellers where he had exchanged some of his nuggets for cash. They noted several other jewellers as they walked. Charles stopped at the Post Office and penned a brief letter to his father, saying that they had arrived safely in Melbourne after an uneventful voyage.

Mrs Simpson interrupted their conversation at breakfast and informed them that their animals and equipment were ready at the stable. "You'll be off then, sirs?"

Alfred replied, with a polite smile. He knew that Charles appreciated not having to make the effort to speak, if one of the others would do so. "Yes,

Mrs Simpson. We'll be on our way north to look for suitable land. We wish to establish a property to breed fine wool for English mills and look for any other opportunities that might arise. Australia at the moment is a most attractive proposition. We have enjoyed your excellent service, especially the food and will recommend you to other travellers. Thank you." He placed two half sovereigns on the table, which Mrs Simpson quickly pocketed before leaving the room. The three men again became engrossed in their discussion. Tom had drawn a map of the way to the Pyrenees and gave estimated distances as best he could remember. Alfred added explanatory notes from Tom's description. This was referred to regularly and Tom reckoned the journey would take at least a week. They decided to pool their remaining money for contingencies. Their funds were better left in the Bank of Australasia.

The animals were ready when they arrived at the stable. Charles checked everything in his usual methodical way. Satisfied, he took the fearsome-looking long-handled stockwhip from the previous owner, who ominously had his left arm in a sling. The whip had a thong three yards long, tipped with a kangaroo-hide lash. The bullocky did not provide any explanation for his injuries but offered to give some preliminary instruction for a fee, which was accepted.

"There's 'Gee up' to start off, 'Gee off' to turn, 'Gee back' to make a full turn and plenty of yelling," explained the bullocky. "And that's about it. Watch me take them through their paces and make sure you keep Blackie in the front left hand position. He's the smart one and leads the others."

Apart from finding that the bullock rig was far more cumbersome than anything he had driven before, thereby requiring a larger turning circle and that he needed to add a list of appropriate expletives to his vocabulary, Charles had sufficient control in just over thirty minutes.

"Well done, sir. It usually takes longer to get the hang of it. Slow and contrary, they be. Don't be afraid to use the whip. They have thick hides."

"Th-Th-Thank y-y-y-you." Charles lifted his eyebrows at the others, who had been applauding his performance. He paid the bullocky and the stableman from the leather wallet attached to his belt. "No-No-Nothing t-t-to it r-r-really."

The others decided to walk for the exercise and so the threesome and the bullock team with the horses and mules tied to the dray, moved slowly down Elizabeth Street to the boarding house, where their personal belongings, provisions and the crates were loaded. They then turned left into Bourke Street, right into Spencer Street and were on their way north.

Alfred spotted the notice first. 'Dogs available'. It was tacked to a post at the front of a neat cottage. He called to Tom and told him what the notice said. With a whoop, Tom ran down the drive and hammered at the door, which was opened by an elderly man.

"Could I see the dogs, please?" The man walked to the fence of the nearest paddock and whistled. Six dogs raced to the call. One was the spitting image of Blitzen. It had some remote connection to the collie breed and was black and white. Tom put his hand over the fence and patted the dog, which barked and then licked his hand.

"He's yours, son. No charge, just look after him. He's a good dog but, as you can see, I've more dogs than I need." The man opened the gate for Blitzen Junior, who walked through and sat at Tom's feet.

"Thank you very much, sir. I'll look after him." An elated Tom caught up with the dray, his new dog running at his heels.

They passed through Flemington and several small settlements, following Tom's directions. The country was lightly wooded and the track reasonable. Additional time was taken to traverse the creeks as Charles was mindful of the problems of bogging the dray but they were able to find a solid base each time.

"G-G-Glad w-w-we ha-haven't got ei-ei-eight b-b-b-bullocks and a wa-wa-gon," Charles said as, with a "Bloody Hell! Move you bastards," he cracked the whip at the bullocks which stood sullenly on the bank.

Tom opened his mouth to say something and Alfred shook his head.

"Give it to them Chas," he called loudly. "Where did you get this language? Not through my tuition, of that I'm sure."

"F-F-From T-T-T-Tom a-a-and the vi-vi-llage k-k-k-kids."

"Who? Me? Never," protested Tom.

Camp was made under a stand of eucalypts on a low hill by the side of a creek. The water was clear, albeit cold. By consensus, they decided not to worry about the tent. They would spend the first night on their quest for gold under the stars. Alfred took over and gave the orders because, as he explained, he had often taken boys on overnight nature excursions and someone with experience in these things should take the lead. The animals were unhitched, hobbled and left to graze and wood gathered. A fire was lit and meat and damper cooked. Before dark, Charles and Alfred had seen their first kangaroos as they came to drink at the creek and heard their first kookaburras laughing at the English visitors. "Enchanting, absolutely enchanting," said Alfred.

After sunset Charles gazed at the brightness of the stars and the huge yellow moon rising in the east and he questioned Alfred.

His old tutor paused, as he had always done while having to think through an answer when Charles was his pupil. "It must be the lack of smoke and fumes. The air is therefore cleaner. The atmosphere is not as polluted as that over the cities of England, so the clarity of your view of the celestial bodies is enhanced."

"Cripes," was all Tom said.

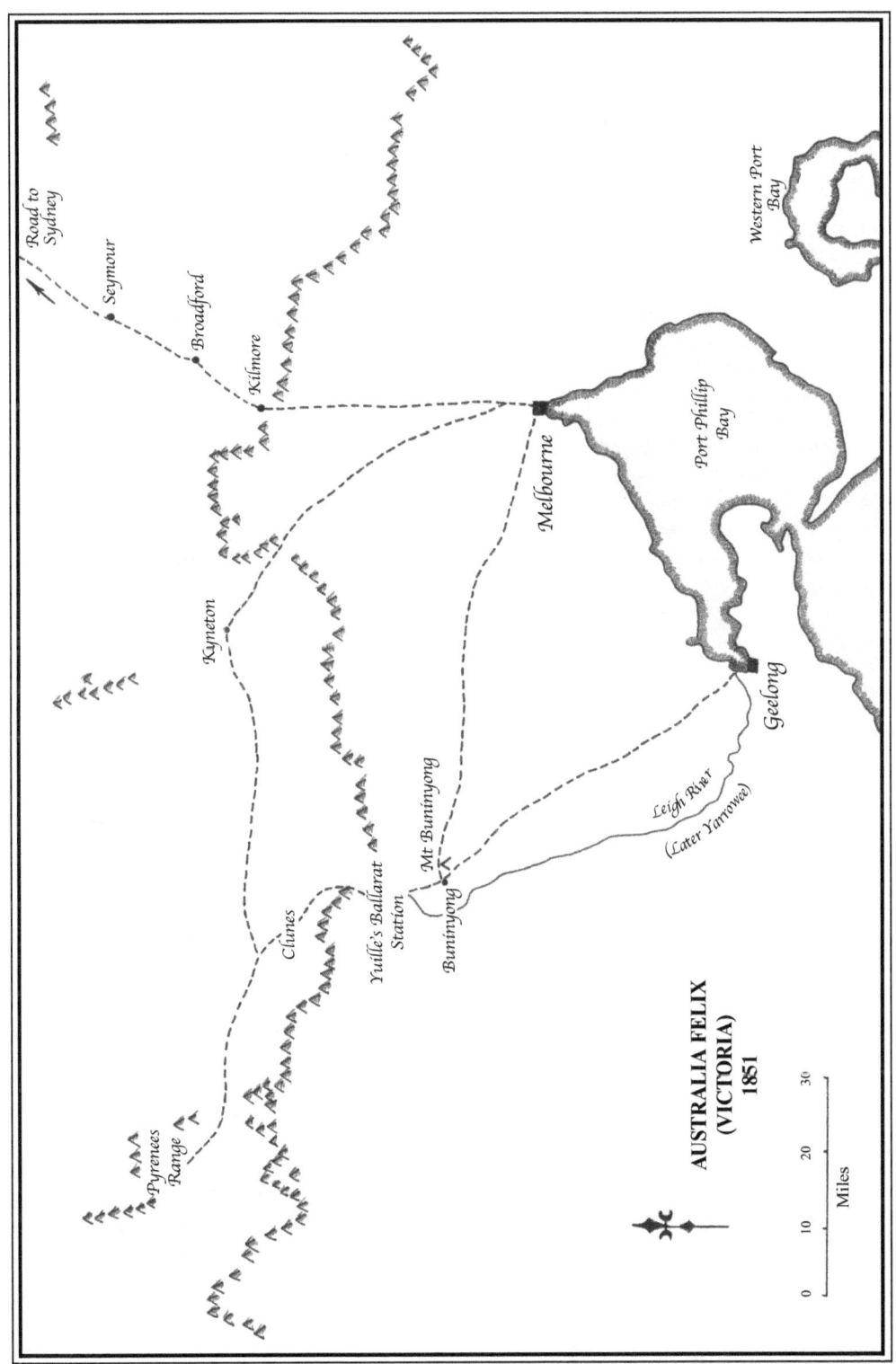

AUSTRALIA FELIX
(VICTORIA)
1851

Road to Sydney

Seymour

Broadford

Kilmore

Melbourne

Port Phillip Bay

Western Port Bay

Geelong

Kyneton

Pyrenees Range

Clunes

Yuille's Ballarat Station

Mt Buninyong

Buninyong

Leigh River
(Later Yarrowee)

Miles

0   10   20   30

The journey was much slower than anticipated. It was an eye-opener for Charles and Alfred, who found much to comment on. They passed no one on the first two days and all enjoyed the solitary nature of the travelling. Alfred spent time on the dray so that he could make sketches of items of interest and he pondered on the high range to their right as they headed north-west. When they stopped to camp on the second day, Alfred asked Tom about the mountain range.

"Tom, how did you travel over the range? It looks very high."

"It is. The Pyrenees are on the other side of that range." He pointed to the range which was now at its closest point so far.

"How will we manage the dray over the range?"

Tom frowned. "There's a track but it will be difficult in some sections. I walked through valleys, sometimes."

"In the winter?"

"No, it was spring."

"Could you draw another map, Tom? Put in the mountains and rivers, as accurately as you can and keep the measurements to some sort of scale. The sketch map was fine but now I need more detail. Can you do that while Chas and I set up camp?" He handed over his drawing pad and pencil to a doubtful-looking Tom.

As he sat and drew, Tom bit the end of the pencil in concentration. Eventually, he handed the pad back and pointed to the features for Alfred to write in the names as Tom remembered them.

When the lamp was lit that night, they took turns at studying the map. Alfred asked Tom many questions. Finally, he made comment. "I'm convinced we would be wise to alter our plans. First, I think we should have gone north and then west, because of the bullock dray. Tom, do you know whether the owners, or lessees of the land travel the way you came back to Melbourne?"

"No. They went east and south. Oh! I see what you mean. The northern pass. I've messed everything up, haven't I?"

"Not necessarily. My second point is that for the past day I've been wondering why there isn't gold in all these mountains. Why go so far, when we've a mountain range just to our north? It's the closest it's been to us since we began. You see, all the travellers through this area would be keeping to the flats or lower hills as much as possible. From what you have told us, the squatters and the shepherds would not be at all interested in the high ground. It's no use to them. Were you on high ground, when you found the nuggets?"

"Hmm. About half the way up the hills. Mr Hall always said I took my flocks higher than the other shepherds. You're right, Alfred. Where I found it, the gold had come down from near the top of a hill. There was a spring and a small waterfall washing over the rock."

"It's a classic situation. The most readily obtainable gold is alluvial gold, which is found on the surface or close to the surface. It can be in the form of nuggets, or specks in the soil, or in the silt of river beds, or in layers of clay. It would have taken millions of years of erosion to have broken down the quartz reefs. Torrential rains and rivers would have dispersed the surface soil and gravel and by a process of attrition, over time the gold would have been released."

"Phew, Alfred. How do you know all that?"

"Because, Tom, I read it in the College library the night after your visit to King's."

Tom and Charles could not contain themselves and dissolved into laughter.

"Y-Y-You're a prankster, b-b-but a kn-knowledgeable o-o-one, Alfred. Wh-Wh-What do you suggest?"

"I am of the considered opinion that tomorrow we should turn north and follow this river to its source."

The following night, they camped on the flats near a creek, below the highest hill in the area and once again slept in the open.

Much barking awoke the men at dawn. Blitzen was confronting another dog, which clearly belonged to a man on a horse nearby. "Good morning to you," he called. "Looks like a fine day."

Charles scrambled out of his bed-roll and rubbed the sleep out of his eyes. "G-G-Good morning t-t-to you, s-s-sir." He reached up with his hand and they shook.

Tom and Alfred were now sitting up in their bedding.

"Just checking. There have been some escaped convicts from Van Diemen's Land seen hereabouts. Haven't caused any trouble as yet but one can't be too careful. We think they have probably headed east towards Sydney. Our settlement is over there behind the rise. You must have been late in last night or you would have seen the smoke from our fires."

Alfred replied. "That we were, sir. It was a long day yesterday. What is the name of your settlement?"

"Buninyong." He pointed north. "And that is Mount Buninyong." He pointed east. "And you're camped on Leigh Creek. The Leigh River arises in the north in the Ballaarat Station area."

The three travellers looked towards a large rounded hill. "Would it be permissible for us to climb the hill and explore around the area for a while?" Alfred asked.

"Certainly. There aren't too many that own any land. It's mostly leased. No one has laid claim to the mount. The only thing we ask is that you are careful with fire and don't interfere with the stock. Good day, sirs." He turned the horse's head and cantered in the direction of the settlement.

The bullocks were hobbled near the wagon. They rode their horses to the hills topped by Mount Buninyong and climbed the lower slopes. The nearly dry bed of a stream was located. Only small pools remained.

"Must be the beginnings of Leigh Creek. It must flow down the mountain after rain," Alfred said. "It's worth a look."

An hour later, Charles cooeed. Without appearing hurried, the others walked towards him.

"Look a-a-at this," he said, pointing to the uppermost side of a barrier of rock that acted as a small dam.

They knelt together and saw the unmistakable glint of gold through the clear water.

"Pick it up, Chas."

Charles rolled up his right sleeve and plunged his hand into the pool. The others held their breath, as he grasped something. He withdrew his clenched fist and displayed his find. It was a gleaming, irregularly shaped gold nugget.

"You bloody beauty," whispered Tom. "Look again, Chas. The water's clearing."

The small pool about a yard across produced two more nuggets, both slightly smaller than the first.

"Eureka!" said Alfred.

"Hallelujah! Hallelujah!" Charles stopped abruptly. "Wh-at's wrong, you two?"

Alfred had a most unusual expression on his face. A combination of surprise, thankfulness and affection. Tom just looked pleased.

"Chas, you're obviously not aware that your stammer has lessened significantly over the past week. It has almost gone. Both Tom and I have noticed it."

"I am, I'm t-t-trying hard. Tell you t-t tonight."

"Back to work troops," said Tom. "We've a lot more daylight yet."

Alfred looked thoughtful. "Perhaps we need to be more systematic in our search of Mount Buninyong. We can't continue coming back and snooping around. It would be too obvious. Let's walk up as far as we can and follow sections of the slope that keep us hidden from the settlement. If anyone asks, I'll say something about geology. Remember, if a nugget is not in water, it is likely to be covered with dust, by vegetation, or partly hidden by detritus."

"What?"

"Loose stones and sand. I'm practising my geological terminology."

"Right," said Tom.

By the end of their first day's prospecting, they had collected several handfuls of nuggets. "Not pure gold by any means," said Alfred. "But close to it. I'd bet these mountains are very, very old in geological terms and that's why the nuggets are so clean so to speak. They've been cleansed by the elements."

Tom nodded sagely and Charles grinned, as they toasted one another with their best brandy after a dinner of tinned beans and damper.

"Now, Chas, what's happening about your speech, except that it's getting better by the day? After all my attempts were to no avail at Lydiard, it seems that the wide open spaces of Australia are doing the trick."

Charles took a deep breath, paused and spoke very slowly and very loudly. "It seems to have something to do with concentrating on my breathing."

Tom and Alfred clapped. "Well done! Bravo!"

He took another deep breath. "It was the bullocks. I could swear and shout as much as I liked. That seemed to help." He took another breath. "And I'm away from my m-m-m-other. You see, sh-sh-she always l-l-laughed a-a-at m-m-me."

"Chas my boy, there is absolutely nothing to laugh at, nor was there ever anything to laugh at. Perhaps your mother's own insecurity was her problem and in some way, for some reason, she was able to transfer it to you. It's over now or will be very soon. We'll have it beaten in no time at all. Here's to it." Some more brandy was splashed into pannikins.

By the light of a rising moon, Tom took out the tool box and fashioned a small box out of their spare wood supply, which he screwed securely underneath the tray of the dray. "Just in case we find so much that it's too heavy for our pockets or money purses." Tom had a very satisfied smile, almost a smirk, on his face.

One more day was spent on the slopes of Mount Buninyong. Several more handfuls of small gold nuggets were found. As they were about to head back to their camp, Chas slipped and slid feet first down a slight slope. His sturdy heels uncovered a nugget the size of a chicken's egg. This was secreted in Tom's box along with the other nuggets.

"That's it lads. Let's move on tomorrow. We've a whole mountain range to explore."

They headed north soon after dawn the next morning, estimating their journey to be about ten miles. The track was rough and it took time to negotiate the bullock team between and around trees. Tom pointed out evidence of sheep having been moved over the track some time ago but they saw no one. When the incline increased, Charles was clearly in his element. He swore and cursed at the top of his voice and cracked the whip. The bullock team responded and so did his stammer.

About noon, Alfred suggested they turn off the track and forge their own path. "We'll find a suitable place, set up a semi-permanent base camp and use our horses and mules to cover the area north. We don't need to hide but we don't want to expose ourselves unnecessarily. Who knows how much time we have before the whole range is crawling with men."

The three horsemen, with two pack mules trailing, spent the afternoon reconnoitring the surrounding bush. They found several creeks. Tom tried panning to assess the situation and glimmers of gold dust appeared.

"Right," said Alfred. 'We look in hilly streams and we look on slopes and we look on barren and gravelly ground with a quartz base or boulders."

"How do you know?" said Charles.

"Because I read an article in *The Times* about the Californian goldfields."

"When?"

"The night I read about gold in the library at King's."

"Didn't you get any sleep that night?"

"No. Just think how much more we'd know if you'd given me sufficient time to research the subject."

"So, Professor. How about finding us an example of such terrain? You always made me give examples."

"Strewth," said Tom. "Talk English, you two."

"Tom, do you want to be a toff? A wealthy gentleman?"

"Yes, of course."

"Then pay careful attention."

Alfred scouted around for an hour, climbing higher and higher until he found what he was searching for.

"This looks like the perfect example you asked for Chas. A barren, gravelly slope with quartz boulders."

"You're r-right again, Alfred." Chas held out two large nuggets at arms' length and even with his strength, it was a strain.

"I agree." Tom was grasping a nugget with both hands. It was larger in size than a grapefruit but elongated and pitted. "It's about two pound weight."

"Alfred, th-th-this is ridiculous. Are you s-s-sure? Could it b-b-be anything else?"

Alfred's eyebrows closed. He was clearly sifting information. "Pyrites," he answered.

"What's th-that?"

"Another mineral but it's not as bright in colour as gold. It's found with quartz but I wouldn't have expected it in this sort of terrain or scattered like this in large lumps on the surface. No, I'm sure, positive, this is gold. It's because the whole situation is like a fairytale that it's so hard to believe. We're here first, thanks to Tom and we have to make the most of it. The hordes will be here soon enough."

Day after day, they traversed large areas and worked like slaves, collecting, sifting, kicking, scraping and pulling vegetation and roots. The creeks were left alone to concentrate on 'their terrain', as Tom described it. Following a shower of rain, the gold could be found even more easily. They each donated a shirt to wrap the nuggets as they were collected before placing them in the horses' saddle bags. The panniers on the mules could take only so much weight.

They were rewarded beyond their wildest dreams. Tom utilised all the spare wood they had brought, building a partitioned false floor in the dray to spread the weight of the gold as they hid it. Alfred kept a tally of the estimated weight of nuggets found daily and recorded the details of amounts and location in his journal. "Don't worry lads," he said. "It's a combination of Sanskrit, Latin and Greek with a few Egyptian hieroglyphics thrown in."

After seven days, Alfred gave his report while they waited for the damper to cook and the tinned soup to heat. "Attention please gentlemen, for our first week's report. To 16th June, the total amount of gold is 6088 ounces. A good start, lads. Let me see. That's approximately 380 pounds, so we certainly won't be overloading our beasts of burden."

"How much is it worth?"

"Thomas, I'll tell you what the good book says. 'Yea, they are greedy dogs which can never have enough and they are shepherds that cannot understand: they all look to their own way, every one for his gain, from his quarter'."

"Sorry, Alfred. I suppose it did sound greedy."

"Ah but listen to what comes next. 'Come ye, say they, I will fetch wine and we will fill ourselves with strong drink; and tomorrow shall be as this day and much more abundant.' At the conservative price of £3 per ounce, it's worth £18,264. Find the wine, Chas. If the Bible tells us to fill ourselves with strong drink and tomorrow will be better still, then surely we should follow the word of the prophet."

"You made that up, Alfred. Any excuse to open the wine."

"Not so, Thomas. Isaiah, Chapter 56, Verses 11 and 12."

And as the good book said, the next day was a bonanza. They found over 2000 ounces in small nuggets and Charles picked up one that Alfred estimated exceeded ten pounds.

That night was decision time. As usual, Alfred led the discussion. The others had come to expect it and he clearly enjoyed the leadership role.

"Gentlemen, your attention please. Today, being 16th June 1851, I would like to announce that our kitty has increased by £6480. Our clothes need a wash, our beards need a trim and we're almost out of food. If we shoot kangaroo, we could draw attention to ourselves from a curious shepherd or traveller. As I see it, we are on the horns of a dilemma. We can leave our mountain of gold and return to Melbourne, or go hungry, or shoot kangaroo and risk someone investigating and stumbling upon us. Of course, we risk the latter anyway. The trouble is that we don't know how long it will be before the rush starts. And start it will."

"W-W-What do you suggest, Alfred?"

'No, Chas. I want to know your views and Tom's views."

"I say we shoot k-k-kangaroo and keep going. If we do attract attention, we can just break c-c-camp and leave. That would throw them off the scent."

"Yes, makes sense. What do you think, Thomas?"

"I agree and I'm happy to shoot, skin and cook the kangaroo, starting tomorrow night. There's something else though. I found all my first nuggets in a stream and so I'd like to follow the river a bit."

"As you wish. It is certainly worth a try."

"Alfred. D-D-Do you know exactly where we picked up the largest nuggets?"

"Yes, I recorded the details by using landmarks."

"Then before we leave, I would like to dig below those areas."

"Good idea."

* * * * *

It being a fine morning, they rode to the river, washed their clothes and themselves in icy water and put on their last clean set of gear. The washing was spread on bushes to dry.

"Don't look like that, Thomas. You're now wealthy and must act as a gentleman would."

Tom grumbled but sat patiently as Alfred trimmed his black beard, while Blitzen kept watch to make sure no harm came to his master.

Within two hours of paddling in the river, they sported beaming smiles. Charles was admiring a nugget shaped like a cat. At least he thought so, even if Alfred couldn't see it.

"I'll take it home as a present for Mama," he said, articulating every word meticulously and keeping a perfectly straight face.

"Cooee." The danger signal from Tom. Blitzen was barking at two men on horseback approaching through the trees. Charles casually put his right hand holding the nugget into his pocket and left it there.

"Hello there. Name's Eastwood," one called. "I'm looking for my shepherd, who appears to have strayed from his usual patch. Have you seen any sheep?"

"No, haven't seen any sheep or anyone," answered Alfred, taking the lead as they had planned.

"Nice day," the horseman said.

"Yes. Looks like a late winter."

"Travelling far?"

"That depends."

"Oh?"

"Depends on the terrain." Alfred heard Tom splutter and turn it into a cough. "We're checking the land for pasture as we travel. Thought it time to do our washing." He pointed at the washing drying on the bushes.

"Your rig down below?"

A surprised, "Yes."

"I'd keep a closer eye on it, if I were you. Well, goodbye. If you see a shepherd, let him know that Eastwood's looking for him." He turned and followed by the other man, rode back the way they had come.

"Phew! Good boy, Blitzen. That could have been close."

Tom stayed closest to the washing, Charles walked upstream and Alfred wandered downstream. When the sun was directly overhead they met and compared finds.

"There's a lot of gold dust if you look closely," Charles said. "Must be gold everywhere in this stream. A good idea of yours, Tom. Altogether a worthwhile exercise. We've beaten yesterday's find already. If we brought the cradles up on the mules, we'd find a fortune."

"Well, we certainly carried a lot of extra gear from Melbourne for nothing. Never mind. It would have given the game away today. I'm mindful of what our visitor said this morning and think we should return to camp early. From now on, it might be a good idea if either you or Tom remains on guard. You're both crack shots and the wagon's worth protecting, you'd agree. I know nothing about guns, thank goodness." Alfred breathed a sigh of relief. "I couldn't shoot someone to save myself."

"All right. I'll take first duty tomorrow and give Tom the opportunity to improve his gold tally."

Tom shot a kangaroo at dusk. Straight through the head with a single shot. After skilfully skinning its rear end, he cut the legs and tail into pieces and wrapped the portions in bark before placing them on stones in the coals of the fire. "Something the natives taught me," he remarked to nobody in particular as he heaped further embers on top. The carcass was thrown well away from the camp for Blitzen.

"Tell me about the natives," Alfred asked, as they waited for the meat to cook.

"Don't know much really. They kept to themselves most of the time. I didn't have any trouble with them. Only saw them when I got my stores, 'cos they knew I didn't smoke and so came for my baccy ration. They always knew when to come. Then they would bring something, such as lizard, snake, possum or kanga and have a meal with me. Quite friendly they were. Didn't touch my sheep either, probably because of the baccy. Some of the other shepherds lost sheep but I never did. Heard stories about blokes shooting the natives after a few drinks but don't know whether it was true."

"How did you speak with them?"

"Sign language mostly. "S'pose the poor blighters will be killed or chased away. Not too many left in Van Diemen's Land, they say. Strange to think I'm only about fifty miles away from my old shepherd's hut."

"Just think how much gold lies between us and your old shepherd's hut, Thomas."

"Just think how lucky we were that I drank a bottle of rum and somehow ended up at the edge of a creek."

"Oh, I don't know, Tom. I'd still be at King's teaching upper sixth form boys."

"And I'd be in London bored out of my mind with flighty adolescent girls fluttering fans under my nose."

A week on a constant diet of kangaroo left them all craving for more normal fare and in particular sweet foods.

"Can't take much more kanga haunch," grumbled Alfred after their night meal. "The prospect of it is starting to turn my stomach. Oh, for some damper with jam, or some fresh fruit." He threw the remainder of his kangaroo into the fire.

"Alfred, why don't you do another tally tonight and see what we're worth? We can't stay here for ever in our treasure trove. I'll be happier when this small fortune is in a bank safe. We can come back as soon as we've reprovisioned. And I must get a letter off to my father, as soon as possible. I'll leave the hard work of my digging idea till next time."

In the circle of lamplight, Alfred spent ten minutes scribbling furiously. He coughed. "Gentlemen, your attention please. I would like to announce to this Directors' meeting, that CAT Mining Company Proprietary Limited of Australia Felix has made an estimated profit of £52,080 in its first month of business."

The bullocks bellowed all the way back to Melbourne. "They certainly object to the extra weight. Move you stubborn bastards!" Charles grinned at the others. "I really think driving a bullock team is very rewarding. It brings out the worst in me."

They followed the plan they had devised on the track. On the last afternoon, they took to the trees and, hidden from view, Tom converted the crates into small wooden boxes. He was skilled with tools and after four hours, fifteen strong boxes stood lined up on the ground beside the dray. The nuggets were taken from their hiding place and apportioned, so that each box was approximately the same weight. The lids were screwed on and the boxes tied with rope. Finally, the screw holes and knots were sealed with candle wax and the boxes hidden under canvas on the tray. All their equipment and gear was concealed in the bush.

"With luck chaps, we might get a few more shots at our range before someone else finds gold and the word gets out."

On their arrival in Melbourne, horses and mules were returned to the stable and the stableman advised that the animals were to receive the best grooming and all accoutrements were to be cleaned and polished. The bullock team would be returned later that morning. Greatly excited, the stableman informed them that the mayor and burghers had just offered a reward of £200 for the discovery of a payable goldfield within two hundred miles of Melbourne.

"Then we'd better be on the lookout lads," said Alfred with a wink. "We could do with £200."

There was one letter waiting at the Post Office. It was from the Earl and Charles related the content to the others. All was well at Lydiard Mansion, except that Lady Powell had complained that Charles' absence seemed to have affected the number of dinner invitations received during their stay in London. His father hoped that they were finding their time in the antipodes profitable and that they were safe and well. He concluded, 'Make the most of it my boy. I am envious in the extreme. I trust the allowance was sufficient.' There was much guffawing at that.

Charles wrote a short cryptic letter to his father.

Post Office, Melbourne
Australia
28 June 1851

Dear Father,

Thank you for your communication. It is always reassuring to hear that all is well at home.

Our stay in the recently proclaimed State of Victoria has been extremely interesting. As you suggested the land is rich and very suitable for grazing although it seems that great tracts of country are already leased by squatters - that's the name they give to the settlers who have extensive runs and huge flocks of sheep and cattle. I shall make appropriate inquiries about land acquisition before I leave Melbourne.

The business has been profitable and the allowance has remained intact. We have decided to return to England sooner than we anticipated, although we are intending to look further than Victoria now that we are here. Both South Australia and Western Australia might be worth our scrutiny. I shall keep in touch.

My regards to Mother and John,

Your respectful son,
Charles

During the next three hours, they purchased new clothing, washed at a bathhouse and visited a barber. Groomed and dressed in their new gear, they walked to the first of the three banks in Melbourne, Charles cracking the whip at the bullocks, as necessary.

At the Derwent Banking Company of Hobart, Charles approached the front counter with a swagger. "I say old boy, could I see the manager. Charles Earl is the name." He pulled his large gold watch from his fob pocket and flicked it open, looking decidedly bored. The manager appeared immediately and Charles followed him into a plush office.

"What can I do for you, sir?" asked Mr Marsh after introductions.

Charles waved a limp wrist around in the air and, using his best upper class accent, explained that he needed a large safe to store some valuables. "At least a month or so, old chap. I might just speculate in some land. Payment will be made a month in advance, of course. Just awful this Melbourne weather, wouldn't you agree?"

After handing over the money and signing some papers, Charles ignored the offer of assistance and returned with Alfred and Tom. They all carried a box with apparent ease. One more trip by Alfred and Tom, while Charles talked inconsequentially with the teller and then with key in pocket, he led them back to the dray and on to the Union Bank, where exactly the same procedure and conversation followed. The final stop was the Bank of Australasia and having off-loaded their booty to safe storage, they returned the bullocks and dray to the stable. The stableman was left with a long list of provisions to purchase. Blitzen looked thoroughly miserable and insulted at being left with the other animals.

"Well, what now chaps? How about we kick up our heels and stay at a hotel for the night? Then I think we should head back to the range before there's a scramble for that reward. What do you reckon?"

"Too right. I need to learn more about being a wealthy gentleman."

"Chas?"

"Yes, lead me to wine, women and song."

That night Charles, Tom and Alfred dined and wined at the Melbourne Hotel before being directed to the red light area of town by a helpful desk attendant. All smiles, they met back at the hotel to join in the midnight celebrations of Australia Felix formally attaining statehood and the name of Victoria. It was the 1st of July 1851.

* * * * *

Late the following afternoon, they arrived at the bush area in which they had hidden their equipment and set up camp. Next morning, everything was reloaded and they moved off optimistically on their journey back to the range.

On arriving at the Leigh River camp site, it was freezing cold and the rain had set in. Winter was at its fiercest. The dray and animals were brought as close to the river as possible for security and their camp established on high ground nearby. The three men worked hard and found a number of nuggets as they foraged further afield but it was miserable trying to keep clothes and gear dry and cooking in the rain was difficult. Often, unable to keep the fire going, they ate leftover meat and damper or cold tinned food while dressed in soaking clothes and then tried to sleep in wet bedding. The tent could not keep out the driving rain and the rivulets running over the hard surface relentlessly found their way under the sides, despite prepared gutters. When the sun and fine weather returned, it was still bitterly cold but so much more pleasant.

Several solitary men passed them, travelling north in a hurry. They didn't stop nor offer any explanation. "The reward has generated interest no doubt," remarked Alfred dryly. "It won't be long now."

After a four day fine spell, Alfred brought out his journal and deciphered his notes, as to the location of their largest surface nuggets and most concentrated finds.

"It's time to dig lads. We're not finding much now on the surface. We've cleaned out the obvious stuff. Might as well make it obvious what we're doing, in a last-ditch attempt to take what we can from this range."

The two mules were at last utilised as beasts of burden. On the first day, Charles dug shafts in the designated areas, Alfred loaded the auriferous gravel and clay into the panniers and led the mules to the river, where Tom emptied the panniers into the cradles and watered and rocked them to separate the gold. Each day they rotated tasks. Alfred explained the importance of sinking the shaft until they reached a thin layer of what was called blue clay, a misnomer as it was usually a chocolate colour and tough and soapy. This layer was rich in gold. When they reached a hard white pipe-clay barrier, they should abandon the shaft and sink another.

It was extremely hard work and for the first week the men were stiff and sore but as their muscles hardened and they grew accustomed to the exertion, they could work at a consistent and sustained effort level from an hour after sunrise to an hour before dark.

By trial and error, they found that the blue clay was closer to the surface on the slopes near the brow of the hills and that reduced digging. The day's taking of nuggets was hidden beneath the false floor in the dray after dark.

Within a fortnight, the dray cavity was almost full. One six foot deep shaft had given up 54 pounds of gold and another nearby 31 pounds. Most shafts in their chosen areas produced over 20 pounds.

"Wonder what they'll call this place in the future?" puffed Tom as he helped Charles empty a pannier into the cradle.

"Probably Ballaarat after Ballaarat Station," answered Charles.

"Must be one of the richest fields ever discovered."

And so it was! The gold seekers had stumbled on what would be aptly named Golden Point. As history records, the Ballarat goldfields of Victoria finally yielded 20,000,000 ounces of gold.

One early morning in late July, Blitzen began barking furiously. A figure with a swag tied to a shovel came into sight along the river.

"Good morning," called Alfred. "Want to join us for breakfast?"

The man hesitated before walking towards their fire.

"Thank you," he said. "Name's Esmond, James Esmond. I am hungry."

Over tea and damper, the man told them that he'd heard a rumour of gold being found at Clunes and was travelling north to try his luck. Alfred was rather noncommittal and explained that they were also chasing the reward but with no success. "Must be in the wrong place, as we haven't seen a sign of any gold."

After thanking them for the meal, Esmond headed off at a fast pace.

Alfred had a grim look on his face. "That's the first lie I've ever told in my life. The gold fever's getting to me."

Over the next three days they found 53, 63 and 48 pounds of gold.

Esmond came hurrying past on the fourth day, neither looking to right nor left.

"Ah, ah! That's it lads. Won't be long now. We've probably a week left, I'd say. Let's make the most of it."

Shafts appeared everywhere and there was no time to rest between dawn and dusk. They were on a countdown and knew it.

With the week up, Alfred brought out his journal and calculated the worth of their gold. "Gentlemen. I would like to report that CAT Mining Company Proprietary Limited of Victoria is now worth approximately £98,126."

"Phew! We're rich! I might not yet be a gentleman but I'm certainly wealthy. What's this CAT business you keep talking about? Who's CAT?"

"It's an acronym for Charles, Alfred and Tom."

'I don't understand what you two are talking about half the time. P'raps I'd better stay a servant."

"You'll do us, Tom. You brought us to the gold. We're now three wealthy friends, without a servant and there's no question about it."

That night they celebrated their gold-seeking adventure and toasted their futures late into the night.

"What will you do, Tom?"

"Build my family a new house in the village, or in Swindon, or London if they want it. Have a stable and horses and a four-in-hand. Learn to read and write and call myself Squire."

"Chas?"

"Go home to Lydiard and find myself a wife, I suppose."

"Alfred, what about you?"

"Back to King's College. All seems a bit mundane after the colonial life. Perhaps I'll do some writing. How about *The Australian Journal of Alfred Carson 1851*?"

There was a long pause while each pursued personal thoughts. "Gentlemen, thank you for your faith in my potential as a writer. I am now about to pass out," and with that Alfred rolled over, asleep.

Tom lasted one more drink. Charles covered his companions with their blankets and lay awake for some time thinking. All in all, he decided he was very thankful to have been given the opportunity to find himself, as he had so desperately wanted. And I have, he said to himself, as he drifted into sleep.

* * * * *

On the return trip to Melbourne, they passed dozens of men travelling north.

"You're going the wrong way," they all chorused, laughing loudly. "Gold's been found at Clunes!"

"Then good luck to you, lads," called Charles.

"What an assortment of gear - or lack of it," grinned Alfred. "Glad we were properly equipped. It's going to be bedlam in the ranges before long. There will be thousands upon thousands of men crawling over our terrain."

Most men walked with a swag and a shovel. Some had wheel barrows. One drove a mule laden with provisions. A rather better dressed man rode a black gelding with a pack horse trailing behind. An old man shuffled along beside a goat, harnessed to the shafts of a small cart, mumbling to himself.

By the time they reached Flemington, Tom had counted fifty-three men hurrying on their way to Clunes, wherever that was.

At the first large general store, Charles purchased saddle bags, valises and small chests. The gold was then transferred into the receptacles and deposited in their safes in the three banks. Tom and Alfred each withdrew cash from their Bank of Australasia accounts and there was a reckoning of expenditure. Charles protested but the others insisted. "We want everything to be square and above board, Chas," remonstrated Alfred.

That they would worry about the sale of the gold later was a unanimous decision.

The dray and animals were returned to the stable and the stableman asked to sell everything as soon as possible. Judging by the exodus of men from the town to all places north and north-west, he didn't think it would take long.

Back to the clothing store, back to the bathhouse, back to the barber and back to the hotel. After a sumptuous meal and many champagnes, it was decided.

"Gentlemen, I would like to bring this meeting to order and to synthesise the previous discussion, whereupon we will vote on our tentative decisions. Our directions will be by majority vote. Have I concurrence?" Alfred looked to his two partners.

"Yes," said Charles.

"Yes," replied Tom.

"Voting will be on the nod. First, we will finalise our transactions with the stable immediately, if necessary taking a loss to expedite matters."

They all nodded.

"Secondly, we will make a booking on the first ship leaving Melbourne enroute for Fremantle via Adelaide. We will spend what time is available in sight-seeing in Adelaide and then travel to Western Australia where we will disembark. We will remain in that colony for a period of time to be decided at our discretion."

The three men nodded.

"Thirdly, in alphabetical order, we will individually empty our safes of gold over the next three days. Tomorrow, we will sell the gold under my name to the jewellers in Melbourne for the best price per ounce that we are offered. That will set tongues wagging. The next day, Chas will off-load the contents of his safes in each bank to that bank for their best price, assuming they are reasonably comparable in their offerings. In each case, one third of the amount will be placed in individual accounts in our proper names in the Bank of Australasia and drafts drawn to be transferred to accounts in the Bank of England in London. Naturally, each of us should retain sufficient cash for personal expenses."

Nods all round.

"Finally, within twenty-hours of the designated departure time from Melbourne, we will remove the contents of Tom's safes from the three banks, seal the gold in boxes and board the ship with all our belongings. We will remain on board until the ship sails to safeguard our possessions."

The final statement received three nods.

"Thank you, Gentlemen. I now intend to visit Fifi in her studio and hope she will be able to accommodate me this evening. Will you join me in my walk to find your own courtesan?"

There were two vigorous nods of agreement.

CHAPTER 38
Henry

One of nature's ways of healing grief is through the repression of painful images. The flashbacks of Yeddi's death continued but slowly the vividness of the mental pictures began to blur. Sara Jane found that if she focused on pleasant reminiscences, recalling her babbingur did not cause her as much sorrow. Most of all, however, she knew that death had been Yeddi's way of coping and he had chosen the final sequence of events, feeling he had no alternative. However, he had made it clear that Sara Jane should look forward and not live in the past and therefore, she began to reason, she must look to the future.

Arrangements for Henry's impending visit were a satisfying distraction. She liked Henry, his company had always been enjoyable and the hospitality shown her at Nine Elms deserved reciprocation to the best of her ability given the rather more primitive circumstances of colonial life.

The topic came up as Sara Jane poured tea. William was on his way to Augusta and the two women had just finished a light lunch. "Elizabeth, I think the very first thing on the agenda should be the preparation of the spare room. Don't you?"

"Yes, definitely, Sara Jane." Elizabeth was grateful for the new found enthusiasm. "Don't you think a new counterpane would add a more masculine touch to the room? The present pink one doesn't look much like your description of Uncle Henry." She had a mischievous smile on her face.

"Elizabeth!"

"Well, I'm only trying to be helpful. Perhaps we should start with a list of things we need to do and activities we need to plan."

"Good idea. Let's do it."

At the end of an hour, three lists had been drawn up. A shopping list, a doing list and an events list. The unknown factor was the arrival date of the *Antoinette*. Sara Jane judged they might have four weeks but couldn't be certain.

"We'll just have to try to complete all arrangements in the next three weeks to be sure and to alert people of planned functions and activities with dates to be confirmed at a week's notice."

* * * * *

Sara Jane was seated at her new desk in the front room of the old Henry Street cottage. The office of Blair Transport Enterprises had been transferred from the Post Office and she continued to attend to clients between the hours of 4 o'clock and 5 o'clock, Monday to Friday. While waiting each day, any record keeping requirements for the business were completed. She rose and filed away some copies of invoices in the cabinet.

"Good afternoon, Sara Jane. May I interrupt?" John Bateman was standing at the door, hat in hand.

"Hello, John. Come in and sit down. To what do I owe this pleasant surprise?"

"Business, or possibly some business, if you're interested."

"Fire away. William is down south but due home any day."

"Have you seen the latest *Gazette*, Sara Jane?" He placed a newspaper on the table.

"No, I picked up my copy this morning but haven't had a chance to read it."

"Thought this might be of interest." John proceeded to read out an advertisement.

Sandalwood ready for delivery to Fremantle
200 tons
For cash payment of £5 per ton
Harold Day
Banksia Farm York

Bateman looked up from the *Gazette*. "Mr Day obviously needs cash in a hurry," he grinned. "Assuming we were paid £10 to £12 a ton in Singapore, we would make a profit of £5 to £7 a ton, less wages and keep for my crew and any incidental costs. With back-loaded goods sold at a profit here, it would be more. My ship could be on its way with William acting as agent, as soon as the sandalwood arrives."

Sara Jane was dubious. "After that typhoon business last year, I would worry so much, John." She sighed. "However, William made it quite clear that he wanted to continue to act as your agent, if the opportunity arose, so I suppose the answer is 'yes'."

"Great! Young John is at home at present. His whaling activities don't begin for several months. I'll send him to York to sign up Harold Day immediately."

Sara Jane had a calculating expression on her face. "Why not offer him £4 a ton to take the lot?"

"Why not, indeed? Who's teaching you these business ploys, Sara Jane?"

"It must be something I just picked up."

Bateman smiled. "Send William around to my office when he returns. Thanks, Sara Jane." He hurried from the room.

* * * * *

When William returned from Augusta, he was exceptionally pleased that Sara Jane had accepted Bateman's offer on their behalf.

"It means I'll get away by early June and hopefully be home by the end of September. And remember that the profits take us closer to our own vessel for overseas trade, Sis."

"It will also leave me to entertain and play host and hostess to Henry. Nevertheless, you made it clear that you wanted to proceed with this venture and you are the skipper." She smiled ruefully. "You will hasten back, won't you, William."

"It's a promise, Sis. I think I'll pay John a visit immediately," and he was quickly on his way.

"Welcome back, William," Bateman said, as he ushered William into his office. "Profitable trip, I hope."

"Yes, the business continues to do well, due in part to Sara Jane's assiduous attention to the finer details, as you would know. There's a lot more to business than most people would ever contemplate."

The men conversed amiably and agreed that William would leave as soon as the sandalwood had been delivered to Fremantle.

"John should be back tomorrow with an answer and providing no one else offered Day more than we did and also wanted the lot, we'll have a shipload." He paused. "William, what would you say to taking an assistant with you. Actually a trainee would be a better description."

"Who is this person?"

"My son, John. For the first time he has indicated an interest in commerce. Said he'd like to go with you and learn the ropes, so to speak."

"But I'm only a novice myself! He should go with you, John."

"At sixty-two years of age, my wife tells me I'm too old for overseas trading and although I pooh-poohed her opinion, I'm inclined to believe it's true. In any case, I've always believed that sons should be tutored by others than their fathers. That's why Walter has done so well under your instruction. Fathers and sons end up competing with one another at every turn. A sort of one-upmanship. I've seen it too often. What do you say?"

"Well, of course I will, if that is your wish."

"Good, then it's arranged."

* * * * *

Two days later the *Antoinette* arrived in Gage Roads. Elizabeth almost ran to alert Sara Jane, when the first boat ashore delivered the mail directly to the Post Office.

"Henry will be landing shortly. I hope it's all right by you but I've let Mr Cooke know that you wished me to accompany you to the jetty, in order to maintain the expected decorum."

"Of course. I'm dying for you to meet him." Sara Jane's heart leapt with excitement, anticipation and affection for this genial man who had so openly offered his love. How to play the part, the role in the soon-to-be-acted performance? The scene was set but the actors were still to enter from the wings.

"Quickly, Elizabeth. I'll fetch my cape, hat and gloves and we're on our way."

Sara Jane need not have worried about any facade or reticence. Henry doffed his hat and waved enthusiastically from the tender as it approached the jetty.

"Which one is Henry?" whispered Elizabeth.

"The one in grey, waving his hat."

"He's very handsome, Sara Jane and looks younger than I envisaged. I think this visit might be more fun than I had expected."

Henry stepped lightly from the tender and ran up the steps. He stood in front of Sara Jane and composed himself. His eyes twinkled and a huge smile spread from ear to ear. He took her proffered hand and lightly brushed his lips to the glove but his eyes did not leave her face. "My dear, you are even more beautiful than I dared to remember."

"Thank you, Henry. I am pleased that you have arrived safely. The voyage seems to have treated you well. Elizabeth I would like to introduce Mr Henry Blair. Henry, my friend Miss Elizabeth Rothwell."

Elizabeth hesitated only a moment, as Henry stepped forward, before offering her gloved hand.

"I am delighted to meet you, Miss Rothwell. This colony seems to have more than its fair share of beauty."

Elizabeth blushed. "Thank you, Mr Blair. It is so kind of you to make such an observation."

Henry nodded to a man hovering in the background and pointed to his luggage on the landing below. "Ladies, will you escort me to my lodgings?"

"Why certainly, sir," answered Sara Jane as she slipped her arm through his, quickly followed by Elizabeth on the other side.

The two young women pointed out landmarks as they walked back to High Street and the Blair home.

"Fremantle received quite a fillip with the arrival of the convicts," Sara Jane replied to Henry's umpteenth question. "And I'm glad to say without any of the predicted catastrophes."

"Yes, people tend to be far more gloomy and pessimistic in their prognosis for the future than they need be. Fortunately, it is not a trait I have adopted. I am always the optimist and to date it has stood me in good stead." He glanced at Sara Jane and smiled. There was no acknowledgment. He turned to Elizabeth. "What about you, Elizabeth? Are you optimistic or pessimistic in nature?"

"Always optimistic, Henry. It is the way to a happy future, I'm sure."

"Quite so, my dear. Quite so," Henry replied, looking straight ahead.

Henry was shown to his room to drop his bags and then around the house, making appropriate comments as they went. "I must say, Sara Jane, that modern houses have many advantages. They must be much easier to keep clean and tidy and one can install more up to date appliances and utilise new ideas. This is both a functional home and a house of sound architectural lines. Altogether delightful. You must be very proud of the result."

William was doing some maintenance on the *Margaret*. He arrived home for lunch and was introduced to their guest. Henry shook his hand heartily. "I've heard much about your exploits, William. All good, I promise you." He whispered loudly to Sara Jane. "Your brother will be a big boy when he grows up." His gaze returned to William, as if sizing up his height. Henry was tall but William was much taller. They all laughed.

Elizabeth made tea and they munched on chocolate biscuits while they caught up on happenings at home and in Cape Town.

"Your mother and father are in good spirits, although becoming progressively frail. They send their love and that's not just a platitude. They talk about you constantly, almost as if they expect to see you walk through the door. Edmund is becoming very forgetful and can't remember where he's left his papers and books. I've designated a young servant especially to attend to him because he becomes frustrated when he can't find his things." Sara Jane dabbed her eyes.

"I've been given strict instructions to sketch every aspect of the new home and forward a package to Nine Elms as soon as possible. Your parents want to be able to visualise you in the house."

Sara Jane could contain herself no longer. "What about the Roberts?"

"Cameron and Jacinta are well and very happy and their son is lively and extremely handsome. I was present for Gurdu's third birthday and can tell you he is a handful. Full of beans. I didn't ever find out what Gurdu meant. Strange name. Must be derived from some African dialect. Anyway, he blew out the candles on the cake and smothered himself in the icing and had a thoroughly good time, as we all did. We celebrated over a scrumptious feast with a superb selection of Madeira Estate wine and you were right Sara Jane, it was the best I have ever sampled." Sara Jane again dabbed her eyes.

"Sara Jane, if you cry at everything I relate, then I will be forced to stop."

"Sorry Henry. It's just that I probably won't see mother and father or the Roberts ever again. I promise I won't cry any more."

Henry was about to say what was on his mind but coughed instead. It was neither the time nor the place. "Well then, smile for me," and he proceeded to tell a joke about an Englishman and an Irishman, who met in Scotland and he soon had everyone laughing.

Bless you, Henry, thought Sara Jane.

That night, their guest insisted on taking them all to the best hotel in town, which William assessed was still the Union Hotel in Market Street. The repartee and laughter continued and any reservations Sara Jane might have had about Henry's lengthy visit were quickly dispelled. She broached several topics and proposed the series of activities she had included in his schedule. True to form, Henry gave an enthusiastic response to all the suggestions.

William was leaving for the Vasse in two days time with Walter as for'ard hand and invited Henry to join them. "You'll have the chance to see some of the coastline and with luck we could meet up with the Bussell brothers, John, Charles, Vernon and Alfred, if they're not in the back blocks. They run a grant of thousands of acres called 'Cattle Chosen'. Not a large property in the colony but large compared with estates in England."

"Curious name to give a farm."

"It seems a cow, lost over twelve months before at Augusta, turned up at their new homestead at the Vasse after walking over fifty miles. Hence the name."

"Then it is a very apt name."

Henry really wished to spend time with Sara Jane but knew he should not press his suit too soon. He also knew it would give Sara Jane some time for the preparations for his stay. "I'd like that, William. And I'll have the chance to learn something about sailing and the business. Just as well I don't suffer from sea sickness."

* * * * *

The *Margaret* returned the following week and William and Henry were banished to the outside pump to wash down before having a hot bath. Sara Jane was surprised and impressed by the rippling muscles of Henry's chest and arms as he scrubbed himself. She could hear the men from the kitchen, where she was instructing the new servant who was heating water for their baths. Patience Murphy was plain, hard-working and hoping for a good reference at the end of her period of employment. Sara Jane thought she'd need to be able to live up to her name to survive the six months of her agreement.

"The stink rather depends on the cargo, Henry," William explained. "Billy goats are the worst, so you now stink as much as you'll ever stink after a trip with Blair Transport Enterprises."

"I suppose that's something. I was sure I was going to throw-up when that black and white animal defecated on my foot."

"Ah but you didn't, Henry. We'll make a sailor of you yet."

"How did I compare with Sara Jane as a for'ard hand?"

William could see Sara Jane lingering in the doorway.

"Not bad at all. She's had more practice but you certainly showed promise, especially when you fell overboard as you dropped the anchor."

"Don't you dare tell Sara Jane about that!"

William slapped him on the back. "Of course not! How are the muscles?"

"They're fine now but after the first day I will admit, only to you, that I could hardly move."

"You were a good crew member Henry and, as you're our guest, can have first bath."

William winked at Sara Jane, as Henry disappeared into the bathroom.

* * * * *

That Saturday evening, a welcoming dinner party was held at the High Street residence of Mr William Blair, Miss Sara Jane Andrews-Blair and Miss Elizabeth Rothwell. The guests were Mr Henry Blair, Mr and Mrs John Bateman and sons Walter and John, Mr David Long and Mr James Dempster, who arrived by himself because his wife could not leave the children alone on Rottnest.

The meal was beautifully prepared. Patience was determined to make the most of her chance and cooking was her forte. As a recently-arrived spinster immigrant of eighteen years of age, she needed continuing employment, or a husband. Beef broth was served with a crusty bun, the entree was baked snapper and savoury haricot beans and the main course roast pork with apple sauce and boiled vegetables, lightly sprinkled with a cheese sauce. Dessert was a choice of apple crumble or trifle with either jelly or cream. The evident enjoyment of the meal would have been enough but to Patience's gratification continuous praise was forthcoming as each course was served.

William, who had been studying a book on wines, took great delight in displaying his newly-acquired knowledge, expertly advising the guests on the subtleties of the best wines from his cellar.

It was a replete and happy group who moved to the sitting room. Tea and port were offered to both ladies and gentlemen as was now the custom and all but Elizabeth chose port. When Sara Jane lifted her glass from the tray, there were a few sideways glances and suppressed smiles. Then animated conversation took over.

Henry might have been the guest but he was also the main performer. It all began when Elizabeth, who had been learning the piano, was prevailed upon to play a few simple tunes, which she did with confidence and feeling. Following applause from the guests, Henry excused himself and slipped from the room to reappear a few minutes later holding two silver candelabra. There were immediate 'ahhs' as he placed them on the mantelpiece. Each candelabrum provided for six candles and the stands were beautifully filigreed.

Henry placed himself strategically in front of the fire facing the guests and cleared his throat. There was immediate quiet. "Ladies and gentlemen, I would like to take this opportunity, while I have such a small and select audience." He inclined his head and there were subdued chuckles. "---to present to my hosts a small gift for their kind invitation for an extended visit to this far flung outpost of our glorious empire. When Queen Victoria, God bless her, was informed of my impending visit to her favourite colony, she asked me to call upon her. Of course, it being a royal command, I attended immediately and met Her Majesty in her chambers." All were desperately attempting to stifle laughter with little success. "The presence of Lord John Russell, the First Lord of the Treasury was immediately requested and he joined us within the hour. Meanwhile, I kept Her Majesty entertained with snippets of gossip from rural England and what I had gleaned about Western Australia of late." Henry's flourishes and poses were superb and he was acting the parts of those mentioned. "Well, as soon as John was informed of the situation, he insisted on the procurement of a suitable gift to be delivered to my hosts at Swan River as a token of the esteem in which Queen Victoria, God bless her, holds for those of her subjects who strive to expand her realm. I bring you this gift." He gestured towards the mantelpiece.

After much clapping and laughter, William stood. "On behalf of the Blair household of the Colony of Western Australia, I gratefully accept the gift from Queen Victoria---." He paused for every one to join in with "God bless her", before resuming, "and thank her equerry Henry Blair of Nine Elms via Swindon for his long and arduous voyage to fulfil Her Majesty's wishes. We hope that his stay with us will be enjoyable. He has already proved himself a competent for'ard hand, even if he is the first of my crew members ever to manage to fall overboard."

Much more laughter.

John Bateman then stood, swaying a little. "Would you please be upstanding and join me in toasting Queen Victoria, God bless her."

Glasses were quickly filled and the toast made. A rowdy rendering of 'God save the Queen' followed, before the laughing guests retrieved cloaks, hats and gloves and braved the chill winter winds.

CHAPTER 39
Houtman Abrolhos

The next day, deliveries of sandalwood began arriving. There was so much of it that it came in batches, some by river barges from Guildford and some by road on bullock wagons. Because John's ship was waiting, the sandalwood was loaded directly onto the *Constance*, which was tied up at South Jetty. William and John Junior supervised the loading with John Senior and Henry hovering and giving advice. In the end, William threatened dire consequences if one more of his orders was questioned and the two older men laughingly left to 'attend to other business' as Bateman described it.

The *Constance* sailed on 12th June, with a fresh south-westerly taking her speedily through the passage north of Rottnest and out to the open sea. William and John Junior were glad to be on their way. There was always the chance of a sudden squall from the north-west while tied up at the jetty and being that close to shore left little room for error if the hawsers snapped or the ship's planking was shattered.

The two men leaned over the rail of the ship, the wind tugging at their hair. John, at twenty-seven, was two years older than William and both had a great deal of sailing experience, although John had largely been involved with whaling. He admitted that his father's interests were expanding so rapidly that he saw a place in the business rather sooner than he had expected.

"My personal view is that Father's expertise is in the retail trade. I'd rather be on a ship going somewhere, at least while I'm young but being the oldest son I'll probably be required to handle some of the paperwork and negotiations for the trading activities. Hence my request to travel with you to Singapore. I know precious little about commodities and their value."

"Well, let's talk about some observations I made on last year's trip." William discussed prices and haggling and keeping face and win-win situations. "What it amounts to, as I see it anyway, is maximising profit without ripping off the client. If you're fair and honest in your dealings, you're likely to be approached for another deal. It is a good business if clients come back for more. And it doesn't matter if you're a buyer, or seller, or providing a service. Blair Transport relies on all three, so I don't want to alienate someone today and therefore lose the possibility of a future deal."

They talked a lot about business over the first two days, which was just as well as events turned out.

On the morning of the fourth day, the barometer fell alarmingly and Captain Masterson warned his two passengers to tie everything down in their cabin. The crew were busy lashing down the cargo in the hold and reducing sail. By early afternoon, the sky was black and the wind was howling from the north-west bringing sheets of rain and hail the size of large pebbles. Visibility was limited to several yards and the ship was plunging and bucking as the Captain tried to hold her into the wind with all sails furled. It was an impossible task and they were now on a side drift.

William was only glad they were so far offshore. One of the first golden rules, he had learned from the seamanship manuals pored over as a youth, was that one had to be wrecked on reef or land and therefore one was safest a long way from any coastline. And they were a long way from shore, or so he assumed, because the Captain had considerable experience.

At three bells in the dog watch, just before the sun's rays were due to creep above the eastern land mass and push away the darkness, the *Constance* was lifted high on the surge of a huge wave, carried over a coral reef on the western side of the Houtman Abrolhos and unceremoniously dumped into the calm waters of a lagoon. She listed slowly to starboard and then gently grounded. Crew scurried below decks and thoroughly examined the hull for any signs of water seepage. There were no leaks and no apparent damage. It was a phenomenal piece of misfortune and an amazing piece of luck.

The only casualty was William, who broke his left collar bone and cracked several small bones in his left ankle on being thrown out of his bunk. John held a lamp while the Boatswain, being the self-appointed medical expert aboard, strapped the foot firmly, put the arm in a sling, grinned at William and said "She'll be right, sir."

With dawn came the abatement of the wind and a miraculous sight. The *Constance* was resting gently on her keel on the sandy bottom of a large lagoon. The swell from the ocean hammered the circling coral on the seaward side but petered out as it crossed the reef. They were safe but neatly trapped.

Captain Masterson called William, John and First Mate Dean Jones to a meeting in his cabin. He was huffing and puffing, as if he either had a sudden affliction of the lung or was trying to assert authority. "Gentlemen, we are in a rather unusual situation."

An understatement and that was sure and certain, thought William.

"Because of your experience, I considered it appropriate to ask you to join me in coming to a plan to extricate ourselves from our predicament."

It will appear as though you are using our expertise in coming to a collective decision but we will consequently have to share the blame if it fails, thought John.

"Can we discuss possibilities and come to a decision."

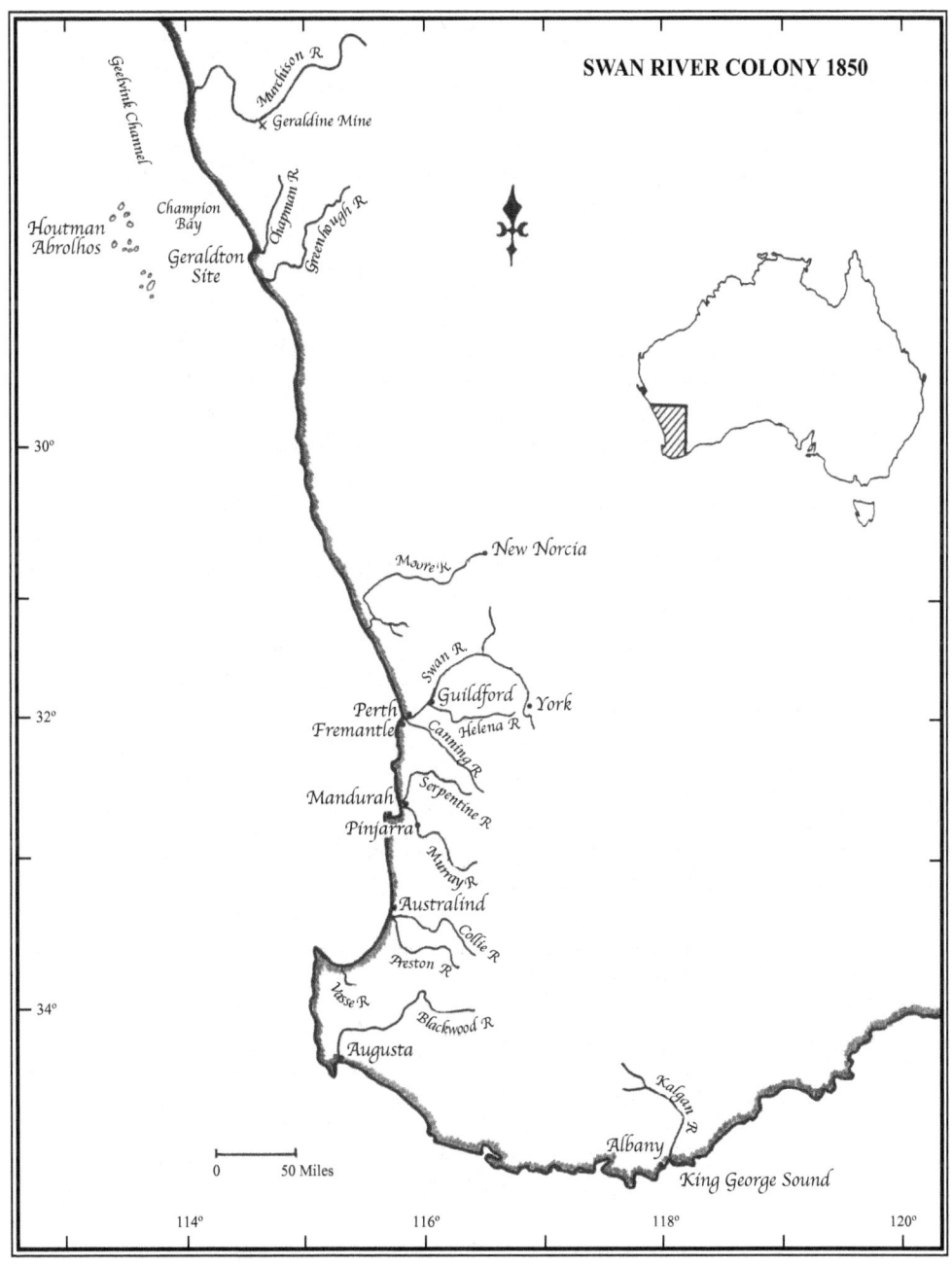

SWAN RIVER COLONY 1850

Geelvink Channel

Murchison R.

X Geraldine Mine

Chapman R.

Greenlough R.

Houtman
Abrolhos

Champion
Bay

Geraldton
Site

30°

Moore R.

New Norcia

Swan R.

Guildford

York

Perth

Fremantle

Canning R.

Helena R.

32°

Mandurah

Pinjarra

Serpentine R.

Murray R.

Australind

Collie R.

Preston R.

Vasse R.

Blackwood R.

34°

Augusta

Kalgan R.

Albany

King George Sound

0   50 Miles

114°   116°   118°   120°

411

Silly old bastard. You haven't made a decision for the last six months. I hope the owner's son has his eyes open. It's about time I took over the *Constance*, thought Jones.

When they emerged from the Captain's cabin, the wind and swell had both dropped and the sun was shining. William followed the others, hopping in ungainly fashion and pretending that his injuries were bearable, when in fact they were excruciatingly painful.

So what did they know? They knew they were safe, albeit for the moment trapped, having made contact with a coral reef on the southern section of the Houtman Abrolhos at about 28° latitude and 113° longitude. They were in fact perched close to the edge of the continental shelf and should have been hundreds of miles to the west of this archipelago. William had been appalled at the condition of the navigational instruments and had made a mental note to have a serious talk with John Bateman Senior, if he ever saw him again. They were approximately forty miles from land and the closest settlement was Champion Bay. They were in an extremely dangerous situation.

William was able to give the others a brief description of the Champion Bay area, because Sara Jane, who perused every *Perth Gazette* and *Inquirer* for business opportunities and took copious notes, had briefed him as events unfolded. It was clearly the next coastal settlement with development potential and therefore of particular interest to Blair Transport Enterprises.

"The Gregory brothers surveyed the area in '48 and discovered lead and copper ore. They also reported good land. Then later that year, Augustus Gregory and Governor Fitzgerald, under military escort, travelled north by ship, to further ascertain mining possibilities. If you remember, Fitzgerald was wounded in the thigh in a skirmish with the natives. Anyway, the upshot was that the native problem was disregarded and the Geraldine Mine commenced operations shortly afterwards. Last year, Thomas Brown drove sheep and cattle north from York and founded a large station between the Chapman and Greenough Rivers. It's rumoured that a town site to be named Geraldton will be surveyed soon. I'm sure we'll be able to get help, if we can reach Champion Bay."

The problem was extricating the ship from her prison. "So, what is your best estimate of high tide, Captain?" William asked. It was clear the younger man was becoming frustrated.

"About 2 o'clock." The Captain seemed incapable of action. He was shaking and stammering and knew that his skippering days were over.

"Well then men, let's get moving," ordered William.

Within the hour, the ship's dinghy had been rowed around the inner rim of the coral atoll. On the southern side, they discovered a gap in the reef and William supported the suggestion by First Mate Jones on his return, that they should try to squeeze the vessel through the opening on the high tide.

"We'll tie hawsers from the two ship's boats to the *Constance* and the crews will row with all their strength on the high tide. There'll be no question about that. The wind will be behind us. With luck we might just make it."

William didn't want to have to suggest it, because it would cost him dearly but knew he had no choice. "Jones, our contingency plan must be to jettison the sandalwood. I will take responsibility for that order if it is needed." He saw John lift his eyes in relief.

The sailors were briefed. Worry was written all over their faces, since few could swim and in any case, they were all very aware of the fins circling the ship. Sharks scavenged for food scraps, vomit and excrement. A human limb would be a rare treat.

By 1 o'clock the ship's boats were in place and the procedure tested. The strain on the cables was considerable but there was no splitting of timbers. Half an hour later, the *Constance* moved back to an upright position as the water ran over the reef into the lagoon. There were cheers from every quarter. Jones gave the order to take up the slack on the cables and yelled "Pull men. Our lives depend on it." The crews shouted and grunted and roared abuse at one another, as if that would help to gain impetus.

For a few minutes nothing happened. Then William felt a shudder. Slowly, in infinitesimal increments, the *Constance* moved. There was a bellow of satisfaction from the two crews and those watching from the vessel. The ship was floating!

It seemed an age before the bow of the ship was nosing into the opening in the reef. All went well until, by William's judgment, she was about halfway through the channel. Then she stuck fast.

"Maintain the strain but don't pull any harder than that," Jones yelled at the rowers from the bow thwart of the leading boat. He waved at William.

John waited for the inevitable order. "Ditch the sandalwood," called William to the crew standing on deck. "And at the double, if you value your lives." Men scampered to their places. They had loaded and unloaded sandalwood many times before but not in a life-threatening situation.

The cargo hatch was already open and now the logs were being placed in slings down below and raised above deck by pulleys attached to a hastily-erected gantry. When the sling was released, crew members picked up the logs, walked sideways to the railing and threw them over the leeward side. The activity was hurried but in unison. A sort of team-like rhythm developed as the sandalwood splashed overboard.

William watched until he estimated that half the cargo had been jettisoned. There goes half my investment, he thought regretfully. The ship did not move. He pulled his watch from his fob pocket. It was 2 o'clock and it was all or nothing.

"Ditch the rest of the cargo," he ordered. Waves of pain were enveloping his consciousness. He gritted his teeth. I can't pass out. I must keep control.

John saw William swaying and slipped away to return immediately with a hip flask. "Swallow this," he said sternly. "We need you, William. You're worth ten of that bumbling Captain."

William took the flask gratefully and swallowed half its contents in one swig. He slipped the flask into his pocket and returned his attention to supervising the task at hand.

When the last log had been thrown overboard, William limped and hopped to the prow of the *Constance* and yelled to Jones. "I'm ordering everyone off the ship. It's our last chance."

Jones shouted his agreement.

"Over the side, men. Stay on the reef and you should be safe from the Noah arks." William saw Captain Masterson disappear into the cabin area. John started to say something but William shook his head. "Let him go. He's no use to anyone."

John and the crew members still aboard clambered down the rope ladders and stood forlornly on the coral. They looked like castaways.

William cupped his hands round his mouth and bellowed. "Push! What are you? Bloody landlubbers? This is your ship."

There was a shout of acquiescence. The men on each side of the boat put hands, shoulders and cheeks to the planks and gave it everything they had. The men in the boats pulled. William prayed.

It was just enough. Slowly, inch by inch the ship moved through the opening, its planks scraping and squealing in complaint. When the beam was through, the sailors climbed back on board cheering. The deck ran red from their bleeding feet. Some were prising coral from their flesh with the point of a knife.

William, his hand clenching John's shoulder, hopped back to the stern. "I'll take the wheel, John. Good job the Captain's in hiding."

"It will be his last command after I report to Father. If we get back," he muttered grimly.

"We'll make it back. We've made it this far. Set topsails, Boatswain."

"Aye, aye, sir," responded the Boatswain, grinning broadly. He was grateful for some authority at last.

"Set topsails," was the call.

When the *Constance* began to move slowly forward under sail, William yelled to Jones. "Drop your cable and keep a lookout. Send the other boat back." The crew on board hurried to haul the cables in and retrieve the smaller boat.

William followed Jones' signals until they were in deep water and a mile from the fateful atoll. "Furl topsails," he said to the Boatswain.

"Furl topsails." There was a flurry of activity.

"Drop anchors." As the lines tautened, the ship swung slowly into the wind. Darkness was closing in. They had made it just in time.

"Three cheers for Captain Blair," called First Mate Jones as the second boat was hauled aboard.

William acknowledged the cheers and then, overcome by waves of pain, closed his eyes and unconscious slid slowly down the wheel to the deck.

* * * * *

He awoke in his bunk to the whisperings of a concerned trio. John, the First Mate and the Boatswain were trying to make a decision.

"What seems to be the matter?" he muttered groggily.

"It's morning, sir. I gave you a little something to make you sleep and bound you up again. Do you feel better, sir?"

"Bloody marvellous. It must have been potent. Thank you, Boatswain. Well, what are you all gawking at?"

"Are you well enough to take command, William," asked John.

"Where's the Captain?"

"The Captain has not emerged from his cabin."

"Well then, the answer is 'Yes' but I won't. I'm sure Jones is quite competent. Neither of us know anything about these waters and he knows the ship better than I."

The First Mate looked doubtful. "All the same, I would appreciate your assistance, sir."

"If that's what you want, Jones, you've got it. What's the plan, John?"

John turned to the others. "Leave us, gentlemen. Prepare the crew to make sail."

When they left, John grinned at William. "You made quite an impression on the men yesterday."

"Things are pretty fuzzy. What did the Boatswain give me?"

"Some sort of opiate, I expect. You went out like a light when the wick is snuffed."

"So what's been happening while I've been out to it? Have you made any decisions?"

"Yes." John took a deep breath. "It is now 11 o'clock. The men have worked like slaves, all morning. They said you saved them and they wanted to repay you. Most of the sandalwood has been retrieved and tied down below decks."

"What!"

"Just as I said. The wood should still be tradeable. It wasn't in the water all that long. While the men were reloading, Jones and I examined the horizon in every direction with the telescope and both came to the same conclusion."

"Yes?"

"We could see dozens of shoals and low islands to seaward. Somehow, we must have drifted quite a way on that nor'wester, missed the main collection of islands and hit an outlying reef to the east. We decided we would be foolish to try to find our way through these treacherous waters to the open sea. We'd be pushing our luck. If another storm blew up, we mightn't be so fortunate."

Well?"

"Have you heard of the Geelvink Channel?"

"Yes. I noted it on the charts, when Sara Jane drew my attention to exploration parties up this way. It heads north out of Champion Bay. Is that the way we're going?"

"That's the way we are going. You are going home."

William tried to sit up but gasped in pain and fell back on the bunk. "Perhaps I need some more of the Boatswain's brew."

"That will be arranged, when you agree to our decision."

William began to argue but John would not change his mind. "If there are storms and you don't heal properly, you might well ruin your and Sara Jane's future. At the least, you might end up unable to pull up a sail or be left with a gammy leg. At worst, you could get gangrene and die. If you go home on the first vessel out of Champion Bay and receive medical attention, you could be back aboard your own boats in a month's time." He frowned. "And surely you would not subject me to the wrath and recriminations of Sara Jane, my family and Elizabeth to boot. My life wouldn't be worth a halfpenny."

William nodded glumly. "You're right John. You're a chip off the old block." He looked at John, a worried expression on his face. "But what about the trading? You've had no experience."

"William, you spent the first two days aboard ship telling me what to do and how to do it, when we arrived in Singapore. I'm a full bottle. Besides, you just said I'm a chip off the old block."

CHAPTER 40
A Social Whirl

In May, Sara Jane had sent off a series of letters, in order to inform appropriate gentlemen that Mr Henry Blair Esq. of Nine Elms via Swindon, brother of the Reverend Edmund Blair, had arrived in Fremantle on a visit and was the guest of Mr William Blair and Miss Sara Jane Andrews-Blair of High Street.

Invitations arrived duly and it seemed that many of the respected citizens were eager to meet with Henry. On purpose, Sara Jane had refused to officially inform Governor Fitzgerald, still blaming him for his recalcitrant stance in regard to Yeddi. However, Fitzgerald pulled rank and invited Henry and senior members or ex-members of government and their wives to Government House for a dinner to honour the visitor. If Henry chose to travel to Perth early, or stay after the dinner, the Governor would be delighted to arrange that he be shown around Perth and adjacent districts.

Two further invitations were delivered, George Fletcher Moore inviting Henry to stay with him at 'Millendon', his property on the Upper Swan and Thomas Peel inviting him to travel to Mandurah to see the Murray River area.

Sara Jane flatly refused to accompany Henry to the Governor's dinner, properly arguing that she was busy operating the business while William was away and that in any case Henry would see far more being hosted around by the Governor. The real reason of course was that she refused to be a guest at the Governor's table. No matter how much Henry pleaded, Sara Jane was adamant and she eventually ended his protracted entreaties by writing in that vein to Governor Fitzgerald.

However, Sara Jane did want to spend time with Henry. In her own way, she felt much affection for him and enjoyed his company enormously. So they walked arm in arm around the town, discussing aspects of architecture and places of historical interest, picnicked on the beach when it was fine, hired a small boat and crew to be taken several miles up the river and attended St George's Church on Sundays. Henry was easy to entertain and spoke politely and sincerely on introduction to individuals. Several of the Fremantle matrons were clearly showing interest in such an eligible bachelor. They hovered after church hoping for an introduction to their daughters and were often seen parading along High Street on fine mornings. At first, Sara Jane was amused and then became annoyed at such manifest attention. Henry was totally oblivious. He had eyes for only one young woman and was biding his time.

After two days of fine weather with light winds and with the barometer showing no indication of a change, Sara Jane suggested a sail to Rottnest. David and Walter had reported in from a trip to Rockingham the day before, so she knew the *Sara Jane* was available.

"Care to go to Rottnest tomorrow, just for the day, Henry?" He was reading in the sitting room, when Sara Jane interrupted.

He covered a yawn. "My apologies, Sara Jane. I was nodding off over 'Robinson Crusoe'. Perhaps I should be apologising to Defoe, except it is my third reading and I am relaxed in front of the fire. What did you say?"

Sara Jane laughed and repeated the question.

"Yes. Sounds like a great idea."

"Good, I'll make arrangements with Walter."

Henry knew Sara Jane could sail, because she had told him so. However, when she appeared for breakfast the next morning in white trousers and a heavy navy blue jumper, with her hair tied back, he looked a little bewildered. "Are you going to be for'ard hand, Sara Jane?"

"I'll take turn with Elizabeth," she answered, "unless you'd like to crew?"

"No, no, my dear. That sounds a perfectly satisfactory arrangement. I'll be a passenger. Besides, I'm prone to falling overboard, remember."

On a glorious, fine winter morning, carrying oars, picnic basket and rug and wearing jumpers and waterproofs, Sara Jane, Elizabeth and Henry walked to Bathers Bay. The dinghy was pulled down to the water, which was freezing cold.

"Push us off will you, Henry," said Sara Jane, securing the oars in the rowlocks.

"Where's Walter?" he replied, looking around suspiciously.

"Oh, didn't I tell you?" she said with a grin. "Walter had some goods to purchase at the chandlery, so I'm Captain for the day. I presumed that would be all right with you, Henry."

"Er---of course Sara Jane. Have you skippered before?"

"Of course, Henry."

Altogether, it was a perfect day. The sun shone and the water proudly displayed every possible shade of blue and green. Carnac Island and the Stragglers were given a wide berth. As they approached the island, the white beaches contrasted with the dark brown reefs and deep blue waters of the channel. Gulls wheeled and screamed at the intruders as they nosed through the narrow entrance from Porpoise Bay to the shelter of Parker Point. Sara Jane pointed out a sea hawk's nest on the rocky point and the coloured coral in the waters below.

"Drop anchor, Elizabeth."

"No you don't, Elizabeth," called Henry, scrambling to the prow. "If I don't get this right, I'll never hear the end of that last episode." He unpinned the anchor and it dropped free. As the boat drifted away from the wind, the slack on the rope was taken up and the *Sara Jane* secured.

"Well done, Henry. You have redeemed yourself."

"Thank goodness for that. And stop grinning you two."

They picnicked and walked and climbed the rocks. They told stories and jokes and sang sea ballads. They played 'I spy' and then it was time to sail for home.

"Thank you for a wonderful day, ladies." He put his arms around them both and gave them a squeeze. "It passed all my expectations. How fortunate you are to have such a beautiful island on your doorstep."

That night, as Patience did the dishes and Henry headed for the bathroom, Elizabeth brought a cup of tea to Sara Jane in the sitting room.

"Have you driven away the demons of the past, Sara Jane?"

Sara Jane looked up with a sentimental expression on her face. "You knew, didn't you, my friend? How perceptive you are. But then one would have to know me and care for me greatly to understand why I needed to go and to go in such company. Yes, his spirit is at rest at Kurannup and so is mine here. I feel free, totally free at last."

Several days later, Henry sailed on a small vessel which plied between Fremantle and Perth. Sara Jane walked with him to North Jetty in the Swan. He carried a leather case and looked quite dejected.

"Henry, don't look so miserable. You're only going for a few weeks and you'll have a wonderful time. You'll be looked after by the elite of Perth and have the opportunity to observe the capital of the colony in action."

"I know Sara Jane and I'm grateful for your arrangements." He put down his case and took her hands in his. "However, three weeks can be a long time and I shall miss you."

"I promise I'll be here when you return. Now hurry up or the boat will leave without you." She waved him goodbye and felt quite nostalgic as the small craft sailed up the Swan.

* * * * *

It seemed like no time at all before Henry was back. He was bubbling with information and had thoroughly enjoyed his stay with the Governor and then with Frederick Irwin at 'Henley Park' and George Moore at 'Millendon'.

That night, Sara Jane and Elizabeth laughed at Henry's descriptions of events, scenery and the individuals he met on his visits.

"Don't worry about London Bridge falling down. The woodwork in your Government House is being systematically devoured by termites and the limestone is fretting away. Ultimately, when the white ants stop holding hands in the ceiling, it will tumble down and probably take a governor with it. The Greek Doric columns at the portico are its saving grace."

"The dinner party was fine. However, I have to say that Patience would beat His Excellency's cook any day. The guests were interesting. A curious mixture. I judged Governor Fitzgerald as shrewd, hard-working and feathering his own nest, Colonel Irwin as astute, caring and overly religious, George Moore as jovial, honourable and determined to make the most of his opportunities, Marshall Clifton of Australind as a nature-loving optimist, Reverend Wollaston as a keen observer of people and events and overly voluble and Peel as ill-mannered and eccentric."

"From what I know or hear that sounds a reasonable characterisation. What about their wives?"

"None would hold a candle to either of you. They all continually play a part. Exactly the same part. It's a shame really. 'Yes, dear. No, dear. Three bags full, dear.' They laughed on cue and looked serious on cue and seldom spoke unless asked a question. I'd prefer the modern young woman, if that's a polite description of the two of you."

"Thank you, Henry. You flatter us unduly, I'm sure but we'll accept the compliment graciously, won't we Elizabeth? Say 'thank you' to the kind gentleman."

Elizabeth fluttered her eyes at Henry and held her hands cupped appropriately in front of her chest. "I thank you muchly for your muchness and likewise your veracity. Your extreme kindness and generosity will never be obliterated from the tablets of my memory."

"Perhaps just a trifle loquacious, Elizabeth," he responded sardonically.

"How do you think they would describe you, Henry?"

"Oh, probably a sanctimonious stick-in-the-mud from Swindon."

He kept Sara Jane and Elizabeth entertained with snippets of gossip and information gleaned on his travels, until Elizabeth could stay awake no longer and excused herself.

Henry could hardly wait to hear her bedroom door close before he flung himself to a kneeling position in front of Sara Jane. "My dear, I can contain myself no longer. I love you with all my heart and have since the day I met you. Sara Jane, will you marry me?"

Sara Jane had expected a proposal but not this soon. She took his hands in hers. "Henry, I sincerely thank you for the honour you bestow upon me. You have made it clear in your letters how you feel and I am privileged to be the recipient of those feelings. You are a gentleman, a fine, upstanding person, who is respected by all and especially so by me. However, I am not ready to marry. I'm not sure whether I will ever be ready. So, please, Henry---."

Henry stood, gently pulling Sara Jane to her feet and kissing her hands and then her forehead. "Then I shall just have to wait, Sara Jane. Good night and sweet dreams my dear. I will see you in the morning." Head down, he turned and walked slowly from the room.

Sara Jane stayed up for a long time thinking.

'You are a fool', her alter ego said.

'But I don't love him', she answered.

'In time you would love him. He is a wonderful man, who would provide you with your heart's desire, if it were possible. You would live in comfort, close to your mother and father, have children and live happily ever after. What more could you ask?'

'I would have to leave Western Australia', she replied.

'You are being very foolish, Sara Jane.'

* * * * *

Several days later, as Patience served lunch to Sara Jane, Elizabeth and Henry, a knock was heard on the front door. She excused herself but was back immediately. "Mr Blair is at the front door, ma'am."

"William?" There was a stampede down the hall.

William was sitting in a large hand cart, normally used for transporting personal luggage from South Jetty. He had a silly, abashed look on his face. His ankle was bound and his arm was in a sling. He was unshaven and filthy.

"William! What happened? Are you all right?"

"You told me to hasten home Sis and I always do what I'm told."

"Stop being facetious, William. And don't stand there gawking and grinning," she said to the porter. "Help him inside."

The stupid grin vanished and the brawny fellow assisted Henry in carrying William to the sitting room, where he was placed on a couch. The man hurried back for William's trunk and was paid off by Henry.

Elizabeth was flapping. Her hero was injured!

"Elizabeth, ask Patience to heat water for the bath. Henry, take that trunk out to the laundry. It's disgusting. I'll light the fire and get this room warmed up."

Elizabeth and Henry rushed back to find Sara Jane and William chuckling. "Calm down you two. It's not a catastrophe after all," said Sara Jane. "A full diagnosis has been completed and I wish to report that William is fine, apart from a broken collar bone and a badly sprained ankle. The prescribed treatment is an immediate bath, some home-cooked food, a glass of wine or two and lots of rest. The prognosis is favourable."

"Tell us what happened William," Henry asked. "Where's the ship?"

William, rather enjoying the attention, related the story of the near disaster at the Abrolhos. "It was a miracle really that we managed to escape. I would have continued on the voyage to Singapore but was outvoted by young John Bateman and the First Mate. They said that discretion was the better part of valour and did not want to exacerbate my injuries and incur your wrath, Sara Jane."

"Very wise of them," remarked Sara Jane, with a touch of mockery, as she continued to unstrap and unbandage various parts of William's anatomy and prod for further, hidden damage.

"The Captain was in a blue funk by then and virtually incapable of making a decision. So we took the easy way out and sailed to Champion Bay. I was off-loaded and they continued north through the Geelvinck Channel. A cart was provided to take me to Wizard Peak and I stayed with Thomas and Eliza Shaw and their son Kenneth. They had travelled on horseback from their York farm to survey 'Glengarry', their new property, not in a technical sense but rather to decide the layout of buildings and such. Their supply ship had just arrived in the Bay. A fortunate coincidence for me. There were several white labourers, three soldiers, who arrived on the ship and some native shepherds at the camp. I was their guest for four days until the ship was back-loaded with ore from the Geraldine Mine and sailed for Fremantle."

"Any prospects for Blair Transport, William?"

"Ouch! Not so hard, Sis. Yes, I would think so. They're surveying the site for the town of Geraldton at the moment. I thought you would be pleased to hear how they're honouring your favourite governor, Sara Jane."

Sara Jane ignored the sarcasm. Henry looked from one to the other but was not enlightened.

"I also met William and Lockier Burges, who are establishing an adjacent property. Oh yes, Sara Jane. I expect that Geraldton will become an important centre. When I'm back on my feet again, I'll make some inquiries."

"Meanwhile, my big brother, Henry will supervise your bathing, I'll make ready an embrocation and bandages, Elizabeth will do something about your clothing and Patience will prepare some of your favourite food."

"Thank you, little sister," he said. "It's good to be home. However, I must admit I'm not looking forward to telling John that one of the Musketeers was wounded in action."

William need not have worried. When John arrived posthaste, he was his usual concerned self and pleased to hear that his son had taken a lead in events. "All in all a remarkable escape from a potential disaster, William. I will speak at length with Captain Masterson on his return."

* * * * *

Later in the week, Elizabeth brought a letter home for Henry. He skimmed the contents. "Sara Jane, it's an invitation from Thomas Peel to travel back to Mandurah with him in three days time. I'll have to hire a horse."

"Hmm. That's not a problem. Is this all men's business or do you consider it would be possible for a woman to be included in the party?"

"Oh, Sara Jane, would you?"

"If it doesn't upset Mr Peel. I'm sure Elizabeth will be more than happy to minister to William's needs. In fact she will spoil him rotten and enjoy the chance to do so. I could show you the location of our farm and where we lived with the Aborigines. The waterways down there are a wonder of nature, although they will be discoloured at this time of the year."

In reply to their dispatch to Perth, Thomas Peel wrote that he would be delighted to host both Mr Blair and Miss Andrews-Blair at Mandurah. Actually, he thought it should make for an interesting few days. He just wished that he had left the house clean. Normally, he wouldn't give a damn but it was hardly in any condition for a female guest. Never mind, they would travel to Serpentine Farm first and he would send someone on ahead to get things ready.

Meanwhile, the *Perth Gazette* reported on the visit of Mr Henry Blair Esq. to Western Australia and the dinner hosted by Governor Fitzgerald. The Governor had remarked on the importance of showing travellers the potential of the colony as an investment opportunity.

"Are you intending to buy some land as an investment, Henry? There's certainly plenty available and it's going at a very reasonable price." Sara Jane looked to Henry after reading out loud the section from the newspaper.

Henry shuddered. "Perish the thought, my dear. I'm settled at Nine Elms and see no reason to extend my interests to the wilds of the colonies with all the worries it would bring."

"Yes, I suppose there's something in that," Sara Jane responded, thoughtfully.

* * * * *

Peel arrived in Fremantle in mid-July and they rode south and then east towards the upper reaches of the Serpentine River. In many places the ground was muddy after the winter rains but although it was hard going and the mosquitoes were fierce, they were compensated with beautiful stretches of water.

They talked companionably as they rode and time passed quickly. The men compared farming procedures in Swindon with the south-west of Australia and discussed the prospects for the colony. Sara Jane, who was riding astride, would occasionally spur on to explore some special natural feature and then return. She could identify almost all the birds and knew both their native and English names.

"It's like having one's personal ornithologist along," Henry said to Peel when Sara Jane pointed out the white-backed male magpies compared with the black-backed females.

At Serpentine Farm, they were greeted by Tom Peel, who was working in the home paddock. From earlier conversation, Sara Jane knew he was the same age as William but he seemed much younger. He was a likeable young man but clearly ill at ease in her presence. They were shown over the farm buildings, which were crude. A recently completed pug hut with verandahs was proudly indicated and Sara Jane was so tired, she thought the accommodation more than adequate. They all remarked on the magnificent backdrop of the Darling Range with the rays of the dying sun reflecting from the granite outcrops.

Tea was a mutton stew and mulled wine in front of a huge fire. "That was a wonderful meal, Tom. Thank you." Sara Jane tried to suppress a yawn.

Tom looked embarrassed at the attention. "My pleasure, Miss Andrews-Blair. I'm glad you enjoyed it. It's my father's favourite."

Shortly afterwards, Sara Jane asked for a lamp and left the men to finish the ample supply of spiced wine.

After another day exploring the environs and riding to the foothills, they left for Mandurah. Tom waved from the gate and looked a lonely figure as Sara Jane called a final goodbye. The threesome headed west towards the Fremantle-Mandurah track.

When Peel cantered ahead to check the state of his home, Sara Jane and Henry continued on and stopped at the old Blair cottage. "This is where we lived all those years. It was quite comfortable really but you can see why I wanted Mother and Father to spend their autumnal years at Nine Elms. Seems to be a store house now."

Henry shook his head in disbelief. "My brother really did have a calling, didn't he?"

It being a rhetorical question, Sara Jane did not reply, although a thoughtful look appeared on her face as she realised the truth of the assertion.

As ordered, Mandurah House had been cleaned and Peel thought it more presentable than it had been since Mary left. Over drinks that night, he talked about his family and the difficulties he was experiencing in trying to return home.

"That's why I've been up in Perth," he explained. "John Levey Roberts, the son of my original partner, arrived from Sydney, having had little success in sorting out his father's financial matters as they related to Daniel Cooper, another ex-convict. Now he's trying to negotiate a settlement with me. Neither of us want litigation, of course. I've had enough law suits to last a lifetime and hope, if we can come to some arrangement, that it could be settled before Christmas. Mind you, with all the toing and froing which will result between the colony and the Colonial Secretary's office, it could be years before it's all resolved and I can return to England and my wife and daughters. Thank goodness Tom stayed." Peel became quite maudlin as he talked about his family.

Sara Jane felt sorry for Peel, whose position she thought quite devastating. He was now virtually a recluse. She missed her mother and father every day but had chosen to return and here was Peel, not able to leave the colony that he had been instrumental in founding. People talked about his failure but Sara Jane had never seen it that way. In her eyes he was just a victim of circumstance. Many others had land and status and no more ready cash than Peel. Besides, she felt she owed him something for the direction of her own life. How lucky that William and I have the business, she thought.

"I sincerely hope that you will be able to return to England and your family, Mr Peel. You have given a great deal of your life to the colony."

Peel nodded glumly and took another swig of brandy.

In the following two days, Sara Jane and Henry packed their saddle bags with bottles of water and food and rode off together. Peel had already settled down and didn't feel any obligation now that Sara Jane was doing the honours.

First, Sara Jane showed Henry where the Andrews' Place had been. A pile of stones, the remains of the chimney, was all that was left. Trees had grown again on the previously cleared land. "It was in a couple of logs on the edge of the river, somewhere about there," she pointed, "that Father hid us from the storm. The fire came afterwards. I'll never know whether Mother was already dead or died in the fire. Father definitely died in the fire, because he went back into the house. Ah well, it doesn't warrant agonising over the past and events that can't be changed."

"How were you connected to Peel?"

"Father was an indentured servant. We all travelled out on Peel's first ship. I don't remember any of that, of course."

Next day, Sara Jane took Henry to the caves area. He was particularly interested in the limestone formations and especially the cavern in which she had discovered the treasure. While he explored the area, Sara Jane slipped away and spent a few minutes at Yeddi's grave. She felt only positive memories and realised she was coping with her loss and could now face the evidence of the most difficult thing she had ever had to do in her life.

They spent that night at Mandurah House and left the following morning for Fremantle. Peel farewelled them. "Give my regards to Reverend and Mrs Blair, Sara Jane, when next you write home, if it's before Henry's departure. They contributed a great deal to this community."

Henry didn't comment but he was surprised at the deference Peel had shown Sara Jane during their visit south. He wouldn't have thought the man was capable of such considerate behaviour after meeting him at the Governor's dinner.

* * * * *

That week, Henry asked Sara Jane whether she would like to accompany him on a walk after lunch. It was cold, wet and windy and anyone in their right mind would be occupying a comfortable chair in the sitting room but William had made it his day room and Elizabeth fussed over him, read to him and played cards with him whenever he desired. So Henry often suggested a walk for an excuse to depart from the house.

They rugged up and walked arm in arm down High Street towards the Round House, through the tunnel excavated for the Fremantle Whaling Company and out onto the beach at Bathers Bay.

"Are you sure you are warm enough, my dear? I'd never forgive myself if you caught cold."

"Henry, I am covered from head to toe in clothing. I'm even wearing my clodhopper boots. It's invigorating."

At that moment, the wind howled and it began to teem with rain. Laughing, they scurried back to the tunnel.

As they peered out at the wild weather, Henry placed his arm around Sara Jane protectively.

"My dear, it is over six months since I left Nine Elms and I should soon be on my way home. This morning, I made a tentative booking on the *Caesar*, which should arrive here sometime in the next fortnight."

Sara Jane suddenly felt very cold. She knew what was coming. Why was she holding back?

"So my beloved, I can wait no longer to ask you again to marry me. My love for you flourishes. I want to spend the rest of my life with you. I cherish and adore you. Will you marry me?"

Sara Jane was on the verge of saying 'yes'. She wanted to say 'yes'. Yet something kept her from doing so. "Henry, I honestly don't know why but I can't give you the answer you want and yet I am not ready to refuse you." Her tears mixed with the windswept rain and sea spray. "I am unworthy of you Henry Blair."

He ignored the comment. "We have until the *Caesar* sails, Sara Jane. I hope you will be able to give me an answer before that."

After dinner that night, Sara Jane signalled Elizabeth to accompany her to her library upstairs. The men were engrossed in a game of chess in the sitting room. Fred, now going grey around the whiskers, was left supervising from the lounge.

"What is it Sara Jane? You look so miserable."

"Elizabeth, tell me how you feel about William."

The younger woman looked decidedly uncomfortable.

"Elizabeth, I know you love William. Describe your feelings to me. It is very important that I understand how you feel."

Elizabeth began hesitantly. "Well, it's a strange feeling. To begin with I would spend every minute of every day with him if I could. I would do anything in this world for him, go anywhere to be with him. I feel a softness for him and yet gain strength from him. I want to touch him, to hold him and to love him."

She looked at Sara Jane questioningly. "Isn't that the way you felt about your babbingur?"

"Yes, Elizabeth, it was exactly how I felt about him. I just wanted to make sure that my love for him wasn't different and perhaps confused because I lived with him and grew up with him and continued to see him through adolescence, before falling in love with him. Thank you, Elizabeth. You have just helped me to make a decision. A very important decision. And with regard to that stupid, unaware, nitwit of a brother of mine, there is no one in the whole wide world that I would rather have as a sister than you."

Elizabeth smiled happily and gave Sara Jane a hug. "We'd better go back to the men. They might like some supper," she said with a dreamy expression on her face. Sara Jane sighed.

The day the *Caesar* anchored in Gage Roads, Sara Jane spoke with Henry. It was difficult, because she didn't want to hurt him and knew she was doing just that. Henry accepted her refusal like the gentleman he was and no one would have noticed any change in their behaviour towards one another.

The *Caesar* sailed for England on the last day of July.

CHAPTER 41
A Chance Meeting

Melbourne and Port Phillip Bay were left behind and Charles, Alfred and Tom settled down to a restful voyage on the *Eagle*, a small vessel of 108 tonnes catering for eighteen passengers. Being August, it was cold and on occasions the passage rough but the partners had so much to be thankful and happy about that they ignored the poor weather and either celebrated in their cabin, discussing their previous months together, or socialised with the ship's officers and other travellers. To cover their tracks, they acted the wealthy young bachelors looking for adventure and excitement in the antipodes, which was an easy role to play, since it was true.

From fellow passengers, they learned that South Australia was a debatable name since it stretched only about a fifth of the way across the continent and its northern, western and most of its eastern boundary bordered onto New South Wales. It was explained that Edward Gibbon Wakefield, a political economist, had been instrumental in bringing about the unique settlement which was based on the three principles of self-support, antitransportation and provision for the appointment of clergymen.

Within three days, after beating into the westerlies, the *Eagle* turned northward and passed Kangaroo Island on the port bow as it took the Backstairs Passage into Gulf St Vincent. In Port Adelaide, an ex-soldier from Hobart was engaged to guard the contents of their cabin and Charles, Alfred and Tom spent the three days on hired horses exploring Port Adelaide and Adelaide and its environs. They admired the view from the slopes of Mt Lofty and marvelled at the symmetry and simplicity of the layout of the future City of Adelaide. They were appalled at the condition of the roads, still all unmade and full of pools of water.

Then it was back on board and they were on their way to King George Sound. Crossing the Great Australian Bight was a horror voyage. Strong westerly gales were encountered and the small vessel was hammered by huge waves. Eventually, she limped into the calm, blue waters of Princess Royal Harbour and anchored off the Osnaburg Street jetty in Albany.

When the Captain had assessed the damage, he called the passengers together. "I am sorry to have to inform you that the *Eagle* requires extensive repairs before we can proceed to the Port of Fremantle." There were groans from the travellers. "The risk of sailing into further storms without caulking is too great and would put the vessel and indeed your lives, in danger." Impatient mutterings followed. "However, good accommodation is available in Albany and I would expect that we should be able to resume our voyage within the fortnight." Sighs of exasperation could be heard.

Alfred leaned towards Charles and Tom and whispered. "My friends, I suggest we take a chance and leave the *Eagle* if we can find alternative passage. Chas, how about you being on the first trip ashore and use your charms and cash to find if there is anything available. We'll stay on board and guard the luggage."

"Good idea." Charles immediately followed the Captain and engaged him in earnest conversation. Twenty minutes later, he was one of the few being ferried to the landing in the ship's dinghy.

"Where do the captains stay when in port?" he asked the helmsman casually.

"At the Albany Hotel, sir, when they stay ashore. It's not posh but the food's good. Bit expensive for the likes of most."

After asking directions, Charles walked quickly along Stirling Terrace up the York Street hill and entered the bar of the Albany Hotel. A stoush was in progress and a tall, handsome man with a skipper's peaked cap was being pummelled by a drunk, while being held from behind by a grinning sailor. Another man lay inert on the floor. The altercation was being vigorously encouraged by the men at the bar.

Charles stepped up behind the drunk and tapped him lightly on the shoulder. The man snarled angrily as he turned his head to see who had the gall to interrupt his sport. Charles swung one punch, a right uppercut and the drunk's eyes glazed as he thumped to the floor. The sailor pinning the man's arms disappeared out the door.

"Shall we leave for the moment, sir?" said Charles. The skipper was shaking his head and ruefully feeling his jaw.

"Yes, let's do that." He picked up the unconscious man and threw him over his shoulder, then led the way out onto the street. "Thanks for your help. They had me at a disadvantage when I went to my for'ard hand's assistance. Let's move down to Ship Inn on the beach front. It's closer to my dinghy. This mob must have been here all day. They're as drunk as lords."

Charles grinned at the simile. "Charles Earl," he said thrusting his hand forward. "Traveller from England."

"William Blair," said William, giving the hand a shake. "From Fremantle."

"Ah, Fremantle. My destination. Are you by any chance a Captain Blair, sir?

"Aye. I sail a cutter by the name of *Sara Jane* this trip. Leaving tomorrow morning for Fremantle."

Charles' eyebrows lifted in surprise. "A pretty name for a sailing vessel, Captain."

"Yes. My sister's name."

The vision of a beautiful blonde-haired woman in a deep-blue dress, which matched incredibly bewitching eyes came back to Charles. Just a coincidence, he considered and dismissed the idea.

There was a moan from the man over William's shoulder. "Thank goodness, Walter. You're as heavy as lead," and he lowered his burden onto a log by the side of the rough road.

When Walter had recovered, they finished their journey and William insisted on buying his rescuer a drink at the Inn.

As he sipped the strong rum, Charles broached the subject of passage to Fremantle. "Otherwise, we're stuck here for at least a fortnight," he concluded.

"Who's we?"

"I have two travelling companions and some rather heavy goods to transport to Fremantle."

"We have no facilities, Charles. The *Sara Jane* is an open cargo vessel. I would imagine you would be accustomed to rather more comfortable quarters," he said, sizing him up.

"How long is the journey?"

"Depends on the winds. Could be four days. I don't have any calls to make at other ports on the way."

"We're prepared to pay well for passage to Fremantle."

"No, no. If you wish to join us, knowing the conditions, it will be my pleasure to transport you and your fellows free of charge. Without your intervention earlier, I fear I might not have been capable of sailing home for some time. I'm only recently mended from injuries sustained at sea."

"Then you're on, Captain."

"Book yourself in at Ship's and organise your goods to be brought ashore. We'll leave soon after dawn. We've plenty of water, hardtack and salt pork."

Charles pulled a face. "Spare me," he said.

* * * * *

By the time the *Sara Jane* reached Fremantle on the 20th August, the five men were on good terms. Charles, Alfred and Thomas stuck to their story and, as by then Tom's use of the English language was quite acceptable, their tale was plausible. William was surprised at the weight of their luggage but it was none of his business and travellers did accumulate odd souvenirs.

Surreptitiously, Charles watched William and became more and more convinced there might be a link with the beautiful visitor to Lydiard but as he couldn't explore the notion without giving away information, he kept his own counsel. It was the colour of the eyes and hair and the same easy, self-assured mannerisms.

On their arrival in Fremantle, Walter made arrangements for the transfer of the visitors and their luggage to the Union Hotel in Market Street and William promised to get back to them with an invitation to his home for dinner when it could be arranged.

"How long are you staying over in Fremantle?"

"I would hope at least a month or two."

"Then that'll give us plenty of time."

"Thanks a lot, William and Walter. Your company made our revised schedule well worth while." Charles shook their hands, followed by Alfred and Tom.

"Oh," said Charles as an afterthought. "We might need the facilities of a bank."

"The Western Australian Bank is the one. It's in the same street as the hotel. Ask for Mr Moore and say I sent you. We're good customers."

A cart was hired immediately and Charles transferred the boxes of nuggets directly to the Western Australian Bank, while the others booked into the hotel.

Mr Moore was his usual, disinterested self until Blair Transport Enterprises was mentioned, whereupon his demeanour became much more politic. When the subject of the safe storage of boxes of gold was broached, he became instantly respectful. What were those Blairs up to now?

* * * * *

That night, Charles, Alfred and Tom were standing at the bar, dressed in their modish Melbournian clothing and enjoying an expensive champagne, when three women, attired in silk and adorned with feathers, sidled up and stood in proprietary fashion next to them.

"Good evening, gentlemen. May we join you?" asked a blonde. Her skirts rustled enticingly and Tom goggled at the exposed cleavage.

"We would be delighted," replied Charles in his polished accent. "Three more champagnes, my good man." Introductions were made. They met Lydia, Marcia and Carmel.

"Shall we retire to a table for a drink before dinner, ladies?" Alfred nodded at a table well away from the bar. The offer was accepted with alacrity.

Everything went smoothly, until a man of huge physique stormed up to the table. "You're with me, love," he said in a thick European accent, as he pulled one of the women by the arm. She squawked with disapproval. It was the blonde, Lydia and she did not look at all pleased.

431

"Go away, my good man. I am with these gentlemen." She fluttered her hand in a dismissive gesture.

"No, you're bloody not! You're with me, Lydia. Remember the arrangement we made last night?"

Charles stood and spoke quietly. "Shall we go outside, sir?" It was spoken as an order. The brute took it as a challenge.

"You're on," he said as he lumbered towards the entrance.

"Fight!" called the man from the next table. "Fight!" came the echo and the room emptied as two dozen men chased them through the double doors.

Tom pressed close to Charles. He knew what was expected of a second. Alfred strolled nonchalantly behind.

The eager spectators made a circle on the road outside the front of the hotel. This was obviously a regular occurrence. The lamplight from the second storey lit up the crowd. Bets were already being taken by a small dapper-looking man, who held a pencil at the ready while flicking over the pages of a notepad.

"Jonesy's the stakeholder," came the call and there was a surge in his direction.

"Will you give me two-to-one on Bruno, Jonesy?"

"You're joking!" someone called.

"How much?"

"Six pence."

"You're on," replied Jonesy. "You're the first and last at two-to-one."

"Evens on Bruno the Bear?"

Several small bets were accepted.

"What's the toff's name?" There was much laughter.

"Charles Earl," called Alfred in his schoolmaster's voice that quietly penetrated the crowd. "What are your odds on Earl?" That brought more raucous laughter.

"I'll give you ten to one on the toff winning, if you want to lose your money," the stakeholder replied derisively. More laughter.

"Done," said Alfred. "My stake is £10."

The stakeholder hesitated only a moment, before saying, "Are you sure, sir?" as Alfred counted out ten gold sovereigns.

"I'm certain, my good man," and Alfred thrust a purse into the hand of the man standing next to the self-appointed stakeholder. "Count it," he ordered.

The man counted the ten gold sovereigns and Alfred received a slip of paper as a receipt. The stakeholder recorded the transaction.

There were now more than thirty onlookers, all urging on the local champion. Filippo Bruno, of Italian extraction, stood to the side with a vacuous smirk on his face as he received encouraging slaps on the back. He had stripped to the waist and presented a formidable sight in terms of bulk and blubber.

Charles gave him a quick appraisal as he took off his coat and shirt and handed them to Alfred. Bruno's size didn't worry him, although he estimated him to weigh 300 pounds. His own style of pugilism was based on the technique made famous by Mendoza, who had beaten the best and biggest fighters in England and had weighed only 160 pounds. Charles was a fit and trim 220 pounds.

Alfred returned to Charles. "Remember Daniel's maxim, Chas. Never underestimate your opponent. Be wary until you gauge the man's weaknesses. You should easily outlast him on stamina."

A tall sad-faced man stepped into the circle and held up his hands. The crowd fell silent. "Does anyone wish to referee this bout?"

There were no volunteers and heads were shaking.

"You do it, Joe. You know what to do," someone called out. There were loud cheers of agreement.

"Do the contestants agree?"

Charles and Bruno nodded.

"Then this bout will be fought under the London Prize-Ring Rules."

Joe held his hands up again. "Seconds," he shouted. Tom and Alfred and Bruno's two seconds stepped forward and a coin was tossed high.

"Heads," Tom called.

"Tails it is," said the referee.

Bruno swaggered to the edge of the light so that his back was to the hotel verandah and began shadow-boxing to warm-up.

"Damn! I've given Chas the light for the beginning of each round," Tom breathed. As Charles turned to walk to his corner, he noticed the three women standing on the upstairs balcony. The redhead fluttered a handkerchief at him. Tom hurried over to kneel as Charles' support if he wished to sit, which he declined and saw Bruno seating himself on the thigh of one of his seconds.

The referee strode to the middle of the road and drew a scratch mark several yards in length.

"This bout will continue until one of the contestants cannot come up to scratch within eight seconds of the call. A foul will be called for head butting, gouging, biting, striking below the waist, or hitting or kicking the man when he's down." He paused momentarily. "Time!"

The barracking began in earnest. Obviously Bruno the Bear was a popular local fighter.

Charles was the first to the scratch mark and took up his pose of left foot and left fist forward. Bruno lumbered to the mark and did the same but Charles noticed immediately that his stance was flawed. Bruno's fist was not in a ready position for attack. It was too defensive. Too close to his face, a little low and his wrist was limp. He was also very slow on his feet. Nevertheless he carried bulk and if he connected Charles knew he would be in big trouble.

The referee dropped his arm and Charles sidestepped a lunge, ducked a swing and weaved out of the way of a wild blow to his head. Then he slid forward on his left foot and jabbed. It was a very strong jab and Bruno's head jerked back. Charles continued to jab. Rat-tat-tat went his left fist. Then with several short retreating steps, he crouched ready.

The Bear moved forward and swung again, missing Charles' head by inches. The Englishman pulled his chin in, made himself as compact as possible and lightly bobbed forwards and backwards. He let loose with another jab which caught Bruno on the eyebrow. It split and spouted blood, as though it had been sliced. Charles danced away again.

"Come on Bruno! Get him!"

"Get the toff!"

With a roar, Bruno swept the blood away with his forearm and charged. His defence was forgotten and he just wanted to hit his opponent to pulp. A mistimed swing left his head wide open, resulting in another series of left jabs from Charles.

Bruno reached forward with his right hand and made a grab at Charles' hair. Pulling hard he made a vicious jab to the eye and then another before the Englishman lifted his forearm sharply to free the grip on his hair and responded with a right jab to his opponent's chin. Reacting to the pain in his chin, Bruno couldn't avoid the three terrible left hooks to his ribs followed by two rights to his heart.

"You bastard! You deserved that!" said Tom under his breath. Hair-pulling was not against the rules but hardly worthy of any prize fighter. Should be kept for gutter fisticuffs.

Charles felt his right eye closing. Must do something quickly to finish this off. He'd only fought gentlemen before and they always fought cleanly. This was the real world. He proceeded to circle the lumbering Italian. Almost dancing, his footwork light and agile, he stayed just out of reach.

"Chase the bugger," someone yelled.

"Should be called the dancer. He's scared to get close. Come on Bruno!"

Bruno, hearing the comments rushed at the enemy, dropping his guard. When the opportunity presented itself, Charles waited until the last moment and then ducked the wild swing and planted a succession of shattering lefts and rights to the face.

Bruno fell to the ground and his second ran forward to haul him back to his corner. Charles walked back to Tom and refused to sit down.

The crowd howled for Charles' blood.

"Damned fool I am. Never considered anyone would go for the hair-pulling trick."

"Watch them, Chas. The more you get on top, the more likely they'll try something. This isn't going to be a fair fight with all but two of the crowd barracking for the Italian."

Alfred joined the conversation. "Sound advice, Tom. No one wants their own champ to lose, especially when there's money riding on the bout." He examined Charles' eye and looked relieved. "It'll be black for a few days but there's no bleeding."

"Time!" called the referee. The men took their positions at the scratch mark. Joe dropped his arm.

The dancing resumed. Charles' footwork was brilliant. Alfred judged it the best he had ever seen and refused to accept that he was biased. Charles hit, sidestepped and jabbed. Swung, skipped away and circled. Jabbed, weaved and retreated.

Exhausted, Bruno fell to his knees after pursuing Charles for several minutes without landing a blow.

"Foul!" called Tom. Under the rules, falling without a blow being delivered, brought immediate disqualification. Charles stepped back and waited for the referee's decision.

Before Joe could make any pronouncement, Bruno's seconds lifted him to his feet and supported him back to their corner. He sat on the knee of one of the seconds, while his face was dabbed with water. The other ran to the referee and began remonstrating and gesticulating. At first Joe shook his head but when the crowd jeered and yelled derogatory comments, he appeared to waver. At last he nodded and walked over to Tom and Alfred. Charles wandered rather aimlessly around in his corner to keep warm.

Tom argued vehemently for several minutes and then hurried to Charles. "Chas, this is a set-up if ever I've seen one. They reckon he fell accidentally. It's ridiculous!"

"Let it go, Tom. I'm rather enjoying myself. Tell the referee that we are prepared to continue. This is the best stoush I've ever had."

Tom strode across to the referee who was trying to assume an impersonal stance, with little success. He was receiving a great deal of heckling from the crowd.

"We'll continue," he said, rather ungraciously for Tom.

"The contest will continue," the referee announced to whistles and cheers.

"Good on you toff. You're a sport."

"Get on with it. I need a drink."

"Time!" the referee called.

That should have given him a good breather, thought Charles ruefully. I'll have to exhaust him all over again.

It didn't take long. Bruno was badly out of form and just couldn't keep up the pace. Charles continued the ride and hide, as Alfred called it, for a few more minutes until Bruno was once again stumbling, then a left jab was followed by a right hook and it was all over. When 'Time' was called, Bruno couldn't walk to the scratch mark in the required eight seconds.

The referee walked over to Charles and lifted his arm high to acknowledge the victor. For a moment there was silence and then cheers.

"Good fight, toff. You showed him a clean pair of heels," some wag called out.

"I'll be betting on you next time, toff."

An outburst of laughter followed. The mob quickly disappeared into the hotel, accompanied by Alfred, who kept the stakeholder in sight as he followed him to collect his winnings. Bruno and his seconds were left alone as so often happens when the favourite is vanquished. Crowd loyalties certainly change rapidly, Charles thought. He pulled on his shirt and coat with Tom's assistance and walked over to Bruno's corner. The ex-champion was becoming impatient with the attention he was receiving from his seconds, who were both fussing. One dabbed the cut on his eyebrow with a none too clean looking rag.

"Thank you for the bout, Bruno. May I call you by that name?" Bruno looked surprised but nodded. Charles held out his hand. Bruno looked even more surprised but took the proffered hand. "Will you join us for a drink?"

"Thanks." Bruno gave his seconds a baleful glance and walked inside with Charles and Tom. The table was already occupied by the three women, who were talking with Alfred.

"Bruno is joining us for a drink," said Charles. "Can I presume that you are buying, Alfred?"

"Of course, Chas." He turned to the Italian with a grin on his face. "You've given our partner a shiner of which to be proud, Bruno. I always did tell him to keep his right guard higher. What would you like to drink?"

CHAPTER 42

Gentlemanly Activities

Champagne Charlie he was called around Fremantle. On every possible excuse, a cork was popped and the bubbly quaffed. Not that anyone minded. Wasn't he the one who had beaten Bruno the Bear and without complaining about a bit of skulduggery on the side?

Who was he anyway? He and his two companions had arrived from the eastern states. Sailed from King George Sound with Captain Blair. What were they doing in the colony? What were they up to? Just seemed to be relaxing and enjoying themselves. Well someone must know something! They've been here a week!

Aha! Perhaps they were bushrangers. Look at that Captain Moonlite fellow in the book. He was a gentleman. Or could they be remittance men, whose presence was no longer wanted in England. Maybe they were confidence men, here to trick people out of their hard-earned money. No! They seemed to be happy sharing their money. One of the luggage porters from South Jetty said their luggage was very heavy. That's what it was! Gold! They had found gold! Where could they have found gold? That notion lapsed.

The sticky beaks and gossips had a field day as they always did with new arrivals but as time went on nothing was revealed. The men were obviously gentlemen and rich. They were also polite and generous.

After a few days of inactivity, they were bored. Alfred was browsing through the *Inquirer* over a late breakfast. "Here we are, Chas. A horse race this coming Sunday. That's tomorrow! All comers welcome. Entry fee is £1 and the prize money, less expenses, will be proportioned to the winners. It says to contact a Mr Forsyth at 16 Cliff Street, Fremantle. The race must be being held here in the Port."

"Well! Who wants to be in it? 'You've got to be in it to win it', my father always says. One, two, three. Right lads, let's check out the details."

"Wait on! There's an article about the fight.

Local Fremantle Champion beaten by London prize fighter. Last Monday evening, an impromptu bare-knuckle fight took place outside the Union Hotel in Fremantle. Apparently, an altercation had occurred over one of the female attendants of the hotel and as a result Mr Fillipo Bruno, the Fremantle fighting champion, was challenged by Mr Charles Earl of London. A bystander reported that the subsequent fight, held under London Prize-Ring Rules, was convincingly won by the visitor, in spite of some rather creative interpretations of the rules and dubious decisions by the referee. The winner, who has been dubbed 'Fleet-of-foot' and 'The Dancer' is apparently remaining in the colony for an indefinite period seeking investment opportunities.

"Chas, you're famous! You've made the colonial press! Pray tell us of the investments you seek?"

"Knock it off, Alfred. You know I'm not seeking any investments."

Alfred turned to Tom. "I say old man, what do you think of Viscount Charles Sebastian Powell of Lydiard brawling in the streets?"

Tom just smiled. He was personally very proud of Charles.

They called on Mr Forsyth that morning. The races were open to any riders. In order, there would be a pony race, a half-breed race and then the Fremantle Cup. All were over half a mile and would be held on South Beach the next day at 11 o'clock. They decided to each enter one race.

"That will be £1 each, thank you gentlemen," said Forsyth cheerfully pocketing the three sovereigns.

The stable couldn't offer much in terms of quality horseflesh but it could fill the required categories. Lucky, a half-breed gelding of doubtful origins, Emily, a pony of doubtful stamina and Devil-may-care, a thoroughbred stallion of doubtful age, stood munching straw in their stalls.

"We'll take them all for two days," said Charles, "with the lightest saddles you have. We'll be racing them tomorrow morning."

The stableboy was also doubtful. He started to say something, then changed his mind when Charles held out three crowns. "Thank you, sir. I'll have them ready in a jiffy."

Alfred pulled out a penny and said, "Call, Tom."

"Heads."

"Your choice."

"I'll take the half-breed."

The penny was handed to him. "Toss, Tom. Your call, Chas."

"Tails."

"You win."

"I'll take the thoroughbred."

"Then it looks as though I'll take the pony," said Alfred.

Next morning was fine but windy. They trotted the horses towards South Beach, all looking forward to the competition, in spite of the fact that a practice run the previous afternoon had not improved their opinions of the animals.

In the middle of the beach, two tall red flags, ten yards apart, marked the finishing line and half a mile to the south another two flags marked the starting line. Chairs and a table were provided for the three adjudicators and Mr Forsyth, who held the purse. A crowd was gathering and bets for the first race were already being taken by a bookmaker.

Sara Jane and Elizabeth stood on the seaside track, holding onto their bonnets. After communion at St John's, they had decided to take an extended walk to South Beach and back before lunch.

"The horse races are on, Elizabeth. I read about them in the *Inquirer*. Let's watch for a while, before we head back." The two women moved down through the dunes to the side of the crowd.

Alfred lined up for the first heat of the first race. The pony stood perfectly still, looking decidedly bored with the proceedings. When the starter's arm dropped and the white handkerchief fluttered down, Alfred took several seconds to get the pony off the starting mark. It was a chase all the way and his opponent held his lead, crossing the finishing line with yards to spare. He waved to the cheers of the crowd.

"Bad luck, Alfred. Emily looked as though she was stuck at the start."

"Ah, well. I think her opposition would have been too much for her anyway." He led Emily away to the drinking buckets.

In the second heat of the second race, Tom was away to a good start but Lucky could not keep up the pace and faded at the finish.

Tom gave him a pat and then a drink, before leading him over to the others. "Sorry, troops. It's all up to you now, Chas."

Forsyth stood in front of the crowd and announced that the Fremantle Cup was to be run along different lines. "As there are only two entrants, the winner will be decided on the best of three contests between David Parkinson from Spearwood on Likely Lad and Charles Earl from London on Devil-may-care."

"It's the toff! It's the toff!" echoed around the crowd. "Bet on the toff."

In the first contest, Devil-may-care surprised Charles in his efforts. He took off with a burst of speed and was leading by a head as they neared the finishing post. Charles could hear the cheers of the crowd, when suddenly Likely Lad's shoulder nudged Devil-may-care's rump. Adjudicators scattered in disarray as Charles galloped past the line on the wrong side of the flag.

'Disqualified', was the decision, as the adjudicators brushed themselves down and tried to regain their composure to the hoots of the crowd. Charles ignored the setback and remained silent, as he trotted his horse back to the starting line.

Two women were standing watching him approach. His eyes met the deep blue eyes of a beautiful woman. He started. It was her! The woman who had rescued the little girl in Lydiard Forest. The face that had remained etched in his memory. Stop staring! He shook his head and kicked his horse into a canter.

The second race was Charles' from start to finish. Devil-may-care leapt forward as if stung and lengthened his lead as the finishing line approached. They won by two lengths. The crowd roared its approval. "Good on you, toff. That showed him!" Parkinson glowered.

This was the decider. Charles had never been more determined in all his life. As the handkerchief dropped, he gave the stallion a kick and Devil-may-care bounded over the line. But his age was catching up with him and, after two races, he was struggling to stay in front. Parkinson had drawn level and was trying to reach the stallion's neck with his whip. "No you don't, you bastard," whispered Charles. Leaning forward, he urged the old stallion on. Devil-may-care gave his all and won by half a neck.

The crowd went wild and Charles was lifted onto shoulders for the presentation of the Cup and the prize money of £5. Afterwards, when he looked around, the women were gone.

* * * * *

On the Monday, a letter addressed to Mr Charles Earl was delivered to the Union Hotel by a sailor from the Perth-to-Fremantle ferry. It was from Governor Fitzgerald inviting Charles and his two companions to attend him at dinner on Wednesday evening and, if it so pleased them, to stay overnight at Government House.

"You must be making an impression, Chas," Alfred said with a grin. "They're treating you like visiting nobility."

"Which he certainly is!" retorted Tom.

"Well, do we go, chaps?"

"I'd like that, Chas. It will prove I'm a gentleman."

"Definitely. We were going to travel to Perth this week anyway," added Alfred.

An acceptance was hurriedly written and given to the waiting mariner for the return trip to Perth.

They decided to travel to Perth a day early to look around, so packed their bags and left Tuesday morning. After booking into the fashionable United Services Tavern, horses were hired and they paid a recently retired pensioner guard to travel with them and point out the sights and buildings. Apart from the newer, two-storey stone buildings for government or commercial business and some private residences, the majority were still of wattle and daub construction. Teams of convicts were paving St Georges Terrace and William Street.

The highlight was the view from Mt Eliza. "What a wonderful site for the capital," breathed Alfred. "That Stirling fellow certainly chose the right spot.

Future generations of Western Australians will be extremely grateful, I'm sure."

The next day, they found a barber and had their beards and hair trimmed before taking to the bath tub. At dusk, dressed in their most formal clothing, they took the hotel's hansom around the block to Government House.

The aide-de-camp noted their names and escorted them through to the sitting room where they were introduced to Governor Fitzgerald. Sherries were served and half an hour later on the chime from the grandfather clock, Eleanora Fitzgerald made her entrance and they removed to the dining room.

Tom found the food plentiful and tasty and the conversation stilted and boring but tried to nod at the right time and ask the occasional question. As usual, Alfred took the lead in the dialogue but since they had played their roles for so long, their stories were plausible and there were no slip ups.

The single point of interest was when Fitzgerald brought up the topic of gold. "Did you hear rumours of gold discoveries in Victoria before you left, gentlemen? I received copies of the Geelong and Melbourne papers only yesterday and they are full of reports of gold. Most are unsubstantiated, as one would expect but the possibilities must be there, following Hargreaves' discoveries in New South Wales and the reward offered in Victoria. One wonders whether there could be gold in Western Australia."

Alfred made some noncommital remark and Tom shook his head and continued eating. Not daring to look at the others, Charles commented, "One never knows with gold, Your Excellency. Eventually it all depends on the terrain." Fitzgerald nodded sagely having no idea what the fellow was talking about.

Over glasses of port, the Governor asked whether they would still be in Perth on Sunday, as a cricket match was planned for 10 o'clock on the Esplanade. "The Perth Gentlemen will play the Fremantle Gallants and I'll be there as the patron of the Perth team. It should be a close game."

"We'll be there then. But I'm sorry to say, sir, I'll be barracking for Fremantle."

"And I."

"And I."

"Ah well, gentlemen, it will all add to the contest and help to reduce the home ground advantage."

* * * * *

When Charles, Alfred and Tom strolled to the Esplanade area, after Communion at St George's Church, it was half past nine. The Perth Gentlemen were sitting on logs at the side of the clearing. Fitzgerald waved. "Your Gallants haven't arrived, gentlemen."

441

"Probably chickened out," someone called. A few ribald comments were added.

"If they're not here by 10 o'clock, we'll claim the prize and have a scratch match."

"And then go to the United Services Tavern." Cheers of agreement followed.

The threesome joined the group. It was easy to see that the game was being taken very seriously. All the men wore whites, right down to white bow ties and high, black beaver hats. The stumps and bails were set up and an umpire wearing a dark coat was checking the width of the bats with a bat gauge.

The umpire walked over to the group. "It's time to toss, Governor Fitzgerald. What do you want to do?"

'Perhaps one of the visiting gentlemen would represent the Fremantle Gallants and call. I can vouch that all three qualify by virtue of their Fremantle residence."

"Thank you, sir." Alfred looked to his companions and then stepped forward. An idea was forming in his mind but its success was predicated on winning the toss. A great believer in fate, Alfred willed himself to win.

"Heads," he called.

"Heads it is, sir."

"The Fremantle Gallants will bat. That is if the Perth Gentlemen will lend us some gear."

There was silence for a moment, as the implications of the statement sunk in.

"Yes. Why not? Good sports all, we are!"

Charles declined to be involved. He had featured in both the *Perth Gazette* and the *Inquirer* in past weeks and reckoned that enough was enough. A bystander was recruited as the second umpire.

Tom and Alfred tied on leg guards, borrowed hats and strode towards the wicket. Alfred was to face the first ball.

"You realise that we must stay in until the others arrive, Tom."

"Aye, Alfred. I do." He had an intent expression on his face.

The bowler used the traditional underarm bowling action and the first ball fell slightly to Alfred's leg side. It was a slow and carefully placed ball, which bounced three yards before the wicket. Alfred stepped forward and hit it squarely in the centre of his bat. The ball lifted cleanly over the heads of two fielders and bounded over the rough ground towards the river where it disappeared into the rushes. They ran seven.

The Captain waved the fielders out and they respectfully took several paces backwards.

Tom faced the next ball. It was much faster and right on line. He waited until the last moment, judged that it was at the top of its bounce and lifted it over the head of the bowler. They ran two.

The next ball hit a clod of earth, bounced past the off stump and flew past the keeper. Alfred called and they ran a bye.

Alfred faced his second ball. The bowler switched to a round-arm action, which momentarily caught Alfred unawares. He quickly adapted his swing to the increased speed and cracked the ball through mid-on. With the overthrow, they made six runs.

The bowler was becoming flustered and let loose a ball which just missed Alfred's ear on the full.

"Wide!" signalled the umpire.

The last ball of the over. Alfred took his stance and square cut it past point for three runs.

"Over!" called the umpire.

While the Captain set the fielders, Tom and Alfred walked to the middle of the pitch and appeared to engage in serious conversation.

"What a lark," said Alfred. "Better than the Masters versus Boys match last year. This bat is beautifully balanced. Wish I could take it home."

"Be serious, Alfred. The reputation of the Fremantle Gallants rests on our shoulders," Tom said with a straight face. "I must admit though, it's a bit more polished than the village green games."

The umpire coughed. The fielding team was ready!

The first ball from the second bowler was delivered underarm. The ball was so slow it seemed to wobble through the air, before it landed, whereupon it spun away just missing off stump. Alfred completely mistimed it. This fellow requires attacking strokes or he'll have my wicket, he thought. The next ball was similar but Alfred was ready. He skipped down the wicket and hit it on the half volley. It sailed over the bowler's head and they ran three on a misfield.

Tom was clearly not comfortable with the spin bowler and blocked two balls before hitting a single.

It was the last ball of the over and Alfred, looking around at the positioning of the fielders, saw a dozen or so men running up Barrack Street from the jetty. They were in whites. It was the Fremantle Gallants. They had made it at last. Alfred cut the ball with all his strength and it raced across the field towards the Gallants with a fielder in hot pursuit. They scampered out of its way and cheered as the fielder crossed Barrack Street towards the Court House. They ran nine while the fielder searched the long grass for the ball.

The umpires called the Captains into a huddle. There was much discussion. The Gallants argued that their vessel had left Fremantle in plenty of time to make the scheduled starting time but as it turned out the Captain was drunk from the night before and had run them aground on Point Walter. The decision was taken that the score should stand but that the two ring-in batsmen should be declared retired not out. They had made 33 runs.

It was a one innings game with lunch to be served following the match. The final scores were Gallants 66 and Gentlemen 64, with Alfred top-scoring with 28.

Everyone walked to the United Services Tavern and Charles shouted champagne throughout lunch and afterwards until the tavern had exhausted its supply. It became a very noisy gathering.

Ken Spencer, the Captain of the Gentlemen toasted the winners and complimented Alfred Castle on his score, considering his short innings. In responding, Lennard Pavy, the Gallants' Captain, thanked the Gentlemen for their good sportsmanship and issued a challenge for a rematch in the Port in a month's time. The Gallants sailed for Fremantle mid-afternoon, more than a little the worse for wear. After they had waved them off, Charles chuckled. "If they managed to ground on Point Walter on the way upstream, I wonder what they might hit on the return journey," he said.

"I'd hate to think, Chas. Everyone cross their fingers." They returned to the celebrations.

The Governor's aide-de-camp, eventually persuading Fitzgerald it was time to leave, was grateful that the United Services Tavern was only a stone's throw from Government House.

* * * * *

William returned from a day at Mews' shipyards. The *Margaret* was up on the slipway for the removal of marine growth and caulking. His injuries had healed completely and caused him no trouble, although he tended to favour his left shoulder when lifting heavy objects.

"Hello-o. Anybody home?" He found Sara Jane and Elizabeth in the sitting room reading.

"Hello, William. Have a good day?"

William nodded. "Aye. Another couple of days should do it."

Sara Jane put down the *Inquirer*. "The papers are full of the exploits of the three visiting Englishmen. They must have reporters following them to see what they do next. They sound much more like the Three Musketeers than we do. I wonder who they are?"

"Read it out, Sara Jane."

"All right, listen to this," and she read.

> *Fremantle Gallants beat Perth Gentlemen. Visitor top-scores in cricket match.*
> *Openers Alfred Castle and Thomas Goldman played well to*

remain not out until the Fremantle team arrived late for their match at the Perth Esplanade, having run aground on the hazardous Point Walter Bank. Castle top-scored with 28, playing some excellent strokes.

"And then they give the details. First, it was the prize-fight and then it was horse racing and now it's cricket. What's next, I wonder?" She paused. "I must admit that Charles whatever-his-name-is rode well at South Beach, particularly as Parkinson was out to win at all costs. Mr Parkinson certainly had a few unethical tricks up his sleeve."

"Hmm," William hesitated. "Sara Jane, didn't I tell you about the passengers I brought back from the Sound?"

"Yes." She looked puzzled and then suddenly looked askance at him. "William, don't tell me your passengers were the three gentlemen in question?"

"Well, yes." He looked embarrassed. "But what's more, I've just remembered I said I'd invite them to dinner."

"William!" Sara Jane and Elizabeth spoke simultaneously.

"Here we have the toast of the town waiting to be invited to our home. What a good excuse for a party!" Sara Jane's eyes sparkled. "Where are they staying?"

"Walter arranged for their luggage to be taken to the Union Hotel. I guess that's where they'll be."

"Well then, big brother, you'll deliver an invitation first thing tomorrow. Won't you? If they accept, we'll arrange a party. We haven't had an excuse before but now we have. What do you think, Elizabeth? About twelve to fifteen people should make a good-sized but not too large a gathering."

Elizabeth's eyes lit up. "It's a lot of people! Would be our first party."

"Sounds like a good idea, Sis. What's the difference between a dinner party and a party?"

"The guests come after the evening meal and one serves drinks and a buffet supper," answered Elizabeth. "Therefore we can have more people."

"Sounds like a good idea. I'll call on the gentlemen tomorrow morning."

It was all arranged for Saturday week. Invitations to other guests were delivered and Patience, whose term of employment had been extended indefinitely, cheerfully drew up a list of possible supper dishes.

* * * * *

Meanwhile, urged on by Sara Jane, William planned a voyage to Champion Bay to investigate the mining position and assess business opportunities. In July, the *Inquirer* had reported that Francis Pearson, a smelter, recruited from

445

Newcastle-on-Tyne, was due in Fremantle shortly to take up a position at the Geraldine Mine and Sara Jane reasoned that this meant activity would increase. When William met with Charles, Alfred and Tom to invite them to his home, he mentioned it and they begged to go.

"We'd like to see as much of Western Australia as we can. We'll probably never get back again, William," Charles said. "And Alfred is a bit of a geologist and would be interested. Wouldn't you, Alfred."

"Very much so."

Tom nodded assent.

"Well, you're all welcome. I'm leaving with Walter the day after tomorrow, as I must be back for a party we are holding in our High Street home for three visiting English gentlemen."

They all laughed.

* * * * *

The next day, William took the ferry to Perth and visited the Colonial Secretary's Office. Maps were made available to him and he sketched and recorded the information he needed about the Geraldine Mine, which had been operating since just before Christmas the previous year. The mine was on the banks of the Murchison River about sixty miles north of Champion Bay. Gantheaume Bay, at the mouth of the river was charted and the obvious anchorage for a small cutter.

They sailed north on 15th September, rugged up against the elements. Tom became the assistant for'ard hand, Alfred prepared the food, such as it was and Charles was the lookout. William stayed outside the three mile reefs but in sight of the coastline. In a boat the size of the *Margaret*, they couldn't take the risk of being too far from land.

William was consistently ribbed by Charles, who asked him about the coming party and the guests and about his sister. Abashed, William said little.

Walter, determined to have his say, described Sara Jane as beautiful, intelligent and caring and Charles surmised that Bateman was enamoured of her. Nevertheless, if she was the woman he had met at his Lydiard home, it was an apt description.

When William admitted that another young woman lived with them as a house guest and Walter added that Elizabeth was also beautiful, he was ribbed even more. William took it all good-naturedly but disclosed little. He was surprised that he felt so protective all of a sudden.

After three days, they passed Champion Bay, entered the Geelvink Channel and travelled northwards well to the east of the Houtman Abrolhos. William did not want any more misadventures on that archipelago of Sirens.

446

The distinctive, red bluffs, characteristic of this section of the coast, came into view in the early morning and they reduced sail in order to reconnoitre the reefs and mouth of the Murchison.

William tugged on his blond beard thoughtfully. "We're of such shallow draft that we should be able to get over the sandbanks without any trouble and anchor in the river. Judging by the colour of the surrounding ocean, it's still flowing out to sea and has washed out a channel. We'd be safer."

"What about getting out again if the winds stay from the west?" asked Alfred.

"You've hit the nail on the head, Alfred. It's a chance we'd have to take. Spring can be so variable. Highs with fine weather and easterlies, followed by lows and onshore winds. What's the decision to be, gentleman?"

"What's the barometer saying?" came the next query from Alfred.

"It's rising."

"You're the skipper, William."

"Then let's give it a go."

The next half hour was spent carefully manoeuvring the *Margaret* over the bar and through the main channel to calm waters. Two anchors were dropped.

Walter remained on board as guard, while the others, with provisions for two days. set out following the left bank of the river. At first it was easy-going but after about five miles it became much narrower and rocky and the gorge was crowded on both sides by high walls of red rock.

Mid-afternoon, sweaty and tired, they turned a corner in the gorge and came upon men digging. "Ahoy," called William, not wanting to be blasted by a nervous soldier. "Is this the Geraldine Mine?"

A man came hurrying forward.

"Captain James, I presume," said William holding out his hand.

The Captain brushed his palm down his trousers, before shaking hands. "At your service. And who the devil would you be, sir?"

"William Blair, sea captain from Fremantle and these gentlemen are Charles Earl, Alfred Castle and Thomas Goldman from London." The men shook hands. "We arrived this morning by cutter, which is anchored in the river. I am interested in any opportunities for the transporting of ore or metal. The *Inquirer* reported that a smelter was on his way and I assumed that would mean less quantity in ore even if it's more weight in metal."

James laughed. "Striking while the iron is hot, eh?"

"Any traces of copper or silver?" Alfred asked. "They are often found in galena. Galena is actually a sulphide of lead and the metal can be extracted by heating. Quite a simple process really."

"Could be. I'm just the manager, not the geologist. Come and see the Geraldine Mine, gentlemen. It's not much."

There were a few huts and tents and a company of six scruffy and dirty convicts commanded by Captain James. "We've taken out a few dozen tons of ore but getting it south costs almost what it's worth. At the moment we're just stockpiling and waiting to see what Mr Pearson, the smelter can do, when he arrives."

"How large is the vein, Captain James?" asked Alfred.

"I'll show you." They followed him to the river's edge, where the miners were leaning on their picks and shovels watching the proceedings. "Back to work men. You've another hour yet," James yelled. "Unless you want some overtime."

The men muttered but returned immediately to their allocated tasks.

"See, here is part of the vein. It covers over three hundred yards, following the river bed and is anything up to two feet wide. Trouble is, the river is still flowing at present and so most of it is covered with dirt and several feet down. By the time the river drops appreciably, it will be hot, very hot working in this gorge. My term will be up next month. I'll see Pearson settled and then be on my way. It's a miserable existence."

They hung around and watched operations until it was stop-work time. Alfred threw in the occasional question, which James was happy enough to answer. William became more and more pessimistic about the possibility of any connection with this particular venture.

They left at 4 o'clock, declining James' enthusiastic invitation to stay over. "Thanks, Captain but we've seen everything we need to see and I don't think that our transport business would make much of a profit, even if we were invited to become involved. Looks as though the Mining Company would remain better off with its present plans. Good luck to you, sir."

They arrived back at the river mouth a few hours after sunrise, having camped overnight on the way. There was a slight problem. The tide was very low and they couldn't risk trying to traverse the bars at the mouth. It was four hours before they managed to negotiate the entrance.

'Well, William. What have you decided?" asked Charles as the *Margaret* headed south.

"That we'll stay with agricultural produce," he laughed. "At least for the present."

"Yes, I'd have to agree with you," Alfred remarked. "I have a feeling that the Geraldine Mining Company may be overextending itself financially for no guaranteed future. That's the trouble with absentee landlords. By the by, who is 'we'?"

"We? Oh, you mean Blair Transport Enterprises? It's a partnership. Sara Jane and I are partners."

Alfred was becoming more and more intrigued but would wait for the party to find out more about this singular woman.

"All in all a very interesting voyage, thanks William," Charles said, as they approached the anchorage in Bathers Bay. "Our family shipping company might be interested, if there was a turn around in fortunes. You know the sort of thing. Goods to Fremantle, lead and sandalwood to Asian destinations, silks and spices back to England."

"You didn't tell me you were in shipping!"

"Well, I'm not involved personally but shipping is a peripheral activity of our family and has been for several generations."

Alfred and Tom both lifted their eyebrows.

CHAPTER 43
The Recital

Sara Jane and William met their friends at the front door of their High Street home. Patience hurried away with coats, hats and gloves and Elizabeth showed them to the sitting room and provided refreshments. As protocol demanded, the three Englishmen were to arrive later to be greeted by the assembled guests.

First to arrive were Mr and Mrs John Bateman and sons John and Walter, who appeared promptly and smiling on the doorstep at 8 o'clock.

"John! When did you arrive back?"

"Only yesterday. What a trip we had. I've slept for twenty-four hours. Must go down in history as the longest round trip from Fremantle to Singapore on record."

"But highly successful," said his father proudly. "Thanks to each of you, now I've heard both sides of the story. I've asked Masterson for his resignation."

"Come, John dear. Business can wait until Monday," Mary Bateman remonstrated, tugging at his sleeve and leading him down the hallway.

The Batemans were followed by Mr and Mrs James Dempster, who had left their brood in the capable hands of the Back family on Rottnest and were staying over at the Union Hotel. Mr David Long arrived alone soon afterwards and was his usual bashful self. Sara Jane always jollied him along and tried to make him relax but it just seemed to make him more uncomfortable, so tonight it was Elizabeth's turn. She linked her arm with his and guided him through to the others. It was a cool September night and a friendly fire glowed in the grate.

Right behind were two others, whom Sara Jane had yet to meet. William introduced his sister to Mr and Mrs Thomas Brown from Grass Dale via York. Sara Jane smiled at the couple as she shook their hands. "Thomas and Eliza. May I call you by your Christian names?"

"Of course, my dear." Mrs Brown was a bubbly, motherly sort.

"I'm glad to have the chance to thank you personally for your hospitality in caring for my accident-prone brother at Champion Bay. Whoever heard of a seasoned mariner falling out of his bunk?" She looked at her new guests and then at her brother with one raised eyebrow and they smiled politely. Elizabeth returned to meet the Browns and escort them through to the sitting room.

"I wonder where our guests of honour are?" Sara Jane asked William. "No one could lose themselves in Fremantle."

Into the lamp light stepped three men. "Good evening, William," said Charles.

Patience stepped forward to collect the superfluous clothing.

"Good evening, gentlemen. Come into the foyer. We were worrying that you might have managed to lose yourself but we weren't sure how that would be possible. Anyway, you're here now and that's the main thing. We won't have to send out a search party." The men shook hands.

"Sara Jane, may I introduce the three infamous, publicity-seeking gentlemen from London. Messrs Charles Earl, Alfred Castle and Thomas Goldman. Gentlemen, my sister, Miss Sara Jane Andrews-Blair."

"How do you do, gentlemen." Sara Jane held out her hand and Charles took it, bending forward. The others followed. "Ignore my brother's facetious comments. He is overly eager to sample his latest cellar acquisitions, as I'm sure you are. May I introduce our friend Miss Elizabeth Rothwell."

In turn the three men greeted Elizabeth.

Charles turned to his host. "You do not play the game fairly William, keeping two such beautiful young women for your own company."

Sara Jane had a pert expression on her face. "Not so sir. We are both of independent means. Now, please follow me gentlemen." She chatted easily as she led them through to the sitting room.

Charles couldn't take his eyes from Sara Jane. He was elated. It was the woman he had met at Lydiard. The woman with the bluest eyes he had ever seen. The woman who had delighted his father and actually received the approval of his mother. It was William's lack of a hyphened surname that had thrown him. Stepping lightly in anticipation, he followed.

After introductions and a punch, sherry or brandy or two, the guests relaxed and conversed easily. Sara Jane's calculating eyes made quick assessments of their new visitors.

Eliza Brown was a gem. Eager to assist with drinks and savouries, a caring and capable woman, clearly taking everything in her stride. She even managed to animate her rather taciturn husband, who appeared to be embarrassed by attention from any of the females present.

Thomas Goldman was dark and good-looking in a craggy sort of way, wooden in manner and seemed to think himself socially inadequate, which he wasn't. He waited to see what his two friends did before he responded and yet Sara Jane gauged his inner self to be warm and out-going.

Charles was tall and extremely handsome, with in-built good manners and a casual confidence. He listened carefully to whoever was speaking, asked intuitive questions and put everyone at ease. His attire was immaculate and his broad shoulders rivalled William's. Close-cropped, fair curly hair and beard added to a clean-cut, outdoors appearance. Sara Jane considered him absolutely delightful.

Alfred was taller than Charles but slimmer. He also wore his fair hair and beard short. There was a continual sparkle in his eyes, as if the world was a wonderful place and he was lucky enough to be at the centre of it. His clothes were a touch loose and cut for comfort. He deferred to Charles and yet Sara Jane reckoned he was ten years older than Charles and Thomas. There's more to that one than meets the eye, she thought.

A buffet supper was served in the dining room and guests carried their laden plates back to the sitting room and stood or settled as was their wont. For convenience, small tables had been placed for glasses and plates. Patience had surpassed all her previous culinary efforts in the preparation and presentation of the meal.

"I mean to steal her away, Sara Jane. She can demand her price," said John Bateman Senior loudly.

"My dear, I doubt Patience would consider leaving the Blair kitchen for ours." She turned to Sara Jane. "I keep reminding John after each of your kind invitations, Sara Jane, that our kitchen facilities need some urgent upgrading."

"This time, Mrs Bateman, I promise."

"This time, my husband, I have more than enough witnesses. You may all be called to attest to the truth," she said, eyeing each guest. Everyone laughed and William refilled wine glasses.

Dessert comprised a variety of jam, custard and fruit tartlets with fresh cream, which Patience offered from a platter.

"Delectable," said Charles.

"Delicious," added Alfred, taking another.

When the plates and glasses had been cleared, Patience returned with a tea tray. She was followed by William, carrying a tray with glasses and a bottle of Madeira Estate port.

"For the benefit of new guests, I would like to announce that we differ in some aspects of our code of social behaviour from most contemporary households. In our home, it is acceptable for both ladies and gentlemen to choose either tea or port, or be served both. In fact it is now tradition, isn't it gentlemen?" William turned to the Batemans and David Long, as he placed the tray on a side table.

"Quite correct, partner," answered John Bateman Senior.

"Wholeheartedly supported," winked Mary Bateman.

"Aye, aye, Captain," responded David, John Junior and Walter in unison.

Charles added his piece. "Damned civilised, I'd say, if the ladies will pardon my expression. Our conventions are habitual and allow little freedom of choice. I'm all for it. In fact, I don't enjoy port - unless it is of the finest quality. Usually I partake of tea."

William focused his eyes longingly on the bottle of port, before turning to his sister. "Sara Jane would you like to say something about the contents of this bottle since you have a more intimate knowledge of its making, than I."

"Thank you, William. Yes, I would like to describe this particular port, since I was a guest at the winery on two separate occasions and imbibed it with relish."

Thomas Brown looked shocked. His wife patted him on the arm in an understanding fashion.

Sara Jane began. "This vintage Madeira Estate port is made from a blend of specially selected shiraz and cabernet sauvignon grapes. The grapes are crushed, de-stemmed and fermented until they have consumed half the original sugar content. The skins are then removed and alcohol added to raise the strength to 18 percent by volume. The pressings are returned to the vat with the free-run wine. The port is then mixed, filtered and transferred to oak casks to mellow and develop the fruit characters. After two years it is fortified with a high-flavoured brandy spirit, bottled and kept for at least twenty years."

Charles stood. "I'll have one."

The evening concluded with singing around the pianoforte and Sara Jane and Elizabeth took it in turn to play such popular songs as "Ye banks and braes', 'The knights of the golden crest', 'The merry month of May', 'The King, God bless him', 'The sea, the sea, the open sea' and 'Away, away to the mountain glen'.

Charles then took possession of the piano stool and to Sara Jane's delight played the music from 'Don Giovanni' superbly. William fetched his flute but, not having played it for many years, gave up and placed it on the top of the piano.

"May I?" On William's nod, Alfred wiped it with a clean handkerchief and accompanied Charles. He was clearly an accomplished flautist. Sara Jane was in her seventh heaven. She had longed to be able to entertain guests in her own home and be satisfied that they were enjoying the occasion. And enjoying it they certainly were. Even David and Thomas were bellowing out the tunes!

It was 2 o'clock in the morning, when the visitors reluctantly took their leave.

As Alfred said good bye to Sara Jane, he added, "Music, the greatest good that mortals know---."

But before he could finish, a radiant Sara Jane concluded, "And all of heaven we have below."

* * * * *

William left early for Bathers Bay. He had some work to do on the *Margaret* and needed to be back for the 11 o'clock service at St John's. "Oh, my head! Did you spike the tea, Elizabeth?"

"You didn't have tea, William. However, you did consume several glasses of your favourite port."

"I'll probably not survive the day. You two are devoid of sympathy." He lifted the handles of his overloaded wheelbarrow and trundled it off down the street.

The two women lingered over breakfast. Every minute of the previous night was recalled and discussed. Neither had ever enjoyed herself as much and both were extremely pleased with their first party.

"The musical finale made the evening," Elizabeth concluded. "Charles was an impressive pianist, as was Alfred an excellent flautist. Not only did everyone join in but it was actually a sound duet. Did you gain the impression that they had performed together before?"

"Definitely. It was too polished to be impromptu. Wonderful, really." Sara Jane had a dreamy expression on her face. "I wish we could arrange such evenings on a regular basis."

"Nothing to prevent you inviting the gentlemen again. I'm sure they enjoyed themselves as much as we did."

Patience answered a knock on the door and, after a brief exchange, returned with two letters and a twinkle in her eye. "From the Batemans and the Browns, ma'am."

Sara Jane read the messages aloud.

Dear Sara Jane,

Thank you for a delightful evening, which we all enjoyed immensely. John had such a good time that he has made a firm commitment to upgrade the kitchen. At long last we will then be able to reciprocate your hospitality.

In appreciation,
Mary Bateman.

Elizabeth grinned. "Well, that's certainly good news. Mary's been waiting for ages for a new kitchen. What does the other one say?"

William and Sara Jane,

Both Thomas and I agree that last night was quite the most enjoyable musical evening we have ever had the pleasure of experiencing in the colony. My ardent wish to own a pianoforte has moved much closer as a result.

Bless you both,
Eliza Brown.

"Heavens! I wonder what it achieved for Mrs Dempster?"

As if on cue, there was another knock on the door.

Sara Jane read the third message. "It's from the United Hotel."

Miss Andrews-Blair,

James and I thank you sincerely for a wonderful evening. Every moment was held dear by both of us. Our isolation on Rottnest has prevented us from socialising and James now acknowledges that we need to make the journey to the mainland more frequently. That acknowledgment is very precious to me.

Sincere thanks,

Ann Dempster.

"All in all, Sara Jane, I tend to be of the opinion that the party must be considered a complete success."

"Thank you, Elizabeth. For once, we are in total agreement."

William was late as usual and the Blair household entered St John's a few minutes before eleven o'clock. They nodded to the Batemans and Browns before entering their pew and kneeling in prayer.

As she sat back in her seat, Sara Jane was disappointed that their new English friends were not in attendance. She now realised how much she had been looking forward to seeing them again.

* * * * *

Elizabeth had just left for the Post Office on Monday morning, when a huge bunch of roses was delivered by a young footman from the Union Hotel.

"If it's all right, ma'am, I'm to wait for an answer."

Sara Jane nodded and looked very pleased with herself. She placed the flowers on the table, as she walked through to the sitting room. The enclosed note read:

William, Sara Jane and Elizabeth,

We thank you for your hospitality last night and sincerely wish to report how much we all enjoyed ourselves. The spontaneous nature of the musical part of the evening was the final unique touch on top of fine food, fine wine and fine company.

Alfred Castle and on behalf of Charles Earl and Thomas Goldman.

PS. We extend an invitation for you to join us with other special guests for dinner next Saturday at the Union Hotel at 7 o'clock. This will be followed by a recital at 9 o'clock to be held at the recently established Fremantle Literary Institute in the

Mechanics Institute building in Cliff Street. If you are interested in participating in the recital, I will inform you of individual responsibilities for recitation in due course.

Sara Jane was unable to keep the contented smile from her face as she penned the reply.

Dear Alfred,

We accept with pleasure your kind invitation to dinner at the Union Hotel at 7 o'clock on Saturday 1st October and would all be delighted to participate in the recital to follow.

Sara Jane Andrews-Blair.

Within an hour, the footman returned with a sealed letter.

"Do you need to wait for an answer this time, young man?"

"No, ma'am." He twisted his cap in his hands and was clearly bursting to speak. "Can I say, ma'am, how pleased the gentleman was when he received your reply," and he ran off down the street, fearful of his own audacity.

When Sara Jane broached the subject at lunch, Elizabeth was delighted and William horrified.

"Sara Jane, I will not recite poetry. I flatly refuse. In any case I would never remember the words."

"Your recitation is not poetry. It's a piece from 'Hamlet' and it's quite permissible to read it. You'd be performing with Elizabeth. Didn't you expect our party guests to join in?"

"Well, yes. But that was different!"

"No, it wasn't. Was it Elizabeth?"

Elizabeth hesitated. A direct answer would hardly be prudent here. "Don't worry, William. I'll help you."

"William, it's a strong male part and you have a fine voice. Remember how Father praised your reading and recitation skills."

There was much mumbling and muttering for an hour or two, before William called from the upstairs balcony. "Elizabeth, come up to the library and keep your promise. I can't pronounce half the words." By the look on Elizabeth's face, it was going to be a labour of love.

At every spare moment, lines were practised and after dinner each night individual pieces were recited and critiqued by the others.

Came Saturday night and William, Elizabeth and Sara Jane, each with some apprehension not revealed to the others, were collected by the hotel coach. The women wore their best and most fashionable clothing but were aware they were probably very much behind the times. There was little reason to keep updating their attire, when there were so few occasions to wear formal clothing and it was always at least six months out of date with London fashions anyway. Still, Sara Jane looked stunningly beautiful in her full-length blue gown with flounced skirt and Elizabeth enchanting in her long gown of carefully chosen shades of mauve, also with a flounced skirt. William wore his year-old dark grey frock coat and matching trousers, with a new white shirt and white bow tie. He carried their allocated pieces for the performance in his leather document case.

When they arrived at the hotel, a liveried servant met the coach and led them through to the entrance of the large dining room. It was the cheeky young footman who had delivered the messages. "Evening, ma'am," he said to Sara Jane and doffed his cap. William glared at the impertinence.

Charles was obviously the designated host and received the guests, with Alfred and Thomas standing to his left. Their formal wear was well beyond the fashion of Fremantle at the time and they looked splendid in black, narrow-waisted, tailed coats with long, narrow-legged black trousers, black waistcoats, white shirts with bow ties and pointed, black shoes. Charles bent over Sara Jane's and then Elizabeth's hands and gave a short bow from the waist to acknowledge William. "We are especially pleased that you were able to attend this evening's function," he said, with twinkling eyes.

"Captain William Blair, Miss Andrews-Blair and Miss Rothwell," the now formally-attired hotel manager announced. This was all very new to him but for the price he was being paid, he would do exactly as ordered.

They walked into the room. Guests were gathered in groups, sipping sherries or punches and some turned to acknowledge the newcomers. John Bateman waved and they joined the Bateman family group. Sara Jane saw Captain Daniel Scott, Chairman of the Fremantle Trust and his wife, Frances, the Reverend Spencer, who was staring in her direction, Mr William Pearse, whom she knew to be a Director of the Geraldine Mine and his wife, Susannah, Mr George Leake, a lawyer and his wife, Rose and Mr Lionel Samson, importer and auctioneer and his wife, Fanny.

"Ladies and gentlemen, would you please take your places."

Sara Jane had already seen her place card and knew she was on Charles' right, the privileged position. She saw him approaching.

"Would you do me the honour, Miss Andrews-Blair?"

"It would be my pleasure, Mr Earl," she replied, as she took his arm.

Thomas Goldman approached Elizabeth and whisked her away to the table leaving William looking both surprised and dismayed. There were more men than women in the room, which was usual at colonial functions and when William walked to the long table, he found himself between Lionel Samson and Walter Bateman. He looked to see Elizabeth seated between Thomas and

Charles. It was getting worse. Why, Elizabeth should be with him! Everyone should know that! She was smiling at Thomas. That beautiful smile. The white bow in her shining black hair was bobbing as she agreed with something he was saying. This was not right! She should be sitting next to him. He began to push his chair back but then stopped and slumped in his seat. Elizabeth was not his to command. What a fool he was! Something must be done about this decidedly unfortunate situation as soon as possible.

The guests were now seated. Sara Jane looked to her right. There was no place card and the seat was empty. She turned to Charles with a questioning look but he just smiled and continued to give orders to the chief waiter.

Glasses were filled with champagne and everyone looked to the host, who was now engrossed in a conversation with Sara Jane. He must be waiting for the last guest. How rude of someone to be late! Ah-ha, that explained it! He had just arrived and was about to be announced.

"Mr Thomas Peel."

Peel blustered into the room, looked around, shook hands with Charles, who stood on his entry and sat down next to Sara Jane, ignoring everyone else.

"My dear, how lovely you look."

Charles picked up his glass. "Ladies and gentlemen, would you please be upstanding for the royal toast." He paused to allow time for his guests to stand before lifting his glass and saying, "Queen Victoria."

"Queen Victoria," echoed around the room.

The meal was superb, which was not surprising because Patience had been borrowed for two days to prepare for the special dinner. French onion soup was followed by baked snapper, roast chicken and vegetables and steamed pudding with custard. Superb white wines were served with each course. It was clear that Charles was sparing no expense.

Sara Jane had a marvellous time. She was so proud to have been chosen to occupy the seat of honour and Charles was considerate and charming. When Peel demanded her attention, she found that she could converse with him easily on most topics. He seemed to know exactly what was happening in London as well as in Western Australia. It appeared that his family was connected socially with Charles', although the connection was not made explicit. As she took a mouthful of the delicious pudding, she suddenly came to the realisation that she was catching up in time and maturity. An interesting thought!

Following the removal of the dessert plates, Charles stood. There was immediate silence.

"Ladies and gentlemen, could I beg your leave to say a few words." Nods from the gentlemen around the table. "Alfred, Thomas and I have now been in Western Australia for over six weeks and every week seems to bring a new adventure. Sailing with Captain Blair, who rescued us from Albany and also took us to the Geraldine Mine. I've been informed by your newspapers that it was to investigate investment opportunities." Polite nods and smiles at William. "Bare-knuckled prize-fighting, horse racing and a cricket match, when we showed the colonists that we could mix it with the best of them." Appreciative laughter. "Wonderful hospitality shown us by families here tonight and kindnesses given in many ways by others. Miss Sarah Jane Andrews-Blair, Mr William Blair and Miss Elizabeth Rothwell were not only responsible for a party in our honour last weekend but have lent us their cook extraordinaire to organise this evening's dinner." Polite clapping. "Their musical interest fostered the idea of tonight's recital, which will be presided over by Alfred. Tea and port will be served at the Institute. Please share transport or take the hotel's coach, which is at your disposal. I thank you."

The gentlemen glanced around the table but it was John Bateman who rose first. "On behalf of the guests, I would like to take, - nay seize, the opportunity to thank you, Charles, for hosting this fine dinner tonight. We look forward with pleasure and anticipation and I suspect a little fear and trepidation, to the second part of the evening, when we'll show Perth that Fremantle is also a centre for cultural activity." Laughter and applause from all.

When the guests arrived, the Institute was already lit by lamps and set up with twenty chairs and a dais. A black curtain, hung as a backdrop, gave the area the appearance of a stage. The guests took their seats and there was a buzz of excitement as sheets of paper and books were retrieved from pockets and bags. Sara Jane looked for Thomas Peel but he did not appear.

Alfred spoke from the dais. "Ladies and gentlemen, could I have your attention." He waited for the polite hush that followed. "As you would be aware, some of those present have elected to recite tonight. However, it was not an open choice and one had to accept to perform the nominated piece. Therefore, unless one had an extensive reading and recitation background, one had only the five days in which to prepare. To those persons who offered to recite, I wish you well and promise, on the audience's behalf, that we will treat you kindly."

"The first part of the evening's proceedings will be selections from 'The Tragedy of Hamlet, Prince of Denmark'."

William Pearse took his place on the dais and read:

"O, that this too too solid flesh would melt,

Thaw and resolve itself into a dew!....."

Pearse completed the soliloquy with only one reference to the book he held and received a vigorous round of applause. He sat down, red-faced but looking very pleased with himself. Susannah patted his arm.

The Reverend Jonathon Spencer walked to the dais, cleared his throat and recited:

"To be, or not to be: that is the question:
Whether 'tis nobler in the mind to suffer
The slings and arrows of outrageous fortune,
Or to take arms against a sea of troubles,
And by opposing end them......"

The second soliloquy was completed without a pause or stammer and Spencer walked to his seat amid loud clapping.

It was John Bateman's turn and he read a short piece.

"Alas, poor Yorick! I knew him, Horatio:
a fellow of infinite jest, of most excellent fancy:
he hath borne me on his back a thousand times;
and now how abhorred in my imagination it is!
my gorge rises at it....."

His facial expressions and gesticulations had the audience chuckling throughout and they gave him an enthusiastic response.

The last Shakespearian piece was a conversation between Hamlet and his mother, concluding in the killing of the concealed Polonius. It was recited by William and Elizabeth.

"Now, mother, what's the matter?"
"Hamlet, thou hast thy father much offended."
"Mother, you have my father much offended."
"Come, come, you answer with an idle tongue."
"Go, go, you question with a wicked tongue......"

It was well practised and cleverly done, with voices modulated to convey the alternate underlying expression of Hamlet's scorn and the Queen's puzzlement, tinged with fear.

They received appreciative looks and respectful applause. It was interval and William headed straight for the port bottle.

After a fifteen minutes break, Alfred returned to the dais. "Ladies and gentlemen, would you take your seats for the second part of the recital, which will include 'Meeting at night' from Browning, 'Morte d'Arthur' from Alfred Tennyson and last but not least, three nonsense rhymes from Edward Lear."

Sara Jane took the dais. Her heart was fluttering and yet she relished the opportunity to recite her favourite poem by her favourite poet. It was only two stanzas and yet it said so much.

"The grey sea and the long black land;
And the yellow half-moon large and low;
And the startled little waves that leap
In fiery ringlets from their sleep,
As I gain the cove with pushing prow,
And quench its speed i' the slushy sand.

Then a mile of warm sea-scented beach;
Three fields to cross till a farm appears;
A tap at the pane, the quick sharp scratch
And blue spurt of a lighted match,
And a voice less loud, thro' its joys and fears,
Than the two hearts beating each to each!"

This was the first love theme and took the audience by surprise. They hung on every word as the pictures were painted in their minds. The applause was thoughtful and many of the couples glanced at one another with soft eyes.

The next performer was Alfred and he gave a brilliant rendering of the first and final stanzas of 'Morte d'Arthur'. He ended in sonorous voice:

"Long stood Sir Bedivere
Revolving many memories, till the hull
Look'd one black dot against the verge of dawn,
And on the mere the wailing died away."

As Alfred's voice trailed off, the clapping commenced.

Captain Daniel Scott concluded the programme with the third of three verses.

"There was an Old Man who supposed,
That the street door was partially closed;
But some very large rats, ate his coats and his hats,
While that futile old gentleman dozed."

The clapping commenced in subdued fashion but gained momentum, until individuals began standing. Soon all were standing as performers were acknowledged.

Alfred returned to the dais and held up his hands for attention. The applause died away and the audience resumed their seats smiling and nodding.

"Ladies and gentlemen, thank you for your attendance and participation this evening. Please join us in a light supper."

Everyone was laughing, as they moved to the trestle tables for tea or port with biscuits and cheese.

"Thank you, Alfred," said Lionel Samson. "It was a most memorable night all around. Next time, I'll not be afraid to put my name forward as an active performer. If there's enough interest and I don't doubt there will be, I'll organise another evening myself."

Sara Jane took Alfred's arm. "How did you know that 'Meeting at Night' was my favourite poem, Alfred?"

"I didn't, Sara Jane. It just happens to be mine."

* * * * *

461

Alfred arrived the next morning to escort Sara Jane to the 11 o'clock service at St John's Church, as he had arranged with William.

At first, Sara Jane was surprised but when she saw the expression on William's face, she realised what had happened. "Good morning, Alfred," she welcomed him, as she picked up her gloves and hat from the hall stand. "So nice of you to call for me. Shall we go. We don't want to be late for the service," and she took his arm.

Elizabeth was ecstatic. She now had William to herself. But then, she need not have worried. After a sleepless night, William had come to the indisputable conclusion that he was a total fool. He loved Elizabeth and promised himself, that from this Sunday morning onwards, he would make sure that his intentions were quite evident, even if it meant wearing his heart on his sleeve.

When Thomas came to the door a few minutes later, William made it patently clear that two was company and three a crowd. An embarrassed Thomas retreated in haste. William returned to the sitting room and gave a short bow. "May I escort you to church, Elizabeth?"

* * * * *

Sara Jane sat back in the pew after her silent prayer and watched the fair-haired man kneeling beside her. She was suddenly overcome with a feeling of such intensity, such warm affection that she blushed and turned away, sure that the emotion must be obvious to all.

What was it about him? She decided that it was mostly because of his pleasant nature. He had such a wonderful, caring disposition. No, not only that. He was also talented socially. And intellectually. And musically. And in the manly sports.

But who was he? Sara Jane decided that she knew very little about Alfred Castle.

Sara Jane acknowledged Charles and Thomas as they arrived and sat in an adjacent pew and smiled knowingly at Elizabeth as she and William took their usual seats next to her.

The service commenced and they all stood. Reverend Spencer led the congregation in a hymn. There was something very different about singing in church and Sara Jane always found it uplifting. The sermon was on generosity of spirit and the Reverend spoke strongly and convincingly. He added some pointed remarks in conclusion, suggesting that generosity was also of paramount importance for the material welfare of the church and requested that parishioners dig deep into their pockets to boost the flagging organ fund. The gathering was reminded again, as it was each week, that St George's Church and Wesley Church in Perth possessed an aeolophon and pipe organ respectively.

Alfred escorted Sara Jane home and she invited him to dinner the following Saturday night. He looked lonely as he wandered off down High Street.

William and Walter left at dawn the following morning for Rockingham and Charles, Alfred and Thomas went with them. They were carrying hardware for the store and would back load with farm produce for sale at the Fremantle markets. As it was not far, William suggested firstly anchoring in Safety Bay, two miles further on and landing on Penguin Island to watch the local inhabitants. This they did and were amused by the endearing blue and white penguins, swimming around the boat and scampering for cover on the island as the intruders approached. Several snapper were caught while they drifted beyond the off-shore islands before returning to Penguin Island for the night. The fish were pan fried in butter and eaten with crusty bread washed down with a local ale, kept cool at the sea's edge. It was a balmy November night and they slept wrapped in blankets under the stars. Next morning, they transacted their business and headed for home on a fresh sou'westerly.

"You know, William, you really have a paradise here in Western Australia," Alfred reflected. "It could be described as a Utopian existence."

"Life is what you make of it, Alfred. I just happen to enjoy everything about my lifestyle."

Alfred pondered over William's words.

CHAPTER 44
Game and Match

On Saturday evening, Alfred arrived for dinner, impeccably dressed, with a bottle of excellent champagne and a bunch of red roses. He also presented Sara Jane with a beautifully-wrapped gift.

"Now, Sara Jane, you are not to open it until I have gone," he said sternly. She took it upstairs and placed it on her bedside table, eyeing it with great curiosity.

Dinner was relaxed, as they ran through the events of the previous Saturday night, laughing as they recalled the initial discomfort of the performers and later the polished recitations and readings.

"It was a wonderful evening, Alfred. They do that sort of thing in Perth but we've not had anything of that magnitude in Fremantle before."

William smiled. Hidden by the damask cloth, his thigh just managed to touch Elizabeth's under the table. "Well, Sis, I wouldn't mind betting that it might be followed by a similar night sooner rather than later. Remember Lionel Samson's offer?"

They played whist until 11 o'clock and Sara Jane and Alfred won so consistently in the early stages that they changed partners and then Elizabeth and Alfred won.

"Our guest is obviously the key to winning," said William with a sigh. "What's the secret, Alfred?"

"No secret, William. One just has to remember which cards have been discarded and guess who has the remainder by the way they play their hand."

William sighed. "Thank you, Alfred. I should have known you'd say something like that."

When the farewells were over and Alfred had gone, Sara Jane opened her present. She found a copy of 'The personal history of David Copperfield', exquisitely bound in dark green leather. Inside was a card. It read:

Dearest Sara Jane,

In appreciation of your charming company.

Kindest regards, Alfred.

Clutching the book, Sara Jane ran down the stairs and called softly. Elizabeth opened her bedroom door. "What's the matter? You look as though all your Christmases have come at once." She pulled Sara Jane into her room.

"Elizabeth, look what Alfred gave me tonight."

"Oh, what a beautiful gift! How did he know you loved Dickens' work?"

"He must have guessed. I haven't said anything."

"Sara Jane, I fear you might be heading for another proposal. If so, you'll have the same problem you had with Henry, of having no alternative to going to England to live. You'll have to head him off."

Sara Jane slumped onto the bed. "I don't want to head him off."

"Then encourage the poor man, for heaven's sake!"

"But I don't want to live in England. It's cold and crowded and women are to be seen and not heard."

Elizabeth sat on the bed and hugged her friend. "I'm afraid that only you have the answer to this dilemma, Sara Jane."

* * * * *

The following morning, in order to give Sara Jane and Alfred more time together, Elizabeth insisted that William go with her to 8 o'clock Communion. There was much moaning and groaning but of course he agreed. Elizabeth was to be protected, if not guarded, until he was able to pull his thoughts into some sort of order and pluck up the courage to tell her how he loved her, needed her and desired her. It really was ridiculous! Why did he have to go through this heartache and anguish? Why didn't she just know how he felt?

Alfred called for Sara Jane at half past ten and, as they walked to St John's, she thanked him for his gift.

"How did you know that Dickens was my favourite novelist, Alfred?"

He looked into her eyes and smiled. "Because he is mine, my dear."

Sara Jane smiled back demurely and said nothing.

At the conclusion of the service, an animated Reverend Jonathon Spencer announced that an anonymous donor had placed £500 in a bank account, opened with the Fremantle Agency of the Western Australian Bank, for the purpose of purchasing an organ for St John's.

"Hallelujah!" someone called from the back of the church.

"Praise the Lord!" was the answering call.

"Let us pray," said Reverend Spencer. The congregation knelt. Sara Jane peeped at Alfred from the corner of her eye but he wore an inscrutable expression.

"Lord God Almighty, giver of all things, we thank thee for thine divine intervention in providing this benefaction, that we may better glorify thy name in joyous song. Amen."

"Amen," echoed the congregation.

As the parishioners congregated outside the church, there was much speculation about the identity of the mysterious benefactor. No one knew anyone in the colony at this time who would be willing to donate such an amount and even if someone had seen the light, why on earth would he demand anonymity?

* * * * *

When Elizabeth arrived home for lunch on Monday, she carried a letter. "It's for you, Sara Jane. In default."

The letter was addressed to 'Mr Henry Nicholas Blair Esq, Fremantle, Western Australia' and marked 'Urgent Delivery'. On the back was a note saying: 'If Henry Blair is unable to be contacted, please make every effort to deliver to William Blair or Sara Jane Andrews-Blair.' The wax seal was elaborately ornamented.

Sara Jane hurried for her letter opener and slit the envelope. She read:

> *Lydiard Estate, via Swindon*
> *10th June, 1851*

> *Dear Henry,*

> *I am writing to you in the hope that you may know Charles' whereabouts. As you would be aware, he left for Melbourne, which I have ascertained is in Victoria, in mid-January to search for gold and we have received no communication from him to date, although Oswald wrote to him in February. It is highly probable that our correspondence has crossed.*

> *Last week, the Earl sustained injuries to his right hip and arm, resulting from a riding accident, which although not debilitating are of sufficient concern to the surgeon to prompt me to inform our son of his condition.*

> *The Earl has told me that Charles is journeying with Alfred Carson, his old tutor and Tom Chapman, a local villager and my problem is that they are travelling incognito in Australia as Earl, Castle and Goldman. The Earl says he is bound to respect this confidence and their identities and insists that I hold to that agreement, otherwise I would write to the Colonial Secretaries.*

> *If Charles is in Western Australia, I'm sure you would know and will inform him immediately of the situation. Otherwise, I have no alternative but to wait for a letter from my son and correspond forthwith.*

Oswald asked that Tom Chapman be informed of the death of
Ted Foster in a village brawl. I do not know the significance of
this message.

Yours sincerely,
Lady Eleanor Powell

Sara Jane stared at the letter with disbelief. Charles Earl was Viscount Charles Powell! That pasty-faced, insipid milksop she had met at Lydiard Mansion, with presumably the worst stammer in the English nobility, had undergone a metamorphosis into Prince Charming personified!

And Alfred was a tutor! That explained a lot of things. His knowledge, his talents and his caring nature. She felt she understood and knew him better already and was glad of it.

Tom had certainly learned to play his part. He must have followed the lead of the others, so that their game plan remained intact.

Sara Jane laughed out loud. If any trio should be dubbed the three musketeers, it was Charles, Alfred and Tom. It fitted them to a T. What an adventure they were having! And it now appeared probable that they _had_ found gold and were living it up before returning home.

So where does this place me? Out on a limb? Up the proverbial tree? However, she knew one thing and one thing for sure, she must inform Charles immediately.

"Elizabeth," she called. "I'm going down to the Union Hotel to see Charles. Won't be long. The letter's really for him."

"Fine. See you soon."

Sara Jane put the letter into her handbag and, pulling on her bonnet, hurried from the house. She found the three men in the hotel lounge. Alfred was playing draughts with Thomas and Charles was reading a book.

"Good afternoon, gentlemen," she said, as the men rose hastily to their feet. "I apologise for interrupting your leisure but I need to talk with you privately, Charles. It is a matter of some importance."

"Of course, my dear. Shall we go for a walk?" He took her arm and they left. Alfred looked both wistful and puzzled.

After a ten minute stroll, during which they discussed the weather and other inconsequential matters, Charles steered her to the Esplanade area and chose a log under a huge gum tree. He took her hand, as they sat. "Now my dear Sara Jane, what is the reason for this tryst?"

"Charles, I received a letter this afternoon and thought it to be of such significance that I should apprise you of its contents immediately. When you read the letter, I'm sure you will agree with my judgment." She drew the letter from her bag and passed it to him. He glanced at the name and message on the envelope, recognised the handwriting and withdrew the single page.

Charles quickly scanned the letter. "Ah," he said. "I am called home."

"I hope that your father is recovered and that you find him well on your return, Charles."

"Father is old, Sara Jane, as well you would remember," he said wryly, "but he is made of stern stuff. I don't doubt that he will be waiting for me in the library with a glass in his hand and will greet me with something like "Welcome home, son. I've missed you. Have you sown your wild oats?""

He picked up her hand again, as if to comfort himself. "You see, Sara Jane, Father knew I must go. I told my mother that I must find myself. It was true and I have. My father understood all along."

"You certainly have changed Charles, from the man I remember."

"Ah! But I needed to change, Sara Jane."

"Can I be impertinent and ask a question, Charles."

"Of course, my dear. You are now a friend and confidante."

"Charles, what happened to the stammer you were purported to have?"

"I left it with a bullock team in Melbourne," he answered, with a beatific smile.

CHAPTER 45

Nuptials

Alfred knocked on the door of Blair House within the hour. He was dressed in a well cut dark grey suit and had a worried expression on his face. Patience showed him to the sitting room and he greeted Sara Jane on entry and sat down next to her on the sofa, where she was embroidering.

She had been waiting expectantly for his arrival.

"Sara Jane, I came as soon as I heard the news. Of necessity, Charles must return to the ancestral home as soon as he can arrange passage. Tom has said he will return to his village. Mrs Foster was the woman he had hoped to marry and, with the demise of her husband, he will ask for her hand." He paused and then rushed on. "I have come to ask your forgiveness."

"Alfred, you do not need to apologise. I understand that you will want to leave with your friends."

"No, no, Sara Jane. You don't understand. I am here to apologise for not having been open and honest with you since first I began keeping your company. My behaviour has been indefensible. I have led you on, letting you believe I am a gentleman of background and means." He was wringing his hands and looked thoroughly miserable.

"Alfred, please." Sara Jane felt her whole world tumbling down. This was the man she now indisputably loved and with whom she could happily spend her life. If only---. She sighed. "Alfred, I understand why you would want to return home. I do not ever want to live anywhere except here in Western Australia. Some individuals and some peoples are tied to their land by their hearts and their spirits."

"Sara Jane, would you listen to me." Alfred rose from the sofa and knelt in front of her. He placed her embroidery on a side table and took her hands in his.

"My dearest, would you marry me and live with me in a house I will build for us in Fremantle? I love you with all my heart and mind and soul and will live my life to make you happy."

Sara Jane covered her face with her hands.

"I'm sorry, Sara Jane. Don't cry. I should not have been so presumptuous."

"I am not crying, Alfred. I am praying. I am giving thanks. Of course, I will marry you. I love you so much and would be pleased, proud and enormously happy to be your wife."

Alfred stood and gently pulled Sara Jane to her feet and towards him. He held her in his arms and kissed her. "You have made me the happiest man in this world, my dearest."

William, who was seeking his sister's whereabouts to discuss a business matter, stood momentarily at the door, before creeping away to find Elizabeth. It was about time that he initiated some action of his own on the home front.

* * * * *

The banns were proclaimed the following Sunday and members of the congregation offered their best wishes and congratulations to the couple after the service. Sara Jane wore a beautifully-crafted diamond ring, which was chosen by Alfred when he, Charles and Thomas had travelled to Perth the previous Wednesday. Alfred had been in a quandary about his alias, because he naturally wanted to marry in his legitimate name and yet his bank account in Fremantle was under his assumed name. They visited His Honour, William Mackie, the Commissioner for Courts and explained the rather delicate situation. An hour later they rejoined their hired craft and sailed for Fremantle. Both Alfred and Charles had in their pockets a document signed by Alfred Carson, Viscount Charles Powell and Thomas Chapman and witnessed by William Mackie and George Stone, which the lawyers agreed should facilitate satisfactory transactions at banks in both London and Australia.

Mackie chuckled as he shook their hands in farewell. "This is not a rare or even an unusual occurrence, gentlemen. Aliases are common in the colonies. They are mostly confined to well off adventurers or vagrants, for obvious reasons. I'm glad you are all of the former category."

Alfred was to be left with one small box of nuggets to sell in Perth for cash as necessity demanded. His bank account was healthy and he still had the substantial bank draft. Charles promised to sort it all out on his arrival in London when the remaining gold would be sold. He assured Alfred it would be a lot easier from that end and Alfred agreed.

On their return to Fremantle, Alfred left the others and walked to Blair House to see his fiancée. He grinned at the title. How things had changed! Charles might have found himself but Alfred had found a whole new life. He was greeted at the door by an exuberant Sara Jane.

"Alfred, I'm so glad you're back." She pecked him on the cheek and gave him a quick hug. "Come inside and congratulate William who is decidedly tiddly, as are the Bateman men. Elizabeth is serving an early dinner to get some food into everyone. William proposed to Elizabeth this morning. Isn't it wonderful?" and she danced away down the hallway tugging him by the hand.

Patience was sent to the Union Hotel and to the Bateman residence with messages from Sara Jane. Charles, Thomas and Mary arrived simultaneously and the party began again.

* * * * *

It was a sad farewell. Sara Jane was beginning to hate goodbyes and now it was Charles and Thomas, who had added so much to their lives in such a short time.

As with the usual feeling of an impending loss and not knowing what else to do, they shook hands, slapped backs and gave hugs and kisses as was appropriate. On the cliff next to the Roundhouse, Sara Jane, Elizabeth, Alfred and William waited until the *Esmeralda* was no more than a tiny speck on the horizon.

"You'll miss them a great deal won't you?" Sara Jane and Alfred were strolling arm in arm back to High Street.

"Yes Sara Jane I will, but they return to England to their future and I remain here with you to live ours. From now on fate, destiny, kismet, God's will or whatever one believes in, awaits us."

"What do you believe in, Alfred?"

"Hmm. A combination of common sense, sound planning and good luck, I think would explain my philosophy."

"Close enough," Sara Jane said.

* * * * *

That evening, Sara Jane was firm. "No cards tonight," she said. "We're going to talk about weddings. The ceremony is only just over four weeks away and we've done precious little in the way of preparation."

"I give in," said William. "Where's a pencil and paper?" The inevitable list was started.

"Who will give the brides away?" Alfred asked.

Sara Jane gave a secretive smile. "That is one thing that Elizabeth and I have been discussing and we think we have two very appropriate gentlemen to invite to do us the honour. Both have had a great deal to do with the Blair household in one way or another. If they accept, you will naturally be the first to know."

* * * * *

The following month was one of the happiest and rewarding periods of Sara Jane's life. She and Alfred took every opportunity to spend time together, as they discussed their lives and families and their likes and dislikes, in order to gain a better understanding of one other. The time was precious for Sara Jane, for as she came to know Alfred, she discovered that every attribute, every facet of his personality and especially his sensitivity made her love him more. He had a wonderful sense of humour and a dry wit but never used either to put another at a disadvantage. He was a deep thinker and more than equalled Sara Jane's own thirst for knowledge. It was a meeting of the minds, as well as a meeting of the hearts.

Elizabeth summed it up on a warm morning as they packed some of Sara Jane's belongings. She and Alfred had decided to move to Henry Street after the wedding, until their new house was built on a block Alfred had recently purchased further down High Street.

"He's his own person, Sara Jane. Contented in himself, complete and predictable and yet with the softest heart and nature of anyone I have ever met. You complement one another." She smiled. "My dearest, you have met your match and I know you will both be very happy."

Tears moistened Sara Jane's eyes, collecting in the corners until they ran down her cheeks. She dashed them away and fussed with her packing. "Elizabeth, I cannot bring myself to tell Alfred about Yeddi. I feel I am cheating the man I love. Is that the way to begin a life together?"

"My dearest friend, if and when the right moment comes to relate that part of your life to Alfred, I assure you he will understand and love you even more. If that were possible."

* * * * *

The pianist played light classical music as the guests arrived at the church and took their seats. St John's filled rapidly and it seemed to Patience that all of Fremantle was interested in the nuptials. She had assisted in the decoration of the church that morning and masses of red roses adorned the altar and bunches of white daisies hung from the aisle posts. When the young footman from the Union Hotel was informed by the senior maidservant of the need for red roses, he disappeared for an hour and returned with a barrow full of blooms for Patience. She dared not ask the obvious question.

A new piece was begun as Reverend Jonathon Spencer solemnly entered the church, followed by Alfred and William. They could be brothers, Patience thought. They wore identical attire, dark grey cutaway coats, stiff white shirts with wing collars, white waistcoats and bow ties, black pin striped trousers and white buckskin gloves. With their fair hair and beards and similar heights, they only differed in the length of their hair. She shook her head. Why did Captain Blair insist on wearing his hair in a queue? Ah, well, he did look very handsome. Her eyes moistened and she wondered whether she would ever receive a proposal of marriage.

The introductory chord for the Wedding March demanded everyone's attention and the congregation stood as the processional commenced. First came Sara Jane on Thomas Peel's arm and then Elizabeth on John Bateman's arm. There was a murmur of surprise at the identity of the stand-ins for the fathers of the brides, followed by gasps of admiration. The two women were dressed identically in long-sleeved, white satin gowns and coiffures, with elegant stiffened veils making their own designs as they floated around masses of curls. Hands held dainty bouquets, blue for Sara Jane and mauve for Elizabeth, each tied with long white ribbons.

They look gorgeous, absolutely gorgeous, thought Patience and not a person present thought otherwise, as the beautiful women took their places next to their betrothed.

Reverend Spencer intoned, almost sadly: "Dearly beloved, we are gathered together here in the sight of God and the presence of these witnesses, to join together these two couples in holy matrimony....."

He then positioned himself in front of Sara Jane and Alfred. "Alfred Carson will you have this woman to be your wedded wife, to live together in the holy estate of matrimony.....?"

"I will."

"Who giveth this woman to be married to this man?"

"I do," said Thomas Peel with obvious pride. He took Sara Jane's hand and gave it to the clergyman who with deliberation placed it on Alfred's.

Reverend Spencer then stepped to face Elizabeth and William. "William Blair will you have this woman to be your wedded wife, to live together in the holy estate of matrimony.....?"

"I will."

"Who giveth this woman to be married to this man?"

"I do," answered John Bateman, a pleased expression on his face and Elizabeth's hand was passed to William's.

The two couples followed the clergyman to the altar for the exchange of vows. There was a moment of fumbling, as Alfred and William each produced a ring from his fob pocket and exchanged it for the other. Rings were slipped onto fingers.

The Reverend Spencer then made the dual pronouncement.

"Forasmuch as Alfred and Sara Jane and William and Elizabeth have consented together in holy wedlock.....I pronounce that they are husband and wife together, in the name of the Father and of the Son and of the Holy Spirit. Those whom God hath joined together, let no one put asunder. Amen."

Veils were lifted and kisses gently exchanged.

The pianist began the recessional and Mendelssohn's March from 'Midsummer Night's Dream' filled the church. Alfred and Sara Jane led

William and Elizabeth down the aisle. All looked radiantly happy. Two couples each so much in love. A double wedding with a double future.

It was Christmas Eve, 1851.

As Patience left the church to join the congregation in wishing the newly weds happiness, she found the young footman walking beside her. "Could I see you home, miss?" Without waiting for an answer, he added, "I'll be back when it's time," and he vanished around the corner of the building.

* * * * *